CHIMES
OF A LOST
CATHEDRAL

CHIMES
OF A LOST
CATHEDRAL

JANET FITCH

Little, Brown and Company
New York Boston London

Copyright © 2019 by Janet Fitch

Hachette Book Group supports the right to free expression and the value of copyright. The purpose of copyright is to encourage writers and artists to produce the creative works that enrich our culture.

The scanning, uploading, and distribution of this book without permission is a theft of the author's intellectual property. If you would like permission to use material from the book (other than for review purposes), please contact permissions@hbgusa.com. Thank you for your support of the author's rights.

Little, Brown and Company
Hachette Book Group
1290 Avenue of the Americas, New York, NY 10104
littlebrown.com

First Edition: July 2019

Little, Brown and Company is a division of Hachette Book Group, Inc. The Little, Brown name and logo are trademarks of Hachette Book Group, Inc.

The publisher is not responsible for websites (or their content) that are not owned by the publisher.

The Hachette Speakers Bureau provides a wide range of authors for speaking events. To find out more, go to hachettespeakersbureau.com or call (866) 376-6591.

All of the Russian poems used in this book are original translations created for this volume by Boris Dralyuk, coeditor of *The Penguin Book of Russian Poetry* (Penguin Classics, 2015) and editor of *1917: Stories and Poems from the Russian Revolution* (Pushkin Press, 2016), except for the following: "The Bronze Horseman" by Alexander Pushkin, translated by Stanley Mitchell, used by permission, Stanley Mitchell estate. "Twilight" by Fyodor Tyutchev, translated by Babette Deutsch and Avrahm Yarmolinsky in *Modern Russian Poetry: An Anthology,* in the public domain. "My Talent Is Pitiful, My Voice Not Loud" by Evgeny Baratynsky, translated by Peter France, used by permission. "The Gypsies" by Alexander Pushkin, translated by Antony Wood, used by permission. Passages from *Notes of an Eccentric* by Andrei Bely are original translations for this volume, contributed by Brendan Kiernan, PhD, and used by permission. Passages from Trotsky's speech "The Fight for Petrograd" from *Leon Trotsky's Military Writings,* volume II, speech to the Soviet, October 19, 1919, New Park Publications Ltd. Translation from the Russian by Brian Pearce. Used by permission.

Civil War Russia map by Jeffrey L. Ward

ISBN 978-0-316-51005-9 (hc) / 978-0-316-45419-3 (large print)
LCCN 2018964644

10 9 8 7 6 5 4 3 2 1

LSC-C

Printed in the United States of America

For Andrew

We'll meet again in Petersburg,
As if we had buried the sun there,
And for the first time we will utter
The blessed, senseless word...

— Osip Mandelstam,
"We'll Meet Again in Petersburg,"
November 1920

Cast of Characters and Notes on Events from *The Revolution of Marina M.*

The Makarovs

Marina Dmitrievna Makarova: Poet. Born 1900, daughter of a prominent Petrograd intelligentsia family. Breaks with family October 1917, joins a circle of radical poets. Marries poet Genya Kuriakin 1918. Her various aliases include Marusya, the deaf-mute, and Misha, boy hooligan and railway apprentice. Pregnant by estranged lover Kolya Shurov, she has just fled the cult of Ionia, February 1919.

Dmitry Ivanovich Makarov: Marina's father. Jurist and Kadet member of the Provisional Government. Presently in Siberia, joining forces with anti-Bolshevik groups. Named Marina a Bolshevik spy rather than risk endangering his movement.

Vera Borisovna Makarova: Marina's mother. Artistic society matron, a spiritualist seeker. Aristocrat. Currently the mystical figurehead of a cult based at her estate at Maryino.

Sergei (Seryozha) Dmitrievich Makarov: Marina's beloved, artistic younger brother. Died in the defense of the Moscow Kremlin, October 1917, as a military cadet, a post secured by his father against Marina's protests.

Vladimir (Volodya) Dmitrievich Makarov: Marina's older brother. An officer of the tsar's army, now fighting with the Volunteers (Whites) under Denikin in the Don.

Avdokia Fomanovna Malykh: Elderly nanny to the Makarov children, and to Vera Borisovna before them.

Ginevra Haddon-Finch: Marina's governess. Returned to England after the October Revolution.

Basya: The Makarovs' housemaid. Clever and vengeful. Becomes chairman of the apartment house committee (*domkom*) on Furshtatskaya Street, a position of power, from which she persecutes her former mistress.

Marina's Friends

Nikolai (Kolya) Stepanovich Shurov: Marina's first and great love. Former officer, Volodya's best friend. Speculator and adventurer. Their relationship ruptured following his infidelity with a peasant woman, Faina. Unaware Marina is pregnant.

Varvara Vladimirovna Razrushenskaya: Marina's brilliant school friend, a radical Marxist and committed Communist, later a Cheka officer. Ruined Marina's relationship with her family by revealing her to have spied on her father for the Bolsheviks. Briefly Marina's possessive lover. Marina abandons her to run away with Kolya.

Wilhelmina (Mina) Solomonovna Katzeva: Marina's childhood best friend. Chemistry student at university. Forced to leave school when her photographer father dies. Now running his studio. Briefly Kolya's lover. Hires Marina, as "Misha," to be her photographer's assistant. Marina abandons her for Kolya during the first anniversary of the revolution.

The Katzev Household

Both Seryozha and Marina, as well as Marina's poet circle, are close to the Katzev family.

Solomon Moiseivich Katzev: Mina's father. A well-known Petrograd photographer. Championed Seryozha. Dies from the hardships following the revolution.

Sofia Yakovlevna Katzeva: Mina's mother. A kind woman with a soft spot for the Makarov children.

Uncle Aaron and Aunt Fanya: Solomon Moiseivich's elderly brother and his wife. Anarchists. Formerly lived in America.

Darya (Dunya) Solomonovna Katzeva: Mina's younger sister. In love with painter Sasha Orlovsky.

Shoshanna (Shusha) Solomonovna Katzeva: Mina's youngest sister. A great admirer of Marina's.

Roman Osipovich Ippolit: Mina's fiancé. Medical student.

The Poets

The Transrational Interlocutors of the Terrestrial Now, many of whom lived together in a loose collective called the Poverty Artel on Grivtsova Alley.

Gennady (Genya) Yurievich Kuriakin: Marina's lover, later husband. Futurist poet, Bolshevik. Charismatic center of the poets' circle. Departs for Moscow with Zina Ostrovskaya to act in films after breakup with Marina. Creates a radical theatrical group.

Anton Mikhailovich Chernikov: Leader of the Transrational Interlocutors, editor of the journal *Okno,* Genya's best friend and mentor. Difficult and critical of Marina. The sole legitimate tenant of the Poverty Artel.

Zina Ostrovskaya: Radical poet. In love with Genya Kuriakin. Creates an opportunity for Genya to move with her to Moscow.

Gigo Gelashvili: Georgian poet, slightly mad.

Sasha Orlovsky: Constructivist painter. Friend of Genya's. In love with Dunya Katzeva.

Galina Krestovskaya: Actress and would-be poet. Benefactor of Anton, *Okno,* and the Poverty Artel. Her apartment was the gathering place for the poetry circle.

Andrei Kirillovich Krestovsky: Galina's husband. Owner of theater snack bars in Petrograd, source of the funding for the Poverty Artel. Killed during Red Terror, 1918.

Petya Simkin: Poet, university student, musician.

Oksana Linichuk: Poet, university student. Brought flowers to Marina's wedding.

Arseny Grodetsky: Poet, young disciple of Genya Kuriakin's.

The Criminals

Baron Arkady von Princip, the "Archangel": Petrograd crime boss during the revolution. Unstable and brilliant, obsessed with Marina and with Kolya, who double-crosses him in a deal involving Dmitry Makarov's counterrevolutionary conspiracy. Holds Marina captive in an apartment on Tauride Street before she escapes him during a meeting of the counterrevolutionaries.

Akim, the "Kirghiz": Arkady's lieutenant. Tends Marina while she is in captivity on Tauride Street. Discovering her working as "Misha," he informs her that the Archangel has become unhinged.

Gurin: Arkady's driver.

Borya, "Saint Peter": The muscle in Arkady's gang.

The Counterrevolutionary Conspirators

Dmitry Makarov's colleagues, planning the uprising of the Czech Legion, 1918. Met with Von Princip in a dacha in the woods near Pulkovo, where Dmitry accused Marina of being a Bolshevik spy.

Ivan Karlinsky: SR Party, leader of the conspiracy.

Viktoria Karlinskaya: Karlinsky's wife and Dmitry Makarov's mistress. Insists that Von Princip "get rid of" Marina, considering her a Bolshevik spy. Marina reveals Karlinskaya's identity to Varvara while in Cheka custody.

Commander Fielding Brown, the "Englishman": a British military attaché.

Konstantin, the "Odessan": a famous English spy.

The Five

Astronomers at Pulkovo Observatory, where Marina sought refuge as the deaf-mute Marusya.

Aristarkh Apollonovich Belopolsky, the "First Ancient": Astronomer, director of the observatory. Discovered the nature of the rings of Saturn.

Boris Osipovich Bondarin, the "Second": Astrophysicist.

Nikolai Gerasimovich Pomogayush, the "Third": Chemist and astrobotanist. Marusya's mentor.

Valentin Vladimirovich Tipov, the "Fourth": Astrophysicist.

Ludmila Vasilievna Bredikskaya, the "Fifth": The *starushka*. Physicist and spectrum analyst.

Rodion Karlovich Mistropovich: Young astronomer. Returns to the observatory with his sick wife and children during the height of the Petrograd cholera epidemic, spring 1918.

The Aristocratic Communards

Princess Elizaveta Vladimirovna Gruzinskaya: The "white mouse." Elderly aristocrat cultivated by Kolya Shurov. Foresaw collectivization of Petrograd grand apartments and preemptively formed a "collective" of her aristocratic friends, Emilia Ivanovna Golovina, Viktor Sergeevich Golovin, and Pavel Alexandrovich Naryshkin.

The Ionians

Spiritualist cult at Vera Borisovna's family estate at Maryino—rising from the ashes of a failed experiment, the Laboratory, a large commune in Petrograd. Vera Borisovna lives in seclusion there as the "Mother," the spiritual figurehead of the cult.

Taras Ukashin, the "Master": Charismatic leader of the cult of Ionia. Following his teaching of *inflowing*, taking energy in through the skin, his followers nearly starve.

Andrei Ionian: The "intelligent." Ukashin's court jester. Formerly the publisher Andrei Alexandrovich Petrovin, a friend of Vera Borisovna's and one of the founders of the spiritualist group before it was overtaken by Taras Ukashin and moved to Maryino. Commits suicide.

Other Ionians: Magda Ionian, the "gypsy"; **Bogdan Ionian,** former dancer at the Mariinsky Theater, Marina's friend; **Natalya Ionian,** former dancer, Marina's friend; **Katrina Ionian,** singer, object of Ukashin's desire, secret lover of **Pasha Ionian; Gleb,** Pasha's rival; **Ilya, Lilya,** and **Anna Ionian.**

The Maryino Villagers

Lyuda: Avdokia's niece and Marina's girlhood companion, whom she taught to read, married to the blacksmith and currently representing the village at the regional soviet. Protecting Ionia from the Cheka.

Olya: Avdokia's half sister, instrumental in Marina's escape from Ionia.

CIVIL WAR RUSSIA 1919

0 Miles   300

0 Kilometers   300

Vyatka

Glazov   Perm

Izhevsk   Ekaterinburg

Kambarka

Kazan

KAMA

Ufa

Samara

Orenburg

Ural Mountains

K O L C H A K

S I B E R I A

Omsk

KEY

——————— Furthest extent of White Siberian Armies under Admiral Kolchak, May 1919

• • • • • • • Furthest extent of North Russian White Army, English and Allied Expeditionary Forces, May 1919

— • — • —• Furthest extent of Southern White Army ("The Volunteers") under General Denikin, October 1919

— — — — Furthest extent of Northwest White Army under General Yudenich (and Poles and Letts), October 1919

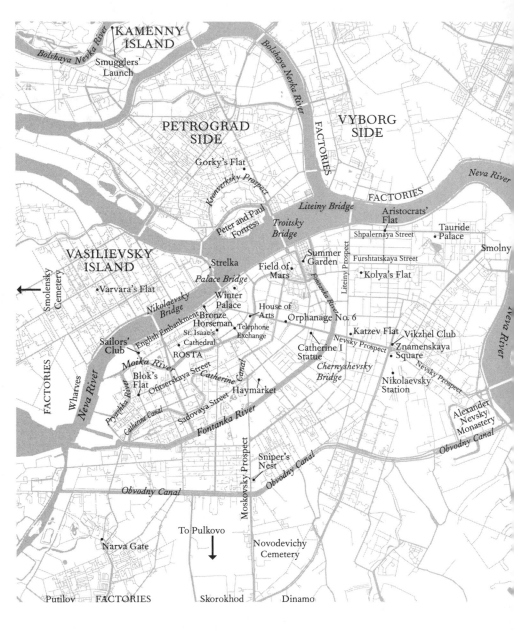

KAMENNY
ISLAND

Bolshaya Nevka River

Smugglers'
Launch

Bolshaya Nevka River

PETROGRAD
SIDE

VYBORG
SIDE

Gorky's Flat

Kronverksky Prospect

FACTORIES

Neva River

FACTORIES

Liteiny Bridge

Aristocrats'
Flat

Peter and Paul
Fortress

*Troitsky
Bridge*

Shpalernaya Street

Tauride
Palace

Smolny

VASILIEVSKY
ISLAND

Strelka

Palace Bridge

Field of
Mars

Summer
Garden

Liteiny Prospect

Furshtatskaya Street

Smolensky
Cemetery

Varvara's Flat

*Nikolaevsky
Bridge*

Winter
Palace

House of
Arts

Fontanke River

Kolya's Flat

Neva River

English Embankment

Bronze
Horseman

St. Isaac's
Cathedral

Telephone
Exchange

Orphanage No. 6

Katzev Flat

Vikzhel Club

Sailors'
Club

ROSTA

Nevsky Prospect

Catherine I
Statue

Znamenskaya
Square

Moika River

Blok's
Flat

Ofitserskaya Street

Catherine Canal

*Chernyshevsky
Bridge*

Nevsky Prospect

FACTORIES

Wharves

Pryazhka River

Catherine Canal

Sadovaya Street

Haymarket

Nikolaevsky
Station

Neva River

Fontanka River

Alexander
Nevsky
Monastery

Obvodny Canal

Sniper's
Nest

Moskovsky Prospect

Obvodny Canal

Obvodny Canal

Narva Gate

To Pulkovo

Novodevichy
Cemetery

Putilov   FACTORIES

Skorokhod

Dinamo

PETROGRAD
1919

Part I
Iskra, the Spark

(March 1919–September 1919)

1 *Tikhvin*

I WAS RISEN, risen from the dead. I had escaped the house of snow and lies, I had been spared.

An icy fog obscured the road the day I left Novinka on the back of the old man's sledge piled with logs, heading for the market town Tikhvin. The countryside revealed itself in the foggy gaps, opening and closing like curtains. The load shifted dangerously underneath me, wooden runners jolting in the ruts. The old man smoked his pipe while I made plans that blew away like snowflakes, into the drifts and gone.

Five days we rode, stopping in villages, sleeping in straw, the child alive and moving within me. It was stubborn, like its mama. My celestial egg. Gathering strength for the jailbreak.

> *And out rushed oceans*
> *Himalayas*
> *Krakatoas,*
> *warring nations . . .*
>
> *Rocketing red and fiery across the dazzled brow*
> *of Nothingness*
>
> *Till Nothing itself became a memory.*

At last, we descended into Tikhvin, a crossroads for centuries, with its river and its railroad, the point of arrival and departure where I'd last left my one and faithless love. His tears had run, but I had not been moved. That vain girl, walking around with her eyes shut tight, thinking that life should be straight and good, that she could pick and choose, like plucking stones out of a handful of rice. But now I was five months along with his child unborn, and

3

had learned that imperfection was part of the weave of the world. I would return to him if I could, and pick up the stitch I had dropped.

Tikhvin was a substantial town of some twenty thousand souls—a number I once thought negligible. Now it was dizzying. So many streets, people, houses, fences, and carts...The giant Uspensky Monastery loomed with its five-towered carillon, its ancient fortress walls, which had once protected the entire population from Swedish invaders. Now Russian soldiers held the town in their grip, hanging about on street corners in their greatcoats, with their rifles and grisly bayonets. A gang of recruits marched toward a barracks, accompanied by shouts and curses. This was the current reality, the sound of the year 1919, the crash and clang of war. Time was bringing me into its brazen dance, leading me by the hand.

After days of nothing more urgent than snowbound forest and the bony rump of the horse, Tikhvin's sprawl and energy unnerved me, and the child recoiled inside me. Like a country simpleton, I marveled at every small sight—the town seemed a metropolis, a terrifying wonder. Every sound amplified, every movement a jolt. I flinched at a carter banging crates to the ground, startled at a shout from a doorway. Now I understood the peasant's terror when he encountered mighty Petersburg for the first time—the din of Nikolaevsky station, the bustle on Nevsky Prospect.

As the sledge scraped along toward the station, I couldn't help but read the signs and portents. I hadn't spent months at Ionia, trapping and hunting, without learning to read the news in sticks and hairs and tracks in snow. All the signs were bad. I saw it in the lean, blue-tinged faces of the arrivals struggling up from the station. Two sallow, soot-eyed women in black coats and too-thin shoes dragged a heavy suitcase between them, loaded no doubt with silverware and bric-a-brac to trade with the peasants for food. *He who trades on the free market trades on the freedom of the people.* A grim-jawed, silent group of workers following them had to be a food-requisitioning brigade. They neither spoke nor joked—they knew their assignment: to relieve peasants of their grain without recompense so they could feed their own starving brothers. I could see them pulling into themselves, hardening for the job ahead. A number of workers traveling alone walked up the main road, collars raised, a self-provisioning holiday. Their faces told me everything. *No food in the city, no help, no end in sight.*

Behold, the station. The old man helped me down from my throne of logs, the horse snorted its clouds into the white air. The days of hard travel had taken their toll on my body, I moved like a woman of eighty. Pine pitch and splinters stuck to my sheepskin and squirrelskin gloves. I held on to my snowshoes and game bag, unable to adjust to the assault of so many people. Travelers pushed past me as if I were a turnstile.

I gazed up at the arches. Here was where I went wrong. Here was my chance to begin again.

I shoved my way through the station and out onto the platform, where a train stood steaming, stinking, its wheels terrifyingly outsized. After the timeless introversion of the countryside, the noise scoured my ears, the child's jerking alarm took my breath, and I clutched my snowshoes to my breast. First- and second-class passengers paced the platform, stretching their legs and doing furtive business with the peasant women selling *piroshky* and roasted sunflower seeds, while third-class travelers huddled in the barn doors of the boxcars, not daring to leave the train, their wooden bunks rayed behind them like shelves in a poor shop. Everyone heading east, east, east, away from Petrograd, into the snowy countryside, toward the Urals, escaping the turmoil and starvation in the capital of Once-Had-Been. My determination wavered. It slipped, shattering against the train's iron wheels.

Perhaps the boy I'd been—Misha, that cheeky lad—would have chanced it. He had his way of staying afloat, but I couldn't conjure him now, not with the child on the way, my face gone round, my breasts past binding. I was a woman in full and there was no escaping it.

Wisdom does not consist of making the best choice among many. Wisdom is understanding when there is no choice and taking the step that must be taken, without complaints or sighs.

Hoisting my small bag higher over my shoulder, I walked to the platform's end and climbed down, strapped myself into my snowshoes, and followed the rails through the fog.

A switchman's shack emerged from the milky white. I knocked at the poorly made door, the pearly gates of this sooty heaven, and swung it open without waiting for an invitation.

Inside, a blackened stove warmed the small hut—no better than a wooden crate—where four men seated on boxes played cards. The kettle boiled. Steam coated the one greasy window. But which was the switchman, the one in charge? *Him*, I decided—the bald one in spectacles, pencil behind ear. The other three, railwaymen: a pensioner—a little bantam cock—and two burly men, one missing an arm, his coat sleeve pinned up neatly. Firemen or mechanics, I thought, the one-armed man wounded in the line of duty, and still drawing rations. Oh, to be the boy Misha again! Misha would know how to talk to them. He would swear, tell a dirty joke. *Eh, brothers!* But trapped in this irrevocable female form, I had to appeal to mercy, if I could find it. I hated negotiating from weakness, but I could do it if I had to.

"Comrades. Forgive me." I spoke quickly, holding my hands in the universal language of wheedling. "I don't want to trouble you, but I don't know where else to turn. My brother was a Vikzhel man, an assistant engineer. He said if I ever needed help, to turn to the railwaymen." I rummaged in the sack and pulled out Misha's papers, presented them to the switchman. "I lost my position, a cook in a boarding house. The woman's daughter came home from Petrograd and took my place."

The bald man peered at Misha's documents. "Assistant engineer? It says he was fifteen years old." He tried to hand them back to me but I shrank away. My fictional brother was Vikzhel, a union man. They took care of their own.

"He was a good boy." I had no problem staining my face with tears. Poor Misha! "He gave me his pay. It kept us going. But he died, four weeks ago. Now I have nothing."

The switchman held the papers awkwardly, he didn't know what to do with them if I wouldn't take them back. "So what do you want from us, little comrade? We can't put you on as a fireman."

The others chuckled. Oh, so funny. How I hated men who thought what a woman did was ridiculous, what a woman needed. I wished I could pull the gun from my pocket, show him who was ridiculous. But I had to bite my tongue. "I can shovel snow, keep the tracks clean," I said, pushing on. "Cook, wash. Read. Look, I'm not asking for charity." I drew myself up to my full height, trying to appear healthy and robust, not like a pregnant girl who'd been breathing her last calories through her metaphysical skin. "I can water trains. Clean the station." That made them laugh—you were more likely to see a pig fly than a clean *vokzal* in Russia.

They exchanged glances as if they were passing cards. The old man pulled something from his pocket. "Here's some chocolate, *devushka*. Take it. Don't be shy."

Now I felt bad that I'd wanted to shoot him. I took the chocolate and let it melt on my tongue like a consecration—dark and sweet, like a drug. Over the switchman's shoulder, a calendar hung next to train schedules posted on nails. Its pages were roughly torn back to *28 Fevrail 1919*. I counted the months on the roof of my mouth. *March, April, May, June . . .* The months had never felt so urgent. The burly man with one arm leaned back, hooked his cigarette in his mouth, and with the same hand, threw a card onto the little box that was their gaming table. "Maybe Raisa Filipovna could use her."

The old fellow puffed out his cheeks, his eyes full of news. "That girl was already halfway out the door. Yulia. Bun in the oven, you ask me." He cackled, oblivious of the insult he was offering.

The bald man flushed. Had he noticed my condition? "Pardon him, he's our village idiot."

"Who's the idiot, you apparatchik." The old fellow held up a bony fist. "*Burzhui* bastard."

The two-armed man threw a one-eyed jack. "You playing or what?"

Bun in the oven. I wished now I had a ring. Still, I could legitimately present myself as a married woman. Between the chocolate and the chance at work, I was already feeling hopeful. I licked the last of the sweet from my lips. "Where can I find this Raisa Filipovna?"

"A big wooden house on Orlovsky Street," said the one-armed man. "Number 8. Korsakova's her name. Tell her about your brother. She has the heart of a kitten. Tell her Styopa sent you."

"I knew the husband," said the old man. "A shame. Tomasovich."

Styopa threw a card. I admired the dexterity with which he used his single hand. "A good man. Eternal memory."

The bald man glanced up at his calendar, and tore the last page off to reveal *1 Mart 1919*, opened the stove door and threw February into the fire.

I set out for Korsakova's. I didn't know Tikhvin well, only the station and the monastery, and the one inn where we used to stay on our way to Maryino. Where we'd stayed the summer of 1917, between the revolutions, when my father had sent us into the country, and Seryozha to the cadets. I asked directions of a woman who walked with the assured step of one who knew where she was going and was in no hurry to get there, and following her instructions, I passed Sovietskaya Street, Karl Marx Street, Svobodnaya Square—*Freedom Square*—a snow-clotted commons. The revolution had certainly brought its passion for renaming to Tikhvin, best known for its icon of the Virgin, and as the birthplace of the composer Rimsky-Korsakov, whose house my artistic mother liked to point out as our carriage jounced through the dusty streets on the way out of town. *Korsakova*—I wondered if the woman was some relation.

I found her house on a snow-filled lane—sagging but not the worst on the street, a big two-story wooden structure with a long balcony looking out upon other houses across the street, equally run-down but not so large. I rang the bell, tested the door. It was locked. It had started to snow again, but if I could spend a night in a blizzard in a forest halfway between nowhere and never, I guess I could wait in the doorway of a Tikhvin boarding house until the landlady came home.

Removing my snowshoes and tipping them up against the dark shingles, I took out Genya's little book and reread his poems, hearing his voice, that concatenation of basso and boyishness:

> *I know what it's like*
> *to be fed paper*
> > *when what one needs is*

> *Bread, wine*
> > *love.*

I wondered if he still felt the same way. If I hadn't left with my delightful man that night, if I'd met Genya after his avant-garde play, I might be in Moscow right now, surrounded by poets, instead of starving, pregnant, and looking for work in Tikhvin. It was too depressing to consider. I closed the book, ate the sausage in my satchel, a bit of bread. The doorway arched over my head. I touched the rough shingles. Would I have my baby here? Would Korsakova take me in? And if she didn't, then what? Death was no conjecture these days, no distant rumor. It was all around, just waiting for me to make a false step. I thought of the romantic idiot who had once strolled among the graves at Petersburg's noble Alexander Nevsky Monastery, imagining my own beautiful, famous corpse. My funeral procession, the inconsolable thousands who would carry me, the great poet, on their shoulders to my final resting place.

But death wasn't at all like that. It was my brother Seryozha, cut down halfway to manhood. It was the student shot dead before me by government troops at Znamenskaya Square. It was a boy-thief beaten to death by the mob, dying in Genya's arms in his grubby apartment. And the astronomer's son, in the cholera epidemic, shitting out his life in the grass. I thought of all my dead — Solomon Katzev, Andrei Krestovsky, Andrei Petrovin...Death was no velvet shadow. He was a worker in a cold brick factory, short on materials, churning out a tatty product — typhus, cholera, civil war. A robber, waiting in alleys and stairwells, a sign painter even now painting the blue faces of the Formers in the Tikhvin station and hovering around the reeking invalids of war. He was circling the rooftops at Maryino, where the Ionians were still *inflowing* in the back parlor with their shining doomed eyes.

Would this damned widow ever return? I clapped my hands together, stamped my feet as I watched more amateur speculators propelling their suitcases up the badly cleared street. How desperately we clung to life, each one of us. Where did we find the energy to carry on? I used to think the dead were hopeful for the living, like benevolent old ladies watching young people at a ball. Now I thought they just pitied us.

> *Two crocuses once bloomed*
> *Between the rails*
> *Of a tram.*
> *The wrong time.*
> *The wrong place.*
> *Once I imagined*
> *A great death.*
> *Plumes and garlands.*
> *But it's all death, my brother.*
> *We vanish just the same.*

At last, a tall woman dressed in black turned up the unshoveled walk, a basket in her arms, already watching me with suspicion.

"Raisa Filipovna?" I called out. She raised skeptical eyebrows. "You don't know me, but Styopa from the switching house sent me over." Who should I be? *Makarova? Shurova?* "Kuriakina. Marina Dmitrievna."

Korsakova hooked the basket over her arm, fished a key from her pocket, and unlocked the front door. "And how do you know Stepan Radulovich?"

"I don't." I vowed I would tell the truth when I could. "I went to the station this morning, looking for work. He told me to come up here." She opened the door. I wasn't sure if I was supposed to follow her, or if she would slam it in my face. "They said you might need someone. That you lost your girl."

She turned back to me then, a firm-faced, dark-haired woman about forty. "Well, don't just stand there."

Inside, her house was warm, simple, and clean. Hooks by the door, wood walls, a little cabinet, a braided rug on the floor of the sitting room so old you couldn't see what color it had been. Clean, wide-planked pine floors, solid, worn furniture smelling of men—a bit sweet, a bit acrid, the strong scent of tobacco. A workingman's boarding house. Badly printed woodcuts, peasant *lubok* style, a couple of silhouettes. She hung up her coat and hat, removed her boots, and slid her feet into felt slippers. I was careful to keep my coat folded in, so the gun would not reveal itself as I hung my coat and my fox hat and took off my boots. She gestured to a pair of worn felt slippers and I put them on.

A long, rough table dominated the dining hall, a table that had never seen a cloth in any era. There we sat on long benches and I told her my tale, as much as made sense. She gazed at me with keen, dark eyes while I spoke, as if judging the weight of a goose under its feathers. "When is the child due?" she asked bluntly.

Seeing she'd lost a girl to a sexual escapade, I was careful to explain about my husband, the poet Gennady Kuriakin, who had moved to Moscow last autumn.

She grimaced, as if she'd just bitten into something sour. "He left you in this condition?"

For some reason, I wanted to defend Genya, even in the course of this elaborate fabrication. "It wasn't his fault. Really, he didn't know. I didn't tell him. I didn't want to make him stay if he didn't want to. He's a very ethical person."

She cocked one of her mobile eyebrows and shook her head wearily, as you would if someone told you they'd just bought a handful of magic beans. "Styopa said you might have a job." I brought the subject around again. "Said your girl left. I'm a hard worker, and... *the condition,* well, it'll be months before it's a problem. I don't need much. Just give me a chance."

"The *girl* was my eldest daughter," she said wearily. "Yulia. Well, you can't keep them young. Eventually the wheat will spring from the earth." Her gaze fell upon my weathered hands. "Why don't you wear a ring?"

My ragged hands, the broken nails. I hadn't had to cut them since I left Furshtatskaya Street, they just tore off. "We married at the district soviet," I said. "When the Germans were attacking Petrograd. He was leaving in the morning. There was no time for rings." Our Red wedding. I could only remember Oksana's geraniums, the petals shedding like little drops of blood.

"Romantics..." The widow Korsakova smiled, and pushed a loose strand of hair back into the black topknot. "I'm glad that's not dead." She surprised me. I'd have thought the landlady of a place like this would be a hard-nosed kopek pincher, counting the linens. "Well, all right. I'll give you a try. But remember, I run a quiet, respectable house. I hear the least breath of scandal, that you're drinking, running around, you're out in the street. Baby or no baby. *Ponimaesh?*"

I was in! It was all I could do not to leap and twirl down the hall as she led me to my room. Only her extreme sobriety discouraged it. We climbed the stairs, walked down a long creaking hall wallpapered in a pattern of tiny flowers the color of old teeth, then up a second, crooked back staircase to a small third floor. She showed me a room with two narrow beds. Cheerful half-curtains of printed calico softened the windows. "That was Yulia's," she said, pointing to the bed under the window. "And this is my younger one's, Lizaveta. She's at school now."

After the disorder of the last years, the lunacy of Ionia, I wanted to kiss the hem of her skirt. Such peace. The good order of family life. Thank God for this plain, sensible Russian woman who was making a home for her daughters. Perhaps I would be like this in a few years, streaks of gray in my hair, calm and competent, able to keep other people alive.

She stood in the doorway in her black dress. There was something Akhmatovian about her, her height, her hair, her somber countenance. My savior, my saint. "I'm sorry about your brother," she said. "We have to cling to each other very tightly these days."

And so I took up residence at Raisa Filipovna Korsakova's. After my duties in former lives—as the servant Marusya at Pulkovo Observatory, as Marina Ionian these last months—I well knew how to make myself useful, and oh, three lovely meals a day! The widow and I worked side by side as she instructed me on the niceties of the domestic arts. It didn't bother me that she was on the taciturn side unless actively illustrating some task. I had learned to appreciate silence.

Eight railwaymen lived in the house, including one-armed Styopa, who watched me tenderly as I carried pots and passed food, even helped me clear the table. He whispered to me, "Come to me when the lights go out. Fourth door on the right." I smiled, neither refusing nor accepting. But it made me happy. He was a kind soul, robust and not unattractive, his hair and moustache had some gray. His gray eyes accepted his fate with the simple courage I'd seen in the military hospitals in Petrograd. God knew it had been a long time since I'd had a man. But I would not push my good luck at finding this position. He watched me as I sewed buttons onto trousers and darned socks on a wooden egg.

Fortunately or unfortunately, I rarely had a spare moment. Korsakova ran the place like a German. Monday was laundry, Tuesday the floors, Wednesday the windows, Thursday the stairs, and so on. When I wasn't scrubbing pine floors with lye soap or boiling acres of laundry, hanging hectares of heavy corduroys in the kitchen, making beds or roasting kasha or grinding oats or peeling potatoes, I was standing in miles of queues for bread and flour and fuel and matches, and Liza's milk ration. Was I complaining? Not I. Our tenants' Vikzhel rations were generous, first category. They even got fabric and galoshes—theoretically. I ate like a queen—at least a Soviet one.

This was my life. I had no friends besides thirteen-year-old Liza, Styopa Radulovich, and the other boarders. I avoided befriending the women in the queues. It was a gossipy town and they asked all kinds of pointed questions about Korsakova and Liza and the way-ward Yulia. You couldn't give women like that a toehold. Oh, the hours of listening to their chatter! Whose daughter was sleeping with soldiers behind the barracks for a piece of their Red Star rations. Whose daughter had been raped last Tuesday and left for dead. She never could identify the rapist. They wanted to know things about me, where I was from, did I have a sweetheart. It made me wonder why they didn't join the Cheka if they liked interroga-tion so much.

So although I was lonely enough to howl, I kept to Liza and the guests.

Spring crept closer, then arrived, turning the world to mud. The un-paved roads transformed themselves into deep brown rivers. Icicles crashed from eaves of the wooden buildings, and now the poor city folk had to struggle ankle-deep in mud with their offerings, their patched clothes spattered with Tikhvin. Workers with their sad plunder, and out-and-out bagmen groaning under huge sacks of flour and potatoes, headed for the station, where they'd boldly load the bumpers between cars for the trip back to Petrograd. The air crackled with anxiety—anyone could be shot for speculation, and yet, no one could survive without it.

I put off registering my presence with the authorities. The more invisible my document-poor life, the better. But eventually, Korsakova too was visited by the local Chekists. Searching—for what, food, weapons, counterrevolution? Or more likely, just to harass the Vikzhel men. Trade unionists tended not to be Communists. Everyone was turned out of bed—the railwaymen, Raisa Filipovna. Every room had to be searched, even the little girl-ish one at the top of the stairs.

Luckily we heard them beating on the front door. I turned on the lamp. "Liza," I whispered. "I need to hide something."

She sat up, her innocent face eager for secrets, her hair all tangled above her braids, as fine as thistle floss. I reached under my mattress and showed her the bundle of cloth in which I'd wrapped the ugly hunk of metal that had taken Andrei's life. "Is it a gun?" she whispered excitedly.

I could hear the men arguing downstairs now. Trade unionists and Bolsheviks made a volatile mixture. "I'm sorry, I was traveling. I didn't think——" Strangely, I'd forgotten there was an outside world, with Chekists combing every corner for counterrevolution.

Liza jumped out of bed and knelt, scrabbling at the floorboards under her bed with her fingernails. She pulled up a board, grinning. I saw something pink in there—a blouse? And books! I'd forgotten, children were natural spies, they always had their secrets. I threw the gun in with them and she quickly replaced the plank.

We could hear furniture crashing on the second floor, men shouting. Liza rounded her eyes at me, her sharp little chin, her blankets up around her neck. "They're coming."

"Don't worry, they're not looking for schoolgirls."

The search was messy and frightening. They finally reached the third floor, burst through our crooked door. Liza and I clung to each other as a flat-cheeked dullard with pale blue eyes searched our room, pulling the mattresses off the beds and the drawers from the chest, making a great racket as the men shouted on the floor below. I was as frightened as Liza, but trembling as I was, I noticed the search wasn't as careful as Varvara's would have been. He didn't even look behind the *lubok* print of the Donkey, the Bear, and the Fox, or run his hands over the wallpaper, feeling for seams, let alone check for loose floorboards. I could have hidden half the Committee for the Salvation of the Fatherland in here and he would have missed them. They had no idea what they were looking for, just throwing their weight around to terrorize the populace.

They herded us down to the dining room and made everyone produce their papers, and thus I was found out. No labor book. No travel *propusk*, no registration with the housing committee. It was a problem for both me and the widow.

Styopa Radulovich in his nightshirt, his thick strong hairy legs.

"Doesn't the Cheka have anything better to do than harass house-maids?"

"Tell us why we shouldn't arrest her right now," said the Chekist in charge, a lean small man with one drooping eye. "And you too." He turned his good eye on Styopa and the bantam and the mechanic Berkovin. "I don't like the looks of any of you. You Vikzhel men are getting too big for your pants."

"She'll come tomorrow," said Korsakova, deflecting the attention from her precious boarders. "I'll make sure of it, Comrade. You have my word." She was as white as white paint, there in her dark shawl and her nightgown.

"We know where you live," said the lead man. "All of you." They left with a great clattering on the bare wooden stairs, a crash as they knocked one of the prints down. The statement hung in the air long after they'd gone.

2 *The New Soviet Woman*

The Tikhvin Soviet was housed in a fine yellow building on Svobodnaya Square, a surprisingly elegant structure. Clearly Tikhvin had once been an important commercial center before its present decline. I languished there for most of the day, standing in long queues, leaning against the walls, my ankles and calves killing me. People coughed, they scratched surreptitiously. Would I be able to get papers as a proletarian this time? Marina Kuriakina? Allowing me a life of some kind or condemning me forever—no rations, my child permanently branded as a member of a counterrevolutionary class. Or would I simply be arrested, taken away to some Cheka cell? I couldn't bear that again, not ever.

Dusk had gathered outside the windows by the time I received my permission, my *propusk,* to move to the desk at which I would receive my labor book. I didn't complain—I just prayed I wouldn't have to come back tomorrow. *Propusk* in hand, I approached the wooden desk of a humorless woman behind a typewriter and, more importantly, the tray bearing its array of precious rubber stamps. After standing all day, my legs felt like watermelons, my ankles like logs. There was only one chair and the woman was sitting in it. Her mouth was wide but pinched, it looked like her teeth hurt her.

Slowly, carefully, I answered her questions. Sticking to the truth in all the small details, lying only in the large ones.

Familia:

Kuriakina.

Imia:

Marina.

Otchestvo:

Dmitrievna.

Mesto Rozhdenia:

Petrograd.

Data Rozhdenia:

3 February 1900

Obrazovanie:

Primary.

Professia, spetsialnost:

General Labor.

Klass:

Proletarian.

Semeinoe Polozhenie:

Married.

Sweat poured off me in rivers, even in this unheated office. The woman worked in knitted gloves, coat and hat, the tips of her gloves cut off. In demeanor, I did my best to straddle the line between Bold Proletarian and Supplicant Peasant as I described the robbery on the train from Petrograd. A bourgeois bagman (describing Kolya in every specific) had made much of me, and then stolen everything—my papers, my money. I hadn't even known it was gone until disembarking at Tikhvin, when I found a bag of small rocks and an old calendar instead of my belongings. To weep for this woman was no difficulty. Then I praised the widow Korsakova in quasi-religious tones, which I then "remembered" was un-Bolshevik. What a performance. Komissarzhevskaya herself would have called for an encore.

"And where is your husband now?" asked the woman, who looked like a raw-boned cow.

I shrugged. "Don't know. He was leaving for Moscow last time I saw him. Looking for work in the Information Section. He has a friend there. He was going to send for me, but I waited and then got tired of it. Maybe he's in the army now, who cares. Anyway, I thought, it's a new world. I can go places too, can't I?" Trying to breathe energy through my pores. The class-winnowing process had reached the provinces, and I had to consolidate my proletarian status. My mouth was dry, my hands shook. Three nights ago, I heard in the queues that the local Cheka had boldly arrested six monks from the Uspensky Monastery, suspecting them of being nobles in hiding. Was no one safe?

"What are you doing in Tikhvin?" Her watery eyes, that frizzy hair. Her mouth was a line, protecting bad teeth.

"My factory closed," I said. "People said things were easier away from the city. Thought I'd give it a try. Though there's nothing here either, just charwoman." I craned my neck to see what she was typing, the way illiterate people did, in awe that someone could put one letter after another. "Not that I'm complaining. Work is work and the widow's fair."

"You didn't come for speculation?"

Why else would anyone move to this godforsaken burg? I wanted to yell. But a certain story was called for here, and I had to tell it, keep the mournful look on my face like a beggar pretending to be blind. It was Kolya's peasant wife all over again. "I wanted to try my luck. But it's all the same. Nothing in the foundry. I got this job, good as any. Place to live...The Cheka came and threw some furniture around. She said I better come over and do the necessary."

The woman was unimpressed, her wide mouth set. There was something bothering her about me. My palms sweated, my eye twitched, but I resisted swallowing or biting my lip. I had to win her over. How? She saw liars every day. It better be good. Not too baroque. Maybe she liked it here, maybe she was proud to be from Tikhvin. "Sometimes I think I should've gone to Moscow with my old man. But I don't think Moscow's any better, do you?"

Wrong. Her expression of tired suspicion turned to one of open-mouthed astonishment. Exactly the way one of Chekhov's yearning sisters would have responded, had someone ventured such a ridiculous notion, preferring this railroad backwater to the capital of Soviet Russia. I *saw*. She had hoped for something better in life. She had yearned, dreamed, and ended up here, behind that typewriter, with her wide, sad mouth, and the power to refuse lying little cheats like myself entry into the working class.

"I'm not complaining," I backtracked. "If only I'd never met that lying, thieving son of a whore—I hope he falls off the train. Men like that, they think they can just take what they want and leave you for dead." She was nodding, ever so slightly. Now I saw how the land lay. *All men are lying bastards.* Okay, Comrade, I could sing that song. How Kolya would have enjoyed all this, he would have laughed himself sick. "And me in the family way—I mean, what kind of soul does a man like that have?" My belly fluttered. I had to pee. I put my hand on my belly for the extra sympathy. I couldn't have knocked myself up just for proletarian papers, could I, Comrade?

Finally, I heard those musical sounds, the loveliest in the world, the sound of round blue stamps striking the pages of a brand-new labor book. *One, two, three.*

"Now you can register your housing," she said, holding out the little pamphlet that meant a new life for me. "There are lectures for our Soviet mothers at the Women's Club. They're very educational. I hope you'll come."

"Oh, I will! Thank you, Comrade."

Of course, I avoided the Women's Club like typhus. I didn't relish the prospect of running into Lyuda the new Communist or someone else who knew me as Marina Makarova, *barynya,* granddaughter of landowners. And I had plenty to do at the boarding house. Korsakova might be a good woman, but she wasn't exactly kitten-hearted as advertised. Pregnant or not, I worked like a mule. Boiling sheets and tending to the single toilet we all shared—beyond execrable. But for me, the worst was beds. *In the Republic of the Future, there will be no beds. We will sleep standing up, like horses.* So many beds, heavy and awkward, mattresses that needed beating, frames that needed wiping. The widow was a crusader against lice, a veritable Chekist, Dzerzhinsky himself. It was downright heroic of her to even attempt to run a clean household, let alone succeed in keeping house and tenants free from insect incursion. But it was my back that did the lifting.

Making beds perpetually frustrated me. Sheets never lay flat for me the way they did for other women. It seemed a judgment on my womanliness that I could not make a bed that didn't look like it had already been slept in. As a child, I'd often watched our maid Basya lay out a sheet with a simple snap of the wrist, making it float over the bed like a cloud, hovering for an instant before it settled perfectly. For me a sheet became a white dragon, twisting and bucking before coiling itself in a sullen heap. How I resented beds. What a waste of time, when they'd be ruined all over again in the morning. The entire category of housemaid was the most reactionary of professions. My back hurt, my hips and my legs.

Every morning before dawn, I joined the others, ready to measure out my next hours in three-foot intervals from the end of the queue to the blessed splintery counter of the bakery, each of us clearly the least valuable members of our households. Grandmothers, maiden aunts, teenaged daughters, cripples. We freed the able-bodied for worthier tasks. In some glittering Soviet future, you wouldn't have to wait like this, you'd sign in on a sheet and go to work, come back to find your rations all wrapped and waiting for you.

But that was a dream born of useless hours, weight on one leg, then the other, trying to relieve aching hips and backs. Rations would always be too valuable to entrust to bakery workers, or really (considering my hunger) anyone besides a family member. You had to keep a sharp eye on every bite. Each gram of bread was the difference between queasy health and weak, shivering faintness. *Give us this day our daily bread,* and you hoped it didn't have too much straw in it. Also our daily *vobla,* that little bony fish, if you could digest it. We had no fragile people living at Korsakova's, only workmen with good rations. I shuddered to think of the old people, like the Pulkovo astronomers, or the chronically ill, like poor Solomon Katzev. The cereal cut into our guts. And there were no fat rations at all. I still had to go to the illegal market by the east wall of the monastery and trade for small bottles of oil from local peasants. If I were arrested, no one else would go to jail, no one else would be interrogated as a speculator. Only the least valuable member. Me. And who knew what would even be in those bottles—sunflower oil, hempseed, linseed, castor—a couple of times I'd sworn it was kerosene. In exchange, I offered bits and pieces of hardware the men brought home from the railroad—nails mostly, rivets, every worker managed to take a little something. A wonder there was a railway left to run, considering the pilferage, but the peasants didn't want your money, they wanted hard goods—fabric, metal, anything manufactured. Such was the dearness of fats, you always wondered when you fried the potatoes, the bits of sausage, whether you'd poison everyone in the house. Once I was so hungry, I drank an inch of cod liver oil right in the street and struggled not to belch in front of the widow.

I stamped my feet in the queue and exhaled white breath, waiting for dawn, in boots that had been resoled by Bogdan Ionian, and tried to keep my legs from cramping. I wished I had a book to read. I wished it as much as you might wish for a nice steak with a pat of butter on top. Not a newspaper—Zinoviev thundering away—but a real book. A novel, a big fat one. Tolstoy. Or Dickens, I would die for Dickens. I'd read everything at Korsakova's—the ragged Nat Pinkertons in Mikhail Gendelev's room, and Berkovin's copy of Gorky's *Luckless Pavel,* all of which I'd "borrowed" several times. Perhaps Korsakova had something in her room, but I'd never been invited in. Aside from the men's reading, I fed off Liza's small threadbare cache of schoolbooks: an old biology text written about the time William Harvey cut up his first frog, a basic mathematics, a collection of Afanasyev's folk tales illustrated by Bilibin, Pushkin's "The Bronze Horseman," and a book of morning and evening prayers, which I never saw her open. I impressed her by reciting the "Horseman" from beginning to end from memory as she followed along in the book. *"I love you, Peter's creature / I love your strong, terrifying gaze..."* And better, I had a chance to examine the collection beneath the floorboards: a clandestine copy of *The Tale of Warlord Dracula,* Mary Shelley's *Frankenstein* in a cheap clothbound edition, and a translation of Edgar Allan Poe by Balmont. No wonder Liza had trouble sleeping.

Now, in the cold half-light pushing toward dawn, I had nothing but my heartbeat and Pushkin to keep me company: *I love you, Peter's creature...* But I wouldn't be going back to Petrograd anytime soon. At long and blessed last, the sun rose, and in the morning light, like warming birds, the sound of women's chatter began to fill the silence. Somebody was making eyes at someone's husband. A commissar's wife was taking French lessons. Somebody was pregnant again. Someone's baby was sick. Someone's daughter was running around with a mechanic. I didn't know anything, and if I had, I wouldn't share it with these old girls for love or money. Why hadn't I gone abroad when I had the chance? I could be at Oxford now, studying English literature and publishing my poems.

Abroad. Was it still there, *abroad*? My nightly fantasies swirled around the sound. Not *in three years* when this war would certainly be over, the way Varvara and I had dreamed it, after the world revolution. But *abroad* as it always had been for us—everywhere that was not Russia. The place where people were educated and read new books and hadn't had a reactionary monarchy sitting on their heads for three hundred years.

I saw myself at twenty-one at a café in New York, the bourgeois young lady, wearing a coat that was sometimes sable, sometimes gray chinchilla, eating a steak fried in butter. I imagined myself half naked in California, sunbathing on a rocky shore. Or in Buenos Aires, dancing a tango with Kolya Shurov, finally together the way we should always have been—not in a wagon scratching our fleas but in the great world. In my fantasy, how he begged my forgiveness, how he wept on his knees! And eventually, when I did forgive him, we would laugh to remember how we'd been peasants together, a world ago.

But I could not put the baby into that picture. With the baby, there should be a promenade by the sea—Yalta, or Nice. The Lido at Venice, why not? The baby—no, a child by then. Nicely dressed, a laughing boy, running after a ball, followed by a small, bright-eyed dog. A boy in a white sailor suit...

I groaned at my own bourgeois longings. What had happened to my revolutionary fervor? Equality and good conditions for all? Why not picture a bold and rugged boy, sticking up for his little comrades, skillful and useful and practical? But it was harder to picture than the Ligurian seashore. Why? Because I could not see the end of it, only this blasted queue, the eternal waiting, and I had to pee. I asked the woman behind me, a woman with a small girl, if she would hold my place.

What madness, I thought, squatting on the far side of the depot, teetering and struggling not to fall into the snow or wet myself. Flailing like a goose, I lost my balance and fell anyway. I cursed the world as I lurched to my feet, my derriere and skirt wet through. What kind of irresponsible God would give me a poor innocent baby to care for?

"Thanks," I said to the woman when I finally came back into line, my clothes freezing to my backside. How somberly the woman's child looked up at me, big-eyed and blue with cold, half-starved already. This was what I was bringing into the world. Not that rosy-faced boy in the sailor suit. Just another starveling. Someone who would never know a good meal, the thrill of a winter's gallop in a sleigh nestled under a fur rug. No, he would attend a school much like Liza's with its out-of-date textbooks, and potatoes cooked in castor oil. He would have cracked shoes and be inspected for lice. No Avdokia to take tender care of him. How I envied my mother, how I envied my younger self.

Now I was the servant. And mine would be a servant's child, that most expendable of expendable human commodities. I smiled at the little girl, tried to get her to smile back. Suddenly it seemed of absolute importance to see if I could get that child to grin, or stick out her tongue. I touched my tongue to my nose, whistled like a dove through my hands, pretended to insert my finger to the first knuckle into my nose, but she just stared, drawing closer to her mother. I had to stop. There just wasn't a smile in her. She was like a somber little woman, suspicious of my oversized child self and my antics. No childhood for these children of the revolution.

How selfish I was, to have this baby. So stubborn. What a romantic. Every bit as foolish as the foolish Yulia chasing her man to Tver.

At last, the line lurched on, the shop opened. After a time, I peered back at the shy little girl from between my fingers, like a mask. She clung to her mother's hand, staring at my odd Ionian clothes. Had she never seen a clown before? She was what, four? Five? What had she known but hunger, the hunched, resigned shoulders of women in their kerchiefs and shawls, their bags and worn boots and patched coats. But these women had been young once, had laughed, had danced, had teased a handsome man. There had been joy in Tikhvin, once upon a time.

I took my notebook from my bag and began to write something about the wasted time of all of us women, "A Poem to the Queue."

The little girl with the somber face had inspired me. I was tired of the clumsy drabness of my own thoughts. Fun was rarer than peacocks. It made me laugh. Not a sound much heard in a morning bread queue. The old woman in front of me, fragile shouldered, in a heavy scarf, turned my way. "What are you writing, *devushka?*"

I shrugged. "Something I was thinking."

"Something funny? Read it." She nudged another woman, a broad-shouldered *baba* with a faint moustache. "Listen, she's written a funny joke."

"Well, let's hear it," said the bigger woman. The lines on her face were weathered hard, like ironed taffeta, I swear I could hear her face crinkle when she spoke. "God have mercy, I could use a laugh."

"It's not done yet," I said. Tickled that someone would want to hear it, especially this crusty old girl.

"Go on." She squinted to read the tiny scrawl.

I couldn't resist. "A Poem to the Queue," I began.

> *Attention, comrades. Podrugi.*
> *Sisters, mothers, aunts.*
> *(You too, Granny.)*

"Snothead," the solid *baba* murmured good-naturedly.

> *It has come to the attention*
> *Of the regional soviet*
> *A widespread speculation*
> *In the matter of queues.*

They were listening, the two *babas* and the little girl's mother.

> *Look at these hours DAYS Weeks*
> *Squandered!*
> *You, sisters.*
> *Standing like tired horses*
> *Stamping before the station*

your steamy breath
Knee-deep in snow, in mud.
The waste of precious Soviet time!

Now they smiled, recognizing the official Bolshevik/*Pravda* tone, understanding it was a joke—a poem for them! More people turned to listen, a girl behind the woman with the child.

It must be
Capitalists! Foreign imperialists!
Wreckers. Take warning!
From now on
Time
Will be closely rationed by Narkompros.

Outright chuckles. I held my finger up to my nose, and then pointed, discreetly, at each one, a village admonishment. Laughter was like water in this desert. The *baba* with the moustache murmured, "Why not? They've rationed everything else." The woman with the child unconsciously stroked her long plaits.

This is not your old bourgeois time
Served up with lace and opera capes.
This is Soviet time you're wasting.
Soviet women
Measuring time in bread and sweat and shoe leather.

Therefore it's been declared
only a pood and a half of time
per family per week!

Now they were laughing openly, the woman in the wool scarf clapped her mittened hands to her cheeks.

The hours of your beautiful red blood

flow out with the hands of the clock.

Nobody's getting any younger,

> *Four hours in the queues?*
> *Such extravagance!*
> *And in wartime?*
> *It's counterrevolutionary*
> *Anti-Communistic!*
> *Down with the capitalist, piecework queue!*
> *Wrecking our days*
> *Digesting us whole*
> *consuming our Soviet dreams.*

Now I had come to the end of the written poem, but was caught up in the joke and the rhythm of the thing. I kept going, making it up like Misha's *chastushki.*

> *Slaves of the queue!*
> *I propose we*
> *declare this*
> *the International Day of Waiting.*

> *Sisters, we should demand speeches!*
> *Where are our medals?*
> *Our slogans?*
> *Our Internationale?*

We demand a newspaper
The Stander's Gazette.

"Call it 'My Varicose Veins,'" said the woman with the kerchief.
"'My Aching Feet,'" said the little woman with the patched coat.
Oh, the beautiful, phlegmy music of their laughter! I hadn't realized just how tired of creeping around like a kitchen mouse

I was, scuttling across the floor ahead of the housewife's broom. To touch for one moment these tired, hungry women, to lift their spirits, knowing we were not crazy, laughing together at the life we all found ourselves living, this ridiculous world that had us all by the throat.

A woman with two loaves had stopped to listen.

> *Our slogan —*
> *"Those who do not Stand*
> *Do Not Eat."*

I thought it was very good, but my sisters suddenly faded back into the submissive postures of the queue, freezing like jonquils caught in a late frost.

"Who are you?" demanded the woman with the loaves. "I haven't seen you here before."

"Just a joke, Alexandra Sergeevna," said the woman behind me with the little girl. "She wrote a poem."

The woman turned her flat-cheeked, gravel-eyed face to me. "A fine time to criticize our struggling Soviet system. Too bad about your petty-bourgeois dissatisfactions. This"—she waved at the queue, raising her voice like someone on a podium—"is no joking matter. We're fighting for our lives here. Our soldiers are spilling blood that's quite real. And we women are doing our part."

Sober morning gray returned to the faces of my listeners. There was nothing the least bit funny about being alive in the bread queue on Ulitsa Truda, *Labor Street,* in early spring 1919. I had forgotten myself. The day when one could safely stand on a street corner and proclaim poems to workers was over.

"Who are you?" she demanded again.

"Kuriakina," I replied. Did she need to see my labor book?

A woman in a felt hood said, "She's the new girl over at Korsakova's. She's took the place of the daughter."

The officious woman eyed me closely, as if memorizing me for a police report. I felt myself stiffening. I wanted to argue with her, defend my rights, my labor book securely in my pocket, but I'd grown cautious—something to do with my encounter with the Cheka, at Pulkovo, and in the cells at Gorokhovaya 2. With her self-righteousness, this puffed-up woman had to be a big local Bolshevik to dictate so freely to the others.

I shrugged. "Just a poem, Comrade. Having some fun. Making the time go faster."

Having told me off and spoiled the moment, she settled herself importantly, like a hen who'd been disturbed. "I could report you. Stirring people up against the government."

Oh God. "A little joke makes people feel less alone, Comrade," I said.

"Alone?" The woman hoisting her bread under her arm. "Does this look like you're alone?" She gestured to the queue, front to back.

"She's pregnant, Alexandra Sergeevna," said the woman with the little girl. "She's been standing a long time."

I touched my belly through my coat, wanting to hide him from this sour woman.

Her eyes narrowed, circled in black around the iris like a bull's-eye. "Why haven't we seen you at the Mothers' Course? We have an excellent Women's Club here. We're not some benighted village, you know."

Oh, the infernal Women's Club! "I'm just so tired these days, Comrade," I said. "I don't sleep well."

"We're building socialism, *devushka*. We have to take our place, mothers and grandmothers, and not grumble in the breadlines. There's a lecture tonight. 'The Future of the Family.' Seven o'clock. I want to see you there." She turned and briskly walked off, having done her socialist duty. It looked like I would be attending the Women's Club of Tikhvin after all.

The sun had come up, and the frost on the stones rose as mist into the sunlight. Although the sour woman had taken the steam out of the moment, a wisp of good cheer remained. I could smell it off the other women, just a hint of it, the way woodsmoke clings to your coat. The girl with the hollow eyes peeped out at me from behind her mother's legs, still staring.

3 *The Future of the Family*

After the men's dinner was cleared that night and my own portion consumed—devoured—I scrubbed the table, and Styopa helped me put the silverware back into the pantry. I would have liked to crawl upstairs to bed, but instead, I forced myself back into my coat and boots for the hike over to the old Duma building, the long yellow structure of the Tikhvin Soviet. What choice did I have? I had to live in this town, and now that I'd taken the risk of becoming known, I had to fork over my pound of flesh.

"You shouldn't go alone," said Styopa. "I'll walk you. It's dangerous out there."

I looked over at Raisa Filipovna. "She'll be fine," she said. "Just be careful. And watch your tongue." The thing I hated most. I clapped my fox hat onto my head.

I steeled myself as I approached the loitering soldiers under the one operating streetlight of the square, men who knew nothing about the New Soviet Woman, and were desperate for sex. "Hey, girl, come with me, I've got chocolate." "I've got some dynamite and it's about ready to explode." The chocolate was tempting but the syphilis held me at bay. If I were Misha, I'd point out they would have their share of explosions when they faced Admiral Kolchak and the Whites. But if I were Misha, I would not have to listen to this at all. Our poor, rude, ignorant Red heroes. Half the women in town wished they were dead already. Korsakova had to collect Liza from school herself, or I had to do it, you couldn't have a thirteen-year-old girl walking through a town like this by herself. I wished I'd said yes to Styopa Radulovich despite Korsakova's disapproval. My pregnancy didn't shield me—they would be happy to have me. We were coarsening like abused beasts, the whole country. We thought only of food, and sex, and sleep, of warmth and safety. No more morality, none of those *burzhui* niceties. I shut my ears and hurried toward the lit portal of the soviet like a small boat tacking toward a dock on a dark night.

A hand-lettered sign indicated ROOM 145, TIKHVIN SOVIET WORKERS' AND PEASANTS' WOMEN'S CLUB. LECTURE TONIGHT. Oh, were there any happier two words in the Russian language?

The Women's Club occupied two cold rooms toward the end of the hall, past the printing press and a classroom in which a potato-shaped woman was wearily teaching people to read. Her adult students sat, fist to forehead, as if in pain with the passage of a new idea, like they were passing a kidney stone.

In the first room of the Women's Club, a girl in a white scarf with a face like a pancake handed out tea with saccharine. A number of children played quietly under the eye of two other girls—too weak to make much of a racket. In the second room, fifty women assembled on benches and sills of the windows, some with babies in arms—an impressive turnout. The panes were frosted with their breath. The soviet clearly didn't consider the Women's Club worth sparing the firewood for. I saw the woman in the felted hood who had told the Bolshevik where I lived, and stayed away from her. The woman who'd had the little girl in the queue waved me over, opened a space on the bench for me.

"Get your maternity ration after," she advised.

Well, that was something to look forward to.

The Bolshevik woman came out with an armload of papers, wearing her coat against the cold, a red kerchief on her head, self-consciously echoing the Communist poster on the wall behind her. She rose to the lectern, puffing up to a round of applause.

"The commissar's wife. Alexandra Sergeevna," the woman next to me whispered. Followed by a derisive exhale.

Sergeevna cleared her throat and opened a pamphlet. "Last time, we talked about the four categories of housework doomed to extinction. Does anyone remember what they were?"

I worried a loose tooth—lower left canine. There was no hope of finding a dentist—anyone with any medical training was doing surgery at the front. I'd told Korsakova about it, but she'd shrugged, saying a woman lost a tooth for every child, it was normal. How privileged I'd been, I hadn't even understood the distance between my life and that of an ordinary woman. Now I would lose a tooth. Now I would truly become what I'd only been pretending to be, a nineteen-year-old proletarian on my way to becoming an old woman as the baby leached the precious calcium from my bones. I was being eaten alive. The Drops of Milk campaign would be a god-send. I shouldn't have waited this long.

"Four categories of housework are doomed to extinction with the victory of Communism," she read. *"In the future, the Soviet working woman will be surrounded by the same ease, hygiene, and beauty as the rich once had under Capitalism. Instead of spending her free hours in a private kitchen and laundry, she will have public restaurants and communal kitchens, collective laundries and clothes-mending centers, at her disposal."* She received a polite, apple-polishing round of applause. "Questions?"

A woman perched on the windowsill raised her hand. She had strange shiny blue eyes that contrasted oddly with her drawn, hungry face. "How'll they know whose clothes are whose if we all take 'em to the same place?"

Sergeevna frowned, blinked. It was not a question she'd expected, and clearly not one she welcomed. "I don't understand."

I actually felt sorry for this officious woman, trying to inspire these tired Fraus into envisioning a new socialist future, and having them worry about how they were going to reclaim their clothes at the nonexistent repair center. Women who had never taken their clothes to a laundry or a tailor, they couldn't imagine such an exotic exchange.

"At the mending center," the woman tried to explain. "How will they know whose are whose?"

The commissar's wife let out an exasperated sigh. "They'll fill out a ticket for you. And you'll bring it when you pick up the clothes."

"What if I lose the ticket?"

The speaker leaned on her stack of printed material and pointed to the poster behind her, a firm-faced Soviet matron before a series of upright shapes that could have been smokestacks and could have been rifles, the whole thing boldly titled FREE WOMEN BUILD SOCIALISM. "What's the point in having a hundred women at home washing their own individual clothes, when five women could have a paying job working in that laundry? With rations and a crèche. Leaving ninety-five women free to contribute to society. *Capitalism outmoded the family as a unit of production. Communism makes its domestic arrangements obsolete.*"

But the words she was using were meaningless to them: *unit of production, domestic arrangements.* She was making sense, but not to this audience.

She opened a pamphlet, smoothed down the pages. *"What of the mothers?"* she read. She pointed to another poster behind her on the wall. CHILDREN ARE EVERYONE'S RESPONSIBILITY. On it, two women, a peasant and a worker, stood with their children, a barn behind one, a factory behind the other.

"Society needs more workers and rejoices in the birth of your child," she valiantly read on. *"You don't have to worry about its future. Your child will know neither hunger nor cold. Society will feed, bring up, and educate the child. The joys of parenthood will not be taken away from those who are capable of appreciating them. But the old type of family is withering away, not because it's being forced out of existence but because it is no longer necessary. The task of raising children is passing into the hands of the collective."*

I tried to think of a country where people were free of the family. Of Father who leads and Mother who bows. Imagine that kind of freedom for women. Poor beaten Faina could leave her husband and make a life for herself.

"It used to be that you didn't worry about my children, and I didn't worry about yours," she explained. "But in our socialist society, any child in need is everyone's responsibility. Every mother's welfare. No mother, married or single, will be left on her own to care for her children."

The women shifted nervously, not completely ready to accept that they need not devote their lives to wiping children's noses and washing their clothes, that it wasn't the highest function of womanhood. A woman in a patched jacket stood. "I work over at the lumberyard, and I pay a third of my wages to a woman who watches my kids. When are we getting one of those kindergartens here, like you said last time?"

The commissar's wife flushed, that someone noticed there was a difference between the dreams of the spacemen and the facts of life in the streets and squares of Tikhvin. "We're not magicians, Comrade. I don't have to tell you we're in the middle of a civil war. We already give the children hot meals in school. Step by step. Any other questions?" She opened her book, clearly impatient to move on.

Another hand came up. "They say they're going to take the children away from the mothers. Is that true? Who can better care for a child than its own mother?"

Sergeevna's flat cheek flexed. "We're not taking children from their mothers, Comrade. We're offering the woman an opportunity to engage in the economic and political life of the socialist society. We don't need a hundred women each cooking dinner and ministering to individual children. It's economically regressive, when six women could free the rest for meaningful work."

These women didn't understand that the soviet was offering working-class women the labor arrangements that aristocrats had known for centuries. When was the last time an upper-class Russian woman raised her own children? Vera Borisovna certainly hadn't. I would be the first woman in my family to attempt it — my useless, incompetent self. I remembered the mess I'd made at Faina's, just trying to diaper her baby. We'd all been raised by governesses, tutors, and nannies, but it was a shocking, foreign idea among these peasants and workers, these provincial petite bourgeoisie. To release women from their position as family serfs, there had to be some way to care for the children. Nothing was going to change without it. I had been so ready to dislike this woman, but now I felt sorry for her. I couldn't help but see what a hard job she had ahead of her, trying to get the benighted womenfolk of Tikhvin to understand that there was more to life than motherhood and wifedom and pregnancy every spring.

"Think of being able to go to work without worrying about your kids," I blurted out. "Without paying half your earnings to some crazy old person who waters the milk. That's what she's talking about."

The speaker almost toppled with gratitude that someone understood what she was trying to say. "Thank you, that's exactly right."

"But what if they beat my kid?" asked the woman perched on the windowsill. "He's a brat but I wouldn't want no stranger beating him."

"Nobody's going to beat your child, Comrade. Abusing children is reactionary. We must never beat our children. Any other questions?" She looked around desperately, hoping someone would ask a question about the woman's place in future society.

"But what if they did?" insisted the woman. Now I recognized her, she was one of those busybodies in the queues who had wanted to know all about Korsakova's daughter.

I couldn't keep my mouth shut. "Well, what if you beat your own child? Is that any better?" There must have been something I didn't know about this woman, for the hall erupted in laughter.

"Well, it's my kid, ain't it?" she said defensively. More laughter followed.

"That's the point, Comrade," Sergeevna jumped in enthusiastically. "It's not *your* child—that's done. *My child, your child,* that's the capitalist way—I take care of *my* children, make sure *they* have everything I can possibly give them, but to hell with *your* child, even if it's starving, freezing, crying on the side of the road. *My* child, *my* property. What if my husband thinks of me that way? *I can beat her, she's my property, just like my horse.*"

"I'd like to see him try," whispered my seatmate. "I bet she rules that roost. I bet he has to sing for his supper."

"In socialist society, we've gone beyond all that." She pointed again to the poster, CHILDREN ARE EVERYONE'S RESPONSIBILITY. "Our children belong to all of us. We all have a stake in the future of the working class. Socialism's job is to lessen your burden, so you can make your contribution, knowing your child is properly cared for, not running around loose on the street or in the hands of whatever provision you can make. You are valuable to us, and so is your child."

My seatmate whispered, "I wouldn't give her a chicken to raise."

"I don't know. I could use the help," I said.

She patted my arm. "Wait until you have the baby. Then you'll see. Mothers aren't going to give up their children without a fight."

I couldn't bear the stubborn stupidity of the woman. "But wouldn't it be nice to know you could live your life without worrying, *Oh, if I leave my man, what will I do with my children?* You wouldn't be such a slave." *Like a tethered cow.*

"And maybe pigs will fly," the woman told me. "And shit bacon." Laughter all around us.

Sergeevna raised a hand to quell our un-Soviet mirth, and went on to read from another pamphlet, about a woman's duty to have children to strengthen the working class. Clearly written by a man, for what woman ever decided to have children out of responsibility to the collective?

In response, I felt the baby flutter within me like a flag, deep inside my body. Just a flutter, like a butterfly or a rustle in the trees. The revolutionary words had stirred it. "It's moving," I whispered. The woman smiled. The baby was telling me that it was ready for this new world. Girl or boy, it would grow up into a very different world than any of us could imagine. A brave girl, maybe, a real firebrand.

At last it was over and we rose to return to our homes. Sergeevna stopped me at the door, shook my hand. "Thank you for coming. I so appreciate having someone who understands what we're trying to do here."

I shook her hand and pretended I'd rarely spent a more fascinating interlude after a twelve-hour workday. "Women in the future will have more to live for."

She released my hand. She leaned toward me. "Perhaps you'll help us, a poet like yourself. We could use some slogans. 'Women, Take Care of Everyone's Children,' something like that. See if you can think of some. See you Friday."

The idea that there would be a Friday, and slogans, and Sergeevna on a returning basis, turned me to stone. The clamminess of her hand. The tremulous smile with which she regarded me. I hated people who had plans for me, even if it was with the best intentions. I could see her Bolshevik wheels turning. Maybe I could be roped into teaching literacy classes, or saddled with babysitting duties. My back ached, my legs, I wanted Liza to rub them, and I had to pee like a typhoon. "Thank you, Comrade. I'll see what I can do."

"And don't forget your maternity ration," she added.

Lord knew I wouldn't forget that.

4 *Stepan Radulovich*

After many advances and retreats, spring's troops at last broke winter's lines. Ice cracked in violent retorts on the Tikhvinka. It put everyone on edge, it sounded so much like gunfire. Admiral Kolchak, the head of the White Army, had emerged from his Siberian stronghold and smashed through the Urals. Kolchak was on his way. The railwaymen knew everything, what a relief to have access to the news again!

Styopa Radulovich and I lay in his bed in his single room at the end of the second-floor corridor—the room I'd begun to visit at the very end of my endless day. I had sworn I'd stay away from him, but had finally succumbed to the pleasure of a man's body up against mine, his rich, loamy smell, his kindness. His easy silences. He reminded me I was still young, still desirable. I was already pregnant, he couldn't do me any harm on that account, and I was lonely. He was modest in his sexual needs. It was wonderful just to have someone to talk to. When he wondered at the scarring on my back, the Archangel's souvenir, I told him it was something I didn't want to discuss, and he let it go.

After making love, knowing I liked it, he propped his map of Russia up against the blanket and traced the progress of the White advance for me with his one hand, scattering cigarette ash over the soft paper and the blanket like a weather report of light snow. It was better than any newspaper—especially now that only Bolshevik papers remained, where even defeats were presented as victories, or drumbeats to inspire further effort. But Vikzhel had the telegraph, they knew which trains carried troops and how many, where they were now and which way they headed.

I ran my finger along the eastern front, where Admiral Kolchak and his Siberian Cossacks had broken through the Urals. They'd just taken Ufa, the stronghold of Komuch, the Committee of Members of the Constituent Assembly—my father's people. But now it was just Kolchak, monarchy, and reaction. So much for liberalism. "Voted themselves out of office, and next day the Supreme Leader and his Cossacks marched in singing 'God Save the Tsar,'" said Styopa. I traced the long jagged line to the west of the mountain range that separated Asia from Europe, the Kolchak front. Every day, the Whites moved twenty-five, thirty miles closer to the Volga. It wouldn't be long until they took Samara and Kazan, on their way to Moscow.

I traced my finger down to the Denikin forces in the Don. Denikin's troops, reaction and pogrom. And my brother Volodya, whatever he was doing now. "Will Kolchak and Denikin join up?"

"They'll try," he said.

I nested my head on his shoulder, the one without the arm. He was always careful to conceal the stump, wore a nightshirt, that sleeve neatly knotted. His smell was of machines, of oil and cinders. "We're losing, aren't we?"

Soviet Russia, what was left of it, a tenth of what had been. Red in the center, like a heart, in a sea of White.

"But they've got a weakness," said Styopa, dropping ash on the map. "Sure, we've lost a lot of territory, but we're fighting back-to-back. That's the way you want to fight. Short supply lines. We can move men wherever we need them." He sketched quick zigzags back and forth across the heart of Red Russia. "See? Kolchak's got to send out all the way to Omsk for his laundry and shoe polish." His finger traced a straight line six inches east of the Urals. "Easy to cut anywhere along the line." The Trans-Siberian—always that train. My father saw its importance from the beginning. "The peasants are already rebelling behind the lines, in Irkutsk, and the Transbaikal." He pointed to areas in the Far East, places so remote I couldn't imagine them except in one of Ukashin's tales about hidden monks and their ancient rites. "Those atamans out there are as crazy as bedbugs. Even the stupidest peasants are unrolling red banners. The Red Army doesn't have to win, it just has to survive. The people will do the rest."

He folded the map and put it on his little bedside table. Berkovin coughed in the next room, reminding us how thin the walls were. Styopa rested his coarse hand on the mound of my belly. I knew he liked the way it felt, hot, like rising bread. Sometimes it irritated me, to be enjoyed in such an animal way, sometimes it felt reassuring. We lay in the light of his kerosene lantern, watching his cigarette smoke rise in the spring-scented night. The house was so quiet I could hear the ticking of his watch. He burrowed his unshaven face into my neck. It must have felt good to him, but it left me with a rash. "Do you love me at all, *lisichka?*" *My little fox, my redhead.*

I sighed and sat up, straightening my nightdress—sewn by myself out of a torn sheet Korsakova had given me. I was reluctant to lie, though he clearly wanted me to say yes. I whispered. "I love being with you. Can that be enough?"

He smiled, a little sadly, pulled me in for another kiss.

"Tomorrow?"

"I'll try." *Poor Styopa,* I thought as I left his room, closing the door so very gently, not to alert Berkovin. If only I could have warned him not to fall in love with me. But who ever listened to such a warning?

The night was full of snoring, one man so buzzily sonorous—Gendelev? Zhubin?—I could have hopped the whole length of the hall singing "La Marseillaise" and not have been heard. Yet still I crept down the hall in my felt slippers, skirting the noisier boards, thinking that this was how the world worked. How interchangeable we were. *Lost your man? Well, here's another, nothing wrong with him,* and his one arm would keep him out of the army. *Bozhe moi.*

I inched up the creaking staircase to the third floor, where Korsakova slept in the room opposite ours, listening as I held my breath and lifted our door by the knob before swinging it open—fast—and slipping inside. Closing it—but not all the way—and placing a slipper behind it to keep it from swinging open again.

I'd certainly become pragmatic. *How do you like that, Varvara?* Pregnant with one man's child, married to another, and sleeping with a man who got me a job in a boarding house—five arms between them. I shed my shawl and slipped into bed, Liza's braids ribboned on the pillow opposite. I tried not to think about how crude I'd become. I'd once wanted to live in a poem, but this was the real world, without grandeur or heroics. I needed a gentle man to hold me, a kind man with a ration card who didn't mind massaging my aching legs with his one strong hand.

Moonlight fell across my bed over the tops of the curtains. Although I was exhausted, the moon tugged at my blood. I wondered where Father was, now that Ufa had been taken. Was he dancing with his bright-haired mistress to "God Save the Tsar"? Were they together again? Was she passing information on their every move back to Moscow?

I thought about Siberia, the vast sweep of it. Beyond Omsk, Kolchak's capital, lay the terrible lands commanded by the Cossack atamans. Styopa said they flayed prisoners alive, men and women.

Disemboweled them. Tortured them in ways that made them no longer recognizable as humans. And through their territories laced the spider thread of the Trans-Siberian, which Papa's Englishmen had coveted like a string of diamonds. Maybe my father was on that train right now, heading for China. He and his horrible woman. Though someday, when my soul was placed on the great scales, I knew that I would be called to account for naming her. And she, for her own perfidies.

Walking together in the long spring twilight up by the ponds, Styopa and I attempted to talk, get to know one another. He talked about the loss of his arm, his former work as a mechanic, his current job in the station yard maintaining signals. He was resigned about the loss. "Just one of those things, *lisichka*." He talked about his family, all railway workers—father, a section boss on the Vologda line; his brothers and how they went fishing; his dear mama; a fragile girl he'd loved who'd died of a bad heart. The light lingered like a lover, reminding me of Kolya. *Little feet, where are you now?* The railwayman and I sat in the twilight where we could look back at the Uspensky Monastery with its massed cupolas and five bell towers like teeth of a comb, looking so much like that enchanted city under the lake. I waited to hear the bells from the tower, but they never rang anymore. The bell ringers were gone, the monks scattered, arrested, or hunkered down in the cloisters. The trees now covered by the mist of pale green.

I told Styopa I was married to a poet, who had left me for Moscow, that I was drifting, that he didn't know we were having a child. I said that my father was a typesetter, that my mother was very religious, that they quarreled. "There really are poets nowadays?" he asked.

"That's what I'm doing with the Women's Club. 'For children's sake, your help they need, / Soviet mothers, learn to read!'"

"Hey, that's good," he said, his weathered face smiling, potato-nosed. A kind and honest face. "You think of poets as guys in tight pants talking about clouds."

"All kinds of poets," I said. "Some aren't even guys."

* * *

Draftees thickened the streets like flour in gravy. They marched in groups, their heads newly shaved, they looked like so many taste buds reaching out to lick the air. It tasted raw and smoky, the tang of mud, the bitterness of spring. Peasant boys mostly, in rough clothes and bast shoes, herded in from the countryside like sheep rounded up from scattered meadows. I thought of village vengeance, how the peasants offered up the families they liked the least, pointed them out as hoarders and kulaks—*At least they left the family. Except Motka, they took him for the army.* No wonder the Red troops melted away at the first sight of Kolchak.

I dropped off the slogans at the Women's Club. Not exactly Blok, but it kept Sergeevna satisfied. I had to be careful with her—the appearance of reinforcements, anyone with a pulse, would be seen as water in the desert. As it was, she hinted that she would sponsor me for party membership, if I'd study and prepare. "Such a waste, a girl like you scrubbing pots." But the idea of becoming a party member, signing my life over to the Cause, turned my blood to water. I agreed with much the Bolsheviks were trying to do, but I did not *believe* anymore. I had used up my stores of belief, my cupboards were bare. I could hope that the Bolsheviks would achieve what they set out to do, but my heart and soul remained my own. If only I could squeak through the cracks of all ideologies and loyalties and demands and dictates in this life, with a little beauty intact, a little poetry, it would be enough.

In no hurry to return for pre-dinner duties, I strolled under the unfurling lindens, enjoying the symphony of birdsong, when I heard a gang of new recruits being marched to the barracks. I automatically stepped out of their path. "Marina!" someone called. I glanced up. Amid the usual pale, desperate faces of the draftees, among their patchily shaven heads and homemade caps, a tall recruit was waving at me. His dark eyebrows met in the middle—Bogdan! And there was hatchet-throated Ilya Ionian, and sandy-haired Gleb—marching together in a group of maybe twenty conscripts. I ran after them. "Bogdan!" I didn't care who saw me. He tried to run back to me but was stopped by a soldier's rifle.

"Look at you!" he grinned. "We thought you'd gone back to Petrograd!"

I could see the blood near his ear where the shaving had nicked him. "No one's going to Petrograd. Only leaving. How did they get you?" I was trotting alongside as the soldiers pressed them onward.

"The village turned us in."

Yes, Lyuda had warned me. *They're not all that safe there at Maryino. It's only a matter of time.*

"They burned the house to the ground."

A numbness came over me, dull and thick like a stifling quilt. A roaring in my ears. *Maryino.* The big dacha...my childhood and my mother's. My grandparents, my brothers. That lost world. I thought it would survive—that someone would always live there, even if I could no longer return.

"They roughed up the girls," Bogdan said. Meaning raped. Meaning beaten. But left alive.

"The Mother is safe," Ilya added in his deep singer's voice. "They got away. The Master. Magda."

The smoke, I could smell it. Burned it to the ground.

"Of course they would," I said. "Where did they go?"

Bogdan shrugged. That familiar gesture. Oh, for something familiar, I didn't realize how I would miss it! "I don't know. We woke up and they were gone."

"They'd been planning it all along," Gleb broke in. "Just like the Petrograd dacha. Left us there with our dicks in our hands."

"And Avdokia?"

"The old lady too." They'd taken her with them, and headed out, probably behind the Urals. How would she survive? She'd wanted to be buried in Russia, in the yard of the village church. I imagined my mother and Ukashin heading east now, into the madness of Siberia. And I would never see Avdokia again. I clung to Bogdan's rough sleeve, letting my tears slide down my face. Maryino, all gone, the big logs, the deep porches. Why cry? When I'd gotten out by the skin of my teeth. Knowing I'd never see it again. But I still thought it would exist. I *could* go back, someday. But the world wasn't made that way. It burned itself behind you.

"Enough," the guard said, tearing my fingers from Bogdan's sleeve. "He'll be back someday, girlie, if he's lucky." He shoved Bogdan ahead with his rifle.

"What happened to Pasha?" I called after them. "And Katrina?"

"They got away," my friend shouted back as Gleb lost himself among the other recruits. Katrina's love for her Pasha had saved her. As Gleb's would not have. Sweet Bogdan turned and waved once more. "See you back in Petrograd," he yelled. "I'll be dancing at the Mariinsky!"

"See you there," I called after him, as they marched away down the avenue.

So there it was. The end of Ionia. Drafted, abandoned, defiled, the house burned, and the Family of the Future flung to the five dimensions.

I felt time, the iron thing, groaning. Bogdan, turning the corner, disappeared. That sublime dancer—in the army. Like harnessing a prize thoroughbred to a caisson. Why couldn't there be a place in this world for someone not a soldier? The sweet, the gullible, the beautiful? Bogdan and Natalya, Andrei Petrovin, Seryozha. Only the Ukashins left standing, the Kolyas, the Arkadys, fanatics and criminals. I waved to the empty street, knowing we would never meet again in this life or the next. All of us disappearing into the tunnel of the terrible year, cloaked in thin sunlight.

5 *Dom 13*

May came in its robes of green, squeezing the darkness back. The baby wouldn't let me sleep. I did nothing all day but pray for night, but now in the brief dark, in the narrow child's cot across from sleeping Liza, I sweated and tossed. The only reality was this child, growing within me, my belly taking me hostage, commandeering me like troops on the move, requisitioning my reserves, billeting its soldiers within a body no longer my own, but collectivized. It was getting hard to breathe, I was exhausted all the time.

I imagined childbirth. They talked about it in the Mothers' Course, but a woman is not a cow. What if I died? I was only nineteen. Who would mourn me? Styopa Radulovich. And the child, if it lived. I should write something for him, or her, try to explain myself. I thought of Pushkin, the crowds that gathered outside his house as he lay bleeding on his divan after the duel with D'Anthès. The immortal Keats, dying of consumption in Rome.

> *Alas! that all we lov'd of him should be,*
> *But for our grief, as if it had not been,*
> *And grief itself be mortal!*

To have earned such a mourner as Shelley. The one-armed railwayman would write no elegies. What would remain of this unique sensibility that only I possessed, that would never come again? I crammed the pillow over my head, so Liza would not hear my weeping. What had become of my courage? I heard the lines from Tsvetaeva in my head:

> *For my poems, written so early*
> *That I didn't even know that I was—a poet.*
> *Breaking free like spray from a fountain*
> *Like sparks from a rocket...*

She was only sixteen. I was three years older, and had done nothing with my life but make terrible mistakes.

The baby roiled at the most impossible time, at midnight, hungry, craving more of that sunflower oil I knew was in the cabinet downstairs. I tried to find a more comfortable position in the narrow bed, a bit of unsoaked sheet, and thought about Dom 13, Moskovskaya Street.

I had been delaying my return to Korsakova's this afternoon—as usual—my bare feet enjoying the silky dust of the road, when I passed a sagging wooden house, not so very different from this one. In Petrograd they would have already pulled it down for firewood. I'd stopped to take a sip from the bottle of oil I'd just bought in the illegal market. I called it my *tip*, praying it wouldn't be tainted with kerosene. Sunflower, thank God. I could feel the calories surge into my blood.

"You know about this house?" the old man on the porch called down to me. I quickly capped the oil. Couldn't a person steal a sip of oil in peace? Was there always someone spying? "It's a post house. To the penal colonies. The Decembrists stopped here in 1826." His little cracked voice. "Fyodor Mikhailovich was here in 1849. On his way to exile in Siberia."

I hated when old people talked like this, like they were there in 1849 and knew Fyodor Mikhailovich. "That's a long time ago, Granddad."

"Fyodor Mikhailovich *Dostoyevsky*. Russia's greatest writer, you great ignorant redheaded cow."

I touched the splintered shingles, silvered with age. Dostoyevsky had stayed here on his way to Siberia. Right here. Of course I knew the story, about how he'd been hauled before the firing squad at the Peter and Paul Fortress, only to be reprieved at the last minute and sent to Siberia. The tsar's idea of a lesson.

"House 13, you've never heard of it?"

I stroked the shingles, pressed my lips to them. To think, in one of those sagging wooden rooms above me—maybe that one, with the broken window—had lain the greatest student of the mystery of man the world has ever known. Would ever know. I imagined him on the floor, his coat around him. Perhaps trembling with fever. On his way to Siberia, three thousand miles. *Peshkom—on foot.* I knew he wouldn't have been alone, but I felt his loneliness.

I never knew Dostoyevsky had stopped here on his journey, that lonely road to Siberian mines and wastes. Levitan had painted it—the famous *Vladimirka*. It was a testament to his elegant taste that he had painted it empty. No prisoners in shackles, just an empty country road under a heavy sky, a distant church at its tragic vanishing point. Only the title intimated the suffering that road represented. Each posthouse on the long journey to the penal colonies in the east bore a number, each one day's walk from the last. That road went through every Russian town, the road to exile and servitude.

And one of its Stations of the Cross was right here in Tikhvin, in a crumbling old wooden house on Moskovskaya Street.

Now moonlight glared in through the calico half-curtains, like the gaze of some goddess I'd somehow offended, determined to blow my ship farther and farther from my native shore, into this mundane exile. Dostoyevsky would understand me. Dostoyevsky, with his devils and desperate men. Raskolnikov too had turned at night like a chicken on a spit. Was I not a superfluous man? And whether he had become a monarchist and a reactionary or not, he spoke to our conflicted souls.

Across the gap between our little beds, Liza snored lightly — she had a slight cold. Gripping her old doll Ninochka tight, probably dreaming of the Warlord Dracula. Then in the morning, she'd throw Ninochka aside, ashamed to be caught clutching it. It made me smile — that odd age of shame. Perhaps I would have my child here in this very bed. Torn from my flesh, no Avdokia to rub my back, to pray, to tell me what to do. I could not stop thinking of those hospitals I'd visited, those ignorant nurses, no doctors at all.

All day, I could be brave, but sleepless in the silence of the house, I lost all courage. *Kolya, think of me.* I hoped my face haunted his nights. But I was sure he had forgotten me. He was no sentimentalist, only liked the flavor of love. Tried it on as he would try on a coat, and laugh at himself in the mirror.

The baby was hungry. *Get me something!* Bread, oil, there had to be something left unlocked.

I put my dress on, found the screwdriver the railwayman had lent me, and padded barefoot down the stairs, already guilty, slipping silently past the doors where men farted and snored, the air smelling of quiet grief and stale smoke, past Styopa's little room as he dreamed of railway switches and fish.

On the first floor, I searched the dimness of the kitchen for something to swallow, quick, like a dog. A mouthful of bread—the baby was ravenous and would not be satisfied. Kolya's greedy child. The cabinets were locked, the widow wouldn't have been so careless not to lock up the larder. But it wasn't hard to unscrew the hinges... Careful not to break the hasp, I lifted the small door away, slipped the bottle of oil out, and drank a hefty slug. Then another. Forced myself to rescrew the cabinet hinges. A perfect crime.

But I couldn't force myself back to our little room at the top of the stairs—like a coffin. I sat at the men's long table, my pale feet dirty, my ankles swollen like cudgels, my belly pressing high on my heart, which thumped like a woman beating a rug. I started to cry. For myself, for this lump of flesh, accidentally conceived. For this I'd given up my flame, this life. What of my grand destiny? What of my passion, my soul?

"Marina, what are you doing down here?" Korsakova in her nightdress and shawl, a candle in her hand. "Are you all right?"

I nodded, wiped my eyes, tried to look innocent, tried not to belch. Good-hearted Raisa Filipovna. How wretched of me to drink that oil. Would she notice? But no, she brought out a box of tea, lit the battered samovar, sat down at the scrubbed table. She looked like she'd slept no better than I had, her skin creased, her eyes grave. "I've been thinking, Marina. I've been thinking a lot, about the future. About the house, and Liza."

"I can't sleep either," I said, the oil rumbling in my gullet. "As soon as I lie down, the baby starts jumping. I swear she's going to be a dancer."

Korsakova bit her lip. "Listen. Listen, Marina, and try not to take this the wrong way. But your coming here, it was a mistake."

I blinked, trying to absorb what she was telling me. I'd grown stupid with my pregnancy. Panic clutched me. She knew I was stealing... oh God! "Was it something I did?" I tried. "I work hard, don't I?"

She wouldn't look at me, just wrapped her shawl tight around herself. "You're a good worker. It's not that." Her softened jaw, the subtle lines around her lips seemed deeper now.

"What is it, then?" *Please, God, I will never steal anything from her ever again, as long as I live!*

"It's impossible." Now she looked up, and her eyes, so unlike her fun-loving daughter's, like the sorrowing Virgin's herself. "Try to understand. She's such an impressionable girl, and she idolizes you. *Ponimaesh?*"

Liza? Was she talking about Liza? I knew I had done nothing wrong there. I encouraged Liza to love books, to recite Pushkin and Lermontov. I made her do her homework. What was troubling about that? That she had become more outspoken? More defiant? Oh, damn politics! What was I supposed to do, creep around on my knees, perfectly silent with my eyes trained on the ground? "They're revolutionary times…"

Raisa Filipovna's dark eyes looked so mournful. She ran her long hand against the lip of the well-scrubbed table. "Really, I don't believe you're married. I don't think you even know whose baby it is."

I tried to keep my mouth from falling open. *Children are everyone's responsibility.* How to even begin to defend myself. "I am married, I swear! And anyway, this is Soviet Russia—it shouldn't even make any difference."

She massaged her knuckles, her wedding ring was far too big. She hadn't had to sell it yet, though she'd been widowed for years. "Carrying on with Stepan Radulovich right in front of everybody, that does make a difference. Even in Soviet Russia. I can't have that again. I can't have it." Her ring, she was twisting her wedding ring. The thing I didn't have.

I tried to concentrate but it was like listening to voices when you swam underwater. Perplexing sounds from another element.

"She admires you. I hear your voice in hers. 'Marina says. Marina says marriage is outdated. Marina says children belong to everyone. Marina says, Marina says.' And you, sneaking down the hall at all hours of the night. You think we don't know? You think we can't hear you?"

The shame of it rose within me. Had they all been listening to me and Styopa make love? The whole house? No, it couldn't be. She would have fired me weeks ago.

"I'll give you a week to find a new position," she said firmly.

The heart of a kitten. I could see by those bruised, sleepless eyes, she didn't like doing this. But she would. She was a reactionary. The world was changing, and in her rigid, mother's mind, she wanted it to stop. She didn't understand it, and she was going to do what she could to keep it still.

I sat at the table, my mind an empty steppe. The Vladimirka stretched before me. Exile. The last thing I'd imagined—the Cossack army descending! Unsheathed bayonets flashing red gold in the lowering sun. Losing my place? This awful place? This narrow bed, these rough hands? These sleepless nights? My back, kinked with work, hips that groaned with stiff complaint, my aching knees, kneeling on these very boards? Losing all this? I wanted to laugh. I wanted to scream, *Take it, then! Who needs it? Your pots and floors and queues and rugs. Is it my fault Yulia was a slut?* But I had no idea where I would go. I had no money, no friends. It was difficult enough to find a roof and a job to keep rations coming, but without friends...I thought of Styopa, up there snoring away. How would he like this kitten now?

What would Sergeevna say if I told her Raisa Filipovna had thrown me out? I could denounce Korsakova as counterrevolutionary. *Look what she's done to me, a poor pregnant girl with Bolshevik sympathies. A landlord, a bourgeois!* But I could never do such a thing. Even I had lines I would not cross. She was just trying to protect her child in her idiotic way. It was true, Liza did listen to me, watch me, pepper me with questions, imitate my intonations, my expressions. "She's a smart girl," I argued. "I don't think becoming a pregnant housemaid is part of her plan."

"Keep your voice down," she said.

My tears spilled out, confusion and shame. "Raisa Filipovna, please. I won't deny it. I was lonely, and he was kind..." This poor widow, twisting her ring. Poor Korsakova, listening to us eke out our meager love. Did she envy me my puny pleasures? My one-armed railroad man? If I wasn't pregnant, I'd walk out right now. I hated having to beg, and yet, what else could I do? "I'll give him up. I didn't realize...Please, give me another chance." She looked so miserable. "I'll tell him it's over. You'll never have cause to doubt me." I'd earned my respect for the out-of-doors. I needed her more than I needed Styopa. More than I needed Sergeevna or Lenin himself. "Just two more months, I'll have the baby and be out of your life forever." Like a shot. Back to Petrograd or whatever was left of it. I'd find my faithless, worthless knight, someone who knew me, who understood my nature, who could even embrace it.

"No," she said, stiffening her back, drawing her shawl around her. "It's happening too fast. She'll be lost by summer. The men already joke behind your back, call you Styopa's barefoot bride. Liza's old enough to understand."

How could this be happening now? The ringing sound of my resistance to this was all I could hear. I wanted to scream, but instead I whispered, "The mother of a child, you wouldn't really toss me into the street like so much garbage."

She laughed, just one short bitter *churt*.

I imagined her, sitting up in bed, listening to me creep down the stairs, knowing that the railwayman and I would be making love as she held her book of morning and evening prayers. I wondered how long it had been since anyone had kissed her. "I'm sorry," I said. "Forgive me. Please. I'll give him up. I'll be a model citizen. I'll set a better example." In one last hopeless gesture, I threw myself at her feet, I grabbed her hands and kissed them. I felt like a character out of Dostoyevsky.

"Stop it. Get up."

How had I not considered her terror that her remaining child would turn out like the other? When, of course, she would, eventually. All girls grew up. But this was my neck we were talking about. My baby.

"Please." Wetting her hands with my tears. Everything was going against me. I was a gambler on a two-year losing streak. How in the world would I survive? *Mother, Don't Abandon Your Baby!* Women everywhere making the same desperate choice.

She pulled her hands away from me. "I run a respectable house. I know that means nothing to you. Nothing means anything anymore. But it does to me." Talking to her daughter as much as to me. *Respectable.* That relic. But everyone needed a line they would not cross.

"I promise. I won't do anything to upset you." I clutched her hem in my hands, twisting it, crumpling her gown. "You've been so good to me. I'm sorry I disappointed you. Your trust."

"I have to think of my own family." She rose, breaking my hold. Now she met my gaze. And I could see in her eyes, I was already becoming a stranger. She, next to whom I'd beaten rugs and ground grain, she who had told me the child would be a boy, was already tearing the thousands of silken threads that connected us. The second Fate, who bore the scissors, cut.

6 *The Barefoot Bride*

She'd given me a week. I had to think of something. I got up in the morning to stand in the bread queue, heavy-eyed, still not quite believing my time at Korsakova's was over. What was I going to do? I could no longer work as a porter. Anything I did, my pregnancy would make me look like a whore. Who would hire me now but soldiers? When I got to the head of the queue, I asked if there was any work at the bakery, and they looked at me as if I were speaking Japanese. I returned to the boarding house, silently served breakfast, not being able to look anyone in the eye—especially Styopa. My God, *Styopa's barefoot bride.* I blushed whenever I thought of it. I cleaned up, but would not talk to Korsakova, though she eyed me pleadingly. *Understand.* Well, I understood, but I didn't have to like it.

After dinner, I asked Styopa to take a walk with me, down by the river. The late sun glazed the water, its polished surface erasing the monastery's reflection, its cupolas and walls. I told him what had taken place in the night with the widow, that they all knew about us, what she had said to me. I had to look for a new position, but work was rarer than beefsteak. "All I can think of is joining the party and letting them ship me off somewhere."

"Don't cry," he said, wiping at my cheek with his thumb. He took my hand in his, drew it to his lips and kissed it. "Let's move in together. Find a little place. Hell, I should have thought of it sooner." His eyes were shining. "I get good rations. You wouldn't be the servant anymore, you'd be mistress of your own house. Put your feet up when you like it. You'd be a queen! What do you say? I've had it with the bachelor life. We'd get along fine."

I wasn't sure. It was true, we got along well. He was easygoing and kind. Lovable, even. It would be a safe haven. I could see no better option, no other options at all.

We found a place close to the station. A flat above what was once a tavern, abandoned now. And just as he said they would be, things were immediately easier. My chores were light—cleaning and cooking just for the two of us, making our single bed. I queued for bread, brought him his lunch down to the station in a bucket. I sat when I wanted, put my feet up. Like a queen, just as he'd said. And the privacy was truly glorious. I could sit for hours just watching the May clouds lick the blue sky. How delighted he was to come home in the evening simply to find me there, the place clean and orderly, clothes hanging on the line, a bath waiting in a tin tub, dinner scenting the air. I'd wash his hair and pour water over him as he told me what was going on in the war, where the troops were, what went on at the station that day. It didn't take much to please him. I could make a life here with my railwayman. Styopa's barefoot bride.

"You should divorce him," he said, looking at me over the rim of the tub. "Divorce him and marry me. The kid'll have my name. We could have other ones. I like kids."

The doves cooed through the open window in the warm evening. He wanted me to really do this. Marry him, have his children, spend the rest of my life here in this railway town. I could. I was one false step away from losing my life here. I tried to keep the panic from my voice. "Let's see how you like this one first," I joked, stroking my belly. I was playing house with Styopa now, but marry? He really thought I would divorce Genya and marry him. That would be the natural course of events, settle down with him in Tikhvin and become Marina Radulovich. I cared for Styopa, he was dear, but I did not love him. I rolled him a cigarette with shaking hands, tore the paper, took another one and managed to get it rolled, and stuck it in his mouth below the thick moustache, lit it for him as he steadied my hand with his wet one.

"You think I'm not serious?" he said.

"I know you are." I washed him with a sliver of soap. My heart squeezing itself into a walnut shell.

He came home a few days later with a serigraph of a mother and child. She was tying its shoelaces, and both their cheeks glowed a burnished red. He hung it over our bed. How he loved to look at it when he sat at the table drinking a glass of the *samogon* his friends brewed down at the machine shop. That picture! I could hardly bear to look at it, that awful *poshlost*, that treacle. A promise I never made to him. How it rebuked me. Now he wanted to know about my family, my past. I hated to lie to him, just begged him not to ask so many questions. A person had to have something of her own. We talked about his childhood, he talked about our future. What a good mother I would be, how smart my children would be, how handsome. Even minus an arm, he was the luckiest man in the world.

"I'm not that good a bet, Styopa," I tried to tell him. But I couldn't tell him why. That I was just biding my time, waiting to have the baby. That I really did care for him but would never love him as a man should be loved. Couldn't we just go on as it was? It was sweet between us that spring, and I didn't want to interrupt his delight in everything that had befallen him. He embraced what had been a relationship of convenience with the zeal of the believer. A new sun was rising on a new land, a new breeze blew through the greening trees.

In the evening, when the mosquitoes came out and the frogs chirped like a chorus of creaking doors, we walked up to the ponds to fish. We parked ourselves on boxes under the grieving boughs of the willow trees, and he baited his hook with his rod braced between his feet and knees. While he fished, I watched the reflection of the monastery hanging upside down in the green water. I kept waiting to hear the bells—but nothing ever broke the silence except the occasional splash of water, birdsong, sometimes the whistle of a train—people arriving or departing, their satchels heavy, bulging with foodstuffs, pockets tender with eggs and cheese. Tickets in hand, ready to brave the return to Petrograd with all its inherent dangers—confiscation, arrest.

I envied them. Just the sound of it: *return to Petrograd*.

What irony. Though I was living with a railroad man, I was the last person in Tikhvin who would ever climb onto a departing train now. Styopa would never help me leave, and he would thrash any of his friends if they so much as thought of helping me. *Petrograd!* I could taste it, the sea air, the big wide rush of the Neva, the sound of the gulls. Its wide paved streets, its three hundred bridges, I could feel their iron railings warm under my hands. The trees in the Summer Garden would be in leaf now, the statues unboxed. People who had read a book, who could talk about poetry, who cared about art. I craved it like a mineral missing from my diet.

"You should get that divorce," he said on his box. "Before the baby comes."

A splash, out on the pond. "Plenty of time," I said, brushing a mosquito from my forehead. "It's not due until July."

He reeled in his line, cast again. "Don't you want to?"

No, Styopa, I did not want to. I didn't want to look at that picture for the rest of my life. I didn't want to talk about the babies we would have together after this one. "It all seems pretty unreal," I said. "I feel like I'm in a dream. The baby. Everything."

He smiled. "It'll be real soon enough, little fox. Soon enough."

* * *

I lay in bed next to him, unearthly light flooding into the room through the uncurtained window. He snored next to me, low and regular. I tried to find a better position. Heartburn was eating me alive. I was sleepy during the day, but when I lay down for the night, no position would give me a second's respite. The baby had taken my body hostage and now it was in control, pressing up on my heart and lungs, down on my bladder, crowding me physically as my railwayman was crowding me with his hot, solid body, the arm he liked to throw over me as he slept.

What had I done to myself? I could feel the ground eroding from beneath me, like a riverbank collapsing. I had nowhere to run to. I needed Styopa to keep a roof over my head, a place to have this child. I liked him, and that would be enough for most women. I would think of something. If I left him, he'd be all right. There were so many women alone right now, and so few men, one-armed or not, he would have no trouble replacing me. But what of the child? That idea sank away, leaving me with the reality that I had no better option than this. Sooner or later, I would divorce Genya, and become Marina Radulovich, and raise my little son here in Tikhvin. I had to give up on the idea of flight. He would fish with his father, he would catch frogs. Forget the books I wanted to read to him, the things I could teach him about dreaming. He would become a simple provincial boy, no better or worse than any other. It would be the end of the Makarovs and all our culture and pretensions.

And what of me? How many little Raduloviches would I bear before I had enough? Before I forgot who I was and where I came from? Would I end up in the river, a bloated provincial Ophelia?

Styopa threw his arm over me, drew me close to him. I fought him off, it was too hot, and I could hardly breathe as it was. This tenant, crowding me out of the collective apartment of my own body. Kolya's precious child.

Much as I wanted to murder that man, what I would not give for a half hour with him. We wouldn't even have to take off our clothes. If only Styopa would stop talking to me! His favorite topics could be listed on ten fingers. One, fishing. Two, ice-fishing. Three, fishing from a boat. Four, the legendary pike he had caught twice but never landed. Five, his sainted mother. Six, the war. Seven, drunken antics with his friends. Eight, the one time he went to Petrograd. Nine, his little brother Toma, who died of scarlet fever. Ten, our family to come. How much better it had been when we had talked only about sex and troop movements.

I got up and used the chamber pot, pulled a chair up to the window and sat with my shawl around me, gazing into the beautiful, weary, light-filled night. In the bed, Styopa stirred, then settled. Even his snoring fell into a pattern. To think that once I'd sworn off rooms. And here I was again. In truth, life was nothing but rooms. I had not been back to the Women's Club since I'd come to live here, but I was tempted to return, just for the variety of it. This room, this waiting, the growing thing under my ribs, the incessant urination, the endless heartburn.

The sentimental mother and child across the room glowed in the unearthly light, rebuking me. If I ever burned this room down, I'd start with that picture.

7 *Agitprop*

June. Heat, green. I could not stay awake. I fell asleep on my feet in the middle of chopping a cucumber, my head drooping at dinner. I couldn't keep my eyes open. If only I could sleep, and never wake up. At night, I had bad dreams. I dreamed Styopa was rowing me and the baby on the ponds, rowing around in circles with a single oar. I dreamed I had the baby but it was a kitten, and then a doll as big as my hand, a crude doll made of burlap.

I sat staring out the window one day, when I noticed people hurrying down the street, running toward the station. No one ever ran in this town. Had there been an explosion? A fire? Not just barefoot boys but kerchiefed women, and children, men in caps and leather aprons from the foundry. I rose heavily and thudded down the splintery stairs, out onto the road, dirt under my bare feet. "What's going on?" I shouted.

"Lenin!" a man shouted.

Lenin? I doubted it, but just to be sure, I hurried along with the others, jouncing as fast as my swollen body would allow.

A woman called over her shoulder to a tiny boy standing in the middle of the road, his finger in his mouth. "*Davai,* Fedya!"

The station swarmed with people, more people than I'd ever seen in this town. And here was the reason. A great train steamed at the platform on red-painted wheels—a train the likes of which had never been seen in this dusty backwater or anywhere else. Boldly painted, car after car, with modern constructivist designs—strong silhouettes of arched-necked horses bearing cavalrymen, figures in black and white facing off red obtuse triangles and black circles. It bore the lettering, LITERARY-INSTRUCTIONAL TRAIN RED OCTOBER.

The last time I'd seen anything like it was in Palace Square on the first anniversary of the revolution—the same bold ardor, the same visionary energy. Now it had come to us. For the first time in months, I felt awake. Futurist designs blazoned every car. What a spectacle! Abstracted armies, bold Red soldiers with machine guns, workers with banners, or were they flames? Factories with smokestacks that might be cannons. The Guest from the Future had arrived, shaking our falling-apart town to life. Children raced around like gulls, clamored to be lifted up. The revolution had come to Tikhvin.

Ever more people crowded onto the platform to see the magical beast. They pushed and pulled like the sea. How had I forgotten this, the power, the vision, the possibilities of our time? Those endless dull meetings at the Women's Club, the days sweeping out our tiny flat, cooking, cleaning. The revolution was not about the four categories of housework! *This* was the revolution—iron and thunder, the Future.

The doors flew open, and people in white blouses spilled out of the cars wearing thick belts like acrobats, men and women too. A man in a leather jacket stalked up and down the platform before the cars, examining our faces as if memorizing us. Soldiers sat on the rooftops of every car, their legs dangling, joking, calling down to the crowd. A man in a white blouse began walking on his hands. I wondered if someone would begin to juggle or eat fire. It was a circus—a Literary-Instructional circus on wheels. Exactly what Lunacharsky had meant when he talked about the Revolutionary Carnival. This elation, this moment of glorious non-Styopa! For a brief instant, I was free from guilt and expectations, that possessive arm, his eternal fish and plans for our matrimonial future.

I spotted Liza in the crowd of schoolgirls and boys, chattering excitedly, reading the slogans, admiring the figures on the sides of the cars—no way the widow could blame me for this. It struck me—these murals were the Soviet equivalent of the iconostasis. Instead of Christos, the oversized figure was a worker with his banner. The gathering forces representing the eternal fight between good and evil being conducted right now, raging between the Volga and the Urals.

A soldier with an accordion on the roof of a car struck up "Dubinushka," *Little Hammer,* the old work song, and everybody knew the words: *Ekh, dubinushka, ukh-nem! Ekh, zelyonaya sama poidyot.* I joined in too—why not? I never felt myself more than simply a sojourner here, but as the strength of our voices grew, I felt proud to be among these people—citizens of Tikhvin. Russian citizens. Soviet people. We sang out to prove something to those soldiers on the carriage roofs. We too were the revolution. I even caught some of the railwaymen singing, despite how they felt about the Bolsheviks and their opposition to labor unions. I could imagine Styopa somewhere, singing under his breath. He too knew the feel of a hammer in his hand. The accident that kills the worker in the song, he had personally felt that blow.

The soldier on the roof didn't waste any time but launched right into the next tune, "The Cliff on the Volga," then some soldiers' songs: "Ogonyok" and "Wait for Your Soldier." And a new one most didn't know, though the soldiers on the train and the soldiers in the crowd taught it to us:

Again they prepare for us the tsar's throne.
But from the taiga to the British seas
The Red Army is strongest of all.

We were hungry for inspiration, as much as for bread. I realized that we had all unconsciously accepted the inevitability of Kolchak's arrival. Despite the best efforts of *Pravda* and the Tikhvin Soviet, we'd been steeling ourselves for defeat. This train was performing a miracle—breathing purpose back into our lungs.

Down the platform, a painted canvas bearing the slogan EVERY-THING FOR THE FRONT! and SOVIET PEOPLE'S THEATER rolled up, revealing a boxcar converted to a simple stage. We moved down the platform. I stood on tiptoe to see the play unfold. In swaggered Admiral Kolchak, in his customary white uniform covered with a fat tricolored ribbon, a medal as big as an ash can lid, and gold epaulettes a foot long, a bottle of champagne tucked under one arm. He was followed by three fat men in dress jackets and top hats. Each hat bore a flag—France, England, the United States. A fat priest with a long beard swung a censer as the Entente pulled money out of bags and crammed it in handfuls down Kolchak's coat and into his cap as fast as they could.

"That's right," the man next to me said. "He'd fall apart in two seconds without the English."

"Down with Kolchak!" people shouted.

Kolchak mounted a tall-backed chair, transformed into a throne. The Entente and his own generals were about to invest him with a tsar's crown and ermine.

"The Supreme Ruler of all the Russias," the assembled actors called out, and began to lower the crown amid the crowd's boos and hisses, when a group of Red Army soldiers burst in.

"*Urah!*" the crowd shouted. The old man next to me on his toes, yelling in my ear.

The Entente stole away, leaving Kolchak and his White officers to battle the Red Army—identified by their familiar pointed felt caps with the red star, their bayonets fixed.

"Get them!" the schoolboys called out. "Kill them! Get the Whites!"

As the Red Army men advanced, Kolchak and his generals scrambled away, until, at the decisive moment, Kolchak slipped and fell on the scattered money, and knocked himself out on the floor. Great howls of laughter from the crowd. The generals went running, one of them smart enough to bend over and retrieve the champagne.

The few remaining White officers, also marked by giant epaulettes, attempted to protect their leader, but our Red soldiers easily overpowered them and ran them through. Finally, the Red Army men stood center stage, one with a foot planted on the pile of dead Whites, and broke into "The Red Army Is Strongest of All," and now we knew the words. I wondered if Korsakova was here, if she could see Liza singing along. *A different world's being born, Raisa Filipovna.* Her daughter would be part of it, and my son as well.

And then I saw him again, the boy in my dream, the brave little boy with whom I had run in the streets of Petrograd in the rain, hand in hand. His sensitive spirit, his courage. I felt him take my hand. There might be a future, for me, for him. And where was my courage, where had it vanished to?

The next agit-play illustrated the dangers of speculation and hoarding grain. Aptly chosen, as the town was a real hub for it. The set quickly converted into a factory, a few boxes and uprights nailed together, an old wheel, a shelf out of a wide board. Actors hammered on the bottom of a washtub and a big can to symbolize metalwork. Our brave workers in the city, weak with hunger. One hungry worker collapsed at the bench, while the others gathered around, pulled him up again.

> *I must produce this engine fine*
> *So the trains will run, and the peasants down the line*

Will get their scythes, their hammers and harrows.
But so little food, the rations get smaller all the time.

Another, holding a hammer with a hand that honestly looked like it had never held so much as a can opener:

I don't know why the worker must starve.
We're the ones who unseated the tsar.
We braved the bullets in '17.
We gave them the revolution.
But all we have is a heel of bread.
Who is it starving the nation?

In the next scene, we saw who. A fat peasant family, their clothes stuffed with straw, ate away at a huge loaf of bread, bags of flour piled in the corner. The kulaks. I hated this black-and-white simplification. Of course the peasants were hoarding. It was inevitable. When people didn't know what the future had in store, naturally they held back. When the detachments paid nothing, when the peasants couldn't buy anything they needed, who could blame them for hoarding? But on the other hand, the workers were starving—that was true as well. Scarcity, setting city against country. How were they going to solve that with caricatures and antics?

A knock on the izba door—the speculator. Boos from the audience as he bought a huge bag of flour, and the conspirators drank a glass of vodka all around.

A second knock on the door. The Committee of Poor Peasants, in their rags. "Go away!" the fat peasant called out, as the family scrambled to hide the grain under the tablecloth. The committee threw their shoulders against the door as the peasants on the other side resisted them. Finally, they knocked the paper door down, as well as the wooden doorframe it hung from. All around me, people laughed and cheered.

A big peasant from the committee pushed to the fore. Beard or no beard, I would know him anywhere.

All around me, the crowd yelled to the big man, "It's under the table!" "They're hoarding, the kulaks!" "They sold it to the bagman!" "They had plenty enough for that rascal, didn't they?"

How well my husband looked. Well fed and strong, grown up—so much less unformed than he'd been on another platform, before another train, when he'd fled to Moscow with that little mink Zina Ostrovskaya.

"Who gave you the land?" he boomed. *"Who got rid of your master?"*

I couldn't believe he was here, just a few yards away, wearing that ridiculous beard. Planting himself across the stage like a tree. The kulak wife simpered, tried to distract him, arching her back, twirling her braid. She reminded me of Faina.

His rich voice rolled like a train.

> *In the year '17,*
> *It was us, not God, who gave you this land.*
> *The poor, the worker, the soldier.*
> *Now your brother workers are dropping from hunger*
> *On the front, your brothers are fighting for you,*
> *Keeping Kolchak from your hut and your wife.*
> *Do your part, peasants!*
> *Be part of the new world!*

"Watch him!" the crowd yelled. "Watch him, now!"

The short, tubby kulak husband began sneaking out with a bag of grain over his shoulder. Genya seized him under one arm and lifted him off the ground as his legs ran in the air. The crowd roared with laughter. The Red Army soldiers came in, and Genya and his peasants handed over the kulak and the grain, and then everyone sang "The Internationale," arms resting on one another's shoulders.

All the things this man meant to me. I took off my scarf. I was not afraid for him to see me—huge, cornered, having made every bad decision. I wasn't the girl he'd met at the Cirque Moderne, but he wasn't that boy either. Where was my art, my beauty, my love?

I'd taken my choices all the way, and this is what it had come to—a barefoot bride about to have a baby in a railway town.

"Comrades," Genya spoke to the crowd. "The revolution is in your hands. The army needs to be fed if they're to protect you from the Whites. The workers can't make guns, they can't repair trains, if they're starving. Everybody must pay his share. There's no yours or mine now, only ours. Long live the Soviet Socialist Republic!"

The roar of the people. "Up with the Soviet!"

"Down with speculation! Food for the workers!"

Yes, people needed to be reminded that the land was only theirs by virtue of the revolution, and it could be lost as well as gained. If this agit-train couldn't do it, I didn't know what could.

Now people moved down the platform toward the doors of the People's Kinotheater. I watched Genya edge his way up toward a car painted with a rising sun. I began to push my way toward it. But now I saw Styopa, scanning the crowd for me. Quickly, I tied my kerchief back on—peasant style, under the chin, hiding my face—and traced a half-circle around him, my eyes on the car into which the actors had retreated. Keeping my head down, I marched up to one of the carriage doors where three soldier-actors lounged, smoking. Or were they real soldiers?

Oh yes, I recognized that air of threat, the joking potential for violence.

"I have to see Gennady Yurievich," I said, gripping the hand-hold, but a soldier pushed into my path, blocking my way.

"I bet you do, little mother. All the ladies want to meet him. He's a regular Chaliapin." His ugly face close to mine, leering.

"Tell him Marina is here." My spine straightened, I had not made it this far to be wiped off like mud on one's boots. But the soldier made no move, just leaned against the car like a man outside a tavern. "Go tell him! He'll want to know."

"Which Marina?" the soldier drawled. "Camp-follower Marina? Maybe that's a bomb under there." He tried to lift my skirt with his rifle. The others laughed as I slapped it down.

"Kuriakina," I said sharply. "Quick! I don't have much time." My heart thudded like a perch in a bucket, my breath tight with what room the baby had left for my lungs. My heartburn flamed. Oh, hurry, Comrade Son of a Bitch! I glanced around for Styopa. Finally, the soldier with his knobby forehead retreated into the depths of the car. The others watched curiously.

A moment later, down the platform, Genya burst from the last door of the car like a man hurtled by an explosion. He shoved his way through the people who wanted him to stop and talk to them, fighting his way through to me, and then his arms were around me, lifting me into the air. He was crushing the baby.

"Stop, Genya!"

That's when he realized something had grown between us. He put me down, backed away from me, and now he could see how it was. My belly, my ragged clothes, my bare feet, my hollow cheeks, the wear of sleepless nights.

He came back and embraced me tenderly, his head on top of mine. He remembered me. I was saved.

"Whose is it?" he whispered.

Oh God, not that. I was sick to death of lying. What did I do every day from sunup to bedtime? It made my very bones hurt. "It's mine," I said defiantly. "Please don't ask me anything more."

We gazed at one another. *God, please give me another chance,* I prayed. Could he see my desperation? I needed him. *Help get me out of this place.* I glanced behind me, searching for my benevolent dictator, my relentless Tikhvin husband. "Can we go inside?"

He hesitated just a moment, unsure, knowing from experience that I wasn't to be trusted, and yet longing for me just the same. That hadn't stopped. He led me by the hand into the carriage, past the skeptical soldiers, who now stepped back, tipping up the brims of their caps the better to see and wonder. Inside the car, actors changed clothes in the compartments, and soldiers loitered in the corridor. It smelled like powder and sweat and old boots. The tall blond woman who'd played the kulak wife sat in a compartment knitting. She stared at the way Genya was holding my hand.

"Everyone!" he shouted, his arm around me, holding me against his side like a newly emerged Eve. "This is my wife, Marina Dmitrievna Kuriakina. She's coming with us!" Playing to the house. Same old Genya. He looked to me. "Right? You're coming?"

My heart popped in my chest like a thin-skinned grape. *Yes. Yes yes yes.* "Give me fifteen minutes. I have to get a few things." I'd worked too hard to get those papers. I would not leave them in that hot little room—my clothes, my gun.

"I'm coming," he said. His face, familiar yet different. No longer any traces of boyishness. The broken nose, the hazel eyes. "I'm not letting you out of my sight. Not to sleep, not to take a shit. I'm going to be there for it all now."

Together, we climbed the rickety stairs to the little room I shared with Styopa. I thought the staircase would collapse under our weight. Genya's presence shrank the room to the size of a mouse-hole. Had I really diminished myself so much that I could even exist in such a place? This bed, these blankets, that cupboard, this table.

He peered at the serigraph above the table. "Nice," he said. "Is it an early Kandinsky?"

"Malevich," I said. I threw my few things into my old game bag, my labor book, my journals, fished out the gun from behind a loose board in the wall. I took my sheepskin and my boots and my fox-fur hat.

I stopped to press my head against Genya's, forehead to bony forehead. "Tell me I'm not dreaming."

He pulled me into him, his two big arms, his two hands. Crushing me, kissing me. He still smelled of himself, leaves and moss, and hay. "Just don't wake up."

I was shoving my swollen feet into my boots when the door banged back, and Styopa stood in the doorway. No, we weren't dreaming, because Styopa wouldn't be in it. Oh God. I had hoped to leave a note and be a hundred miles away before he found it. But here he was, big as life, looking like he'd walked into a wall. I felt myself shriveling like a snail you'd just poured salt on. I didn't want to hurt him. He'd built up all his plans, his dreams, around me and my child. How cruel were the gods. The terrible bewilderment on his face. "I was just coming to get you."

I knew how this would look—like I was running off with the first handsome Bolshevik who'd passed through town. But would the truth be worse? Would it make sense?

"Styopa, this is my husband. Gennady Kuriakin."

He turned his gaze to Genya, and the bewilderment began to smolder. "The one who left you for Moscow? The one who abandoned you?"

"Wait just a minute, pal—" Genya said.

Before either of us could see what was coming, Styopa stepped in and punched Genya in the gut. He might only have one fist, but my God, it was an iron one. Genya doubled over, and as he came down, Styopa kneed him in the face. When he dropped, Styopa kicked him brutally.

"Stop it!" I threw myself between him and poor bleeding Genya before he could kick him again. God, what a mess. "He's my husband. Please, try to understand."

"You whore! She said you were a whore. She told me to watch out for you!"

Genya was still writhing on the ground, trying to catch his breath. "You told him...I *abandoned* you?" he wheezed.

"We're going to get married!" Styopa wept, a grown man. It was the most painful thing I ever saw. "Raise the kid, it's all going to work out. And then this scum shows up and nothing ever happened? You big dumb shit. Why don't you go back to Sovnarkom or wherever you came from and steal somebody else's wife." He got in another kick before I could stop it.

"Styopa." I tried to pull him away from my wheezing husband. "We're not getting married. It's over." Ah, how horrible, but how liberating, to tell the truth. I could hardly bear to see his face, still full of fury but now crumpling like an old paper bag. He had finally heard me. He stood with his one arm pressed to his eyes, shaking. I thought he might have a seizure. "I'm sorry. Please, try to understand—I never thought I'd see him again."

"You filthy whore!" He was sobbing unabashedly now, his moustache sagging, his lashes dark with tears. Then he threw himself on me, kneeling, and clutched at my dress. "Don't leave me. I'll kill myself if you leave me."

He was tearing my heart, I could feel it shredding, and yet, I could not stay. "You're better off without me, and that's the truth." I wrested myself free from his grip, grabbed my sack and helped Genya, still retching from the blows, to his feet. Watching Styopa's right hand clench and unclench. "I've got to go. Find another woman. You'll regret it if I stay, you know you will. You'll never forgive me." Everyone regretted me sooner or later.

He wiped his tears on the back of his one arm. If only there was something I could do to lessen his suffering, but I didn't know how to save him and save myself too. "Beat it, before I kill you both. You bitch. I should throw you under that fancy painted train. Damn you and Lenin too."

And so we left him there, weeping in the steaming ruins of his life, another luckless soul dearly wishing his path had never crossed my own.

8 *On the* Red October

Ah! To be moving! The wind in my face, the rumble of ridden thunder, rocking me, shaking the dust from my feet. The speeches of the giant wheels declaiming the miles, fire and steel, hurtling me away from Tikhvin and all my compromises, Styopa's heartbreak, floors and brooms and kitchens. I felt like all the clocks in the world had started again. At a time when any ratchety milk train creaking and screeching its way back to Petrograd would have been enough to fill my heart twelve times over, this was the Literary-Instructional Train *Red October*, a demon, a carnival, a smoke-belching volcano of the Modern. Soldiers from Tula and sailors from Kronstadt caught rides with us, heading for the front—the very sailors who had brought the *Aurora* up the Neva to train its guns on the palace, the vanguard of the revolution. We had hard-bitten Bolshevik politicals, we had actors and journalists. And everyone was enlivened with determination, even vision. Hope unfurled like a flag—now I remembered it. No longer was I sidelined in Tikhvin or Ionia or East Mudhole, Wretched Hut Oblast, I was back on the train of the revolution, from which I'd somehow fallen, hauled aboard by Genya's strong hand. So many things had come between us, I thought as I slept tucked under his chin in his compartment, listening to the song of the rails, *clickety-clack*. Vera Borisovna, Kolya, my life's nightmare turn, the months at Ionia, my tenure as the barefoot bride—yet somehow I had risen, again breathing the shocking air of the Future, like Persephone walking into the sunshine after her months in the underworld, blinking to find that color had returned to the earth. Lupine and cornflowers surrounded us as we raced through the fields of June. Again, there were sounds! Train music and meadowlarks, accordion and guitars, Genya reciting his verse, actors with their thrilling voices, the new songs the soldiers sang, bawdy *chastushki* and rousing anthems. How muffled Tikhvin had been, wrapped in cotton, my ears packed with straw.

Genya, my Genya, sweet. Pulling me aboard his life just as he had in 1917. And away we rode, hurtling across Russia toward the front, where the civil war raged. Was I afraid? I was more afraid of Styopa, of the Tikhvin Women's Club, dirt of a stalled mediocrity filling my mouth, packing my nostrils, muddying my eyes, as I disappeared into the ground. Our sailors and soldiers gave me strength. Truthfully, we wouldn't be the ones up against White bayonets unless the train itself was attacked. But a fight to the death would be a finer fate than moldering to the end of my days, eating my way in a circle around a peg in the ground. Racing across the green fields on the agit-train, I felt free. Like some crazy giantess, I could stand astride continents. I needn't cut myself down to fit Styopa's bedframe any longer.

As we made our way through the countryside, I eyed the sailors and soldiers smoking on the roofs of the cars, taking in the sun like seals, the sound of their easy laughter—protecting the *Red October* clearly a plum job. How I envied them riding up there in the fresh air like kings. Though there was plenty of room inside the train, many of them preferred it on top, for the view and probably the freedom from the eternal speechifying of the politicals, their dead earnestness, not to mention the artists with their theories and the actors rehearsing and squabbling, talk they said made their heads ache.

At one agit-stop, as the train prepared to leave, I could resist no longer. Making sure Genya wouldn't see me—he'd grown so protective!—I grabbed the hot iron ladder and climbed, glad I was wearing my boots. Though bare feet would have given me a better grip, they would have burned. The baby unbalanced me, making even that little ascent a challenge. Where was Esmerelda the tightrope walker? One of the sailors, Slava, from the fortress island of Kronstadt, leaned over the edge and saw me. "What are you doing, little mother?"

"Need some air, Comrade," I shouted up to him. "You can't hoard the view, it belongs to everybody."

"Don't fall, then. We're about to leave. Steady." Strong arms and cheerful faces handed me along, across to the rooftop platform on which they sat, and they cleared a place for me.

As I took my place among our sailor escorts and the hitchhiking soldiers, I felt as I had when I'd climbed into the boat on the Rostral Column, that soar of spirits I never expected to feel again. The train jolted, and I shrieked and clutched Slava's arm. The train was moving. "Hang on, little mother!" He grinned.

The smoke made me choke until we picked up good speed, then it thinned out, chased away by the wind pounding my face, howling in my ears. I quickly retied my scarf under my chin as the sailor held on to me. It was glorious, terrifying. The sound—the speed! I'd wanted to ride up here since I'd first seen them, and now I was on top of the world, clinging madly to the striped-shirted sailor. Ah, the rush, the sweep of the horizon, this enormous country headed into its future! I felt like I was riding time itself, the sun on my face, the freshness of the fields, the great green expanse of Russia in the blue bowl of her heavens.

And my husband down below, hard at work in the old dining car, writing, discussing a pamphlet with the printers, making plans with Marfa Yermilova, our grim-faced political officer, the oldest of them all and senior in command. But he might as easily have been writing a speech or rehearsing a new sketch with the Communal Theater of the Future. I knew I should be down there with him, helping in some way, proving I wasn't just a drain on resources, Genya's barefoot bride. But I craved the wind and the open air the way some craved wine or a lover's touch.

Suddenly we were slowing—the hollow grinding of wheels, the pitch dropping, the shockingly loud whistle crying out into the blue day, smoke back in our faces. I held tight to Slava, a sailor far from the sea.

"Hurry up, brothers!" Slava called out to peasants, running toward us across their plowed fields, their green wheat, stumbling and scrambling to get word of the war, of the outside world. *We* were their newspaper, their telegraph, their harbinger of spring, dressed in the bright plumage of their wildest dreams. What a visitation we seemed to them, what an apparition. "Greetings from the revolution!" I shouted into the wind. We slowed but did not stop, while from the open doors of the press wagon two cars ahead, pamphlets flew out like birds escaping from fallen cages. "Down with Kolchak!" we shouted, shaking our fists. "We'll win it yet! Good harvest!" And they waved back, clutching the white sheets in their hands. They grew smaller and smaller. One boy ran after the train, then stopped, watching us leave. I knew that heartache, watching the future leaving without you.

Now Genya's head poked up at the top of the ladder—his tawny hair close-cropped under his cap, face dark with worry. Spotting me, big belly in my lap, sitting happily among the soldiers and sailors, his anxious expression fell away, replaced by a quick grin, heavy-boned, handsome face alight, and then the clouds returned. "What do you think you're doing up here?" he shouted as he crawled up onto the roof. The sailors and soldiers shouted when they saw him, helping pull him along. They all wanted to touch him, thump him, steady him—a man just like them, and yet, possessed of this song, a bargeman-Keats, giving voice to things they had dreamed but never expressed. They treated him as they would a popular sergeant, and he could have been one, if you didn't know him better. For all his talk about smashing this and beating that, I knew he couldn't even kill a spider, let alone the bourgeoisie, Whites, or the kulaks whose blood he was clamoring for. His tenderness was our secret. "Are you crazy?" he shouted to me. "Don't you have one atom of sense in your head?"

My father used to say the same thing. But Genya was the one climbing along the top of the train while it was still in motion. He cautiously settled next to me, steadied by the sailors, who moved over to make room for him.

"Would you let your woman ride on top of a train?" he accused Slava.

Slava shrugged. Generally, the civil war attitude was every man for himself. "You should be proud. A woman who isn't afraid of her own shadow. It'll be good for the kid."

"Why didn't you tell me where you were going?" Genya was still upset. "I couldn't find you. I thought we'd left you behind," he shouted into the wind. "Olga said she'd seen you come up here."

"It's glorious!" I leaned against him, my face to the wind. "What are *you* doing up here? Don't you have speeches to write?"

"I had to find you. I couldn't wait." He pulled off my scarf and let my hair blow wild, whipping his eyes. "Had to see that flag flying."

I snatched my scarf back and with some difficulty got my hair back under it.

"You are the craziest woman I've ever met." He crammed his cap tighter on his head, touched my cheek with his enormous hand, the other circling my round belly, as I sat back against him. "There's nobody as crazy as you. Other people listen to me now, in case you haven't noticed. But you still treat me like that kid back on Grivtsova Alley."

And they did listen to him, asked him questions: *Comrade, how should we word this? Comrade, news from the front*. He was the one with the *propusk* from Lunacharsky himself, putting him in charge of the train's theatrical-propaganda mission. The very idea that people thought him wise, that they turned to him, that they asked him things, not knowing who this was, made me laugh. A futurist poet, running a train during a civil war? It took some getting used to. But I thought of Varvara at Smolny, when I'd visited her to get help for my mother, how they'd pestered her for decisions, a nineteen-year-old girl. The revolution sped people along.

"You need to grow up," he yelled. "And stop pulling stunts like this. I have to concentrate—I've got other things to do besides worry about you." He pulled me against him, kissing me, his shaven face rough against my neck and cheek. "You've got to start thinking like a mother, and not some wild girl."

I couldn't believe what was coming out of his revolutionary mouth.

"What if you slipped? What if you fell?"

"Yes, Avdokia." How boring. It was the worst thing about carrying a child, people were always telling me what to do. The merest stranger imagined he had the right to tell me how to live and when to breathe. As if I had become less adult for being a woman, a mother-to-be. "You're more likely to fall than I am. *Buivol!*" *Buffalo*. "You're an unstable character."

We rode along, enjoying the sun and the wind and the roar, happy to be together again, as we always should have been. Then the wind shifted and gave us a face full of smoke and cinders, everyone covered their noses and mouths, coughing, eyes stinging, before it cleared out again. Ah, the song of it all, the train, the fields green, the tiny villages nestled against the forest way out in the distance. The engineer pulled the whistle, and though it deafened you, the villagers would hear the train, and see us, bright on the horizon, and know they hadn't been left out here all alone, that the revolution hadn't forgotten them. They too were part of the Future. That was our task, to move behind the front and remind the peasants they had to keep the Red Army fed, to support what was being done for them, and not turn on our troops, not weaken us from the rear.

I wondered when we would get to the front. Hard to know. We should have already been there, but we'd been sidelined again and again in favor of troop trains, or else our destination revised overnight due to a sabotaged bridge or track. In the end, what did it matter where we were or when we got there? "The villages are more important than the towns," our commissar, Marfa Yermilova, inevitably reminded us. "The workers already know which side they're on. Kolchak's troops check the palms of prisoners, and hang the ones with calluses. It's as good as a party card. But the villagers can go either way."

At the moment, Kolchak and his general, Gaida, were being pushed back to the Urals. The revolution had them on the run, but the war moved like the waves, fronts were fluid, anything could happen on any day—the fleetness of cavalry, the surprise of local partisans. And you could never put aside the potential for pure peasant revolt against whoever's troops were most recently marching through. A far cry from the trenches of the last war.

And now we were riding into the thick of it, as full of fire as the locomotive pulling us eastward. My heart crashed in perfect time with the heartbeat of the *Red October*. Me and Genya, together again, heading toward the battle zone, his chest supporting my back, which didn't even ache anymore, not at the moment, the shaking of the train loosened all the knots.

"I'm so glad I found you," he was saying in my ear. "And in that shithole. I hate those towns. They make me feel like I'm suffocating, just the look of them."

He understood. He came from a town smaller than Tikhvin. People thought it was safe in little burgs like that, that they could escape the chaos of the cities, but it was so stifling, without any of the city's expansive joy. Lock the doors and the windows, then peek out from the curtains...Korsakova, Sergeevna, all of them. I still couldn't believe I'd escaped.

"The look on that guy's face." Genya laughed, nestling his cheek against my kerchief. *"Don't leave me, you whore!"*

Poor Styopa. What a nightmare. I couldn't bring myself to laugh at his misery. "He wanted me to divorce you," I said over my shoulder. "He was quite a catch around there. Category 1 rations." Marrying someone for his rations, what a world. How near I'd been to giving up. *That was the real world, Genya, a match like that more common than love.* This was the dream.

"You wouldn't really have married him, would you?" Insecurity creeping into his voice.

So many choices I'd never thought I'd have to make in this life. "I was hoping something else would come along."

"You wouldn't have, though. Not in a million years."

As if he really knew me, knew what I was capable of doing with my back against the wall. Who ever knew another person so well? Not even we ourselves. I'd been a half-dozen different people since the day he crushed that silver-framed icon on the floor of the Poverty Artel.

"Honestly, I don't know who I am anymore."

"You're Marina Makarova," he said, kissing my cheek. "The girl I met at Wolf's in the green coat with a white fur hat, dogged by her disapproving English governess."

I blushed, hoping the sailor hadn't heard. My labor book said *proletarian*. That day at Wolf's bookstore with Miss Haddon-Finch... If anyone had told me on that day that in five years I would be pregnant and riding on the roof of the agit-train *Red October*, wedged between my poet husband and a Kronstadt sailor... *You're an adventurer*, Arkady had once said. Was it true? That brave, thoughtless girl? It was a long way from that girl to this one, a long, winding road. And a long way to go.

All around us the soldiers were lounging, smoking, lying on their small packs, their guns tucked under their arms. They didn't talk much, they sang or watched the horizon or slept on their rolled sheepskins. At night they made a fire away from the train, and I could hear their songs and laughter. Sometimes they went into a village for food and women. I hoped they paid for it, or at least didn't attack anyone. But there was always that possibility. Even to us they always seemed a little dangerous, like a dog who was good when its master was around but you could never wholly trust on its own. Their faces were too similar to those I'd seen in the villages, to the ones who had taken Maryino, their cruelty as ready as their generosity.

Genya shouted in my ear over the roar of the wind. "I should never have abandoned you, that day at the station. I've had plenty of time to regret it."

"I wish I'd gone with you." With all my heart. I wanted to tell him something true, my big tender boy-man, something real. "I saw you after that. At the Miniature Theater. During First Anniversary."

His hands clutched me and I found myself looking up into his wild face, his deep hazel-green eyes searching mine like a man studying an icon's fabled tears, trying to decide if they were real. "You were there? Why didn't you stay? I came to Petrograd to find you!"

Of course I couldn't tell him why. "I got lost." That was the truth.

"What do you mean lost? How far was it to the stage?"

"Farther than you can imagine," I said. I hated being interrogated, hated it with the fury of someone without an alibi.

"Why are you being so mysterious? I hate mysteries!" He shook me like a man shaking sand from his boots. "Have you been planted on this earth to torment me?"

"Easy, brother," said the sailor.

Would he hit me? Would he throw me from the train? "God, I hate mysteries!" he shouted again, and let me go.

The sailor glanced over, his pale blue eyes grinning. "Then you better forget about women, brother." The other hitchhikers laughed. "Might as well give in and enjoy 'er, we'll all be dead soon enough."

Genya's fit of temper seeped away. He was like that, his rages flared and subsided, but the ruddy tone of his face had drained to ashes. Well, perhaps that was what I was on earth for, to be the chaos in other people's lives. Who can know what Fate has in store, the effect we'll have on the lives of others, even the ones we love most dearly? Especially them. I took his great hand, pressed it to my cheek. It smelled of graphite and printer's ink. "Look, for some reason we've found each other again. Let's not quarrel."

"I came to Petrograd to find you," he said again. "And you were there, and you just left?"

I kissed his palm. I had to find something to distract him, like a mother substituting a toy for the sharp object in her child's careless hands. "I saw you at the *kino* too. I went with Mina. You were a regular Fairbanks!" I knew I shouldn't laugh, but I couldn't help it. "Our *Charlie*."

There it was, his bashful grin. "It was shit. A stupid stunt."

"I was proud of you."

He sighed. "But did you dream of me, Marina? Did you lie awake at night, groaning with thoughts of how you tormented me? I haven't gone a day without thinking of you." He crushed me to his breast, speaking fast in my ear. "I'll love you forever, you know. No matter what. Kick me like a dog, I'll come crawling back."

I could see the sailor, his beret set back on his head, gazing up to heaven, as if praying God would come down and knock some sense into this poet.

"This is the girl," Genya announced, "I've been waiting for all my life." He struggled to stand in a sudden rush of passion. We grabbed on to him, men bracing his legs, another holding on to his belt as he sang out to the sun:

> *You! Redhead!*
> *You*
> *who laughed when the others*
> *bolted like chickens*
> *before the rumble of*
> *my iron wheels*
> *the roar of the furnace in my belly.*

They scattered
    Like horses
  before the black diabolical breath
        of my smokestacks.

"*Urah!*" the soldiers shouted, the ones who could hear and the ones who couldn't.

    You!
    without a whip or chair
        marched into my bearish den
Unarmed,
        and clapped your little flower-hands
            ordering me to
        Dance, Bear!
                Dance!

For you alone I dance
    in my cloddish way
        Baring my yellow teeth
                    roaring
        my threadbare pelt
            rich with fleas,
    though I wanted to appear to you

            magnificent!

He threw his arms wide and the men struggled to keep their grip.

            You clapped out a mazurka
    a waltz
        then stepped in for —
                a
                    tango.

"You're not afraid?"
     The young girls trembled.
"You're not appalled?"
     The old maids hissed.
But I was the one
    This bear in your arms
     Who loved
       and feared you the most.

Only Genya could love like this, only he had enough heart for it. We held him there as he rode the rushing train, a Colossus reciting into the wind, superhuman, forgetting everything but his love, his greatest madness.

Finally, he lowered himself back down to the roof, flushed with triumph. "Now tell me you didn't dream of me."

I held him close, printing his rough woven Russian blouse and its button into my cheek. "Yes, you and all of this."

"This?" He pressed my hand to his chest, I could feel the bones, the muscles through his shirt. He grinned—his thick, strong brow, his big jaw. "It's not a dream." He shook Slava's shoulder. "Or else we're all dreaming it. The whole world is dreaming us now."

We lay on the lower bunk of our compartment after the train had stopped for the night. I missed the wind, the swaying of the train. We slept with the window down, batting at mosquitos that longed for our blood, our naked bodies fragrant from making love. At first, he'd been afraid of hurting the baby, but the baby liked it just fine. "Let me guess. You and Apollonia." The blond actress.

"Why not?" he said. "I didn't know that I'd ever see you again. Did you save yourself for me?"

"Of course." It made him laugh, that wonderful deep sound. His hand on my belly. "I assure you, the conception was immaculate. Your girlfriend's taking it pretty well, I have to say. She's only spilled hot tea on me three times." Apollonia regularly bumped into me in the canteen or in the corridor, especially if I was carrying something hot. Well, I couldn't blame her for it. I could deal with her false smiles far better than Zina Ostrovskaya's sharp-toothed attacks in the days of the Transrational Interlocutors of the Terrestrial Now.

"She'll be okay," he said, reaching over me for a cup of tea on the floor, drinking, the liquid spilling down his chin. "You're my wife. My very pregnant wife." He tickled my belly with light fingers and the child writhed under his hand. Our child.

I snuggled back against him. Hot, but oh, such a pleasure. My body remembered him. *Mine.* "Whatever happened to Zina? Why isn't she here? Did you finally kill her off?"

"You never liked her," he said. "I couldn't understand it. Too much alike, maybe."

My turn to laugh. That jealous, spiteful little ferret? Was he even serious? "Idiot." I tried his forearm with my teeth, it was salty and hard, like a gnarled tree root.

We could hear the actors in the next compartment, arguing about playing Sorin in *The Seagull.*

"Was it another woman who finally drove her off?"

He buried his nose in my neck. "Woman? *Woman?* How could I have replaced you with a single woman? I needed boatloads of women. Whole cities of them. Sometimes the flat looked like Nikolaevsky station."

I wrapped his arms tighter around me. Finally, I was content. Though I still suffered from heartburn whenever I lay down, it was bliss to be here with a man who knew me, remembered me, loved me—*my husband.* To be together again, doing something purposeful, something exciting, with our future on the way in several dimensions. "How about Marfa Yermilova?" I teased him. "I sense something there."

Our political commissar, with her drooping mouth and unimpressed eyes, her black cigarette holder. I stayed out of her way as much as I could. When I first came onto the train, she and Genya had argued. I heard them in the corridor. *There's no room here for fellow-travelers.*

She's not, she's my wife. She's reliable. I vouch for her.

But what if you have to choose? One day you may have to put the Red October *into harm's way. Which will you protect, the revolution or your pregnant wife?*

I'm a Bolshevik. I know my duty, he responded. *Don't worry about me.*

I hoped it would never come to a choice. In any case, the front was still far away, and we were here in each other's arms in the half-light of a northern June midnight, growing together again, the baby dancing under his hand.

Jolting along in the hot afternoon in the train's canteen car, the baby lay still, as he always did when something was going on. I could feel him in there, listening. He had finally dropped, lessening the pressure on my lungs but making me clumsy. I swayed like a sailor when I walked. I could no longer navigate the ladder to the roof of the train, the sailors wouldn't help me anymore. They said Genya didn't like it, and for once, I didn't argue. I made myself useful, mostly by staying out of the way. Usually I ended up camped out in the canteen car where the journalists gathered to bang out their stories on typewriters or scribble their impressions in notebooks to be wired back to their respective newspapers. They came from Moscow and Petrograd, as far as Kiev and Warsaw. That day, the young reporter from Kiev was especially glum. He hunched over his typewriter, his head caged in his hands as if birds trapped inside his skull were trying to peck their way out.

The others ignored him, but I sat down next to him. "Matvei, you okay?"

He shook his head.

"It's a pogrom," said another journalist, Kostya, from Petrograd *Pravda*. "The Ukraine's breaking out like smallpox."

Pogrom. The random community violence against the Jews. And he was a Jew, Matvei Grossman. He must be worried about his family back home.

"Kiev's a White shithole," said Grigory something, a sharp-tongued man from *Krasnaya Gazeta*. He rolled a *makhorka* and lit it, preparing to fumigate us in the hot car. "What a sty."

Matvei groaned, sighed. "It's not just Kiev. It's the whole Ukraine. Kiev, Kishinev, down to the smallest village. They're throwing us to the wolves." He drank from the battered metal cup at his elbow.

The train swayed, the tea swayed, the hot wind blew through the open windows but cooled nothing. Gradually the typing began again. A group from the propaganda car came in, not Genya but three of his writers, plus Marfa Yermilova and her deputy, Antyushin. Originally from a peasant family, the commissar exuded confidence and capacity. I knew she excelled at persuading peasants to support the Red cause. She was about forty, a brisk walker, a fast talker, authoritative, and brooked no resistance. "We just had an excellent meeting," she announced, pouring herself tea from the samovar—no shortage of hot water on the *Red October*. "The local peasants seem solid."

"They'll turn on you without blinking," said the reporter from Kiev.

"That's why we're here," she said. "To make sure they don't."

Antyushin smirked. "Worried, Motka?"

"Have you seen a pogrom, Antyushka?" Matvei said, his defiant chin quivering. "I was in Kishinev in '03, during the Easter pogrom. Our neighbors came still damp from the bishop's blessing. There was one woman, Sara Iosifovna, they drove nails into her eyes, and watched her run around screaming. And when they got tired of that, they killed her by nailing them in the rest of the way." In '03, he was probably five. I wished I could hold him, but it was not done on the *Red October*. "They broke into our houses and threw us out the windows. They cut the glazier's balls off—he was trying to protect some girls."

"Yes, yes," said Marfa Yermilova, interrupting him. "They're violent and unpredictable. But they'll feed us if they think it's in their interests."

"Moskovitz," he said, looking down at his typewriter. "The glazier. They castrated him, then they trampled him to death."

"Do you believe in what we're doing, Comrade Grossman?" the commissar snapped.

"It's our only hope," he said.

"Remember that."

I remembered the mob in Haymarket Square, the violence of the bread riot. Varvara scolding the woman in line over that hideous pamphlet — *They're dragging the Jews in front of you like a bullfighter's cape.* And now it was happening again — not just in one village but in hundreds of villages, even in big cities. We had to win this war — the thought of what losing would mean was too hideous to contemplate.

"Denikin's whipping them up," said Marfa Yermilova, perched on the corner of the table with her tin cup, holster strapped across her breast. "That's how desperate he is, trying to catalyze peasant support by serving up rape and murder. It's an ancient recipe."

"So much for your noble Cossack," said Antyushin.

"Swans," said the man from *Krasnaya Gazeta*. "So poetic."

I thought of Volodya in the Denikin army. Would he be part of a pogrom? I hoped he had deserted and joined the Red cause, or just slipped away across the border. Though I suspected he had not. I imagined he, like Father, had made some strange peace with his conscience. All for the noble cause. Like a frog in a pot of water, simmering slowly — it didn't have a moment where it decided *This is too hot.* One adjusted and adjusted, bearing each new disgusting compromise until it was too late. I felt suddenly ill, but didn't have the energy to get up. I wished someone would make me a cup of tea. I moved closer to the window, hot wind in my face.

"Wait till the Siberians come," said Grigory. "They make Denikin's atamans look like schoolchildren. When they took Omsk, they flogged people with iron rods until the flesh tore right from their bodies."

The heat, this talk...and we were heading right for them, not to Denikin but to Kolchak and the Siberians. Suddenly I pictured my belly ripped open, the baby flung out onto the tracks. I had not really considered what would happen if the agit-train were taken. Would I be raped before I died, my head cut off? I felt a dark wave of nausea rise up, and then I was falling backward.

Matvei caught me. "Sorry," he said. "I shouldn't have started. Could someone get her a cup of tea?"

Kostya brought me a cup, sweet with saccharine. But the talk of horrors continued: how Ataman Semyonov in the Transbaikal decorated the perimeter of his barbaric capital with hanged men and women like banners at a country fair. Freight cars of people were machine-gunned along the railway, buried in mass graves or not even buried, just left for the ravens. "Not even Bolsheviks," said one of Genya's sloganeers, Tudovkin. "Just peasants, anybody who gets in the way."

Matvei was holding my hands. "Should I get Kuriakin?" he asked softly.

I shook my head, leaning against the half-open window, sipping sweet tea with its bitter undertone. There was a metaphor.

"They'll live to regret it." Marfa Yermilova's sure voice rang out. "When they've got peasant revolt behind the lines, and us in front of them, they'll understand that they dug their own graves."

"Unless they get to us first," Matvei said under his breath.

I had not been taking this seriously enough. It was up to us to make sure the Soviet Republic survived. Everyone, man, woman, child, sack of grain, scrap of fuel, and Soviet bullet, had to go into this. It was our job to reignite revolutionary hope in the hearts of workers and peasants, soldiers who could so easily desert if the war went badly. As I gazed out at the wide green land spread out under the blameless sky, lines of trees in the distance, the green of June, it was hard to imagine how badly the war might be going. How much misery this beautiful land had already absorbed, how much blood. Mongol and Slav, peasant and soldier. I couldn't stop thinking about the pogroms—what cynicism, to buy the allegiance of peasants with the coin of unbridled violence, as if it were a tasty treat! Indulging hatreds as if it were a glorious and righteous thing. Did they really think it was? Or did they know it was evil in their hearts, and rejoice in being encouraged to evil? *Still damp from the bishop's blessing.* There was certainly something perverse in human nature — and dangerous to believe it was not there.

I couldn't stop thinking of *Rech'*, the Kadet newspaper, and my father and his friends, who were rationally deciding to use pogroms as an organizing tool. What happened to your English sense of fair play, Papa? Your John Stuart Mill? I knew what he would say. *It's terrible, but what else can we do? Once we've stopped the Bolshevik madness, we'll find a way to put things to rights.*

But you could not reclaim your soul once you'd sold it to the devil.

What was it in human beings that delighted in viciousness? Those crowds in the Ukraine that Easter, gripped by the miracle, their dazzled eyes falling on those who resisted salvation. Foreigners for hundreds of years, never accepted. Falling on them like wolves. Served up to distract from the master's true ends. *Don't look at our failures! Look over there, those are the ones.* The weak, the unprotected, the different.

But our side was capable of the same. I'd seen the Podharzhevskys digging in the snow. I'd been in the cells of the Cheka. *Go ahead, we'll look the other way. No, we'll applaud you!* Something inside us gloried in cruelty. Dostoyevsky would say this is why we needed Christ. But religion was its birthing place, and belief the rails it ran upon. What we needed was more pity and less belief. Wasn't it Kolya who said that idealists were the most dangerous ones? Yes, but also dangerous were the ones who believed in nothing. I'd once believed human beings were intrinsically good. But now I knew, decency and goodness were things you had to fight for, cultivate and protect, precious crops you had to water and guard and feed and nourish, to absorb the soulless viciousness that also lay dormant within the human breast.

Genya and I stared out the window in the corridor at the thousands gathered on the platforms at Nizhny Novgorod, his arm around my neck. I had not yet visited such a big city with the *Red October*. I was aware of how we looked together, the strapping Soviet hero and me, the Red Madonna in my kerchief, our determined profiles. Like figures painted on a train. And how he loved this, waving from the window. And why shouldn't they cheer? Nizhny was a Soviet citadel. The workingmen of this Volga metropolis knew very well what awaited them if they lost. Even as they cheered the *Red October,* I suspected there would be those here who could just as easily turn into a mob, become a pogrom. But we were here for a specific job, to solidify the populace for the revolution, not to fight a cosmic war against the forces of unreason.

There were cheers, but I felt their fear underneath, their desperation. An edge of panic, though the front was still far away. Could we reassure them? No, but that was not our purpose here. It was to steel them, anodize their fear into a reckless courage.

And then came the practiced readying of the train for the literary-theatrical agitprop show.

I stood in the crowd, watching Genya take center stage in the boxcar that was the Theater of the Future.

"Comrades!" he shouted.

> *Who's the shadow on the wall?*
> *The one who crawls*
> *Under the bed. Behind the shed?*
> *The one they said*
> *Except for him, or him,*
> *or her—*

He pointed at members of the crowd.

> *We might have saved it all.*

People glanced nervously around themselves, as if to say, *Not me. I'm here.*

> *When your grandkids ask*

Where were you
when Kolchak came to call?
You want to be the one to say
"I hid in the cellar, mal'chik.
I saved my skin but not my soul."

"No!" they began to shout. "For shame!" Was it the crowd or our
actors, wandering among them, stirring them up?

Now he opened his arms, as if to embrace them.

Without you, there's nothing.
No grain in the sack
No bullets in the guns
No trains on the tracks.
Without you, the sun won't rise in the sky!
Without you, the moon won't glow!
Who is walking with us?
Who will fight by our side?

The roll of thunder shook the ground. People waved their caps,
held up their babies as if to be blessed. How brave they were, with
the front still five hundred miles to the east.

I made my way to the *kino* car, to prepare it for the screenings.
Inside, the projectionist was readying himself for the rush after the
speeches with his usual deep knee bends and great exhales, shaking out his legs as if he were about to run a race. He checked his
films, while two soldiers and I straightened out benches, opened
the windows, and pulled down the shades. I settled the first of the
gramophone disks onto the turntable and went forward to use the
privy in the next car one last time. Since the baby dropped, I was
peeing a hundred times a day.

When we heard them sing "The Internationale," we knew it was
our turn. We opened the doors of the darkened carriage, signaling
we were open for business. The soldiers got the people lined up and
I helped them into the car—children and mothers, working girls

and machinists, prostitutes and soldiers and peasants who might never have seen a *kino* before, packing them onto the benches. A woman had chickens in a basket. Should I make her leave them outside? No, she would just set them in the front with me. "There's room for a few more," I shouted. "Squeeze in a little there." Just as Misha had done in a far different life, packing sitters onto benches for Mina's camera, but without this enormous belly—it grounded me, it gave me a certain authority. Finally, we were at capacity. "No smoking, Comrades. Film can burn in a glass of water." Amazing how many bodies we could squeeze into the train car, knee to rump all the way to the back. The lowered shades on the windows glowed golden as we shut the doors. I prayed no one would panic. Soon the air grew pungent with the stink of hot, unwashed people.

As the film flickered through the gate, I stayed close to the door, cranking the gramophone to accompany the showing of *Day One of the Revolution*. The first time I saw it, I'd been startled to find they'd used Solomon Katzev's photographs of the Pavlovsky regiment marching behind their band in Palace Square, and the red flag flying over the Winter Palace. Near the end, a shot from the first anniversary left me speechless—a spectacular though somewhat blurry night shot of a hydroplane flying low over the lighted ships on the Neva. It never failed to give me a shock. My photograph had made it all the way from the prow on the Rostral Column to this steaming *kino* in Nizhny Novgorod.

Sweat dripped down between my shoulders and pooled into the waistband of my skirt, soaking my blouse. The air was as thick as felt. Yet I never got tired of seeing the people's faces as they watched the films. Some watched dumbly, fascinated by the flickering display. But with others, you could see the cells of their brains putting connections together, realizing *they were a part of this*. They were watching their own story, major players in the drama that unfolded not only in front of them on our little screen but outside the doors of this railway car. It was *they* who were propelling history. Not the senseless violence of pogroms acted out of their own frustration and rage but forward movement, toward a better world. Just

as Lunacharsky had hoped from his Revolutionary Carnival. Entertainment and enlightenment together could work to defuse mob rule
and transform it into a citizenry. I found my script and read to them
an excerpt from Lenin's speech at the dedication of the Marx Memorial last October, and then we showed one last newsreel about the
battle to preserve Soviet Russia—and had to open the doors. It took
about seven minutes in all. No one fainted, no one burned to death.
Only six more hours to go.

Outside on the platform, our sailors made speeches to local soldiers and played recordings of Trotsky and Bukharin on gramophones. Listening to that cacophony, I couldn't help wondering
whose gramophones those were. In what rooms had they sat, what
waltzes and tangos had they played? What had become of Kolya's
gramophone, to which we'd danced the tango? *Ah little feet, where
are you now?* It was probably performing hard service on a train
platform just like this, the RCA dog with the cocked head...His
Master's Voice. How funny to think of his perplexity at hearing
Trotsky's rousing voice coming through His Master's bell. All that
was a century ago—no more tangos, only speeches and choruses
of "The Red Army Is Strongest of All." I felt tears upwelling, and
shook myself. I was an agitator on the *Red October,* how dare I be
nostalgic for such things. Only I'd gotten so sentimental lately. It
must be the pregnancy.

People were watching me. It was important how we conducted
ourselves. Women needed to learn *how to be* in this new world. They
needed our example. I had thought that bigheaded at the time, when
Sergeevna had said it, but here I noticed women eyeing me with
frank curiosity. *This mere girl, part of the* Red October*! And pregnant too. Anybody can certainly do anything now, can't they?* I had
to straighten up, though the June heat was terrific. Strike the correct pose, neither humble nor arrogant, friendly, brave, efficient,
compassionate, but tough-minded enough for war. Like the heroic
woman on the side of the train, posed before the factories with her
firm steady face. As though I expected someone to come paint me.

9 *Izhevsk*

We passed through great cities and little nowhere villages with their primitive stations and level crossings, women selling bread and milk as we moved up behind the lines. Now we were getting close to the battle, and saw the burned-out hamlets. Sometimes we could hear guns. We took on more and more soldiers heading back to their units. The summer raced on, the last few weeks of my pregnancy. Surely I could not get any bigger. All my bravery was gone. I was weary, feverish, irritable. No longer did I help out in the *kino* car, let alone yearn to ride on the roof of the carriage with the soldiers. It was as much as I could bear to simply lie in our compartment, sweating, lulled by the *ta-tick-a-TICK, ta-tick-a-TICK,* and the swaying of the car, listening to the actors in the next compartment arguing and playing cards. I nodded off, dreaming that the car was burning, everyone locked inside.

Genya came in from one of his meetings and sat down with me on my narrow bunk, wrung out a cloth in warmish water and put it on my head. He lay down beside me, squeezing me to the wall. He was too hot, and I was too big, we both were. "The 25th Rifle Division is closing in. Kolchak's on the run," he said, tucking a strand of my sweaty hair behind my ear. "They're saying Trotsky's going to start transferring troops toward Denikin if they succeed. Look, we've got a new poster!" He picked something off the floor, sat up, thank God, unrolled a sheet of paper. A single Red Army soldier in a giant red circle on the left, White officers hiding behind the Urals as if behind a theater curtain on the right. It was good, but I was too listless to join in his excitement and I had to pee again. When I returned from the WC, I crawled back into the bunk and fell asleep as he was telling me about the 25th Rifles. *Ta-tick-a-TICK.*

Our next stop was Izhevsk, a big armaments town, liberated from the Whites just three weeks previously. Representatives from their soviet met us at the station, as well as a good crowd of local Tatars and Udmurts, the latter a people I'd never seen before—so many redheads! I felt strangely at home, stylishly dressed in a new pair of bast shoes I'd bought from a peasant woman back in—what was it? Uva? Kilmezh? I could no longer fit my feet into my boots. Swollen, they looked like monstrous potatoes, my legs like peeled birch trunks. There was no difference between my ankle and my calf. Yet it was important to Genya that I join the others, to stand around endlessly in the summer sun, meeting the representatives of the various factory committees, listening to their speeches and our own. We staged our skits, showed our film—I no longer took responsibility for packing the car or reading the speech but instead found a scrap of shade to huddle into, after which we were hosted by the town soviet for tea and the little pastries made by the local women.

It was marvelous to be inside a building slightly cooler than the train. And we sat down—in chairs! I loved these people. They even treated us to a concert of women's singing. The harmonies were angelic, all traditional songs and not, for once, "The Red Army Is Strongest of All." And they made much of me, pregnant and redheaded. On the *Red October* they ignored me if not regarding me as an unnecessary payload, an embarrassment. But here I was the object of interest and attention. Shameful to say, I lapped it up. Most of all, I was grateful for those savory pies and chilled juices. They withheld nothing from us, they who had been so recently under the brutal White thumb.

After the refreshments, once more we traipsed into the sun as an old Bolshevik from their committee, his face still swollen and bruised from a beating, gave us the tour of the town. He made sure we heard about every moment of the occupation.

"They killed a thousand people, right here." He pointed to gibbets still standing in the square, the poles at angles, cut ropes still attached. "They started with the committee, workers, Bolsheviks, but they got all the way down to students, even schoolkids." The journalists took notes and asked questions, our photographer documented the massacre. I could feel the rope around my own neck, the prickly hemp, my hands tied behind my back. The baby lay like twenty pounds of cement in the bowl of my aching hips. "Then they decided it was taking too long to hang them all. Come," he indicated, "I'll show you."

We set off for a long march through the town, following the old man and his comrades. It was a good-sized city, and it was so hot. Although the man limped from some kind of wound, he covered ground fast. A lake glittered green and blue, tantalizing, but we never got close to it. I found myself lagging farther and farther behind the main party. I could keep only Genya in view, a full head taller than the next tallest man. He glanced back every so often, smiled, shrugged, *What can I do?* Matvei Grossman dropped back to walk with me. We followed them to the great Izhevsk arms plant, the place still humming, unlike the bulk of the factories we'd seen in our travels. No labor desertion here.

Outside the munitions plant, the old Bolshevik pointed to a stone wall. "There. There are the workers of Izhevsk." It was pocked with bullet holes, smeared with brown stains in the blistering sun. No one had to encourage the workers here to beat out rifles and machine guns, stuff shells with gunpowder. They worked double shifts, triple. Their committee, what was left of it, said they were producing five hundred rifles a day, whatever it would take to smash the Whites. Our soldiers were all offered ammunition as souvenirs, the nicest present of the day.

I felt worse as we headed back to the train, something about the food and the heat and the bloodstains, the gibbets. My legs would just not keep up. I had ferocious heartburn, my back and hips ached, and all I wanted to do was lie down. The bast shoes rubbed. I took them off and went barefoot on the hot stones. Now I felt the front—just three weeks ago, they had been right here. The wall, the bullet holes. How foolish I was to think that the *Red October* would be a means of escape.

I fought tears. I wouldn't let them see me, hard-bitten Bolsheviks with a job to do. There would be no sympathy for Genya's fellow-traveling wife. We were both so foolish, I saw it now. He should have refused me, but his defiant optimism had prevailed. He was no more practical than I. Sure they would all love me, sure I would fit in—believing in the image of himself, the giant in seven-league boots, heading for the Future as if into the rising sun. Loping ahead with politicals and the Izhevsk Committee, he had no idea whether I was still with them or had fallen into a ditch or been kidnapped by bandits.

Matvei and I brought up the rear. Aksakov, the train's brakeman, gave me a hand up into the dining car. "The 25th Rifles have just taken Ufa," he told us.

Ufa, the last major White center before the Urals. Now there was only Perm. The tide had turned. Admiral Kolchak was in retreat, back to his Siberian stronghold. The Red Heart of Russia had held. Saved by Chapaev and the 25th Rifles, that division was all anyone talked about these days. "But," Aksakov added, "there's fighting at Glazov. Gaida's leading a counterattack."

In the dining car, the others had already gathered at the map permanently affixed to the wall. A white tack at Glazov, to our northwest, and a red one, the 25th Rifles, at Ufa in the southeast. "The Whites'll have to come back this way if they don't want to be cut off," Matvei said.

And here was our train, a piece of cardboard with a drawing of the locomotive, at Izhevsk, right between them. We were sandwiched between the two forces.

Genya and Marfa Yermilova, Antyushin, the sailors and soldiers, propagandists and journalists, smoked, argued, rubbed their faces, trying to anticipate the next step. Marfa Yermilova in her wooden-jawed voice, declared, "They've taken Ufa, that's the main thing. It's not the first time we've faced this."

"But which way will the Whites head?" asked one of the propagandists. "Will they try to retake Izhevsk?"

We stared at the map as if it were a crystal ball.

"We should go straight to Glazov," said Grigory from *Krasnaya Gazeta*. "See what's happening." Obviously he wanted to get as close to the action as he could, and damn the fate of the agit-train.

"Maybe we'll send you ahead to reconnoiter." The sailor, Slava, settled down in a chair turned backward, took out his cigarette makings. "I've got to think of all these duffers." He waved at the rest of us. "This train'd be a catch for Gaida. Imagine those headlines back in Omsk. That'd be some agitprop."

Everyone was waiting to see what Marfa Yermilova would say, but she hadn't moved, she just kept looking at the map, weighing the possibilities.

Grigory said something about taking Slava up on his offer—though it was sheer braggadocio. They settled into the various chairs and benches, gazing up at the map as if the situation might change if they looked at it long enough, and began to discuss a course of action. Marfa Yermilova was right, it wasn't the first time we had no idea where we were going. A bridge blown, a band of saboteurs, a town already in ruins. Sometimes we lost the telegraph completely.

"Ufa maybe?" said Kostya, more as a question. "We'd be right on the heels of the 25th." The journalists were dying to see Chapaev in action, their heroic leader—there were already songs about him.

"We could," Genya said, sitting on the table, one foot propped on the bench. "Do some agitprop, make sure the locals will feed the soldiers when the 5th Army gets there." Another red tack.

"Perm was our destination," said Antyushin. "Then across to Ekaterinburg if the 2nd gets that far."

Behind the Urals. It frightened me, the point of no return. I waited as long as I could, but it didn't look like they were going to reach an agreement anytime soon. My guess was that we'd end up sleeping on a siding here in Izhevsk. Whether it was Ufa or Glazov or Perm, I hoped Marfa Yermilova and Genya decided to stay away from the worst of it, that we would just go on bringing the Soviet message to peasants behind the lines and avoid being attacked by them. They looked on all of us, Red or White, as invaders. And I prayed that we wouldn't cross the Urals.

Which will you protect, the revolution or your pregnant wife? I remembered Marfa Yermilova asking Genya.

Overcome with fatigue and the heat and my immensity, my roiling guts, I staggered down to our compartment, peed in a chamber pot, and lay down on the bottom bunk. I tried propping myself up, tried lying on my side. I wished I could have gone up to the top bunk, more air, but I could no more have climbed there than fly.

There was not a single position in which I could lie in comfort. A peasant woman in one of those towns had told me the heartburn meant the baby would be born with a full head of hair. A boy, she predicted, as had Korsakova. *Iskra.* It meant *Spark.* A revolutionary name for a child of the revolution. How Genya loved to talk to him, lying with his head in my lap and his ear pressed to my giant belly. He looked like a boy himself, making up poems, telling him how he would march through Moscow on his daddy's shoulders. They would be so tall the domes would look like toadstools, so high that Iskra would have to duck so he wouldn't bump his head on the clouds.

This was the way I liked Genya best—silly, tender Genya with all those sounds in his head. I wished he'd decide whether it was Ufa or Perm and come back here—though to do what? I didn't know. I wished I had a woman friend on the train, but everyone was busy, and aside from Matvei, and Slava, I'd made no friends here. I knew I didn't belong, try as I might to be useful. I was just dead weight—not journalist, or soldier, or actor, just an awkward body to step around. My loneliness and irritation blended together with the terrible buzz of the cicadas outside through the lowered window, so loud I could hear nothing else. Though I knew if I could hear, I wouldn't want to. I knew what I was missing, actors in the next compartment arguing over Meyerhold or Ibsen, playing poker, squabbling over missing belongings, fast fornications, drunken arguments when someone got hold of a bit of local *samogon,* all the topics they pursued when out of earshot of the soldiers and the sober propagandists. That and the heat and my head and the heartburn all combined into one huge ball of misery.

I wadded my sheepskin together with Genya's coat into a bolster and propped myself into a seated position that was halfway comfortable. I'd just begun to nod off when I woke, urgently sick, and vomited into the chamber pot. How sorry I felt for those little cabbage pies, they had been so good! Blubbering like an infant. Why hadn't I realized how hard this was going to get? Normally I didn't allow myself the indulgence of self-pity, but with no one around to notice that I wasn't the stoic I pretended to be, I didn't bother to stop myself. Damn Genya! Damn the *Red October*! I wished I'd never seen either one of them. Why didn't I have more sense? Surely Genya must have known it was no place for a woman about to bear a child. Everyone hated me on this train, no one wanted me here. Couldn't he have known it would be like this? How jealous everyone would be of him? Why couldn't he have had a scrap of sense?

I always thought other people knew things, that was my weakness. Kolya, Genya, my father. And then I was brutally disappointed — over things I should have known myself.

Things I did know, and pushed aside.

I rinsed the chamber pot with water and threw the stinking contents out the window.

It was not just the pregnancy but the flu. My misery was complete. I didn't bother even coming out of the car now when we stopped to deliver our Soviet message, our revolutionary passion play. I felt sick and peevish. The only one I wanted near me was Genya. I wanted him to recite poems for me, and rub my back, and tell me he loved me — and not bring me up to date on the progress of Chapaev and the 5th Army, Ufa and Perm, the gift of a whole goat someone gave us. He brought some in for me, but the smell of it — I made him take it outside. Everything smelled awful, my dirty hair, my own body. At one stop he tenderly washed my hair in hot water from the boiler. I wished I could have just crawled into it.

I lay in a thin nightdress in my bunk and dreamed one bad dream after another. I dreamed I was back at school — that the Whites were using it as a headquarters. They'd won the war, and now we would have to pay the price. They herded us all into the ballroom: Mina, and Lisa Podharzhevskaya, and Natalya Ionian, I didn't know she'd gone there too. Magda Ionian was there, though not Varvara—strange. And they were searching all the girls. I knew it was me they were looking for. Magda had told them I was there, Magda the spy.

Then a woman, an old woman with blue eyes, beckoned me silently to a wall between the windows, where she opened a door, a hidden door. How could there be a door on the outside wall? But she popped it open and helped me through, closing it after me. It was dark, but I found a metal door, and stairs going down, dripping and wet, a maze of corridors with pipes running overhead. I got lost. Which way to Bolshaya Morskaya? The Whites were overhead, they knew I was here somewhere. If I kept going down, eventually there must be a door, an exit...except that water lapped the bottom stairs. The basement had flooded. Rats swam in it, trying to get away.

When I woke, the whole bench was wet, right down to the worn leather. My nightshirt soaked through, the sheet a soggy mess. I lay there for who knew how long, calling for help, but no one heard me. The train had stopped. They were probably out bringing the revolution to some village or visiting a site of outrage. I lay there weeping, sick, inert. No one was going to come. No Avdokia to change my wet nightie and remake my bed, wipe my face and arms with cold water.

Unsteadily, I rose and pulled on my dress—backward, it proved—and with what seemed extraordinary effort, gathered the clammy sheet and wet gown to bundle out into the corridor. Maybe I could wash or dry it somehow, or at least get it off my bunk. I don't know who was doing the thinking. I had the idea I could go outside and hang them to dry—but I couldn't exactly hang them from the line outside the *kinotheater* in the middle of a show. Yes, they were just starting, I could hear Genya declaiming. I stumbled toward the rear of the car, toward the toilets I hadn't visited for days; I'd only gotten up to use the chamber pot and fallen back onto the berth. I focused on the door at the end of the corridor when suddenly I couldn't see it anymore, I was falling, and the only thing I remembered thinking was *At least I have the sheet.*

When consciousness returned, I could not force myself to get up from the floor of the corridor. Now I knew—it was the baby coming. Wouldn't someone help me? I didn't know anything about childbirth, the wet and mysterious roots of life. *Get up.* If I didn't, I might give birth right here in the corridor, lying on a wet sheet. I was afraid to stand, but afraid not to. What if I blacked out again? I called out, "Please. Someone." I could hardly bear to hear my own voice, how weak it was. I could die here in the corridor, and no one would know until they finished their bloody *agitka*. *Oh God, please let it go fast.* But the light didn't change. I couldn't tell if I lay there for a minute or an hour.

Then voices. Matvei, leaning over me. And Genya was here, *thank God.* And Faina...no, Apollonia...They were still in their makeup. Genya apologized over and over. "I'm so sorry, I didn't think—There's always someone around." He looked so terrified and guilty, I would have teased him except that the pain had returned, and shivers, and a flash of unbearable heat.

Genya lifted me up and carried me back into the compartment. Someone had wiped down the bench, put down a coverlet, scratchy but at least it was dry.

"Tell me what I should do," my big boy-husband begged, kneeling on the dirty floor, his face on a level with mine, kissing my knuckles as if I were dead already, wetting them with his tears. "I feel so helpless."

If it was not so ridiculous, I would have laughed. I was on fire, and my lower back ached like it was breaking. I was going to have a baby. What did he have to cry about? "My back," I managed to say. "Rub my back." He tried it, but the rubbing wasn't doing anything, just irritating me. "With your hand, not your fingers. Lower. Yes, there." He rubbed the base of my back with his big hands. He was strong enough to do what I wanted, but he didn't understand, kept massaging instead of pressing, his hands too nervous to stay still. "Just press! With your fist!"

Something was wrong. Shouldn't the pain be in my belly? Or down in my crotch?

"Are you having it now?" he asked. "Is this it?"

"How do I know?" I shouted. "I've never done this before." Useless! And there wasn't one damn woman on the train who'd been through this herself. The actresses, the Bolsheviks. All their useless faces crowding round the open door, looking at me like I was a two-headed calf. I felt like I should fart some pamphlets for them.

Matvei Grossman stuck his head in from the corridor. "They've gone for the midwife."

Thank God someone had a thimbleful of common sense. "Where are we?" I asked. Somehow it suddenly seemed very important.

"Kambarka," said Apollonia. She sat on the opposite compartment bench with her legs crossed, staring out the window, as if she could not bear even looking at me. I must be repulsive, my hair plastered to my head. I could see myself in her eyes, like a gargoyle, like a bloated carcass of a cow ripening in the sun, while she looked so pretty and cool. I could tell she was glad I was suffering. I'm sure she hoped I would die. *Get your spell off me, devil.* All of these people, gaping at me like I was a fish in a tank. My writhing, gasping self, this trembling mountain of flesh.

"It's a very interesting town. It has an important ironworks," said Antyushin.

I shivered, and then came another wave of fiery heat. "Get them out of here," I roared to Genya. "Before I shoot them myself."

He cleared them out for me. There was a soft knock at the open door. Slava, my friend, my lovely sailor, had brought a pot of tea, a glass, and a towel. "The midwife'll be here soon, little comrade. Any minute. You're going to be fine. Just keep on breathing."

Always good advice. He handed Genya the water, and pressed something in my hand. A lump of sugar. Real sugar. I wondered how long he'd had that in his pocket. I popped it into my mouth and drank the tea, sucking the sweetness. My husband sat on the floor, not to crowd me on the bench, and never let go of my hand as we waited for salvation.

Janet Fitch

I rested between cramps, dozed and dreamed feverishly of fish, their unblinking eyes and gaping mouths. I knew I'd never be able to look at a fish again as long as I lived. Fish, and wet corridors—Gorokhovaya 2. And my mother with a veil like a coat of slime. But I finally remembered about breathing. I knew how to breathe—that's all we'd done at Ionia. I breathed through my skin, long skeins of light, keeping a vision of a candle flame in my mind. I breathed and tried to keep the candle steady. I don't know that it helped, but it kept me from screaming. Had any time passed at all? Where was that midwife?

Sometime later—was there still time?—the sun remained stalled in the white summer sky. It had not moved at all. Suddenly we heard arguing outside the train. Heavy boots, then the compartment door banged open. Genya rose and left me, closing the door behind him. My hands felt empty without his. "Genya?" I wanted to get up and find him, but I didn't have the strength. I lay there bound up in my dress. How could I go through with this? I had to beg off. I'd been sick ever since Izhevsk. In fact I'd been sick most of this pregnancy, and now I would be expected to do something—not with my mind but with my body alone. The door slid back open and Genya came in, knelt at my bedside. He was biting his lip. There was something he didn't want to tell me.

The midwife. *There was no midwife.* Oh God, I would have to give birth on this train with no one who knew anything more than some soldier who'd sewn up his buddy once at the front with the needle and thread he'd just used on his pants. "What?"

"There's a problem," Genya said, his forest eyes welling. The skin of his nostrils seemed very thin whenever he was upset. "He said the midwife wants you to come to the village. She won't do it here. Thinks we're devils. Typical religious morons. I say the hell with it. You can have the baby with us just as well as with her."

"No!" I cried out. Oh please, could someone please help me, someone who knew his ass from a hole in the ground?

100

"She's in the wagon outside," said Genya's girlfriend, Apollonia. She couldn't wait to be rid of me.

"I can make her come in," said Slava, lounging at the door. "It wouldn't take much."

Force some little old lady to attend me, with a gun to her head? "And if she refuses? You'd shoot her?"

"Why not?" He shrugged. "You can't fight Soviet power."

And leave a village without its midwife? Shoot her right there from the agit-train? Well, that would certainly change people's minds about the Red cause. Another contraction drove my back into barbed wire. I didn't want to give birth on this train. Better some old lady's izba. "Take me to her." I sat up, tried to rise, but my legs refused to hold me. I sank back down to the bench, but still upright, clutching Genya, shivering in the heat, sicker than I'd ever been in my life. "Take me."

"The hell with these ignorant peasants," Genya said, his jaw dangerously flexed. I knew that face, that mulish expression. He was getting his back up. "You know what it'll be like—priests and icons, holy water. Who knows what they'll do to you to punish you for being with us."

I was willing to take my chances. "Genya, sometimes other people know something too. Now help me!"

Reluctantly, he helped me stand, then lifted me in his arms. The sailor led the way. Matvei and a sparsely bearded little *muzhik* waited by a bony horse attached to a cart. In the cart, a woman in a white kerchief sat stiffly next to one of our Red soldiers, a rifle casually at his side. She sat firm in her seat. If she was frightened, she gave no indication. She was a big woman, square shouldered, in a blue apron, her face pockmarked, wide boned, a rock of defiance. You could have ironed a shirt on her back, it was so broad and straight. She could have been fifty, she could have been ninety.

Genya sighed. "You'd really go with her?"

"Help me up."

With one last baleful look, he lifted me up to the soldier, who settled me into the seat next to the midwife. Genya started to climb in after me.

"*Nyet,*" said the old woman, gesturing *no* with one wagging finger. "Not you."

"I'm not letting her out of my sight," he said.

"Not you," she said again.

"This is my husband," I tried to explain. I began to tremble again. I hadn't been upright this long since Izhevsk. The blood surged in my head.

She put her hand on my forehead, a strong hand, cool and steady. I wanted her to leave it there forever. "You're ill. A fever. How long?"

Just the sound of her calm, sure voice brought tears to my eyes, that hand, just like Avdokia's. "A week, I think."

"Has the water come?" I nodded. "How long ago?"

It was hard to say if it was five hours or fifteen. "Maybe noon."

"And the *suzheniya?*" *Contractions.* "How far apart?" She was very abrupt, but I could see her knowledge struggling with her loathing of us, her deep-seated purpose to bring life into the world getting the upper hand.

"Twenty minutes, thirty. It's my back." I started to cry.

She was nodding coolly. She'd seen all of this before. I loved her already. "And when was your last confession?"

Suddenly Genya was there, grabbing the old lady's blouse like he was going to punch her, yelling in her face with his mighty lungs, "What difference does that make? You old fool! Who cares? No—we're not doing this. It's insane. Marina—"

"A long time," I told her.

"We should get started," the old lady said.

"No. I forbid it. Marina, you can't let her—"

The midwife raised her voice, it was clear, and hard. "Your wife is ill, she's fevered, she's already in danger. She's been sick for a week. You call me insane? You people aren't human, you're animals."

Grigory from *Krasnaya Gazeta* ran out of the train car. "Kuriakin, it's good news. The 3rd Army has just taken Perm. The track's open."

I heard Marfa Yermilova's voice, sharp. "It's what we've been waiting for."

Other voices. Clamoring, all at once, like seagulls.

"Can you just give me a minute!" Genya roared, and knit his fingers atop his head, as if things were falling on it. "Just a minute!" He turned back to the old lady. "Anything happens to her, I swear, I'll kill you."

"If God wills it, so it shall be."

He howled as if it were he, not I, who was experiencing the deep pain of labor. He grabbed his head like it was on fire. "That's it," he shouted at her, scrambling up into the wagon. "You go to your good Christian hell, all right? And take your piousness with you." He was lifting me up. "I'm not leaving my wife with you."

"Stop it, Genya!" I fought him like an animal, wrenching myself from his grip. "I need her. I can't do this alone! Put me down!" I didn't know where I got the energy, but I arched and twisted like a cat. He had to put me down or drop me.

He clutched his head like it was filling with demons. "What are you talking about? You're not alone. Look! You have me, you have all of us!" And he waved his hand toward the comrades of our train, Matvei and Antyushin, Grigory, Dutkov the printer, Slava, Apollonia, Aksakov, Marfa Yermilova, Kostya from *Pravda,* an entire audience smoking, watching our drama. All his spacemen, his propagandists and theoreticians, actors. I'd give all of them for one old *baba* who could safely deliver my child. I didn't care how many icons I'd have to kiss. Maybe I'd want to kiss them. I had stopped knowing who I was or what I wanted. I just wanted to get out of the sight of all these people staring at me and suffer my pain in peace and get this baby out.

"Your wife is very ill," the midwife said to my panicked Genya, speaking slowly and clearly as if he were deaf, as if he would have to read the words on her lips. "She could die. I don't think she will, but it's in the hands of God. I can do more for her than you can, of that I'm sure."

I could die. I don't think I really believed it until she said it, right out loud. I was sick, but I didn't realize how sick, and now the baby was coming. My terror rose into my throat like vomit. It coiled up my spine.

"I'll kill you myself if you let her die," he said, pointing at her, right at her upturned nose, as if he would stab her with the spear of his finger. "I swear to you. I'll come back and burn your whole village."

I went into a spasm of labor, and laid my head in her lap, clutching her apron. "Let's go."

The old lady held me, held me hard, pressing my back with her fist, right where it was breaking, splitting in two. I groaned loud enough for everyone on that train to hear. "Pray," said the midwife. "Pray to Theotokos. *Save me, Holy Mother of God.*" After all my life with Avdokia, I knew that prayer like a song. I whispered it along with her: *"O my All-Gracious Queen Theotokos, my hope who befriends orphans and intercedes for strangers, joy of those who sorrow, protectress of those offended . . ."* And the words rushed over me like a stream. They soothed me. If I couldn't have Avdokia here with me now, I had this solid peasant woman, and the prayer gave me some human sounds to utter. *"Look upon my troubles and see my sorrow. Help me for I am weak. Guide me for I am wandering. For you know my offense. Resolve it as you will, for I have no other help than you, no other intercessor nor good comforter, only you. O Mother of God, may you keep and protect me, unto the ages of ages, Amen."*

"Amen," I choked out. She held me and started over again, submerging me in the steady flow of those old words, like an ancient poem, firm in the center, prayed until the cramping left me. "Where's Genya?" I gasped.

"He's right there, by the train."

I sat up and, yes, there he was, with the others, half listening to Marfa Yermilova, half turned from the cart, crushing his cap in his fist, trying not to look at me. Lot's husband. Poor Genya couldn't bear to see anyone suffer. I recalled the night we spent with the thief, in the little room on Grivtsova Alley.

But that boy had died.

The midwife took my hand. "*Devushka,* say goodbye now. As if it is your last day on earth."

The shock, the fear of it, the reality, sank in the rest of the way. *Death in childbirth.* "You really think I'm going to die?" I whispered. My mouth was so dry.

"You have to submit, to whatever comes. Any holding back will make the birth harder. It is important, this farewell. It is the first of the unfastenings."

Yes, I understood. For once, I had to submit, utterly. This was bigger than me, the war I was moving into, bigger than the train, bigger than the sun, it would blot out the sky. I struggled to sit up-right, she propped me up. I took a deep breath. "Goodbye!" They all looked up. "Goodbye, Genya. Don't forget me."

I could see him struggling with himself, his shock as great as mine. I knew him. He could show his anger in front of his comrades, but not his tears. He knew that everything he did now would be re-membered eternally. He had to act as heroic as the worker painted above him on the side of the train. Perhaps the train was the devil, after all. *Which will you protect, the revolution or your pregnant wife?* He was trembling like a horse, his eyes pleading. *I forgive you.*

"Now your parents," the old woman told me. "Wherever they are. Your brothers and sisters, your friends."

Was I dreaming this? "Goodbye, everyone." Tears streamed down my face. "Goodbye..." *Mama, Papa.*

"Forgive them," she commanded.

Mama? *It won't live.* And Papa, with Arkady that night, playing right into his hands. "I can't, I don't know how."

"Pray for guidance. Ask the Holy Mother to show you. Go on."

Please, Holy Mother, help me to forgive them. Unbind me. I tried to remember when I had loved them most. Mama in her morning dress, arranging roses. *Come help me, Marina.* Brushing my hair with her soft ivory brush, rubbing my cheeks with a rose petal to make them rosy. Papa, letting me lace the links into his starched cuffs, teaching me to play chess on Sunday afternoons. Bringing the box home from the printers, my blue books, their gleaming gold leaf. *Just the first of many,* he'd said.

"I forgive you," I whispered.

The comrades gathered around Genya, the politicals, the actors, side-glancing guiltily at him as he stood among them with his arms folded, his cap in his grip, under the rising sun of the *Red October.* His bright-painted train, his revolution. I forgave him. All of them. Kolya, Seryozha. Papa. Varvara, Genya. I could see the tears dripping down his sweet face.

Here was Slava, tucking my sheepskin roll next to me in the wagon, my boots and bast shoes, as if tucking my things into my grave. The sky was puffy with clouds. Goodbye, Genya. Goodbye.

The peasant slapped the reins and the sky began to move.

10 *Angels and Devils*

The dry rutted road stretched from horizon to horizon, my own Vladimirka. Though I sweated and shivered, dry mouthed, cramping, nauseated, I was grateful to be off the train and in the care of this straight-backed old woman. I lay across her knees as she rubbed my back. She wasn't Avdokia, but far closer than a crowd of dumbfounded actors and slogan-spouting Bolsheviks, not one of whom was acquainted with the bare facts of life. Maybe I'd have this baby right here in the wagon. I just was glad to be moving, grateful for the rocking of the cart, the slight breeze, the silent peasant, the grunting wheeze of the horse. I felt safe, safer than on the bright train of the Future, which, disappearing, already seemed unreal.

The pains came and went, and the midwife murmured prayers and pressed my back, resting her broad hand on my belly. I slept when I could. I dreamed of my mother. She was wrapped in a blue veil, with Ukashin at her side. *What appears to be a straight line is only part of the larger form.* Yes. I'd forgotten. I was in this wagon feeling its rhythmic jolts, but also in the nursery with Avdokia, getting ready for bed. And still under the snow halfway to Alekhovshchina. And watching flakes falling into the Catherine Canal from a white bed, where Kolya smoked a cigar. I was the old woman at my side, and also the child struggling to emerge from my feverish body. Perhaps I was also standing on the Finland shore, breathing the briny air, looking out over a swamp, and saying, *This is where I will build my city.*

Sometime later—an hour? A year?—we entered a village, trees passing overhead, the cries of chickens and children. The cart stopped. The midwife spoke to someone. Would we get out here? I peered over the side. A little hard-baked village, a red cow, women at the well. She told the peasant to drive on.

I groaned. "This isn't it?" We'd been driving so long.

"A little farther. Almost there." She patted my back.

We creaked over the deep ruts out the other end of the village, back into the buzzing green, the jammy scent of hot pine, branches intertwined above us, insects whirring, until we finally pulled up before an izba nestled deep in the trees like a witch's hut. This tumbledown izba, half choked in vines. What was next, hen's legs? Baba Yaga? *Hut, turn and face me.* A young woman waited for us there. She wore the same face as the midwife, and a blue *sarafan* and white embroidered blouse. She helped steady me as I climbed from the cart. So this was where I would have my child, wherever this was... *Zhili-buili, once upon a time...* I'd been transported back to when tsars won their kingdoms through valor, and horses had wings and firebirds made promises.

The midwife handed my sheepskin and bundle to the young one. The silent peasant drove off. "This is my daughter," the midwife said. The young one's braid was blond, while the midwife's was gray, and her cheeks were as round as peaches. Other than that, they were the same woman. I was seeing across time, from youth to age. *There is no time,* the Ionians said. *It's just your place on the spiral.*

They led me, not to the izba but down a path overgrown with grass and starred with flowers, to a pond covered in duckweed. In a clearing stood a bathhouse. *The baba, the woods, the bathhouse.* I'd been brought through time to a Russia that existed before it even bore the name. I vomited into the grass, though I had little in my stomach, a sour thread.

At the threshold, another young woman waited, identical to the first, but wearing a red *sarafan* with a plain white blouse, her braid the same blond, her face the same moon. The bathhouse was crude and dark and I was afraid. I balked, fighting weakly, but the midwife and her daughters shoved me inside. A small wooden hut, the three of them tall and broad shouldered and buxom. Where would there be room for me? Candles lit the darkness, and the floor was strewn with straw and fragrant herbs—such a strong scent after the fresh air, very green, both bitter and sweet, artemisia and chamomile and mint, and it made me feel oddly less sick—a surprise. I hadn't imagined myself feeling better even for a moment.

In the red corner, a lamp glowed before an icon of the Vladimirskaya Theotokos in her black robe, the Child nuzzling her cheek, her face steeped in pity. I glanced back at the daylight as they closed the door. *Goodbye!* The next time I saw the sun, I'd have a child in my arms...if I ever saw it again. So this would be my arena, my gladiator's pit—this bench, this stool, this straw...I wondered how many women had come here for their children's birth. How many had lived? How many had died? Had it been scrubbed since the last time?

They laid my sheepskin on the simple bench. The midwife bowed, crossed herself, and knelt in the herbs, as did the daughters. They pulled me down between them. Together we prayed for intercession, a swift delivery. I noticed a second icon next to the Vladimirskaya, a Theotokos I'd never seen—veilless in a red cloak, long red hair flowing freely over her shoulders. I'd never seen a redheaded Virgin. That had to be a good sign. My lips moved along in silent prayer, my teeth chattering with fever. *O my All-Gracious Queen Theotokos, my hope who befriends orphans and intercedes for strangers, joy of those who sorrow...*

Suddenly the pain returned, and I was falling. They grabbed me beneath my arms and hauled me to the bench, where I shivered and whined through a contraction like a sick dog, I was so tired, shaking. How could it be this cold in July? "My coat," I whispered through my cracked lips. The blue daughter covered me with the sheepskin. Her kindness made me cry. *For Mercy has a human heart / Pity, a human face*... The hard bench was good to press my back upon. The midwife and the red daughter continued their prayers as the blue one pulled off her kerchief and took down her braid, and then her sister's, and her mother's. She unbuttoned my dress, checked me all over, chanting, *"Untie, unloose the knots and chains, take your golden keys, O Theotokos, take your keys and unlock the fleshy gates, may the child come easily."* She took a rope with knots in it and held it over me, untied them one by one.

My own high-pitched moans appalled me, but I couldn't hold them back. I'd always thought of myself as a bold girl, but I'd just been naive. Another lost child in need of salvation. Now the two daughters pulled me up, the blue and the red, and walked me around the stool like a man in a prison yard, like a horse on a water wheel. I couldn't imagine hurting this much. Not even Chekists could have invented such a torture. And women lived through this every day. *Holy Theotokos, make it stop!* I wanted to lie down so badly, just for a little while, but they wouldn't let me. The midwife left me with these twin dolls, her younger selves. "Please don't go," I sobbed.

"I'll be back for the birth." She laughed and the door opened... *Ah, light!* Then it closed again, sealing me into the dark like the lid of a coffin.

Time slipped its track. The hut was a portal into the deep past. All my ideas, all my cleverness, my so-called personality made no difference here. The thing I was, a woman, a body, no more profound than a cow, a mare in foal, a bitch whelping under a porch. Whimpering, shivering. No thoughts, no mind. What good was all our revolutionary dumb show, pamphlets, *agitki* like so many children's skits performed for parents and doting relatives? No manifesto was going to help me now. *Holy Mother of God,* surely the baby was coming soon, surely this couldn't go on... "When is this going to stop?"

"What, you thought it just pops out like a pea from a pod?" My pretty keeper laughed. "You haven't even started."

I wept, sagged in their arms. I couldn't go through with this. It was a mistake. I should have gone back to Petrograd, to the modern mothers' home on Kamenny Island. I remembered how clean it was, the nurses, the revolutionary babies... "I can't do this."

"Well, who's going to? We can't do it for you," said the woman in blue. Were they twins? Twin sorceresses in their *sarafany* and loosened hair and secret smiles? "You have to work if you want the baby to come."

"I can't. I'm too weak..."

"City girl," the red one said. "You should have thought of that."

"She's sick. Mama's gone to get you something," said Mercy in blue.

"I have to lie down." I saw flames shooting up over their heads. *For Mercy has a human heart, Pity, a human face... Unlock, untie...* They couldn't hold me up forever, and finally laid me back on the wide, splintery bench. Hot and dark. I needed air. The scent of herbs was overwhelming—I'd smell it until my dying day, which could be soon... "I can't breathe. Please, open the door."

"It's not done," said the blue sister. Her cheeks were pink. Sweat dripped from her skin. "It's not safe."

"Just for a bit?" I begged. "I'll walk, I promise."

They opened the door. Blue sky! Cornflower blue, and a little breeze nodding the boughs. The trees peered in like shy children. The sisters took up handfuls of herbs from the floor and made vigorous crosses in the doorway, protecting me from some sort of devil, while I drank in fresh air in huge gulps. In a moment the red one slammed the door shut again, as if there were wild beasts that would smell my labor and come marauding. Was that it?

The only light came from the icon lamp and the candles and stray beams from between chinks in the log walls. But true to my word, I walked and walked, like some blind donkey. "Where's the old woman?" Suddenly it was of vital importance that old woman was back in the room. "Where did she go?"

"She has other things to do," the red daughter snapped, while her sister wiped my face. "She'll be back. Don't you trust us?" She cackled. Oh, she was a devil!

"Don't scare her," said the blue one. "She's getting you some milk. For strength. So you can push."

I tried to remember when I last ate. I'd been sick since Izhevsk...those cabbage pies...Though I recalled Genya trying to feed me. Bread, a bit of fish. Nothing stayed down. The next grip of pain doubled me over. One sister held me while the other put a knee in my back. They certainly knew their business, these story-book women.

After a year or two, the midwife returned in a flash of light and a gulp of blessed air before plunging us back into the thick, fuggy dark. She held a bowl to my lips, milk still warm from the cow...Were there still cows? I took a sip but it turned my stomach.

"Drink," she urged me. "You heard him, that devil. Said he'd burn down the village."

"He wouldn't really," I said between sips. Yes, I could feel strength passing into my body.

"Oh, you don't think so?" the old woman said.

But maybe he would. I thought of how he had once crushed the poor Virgin of Tikhvin. He wouldn't understand anything about this hut in the woods, the spells, the knots, the witch and her daughters blue and red. Outside, the sun must still be shining, the birds warbling their summer songs...for all the good it did me. Why wasn't it night already? If I could just hang on until nightfall, I'd have made it through this terrible day and the baby would come. *Theotokos, look upon my troubles...*

The old woman shook me, holding the bowl. "More. You have to try."

I drank a few more swallows before she let me sink onto the bench.

I dozed between pains. A terrible rustling came from the rafters. Angels, hundreds of them, hung from the ceiling above my head, upside down, with wings like leather. I could hear them rustling, trying to get closer. They stared down with big squidlike eyes, blinking, dumb, neither male nor female. No physical bodies, no sex, no idea what we humans suffered. All they could do was gape, trying to get a good view of my misery. I got on my hands and knees, forehead cradled on my arms, my tightening belly resting on my thighs, and endured like a cow. No mind, no self, my name was Woman, my name was Pain. The red daughter pressed my spine with her giant hands.

"I don't want it anymore," I whispered.

"Too late," said the red sister.

It won't live, my mother had said.

If the child was doomed, why even try? It would die and so would I, and we'd be buried in a field in Udmurtia and no one would ever find me. I doubted Genya would even return to the village, let alone burn it. I crouched there, on hands and knees, weeping. Couldn't I just die? Did they have to make me live through it all the way?

"That's enough," said the midwife. "Get her up."

They lifted me to my feet, tried to make me walk. "She can't, Mama," said the blue daughter, blue-eyed, with arms like a blacksmith's. "It's the fever. She's burning up. She can't stand."

The old woman came to me, grabbed my chin. "You're not getting away from me," she said. Her eyes were very blue. Her upper lip was long, her nose was short, her gray hair fell like a waterfall. "Hear me?" She slapped me. "Wake up!" Her eyes burned into me. "You're going to have this baby, Bolshevik. Now walk!" They hauled me and shoved me, shouted, praised, threatened. The old woman muttered prayers, incantations, made signs and symbols in the air. However much I begged them to leave me to die, they held me and pressed me, sponged me, and walked me round and round the birthing stool. "Take me outside. Just let me breathe. I can't breathe!"

Finally, the old woman opened the door, making violent crosses with handfuls of herbs, as the daughters walked me as far as the threshold, where I gulped fresh air like cold, sweet spring water, as much as I could get until the witch slammed the door again. "Satisfied? There are dangers you can't begin to understand. Spirits who would love to kill you and your child." Pointing at me with her bony finger like a prosecutor. "You have to trust me. I've been through this a few times. I have six daughters, all born in this very bathhouse. All living."

"I have a daughter too," said the blue sister.

"And I have two," said the red one.

The witch had daughters who had daughters who had daughters...all the daughters in the world, stretching before us like the mirrored hall at Versailles. It was nauseating. I sank to my knees in the herbs and straw, rocking my hard belly back and forth like a bell. *We shall not hear those bells...* No, we would not. Not those saintly chimes, only mournful gongs and the blatting of car horns. Or worse. The screams and cries of the damned.

The midwife stood, her hands on her broad knees. Oh no, was she giving up on me? I was really going to die. I clutched at her leg. "Don't go! I'll be good. I'll walk. Please."

"You'll be fine. Give her the rest of that milk," she told the red one. "And you drink it." Pointing at my nose. She left me sobbing there on the dirt floor, in the straw. Like a beast in a stall.

"I have to go too," said the blue one, patting my shoulder. "I'll be back in an hour."

"No! You can't..." They were abandoning me!

"Send Sonya," the red one called over my collapsed form.

I lay curled in the straw, weeping and mumbling childhood prayers. *O Holy Theotokos, save us for we have no other help than you.* So this was what it was like to die. You begged for it. I went from sweating to shivering as the angels goggled overhead. I swore at them while the red sister helped me onto the bench, covered me with the sheepskin. I lay trembling so violently I had to hold on to the rough wood not to fall. I faded into sleep. And dreamed of the bathhouse spirit, Bannik, a disagreeable dwarf with a huge nose and chin, sniffing the air. *Where is that baby...* But it wasn't here yet. He would have to wait.

I dozed between contractions, lay on the broad bench watching beads of light through the chinks in the door—a constellation of glowing, elongated ovals projected onto the straw, where they took on a life of their own. I knew they were visitors from other dimensions. If only I could speak to them. Their presence reminded me of Ionia, and all the training I'd had there. I remembered Natalya—*breathe in chaos, breathe out light*. I breathed and thought of her, attacked by soldiers...Did anyone escape this curse of the body? The body, the body...I counted the small lozenges of light like a rosary.

Sometime later—hours, days?—the door opened again. Not the midwife, but another daughter, younger still, her hair braided, wearing a rose *sarafan* with a white apron, carrying a pail. I was shaking so violently I thought my teeth would break. The woman in red spoke to the girl, took her braids down, untied what knots she could find on her, then left us alone, gone before I could gather the breath to beg her to stay. The rose girl could not have been more than sixteen. *Oh God*. She sponged my forehead nervously. I pushed her away, her clumsy touch. I wanted the midwife and her great-armed dolls, blue and red.

Time refused to move. Another wave—an enormous hand, crushing me, cracking my spine. The angels came closer but I snarled at them and cursed. "Stop looking at me!"

"Who?"

I kicked off the sheepskin. Who was this, lying in someone's shift on the bare bones of a bench, in a stink of sweat, her skin on fire? "Is it night yet?" I asked. "Just tell me that much."

"It's July," the girl said. "It won't be night for hours."

Night. Such a beautiful word. A big darkness, not this musty closed-in armpit, everything cool and quiet under the indifferent stars. The richness of night's satin robes, not this straw-filled abattoir. Between the pains, I breathed and whispered the names of the stars in the Moving Group, *Alioth, Mizar, Merak, Phad, Megrez, Alcor*, as the girl stared at me and crossed herself. Did she think it was a spell? The stars, born together, moving together through great time and space. The birth of stars was something to hang on to as my tenders came and left. I could smell food on them, smoke…A world was taking place out there as I was dying. This was life's bitter secret. While someone was being torn apart, dying of fever, flayed alive, the world continued. Icarus fell from the sky and the peasant went on plowing. Not even his ox looked up.

They always left one behind to watch me. One skeined wool, another tooled a bit of leather. The red one came back from dinner, stinking of garlic. Sometimes there were two and they marched me around, gossiping about village happenings. In between pains they asked me where I came from, how I'd gotten so far from home. I couldn't remember. My saviors, my tormentors. While overhead, the angels gawked and rustled their leather wings.

My labor was becoming permanent. I had stopped trying, stopped crying. Every few minutes the pain woke me, pain going nowhere, doing nothing but killing me. Then I fell back into feverish sleep. I dreamed of horrible, pointless things, like pulling hair from the ground, hand over hand. Finding a rusted metal doll left behind in a fire. This was no child, it was a monster. It wasn't even a birth, it was a sentence, like being tied to four horses and pulled to pieces. The angels rustled overhead, like theater patrons with their programs.

At last, the red woman opened the door and I saw darkness. Cool air. She said a prayer to the evening star. It was my last night on earth. This is how death came. Your child wouldn't be born, you were too weak, it was the wrong time, the wrong place. If only I hadn't caught this fever. If only I'd gone back to Petrograd where I belonged. She sponged me with water, poured the milk into me a thimbleful at a time.

No more light beads to count now, only the flicker of the candle. Pain spread out like a stain. I collected it in my mind, forced it back small. Not a country but a pool, not a pool but a puddle, not a puddle but a bowl, a teacup. But just when I'd gotten it small, it flooded out again, a stain, a tide, and my city drowned. The pain erased all that was not me. And then it erased me as well, so only Pain itself was left. And Time. Time my rope, my line across the flood. But these women had no clocks. And the sun once up would never set. I would not outlive this contest. Death was coming.

Kolya, think of me! Could he feel the end of what he'd started? If we were as connected as he'd always professed, could he feel this? Oh, he'd think he'd overeaten, tossing in his bed.

As my minder dozed, I sensed something in the corner opposite the red one. Not the angels. This was a new figure, a somber woman dressed in a black cloak, with sorrowful Byzantine eyes like the Vladimirskaya Theotokos. So gentle, so dear. No Child at her cheek, and her skin was made of gold. *Have you come for me, sorrowful Mother? Have you come to take me, wrap me in your arms? Is it time? Pity me, for I am so tired. You, who birthed a child knowing it would die, you who labored, help me now.*

She didn't speak, but we stared for centuries. There was no time in hell.

I don't ask for life, I prayed to the dark Virgin. *Only for an end to this pointless ordeal. Gentle Virgin of Death, come. Give birth to my end, stop this unholy siege. I surrender.* She was coming near, the gold of her hands and of her face. At long and dear last, the Virgin of Death approached to gather up her weak daughter, with eyes of sorrow, preparing to deliver her final blessing. *Take me, Holy Mother, and give me rest . . .*

But then the door opened, and sun splashed the aperture. Dawn, and with it the horrible midwife. She stepped between me and tender Death. *No!* But my savior, the Dark Virgin, retreated into the shadows. And this old woman blazed in the doorway, blazed like sun on Scythian armor. "How is she?"

The daughter shook her head.

"I was afraid of that. Go get your sister." The old warrior lowered herself to the bench next to me, her hand on my brow, so ugly and mean compared with my golden Virgin. She wiped my face with cool water. "This has gone on long enough, don't you think?" she said to me.

I would have laughed if I'd had an atom of life left in me.

She held out a glass with some tea. "This will make it go faster."

She propped me up, held the rim to my lips, helped me drink. Bitter. I drank it all. Anything that might kill me faster. She let me lie back down. "Sleep a little now."

I dozed for a while, praying for the figure in black to return and fold me into her cloak of night, for this all to be over.

All at once, my body, this tormented forked thing, began to convulse, a pain such as I had not yet known, a pain that bowed me back like a bridge, and it—I—emitted a scream that should have brought the hut down in a pile around us.

The old woman laughed with diabolical pleasure. She really did hate me. How she loved my screaming. "*Now* we're getting somewhere." While my body seized again. Once again I was possessed by raging life, plunged into this battle. *They flogged them with iron rods until the flesh fell from their bodies...*

"Now you're going to work, my girl." No retreat without orders. "Scream all you want, Bolshevik."

I twisted, I writhed in her arms, I tried to get away from her, but she was as strong as five men. My body split open like a great door pushing aside the rust of the ages, like the earth cracking open in a terrible quake. The sorrowful Mother of God, hovering in the shadows, disappeared, abandoning me to this hellish old crone. "Are you ready to have this baby?"

The pain was tearing me open the way a cook dismembers a chicken, and I emitted the high yelps of a half-killed beast. The midwife held me from behind on the bench, the blue daughter before me, massaging my legs. A bedspring of iron screwed its way through me. *No, no, no...*

"Oh yes," grunted the old lady. "Say yes!"

But I could only howl.

The door opened, the bright morning like knives in my eyes. "Getting close?"

"Shut the door!" the midwife shouted as a giant burst of pain tore through me. "She screams like the devil. Pray, *devushka*! *Mother of God, save us. Holy Mother, All-Preserving Queen...*"

"It's coming," said the red daughter, kneeling.

"There you go, Bolshevik," the witch gloated. "You thought you'd outfoxed us, didn't you?"

I wept. "I can't...I can't!"

"It's coming! The head! I see it! The hair. It's a redhead!"

"Push!" commanded my tormentor. Sitting behind me, her arms under mine, bracing my back.

I didn't care about the pain now. I didn't care if I died. I didn't care if I ripped my body loose from my body to trail behind me like a sheep torn open by a wolf. I leaned back against the old woman and turned myself inside out.

"Here it comes!"

"No, wait! Something's wrong!" A hand on my thigh.

"Holy Mother of God, what now?" spat the witch. "Take her!" She handed me off to one of her moons. "Stop pushing, you. Stop it. Turn over." She thrust me down on the straw, on my knees, my head in the red lap, fingers up inside me, digging—was she going to pull the child out of me like a goat? The flat of a hand on my back, the way you'd steady a horse. "I've got it! Yes, now."

Suddenly, arms lifted me to the birthing stool, where I squatted as they held me, pushing my life out.

And a wet

> *hot*
>> *weight*

fell

> *between my thighs.*

Blood slick, the twisted gleaming cord still attached.
A girl, alive.
Eyes open, as green as grass. Full head of hair.
Laughter welled inside me like a spring.
"Look, she's looking at you."
Staring at me in wonder. She wasn't even crying! And how beautiful she was, my daughter! Eyes, upturned at the corners, just like his! Her mouth a little bow, her big cat's eyes. What a beauty,

krasavitsa. No redness, no swollenness, after all that. Nothing was as I'd imagined. It was uncanny the way she examined my face, with such surprise! *So this is the world,* she seemed to say. The air we breathed in her little lungs. "She's not even crying."

"Oh, she'll be crying plenty," said the midwife. "So much trouble for such a little nub." She wiped her forehead on the back of her arm. "I've never worked harder in my life."

They wrapped the cord in a piece of red embroidery thread and bit it off, wiped her, put her into my arms in a clean dish towel.

"I could have a kid like that in my sleep," said the red daughter. "Look at those eyes."

My child, staring at me in wonder. As if I were the miracle.

"The shoulder got stuck," explained the blue daughter.

"Never thought that'd be over. Is there tea?" said the red one, stretching, cracking her spine.

She weighed nothing in my arms, as light as a rabbit. My daughter! Suddenly she opened her tiny mouth and began to wail. Not a full-lunged baby's scream, more a high creak like a cat's cry. "No, no, please don't cry, baby." It pierced me, that tiny high needle of a sound. My child. My sweet disaster. What was I doing wrong? She was as hot as a biscuit. That little mouth, and the bright flame of red hair. Did she not like me? I was crying too.

"What's her name, *milaya?*" said the blue daughter.

"Iskra." My voice was sanded to a whisper. *Spark.*

"It just was the feast of Alexander and Antonina," said the midwife, holding a cup to my lips. "How about Alexandra?"

The milk was sour now. I turned my face away. "No."

Another round face swam into view, the red sister. "You can't call a Bolshevik Alexandra." It was the tsarina's name.

The midwife crossed herself. "May God keep her."

"Antonina, then," said the blue one. "Look, Tonya, there's titty." And put her on my steaming, rock-hard breast. I struggled to stay awake. Her name was Iskra, not some saint they'd just pulled out of a bag! I thought I was shouting, but they couldn't hear me at all.

"At least they can't say we killed the girl," I heard the midwife say. "Theotokos be praised."

Her name is Iskra. But I was too tired to argue, I couldn't stay awake. My red-haired baby, my Iskra, my Spark.

11 *Iskra*

We led our camels, our lop-eared goats, across the dry, hard red plains. Red dust in our hair, in our mouths. Loose shale slid and clacked underfoot on the paths, the sound of the camels' bells purer than water. Our small band of Ionians — Ilya, Anna, Bogdan, Lilya. The skins of water shifted on the saddles, dry bread in our packs, dates. The sun ate up half the sky. *Tam! There!* The red sandstone walls of a great city loomed, blue domed, with massive iron gates, the Master's walled citadel. I knew it instantly. In the center, the Tower, like a giant rook in chess. But he never said how small we'd feel standing before its gates in our rags and coating of red dust, the goats bleating, the sun pounding down like a fist. I couldn't even reach the rope to pull the great bell. How long would they leave us to stand here? We beat on the doors, cried out, but our puny fists made no sound on the enormous gates, and there were no guards to hear us.

I saw a small door, hidden in the large one like a cupboard door — no handle, not even a keyhole. Yet it must open somehow. I began knocking on it in a secret pattern I remembered seeing in Ukashin's papers in his *kabinyet*. It was the knight's move — up two, one across. *Untie, unloose the knots and chains...* I whispered to it, and the door gave way, and cool air streamed out.

The way was too small for the camels. We'd have to leave them, and all our cargo but what we could carry. I slung a bag over my shoulder, filled it with the most precious things, bangles and little statues, but the others refused to leave the camels behind. Who cared about the camels? Didn't they want to enter the city?

"Don't go," Anna wept. Ilya, angry, turned away.

We'd come all this way! I would not stay outside, even if I had to go in there alone. I left my companions behind and entered the red city.

It was a maze of alleys. Women in veils whispered to me as I passed, but I couldn't understand them. They were telling me how to go, warnings, important things, but I had no time. I was late. The narrow streets turned and turned again, you couldn't see more than a few houses at a time. Would I ever find my way?

Suddenly I found myself at the square, the heart of the city. Around the red Tower lay the largest bazaar in the world. Rugs, living pictures, exotic birds, perfumes, spices, fakirs and beggars and wonder-workers of every description. A fire-eater spat flames, a woman wore a cobra like a shawl. On a street of jewelers and coppersmiths, I found a stall selling enamelwork and knew this to be my destination.

Enameled trays, tables, basins large enough to lie down in crowded the dark coolness of the shop. A long-bearded merchant waited on a cushion, smoking a hookah, but he didn't fool me. I knew the Master when I saw him. "What have you brought me?" he asked. I opened my satchel to show him my treasures, but it was empty. Everything had fallen out. All it contained was a thin stream of red dust.

"Look, she's coming around."

A clammy rag wiped my forehead, my neck, blue eyes peered, moon faces, yellow braids. A cup to my desert-parched lips. Church bells rang. Light through curtained windows. Where was my baby? "The baby!" I whispered through parched lips. My breasts on fire.

"She's sleeping. Drink." The cup again. Tea, some kind of potion. They began to sing...and sleep bore me away.

Crows calling. A priest dressed in black swung a censer. The sound of pure cold water. Oh God, I was dead. I hadn't made it after all. Light spilled across its wide waxed floors. It all smelled of beeswax, and bees droned outside. Honey in the walls. The grandfather clock stood in the hall. It struck the hour.

As I stood in the doorway a girl came to my side. Graceful and slim, in a white nightgown, barefoot, her red hair braided in loops as they'd done in Pushkin's day. Iskra! She was alive! But I'd missed her childhood. She was already fifteen. "This is all yours," I said. Mother out in the garden in a white dress, walking among the Queen Anne's lace. Maryino! Grandmère at the piano. I thought the house had burned, but here it was, and we were all here! On the lawn, Seryozha reclined in a lawn chair, his bright hair gold in the sun, in his white sailor's suit. He was doing something with his hands. He turned them over and showed me.

Cat's cradle.

I backed away and knocked over a lamp. The rug caught, the curtains. It lit her nightgown. *Stop, Iskra!* But she ran out through the yard, aflame, toward the woman in white.

"No, *devushka*. Shh..." The midwife.

I fought her off. There was something in her face. Lies painted her brow. "Where's my baby? What did you do with her?"

"She wants the child." Her daughters, the blue and the red.

"Where is she?" I was up on my feet, running around the small room. "Where have you put my baby? What have you done with her?"

"She was sick, *milaya*."

"A tiny thing."

I struggled against their big bodies, the hot arms they were wrapping me in.

"She wasn't very strong."

"We put her in the stove."

"NO!" I shrieked and ran to the oven, still warm from the morning's baking. I opened the door and there she was, like a loaf of fine white bread, wrapped in a bit of blue calico. Her eyes closed. I ripped the calico off her. She was even tinier than I remembered...The midwife and her witches tried to pull me away. I flung them across the room, tuned out their jabbering, the cawing of crows. I held the tiny limp body to my fevered throat, no bigger than a squirrel. Opened her mouth, breathed fire into her. Breathed and turned her over, pressing her with my hot palms. I became a bright ball of fire, *hotter, hotter. Come, Iskra. Closer.* I felt her hovering now, close, very close, a little tremor, like fast-beating wings.

"She's gone, *milaya*. You have to stop."

I roughly elbowed her aside, gathered every last inch of myself and hurled myself into my child the way Ukashin did when he wanted to get our attention, the way he'd taught me.

Felt a twitch. A flinch. As when a sleeper falls in his dream. Was it me or was it her? "You saw that," I shouted at the witches. Blank moon faces.

Again, like a live star.

And she jerked. She trembled, she shook, her little arms shot out, her hands tensed into fists. A little cat's cough, and then—her mouth opened, and out came a high thin cry. I gazed down into her outraged face growing red, pressed her to my aching breasts, and laughed the way the midwife had laughed when I said I couldn't bear it anymore, and she told me she would not let me go. Iskra was mine. I'd scorch the earth for her, until Death himself gave her up.

They fell to their knees in the straw, praying. Thanking the Virgin. Touching me, touching the child. I nestled my crying baby's head under my jaw. She smelled of sweet grass and, ever so slightly, of smoke.

12 *Antonina*

I woke to white curtains blowing in an open window carrying the songs of village women. Was this the hymn I'd heard? Then I realized—the baby! Where was my baby? I shot up to find myself no longer on a bench in the bathhouse but in a peasant izba, ancient and smelling strongly of medicinal herbs. My heart beat wildly until I saw the cradle hanging from the rafters before the stove, like in Faina's hut. Wobbly-legged, I hauled myself up, my torn body burning, leaking, but she was alive, alive, snugged inside the tiny hammock. With those delicate features, so sweet, so perfect—the glossy eyelids, the ginger hair, the slight snore. She was snoring! The most miraculous snore the world has ever heard. They had her swaddled up tight in a dish towel—the flush of her cheeks, her moist curls—and her lips were moving. She was saying something in her sleep. Oh, if only I could hear what she was saying. She still remembered the other place, the world she had lived in before she came here. *What are you dreaming, my love?*

I put my hand on the big stove. Stone cold. But I knew I had saved her, snatched her from Death itself. The tiny aperture of her nostrils was enough to make me weep. I felt dizzy, I had to lie down now, but I needed my baby. Steeling myself for her shrieks, I scooped her up out of the cradle. So light in my arms. She protested, one short mewl, then settled. So warm, and smelling of bread.

Through the open windows, a breeze carried the scent of fields and the jamlike sweetness of the pines. The fight was over. I held my child and gingerly lay down on the bench. I thought of that empty sack, the emptiness of my being, but it wasn't so. I had saved her. She was here. The izba's ancient rough-planed logs reminded me of the midwife. Her shelves sagged with jars and crocks, herbs drying upside down. And on the breeze came that angelic song again... This must have been the choir I'd heard and thought it was church.

Iskra's lips were moving. I turned my ear to her, seeing if I could overhear her secrets, but she gave up nothing. The wonder of her—her breath, her golden eyelashes, her bowed lips, her beating heart. I hadn't known how ferociously I would love a child. I lay with her nestled in the curve of my body, wrapping myself around her. It was so hot, why did they wrap her like that? But I was afraid of waking her.

For the rest of our lives, this creature and I would know one another. It was almost impossible to take in the reality of that. First you were one, then you were two. Crazy, when I was no different from the woman they delivered to the midwife, carried off the train, fellow-traveler and nuisance. And now, mother. This body, with bursting breasts and torn loins, where was the *I* of me now?

There is no you, the body said. *Only me.* This body, these breasts, my flaccid belly—hot, weeping, empty and full, it belonged more to Nature than to myself. You could say there *was* no *me,* ultimately, only this body, and its primal urge to make other bodies. Like the Cosmic Egg—first there was nothing, and then desire.

I had to pee. I needed to get up but wanted to stay here, watching her, smelling her hair. I wasn't ready for time to begin, for things to start happening. Give me a moment to understand. She was frowning, making little sounds. I held my breath. *Don't wake up. Please, I'm not ready...* She would see me buried. What if we didn't like each other? What if she judged me, what if she saw everything that was wrong with me—the gaping abyss of my flaws? And of course she would—what daughter didn't? She squeezed her eyes, wrinkled her nose. Her voice, like a creaking door. *Don't cry, Iskra. Please, God, I don't know what to do with you.*

She fell back to sleep.

Thank God. I could pull her back from Death itself but didn't know what to do with a dirty diaper. I was terrified of her, and my terror made me laugh. This redheaded riddle. Kolya never wanted children, never wanted this permanent tie. Would he be furious? But Genya would love her, protect her. He was a man for the future. He had longed for a child to carry on his shoulders, and would help her touch the stars.

She was talking again. What was going through her newborn mind, that galaxy, what tides did she recall? What dreams could she have? Did she remember the Dark Virgin by an open door, the fallen lantern? That the witches had put her in the oven? I lay curled around her, like a nebula curled around its brightest star.

Thank God to be off the *Red October,* away from the pinched face of Yermilova and the glowering mien of Antyushin, the actors, the politicals, the crowds, and the soldiers and the talk of atrocities. I could imagine Genya, mad with worry. For the first time I wondered, how long had I been here? Were they still waiting for me? Or were they already thundering east through the Urals, bringing the word to the benighted? Genya the Agit-Evangelist.

I leaned over to drink from a jug. That creaky cat's cry. Oh no—her face all crumpled and red! *Shhhh.* Such a little bundle wrapped up like that, her head popping out. Now she was awake and furious, shrieking. What was I to do with her? I patted her back but it didn't help. What did she want? Diapers? Feeding? I started to cry too. I tried to put her on my big hard breast but she kept turning her head and screaming like I was trying to kill her. *Please stop, Iskra. Oh please, baby, your stupid mama doesn't know what to do.* She already didn't like me, this poor thing wrapped up like a little loaf. We both lay there weeping.

Finally, the midwife came in, smelling of hay, sweaty from labor. "Look who's awake," she beamed, washing her face and hands at the basin, drying them on a white towel. Her old face's network of lines grew bolder with her smile.

"What's wrong with her? She won't stop."

"She's just hungry, *milaya.*"

She held the baby snug in the crook of her arm as I used the chamber pot, unsteady. I washed my hands and arms and face while she clucked at my daughter, quieting her. It should have been Avdokia. How I missed her! I imagined my own mother at my birth—had she felt this helplessness? But no, she had been through it before with Volodya. To think that I was even more ignorant than Vera Borisovna...But she'd had the luxury of the Furshtatskaya Street flat, not a peasant's izba, doctors and nannies and relatives all around. Yet this izba was a good sight more comfortable than that breathless black nightmare of a bathhouse...

How alone and very far from home we were.

The midwife guided me back to the bench, my cunt on fire, plumped the pillow behind me, and helped the baby onto my enormous hot breast. Swollen, immense—my God, where had that come from? How could she get her mouth onto that? The midwife showed me how to coax her mouth open with a little milk on her lips, to hold the breast flat with a finger so I wouldn't smother her. We sat watching her feed—an everyday miracle, nothing more mundane or astonishing. The air through the window cooling our damp faces.

"How long have I been here?" I asked.

"She came a fortnight ago Sunday. You were still screaming and raving the Sunday after that. What a week that was, the Lord be praised, we had to wrap you in sheets and douse you with water." She touched her face. There was a bruise. Had I struck her? "Tomorrow comes Sunday again."

Two weeks! And I didn't even know where *here* was. Alone with my newborn, not a ruble in my pocket, not a soul who knew my name.

The big woman stroked my hair with her work-calloused hand, smelling of hay and sunshine. And where was the train?

"Any word from my husband?" Two weeks...he could be anywhere.

She nodded, rose, wiping her hands on her apron. "A soldier came. He brought you a letter. You've been so sick, we didn't want to bother you." Reached up into the red corner, and there, propped against the icon of the Vladimirskaya Theotokos, a wrinkled green envelope. She held it out to me, but I was afraid of dislodging Iskra. I had no idea whether she was even getting any milk, but she had stopped crying, so she must be getting something. "Open it for me," I told her.

She tore it open with a big blunt forefinger and extracted the letter, handed it to me.

It was a poem. In Genya's unmistakable hand. He lettered like a madman, cubo-futuristically.

Funeral for Myself on the Tracks at Kambarka

The bells, did you hear them?
I'm a clown
> *I'm a carnival devil*
> *bells on my papier-mâché hat.*
Who would have dreamed
> *I would*
> *drop*

my own heart
from the gallows
pull the rope myself.

THE
CR
  A
   C
  KK
reverberates
   from Petrograd to
           Vladivostok.

But I did it.
Is it weakness or strength
to
    hang
     your own heart?
It's the hell of it.

Tenderness gets in my eyes.

Now I put on my costume
    GREAT RUS
The part I play
           I wrote the lines myself
It's a disaster
   and yet,
      out of disaster,
  the world.

We're all giving birth.

No, not all of us, Genya. Not all.

Yes, I'm a cold-blooded swine.
  Hate me,
        curse me.
  I'm shit.
Man is a puppet.
              Woman is a mystery.
    I don't know anything about life.
I cut
    my own throat
          here tonight
That's what you're seeing,
    The last of my rich

    r

        e

            d   b l o o d.
Tomorrow I'll look like a man,
    but won't
          bleed.

This is no place for humans.
    Steel and iron alone——
        machines
A train   an army   an idea   a war
    When we're finished
    we'll find the humans.
        Show them
    to their new homes.

Here's a joke:
    Do you know why there are no more horses in
    Petrograd?
Because horses have to be fed.
    Where men can live on just the hope of it.

Doesn't that just split your sides?

I should have left you with One-Arm,
that humorless chump
But I'm a demon of vanity.
I was sure if I said
it would be all right,
it would be.

I see you still
on the Chernyshevsky Bridge,
the moon on the ice,
frost on your lashes.

I lay back on the pillow, looking into the trees, baby at my breast, the midwife pouring milk into a bowl. Long-haired birches streamed. So my Stenka Razin had once again thrown his Persian bride to the deep. Proving his loyalty to his brothers at the expense of his love. He was the tenderest of souls and yet, if vanity was at stake, he would walk into hell itself with his chin held high. I could imagine them watching him—Yermilova, Antyushin—reporting back to Moscow on what he'd done, their poet, their great-voiced embodiment of the Soviet dream. How pleased they must be with their Stenka. The train, vanishing over the Urals, red flags ablaze.

At least he remembered the frost on my lashes!

Genya, Great Rus. Throwing himself under the train—but only in verse. No Anna Karenina. She was a woman, caught as a woman, bearing the full brunt of it, not some full-throated giant in the prime of his life, able to stir the masses like thunder. That overgrown baby! Kolya would never have left me like this, in labor alone in a hut in the forest. He would at least have pressed papers into my hands, money, something I could use, some way to get home. While Genya spent the night writing a poem.

I gazed down at Iskra, nursing, and thought back to how I'd left her father on the platform in Tikhvin. Her mama was a fool indeed.

I had to get up, start thinking clearly. I motioned for the midwife, whose name was Praskovia. She took Iskra, helping me stand, firm arm under mine, as hard as wood. I noticed I was wearing a pretty linen shift that wasn't mine, a dazzling white. I stood at the open doorway, admiring the trees, the birches' long boughs streaming, and watched the old lady briskly change Iskra on the bench. Cleaning her, wiping, the new diaper, folding her back into the swaddling cloth. I would never be able to do this. Never. "Can we leave her free for a while?" I asked. Even my voice was unsteady.

"Free?"

"Unwrapped?"

"Babies like to be swaddled. It keeps them calm." She said it in a way that invited no discussion. I wished Avdokia was here, she was easier to cajole. But where once I would have argued, now I simply watched her wrap Iskra smartly—like watching someone with clever hands make a bed.

I stepped outside—would she stop me? Was there yet some new prohibition I was violating? Some Bannik I was insulting? But the old woman seemed to have relinquished her prohibition on the out-of-doors, and I planted myself on a rough bench, facing the trees. She brought me the neatly wrapped package of my child. *Did you really put her in the stove?* I wanted to ask. Iskra gazed up at me, entranced, or perhaps it was just the sun-dappled light overhead. I felt suddenly like a fraud, bankrupt—what did I have to give this trusting creature but the lostness of myself? My sack was empty. Red dust.

The midwife sat down next to me, her big work-roughened hands splayed on her knees. We stayed like that a good long while, just listening to the songs from the fields and the wind in the trees. There was something she wanted to say, she was turning it around in her mind's hands, trying to find the right place to begin. She plucked at her apron, and tucked the swaddling cloth around Iskra once again, when it was perfectly tight. "What do you think you'll do now?" she asked finally.

Iskra was wondering the same thing, her clever moss-green eyes, so much like his merry blue ones. Was it that the old woman wanted me to leave? After all, I'd been lying here almost two weeks, raving, hitting her, sleeping in her hut, eating her food—yes, I must have been eating, I wasn't particularly hungry. They had their crops to get in. Was she telling me it was time to move on? Fear and regret ran down my head and shoulders like cold water. I wasn't ready to go, I could hardly stand. I had no plan. "Head home, I guess," I said.

"And where is that, *devushka*?" Her face, not unkind.

"Petrograd," I said.

She sighed, gazing up into the trees. "And how will you go so far, with that tiny morsel?"

It was a good question. How would I navigate the crowded, wretched stations, the waiting, the hellish rush for the trains? I remembered well the day Kolya and I watched that tide of humanity fight its way onto the carriages at Nikolaevsky station. Could I do that alone, with a newborn in my arms, no help, no friends, no food—no money? I kissed Iskra's tiny face, her body all bundled up like a cigar, head popped out the top like the bulb of a lollipop.

"There's a woman," the midwife spoke slowly, I could see the cautious lines of her mouth. "Here in the village. I told her about you, about the child."

A strange buzzing in my ears. The wind rustled the birches, the pines nodded sadly.

"A good woman," she said, gently touching my arm. "Her husband's too old for the draft. The baby would be safe with them, dear. It's not Petrograd, but she'd have a good life." She sighed, the weathered crevasses in her skin as deep as canyons. She'd seen her share of the trouble that human beings could find themselves in.

Leave Iskra—was that what she was saying? Walk away from my redheaded baby? She smiled, but her eyes were sadder than ashes. She wasn't asking me to abandon my baby, she was simply pointing out my position, trying to save me and the child both, just as she had in the bathhouse. Trying to say that Iskra would have a chance here. A chance to grow up. A chance to be taken care of by someone who knew something about babies, the type of woman who would never find herself in my situation. This wasn't meanness, I told myself, just pure earthy practicality.

I saw myself as I must seem to her, a headstrong girl, unfortunate, luckless. No money, no people. Planning to drag a newborn child across a vast continent in wartime, taking filthy, crowded, disease-ridden trains to a future that was at best uncertain—and that would most surely involve cold and deprivation in a dangerous city, at a dangerous time. I forced myself to imagine earning my fare and my food begging in railway stations. Perhaps displaying my baby's hideous diaper rash for a few kopeks. Or begging in villages from those who had little themselves. Praskovia's sorrowful expression told me: *When she dies this time, you will have to bury her yourself, with your own hands, in a field.*

But when I looked down at Iskra, mesmerized by the shifting coins of light, I couldn't imagine leaving her. The midwife thought it for the best, Iskra raised by a good Christian woman like herself or one of her daughters—round-faced, upright, clean women. She must think, *What could be better than growing up sturdy and healthy in green fields, swimming in the river, cutting rye into shocks to dry in the sun, singing in harmony with women she'd grown up with, spinning the flax?* The regular calendar of Saints' Days and feasts. Surely that was better than the hardship of life in the city with its inedible food and unheated rooms and poor clothes, typhus and cholera.

But I had visited izbas full of sick children, huts where women sat meekly at the foot of the table while their ignorant husbands intoned their vile, reactionary views. Demanding service and threatening beatings.

Could I imagine my daughter thinking that horned Jews killed the cattle, frightened of devils in the butter churn, monsters in the forest? Kolya's child and mine, growing up without Pushkin or Lermontov, *The Wind in the Willows, Les Malheurs de Sophie,* unaware there was a Europe, or that the moon only reflected the light of the sun, that the earth rotated around the sun and not vice versa. She would grow old and die barely conscious of the out-side world—like the countless millions who had died before us. A short, brutish life in a small, dreary place, waiting for Easter and signing her name with an *X. Don't have children.*

Yet I had to look hard at the reality I'd be subjecting her to. She could very well starve, as could I. She might die of a fever she'd pick up in traveling, or in Petrograd itself. *I* might die, leave her orphaned. She might not live long enough to read her first book. The midwife was offering me the possibility of a stable life for her. This tiny thing, red-faced and sweating, so bound in those swaddling clothes.

I couldn't stand it anymore, and loosed her from the cloths, let her arms and her chest and legs feel the breeze, I kissed those arms, that narrow chest. Our blood, mine and Kolya's—now there was a clever, volatile mix! She gazed up at me with those eyes, and I knew no round-faced Olya or Alya was going to be up to that. With a little luck, I would make some kind of life for her.

"I think we'll take our chances," I said. "But thank the woman for me."

I felt Avdokia somewhere, sighing, exactly as this woman was sighing right now.

The midwife pushed down on her thighs and stood up, heavily. "Well, that's that. May God have mercy on you both. At least she's been baptized, that's a comfort."

"What?!" I didn't want to shout, but it just came out. The baby startled and started to creak.

"Wrap her up, I told you. The arms—she's used to being held tight inside you." She took the swaddling cloth and laid it on the bench.

"You baptized her? While I was sick?"

"Well, we didn't know if the baby was going to make it, *milaya.* So I baptized her myself. Then the priest came—don't you remember?"

The incense, the priest—that was real.

"Put her head there," she instructed, pointing to the head of the cloth. I did it. "Yes, we named her Antonina. I hope you like it. It's a good name. You can call her Tonya, or Nina, or Inna."

She'd baptized the baby herself while I'd been raving. Of all the things to worry about. I looked down into Iskra's face, those eyes, Kolya's mischief already showing there, and my own stubbornness. Already, a child with aliases. *Antonina Gennadievna Kuriakina.* I kissed her. *Iskra. Tonya. Inna. Nina.* "She needs to be bigger to travel," I said. "But I won't take your bread for free. I'll work for my keep."

She laughed out heartily, standing over me. "You've never held a scythe in your life. I bet you've never even used a broom, from the looks of you."

Did I really look so useless? "I've dug ditches, I've built fortifications, I've cleared snow. Everyone works in the Soviet Republic."

"You're a good girl," she said, patting my shoulder. "You rest, I'll think about it." She went back out to the fields, chuckling, leaving me and Iskra outside the izba watching the clouds float across the patches of blue.

Wildflowers bloomed in the long grass. The wind in the birches, their haymaking song on the air. I'd been abandoned, and yet right at this moment, it was enough to be here. It was warm and peaceful under the blue bowl of heaven. I fed my daughter, steering the other massive breast into her small mouth the way the midwife had instructed. I would figure out how to get home when the time came. Meanwhile, Iskra nursed and gazed up at the sky, the clouds chasing one another, a blue it rarely got in Petrograd. A real Maryino sky.

She fell asleep in my arms, wet lipped, drooling. I tucked my breast back into the white slip and rocked her, humming along with the singing. *Iskra, Tonya. Nina. Inna.* So trusting. I was her mother now, I had to make the decisions. I would pay these women back, and once she got stronger, we would go back to Petrograd. She might not have ballet lessons or sweetmeats from Eliseev's, we might live in a tiny room somewhere, but we would walk down the granite embankments of the Neva and read Pushkin and I would teach her the Argentine tango, let her climb the trees of the Tauride Gardens, look at pictures in the galleries of the Hermitage. And see if we could find a certain clever fox.

13 *Chess*

I worked in the fields, my birth-emptied body compacting into something I could count on again, while Iskra grew red-cheeked and flirty-eyed. I had never worked so hard in my life. Being Korsakova's servant was nothing compared to this, not even digging trenches during the German assault. Swinging a scythe, cutting rye with a sickle, binding grain into sheaves with reed grass and standing them up in the fields to dry. I fell asleep as soon as we stopped for a rest, in the shade of a tree or just under a wagon. The village was glad of my help. Their men had all been taken by the Whites when they'd come through in the spring. I learned what it was to work so hard you didn't think at all. We sang those beautiful songs in order to work at the same pace, as one, and keep our minds off the labor. Nothing I'd ever done in my nineteen years on earth had prepared me for the difficulty of peasant life. I stopped to nurse Iskra under the trees and went right back to the scythe, leaving her under the wagon. We both grew tanned and freckled and strong.

Late one hot day, a cloud of dust made the midwife and her daughters stop in mid-swing. All the women fell silent. I didn't know what was happening, but several women dropped their tools and ran for the forest. "Grab the baby," Praskovia shouted, and then she too ran off toward her hut in the woods. I picked Iskra up from under the wagon, and the next thing I knew, a unit of Red cavalry was among us—seven hard, dirty men on small, dirty horses, faces lined with grime and sweat, squinting against the light, here to search for grain, for hoarding, for kulakism and possible antigovernment sympathies.

The women were pale with fear as the izbas and barns were searched. The enemy had been here, had taken their husbands and helped themselves to the grain—it could be construed as supporting the White cause. I stood absolutely still, Iskra in my arms, with Praskovia's daughters, Lilina and Masha and Roza, watching Red soldiers rip through their izbas. "You have guns, *baba*? Guns? Gold?" and I thought of my gun, hidden at Praskovia's, under the steps. Would they find it? Would they consider her a White partisan?

Soldiers emerged from sheds with bags of grain on their shoulders. I saw exactly how the revolution must seem from the peasant's point of view. It was the hardest work anywhere, except maybe rowing a slave galley, just to grow these bags of precious oats and rye—no help from the government, no help from the city—and now grim, brutal soldiers appeared from nowhere, demanding their livelihood and offering nothing at all in return, except the possibility of not being shot. We kept our eyes on those rifles with the long bayonets. I knew they would stab us before they shot us, to save ammunition.

The commander demanded to see the headman. An old *muzhik* with a beard halfway down his chest came forward, hat in hand. "You already came through here once," he squeaked. "We need to eat too. We need seed for next year's crop!"

"I have men who need to eat tonight, Grandpa," said the commander through tight lips. He was a tall man, around thirty, with flat blue eyes like pieces of broken china. "Everything's for the army. Didn't you hear the order?"

Meanwhile, we watched as soldiers moved in and out of the houses. A woman shrieked when she saw her black-and-white cow being led away. "No! Please don't take her!" She ran to the soldier, clutching at him, begging. He shoved her down into the dirt.

"She has four children," broad-shouldered Lilina shouted out to the field commander. "They need the milk!"

But he barked at us to be quiet. She'd get a receipt, there was nothing we could do. Did we want our soldier-brothers to go hungry? Tears streamed down the woman's face seeing the bony rump of her cow behind the soldier, the sway of her udder. I knew the other women were thinking of their own cows, hidden in the forest, wondering when they would lose them. It was a terrible loss. The woman's children pressed close around her like scared chickens as the soldiers loaded the bags over the pommels of their saddles, their short, nervous horses sidestepping. Eight, nine, ten poods—the village's lifeblood.

Suddenly we heard a scream from one of the izbas. A woman's howl—and this had nothing to do with requisitioning in the strict sense of the word. More painful than the grain or the cow. This was one of our women—Galya, pretty, round-faced, the mother of a two-year-old. "Stop him!" I shouted to the commander, Iskra on my hip. "Is this how you represent the Soviet Republic to a Red village? This is your idea of agitprop?"

The hot, irritated commander swiped the sweat from his forehead and squinted at me over his requisitioning book. Those dead eyes. "Who the devil are you?"

"Marina Kuriakina. From the agit-train *Red October*." I held Iskra tighter. I could hear the blood pumping in my ears. "With the Propaganda Section—here to educate these people about the revolution." The woman's screams filled the hot, insect-laden air.

He gazed at me closely, baby wound in cloth on my hip, wondering, I was sure, who this tanned freckled peasant woman was, lecturing *him* about the revolution. I lifted my chin and gazed back, imagining Varvara. Imagining Yermilova. "Where is your commissar, Comrade?"

It was a step too far. He unholstered his Mauser and pointed it at my forehead. "Right here," he said. "You and the kid want an introduction?"

My whole body went cold with shock. But I kept staring back. Now that I'd started this, I had to keep going—you had to meet a dangerous man eye to eye. Would he really shoot us right in front of the whole village? Oh God, those china-blue eyes said he would do it and never think of it again. That moment probably lasted a second, but I would remember it the rest of my life—the breeze in Iskra's hair, the color of his eyes, the absolute silence of the other women. Another shriek from the izba. The unwashed commander lifted and fired his gun into the air. All the soldiers ran out of the huts, their rifles in hand, including the one trying to pull up his pants.

"Ride out," he said. He got onto his horse. He stared right into my eyes, touched the brim of his cap with the Mauser. "Send my greetings to the *Red October*." They swirled away like devils in the dust.

August, September. The oats and the golden rye had been cut and stacked. The sun set earlier each day. It was high time I was on my way. I sewed pockets into my skirts, into my sheepskin, pockets inside and out, I had to leave my hands free for the scramble onto the trains. The women from the village stuffed my pockets with food for the trip, carefully chosen food that I could carry myself. They cut cheese into pieces and wrapped them in waxed cloth, gave me dried apricots and cherries, boiled eggs, sausage, dried fish, and bread. I wept to see what they were sacrificing for me. The best they had. I knew I wouldn't see food like this again for a long time. If I'd been alone, I might have carried a pood of grain or potatoes, *self-provisioning*. But the baby would make it physically impossible. Ironic—half of Russia was self-provisioning, and I, coming from fat Udmurtia, could bring nothing at all. Roza gave me a long cloth she'd woven herself from their own flax, and I tied it into a sling for Iskra, experimenting with different wrappings to keep her secure, even nurse her in it. I could smell the chill of autumn in the air, the grain drying. Soon they would be able to replace what had been taken. It was time to head home.

I was a peasant now, my arms as hard as wood, and Iskra no longer had that compressed newborn face. She was quick and lively, full of ideas and comments, if only I could understand. How the women petted and clucked over us, giving me food and diaper cloths and wagonloads of advice, worrying that I was about to leave the small known world to venture impossibly far. To them, *Petrograd* was like saying *America*.

The sturdy midwife and her daughters Lilina and Masha traveled in the wagon with me, driven by the same silent peasant, back to

Kambarka, where I'd left the train. Praskovia had saved my gun during the search, hid it in the bathhouse with the icons. I decided the safest place for it was under my skirt near my hip—I could hardly wear my sheepskin in weather so hot. I carefully slit the skirt on the seam so I could reach in if I had to, beneath my apron. She'd risked a great deal hiding it for me. Her cousin was a fisherman on the Kama River, I would go halfway by boat, then cross in a wagon. Sad as parting was, I yearned to be off. I was ready. I would fight my way onto those lice-ridden trains. We kissed many times as they put me on the boat.

The Kama was a beautiful broad river, in places as wide as the Neva, and if I stayed ahead of the smokestack, the air was bright and scented river green. I sat on a box with Iskra in my lap as they spent the day fishing around Sarapul, grilled up a midday meal. The fresh fish melted in my mouth. We reached a small townlet at just about dusk, where the cousins of the fisherman took me in and fed me, and I boiled water and washed Iskra's diapers as well as I could, spreading them out on the line, hoping they'd be dry by morning.

The fisherman's wife insulted the baby as much as she could, protecting her from the Evil Eye, extra servings of abuse because she was so beautiful, so extraordinary, like a splash of sunshine in a cave. I was used to it by now. She said things like "She sure is a puny thing." "Hardly worth the milk." She talked about her own little son that way too, a round-eyed, well-behaved child. "Him? That idiot? Who'd want a miserable child like that?" Looking around, as if someone was listening. Layers of superstition, you couldn't turn around without bumping into some rustic devil.

The next day, there was much argument about who would take me to Izhevsk—the honor finally went to a man with a debt he said was owed to him, a welder in the metalworks plant. We got into the cart and he brought a full load of potatoes and grain for sale to the self-provisioners at the station, to make a day of it. As we drove along, looking like a good peasant family—father, mother, redheaded child—I considered my options after Izhevsk. I could go back on the more major southern train line, through Kazan,

Nizhny Novgorod, Yaroslavl, or Moscow—there was more traffic that way. But the chaos of the stations, the crowds—the roadblocks. Because of the self-provisioners, the trains would stop constantly for searches. On the other hand, there was the northern route, through Vyatka and Vologda, the line I'd taken with Kolya last fall. *Cherepovets. Babayevo. Podborovye. Tikhvin.*

His dear face. How he'd wept at Cherepovets. On his knees, begging my forgiveness. It wasn't an act. What a vain girl I'd been. I didn't even know who that girl was now. I was a woman with a child, and life had become something far clearer, something more serious. You didn't play little games of hard feelings just because your vanity was wounded. I saw now the price of sending love to the gallows, pulling the trapdoor. I wasn't Genya. I was flesh and blood, and there was nothing as bloodless as an idea. I forgave Kolya his passion. At least it was passion—he was a flesh-and-blood man. He might make love to another woman, but he'd never give me up for an idea. He lived in this world, not the one of the spacemen. I would go back to Petrograd. It was where I belonged. I would show him his daughter, and let the cards fall where they may. Would he be cold? I knew that he could be hard as well. But whatever it was that fate held in store, I would find out.

The peasant next to me in the wagon sniffed the hot air. "Izhevsk. Can't you smell it?"

I could—the rubbery stink of the factories, turning out Red rifles and bayonets that could point any which way. I only hoped they still remembered me there.

They did remember. At the soviet, they beamed at the baby, laved praise on the *Red October* and on Genya in particular. The bustling redheaded president of the local soviet personally oversaw the drawing up of my *propusk* to return to Petrograd. I warmed to the respect in the apparatchik's yellow-brown eyes when he heard the magic word—*Petrograd*. Whereas, to the women of Praskovia's village, it was the land of fairy-tale tsars and paved streets, at the Izhevsk City Soviet, *Petrograd* meant something quite different. It was the cradle of revolution. It was the *Aurora,* the storming of the Winter Palace. Though Iskra was crying and had pooped her diaper, the clerk still afforded me a full measure of Bolshevik approval.

Again I was brought to the munitions factory, where I met with their committee and gave an impromptu lecture on the further work of the *Red October,* and the situation in the villages—their bravery at bringing in a crop despite the absence of their men and so on—and was given an item that was more precious than rubies, a metal pail. Anything metal was highly prized, and with this pail, I might boil water, wash the baby's clothes. I wanted to go straight to the train station, talk to the men and find out the situation on the rails, but one could not rush this kind of diplomacy. I ate with them in the factory canteen, and accepted a place for the night with the chairman of the committee, who spent the whole time talking about my husband, the Future of Russia, and read aloud to me at length from Genya's second book of poems, *Red Horses.* Oh Great Rus.

It was only on the third day that I was able to conduct myself to the Izhevsk station and present myself to the stationmaster, accompanied by two members of the committee. The tension between the Bolsheviks and the railroadmen was alive and well, even here—I saw it in the way they enjoyed instructing the stationmaster on what he should do with me, their interference doing more harm than good. The stationmaster bristled from the hair in his ears to his gray moustache in the small office decorated with the familiar calendars, timetables, and portrait of Lenin. My escorts urged me to go south to Kazan, and meet the comrades there in another factory, then to Nizhny Novgorod, Yaroslavl... If it were up to them, I wouldn't be home until New Year's. And the train to Kazan was due to arrive soon, just a few minutes. What luck! I kept hoping they would leave me alone, but it looked like they were going to accompany me right onto the train.

"What about Vyatka?" I said. "The Vologda line?"

"The English are up there," said the committee woman, in her skirt of rags and patches. "We heard they made it down as far as Velsk."

I continued to speak directly to the stationmaster. "What do you think, Comrade? What's the word up there? I'd like to take the fastest route, the fewest stops." I didn't want to say *the fewest roadblocks and searches*—he might think me a speculator, with a pood of flour hidden in my skirt.

He smoothed his moustache and then ruffled it up again. "The Vologda line's faster. You might sit awhile in Vyatka, but up there you'd only have to worry about bandits. I wouldn't worry about the *English*." He shot a contemptuous look at the committee woman.

"Our comrades in Nizhny could use a good speaker," said the man from the committee in his worn leather cap. "An agitator from Petrograd? From the *Red October*! The wife of Gennady Kuriakin? It would be a great honor."

I nodded, pretending I was considering it, then sighed. "I have to get back. Orders." Oh, how important I must be! "Another train's being assembled. For the Denikin front." Wherever that was these days. I hoisted the baby on my hip, as if it were the most natural thing in the world, to lug an infant around the agitprop circuit in the middle of a civil war. "What time's Vyatka?"

I waited for the evening train north, nursed Iskra, and ate a little of the bread hidden in my skirt. I glanced up to discover a boy and a girl, no older than four or five, standing before me, dressed in ragged shirts and nothing else—no shoes, no trousers, their hair clotted with dirt and lice. They stood quietly, gazing not at me but at the baby at my breast. Saying nothing, not begging, just looking at her, tied to me in the flaxen cloth. The naked longing in their dirty, drawn faces was so far beyond hunger I couldn't bear it. I offered them bread and one of our eggs. They snatched the food out of my hands and ran away to eat it like dogs. *Mothers, Don't Abandon Your Children!* Where did they come from? Left behind while the families clambered onto trains? More likely orphaned. So many children everywhere in the Izhevsk station, begging, plying the crowd. People shooed them away like pigeons.

What would become of Russia? I really wondered. It had been uplifting to ride the *Red October*, yet every day we passed through stations like this, full of hungry, lost children, solemn, awestruck. Children, despite their terrifying, scavenging lives, crowding into our *kino* car, wanting to see something miraculous—a visit from a dragon or sorcerer in the midst of their unspeakable misery. A group of urchins threaded its way through the crowd, magpie eyes watching for any unattended package, any crust of bread they could snatch from a hand. What would become of them all? Starvation. Typhus. Surely some would live, and what then? Criminals, bandits, prostitutes—if they hadn't already passed that milepost. Soldiers, if they lived long enough.

How dare I feel frightened about making this trip alone! I was privileged just to be an adult. To have an education, a story to tell, some wits about me. Even fatherless Iskra was enviable, my breast in her mouth.

Finally, toward the end of the long northern day, the Vyatka-bound train jarred and shivered into the station. Iskra wailed with the noise, metal on metal—didn't they have grease anymore? A mixed train of twelve cars, both passenger and freight, of varying decades, it was already packed, people sprawling on the roofs, hanging out the windows as more tried to push on, but the blessed stationmaster put me on the train himself, shoehorning me into a tattered first-class compartment with curtains. My compartment-mates seemed resigned—some sort of intelligentsia by the looks of them, three men and a woman. They moved their belongings around to make room for one more. If they were looking for food, they were traveling the wrong way. There would be nothing to eat in the north but wood.

A journey that should have taken two hours took nearly ten, despite my calculations. The train kept stopping, shunted and searched. I got to know my fellow passengers rather well. They were German Marxists, old-fashioned Social Democrats coming from Ufa. My German was not as good as my English, but it wasn't so bad, and one of the men spoke passable Russian, so we talked about the fate of the German revolution, and the imminent proletarian revolution in the West. The Russian speaker, a long-nosed man in steel eyeglasses and shapeless jacket named Blau, said that the German socialists Rosa Luxemburg and Karl Liebknecht had been executed back in January. The Spartacist revolt had been crushed. "Ebert called on the Freikorps to do the dirty work. That so-called socialist." Ebert, the president of the Weimar Republic. But who were the Freikorps?

"Right-wing paramilitary," he said.

Working for a Social Democrat?

"So-called. He was afraid of a Soviet replacing him. The Freikorps also crushed the Munich Soviet. Did you hear about that?"

I shook my head, wiped tears from my eyes. I'd heard on the *Red October* that a Bavarian Soviet had been declared in April. And by September, it was gone.

Blau leaned forward, his bony hands clasped together between his knees like a penitent in a Lutheran church. "Thirty thousand Freikorps, with enough armaments to retake France. The soviet was no match for them."

"And the Kiel sailors? Bremen? The Ruhr?" This was our hope, that these workers' strongholds would come to Russia's aid.

Blau shook his head. Gone.

I sat back in my seat, knocked down by the news. Why hadn't we heard this on the agit-train? No one had told us that the revolution was finished in the West.

"There's still agitation in Turin and Milan," said the woman. "But Poland's gone, Romania——"

"Hungary?"

Four heads shook in unison. "Also the Slovak Republic——the Czechs took it in July."

My head swam with the news. It had been so long since I knew anything of the outside world. I propped Iskra in the crook of my arm, fussed with her hair, trying to take in the enormity of these reversals. "What about America? The miners. The steelworkers. Seattle's general strike." On the *Red October,* we'd drunk in these stories—strikes and struggle worldwide. The textile plants of France and the mines of Wales, the factories of Glasgow and the steel mills of America, the world was rising up all around us. And we'd been sharing this information as fact to crowds in the thousands. Everything that Moscow had been radioing us. All dissolving like a pretty frost.

The German with the knobby face and heavy brow presented his view. "You have to understand the frenzy in France and England to revenge themselves on Germany. Their socialists are either jumping on the cart or warring among themselves how best to use the knout of your Soviet Revolution to win concessions from their own governments."

"And America?"

He grimaced. "As long as the worker in America can buy bread to feed his family, we're not going to see socialist revolution there. We were the closest in Germany, but our timing was off. Comrade Liebknecht said it was too soon, and sadly, our socialists were too willing to settle for what we could get. Now it's over, at least for a while. You Russians, you're going to have to go it alone until we catch up with you."

My mouth filled with dust. No world revolution. No workers of the West coming to rescue us, no flood of industrial goods, no help. We were alone. The only Red Republic in the world. We had been lying to the people all this time. *Because horses have to be fed, where men can live on the hope of it.* All those discussions with Varvara, how the revolution may have begun in Russia, the least industrialized nation in Europe, but we would be the spark, and Europe would catch fire. Without world revolution, what did we have? What were we going to do?

We'd been abandoned by the world's proletariat like children in a train station.

I looked down at the baby in my lap, loosened from her cloth, gazing up at me with those green eyes as if I were the eighth wonder of the world, Hera of the mountainous breast. Then she closed her eyes, her face went red, and I realized I had more immediate problems than world revolution. The poor Germans! The foul diaper had to be removed and the baby cleaned in sight of all, which I accomplished with foreseeable clumsiness. They were so kind, holding their gaze out the window, now full of twilight. But what to do with the remains? The stink was unbearable. Of course, it couldn't be one of the compact variety.

The German SD woman, Lise, volunteered to hold Iskra— *Danke!*—while I went out in the corridor and tried to address the problem. I would have liked to just throw it out the window and been done with it, but I couldn't afford to lose any diapers. It might be years before I could get more.

I waded through the passengers clogging the passageway, hanging from the windows, smoking and spitting sunflower shells on the floor, until I found a family, the woman with an infant in arms. "What do I do with dirty ones?" Holding up Iskra's little present.

She shrugged. "Put it away until the next station," she said.

Not likely. I waited my turn at the unspeakable convenience, where I knocked the remains as well as I could out of the offending linen, poured water from the tap into my bucket, rinsed and dumped it down the hole—you could see the tracks down below—rinsed and dumped again. In the end, it wasn't too bad—stained, but when it dried, it might be useable, and in any case, wouldn't make everyone ill. Halfway through the operation, someone began banging on the toilet door. I hurried to finish, and the moment I opened it, a heavyset man pushed past me, I could hear him vomiting. There was a samovar with boiling water. I threw a little of it into the bucket for good luck, rinsed, burning my fingers, wrung out the cloth and threw the water out the window, hoping it wouldn't spray the people in the next car, before I inched back through the shuddering train to our compartment.

Now Iskra was on the lap of the quiet German. Both were all smiles, she was reaching for his cap. *"Eine was für kleine Miezekatzekatze? Ich habe meine Frau in den Monaten nicht gesehen."* He sighed. *"Meine Kinder. Zhena moya. Deti."*

"You are lucky to be raising her now, in a Soviet society," Lise said over the noise of the car. "Women are going to benefit from this revolution like no women in the history of the world. If only we could accomplish what you have accomplished here." I nodded. It made me proud, but also anxious. I certainly hoped that the Petrograd Soviet had made some inroads into building those crèches and kindergartens by the time I got home. I was going to need them.

The train rattled and screeched and jarred its way through the night.

In Vyatka, we said *auf wiedersehen* to the German comrades. They were taking another train, zigzagging their way to Moscow. I was sorry to see them go. I brought my pail to the engineer, who filled it with boiling water straight from the engine. I gave Iskra's diapers a real wash—God bless the factory committee and their gift of a simple pail. Now I felt bad for being so irritated at their enthusiasm. I laid the cloths in the sun at the end of the platform, weighing them down with rocks, and got talking with the railwaymen, broad-faced workers in grimy overalls, as they serviced the train and loaded wood and insulted the railroad Cheka climbing aboard to search for contraband. Iskra's charm won them all. Funny, I'd only imagined her presence in terms of difficulty. I hadn't realized how everyone would fall in love with my redheaded baby. They invited me to join them for lunch, where, over a meal of soup and cucumbers, I repaid their generosity with stories about the *Red October* and having the baby and working in the fields—making a pretty tale of it. That was me, the Scheherazade of the Russian rails.

Back in the switching house, I noticed a chessboard on one of the shelves by the stove. "Who plays *shakhmaty?*"

I spent the rest of the afternoon playing chess with members of the Vyatka rail crew. I beat the first two, and then excused myself to nurse Iskra, covering her with the long cloth that was also her hammock. I'd bet one of my packages of cheese against three bread cards, and then the bread cards against a lighter, and walked away with all of them. "Where'd you learn to play like that, *devushka?*"

the foreman asked, smoking a pipe, still staring at the board in disbelief, as if the pieces had moved by themselves.

Those snowy evenings playing chess with my father. I was not particularly gifted, but I was the only one in the family interested in playing. I so wanted him to think I was intelligent, that I was worthy of his time. The hours we spent in his study, him cleaning his pipe and tapping it out, all those little gestures, the smell, the closeness, his brown eyes, the neatly trimmed beard, his dimples. We would play the famous games, Marshall v. Chigorin, Rubinstein v. Lasker, starting with the endgames, stopping, discussing. Papa's professorial voice, explaining, until I came to feel in my very bones the power of rooks controlling overlapping rows, the surprise of the knights, the versatile queen. He scolded me on my predilection for lightning strikes and odd impulsive moves early in the game, proving to me again and again how methodical development of one's back row and pawn defenses would win out against startling aggression or whimsy, which soon fell apart for lack of correct placement of lesser men. But in the end, neither one of us had played a very good defensive game, had we, Papa?

I remember how angry Varvara was when we first played and I beat her, not once but every time. She considered me flighty, and yet, who ended up pinned to the edge of the board, or isolated in the center? She hadn't had the advantage of growing up with such a father, a man who worshipped cool intellect and living within the rules. In the end, however, she had won on a much larger chessboard. My father couldn't anticipate what life would deal out in the streets and courtyards of his country, that abiding by the rules would never win against a player who might turn over the board and pull out a Mauser, stick it to your forehead.

The heat lessened with the brief but blessed northern night, and by the time my train trundled into the Vyatka station at three in the morning, I'd won a small pair of scissors, a fountain pen, and a watch that didn't work. I left them a poem:

Redheaded and red-handed
Red Marina and her little Spark.
Thank you for helping them
along their Red way.

They introduced me to the engineer and the conductor. "But don't play chess with her," the foreman warned. "You'll end up without your shoes and a month of rations."

There were no first- or second-class carriages on this train, just third class and miles of boxcars brimming with people. Iskra and I were lucky beyond lucky that the conductor got us into third class at all. It was utterly packed, but at least it was designed for human transportation, with windows and berths. The heat was still awful, but once we got going, I imagined there would be a breeze to cut the ripe stew of unwashed, sweating bodies. I followed him down the teeming central aisle of the uncompartmented car, Iskra sweating against me, picking our way through passengers sitting on their packages and sleeping leaning on one another's shoulders. On either side of the aisle rose three layers of facing berths filled with luckier people who could sleep stretched at full length, heads toward the open windows.

He stopped at a set of berths about a third of the way down and rousted a sleeping boy out of the top berth, up by the ceiling, lifting him down and unceremoniously shoving him in with his mother on the second tier. "Sorry, kid, we got company."

The mother, startled from sleep and half naked in the heat, raked me with her stink-eyes. "Who's this, your whore?"

"How'd you like to spend a couple days on the platform and cool off, eh citizen?" He turned to me. "She give you any lip, you let me know, I'll throw 'er off. Good luck, Comrade."

"Oh, and a baby too." She sighed, glottally, *ekh*, and irritably pulled her ugly son over to her on the narrow bunk. "This is already the worst trip I've ever taken. Now God has to make sure it's the worst I'll ever take."

150

I eyed the thin, hard padding of the eye-level bunk—greasy, cloth-covered, about half an inch thick, up where it was hottest—and wondered how many people had slept on it in the last weeks and months. Fleas at best, lice at worst. I brushed it off as well as I could and put my bundle up there, spread out my sheepskin to lie on. At least it was summer. They said typhus was a winter disease. I couldn't afford to get sick now—Iskra would have little chance of surviving anything we might catch on this train. I unbound her from the sling and put her up in the berth closest to the wall, and climbed up myself, apologizing as I stepped on the lower and then the middle berth. I lay down, loosening my clothes. How I hated to have to lie down on that bunk, but what choice did we have? Sleep sitting up for a week? I was lucky. I'd been lucky the whole way. Iskra was my luck. I could be in a boxcar. I could be lying on the floor with my infant.

"You'd better keep that baby quiet," the woman below me hissed.

"Or what?" I said, turning over to face the window.

The woman proved to be a loud-mouthed, irritable harridan traveling with her husband and child from Perm to Petrograd, her husband a *spets*—*specialist*—in the chemical industry. She harped on me hour after hour, and when I returned from washing Iskra's diapers (no offer to hold her, that was for sure) her kid was back lying in my bunk. He climbed down only under duress. Iskra and I spent most of our time lying in the berth up by the ceiling, sweating and watching the trees pass at almost walking speed as the train shuddered down the track. The middle bunk folded up, and everyone else sat on the bottom one, but there was only room for three people. I didn't mind, I didn't need to socialize. I slept and fed Iskra and assembled my plan for Petrograd. First, I would go down to the English Embankment and see if Kolya had returned. Then I would try Krestovskaya's—that was a good-sized apartment, if the actress had been able to keep it after her husband was shot during Red Terror.

I could try Mina if it got desperate. Her mother, Sofia Yakovlevna, had always liked me and she had no idea that Misha and I were the same person—but Mina would be furious at my abandonment of her. Genya's friend Anton Chernikov was a possibility...he might still have the Poverty Artel. There were still places I could go. And Iskra could see her city. I brushed her damp hair from her face—we were both sweated through—and dried her with the cloth, took the diaper off her in hopes of letting the sweat evaporate. I knew when to expect diaper usage. I hummed to her some of the work songs I had learned in the long hours of harvest.

It was a long way from Vyatka to Vologda, and this train stopped at every little town—Kotelnich, Svecha, Shabalino—and even in between, halting with an unearthly screech and shudder in the middle of nowhere. Another local roadblock, another search. Rough local militiamen in clothes that looked like they'd come off dead people would mount the train and search the cars. I figured it was safer to keep my gun on me, up near my waist behind the baby. Uncomfortable, but they would pat you down everywhere, it was an added bonus of the job.

They searched the cars, demanded everybody's papers, though it was clear the man looking at mine, dirt caked on his fingers and in the lines on his face, could not read them. He found my food, but no surplus, just enough for the journey, and he returned my little packets and began harassing other people. Out the windows, I could see the boxcar passengers herded out into the sunlight, smoking, blinking like moles. Some of them seemed quite ill and lay in the shade of trees, unable to stand. It reminded me to thank the great forces for my berth and my *spets*'s family, irritating as they were. None of them were ill and neither were the men on the other side, two from Petrocommune and a talkative blue-eyed man who told everyone he was an agronomist from Ekaterinburg, though I noticed none of the searchers had searched him, or his berth, or his valise, which he kept under it. In case his hearty confidence and ruddy good health—when we were all suspicious and exhausted—didn't give it away. A Cheka spy. Well, at least he wasn't ill. I would take the woman and her smirking boy, who spit sunflower shells on the floor that we all had to walk on, even the Chekist—me with an illegal pistol digging into my ribs under my skirt—as long as they weren't feverish or scratching with lice. Watching a pale, shaky boxcar woman sitting out the search under a tree with a baby at her breast, her dull eyes staring at nothing at all, I knew my luck was still holding.

The so-called agronomist took out a case and began assembling a cunning little chess set on his knee. "Does anyone play?"

He beat both the Petrocommune men, one in a shameful seven moves, narrating the game the whole time: *Bishop to queen's knight four. Queen takes pawn and checkmate.* "You," he said to the *spets* sitting opposite him. From where I lay in the top bunk, I could just see his shoes next to his wife's heeled ones, and the boy's sandals. "How about it? This tedium's driving me crazy."

"I can't say I ever learned," said the *spets*.

"He doesn't do anything," confided the wife, leaning forward. I could see the black roots of her blond hair. "Just plays with his chemicals. He doesn't even know how to swim. Isn't that right, Ivan Danilovich?"

Her husband said nothing. What a coward. Married to that loathsome woman. I wanted to plug my ears with wax.

"Amazing he knew how to get a kid," said the thick-lipped "agronomist," sitting with his knees wide apart, crowding his seatmates. "Sure it's his?"

She preened at his attention, touching her hair. "You could teach my Yasha. He's a very bright boy."

I could imagine the smirk on that little brat's face. I saw another reason children shouldn't be praised—that was one the Evil Eye could take any time.

"Do I look like a schoolteacher?" said the bull-necked Chekist. "Someone. Anyone. Hey, you up there, Red, with the baby. I know you're listening. Can you play? Give you half a sausage."

Play the Chekist? "Win or lose?"

"Oh, a hard bargainer! Why not? I'll beat you with one hand tied behind my back. Girl chess players. No concentration."

We'd see about that. "But there's no room for me to sit."

"Make room. You, go up there." He held out his chubby paws. "Hand me the baby."

I hated lowering Iskra into those fat hands. I could only imagine how many lives they had ended. But I did it, handed her to him, then gingerly negotiated the climb down from the bunk, hoping my gun wouldn't clunk against my fellow passengers' heads. I settled next to the *spets* on the bottom bunk as the boy clambered up into mine.

Unlike the Vikzhel men, the heavy-jowled Chekist proved a considerable adversary. Good development of pieces, castle on the queen's side. He made no mistakes. But I would change his opinion of girl chess players. The set was tiny, with little pegs that fit into holes in the board so we could hand it back and forth without losing any of the pieces. The way he narrated his moves, like a man playing to a crowd, was odd and intended to rattle his opponent: *Knight to bishop three. Bishop to rook four.*

"How's the harvest looking?" I wanted to throw him too. "Will there be enough rye to plant for next year?" When all he probably knew about rye was cutting it—and not only rye.

"Oh, let's not talk about rye," he said. "A dull subject, even to me."

Naturally. We were silent for a while, jolting and jarring on the untended track, gazing at the board. "How was it in Ekaterinburg?" I said. "Are the Whites still there?"

"Liberated, July 14, 2nd Red Army. And not a moment too soon. They must have shot twenty thousand workers. Even hosted a pogrom on the way out. I didn't think there were that many Jews in Ekaterinburg." He pursed his fat lips. "Pawn to queen four." He sat back, satisfied. "That's how you can tell when the Whites are losing—follow the trail of dismembered Jews."

I shuddered. It had happened on July 14. Iskra had been a week old. I stared down at the tiny board. Twenty thousand. The very same troops who had massacred so many in Izhevsk just a short few weeks before we'd arrived had gone on to ravage Ekaterinburg. Exactly where the *Red October* had been heading. The same White Army that had taken the men from Praskovia's village. Perhaps their husbands and sons had been among the pogromists—who could tell? I was learning one thing, people could go straight from church to hammering nails into a woman's eyes. Nothing would surprise me again.

I took the agronomist's pawn. Though it opened my queen to attack, I would take his as well. Something needed to happen. "So where are they now?"

"Tukhachevsky took Chelyabinsk at the end of July—5th Red Army. They're across the Tobol now. Omsk by October. You heard it here first." He touched his queen, but didn't pick it up. "The English will abandon them soon—they're starting to see their White angels aren't so spotless. You should see the local whores—dolled up in English woolens. The corruption would make you Petrocommune fellows weep." The men at his side were dozing. "The Whites are supplying our armies with half our weapons and food. Trotsky's sending them roses. Kolchak keeps his hands clean, makes a big thing of it, but everyone else is up to their eyeballs. The peasants are raising armies in the east, all on their own." Just as Yermilova said would happen. He moved the queen after all. "Queen takes pawn."

Iskra woke and started to cry. "She's hungry," I said. "Excuse me, I have to feed her. Can we finish later?"

"Feed her, I don't care," said the man, grinning. Those horrible lips, moistening each other.

I jiggled her on my knee. "She can wait."

"Babies shouldn't go hungry. Don't mind us."

But I did mind. Normally I wouldn't, but this man was far too interested in seeing me feed my baby for my taste. He gave me the shivers. But what was I to do? In compromise, I reached up over the heads of the *spets* couple into my bunk for Iskra's cloth—a bit of modesty—only to find the boy reading my notebook, one leg crossed over the other, like a man reading a newspaper. He'd gone through my sack—my meager belongings, that brat! I would have slapped him but I didn't want his mother to get involved. Instead, I took hold of the hand that held my notebook, and squeezed it. Staring him in the eye, daring him to cry out. I'd gotten plenty strong this summer working the fields, I could have broken that grubby paw, but when I saw the tears in his eyes, I let him go, pulled the notebook out of his hands and stuck everything back in the sack, knotted it and pulled my cloth out from under him.

"Play chess," the Chekist called out.

"Right there." I sat back down, put the cloth over my shoulder and undid my dress, put Iskra to the breast.

It was a long game. Torture, with Iskra slurping and smacking under the cloth, drawing the attention of the already too attentive Chekist, while I continued trying to play. He ended up winning, but I made him work for it. No more rude comments about "girl players." As soon as we had finished, he gave me my half sausage, and set the board up again for another game.

The days passed. I learned about the Petrocommune men. One had been a shipping clerk at Eliseev's specialty grocery in old Petersburg, the other had worked for the government in the timber industry. I lay in my bunk, playing with Iskra, and gazing at the passing trees outside the window. I wrote a poem about chess, a city of chess pieces, the chess game of our times. I recited Akhmatova aloud to her, and Blok, and Mandelstam—bathing us both in their verbal coolness. The *spets* woman was complaining about Perm, talking about her sister who lived in Kiev, on and on, I decided to cut a corner from a diaper to stuff into my ears. But when I rummaged in my sack—no scissors. The scissors I'd won from the Vikzhel men. There was no doubt as to what had happened to them.

"Yasha?" I asked, leaning over the side of the bunk. "You didn't happen to see a pair of scissors, did you? Brass, about four inches long?"

He turned his innocent face up to me from the lower berth where he sat with his parents, the father reading, the mother knitting. The boy was holding the skein of yarn.

"No, he hasn't been using your filthy scissors," the mother said. "What are you insinuating? Are you calling my boy a thief?"

Ah, the smile on the brat's face hidden behind his mother told me everything.

"He got into my things. I was wondering if he'd developed a fondness for them."

Her homely face, red-cheeked and sweaty in the heat. "You tramp. You railway slut. Sitting up there with your disgusting bastard. How dare you call my son a thief!"

"Talya, please," her husband said.

She brushed him off like a moth that had landed on her shoulder, and stood, bringing her face up to mine. "Say it again and I'll smack you."

"Your brat took my scissors," I said.

She reached out and slapped my face. The sting of her hand, her ring on my cheek. The Petrocommune men didn't know where to put their eyes, they were embarrassed for both of us.

The Cheka man smoked his cigarette, enjoying the show.

"Don't you speak of my son, you whore, you cheap trash. Women like you shouldn't be put in with decent people. If anyone should be thrown off the train it should be you." Her breath was hideous. Bad dental care, poor food, the whole place would ignite on the fumes if there were a spark. "Apologize to us this instant."

"Ask him if he didn't go through my things when he was up here the other day. Reading my notes, pawing through my belongings."

I could see the part in her hair as she leaned over her son, making her mooing sounds. "Yasha. You didn't do any such thing, did you, sweetheart?"

"No, Mama." But the smirk returned as soon as her back was turned. That little criminal was splitting a gut at this.

"Good, that's a good lad." The Chekist reached across and squeezed the boy's shoulder. "Good lad."

What game was he playing? This man disliked little Yasha. He'd made that clear with the suggestion that he teach him chess. But perhaps he recognized himself in the boy—the liar, the sneak—traits that might end up making a good Chekist. "Never tell them anything. If they want those scissors, they can bloody well search for them, and good luck—right, kid?"

Now the boy wasn't smirking.

"I beg your pardon?" said the mother.

"He's got 'em, all right." Inhaling his cigarette, then examining its lit tip. "Innocent people, see, they get this moment of shock. A moment where they don't even understand that someone's accusing them of something. It takes a second to get it—oh, I'm being accused of, say, taking some scissors." I could see the part of the mother's hair, where the dye stopped and her roots began, and the Cheka man, his legs set wide, crowding the shipping clerk, whom he'd turned to address. "Then they start yelling. You can't fake that kind of outrage. *I didn't take them! I wouldn't touch your lousy scissors. I didn't even know you had any, and if I did, I wouldn't have touched them.* Where a guilty person starts defending himself right away: *How dare you!* They get all puffed up. They overdefend, they attack, they spread it out— *Who are you, some railway whore,* and *We are good law-abiding people!* The innocent person sticks to the facts. The guilty go for pride and honor. And the born thief says nothing. He waits for confusion to rule and slips out when he has a chance. Good for you, kid. If this was the street, this would be your chance to inch for the door and make a run for it." The Cheka man stood. He held out his hand. *"Davai." Give it.*

"I didn't take them," the kid said softly, retreating deeper into the berth.

His interrogator reached in, as fast as a snake, and dragged the kid out of his lair by the arm, shoved him to the floor. "I don't think your dad beats you enough. That's half the problem right there." He unbuckled his pants and started to pull his belt out.

The woman grabbed the man's shoulder, clutching the cloth. "Don't you touch my son!" He shrugged her off. The force threw her back against the window.

On his knees on the filthy floor, the boy scrambled into his mother's sewing basket and came out with the small brass scissors.

I hated that kid but still—the sight of him on his knees holding the scissors out made me ill, the fear in his face, the whimpering of his mother. The man ignored the boy, rebuckled his pants. Did he beat his own children with that belt? Had his father beaten him that way? "Give them back to the girl. Say sorry."

Yasha handed them up to me, the tears in his terrified eyes were real. "Sorry," he whispered.

I nodded. He *was* sorry, that was clear.

The mother ruined the moment by grabbing him and slapping him herself. "How dare you steal, and then hide it in my basket! What will people think of us?"

He sulked the rest of the day, which was fine with me. Even the mother was wonderfully subdued, apologetic. She offered to share some of their food with me. "Raising children now, in this climate. You'll see. Everything's upside down." The thick-lipped Chekist kept me under close surveillance, nodding at me meaningfully.

I took Iskra for a little walk on the platform at Vologda. Though it was still hot, you could feel autumn in the bright air, the birches turning yellow inside the deep green pines.

> *The slight breeze ruffled*
> *a million tiny flags,*
> *capturing your upturned gaze.*
> *What can you see, my dear?*
> *What do you know?*
> *Your laughing eyes,*
> *so much like his.*

Alas, we had work to do. No time for poetry. I handed my pail up to the assistant engineer and asked him to drain off some boiling water for me. I amazed myself, this new mother-person I'd become, worried about disease and rashes and illness, sanitation and linens, a real German housewife. How my father would enjoy this if he could see me now, how Kolya would laugh. Yet I was proud of those clean nappies.

It was a big station, full of exhausted, overdressed Russians with bundles, children, and Komi women selling food. Passengers didn't dare go far, but took turns leaving the train, walking the platform, not to lose their spaces. "Go, go," said the *spets* woman, her name was Natalya Romanovna. "You do take good care of that baby. Honestly, I'm surprised. When I saw you, I thought, *Oh no, and a baby too. It'll just cry the whole time, and stink to high heaven.* But you do a real good job."

As I washed diapers at the end of the platform, leaning over the red feathers of Iskra's hair, I inquired of a loitering mechanic, "So what do you hear about the English?"

"A few sorties up around Onega, but the trains have been getting through," the mechanic said. "The Americans are gone, now it's just the English."

"We'll be done by spring," said the Cheka-agronomist. He'd developed a nasty habit of creeping up on me. Whenever I turned around, there he was, this stocky, lecherous, thick-necked man who now saw himself as my personal savior. "Denikin's the one to beat. He's closing on Tula. He could be in Moscow in six weeks if they don't sell all the guns to us first."

"Yudenich's still there, in Estonia," the mechanic said. "Waiting for his chance. I wouldn't count my chickens yet, brother."

"If the English had given half a hand to Yudenich, Petrograd would be gone already," said the fat man. "That should tell you something. They don't trust him any more than anyone else does." He put his hand on my shoulder in a false gesture of reassurance. He just liked to touch me whenever he could, see if he could get a look down my dress.

I snapped the diapers to get as much water out of them as I could, and laid them in the sun, away from my admirer.

He leaned over to where I was squatting, his shadow shading me. "You're avoiding me, Marina Dmitrievna." I cringed. How could he know my name? From the visit from the railway Cheka? I never used my patronymic on the train.

"I'm just trying to get these diapers done."

"Leave them. Let's go have some *samogon* with some friends of mine. They say it's good for the milk. Makes it flow like a fountain."

The last thing I wanted to do was to go drinking with this man, or meet his friends. I certainly didn't want him thinking about my milk flowing like a fountain. It made me ill to think that he had given such consideration to the condition of my milk. "No, I think I'll live instead," I said. "It's all poison."

He brushed his hand against my shoulder, the tips of his fingers. I shuddered despite myself. "Suit yourself," he said.

The full moon filled the windows of the rocking train. Everyone was asleep, including the Chekist, out cold on the bottom bunk opposite after his party in Vologda, snoring even louder than the train. I recognized everyone's night sounds now—the Petrocommune man from Eliseev's with his whistling snore across from me, and below him, the timber man, who was a tremendous farter. We knew each other all too well. The rising moon was like a small child trying to peer above a table, enormous and white, round-faced.

All I could think of was being back in Kolya's embrace. This same moon was peering in at him, somewhere up ahead. *Dream of me, Kolya. Feel me. I'm on my way.* I breathed, and projected myself into the astral, and flew out across the miles, Iskra in the crook of my arm, west to Petrograd, following the train lines. We dipped over the canals and the vast shining Neva, peeked into windows, looking for him. We landed on a windowsill—Kolya at a desk, the lamp lit, the window open, he was smoking a cigarette, writing a letter. To whom? He looked tired. I didn't like to see him like that. I wanted to rub my palms over his forehead and erase those lines. They didn't suit him. *I'm coming, my dear.*

I needed to urinate, but dreaded the long march to the filthy toilet. Next to me, Iskra lay, her tiny upturned nose, the bow of her mouth. What could she be dreaming? I hated to wake her, but I would not leave her here alone. At least at this time of night, there might not be a queue. I clambered down, trying not to step on the woman and her son, and the husband below, then lifted the baby's sleeping weight out of the berth and snugged her into the cloth. I had about two seconds to quiet her between her awakening and the first shriek. I was getting pretty good at this. Then we began our awkward, jolting, swaying stumble through the crowded car, stepping across people sleeping on the floor with their bags and packages. They slept pretty well considering the clanging and rattling of the unmaintained train and my misplaced steps. God, what a stink. Gas and bad teeth and unwashed bodies worse than any zoo. The longing face of the moon followed me down the car.

I used the unspeakable hole at the back of the train, holding my breath until I could open the door again.

There in the narrow corridor, waiting for me, loomed the Chekist's fat face. He pushed me back into the WC, shut the door. In this stinking hole, he was on me, crushing me to the wall next to the toilet, smashing Iskra between us to plant a repulsive, boozy kiss on my lips, clawing at my dress, popping the buttons from its bodice. His disgusting hands grabbed my bare breast. I screamed, but who could hear me in this coffin over the grinding of metal on metal, the clangor of the train? He clapped his hand around my throat, cutting my wind, and with the other, unbuckled his famous belt. I heard it hit the floor as his pants dropped, God, he was going to rape me right here in the crapper with my daughter tied onto me. She was screaming now that she had the room.

Perhaps wanting a better grip on my body, he reached into the cloth and grabbed her. He was trying to pull her out by her arm! Oh God, her screams. I had no thought but to stop him, stop him from hurting my baby. I reached through the slit in my skirt and pulled out the gun, pressed it deep into his chest. *Do you know what this is, Mr. Cheka?* Without hesitating, I fired.

The impact slammed him back against the door. He slid down, but there was no room to fall, he sagged onto me. I tried to open the door, but he was in the way. The baby screamed and screamed. He was holding his chest, blood bubbling out of his mouth. I had to stay out of the blood. I climbed onto the surround of the toilet, so he could fall against the wood. I put the gun back in my pocket—searing hot against my belly—and pushed open the door into the narrow corridor.

It was full of people. I could see their staring eyes in the moonlight. Boys. Orphans, traveling for free huddled in the filthy corridor. Gaping at me. "Help me open that door," I ordered over Iskra's screaming. "Quick."

A boy reached over and pulled open the rear carriage door. His eyes gleamed with respect in the moonlight.

The sound of the train, the couplings, the fresh air, twice as loud now. I could no longer hear Iskra's shrieks, or the man's chest-shot gurgle, or smell the odor of offal and blood. All I knew was that I had to get rid of this Chekist or they'd come looking for his murderer. I pulled him out of the toilet on the blood-slick floor—my God, he was still alive, wheezing. The blood made the floor slick. "Help me," I begged of them. "I can't let them find him here." First they pulled off his boots and went through his pockets. They took his clothes except for the bloodstained shirt, stripped him fast as one would skin a rabbit. Then they helped me pull him out onto the platform between the cars—the platform, too, was full of beggar children, riding out here in the dark and the wind and the scream of the metal. The bigger boys were the ones who shoved the Chekist out into the rushing darkness, onto the tracks. We stood on the platform among the smaller children, as his naked body disappeared in the moonlight. He was gone. Ten yards, twenty yards. The moon our only witness.

The baby wailed. I came back inside the car, and stood panting, staring at what had to be blood on the floor. Was it on my hands? On the boys? They didn't look too bad. They showed me their hands. We stood outside the stinking hole, listening, waiting to see if anyone would come. You really couldn't see the blood, the floor was so dirty, no one would notice it. I had to bet on it.

The moon leered through the window, a dangerous witness. I tried to soothe Iskra, but she would not be consoled. "What's wrong with her?" one of the boys asked, a tall, tough-looking one with dark eyes.

I sat down, took her from the cloth and had a good look. There was something wrong with her arm. Limp. It was lower than the other. The bastard! My head was on fire. I wanted to scream, to become hysterical, but there was no time. My innocent child. This was my fault. It was up to me, there was nobody else. The moon waited, the train shuddered and groaned.

"He pulled the shoulder out," the boy said. "You gotta pop it back in, *mamenka*." He gestured, a fist into a cupped palm.

"I don't know how," I said, fighting hysteria.

"I do. Here, give 'er to me," said the boy. He looked about fifteen, scabby and mangy. Though my life rested in his hands, I didn't want to give my baby to him. There was no way to know when he'd last washed his hands, what diseases he might carry. But I did it. He sat on the floor and I handed him to her. "So, here's what you do," he said as he settled my poor screaming baby between his bony thighs. "You hold her arm still." He showed me, pressing Iskra's tiny upper arm against her rubbery baby body, as she shrieked and writhed. "Now ya gotta lift the bottom part up." He raised Iskra's forearm. The shrieks!

"Gently, please." Sweat and tears stung my eyes. "Gently..." *Oh God, please let this be over soon, please help Iskra.* She'd been through so much already. "It's going to be all right, kitty-cat. Just another minute. We're going to fix you right up." Hoping I wasn't lying.

"Now you just gotta feel around for where it pops in." He secured his tongue in the corner of his mouth and lowered the forearm and moved it across her body, holding the upper arm tight, completely resistant to her piercing shrieks. Then he rotated it outward, the arm at a ninety-degree angle, feeling, listening with his fingers like a safecracker. *"Vot."* There. She gave one last body-shaking scream—and stopped.

The boy grinned shyly, as if it were nothing, but I could tell he was bursting with pride as he handed her back to me. I held her against my breast, rocking her, begging her to forgive me, thanking him, thanking all of them, and whatever sloppy God was watching and not watching. I wrapped her cloth around her shoulders so she couldn't move her arm, and turned to lift my skirt to remove half the food I was carrying, and pressed into dirty hands—cheese, chunks of bread. "Forget you saw any of this."

"Saw what?" the boy said, already eating. "You think any of us talks to the Cheka? That's nuts."

"Good luck, boys. Thank you."

"Good luck, *mamenka*." Once we'd regained our composure, I carried Iskra back through the crowded car, quietly, quietly, as Ukashin had taught us to do. *I'm a shadow, I'm a figure in your dreams. I'm a ghost, I'm nothing. I'm smoke. I'm no one.* Anyone who saw me would recognize me, the girl with the baby. My shoes were sticky with blood. I could feel the tack against the rubber of the floor. Was I covered with it? The cloth, my dress?

Finally, I knew I was back in my little enclave when I recognized the whistle of the shipping clerk. I lifted Iskra onto my bunk, and clambered up, quick as a monkey, careful as a thief. How long had I been gone? Twenty minutes? An hour? Once in my place by the ceiling, I quickly cut a strip from one of the diapers—with the scissors my victim had saved for me!—and made a brace for her, tying it gently across the arm. *Oh, oh, I know, I know. Please don't start screaming again.* I carefully bandaged her arm and collarbone and swaddled her up tight, then put her to my overflowing breast like a fountain, and lay as quietly as I could, through the thunder of my heart. Someone was dead because of me. And I would do it again. Anyone in this life who wanted to hurt my child would find me as cold-blooded a killer as any Chekist.

I dozed a bit toward morning. In my dreams, I was back at Furshtatskaya Street, tending chickens in a locked room, caring for them among the embroidered chairs and the polished parquet. The next thing I knew, people were talking. I peeked over the side and saw that they'd already put up the middle bunks. I'd been sleeping so heavily I hadn't noticed. Natalya Romanovna was combing her hair. The man from Eliseev's washed his hands and face with a little boiled water poured onto his handkerchief.

"He was stinking drunk last night," said the woman, working out a snarl in her hair. "It was awful. He pinched me when I was getting ready for bed."

They were talking about the Chekist. I pretended to awaken, yawning.

"Maybe he's gone to the toilet," said the *spets*.

"Maybe he found someone to play chess with in another car," said the timber man, whom he'd beaten in seven moves and never played with again.

"Well, good riddance," said the wife. "A very unpleasant man."

The boy said nothing as he stood at the window, ostensibly looking out at the fresh sunlit morning, but he kept stealing looks at me over his shoulder. Had he seen me get up, and the agronomist follow me? I wouldn't know until we were searched again, until the railroad Cheka walked between the rows of bunks, until we showed our papers and answered their questions. Would he blurt it out, betray me for revenge? I had to get rid of the gun. Maybe Mama Natalya's sewing basket? That would be a rude surprise. The man's valise was still under his bunk. Surely they would find it, open it, and ask whose it was, what had become of him. The railroad Cheka would notice any blood. I looked down at my dress, with the torn buttons. It was dark with a pattern of cherries, but the baby's white cloth was spattered in red. I turned it, refolded it so the blood went to the inside. My boots had a line of blood at the sole, I could disguise it if I stepped in some water. I drank from a cup the timber man passed across to me, and saved a bit to wash my own hands and face.

I spent the rest of the day worrying about the gun, and the children, the people who had seen me. Should I throw it down the toilet? Give it to the boys still riding the rear of the car? They could sell it and get something to eat. Each search increased my chances of being caught, and a girl with a gun nowadays would be considered a potential Fanya Kaplan, Lenin's would-be murderer. Who was I traveling to Petrograd to assassinate? I had been raped before, I might not have shot him even to prevent him from fucking me—but he'd hurt Iskra. If he had gotten her out of the cloth, he would have thrown her on the floor, even down the toilet onto the tracks. But now it was he who was on the tracks somewhere to the east of us, where he belonged. Give up this gun? Going to Petrograd, which by all accounts had become an even more dangerous place than it had been when I left it? Where Arkady and people like him still walked the streets? Even if I had to suffer an agony of suspense each time we were searched, I would not give it up. I'd never be able to replace it.

The Chekist never did come back, and no one gave a damn. The *spets*'s family were able to spread out, the boy had a bunk to himself again. It didn't keep him from staring at me at odd moments, though. I sensed he knew something, but I couldn't ask. Every hour that passed, every mile we were farther away from that stretch of track, I felt less terrified. And now the familiar stations began to appear. Cherepovets. Babayevo. Tikhvin.

Tikhvin! I dared not get out to walk, in case my one-armed mechanic was at the station. I thought of Avdokia—how I wished she were here. I ached for her gnarled hands, her pity, her love. But I had to go on alone. Could not retreat to the infantilism of bourgeois motherhood. *Theotokos, have mercy on us all.*

When I went back to the toilet, the children I had seen that night were gone, replaced by new orphans, who stared at me with the same hunger I was used to seeing. The others must have gotten off, deciding to try their luck at other stations.

One more day. My fellow passengers gathered up their bundles, straightened their clothes. I had sewn up my dress with a borrowed needle and thread, fashioning some elegant new buttons out of the hem—cut, rolled, and sewn. Again, the lessons of Ionia had not been lost on me.

As we approached the city—city of my heart, my arteries sluicing under its bridges, Petersburg!—the train slowed to a walking pace, that brutal grinding of metal against ungreased metal. From the window, I could see not only bagmen but ordinary citizens jumping off not in twos or threes but by the scores—falling, rolling, scrambling to their feet and disappearing into the shaggy woods on the outskirts of the city, dragging their bags and suitcases of illegal foodstuffs. Hundreds of people from a single train. *Self-provisioning.* I had a moment of doubt. If the food situation was so bad...But I had made my decision. I stood, hanging onto the open window, holding Iskra and waiting for the first sign of Petrograd to appear. Yes—there! The Admiralty needle, far off in the distance, just a wink of gold catching the autumn sun, just a stitch between sky and earth. The *spets*'s wife and the Eliseev man cried out as well.

"We're home," I whispered to Iskra, kissing her hair. She needed a bath, and her arm was still tender, but she was alive. We were both alive—and going home. I blubbered, letting my tears wet her hair. Somewhere in this maze of a city, Kolya lived. I felt him out there somewhere, making deals, living his subterranean life. *I have your daughter, Kolya. Can you feel us coming?* I imagined him stopping in the middle of whatever he was doing—midsentence, in an office, or a courtyard, as the image of me crossed his mind. While hundreds of miles to the east, a naked man lay on a train track with a bullet in his chest. And in some small railroad town, a boy with brown eyes remembered the red-headed baby he had saved, and her mother's tears.

Before we were able to leave the car, the railroad Cheka arrived. Too late to jump off the train now. We sat on the berths while a sharp-faced man in leather examined our papers. He was quite literate, too bad for me. "Why is your residence in Tikhvin but your *propusk* from the Izhevsk Soviet?" I had to explain the *Red October,* the baby, the agricultural work. I showed him Iskra's baptismal certificate—he sneered at that bit of backsliding. I shrugged. "Peasants." I showed him my hands, the calluses from working the crops, though I didn't explain the scar on my right palm, courtesy of the Archangel. I had, however, replaced my bloodstained boots with my woven bast shoes. My eyeballs burned with the effort of not looking at the agronomist's valise nestled under the bunk across from us, wishing it would disappear. Unfortunately, the Chekist had eyes in his head. He lifted it out.

The generalized sense of anxiety heightened, a twang, like the tightening of a string, as if everyone had been guilty of doing away with him, or was afraid they would be accused of it.

"Whose is this?" he asked.

I should have thrown it out the window, but that would have been too obvious.

"There was a man here," said the shipping clerk from Eliseev's. "He disappeared, after Vologda."

The hatchet-faced Chekist tried to open the bag. Locked. The boy was staring at me. I glanced back as if it was of no interest to me whatsoever, but I could feel sweat trickle down my neck and under my arms. Iskra was sweating too, her red hair plastered to her skull. I kissed her, swayed her a bit in her bloodstained sling. It was airless and hot in the car without the train movement. I sent Yasha the telepathic message: *Nobody beat you, you got your own bunk — do you really want to make trouble? You don't know how far this might go.*

"An agronomist, didn't he say, Talya?" said the *spets*. "From Ekaterinburg. Though he didn't seem like any agronomist I'd ever met."

"A very unpleasant man," his wife chimed in.

I waited. Iskra's good arm came up, playing with my nose, my lip. Her other in its sling. What would happen to her if the Cheka arrested me? *Please, God, get us through this.* I hoped I looked like a sad-eyed redheaded Theotokos. Who would suspect a Virgin and Child of murder? I felt the weight of the gun against my belly. *Please let him not search too closely.* Had anyone, of all these hundreds, mentioned the shot in the night, the recognizable figure of a woman with a child skulking through the car? I could only depend upon the way people minded their own business these days. Why should they help the Cheka?

"*Mal'chik*, what do you know about this man with the suitcase?" the Chekist asked the boy.

I let my eyes rest on the timber man, who was pressing his

abdomen with his fingertips, something not working in his bowels, and steeled myself in anticipation of the *spets*'s son spilling his guts. "He was fat. And he snored," the boy began in an overearnest voice. "He wore a big metal buckle, like a *sheriff*." He pronounced it *sharif*. A Zane Grey fan. Yes, the belt would have caught his attention. It was riding the rails somewhere, around the waist of a Vologda orphan. "He played chess. He had a little tiny set and he beat everyone. He didn't want to teach me." The screwed-up face as the little liar thought of other facts about the man he could share. "He was from Ekaterinburg. Talked about the war. He knew a lot about it."

"What did he say about the war?" the Chekist asked.

The mother was making eyes at him. *Be quiet!* The boy paused. "He knew a lot," he continued. "He said the English were going to abandon the Whites. That they didn't trust Yudenich or he'd have Petrograd already. I think he was a spy. An English spy."

The Chekist was clearly disappointed in the boy's information. "Anybody else know anything about this man?"

"He just disappeared," said the timber man, his breath sour with indigestion. "After we'd left Vologda. I thought he'd passed out, but I guess not."

"He came on the train stinking drunk," added the *spets*'s wife.

"The English were in Vologda," said the shipping clerk. "Maybe he joined them."

"And left his bag?" The sober, thin-faced Chekist clearly didn't like the bag. That's what was troubling him.

The shipping clerk scratched his head. It made me want to scratch.

"Maybe he wandered off at one of the stations and missed the train," I said, not to be left out of the general guessing. Thinking about the dead man's advice, what makes the guilty look guilty. If the innocent were putting in their comments, I needed to join them. Not be the one visibly inching for the door.

"Or maybe it was supposed to be picked up by someone else, like in *Pinkerton*," said Yasha. "His *contact*." Supporting the spy theory. But the way he looked at me, I knew he knew. He was doing this for me.

The Chekist spat on the floor of the train. Where someone would have to sit later. "The simplest explanation," said the timber man, "is that he went for a smoke and fell off. He was in pretty bad shape."

"Well, tough luck for him." The Chekist tucked the case under his arm, and moved on through the car.

In a few minutes, they unlocked the doors, and we spilled out onto the platform at the Nikolaevsky station. I loved every member of this sweating, shoving crowd, the high arched roof covered in soot and fluttering with pigeons, the patched but decidedly urban clothing, the begging orphans. I loved it all. We were back among the living. We were home.

Part II
Petrograd

(Autumn 1919)

14 *My Petrograd*

Nikolaevsky station soared before my eyes, a city within a city, just as I'd left it ten months ago. Dirty and crowded, but a beautiful sight regardless. "Here it is, Iskra. This is where we're from." She gazed up at the rosettes on the smoky ceiling. Perhaps not as impressive as I'd hoped for her first introduction, but what did she know. The station hadn't changed, though the people looked a little sicker than before, skinnier, and more resigned — as if they'd been waiting for centuries. Maybe they weren't even traveling anymore. "Traveling" had perhaps become a permanent condition. Ten months ago, I'd left this station a girl delirious with love, on the brink of a great adventure. Now I had returned, the prodigal, sans swagger, sans lover, with an infant in her arms, the Izhevsk Committee's pail over one arm, all my worldly goods in a little satchel. The Petrograd Soviet had not sent a welcoming committee. I kissed Iskra, checked her arm. "We're home, *milaya*."

Beggar children seemed to outnumber the passengers now, besieging them with their outstretched hands. A woman my own age, perhaps a young teacher, knelt to address two tiny children, holding something out in her hand, trying to coax them closer, the way you tamed animals. She'd almost lured them to her when a gang of them swooped in and hurried the little ones away.

I noted the Petrocommune shipping clerk stride past, determined to ignore the raft of orphans trailing behind him. *Petrocommune* — why hadn't I thought of that? The state's food distribution network. They would receive regular rations if anyone did, and all they could steal besides. I ran after him, trying to joggle Iskra and her poor arm as little as I could. "Hey! Comrade! Is there work in your office? I have my papers. How would I go about it?"

"Go to Smolny," he said, not slowing his pace or turning his head to regard me. "Talk to Gogilevsky. Tell him Strumlin sent you. And God help you." He cast a glance at me briefly. "That was an evil man."

He knew. *He knew!* I wanted to thank him, but he had lost me in the crowd. *Strumlin. Gogilevsky.* That's exactly what I would do. But today, I wanted to show Petrograd to Iskra. I was hungry for the statues, the red granite of its embankments. I wanted to show my daughter this empress of mirrors, its beauty and poetry, the reason I had dragged her all the way from Kambarka.

We emerged into the heat and glare of the afternoon, and I gazed across the great expanse of Znamenskaya Square. How quiet it was. Where had all the people gone? Here, where the Volynskys had once wheeled and slashed, where the soldiers had fired on the demonstrators in '17, I could still hear the gunfire, smell the sulfur…where the student had bled in my arms, and died. But only a single cart traversed the enormous open space. Had everyone perished in some plague?

I touched a wall, warm from the sun. The stones were still pockmarked from those gun battles. *He's dead, Marina. Let's go.* Running with Varvara across the square, where we crouched with the other patrons behind the closed curtains of the restaurant, while braver people hauled the wounded away and left the dead.

Now people walked around me, as if I were a stone in a river, no one said anything as my tears flowed. I was no longer a girl whose appearance drew attention, just another weathered woman in a faded kerchief newly arrived from the country, holding an infant, weeping next to a wall. Where was everyone? Weeds grew in the roadbed in what had been the busiest square in Petrograd. Not a tram in sight, not an automobile, just a few ragged pedestrians, a bony horse pulling a two-wheeled cart. One of the buildings had fallen in, leaving a mark like a missing tooth in a familiar face. Seeing Znamenskaya Square like this was like greeting a father or a brother after a war—the battles had left their mark.

The passersby tended to their business, walking wherever they liked, even down the middle of Nevsky Prospect. I kept touching walls. How the city had changed. So many broken windows, street doors nailed shut with all kinds of junk. I knew every shop, the painted signs boasting luxury businesses that no longer existed. All those clerks and businessmen and women in the latest hats, restaurants and shops, dentists and doctors on the floors above. Vanished, leaving only Blok's light blue vault untouched overhead. I caught my breath at a flash of seagulls, *snik snak,* across the canvas of the sky. Iskra gazed around her, bobbleheaded and astonished, her curls sweaty.

I paused at the corner of Liteiny Prospect, and pointed up to the curved windows at the top floor. "Mama's friend Auntie Mina lives there." I imagined her up there right now, in her father's studio photographing some commissar's girlfriend, her mother getting supper ready — no canteens for them. If Sofia Yakovlevna was still alive. I felt like a ghost. Perhaps in another time stream we were all still sixteen, sitting on the wide window seat up there and sharing a secret, Seryozha sewing a patch for a dress or in the darkroom with Solomon Moiseivich, Dunya in long plaits, Shusha banging away on that old piano. How angry would Mina still be? But who could resist Iskra Antonina Nikolaevna Shurova?

I imagined I smelled burning rubber from the February 1917 barricades. And the flower shop — from my dream of the little boy, who turned out to be this little apple! I would show Iskra Furshtatskaya Street. The broad parkway — I wondered what it would look like now, when there was grass growing even on Nevsky Prospect. I smiled to think what Basya would say if I showed up at the flat with my kerchief and bast shoes. I'm sure she'd love to see how the mighty had fallen. She'd probably give me some wretched hole of a room in our old servants' wing, just so she could bask in my downfall.

But I had papers now. I was the proletarian *Kuriakina.* I wouldn't have to submit myself to that humiliation.

Here was the Fontanka, its quiet looking-glass reflection. I held Iskra up so she could see the river, so gay after the long days on the train. Her eyes lingered on the shifting waters, the pastel buildings admiring themselves in the water — pistachio, peach, butterscotch.

Iskra had never seen such marvels. She had only experienced earth and trees, fields and that eternal train. She gazed down into the water, exceptionally clear these days—no sewage to sully its surface, no oils from boats—no boats. No barges. It was the absence of human beings—the city was returning to its pristine state. No factory smoke smeared the crystalline air. I could see, upriver, the yellow glow from the Sheremetev Palace, and wondered if Akhmatova still lived there. Had she stayed, weathering the storm at anchor? Or had she returned to her childhood home in Tsarskoe Selo, or headed south in search of food? Thought I could not imagine her leaving, not after having written, *I am not one of those...*

The massive bronze horses of the Anichkov Bridge still fought their sandaled grooms as it passed over the Fontanka. I knelt so Iskra could inspect the mermaids and seahorses of the bridge's ironwork. Below us, the waters shot diamonds into our eyes. Metal and stone, water—these things at least hadn't changed, nor did the passion of horses that could never be tamed, no matter how hard the grooms tried. We still flung ourselves to the ground and trampled our saner nature.

Farther on, Eliseev's fine grocer's still stood, with its art nouveau mirrors encased in grime, where once a refrigerated counter stocked every grade of caviar, where we bought our Pears soap and imported wine. Now it was a dingy ration point—Distribution Center No. 3—while across Nevsky, Catherine the Great rose on her bronze pediment, sheltering her courtiers in her bell-like skirts. The weeds sprung up like a field before the classical pillars of the Alexandrinsky Theater, the tree boughs tickled with yellow.

Iskra gazed at it all in green-eyed amazement. How could I have ever left her behind in the village? "See those arcades?" I pointed out Gostinny Dvor, its double rows of empty shops. "That's where your grandmother shopped. And this is Nevsky Passazh." The entryway to the luxury arcade boarded up. The perfumer, the milliner...Zimniye Nochi. *Winter Nights.* I'd had a Zimniye Nochi baby blanket from Orenburg, so warm and light it was like sleeping on a cloud. Iskra would never know a blanket like that. I brushed the soft hair from her forehead. Well, what difference did it make if she never had an Orenburg blanket and soap from Eliseev's? She would have Petersburg.

We continued past the Singer Building, and Kazan Cathedral—site of my terrifying dream, the white wolf stalking me in the forest of its columns. A pang of fear shot through me. The Archangel would be stalking me here. *If you don't like wolves, stay out of the woods,* his man Akim had once said. I would try, but these were my woods as well. And here was the Grand Hotel Europa, site of that last ridiculous lunch with my great-aunt before the February Revolution, a string quartet playing Bach while we ate our soup. It seemed like a century ago. Now a number of ragged children played under the hotel's porte cochere. It must be some sort of school or orphanage now. The forecourt on Mikhailovskaya Street was cracked, no fine automobiles lined up there anymore, no carriages. I could only imagine what the hotel's lobby looked like, that patrician dining room. Was this all that was left of Petrograd—soldiers and abandoned children? I kissed Iskra's sweaty forehead. *Don't worry. We're going to be all right.*

We paused on the Kazansky Bridge over the Catherine Canal, and I pointed to the windows of that green-and-gold apartment, from which I'd once gazed out into the falling snow. "That's where your papa and I made love the first time," I whispered into her small ear. One of the best things about babies was that you could tell them all your secrets. I hummed "Mi Noche Triste" and danced with her in the empty street—the Argentine tango. Its rhythm, its balances, the changes of direction. She already liked to dance. I remembered how careful we'd been in those old days, not to start a child. It made me laugh—and now, the whole catastrophe!

I felt him here. I knew he could feel me too. In some abandoned palace or hotel in this city, Kolya was living his mysterious life. Maybe at the Astoria, pouring the last of the champagne into hoarded crystal. Or in some decayed flat with elegant old people. I knew he'd feel the change in the air, and sense that I'd come home.

The city resonated with our love. I would find him. And then? But I was no seer. I would leave the future to itself.

At the top of Nevsky Prospect, the Admiralty flashed its golden salute, and across the river, the Peter and Paul Fortress returned it. The *kino* was still here, showing an old Kholodnaya film, the placards faded but the ticket window open. I was shocked, really, that such bourgeois trash would still be playing in the heart of revolutionary Petrograd. And yet, there were other songs than "The Internationale," other moods. We were more than just units of work, representatives of class. The wily individual was more stubborn than the forces of history, and our needs, our desires, our deepest dreams, would always rear up and run crazily around our lives like a horse escaped from its stall. The soul knew no politics.

Palace Square lay vast and as empty as an old walnut shell, and silent as snipers, the statues on the roof of the Winter Palace scanned the horizon. The Alexander Column looked taller than ever in that empty circle of buildings, shooting up into the pale northern sky. Grass grew between the stones. I passed the Admiralty with its nautical bas-reliefs, its park overgrown, passed the Astoria, and St. Isaac's Cathedral, along wide Senate Square. I wanted to touch the Neva, and see if Peter yet stood, commanding.

That much had not changed. The man who had created this dream in stone still pointed toward the river. *Here I will build my city.* His only true child. Peter, marvelous and cruel, who had built it from the swamp, leaving forty thousand dead. Their bones creaked under our feet. Now his dream belonged to the masses. Yet the *Bronze Horseman* remained. Without a soul left to follow, he kept his post, his great and terrible purpose locked in his implacable heart.

I strolled along the embankment, feasting on the distances and the gallop of the river, the sea air, wind fanning my face, sun-kissed gulls flitting over the water. Sea wind and Neva spray, the ensemble of eternal Petersburg's classical facades and secret courtyards, shining canals. It was music, it was history, alive despite the silence, perhaps more than before, as now it was mine alone. Not a fishing boat, not even a rowboat, sullied the sparkling surface of the waters.

I could *feel* the Allied blockade just beyond Kronstadt in the gulf. I could see no ships waiting for cargo at the great wharves. We were in quarantine, not from fear of disease but against the contagion of our ideas. I had not forgotten the gloomy news from the Germans on the train to Vyatka—the failure of the Soviets, the death of Rosa Luxemburg. Yet all that could change in a day. The English were backing away from the Whites. Then I remembered who had told me that.

Soldiers did worse on the field of battle, I told myself. In the world's eyes, the Chekist was just someone who died, fell off a train. Iskra, will you judge me someday? I hoped her times would be much milder. I was not going to chastise myself for lack of feeling. Things happened to people in this world, they disappeared, they were arrested, they were packed off in work parties, conscripted, shoved into provisioning units, they died in childbirth. They got typhoid and typhus, they drank bad water and worse. The Chekist had had the bad luck to run into me. Which of us controls his own fate?

I held her upright, taking care not to hurt her arm, so she could better see the wide, whitecapped river, the university, the Sphinx. "She's from Egypt, *lisichka*. Very old and very wise." She always seemed to understand everything I said, waving her little fingers, exploring my kerchief, my collar. I chewed on her fingers. Sometimes I wanted to bite her. I could see why there were so many fairy tales about witches eating children, you really wanted to. I turned around so she could look over my shoulder and pointed to the Strelka, its two red Rostral Columns with green verdigris prows. "When I was a boy, I climbed way up there."

How would she understand the strangeness of my life? She blinked her long coppery eyelashes and made squirrel sounds that turned me to jelly. What she had been through already.

I was sad that she would never know Petersburg as I'd known it, as my parents had known it, my grandparents.

On the other hand, she would never be subject to an imperial will, she'd have no idea what that meant—the entire country at the whim of one person, the aristocracy chewing up the wealth of the nation. She would not take her privileges at anyone's expense. She would vote, make decisions without the interference of fathers and husbands and tsars. What were ice creams and drawing rooms, Orenburg blankets, compared to that? To her, our lives would be as archaic and unimaginable as that which gave birth to the Sphinx.

We just had to live through this time. She gazed into my face as into a tree, her trust absolute in this nineteen-year-old holding her. My Soviet girl. She would be so modern, the life she would live was unimaginable. How dare I be teary for Pears soap and the tango? I sighed. No matter how revolutionary I thought I'd become, my ideas, my beliefs, my very bones, had been marrowed in that old world. It would take another generation to breed these predilections out of us, do away with nostalgia and tangos—perhaps even passion itself.

Though I couldn't imagine that a daughter of my blood and Kolya's would manage to stay free of that curse.

She started to whimper and fret, and I felt my breasts let down their milk in plain view of Peter the Great. I took advantage of the city's emptiness to nurse her up against its foundation rock. She wasn't a fast nurser. She liked to finger my skin, my dress, her eyes closing in blissful reverie. I leaned back on the warm stone. I felt like I was living in a dream of Petrograd where all the people had disappeared.

The thing was to find Kolya, tell him that I was ready to reconsider my decision to leave him. Anyone else would call it quixotic, and perhaps it was. I hummed to Iskra as I nursed her. I thought she'd fallen asleep, but then felt the gurgle, and knew what was next—allowing me the strange experience of walking down the stone steps of the Neva to wash a baby's diaper. What a poor example of Soviet hygiene! Like a peasant woman, I rubbed her laundry on the stones, draped the cloth to dry in the sun. It was heaven to sit on sun-warmed granite by the mother-river in the honeyed light. We slept for a while there, under Peter's disapproving watch. *Go!* his pointing arm commanded—but he was bronze and I was flesh, and in this, flesh emerged triumphant.

Afterward, we walked down to the English Embankment, in search of a certain yellow mansion. It was smaller than I remembered it but its facade glowed like sun through a spoonful of syrup. I tried the street door—locked...but perhaps the service entrance off Galernaya Street, in the back, might be open. From that street, I easily found the courtyard—the big gate was showily padlocked, but the smaller one gave way. The yard was a filthy hole now, filled with all kinds of junk. No sign of black horses, as on that terrible morning when he left me. *Go back to your poet.* Those giant blacks that were in fact Arkady's.

I tried the doors. It was like rapping on panels for a secret entrance. One door was locked, the second nailed shut, but I knew people got in there somehow. Success came in the form of a modest, almost invisible entry at one side of the yard, its wood weathered to silver. I slipped inside.

The cold darkness immediately wrapped us in its ghastly embrace, a zoolike smell. I hesitated a moment—Iskra heavy in her sling—and reached through the slit in my skirt for Kolya's gun, held it against my leg. I was by no means the only one who'd found this door. As I wound my way through the decimated pantries and storage rooms, the stink assaulted me. Everywhere the tooth of wood scavengers had made its mark, gnawing away doors, cabinets, furniture. Light fingered the broken windows on the front landing, dust motes hung in its rays, as still as death. The marble of the grand staircase rose as pale as a nude in the gloom. How cold it had been that winter—even now, its chill was just this side of a grave. I ascended slowly, listening. Iskra talking to herself in her sling. *Shhhh...* I jiggled her.

Last year, the abandoned mansion had just felt empty, but now it seemed occupied by something that skittered in the corners of my eyes as I walked soundlessly, tiger-footed, through the dusky rooms of the bel étage. Shattered bits of upholstered furniture lay across the elegant parquet, or what was left of it—half had been pulled up, darkness gaping through from the next level. I had to be careful in the gloom not to take a misstep and break my leg.

Someone had harvested the frames from the couches and left the springs and wadding like so many slaughtered sheep.

Footsteps. I halted, listening with every hair on my body. Light footsteps running down a corridor. His name jumped to my lips—*Kolya!*—but I stopped myself from calling out. Those were not his feet. I wrapped my fingers around the revolver's grip, slid off the safety. A sensible person would leave—a sensible person would not have entered this desolate place—but I'd long dreamed of this mansion, the perfect hideout, derelict as it was. I remembered the door, flush with the wall. I had to know if he was here. My hands were sweating despite the cold, sweat ran down my back into my homemade drawers. The baby bulky in her sling. I crept toward the small boudoir, that jewel, feeling the wall for the giveaway crack.

There it was again, the sound of running steps. Cats? I shuddered to think *rats*.

There. I had found it, not by sight but by touch, the seam in the wall, and pushed it open, this room where I'd spent those four mad days of grief, my passion blindly bounding, wounded and dripping blood like an arrow-shot deer.

The dirty windows permitted a dull light, the room smelled of smoke. Its yellow wallpaper had been charred black by fire, lit not in the fireplace but right on the floor against the plaster. The corners of the room were littered with civilization's shards and refuse, a torn mattress heaped with rags. I was surprised to see the little chandelier yet hung from the ceiling, as well as a few of the paintings. Hadn't anyone thought to sell them?

The rags moved. I practically shot my own foot off. Not rags but *children*. Huddled together in the corner like a clutch of hedgehogs, three children with gray matted hair and filthy faces the color of their rags, watching me. Listless, inhuman, their eyes the only clean parts of them. I heard running in the corridor, light feet fading away. "Don't be afraid," I whispered, my heart somewhere in my neck. "How long have you been here? Are you alone?" They stared at me as if they'd been deafened by a blast.

Children living alone, burning things in this room, and there were probably more, but these, unlike their more able comrades, hadn't the strength to run. Sick, feverish—these poor little beasts. They needed water, food, medicine—everything I didn't have. I was raked by my own pure helplessness. I put the gun away. The children looked about seven or eight, maybe nine, hard to tell, their clothes so ragged, and they were so malnourished, it was impossible to even guess if they were boys or girls. "Are you hungry?" I said. "Food?" I put my fingers to my lips but they just stared.

I took the bread I had in my pockets and broke it into pieces, held it out to them. I would run low soon myself, but I was strong, and these children might not last the night. Varvara would say I'd be better off feeding their stronger companions, the ones who stood a chance. Yet I couldn't bear to leave them with nothing. They just stared and stared—those glittering, feverish eyes. They didn't even try to take the food. I didn't want to get any closer to them, with their matted hair and grimy hands. *Jesus kissed the lepers. He washed their feet.* Scalps patchy from some kind of mange. But I couldn't just throw chunks of bread at them like they were animals. I bent down and I pressed the pieces into their dirty, dry, hot hands. I couldn't show how terrible I found them, disgusting and frightening and hopeless. "Eat, children," I said in my most musical voice. "You need to eat now."

They ate, slowly, mechanically, not even noticing, as if mesmerized by my appearance in their filthy dreams. One of them—a boy, I could tell now—crawled forward from the pile of rags and kissed the hem of my skirt. His shining eyes. What were they seeing?

He knelt and crossed himself. The other children followed suit.

It wasn't me and Iskra they thought were standing before them, but a visitation of the Virgin and Child.

After the initial horror at their mistaken awe, I felt the urge to give them what they wanted, and if it was blasphemy, so be it. I who had nothing could at least give them that. I could only imagine what Genya would say about what I was about to do.

I made the Ionian sign of benediction over their scabby heads, right hand raised to radiate energy, the left below to collect it, and blessed them with all the somber grandeur I could manage. "Rest and grow strong, little ones," I said, improvising Her lines. "I see you, day and night. I watch over you. I'm there when you sleep. I weep for your suffering, little lambs, my holy ones. I love you so...very much." My throat closed. I didn't know whether I could go on, it was such a disgraceful act. But they were children, and their loneliness must surely be as terrible as their hunger, their disease. "When you close your eyes, I'll be there watching over you, even if you don't see me. Don't be afraid. God bless you and keep you."

And then I had to go, to fly, before I started sobbing. Out in the dark corridor, I heard the scuffling of feet and the particular hush of held breath all around me. The other orphans, the stronger ones, were waiting for me to go. "Get them water, boiled if you can. And good luck to you all, children."

15 *Out in the Cold*

I tried to remember the name of the man I was supposed to see at Petrocommune—*Gogolinsky? Gogolevsky?* I used to have a perfect memory, but after my visit to the yellow mansion my wits had fled. I barely noticed where I was walking. This was what had happened to our beautiful revolution—children living like animals in abandoned buildings. They rode between trains, begged at stations. I thought our purpose was to protect the weak from the strong, not create some desperate Darwinian culling of the herd. Oh, those quaint old-fashioned virtues of mine.

To our leaders, the spacemen, everything that made the revolution more secure was good in the absolute. If it strengthened the revolution, it was good, and if it weakened it, it was the enemy. I knew that's what Varvara thought. But the truth was, the weak could only weaken things, taking strength from the strong. They couldn't help to build a revolution. And yet, this was why the revolution had occurred. To help the weak. The strong would always take care of themselves, but what place in the great machine was there for ongoing suffering, for starving, abandoned children? Their pitiful lives too much of the present, this terrible moment, which was supposed to vanish. I knew one was supposed to lift one's eyes to the glorious future, and not focus on present suffering, but what of these children? The unfortunate baggage of history. Were they to quietly starve to death, die in the walls like rats? Everything that struggled weakened the revolution. My own heartache, my tears weakened it.

I didn't want to walk out to Smolny now. I wanted to go somewhere private with a door that locked, where I could sit down and cry. I wanted to wash and drink boiled water and nurse my baby and, yes, even show her off to someone who knew me. I wanted all these things as another might crave food or water. So instead of treating myself to Smolny's bureaucratic charms, I found myself entering a familiar doorway, still open right onto the street. And here was the sign, KATZEV PHOTOGRAPHY STUDIO. I touched its fingerprinty black glass, traced the letters.

The elevator had lost its function, its safety gates locked. As I climbed the stairs, Iskra—heavy in the home-woven sling—woke and started crying. I sat on the stairs to calm her. People scowled as they climbed past us—this bast-shod vagrant with her bundle and her screaming infant. Only when she was quiet did I begin to climb again. When I knocked on that door, she had to be at her best. They would be the first people who would care that this particular fireball had landed upon the earth.

I reached the door, the black paint, the nameplate. Rang the bell.

Heavy footsteps. Solomon Moiseivich! The door opened, but instead of her father's warm, smiling face, it was Mina's fiancé, Roman Ippolit, the medical student—the same bristly hair, arrogant jaw, his old self-satisfied air. So that was still going on. He took in the sight of me—my pail, my shoes, my baby with her sweaty hair, my satchel. "What do you want?" he asked rudely. Did he think I was a beggar? Thank God he didn't recognize the boy assistant, Misha.

I tried for my most elegant tone. "Excuse me, but is Mina Solomonovna home? Or Sofia Yakovlevna?"

His eyes raced again, from my dusty kerchief to my redheaded baby, sheepskin, and satchel. What could such a creature possibly want from a modern Petrograd photographic studio? A baby picture? "Who wants to know?" He planted himself even more firmly in the doorway. He certainly hadn't gained any manners in the time I'd been away.

"Tell her it's Marina Makarova."

"From the academy? Dmitry Makarov's daughter?" Now he reinspected me, temples flexing, a portrait of Suspicion in a gallery of human venality. My God, he would have made a good maître d'.

"Actually, it's Kuriakina now. I'm married." I shifted my weight and spoke in a soft, educated voice, as feminine as I could muster, in fear that he would recall Misha. "Forgive me, but I've been traveling for some time. May I come in?"

He must have remembered a trace of manners from a few generations back. He let me in. The apartment was the same and yet not. Sparer. Things gone missing. The piano was where it had always been but the clock that had always sat upon it was gone. Also the carpet, and the collection of bric-a-brac on top of the bookcase. The Meissen figurines Sofia Yakovlevna had so loved had definitely lost a few comrades. The crystals on the chandelier were less plentiful. Well, who had not changed? I just wanted to sit in peace with Iskra, grateful not to be eight years old and lying on a filthy mattress dying of typhoid or influenza.

"Mina's with a customer," said Roman. "I'm Ippolit. Roman Osipovich." He extended his hand.

"Good to meet you." I hesitated, aware of my calloused, weathered hands, no longer the academy miss I'd once been, clasping his, which was soft and sweaty. I remembered all those dirty jokes he used to tell, all those awful stories he insisted on imparting to Misha. I fought the urge to wipe my hand on my skirt. He didn't offer me a seat, so I stood as elegantly as I could—like a duchess, waiting for a courtier to pull out a chair. Now I was conscious of how dirty I was after the days of traveling, I could smell myself and Iskra, diapers and puke and the vague suspicion of blood. "Might I use the washroom?"

"Sure." He pointed down the hallway. "Third door to the right."

"Yes. I know," I said.

I carried Iskra down to the bathroom, sat on the edge of the tub, and cleaned her properly. My God, they still had running water! Reveling in the privacy, I ran water into my bucket, cold but plentiful. And soap! I rinsed and scrubbed those diapers. Maybe later I could get someone to boil water for us. Iskra looked so small and clean and pretty, lying on the cloth on the white tiles, looking up at her mama, and the electric light.

I couldn't get those children out of my mind. What a hell this life was for small things. Yet I couldn't help but rejoice in the luxury as I laved my own face and hands, stripped down and washed my arms and armpits and the rest, already estimating the fortunes of the Katzev family in the months I'd been gone. They'd had to maintain enough people to keep the flat private, that was good news, everybody alive and well. If only Mina wasn't too angry at me for leaving that day, maybe she'd see Iskra and relent. Who could resist such a beauty? And I could get work with my new papers, contribute to the household. Perhaps Sofia Yakovlevna would help me soften her up. She'd even liked Misha, and that was saying something.

I came out of the washroom with the newly fresh Iskra, and nearly collided with a tall Negro woman in a modern but unusual dress, wavy hair cinched in a cord like a Greek stele. *"Izvenite, etot tualyet?"* An American accent. She stumbled in her Russian. An American Negro in Petrograd—maybe I'd hit my head in the bathroom. Maybe I was still lying there. *"Tualyet, da? Etot? Etot?"*

"No, it's the next one down," I said in English, pointing to the correct door.

She burst into the most radiant smile, clutching my arm in gratitude. "Oh my God, you speak English. Wait there. Don't leave, promise me you won't leave?" Holding up her pink-palmed hand, like asking a dog to *stay*.

"I won't," I said.

I returned to the parlor with my pail and diapers, Iskra awake and looking at everything as if she'd never been indoors before. She gazed at the light coming in through the curved windows, the colors in the chandelier's crystals. But I didn't have time to share in her delight. A disapproving figure waited for me like a strict, humorless schoolmistress. Arms crossed, one toe raised, heel digging into the floor, as if she would like to crush me under it. I smiled, but Mina didn't. It had been almost a year now, but my hopes that she wouldn't still be angry were overly optimistic. "You look well, Mina." Thin but not starving, her hair in a stylish bob, though I saw circles around her gray eyes behind her spectacles. And her shock—at seeing Iskra.

Roman grinning like a perfect fool.

"Don't you have something to do?" she snapped.

He dropped his chin to conceal his smirk and went across the room, to the divan where Solomon Katzev used to sit between clients. He picked up a large medical book and pretended to study it.

Mina's gaze moved from the baby to me and back again. Her hand went out timidly, to touch my child, the flaming hair, the soft flushed cheek. She extended her forefinger to Iskra's tiny hand and my daughter clutched it. My old friend's gray eyes were full of clouds. "It's his, isn't it? Oh my God, I can see him. It looks just like him."

"Her name's Iskra."

"Is that what happened that night? You found him?"

He. She still thought of him that way. As I did. For us, there was just one *he* in this world, and no *Roman* or *Genya* could stand in his way. How could one man have captured so many? Petrograd must lie awash in our sisterhood, women who had felt this lash, this spell, this drawn knife of pleasure across our hearts. Who felt it still, whenever we thought—*he.* We could form our own sect of wounded nuns. Although I certainly knew him best, having shared his childhood, seen him behind the scenes of his traveling show—borne his child. Even I would never know him completely. The religion of Kolya Shurov was a mystery cult.

"How's Sofia Yakovlevna?" I asked her.

"She's well," Mina said, still staring at the baby, who had her firmly by the finger.

Still alive. Thank God. "And Aunt Fanya? Uncle Aaron? Dunya?"

"Same as ever," she said shortly. "Dunya's seeing that painter, the blond one. Sasha." She danced Iskra's hand up and down, and the baby grinned wickedly, reached for her specs. I was happy for Dunya — someone should be lucky in love.

"And Shusha?" The youngest Katzev.

"School. She's at Insurrection." Mina laughed despite herself. Insurrection, the new incarnation of the Tagantsev Academy. "She wants to be a doctor someday." Never taking her eyes off my child. "God help us all, right?"

Roman spoke up from his books. "Hey, aren't you going to tell her about us? We're engaged. Getting married as soon as I graduate medical school."

"Congratulations," I said, trying for enthusiasm, framing my reaction as it would be if I hadn't already had a bellyful of Roman Ippolit. And trying to keep the extra smile out of it, the horselaugh I was also feeling. Who in the world would marry a jackass like Ippolit? I kissed Mina three times in the traditional blessing. Her eyes widened in unspoken sentences that her pale lips had to hold back. I noticed she'd stopped reddening them.

"How old is...Iskra?" Mina asked me.

"Almost three months. Want to hold her?" I passed her to Mina, who held her uncertainly, as if this small creature might explode. "Actually the midwife baptized her: Antonina. Antonina Gennadievna Kuriakina." Not to rub salt in the wound.

Tcha...that exhalation of exasperation. She touched her fingertips to Iskra's silky hair, the way you'd touch a rose. "Your mama's crazy, you know. She's nuts. Does Genya know about this?" She tilted her bobbed head toward the baby.

I sighed, hoping she would understand. "Most of it."

She used to be so unaware, our Mina Katzeva, but she'd grown up a lot in the last years — as had we all. Now it was her turn for the horselaugh. "Can't you ever do anything right? There's always got to be some drama. It exhausts me just thinking about your life, the way you live it."

I didn't say, *And if I was engaged to Roman Ippolit, I'd want to kill myself, so the feeling's mutual.*

The Negro woman sailed into the parlor like a ship under full sail, freshened and sparkling with energy. She pressed my hand, hers smooth and solid. I regretted my work-hardened paw. I could smell her perfume. She wore a green suit, red lipstick, so much color, I could hardly look directly at her. Who was this apparition? "You speak such wonderful English. I'm Aura Cady Sands." Her hand was warm and long, almost as big as my own, full of electric energy. I could feel her feet through it, her solidity—she would not be one easily knocked over by life. "Forgive me, I don't want to intrude, I was just leaving. But I'm desperate to meet people who speak English, and so well! What's your name, honey?"

"Ma copine, Marina Dmitrievna Makarova," Mina said.

"Kuriakina," I quickly corrected her. "I'm married now. Just returned from the countryside."

"I'm so glad to meet you, Marina Dmitrievna. So glad. Your country, *La Russie! La Revolution!* My God, what you people are doing here, it's incredible. I had to come and see for myself. The energy—the will to change the world! Magnificent!" She was like a wind, and I a field of wheat bowing before it. "Oh, and aren't you precious! Look at this hair, just like Mama's!" She touched Iskra's curls so gently. "And those eyes. She's positively Irish. Can I hold her?"

Mina deposited her happily into the woman's arms.

Aura Sands lowered her nose to the baby's and began to sing "When Irish Eyes Are Smiling" in the most astonishing voice perhaps I'd ever heard. A mezzo-soprano, I was guessing, or dramatic soprano, the rich, round tones. But she sang pianissimo, so she wouldn't scare my redheaded, Irish-eyed Russian baby. One moment I was cutting rye with a midwife and her daughters, and the next I was listening to an African angel sing to my daughter's Irish eyes. I began to cry. Iskra patted the woman's face as she sang.

We could hear, down in the street, the short barks of an automobile's claxon. "Oh, I must fly!" She nuzzled my daughter and put her back in my arms. "Come see me! I'm at the Astoria. I'd love to talk more. Everyone speaks French here but it sure would be nice to speak some good old English. And you..." She tickled Iskra, pressing a strong, manicured forefinger into the baby's tiny chest. "You be nice to those men. You're going to drive them insane!" The baby reached for her earring, gold, and I caught her just in time. What one could get on the street for just one of those earrings. "*Merci, Mina Solomonovna, pour les belles photos.*"

"But you haven't seen them yet," Mina said. Her French was all right, but it was a third language. She preferred German, the language of science.

"I'm sure they'll be wonderful. I can always tell an artist." She switched to English. "And you come see me, Marina Kuriakina. Please don't let me down. Room 223, Astoria Hotel. Afternoons are good, I don't wake up so early. We can have lunch. This is wonderful, what a lucky day!" She kissed me and the baby and left like a hurricane, blowing herself out the door.

"Who in the devil was that?" I asked. Iskra was starting to fret. Hungry, or just missing the dark lady with the shiny earrings.

"A singer. As you no doubt guessed."

"Famous?"

"Well, she's at the Astoria... Yes, I'd say so."

"I've never heard of her. I didn't think Americans were so advanced."

"Probably that's why she left," Mina said, as if I were missing the obvious. "I'm photographing her for Narkompros." The Commissariat of Enlightenment.

I was happy just to be talking to her again, two old friends. "Do you mind if I sit down?"

She didn't look happy about that, but I moved to the old window seat, in the great bay window from which we'd watched the revolution unfold. One of the upper panes still had its bullet hole from the shooting—the sniper on the roof—stuffed with wadded paper. Iskra immediately started fussing. I unbuttoned my dress behind her sling and discreetly latched her onto my breast. I usually liked to watch her nursing—her druggy happiness, it made me feel like I was the Goddess of All Things—but I didn't think Mina would enjoy seeing me nursing Kolya's offspring.

Outside, the sky was darkening, the pale blue becoming luminous over Nevsky's ranks, the buildings shouldering inward. This city was made for twilight. I had missed this more than I had known. Mina joined me in the little nook where we'd sat so many times—half hidden away, our legs tucked up under our skirts—and shared our dreams, outrages, ambitions. Now she kept her feet firmly on the floor, her lips tight, trying not to hear the noisy smackings of Iskra under the cloth. "What are you doing here, Marina? What do you want?"

I didn't answer. Instead, I said, "You know, I saw the photographs, from the first anniversary." I didn't want to say, *The ones I took*. Roman was listening to our every word. "I saw them on the agit-train with Genya. Moscow's using them in *agitki*—did you know? They even used the ones from the Rostral Columns." *Give me credit at least for that*.

"I know what you're doing," she whispered nastily. "It's not going to work."

I thought girls were supposed to grow up to resemble their mothers, but she was nothing like round, cozy Sofia Yakovlevna.

"What am I doing?" I said innocently. "We're just sitting here having a conversation."

She sank back into the cushions, so that she was half hidden by the alcove's striped curtain. We'd even unconsciously taken the same sides we always did, me on the right, her on the left. "I *know* you," she whispered. "You want me to tell you how good those photos were. How important. How the studio came into a bit of favor for your having shot them. Which will lead to a request to hire you again, let you live here with..." She nodded at Iskra. "You think

I'm stupid? I was always smarter than you. And you don't intimidate me anymore."

Oh no. She hadn't forgiven me anything.

"You've got that kid, you need food, a place to live," she hissed. "Well, the answer is no. *No.* We barely feed ourselves these days. You've got two husbands, let one of them support you."

The light illuminated the front of Mina's ash-blond hair, washing the front of her glasses so I couldn't see those eyes I knew so well—their gray irises flecked with white, the white-tipped lashes. *My two husbands*...Why not three, or ten? Useless to me now, both of them. Out the window, the city was so heartbreakingly lovely, the regular pattern of window and stone, arches and caryatids. Below us, Nevsky Prospect was like a street in a diorama in a museum—small, perfect, and empty. Without its shops, I supposed no one had a reason to stroll, even in the warmth of early autumn. And here was my best friend in the world, so close I could reach out and touch her—except that she would have slapped me if I had. This was exactly where I'd wanted to be, and the only thing standing in my way was this angry woman who knew me too well, whom I'd taught to despise me. Surely there must be a shred of forgiveness somewhere in her stony heart, the daughter of the kindest people I'd ever met.

"Don't you turn those big brown eyes on me," she hissed. "Where are you when anybody else needs you? Gone, gone, gone. You've proven yourself to be a complete moral bankrupt. I pity that kid. Grow up, Marina. I had to. You can too."

Grovel, that was my plan. I supposed it was time to implement it. "Just a few days, Mina. Until I find some work, get my rations, a housing assignment. I have an in at Petrocommune."

"I'm supporting three old people, plus my sisters, plus—" She gestured with her head toward Roman. So he was living here too. "You have no idea what we've been through. We almost lost Shusha and my aunt and uncle to typhoid last winter. Dunya got arrested for stealing firewood. Boards off a fence. You can't take wood. It all belongs to the state now, even if it's just a goddamned fence. The bread—you can't imagine. And now you show up like Katya the milkmaid, with a kid, thinking you'll just give me that smile and I'll forget everything?" Now she cast a disparaging look at the cloth covering my suckling child. "I'm not a man. It doesn't work on me. I'm not going to let you stay."

"Not even for a few days?" I said, low. "For God's sake, Mina. Two days. That's all I ask. I have a couple days of food. Just don't make me sleep in the hall."

"No, no, no. I know you. Two days'll become three and then a week and then you're in for the duration. You're a leech. A tick." She said it as if it were a scientific fact, pushing her specs up on her nose. "I won't do it."

I expected her to be angry with me for running away with Kolya instead of working her rounds of factory demonstrations and greetings, but not for her to out-and-out slander me. "You know that's a lie. I've never taken one scrap of food from your mouth, or anybody else's. I just finished harvesting the fields to pay off the midwife. Look!" I held out one tanned hand, so she could see the calluses, the muscle and sinew of my forearm. "Leech? Of all the horrible things. Call me what you like but I'm no parasite."

"Unlike you, I can think a week or two ahead," she said. "And that's what's going to happen. For instance, how are you going to work with that kid around your neck—for Petrocommune or anyone else? It can't even hold its head up."

"I'll think of something," I said. My peasant stubbornness was digging in.

She rubbed her forehead. I was giving her a headache. She tended to have them ever since she was little, and now that she was doing so much darkroom work it must have gotten worse. Well, good. That would serve her, calling me a leech.

"Well, let me finish nursing her—can I do that? Or does that make her a leech too?"

"Fine. But then clear out. I've got to finish those photos. Let yourself out. You know the way."

She got up and left me there, alone with my empty evening. I sorted through ideas of where I could go, what I could do, like hands at cards, all of them unappealing. Roman pretended to be working at his medical books, but I could tell he was enjoying the show. "You must have really done something to irk her," he said.

I sat nursing Iskra, thinking of my options. The Krestovsky apartment. The collective flat on Furshtatskaya. The Poverty Artel. I still had friends in Petrograd—but I was shaken by how angry Mina was. I never expected people to be angry with me. If she was so mad, what would Varvara be like, let alone a darker form in the shadows...No, tomorrow I would go to Smolny. I should have gone today. I would find something, Iskra around my neck or not. Hopefully a few of those crèches had been built. If not at the Petrograd Soviet, where?

As Iskra finished her meal, I calculated how much food I really had left. Enough for one more meal, maybe two. In my aristocratic largesse, feeding the orphans of Russia, I hadn't kept enough for myself. Not thinking ahead, as usual. Such a chess player. I wiped my eyes on the back of my hand. I would stall as long as I could...Worse came to worst, I'd sleep in the hall and let them walk over me, shame Mina into giving way. Now I wished I'd taken that bath when I could. Maybe I'd go over to the Astoria and see what Aura Cady Sands had to offer. I could present myself—"Oh, you didn't mean tonight?" I had to handle that one carefully. I didn't want to appear too needy, too desperate, and scare her away.

The key turned in the lock, the door opened, and Dunya Katzeva stepped in. Dunya, so beautiful! All grown up, in a neat but worn dress printed with flowers. I pushed the curtain back and she shrieked and ran to embrace me. How good to see her, to embrace her with my one free arm, her fresh girl's smell. Dunya, the opposite of Mina—warm where her sister was cold, happy where the elder was resentful. I put a good face on it all, as if Mina had said nothing. It wasn't hard to put my sad mood aside. This was the homecoming I'd imagined. Dunya made a great fuss about the baby, her conversation full of sly innuendo for Roman's sake about my hair having "grown out," and how *womanly* I had become—since being Misha, yes, certainly. She was a regular *Sovetskaya barynya* now, a *Soviet young lady,* working at the Zubov Institute of Art History and spending time with Sasha Orlovsky, who was doing public projects now and teaching. "Wait till he sees you, he'll go crazy. How's Genya? Where's Mina?"

"She's in the darkroom," I said. "She's still mad. She says I have to clear out."

"Well, forget that. You're staying. Our *tsarevna,* she's a *very* important person now," Dunya said. "I'm surprised she didn't make you take an appointment."

"They had a fight," Roman said. "Mina's furious."

Dunya sighed. "Mina's always furious these days. Don't pay any attention to her."

I talked her into boiling some water for me and holding the baby while I had a bath. Ah! Alone in warm water, the dirt just rolled off my skin. I washed my hair, washed the train from me, the guilt, the blood, the miles, the orphans, the dust. I would have washed my dress too if I thought I'd be staying, but there was no way to know where I was sleeping tonight. I didn't want to have to sleep in wet clothes if I was going to be in a doorway or a stairwell.

When I emerged, a new Marina, Shusha had returned from school. Her enthusiasm for my homecoming exceeded even Dunya's. Taller, her face less babyish, her hair cropped, the skirt of her school uniform too short, she was as leggy as a young horse. She regaled me with the doings at Insurrection, where she'd been elected to her class committee, was also the chairman of the drama club and had won first prize for a poem she'd written. I made her recite it to me.

From far away the soldier heard his death.
It called to him with mouthy cannon's speech
And punctuated now with dying breath
his comrades take his gun and breach
the enemy's forward lines.

I especially liked that mouthy cannon, and the short last line. Shusha insisted on holding the baby, though after feeding, she always slept for a good hour or two, and was content in Dunya's arms. Feeling herself changing hands, she just opened her eyes to slits and went back to sleep. Shusha loved the name Iskra. "I'm thinking of changing mine. Shoshanna's so biblical." She made a sour face.

"Shame on you. Our grandmother's name," Dunya chided.

"Yes, I'm the one who gets to stand naked before nasty old men. *Nyet*." She sat down at the table, Iskra in her lap. "I was thinking *Viktoria*."

"That's not so revolutionary," Dunya said.

"It's the sound," I explained. "*K. Vik*. The hard consonants, *Te*, and the drumroll of the *errr*."

"Exactly. I'm sick of all those *shhushes*..." the young girl said. "Like walking in slippers, like you're being careful not to wake anyone up. Speaking of."

The aunt and uncle, Fanya and Aaron, emerged from the back hall. They must have been napping in their room. Aaron's hair was a white cloud. Their smiles were warm, but they'd both lost teeth in the last year, and their hands trembled as they clasped mine and kissed me three times. They smelled musty as old pillows. Lucky to be alive after typhoid. A hard winter for the old people. I could understand Mina's fears. But I wouldn't be a drag on their household. I could work, I could add to their income, I could get rations, Drops of Milk. I could steal wood. They could use another able-bodied person around here.

We sat around the table, talking, laughing, Shusha holding Iskra. How I envied Mina in this. She still had a family. Educated people, soulful—a living, breathing organism. My family had not survived the stresses of the revolution. How was it that theirs had? The samovar boiled and Dunya made tea. She poured it out, a pale green. "Chinese?"

"Celery."

Shusha added, "Exclusive to the Yellow Emperor."

It was dark when Sofia Yakovlevna returned from the queues, a

199

little frail, her sack heavy with provisions. She was thinner and more lined than last year, more bowed, but how happy she was to see me! She hurried to put her sack on the table and embrace me. She still smelled of chicken, though I couldn't imagine they'd had a chicken in years. Such a warm welcome, and the shock when she saw Iskra in Shusha's arms. "Yours? It can't be! Oh, this precious child! Let me hold her. I must." She immediately took her. "Sweet adorable thing!" As if Iskra were her own granddaughter. Asking her name, her age. "Iskra? *Iskra?* Like a box of matches? *Akh,* this revolution, it doesn't know when to stop!" The baby just kept sleeping. "We're so glad to have you back in Petrograd, dear. Both of you," she addressed the baby. "Like old times. I wish Papa were here. Where are you staying?"

"I don't know yet," I said. "I just got back today."

"Is your mother still here? Up next to the Romanian ambassador?"

It was funny, that's how she recalled our place on Furshtatskaya Street. Though Mina was invited hundreds of times to our house, our parents met only at school functions. "No. My mother's gone—followed a mystic. Probably heading for Bukhara by now." The rook, the labyrinth, the treasure.

"And your father?"

I sighed. "Off with Kolchak's lot, I think."

"Then you'll stay here. I insist on it," Mina's mother said firmly. "Have some more tea, dear. I'll get dinner on." She put Iskra back into Shusha's arms—"Watch her head, Shushochka"—and picked up the sack from the table.

In time, Mina reappeared through the black cloth curtains from the studio, saw me chatting with her sisters, my damp hair. "Are you still here? I thought I made myself clear."

"I was just going when Dunya got home," I said, "and I was chatting with everyone. Your mother invited me to stay." I tried not to smirk.

"I don't care what my mother says. Get out and take your brat with you!"

"What's gotten into you?" said Aunt Fanya. "This is your best friend."

"No," she said. "That's done."

Sofia Yakovlevna appeared from the kitchen, drying her hands. "We'll have dinner in ten minutes. Such as it is. Set the table, Shusha."

Mina was boiling. "Mother, I made it very clear to Marina that we have no room for her here."

You could hear the chairs squeak. Her mother stood in the doorway, towel in her hands, the same frizzy hair as Mina's, only tucked back in a large chignon. "Why would you say such a thing? What's wrong with you? She's been gone for a year—"

"Let her own family take care of her," Mina said.

The piercing unfairness of that.

"Why would you say such a thing, Minochka?" her mother said softly.

"Because I don't want her here." She was trembling with rage.

"What happened between you girls?" Her mother looked from her daughter to me and back. "You were always such good friends." She tried to touch her daughter's cheek but Mina swatted her away. Her face was gray-white with perceived injustice, yet she was unable to tell her mother what the trouble was. *I'm in love with Kolya Shurov, and this is his baby. I can't stand to look at her. Marina ran out on me, she took my man, took everything. She gets everything she wants, but she's not getting this.* No, she would be ashamed to admit it was jealousy. And though she was throwing me to the dogs, I could not bring myself to tear the skin off her shame.

"Let's vote." Shusha stood next to me. "How many people want Marina to stay? Show of hands."

My heart in my throat. The hands went up. In my favor, Dunya, Shusha, Aunt Fanya, and Uncle Aaron. It was a majority, by anyone's count.

"Stop it, Shusha." Sofia Yakovlevna clapped her hand over her mouth, and turned away. "My God, what is happening to us?"

Roman stood up, as he would stand to give a speech in a student meeting. "I vote no. Think, Katzevs. You really want a baby in the apartment, crying at all hours? Stinking diapers on the stove? Some of us have to work. It's just impractical. Less to eat, no sleep," Roman said. "I say, Mina's working her heart out, she should have the final say."

Mina smiled at him gratefully.

"We all do our part, Roman Osipovich," Sofia Yakovlevna said, stiff as a British dragoon, but I could hear the tears in her voice. "Each in his own way. That's what a family is. When you have babies, you'll see."

"We won't be having any," said Roman. "Neither of us wants 'em."

The older woman shook her head as if to clear water from her ears—a bit of news she had not heard, that they'd decided not to have children. Too many blows at once. She lowered herself into a chair and buried her head in her hands.

"All this is beside the point," Mina said. "Who keeps a roof over all your heads? Me. Who left university to keep this family together? Me. And I'm saying I won't have her living here. End of discussion!"

Dunya wiped up the spilled tea with her napkin. "Mina, you're being a perfect beast. It's like you're not even a person anymore, you're some kind of golem."

"Mama sides with us, don't you, Mama?" Shusha said, smoothing her mother's hair. "Please don't cry, Mama. She's just being a donkey."

I wanted to sink under the floor. The last decent family in Petrograd, and I had them at each other's throats. "Listen, I'll go. This is no good. Look. I'm leaving." I took the baby from Shusha, snugged her into the sling.

But Mina wasn't hearing anything except the blood pounding in her head. "Listen, big shots, you all want to take my place?" She leaned over the table to her sisters, white around the mouth with rage. "You think this is so easy, Shushochka? Fine, why don't you quit school and you stay here all day? *You* take the photographs. *You* keep the studio running. *You* get in with Narkompros. *You* keep the film coming, and the chemicals, and coat the papers and develop the negatives and do the printing." She was weeping. "And I'll go to school and be in the drama club and write poetry about our brave Red soldiers."

"How can you be so selfish?" Dunya said.

Mina was speechless for a moment, shaking her head. "No. No. That's the living end. You can leave with her. Who needs you either?!"

This wonderful family, it wasn't supposed to go this way. Why had I ever come here? Why had I started this?

Her mother looked so frail, as if the sound of her family's quarrelling had sucked the flesh from her bones. I was ashamed I had brought such misery here. She shook her head wearily, gazing at the younger girls, and rose, putting her hand on Mina's shoulder as she wiped her tears. "Whatever we think about this, your sister has given everything to keep a roof over our heads. More than all of us combined. She's taken your father's responsibilities on her own shoulders. And if she says no, it's got to be no." She looked me in the eye with such regret. "I'm sorry, Marina. But these are terrible times."

A silence dropped over the assembly. Aunt Fanya and Uncle Aaron looked down at their hands, knowing that they were the ones who were the biggest burden. It was horrible. I wanted to protest, *I can bring in rations. I can help in the darkroom. With someone to care for Iskra, I can work.* But what was the point? It was over. This was what families did, this was how they survived. They tightened ranks, took care of their own. Much as the Bolsheviks wished to do away with these ties, they were the only ones left. I just wished I was part of it. They were kind, but my membership in their circle had just been a visitor's pass. I was as much an orphan as any little beggar working a train station. When I'd taken off with Kolya that November night, I had gambled our friendship. Now I had to leave the casino, busted, my heart's pockets turned inside out. I gathered up my bundle, my pail, my sheepskin, collected Iskra from Shusha, whose face streamed with tears. My baby slept on.

"Let us do something for you," their mother said sorrowfully. "How can we make this easier?"

There was a part of myself that wanted to walk out a complete martyr, trailing my blood behind me, see if I could increase their shame. But what good would that do? Who cared about my pride now? I asked for a bottle of boiled water. I felt like some character in the Bible, being sent into the desert. Shusha ran to fetch a bottle, and Dunya poured the contents of the samovar into it. Their mother handed me a hunk of bread out of their meager rations, a slice of hard cheese, and a piece of herring, all wrapped in a page of *Pravda*.

I descended the stairs and emerged into the city, now dark. I would never have a reason to climb those stairs again. The thousand and one times I had gone up in that elevator, anticipating the sights and smells of their homey flat, the sweets her mother would have for us, the mysteries of her father's studio, the sanctum of the darkroom. How kind they'd been to us. How they'd loved Seryozha. What would Solomon Katzev say if he'd been there today, and seen the choice that Mina had made? What she'd pulled in wax, that key—locking the door, barring her heart. I remembered the day we'd followed that lovely man down to the Neva to see the *Aurora* opposite the palace. I remembered the dresses Sofia Yakovlevna had sewn, her magic lantern, Vasilisa the Beautiful...I couldn't stop seeing Mina's face, the way her chin stuck out, the smallness of her bitter mouth. The book of the past had closed. There was nothing left but this—the book of the city itself.

16 *The Astoria*

I took a brave turn in the streets, but the ravaged revolutionary city was too unnervingly empty to spend a night in a doorway. I swallowed my pride and curled with my infant in a jog in the Katzevs' hallway, still hoping against hope that Sofia Yakovlevna would creep out and usher me inside. I'd dreamed for so long about my return to Petrograd, but I hadn't expected this.

"We'll figure this out," I promised Iskra, as she nestled inside my sheepskin. I ate some of their bread. It stuck in my throat. Maybe I would have been better off staying in Udmurtia, where there was still kindness, and work for my hands, room for a woman with a child. But who could tell good luck from bad now? You couldn't know what might lead where. There was only fate, and this was mine tonight.

And I still had Aura Cady Sands hidden in my pocket, my ace in the hole.

I slept fitfully, and dreamed of a ship in heavy weather. I clung to the rail, trying to inch my way to my cabin, but I'd lost track of the baby. The ship spiraled in the churning brown water, the crew struggling to keep from capsizing, while the mad captain ordered it onward, into the storm. We were traveling right into its arms, debris flying through the air as I scrambled to my cabin, *but where was my daughter?* The ship lunged and heeled, taking on water, sluicing the corridor, coming under the doors. The cards I'd been playing flew off the desk. I didn't want to drown on this ship, but the mad captain had bolted the doors.

Someone was shaking me. Mina? Had she changed her mind?

I opened my eyes, saw broad shoulders, a shaved face. "Clear off. This isn't a boardinghouse. If you're not gone in five minutes, I'll call the *domkom*."

It was still very early, the sun rising through mist. The beauty of the unfolding day stopped the breath in my chest. I had forgotten this, the light of Petrograd on the long straight Prospect, the unchanging forms of stone and iron, the mist hanging. Everywhere were the quiet faces I had craved—the benign visages of statues and friezes decorating windows, balconies, archways. They knew me, if no one else did. I imagined they pitied me as I passed by. I stopped to use the convenience of a courtyard off Kazanskaya Street, and drank some of the water Sofia Yakovlevna had packed for me. From there

I made my way up to the sleeping Astoria, its sentries smoking by the door. But it was far too early to disturb the singer. I moved off into the haze like a light inside a paper lantern toward the red pillars and dome of St. Isaac's Cathedral. I climbed to its granite porch and gazed out between the columns as through the legs of a giant, appreciating the rhythm of pillar and pediment across Senate Square like a stately music. Such beauty, everywhere I turned my eyes.

And there, gazing out at the Neva, stood Great Peter, and Pushkin's words bubbled up within me:

> *Here granite borders the Neva*
> *and bridges hang above the river;*
> *and dark green gardens lay a cover*
> *upon each island near and far.*
> *As the young capital unseats her,*
> *old Moscow fades, no more prevails,*
> *just as before a new tsaritsa*
> *a dowager in purple pales.*

At this hour the city was mine, mine and the urchins', curled up against the walls, and a few sleepy streetwalkers', heading home after a hard night's work. I nursed Iskra and gazed out at the ensemble of buildings, the Senate, the Admiralty, the Horse Guards' Manège, and waited for morning to properly age. The leaves on the trees of Horse Guards Boulevard were shedding in yellow pools. I had picked one up to show Iskra, now spun it around between my fingers, tickled her face with it as she nursed and I sang "When Irish Eyes Are Smiling."

A group of little boys gathered on the steps nearby, smoking vile *makhorka* cigarettes to staunch their hunger, and pretended not to listen to my song, as they moved closer, like tramps warming themselves at a fire on Haymarket Square. I shifted to "Fais Dodo, Colin" and "The Little Bell" and "In the Valley" to see if I could prolong the spell.

What a bore to live alone,
Even for a tree!
Ah, a lad without a lass
Is wretched as can be...

When I finished, I asked if they knew any songs, throwing the question in their general direction without looking at them. They were *dikiye, wild,* and like any hungry, wild pack, they could turn in a moment, throw rocks or swarm me for the food I might be carrying, my boots, or, God forbid, my coat. But right now, they were children, and I was the adult. A mother. Whose comfort and care and tenderness they yearned for.

One of them, a dirt-smeared urchin of about twelve with a brutally upturned nose, spoke up over his evil-smelling cigarette. "Patches knows some."

Patches proved to be a painfully thin boy with bald spots in his bristly hair.

"Sing us a tune," the older boy commanded, and kicked him.

Patches began to sing a song I had never heard:

Forgotten, neglected
in my youthful state
I was born an orphan
And misery's my fate.

"Pretty good, huh? And if they don't fork over, he goes into this one," said the chief.

The poor half-bald boy looked even more mournful and sang,

Because of you, I suffer.
Because of you, I'll find my grave...

The song was wrenching, his voice high and true.

"It's his scam," said their chief. "On the trams."

"Are there still trams?" I hadn't seen one since I'd been here.

"Not many, but they're crammed full. All the better pickin' for us. Right, boys?" His friends nodded. "Didja just come inta town?"

They were like a pack of mangy dogs who somehow remembered human caring, human compassion.

"I just got back. I'm from here," I said. I kept it vague in case any other of their brothers had been on a train that night on the Vologda-Petrograd line.

Iskra squealed and wanted to be played with. I tucked my breast away, let her grip my finger. "I love this place. I don't have a place to put my head, but—" and I recited a bit more of "The Bronze Horseman":

> *I love you, miracle of Peter's,*
> *your stern and graceful countenance,*
> *the broad Neva's imperious waters,*
> *the granite blocks that line your banks . . .*

"What's that?" asked their leader.

"It's a poem. Something I heard once." As if Pushkin's masterpiece was just something I heard in a breadline. "You know the statue of the guy on Arts Square?"

"The guy checkin' the weather," said their leader, imitating Pushkin's posture, palm upturned.

"Pigeons shit all over him," said another boy, emboldened. The same age as the leader, he grinned through teeth already ruined.

"Yes, that guy," I said. "It's an old poem, just so you know."

"Go 'head, say it," said the leader. I was Patches, here for his entertainment. I hoped he wouldn't kick me.

Iskra was squirming. She liked the morning. I stood up so I could rock her on my hip as I began to unfold for the orphans the tale of their own city's mythology, a story they needed to know. Even if they were homeless, they were still citizens of St. Petersburg, and more so than most, as they slept on its stones.

"It's about the great flood of 1824, right here, a hundred years ago," I said. "But it starts in . . ."—what did they care about dates? — "with Peter the Great founding…this city. That Peter." I pointed to the Falconet statue, the horse's great haunches, rearing on its stone. "He's called the *Bronze Horseman*."

And I began:

> *Where desolate breakers rolled, stood* he,
> *immersed in thought and prophecy…*

My recitation was by no means perfect, but none of these urchins had ever heard of Pushkin, and oddly, their attention flattered me more than any silver ruble my Makarov grandmother could have bestowed. All the while, I kept a good watch on my coat and my bundle. And by God if they didn't listen until the very end, until poor mad Evgeny had lost everything, city, love, home, chased to his death by that brazen statue come to life. And for a moment, we all sat together, and looked out toward the grand, treacherous monarch, and over his city, dramatic, tragic, deadly. Our city, mine and theirs, Iskra's and Pushkin's. We citizens along with every poet, every poor clerk and water carrier and nurse. Whatever the fate of this place, I would be part of it. I wouldn't be mindlessly grazing in a field like a cow chewing its cud.

Later, the children melted into the morning, following their leader, off to steal and beg or whatever it was they did to get their daily bread. I still had hours to go before I could safely visit the singer. Now was the time a reasonable person would go and queue at the district soviet, take the next step in my official future. Find some sort of job, any job, and a corner in a collective apartment. I had come back of my own free will, hadn't I? Nobody had forced me, I had no right to cry. I should have known Mina would hurt me if I gave her the chance. But the idea of Aura Cady Sands glittered before me like a lamp, a way back into the world. There were still giants here in Petersburg, the sons and daughters of Pushkin and Tolstoy. I would not miss the chance to bask in their light, pale moon that I was. It was worth another night in an unguarded hallway.

I chewed on more of the Katzevs' bread and went for a stroll along the Admiralty Embankment. I wondered what was housed in the Winter Palace now. I remembered the orgy in the tsar's wine cellars during October 1917—whole battalions lost down there, the confusion and gunfire in the halls, and how we stumbled into the room where the ministers had just been arrested. Genya's excitement over Kerensky's pen—I never asked if he still had it. The palace showed its neglect now, weeds growing everywhere, broken windows boarded up or not, the corner that had been bombarded by the Peter and Paul Fortress still unrepaired. Would it really have been so bad if we'd stopped with Kerensky and the Constituent Assembly? The Kadets, the Right SRs? Though it was counterrevolutionary to think it. Better for the bourgeoisie, the intelligentsia—but I knew quite well the capitalists would have kept a tight hold on the reins of power, and the workers would still exist only for their labor, their needs disregarded. No, we needed this, a complete overturning of everything, even if we privileged classes suffered for our former greed and arrogance.

I squinted up at the Admiralty spire, surmounted by its golden ship as the mists cleared and the bright day sparkled on the river. I felt hopeful again. I would find a way of ingratiating myself with the singer, convince her she needed Marina Kuriakina as translator, guide, housemaid, friend. But I had to approach this songbird with care, to lay a snare without frightening her, having her fly away. Worst would be to appear indigent and at my wit's end, throwing myself at her like a scabrous beggar with my sheepskin and my infant. No, I had to act as if I was just dropping in, that her friendship was all I sought, a pleasant half hour with a fascinating foreigner: *Oh! I forgot my calling cards!* I hoped she had more than one room, wondered how famous she was. Perhaps she knew Chaliapin, or Gorky.

Across the river on the rock where the city was founded rose the Peter and Paul Fortress, as grim and solid as ever. How many people from my past were now imprisoned behind its stout walls, locked in its dank and cramped cells? How many hostages against Yudenich's attack had been imprisoned there, Denikin's officers' wives and children? A lone man walked across Palace Bridge. There were so few people, I could watch him all the way across.

At last, it seemed late enough for us to visit. Should I wear my kerchief as *worker* or *peasant,* or try to upgrade my appearance to *displaced intelligent?* I chose the last, pocketed my kerchief and smoothed my clean hair with my fingers. Chin up, I approached the hotel—dark and grand on St. Isaac's Square. I'd come here as a child, whenever my mother's cousin Tamara visited us from Paris. She carried a white Pomeranian with red-rimmed eyes, Rupert, and wore a coat of black monkey fur that was almost like feathers. I strode across the cobbles as if I had breakfast at the Astoria every day of my life. A heavily armed sentry stopped me before I even got close. "*Propusk,* Citizen."

Citizen. I should have worn my kerchief. I showed him my labor book, and my *propusk* from the Izhevsk Committee. He shrugged and handed them back to me. "Where's your *propusk* to enter the First House of the Soviet?"

The members of the soviet were ensconced at the Astoria Hotel? "But I was invited. To visit the singer Aura Cady Sands. Room 223. Call her, see for yourself." The tightness in my gullet, the weight of the gun under my clothes, heavier than the moment before. If they caught me, they would assume I was another Fanya Kaplan, looking to assassinate Zinoviev or Radek or whoever was living here now.

"What, do I look like a desk clerk?" His face was rough, his little eyes stupid and willfully so. "No *propusk,* no entry."

I started to feel tears come. Why didn't she mention a *propusk?* I remembered going into Smolny itself without having to show so much as my labor book. "She told me to come this morning. She didn't say anything about a *propusk.*"

"Well, what did you think, you could just walk in? Who are you? Nobody, anybody. Where do you think you are?" He was shouting at me now. "You could have been sent here by Yudenich. Kolchak. The Entente. You might have a bomb."

This was going all wrong, the other sentry was becoming curious, what a nightmare. I watched my dreams crumple like a wad of cheap newsprint. "Maybe the baby's got a bomb. She's a regular counterrevolutionary."

"Move along before I shoot you both," he said.

I had no choice. I moved away.

So I made the journey out to Smolny, hauling Iskra and my bag, pail, sheepskin, aware of my dwindling supplies, but it was the same story as at the Astoria. No *propusk*, no appointment, no entry. When had that started? Since the assassinations, most likely. "What's your business at Petrocommune? You have potatoes under that skirt?" He started poking my skirt with the barrel of his gun. To him I was just another *baba* from the provinces, there to beg or steal or God knew what. With that gun on me, I couldn't stand a search. So much for the free wandering in and out as we had in the early days. No more democratic free-for-all. It burned, the way they dismissed me, as if I were a beggar.

"This is how you treat the proletariat and the revolutionary peasantry?" I shouted for the benefit of all the others climbing the steps. "*Propusk, propusk*...You're drowning us in bureaucracy!"

One of the soldiers shoved me, and I almost fell down the stairs, baby and all.

"Such a shame," a man said, helping me up, handing me my pail, which had clattered to the ground. *Jack and Jill went up the hill*...Of course, Iskra was bawling by now.

So back I went to the labor exchange at the district soviet, squeezing us onto a tram, holding on with one hand. I chose the Second City district, out of allegiance to my days in the Poverty Artel. The last time I was here, I'd gotten married. Nothing but queues—to get housing, to get work, *propuski* for travel or blowing one's nose. It looked like everyone still living in Petrograd had decided to cram into the Second City Soviet, coughing and weary and spitting on the floor. There were other districts to be sure—Liteiny had more job potential, but too many people knew me up there. Here I could say the Poverty Artel was my last address, not Furshtatskaya Street.

Marina Kuriakina was plausible, though not without holes in her story. In any case, I didn't want to run into anyone I'd known before Genya. He might have been the wrong man, but I was grateful that I could use his name and his all-important class category, *proletarian.* He did me that much of a favor. Without that, there would be little work and little housing for me and my child.

A painful wait. The fat-faced Communist bureaucrat behind the counter at the labor exchange glanced at the papers of the petitioners, her mouth in a frozen sneer, not even looking at their faces — mostly ragged Formers of varying ages — telling each in turn that there was nothing for them. "How are we supposed to live?" wailed one middle-aged woman, thin as paper. "Really, you're trying to starve us out of existence."

"What do I care if you starve or not?" she said. "Lousy *burzhui.* Why don't you go sell your silver?"

"I'm an educated woman," she continued. "I graduated from the Bestuzhev Institute. I could teach, I could be a clerk."

"Move along," said the fat-faced paper pusher.

"My husband's ill," the woman begged. "Please. Anything."

"You're holding up traffic."

The woman didn't even cover her face, just let the tears spill down as she left the office.

"Next!"

I reached out as the woman passed by me, and touched her arm. "You'll find something," I said.

She pressed my hand. "I've been coming here every day for two weeks. I don't think we're going to make it. My husband's talking about killing himself. He can't stand the humiliation."

Yes, it was worse than the hunger.

A bald man wearing a jacket black with dirt, and no shirt cuffs under the sleeves, approached with his hat in his hand. "There has to be something," he said. "I'm an editor. Anything. Proofreader, clerk."

After him, another Former.

Then it was my turn. The *apparatchitsa* opened my labor book at the high counter. I felt like a child, peering over a table. "I read, I write, I'm not bad with numbers," I said.

"The telephone exchange is looking for someone."

Well, it was something. "Do they have a crèche?"

"A what?"

"A crèche. A baby nursery."

"You're joking." She held up the chit. "Take it, or leave it, it's all the same to me."

"But my baby, she's only three months old," I said, opening the cloth so the woman could see Iskra, asleep inside it like a peanut in a shell. "I can't just leave her in the cloakroom." Surely they had crèches somewhere in the capital! Peter's great city, *birthplace of the revolution,* et cetera. "What am I supposed to do with her?"

"What's anybody do?" the woman said, her mouth twisted and sour. "Look around your building. Or go to some mother's home — what do I care? You want it or not? It's all the same to me." She held out the slip of paper.

I took the information, moved away. It was a good job. I was lucky, I told myself. Yet I remembered the chaos of our collectivized apartment on Furshtatskaya, could only imagine my child left in that milieu, with one of the mothers deputized to take care of her. Letting her cry, or shaking her, or watering the milk, or using it to feed her own children. I realized I had believed the propaganda. Jam tomorrow, jam yesterday.

I left the building with the chit in my hand and a heaviness in my stomach. I'd thought I could come back and find my way somehow. Stay with Mina, and find Kolya on the second day. Ah, the Lord would take care of holy fools. But why would he? He was letting everyone else die. It was twilight, too late for the telephone exchange, too late to look for housing. It would be another night in Mina's hallway.

As I walked up Nevsky, I couldn't stop thinking of the midwife Praskovia, and the village in the trees, the women preparing for winter, threshing the grain. A baby was no obstacle there. In the countryside, at least, there was room for women and children, the needs of an infant one of the many duties of a peasant wife. But I had wanted a civilized life and here it was. No place for the most elementary need — to care for one's child. It was just one box inside of another. Now I had the possibility of employment, but in exchange I would have to leave my tiny baby with some distracted hausfrau, some half-witted crone. Everything in me screamed out in rebellion. I did not save her life to offer her to the carelessness of an arbitrary stranger.

I argued with myself. This happened every day. People worked, they left their babies with near strangers, the children lived. At least most of them. But my mother's curse rang in my ears, and memories lingered of those hard-faced harridans, those beaten-down women. There was no one I'd met I would trust with a dog, let alone Iskra Antonina. No. Whatever I did, I would not be separated from her. There had to be another way. It was too late for me to become a *Sovetskaya barynya* at the telephone exchange, but surely there was another answer.

I passed the Former woman down by the Moika, just leaning on a lamppost, gazing down into the water. I'd never seen such sadness. Even my own paled by comparison. "Here," I said, handing her the chit. "It's for the telephone exchange."

She looked at me as if waking from a dream, utterly confused, her worn, intelligent face.

"I don't know if you can use it, but give it a try."

She wiped her eyes on her sleeve. "You're not taking it?"

"I can't leave my baby," I said. I closed her hands around the slip of paper.

"Thank you," she whispered. "Oh God, thank you." She began to weep in earnest, covering her mouth. "Sometimes I wish we could all just die. That the Cheka would come and put us out of our misery. I look at the horses that fall in the street and I feel just like that. And no amount of lashes will ever put me on my feet again. But my husband, I can't let him see me — he's in an even worse state. Frankly, I come looking for work just to get out of that room." She took my hand and pressed it to her cheek.

17 *Hotel Europa*

A group of tattered boys loitered in the porte cochere of the Hotel Europa, smoking and watching my progress up Mikhailovskaya Street. It was six o'clock, the twilight smelling of water. I entered the vast lobby stinking of mold and old soup, sour cabbage. Who would have guessed how quickly a grand hotel could become as squalid as any Haymarket Square tenement? A few years ago, the lobby would have been filled with elegant women and polished men, bellhops squiring mountains of luggage. Now the chandeliers were dim and the unwashed mirrors reflected only ghostly forms of those long-ago guests. The moldings on the wooden pillars had been savagely broken, and the marble underfoot was so black that you would not suspect its former honeyed hue. Iskra was awake, taking it all in. Groups of children hovered by the pillars, watching. One of them said something, making the others snicker. A dark and dangerous place, a place you'd never permit a child to enter, but I was the stranger here, and they the tenants. An orphanage, a hotel for the abandoned.

An older woman in a white kerchief worked the front desk behind the amber marble top, now pitted and brown. I sighed in relief just to see a face over eighteen. As I waited for her to look up from the heap of papers she was sorting, I had the uncanny vision of myself tapping on a polished brass hotel-desk bell, a grande dame in hobble skirt and huge hat with a veil. Signing the register, the glossy pen in my soft kid glove with little pearl buttons, while behind me waited servants with my trunks and a maid holding the leash of a tall feathery dog.

"Excuse me, Comrade," I said.

She still didn't look up. "Infant Department. Second floor, to the back."

It took me a moment to realize—she thought I was here to abandon Iskra! Assumed it! Was I so desperate-looking? Did it happen so often? "I'm not leaving her. I'm looking for a job."

Now the woman lifted her gaze, sheaf of papers clutched in one hand, her pince-nez uncomfortably clamped to a long narrow nose. She took it off and rubbed the indentations. "Can you read? Know your letters?"

Certifying my rusticated appearance. "A, Be, Te, De, Er," I rattled off as a joke. "Something like that?" But the expression on her face, weary and exasperated, told me she was the wrong person to joke with. "Sorry. Yes, I can read, write, alphabetize, do calculations, cook, and scrub up if necessary."

"It won't be up to me," sniffed the woman. It occurred to me, there were some people made sour by life, and others who were sour and tired of life from their very birth. I wondered which one she was. "But there is a vacancy, lucky you. They're taking applications." She indicated the heaping piles of records. "Commissariat's got a new idea. Wants the files redone. As if I didn't have enough to do. There's no one here right now to talk to you, but Matron'll be back in the morning." She scrutinized me more closely. A tall, rangy woman, she had at one point been beautiful, but life had proved brutally disappointing. "It's night work, I'm afraid. We had someone, but she disappeared. After that, nothing but thieves or complete simpletons."

Imagine, someone had walked away from this gloomy hole. I hoped the missing woman had found something better and not fallen afoul of dark forces. "Nights, days, doesn't matter," I said. "I just have to have the baby with me."

"No family, no husband, is that it?" She smirked. You could see how she hoped that's how it was. So that she could feel superior.

Well, fine. If it made her like me, gave her confidence to think she knew me, all the better. I would have trotted out my husband with the agit-train, but she seemed to so enjoy my sinful suffering, I didn't want to disabuse her. Anyway, I was sick of that story. I shrugged and sighed. "They say, *He who does not work, does not eat. So here I am.*" It was in our labor books, even on the ration cards.

She considered me again—bundle, sheepskin, baby, pail, the architecture of my face, my rough hands. "Read this." She handed me a piece of paper from the monstrous pile.

"Commissariat of Social Welfare, Department of Motherhood and Child Welfare, Northern Commune, Petrograd Orphanage Number Six, Notice of Transfer—"

"Thank God." She exhaled deeply. "You should see the illiterates who've been marching through here." Now she looked upon me with a bit more enthusiasm. I handed her the page. It was a notice of transfer to another orphanage for *Shushkin, Gavril. Age 4. Date of birth, 17 May 1915.* Age four, and already the subject of such documentation. I could imagine Gavril, his dirty snotnose, his rags. Lost and terrified. Transferred to a children's home in Detskoe Selo, Children's Village—once the elegant town of Tsarskoe Selo, Tsar's Village, where Akhmatova had grown up and Pushkin had attended the lycée. Now orphanages.

The sharp-chinned woman continued filing papers. "A nice mess, eh? They want it all refiled on a new system—how that's going to get any more of these little brats off the street, I can't imagine, but nobody asked me. Look, give me a hand with this tonight, and I'll put in a good word with Matron in the morning. I've been on since six a.m. and I'm ready to drop off this stool." She glanced up at the clock in the old cashier's booth—miracle, it was still working. "They're feeding the animals now—if you don't mind the noise, I'll have them give you something to eat." She lowered the grate with a bang, startling the boys in the lobby—purposely—and locked it. "Don't leave anything you don't want to lose," she said. "There's no private property anymore—in case you haven't heard."

Her name was Alla Denisovna, a blonde of forty with a long-legged stride—yes, she must have been quite the beauty twenty years ago. She led me through the blackened lobby, absent the potted palms and carpets, past languid gangs of boys with whom she exchanged a look of mutual loathing. "Hooligans."

"Dried-up hag," a boy called back at her.

"Bow legs," another one chimed. "The wind's whistling."

"Degenerates."

She led me down a wide corridor into what had once been the hotel tearoom. The wallpaper was faded and stained and the floral beams too dirty to distinguish their patterns. It had been a pretty room, an afternoon gathering place for the ladies, known for its dance floor and small orchestra. Now the floor was black with grime, and little emaciated bodies with shaved heads crowded around rough tables. Some had to stand. She hadn't been joking about the noise. The din would deafen a railwayman. But Iskra didn't seem at all worried. She was gazing about her with fascination.

"They feed them in shifts," Alla shouted. "This is the last one." There were seventy or so children here of youngish school age, all boys, crowded onto benches. They ate out of tin mugs, with spoons or their fingers. A group of red-cheeked women in stained white aprons and white nurse's kerchiefs sat at a table of their own at one end of the deafening, airless room, smoking and jabbering away. They moved over to let us sit down.

"Hey, Polya." Alla Denisovna called to one of them, a short-nosed peasant with the exposed nostrils of a skull. "This is my new assistant on front desk. I've got to get to the queues before the bread runs out. Give her something to eat, will you? She's got to make it through the night, and feed the baby."

The woman Polya brought me a dented cup of *vobla* soup, and a plate with kasha. Alla perched on the end of the bench, lit a cigarette and sat smoking, watching me eat, her leg bouncing up and down with impatience. A sullen girl about my age, her face coated with pancake makeup—makeup!—grumbled, "She's not getting that job, you know. I got a friend up for it, and she's in the party."

"That cross-eyed tart from Tula?" laughed another woman, short and wide, with a beauty mark next to her surprisingly pretty mouth, like a star hanging from the moon. "I hope she doesn't have to take the medical exam. I heard she's the darling of the fleet."

The women snickered.

"I'm sure Matron will make her own decisions," said Alla Denisovna. She was at least fifteen years older than any of them, except for the peasant woman Polya, and clearly had no interest in being liked.

A scuffle broke out at one of the tables, a fury of fists. I was amazed to see that none of the women did anything about it. At another table, a boy wrestled a cup away from a smaller boy, who now just sat, silently weeping. "Did you see that?" I asked Alla. "He just grabbed the other kid's food."

"Degenerates," she said. "Dog eat dog."

With Iskra on my hip, I marched over to their table and twisted the stolen cup from the perpetrator. The shock on his face was worth a thousand words. "That's not yours," I said firmly, and I gave it back to the silent child, who wouldn't look at me, but grabbed it and devoured what was left in the cup.

I rejoined the women. I tried not to accuse anyone, I wanted to work here, but my God, what a lot of apparatchiks.

"You think we're heartless," said the woman with the beautiful mouth. "But he'll beat that sniveling runt up tonight when they go to bed. They have their own ways. Better to stay out of it. I was like you when I first came here. What went on here made me sick. Now I just live and let live."

"Come on, Sister Charity." Alla hooked her finger into the cord of my bundle, strapped over the shoulder opposite Iskra.

As she led me back to the Sisyphean mountain of paperwork, I wondered what kind of a hell I'd wandered into. There was little light in the hallway, children slipped along like shadows. I supposed I wouldn't want orphans kept under lock and key like in a Dickens novel, and yet, should they really be allowed to prowl the orphanage at will, coming and going out the front door as they liked?

Alla led us back behind the door of the front desk, and locked me in. I didn't blame her. You wouldn't be able to concentrate for a minute otherwise. On the counter sat the monstrous pile of paper. "We've been keeping records by category. Children still at the center." She touched one messy pile with the flat of her hand. "Children who've been transferred." She gestured down the counter. "Children who've run off. And so on."

And so on? A shiver went through me like a knife blade. *And so on...* It was an ocean of suffering, a galaxy, neatly captured in bland words on official paper. I held Iskra tighter.

"Now the Commissariat's decided it wants us to file alphabetically, by last name of child." She said *the Commissariat* in a disgusted tone, and indicated the wash of files, rising up against the grate protecting the desk from the shadowy lobby. "And who are we to question the Commissariat, eh? Well, as long as I get my rations, I don't give a damn if it takes from now until Judgment Day. Oh, and we get our rations Thursdays, first and third of the month." It was Saturday, the last week in September.

"They let that child steal the other one's food," I said. "They just watched it."

She sighed, considering me with a certain measure of exasperated pity. "Are you still worrying about that?" A child screamed in the echoing lobby. She looked over at him as he burst into sniggers. "One week working here, I promise you, you won't notice the hand in front of your face." She shrugged. "Just paper and more paper. If they run—paper. When they're transferred—paper. If they die, more paper."

"Do you have children?" I asked her, looking into Iskra's face. She was goggle-eyed in the strange place, not knowing where to point her nose.

Alla lost what little animation she'd had. She curled her lower lip. "Lost them. 1915. Scarlet fever." She sighed. "Both in a single month." Then she straightened her back, picked up her handbag. "So that's it. See how far you get. And don't let anyone back here no matter what. I'll see you in the morning." She took off her white nurse's scarf and put on her hat.

"What if I have to use the toilet?" I remembered to ask.

"There's a chamber pot in the broom closet. Boiled water in the pitcher. Breakfast at seven. Good luck."

* * *

221

And so I began. I swore I wouldn't read the files, simply alphabetize them. I set Iskra on the floor on my sheepskin, but she howled. I made a nest for her on the counter, so she could watch the children in the lobby. I tried not to read the files, but I couldn't help seeing the ages on the forms, the fates of the children. Sent to a *detsky dom* was a common fate. They all seemed to be in the suburbs—Detskoe Selo, Kamenny Island, Narva. I hoped the children fared better there than at Orphanage No. 6.

The runaways were mostly older children. Or *Disappeared*. Or, if it was indicated they had living relatives, perhaps they'd gone home. What a look into the life of the second year of the revolution. Reading through this Everest of paperwork reminded me of the boxlike viewers Papa had bought us to look under the surface of our pond at Maryino, to see the tadpoles. Reading, I could peer into the heart of the city, what was going on beneath the surface of its empty streets. I avoided the end of the counter holding the *so ons*. Here were transfers. You had to hope for the best—boys, a few girls, and babies, so many, transferred to the Kamenny Island Orphanage No. 12. It must be an infant facility.

So many abandoned children. Orphaned in the waves of disease, or simply left behind, coming in from all over Russia, riding the trains into the former capital. What would become of them, with women like Alla and the pancake girl caring for them?

"Hey," said a child's voice through the grate of the front desk. "There's something wrong with my tongue. Could you look at it?"

I glanced up. A girl about thirteen, skinny with stringy straw-colored hair, leaned on the desk, sticking her tongue out at me. She and her friend burst into giggles, joined arms, and skipped out the front doors of the lobby, into the night. Probably to find some men who could give them food or money or something else worth having. The disease rate among them must be terrific.

And so on.

Worse, when I saw those girls again, they'd brought their "dates" right into the orphanage, leading them through the lobby like grown prostitutes at railway hotels. How could this be allowed? Couldn't the government find a single Red Guard to stand watch over an orphanage with hundreds of children? No wonder Alla had locked me in. The girl who'd stuck out her tongue had a particularly stupid-looking man about twenty-five in tow, with small but wide-set eyes and no chin. Her friend, with pimples like boils, led a soldier, a mean-looking blond, about nineteen.

I called out to the men from behind the locked grates. "Comrades, these are children. Have you no shame? No pity?"

"Have you no pity?" the girl mocked me. "Keep your pity to yourself, pitty-pat."

Her man laughed and followed her up the stairs. I was glad Iskra had fallen asleep. Certain things even a baby should not have to see.

Late in the night, a group of boys, the ones who'd catcalled Denisovna, returned from their adventures to climb the wide marble stairs to their own floor, pushing and laughing. The place, I could see, was no better than a flophouse. Perhaps the younger children had some supervision, but these older ones...I wondered if the Commissariat knew what was going on here, or were they only worried about their record keeping.

I nursed Iskra, tried once again to tuck her under the desk out of sight, but she wouldn't have it, started to howl, she wanted to see what was going on. For some reason, I didn't want the children to see her. I feared their envy—like a peasant worrying about the Evil Eye, calling her child stupid and ugly. Now I understood the superstition. The danger didn't spring from devils and sorcerers. It was the mean and envious you had to watch out for. It could be as simple as a child who was humiliated in front of his mates, or a girl who lost a trick because of you.

In the end, I could not help approaching *and so on*. I had to know. The records seemed banal, benign, until you assembled the picture behind the bland language.

Cause of death: Cholera. Typhus. Typhoid. Scarlet fever. Measles. Smallpox. Concussion. Contusion. Hematoma. Alcohol poisoning. Malnutrition. Pneumonia.

Sent to hospital.

Returned from hospital.

Death certificate.

The deaf, the blind, the crippled.

And the dates! Infants of a few months, or hours, *abandoned, admitted,*

deceased.

I could not read anymore, I could not stop reading. I held my head back from the pages so that my tears wouldn't make the ink run, wouldn't blot out the names. I dried my eyes on the shoulder of my dress. Starving children, stronger ones taking their food so that they could grow stronger while the other ones died. Syphilis, gonorrhea. *Parfentiev, Matvei. Age 9. Cocaine addiction, transferred to Orphanage No. 15.* Drug addiction. Habitual degeneracy. Criminal activities. Juvenile detention. *And so on.*

When I thought it couldn't get any worse, I found the suicides. *Lapikov, Pyotr Ivanovich. Age 11. 17 July 1919. Cause of death: Fall from the roof.* Just this summer. *Mordukov, Nestor. Age 9. Cause of Death: Hanging.* No investigation, no follow-up, no attempt to establish the circumstances, to find out who might have been responsible. *Chuzhova, Anastasia. Age 13. Cause of Death: Drowning.* Drowned herself in the Fontanka. No interviews with her friends, nor the attendants. I was loath to bury these files, the fate of these wretched souls, in among those alphabetically related, who'd had half a chance—the housed, the transferred. So many children, eaten alive by the cruelty of our times. With no visible effect upon its appetite. I was unable to shrug and say live and let live. *And so on.*

In the morning, Alla Denisovna returned to unlock the cage she had put me in. I went to eat with the children, this time slot set aside for the little ones, four- and five-year-olds, boys and some girls. Shunning the bland evil of the adults, I found a place at one of the children's tables. "Mind if I sit here?" They all stared at me and Iskra. None said a word. All those faces, those little shaved heads, they were so small. I knew their stories before they were written. I ate the kasha, and although I was exhausted from the long night, I told them a story as they ate, about a cow from Novinka.

18 *Shpalernaya Street*

In the empty light of morning, I recognized the pale building on Shpalernaya Street, its majestic, ruined facade, brawny male cary-atids holding up its balconies. I was terrified to be in this neigh-borhood again, across the street from the Tauride Palace, the neighborhood where I'd spent my days with Arkady von Princip. I kept my kerchief pulled over my hair, my head down over the baby's sling. It made the scars on my back itch. And yet, this was where my trail of Kolya Shurov left off, in the flat with the ancient Golovins and Naryshkins. Although the building still maintained its stately facade to the street, from the courtyard it could have been any broken building in Petrograd, the yard weedy and silent. I didn't worry that the old people would recognize me—I'd been Misha then, and today a bast-shoed peasant with a baby in arms. I climbed the toothless stairs to the bel étage, remembering the state in which I'd last climbed these flights with Kolya, our passion a glowing red bonfire popping and crackling and shooting sparks high up into the night. *And one found its place, Kolya.*

I located the door in the gloom, rang the bell. Listened. Yes, I heard it sound out. But no answer. Rang again. I couldn't imagine all of those old people had gone out at once. No, they would take the streets two at a time, the others waiting anxiously for their safe re-turn. Then I remembered the secret knock—the first five notes of "Ochi Chornye"—*one, two, three...fourfive.*

That did the trick. Here was the same white mouse, peering through the slit in the door, held close by its chain. "Who is it?" she hissed. She must have been hovering just behind it, terrified it was the Cheka coming to call, or a labor conscription from the district soviet. The old lady—what was her name? Eliza-veta... *Vladimirovna*. She clutched her shawl around her throat as if I might try to strangle her.

I positioned Iskra out of sight of the narrow slit. I had to play my pieces judiciously. A good development, slow and correct. The piercing eyes scrutinized. "I'm looking for Elizaveta Vladimirovna. I'm Shurova, Marina Dmitrievna. Nikolai Stepanovich's wife. I know this is terribly awkward, but I was hoping to find him here."

I could hear someone in the apartment behind her, coughing. "You are no such thing," she croaked.

"But I am, as unlikely as it might appear."

"He would have told us himself."

Joy surged through me like water up through the earth, emerging as a sweet spring. "He's here? You've seen him?"

She smiled sourly, her pale blue eyes at the height of a child's. "Of course he's here," she said. "I thought you were his wife. I might be old but I'm not feeble, young lady. You might *know* him, but you're certainly not his wife. Good day."

She started to swing the door closed, but I stuck my foot in the aperture. "Wait! Please. He told me to meet him here if I managed to come back to the city. Please." I spoke quickly. I let a tremor come into my voice, which was not difficult, it had been a trying night. How lovely it felt to just let that tension flow out. I brought Iskra into view, kissed her sweet hair, let the old noblewoman see what the situation was. "He said I should speak to his dear friend Elizaveta Vladimirovna, that she would take care of everything. I've been trapped in the east, near Perm. It's taken me a month to get here. Please, just tell him I'm here. Marina Dmitrievna."

The lines in her brow softened. Her initial horror that I might be his slut weakened by the possibility that she'd misjudged the situation. "We have young ladies here. We're decent people."

Young ladies? I only remembered old people. But there might have been others... She was trying to protect them from my *shame*, as they used to say in Victorian novels. I'd had no sleep in thirty-six hours, the devil was tickling me, I almost broke into laughter. Imagine, in 1919 Petrograd, this old dame was worried about exposing noble young ladies to the coarser aspects of life! When they were probably shitting in the courtyard, and bathing over a basin.

"Of course," I said. "More important than ever." Where had I picked that up from? I sounded like one of my mother's friends, in a feather-bedecked hat, nodding over tea on one of her Thursday afternoons.

Finally, she made a decision and unlocked the chain, pulled me inside and locked it behind me. "I am Princess Elizaveta Vladimirovna Gruzinskaya. Please forgive my suspicions, child. The amount of criminality in this city is absolutely staggering. Staggering! So our Nikolai Stepanovich has been made an honest man, the rascal." She gazed at my baby with an expression half shrewd, half wistful, but made no move to touch her. "Never said a word. Not one word!"

"For our protection," I said. "A pleasure to make your acquaintance, Elizaveta Vladimirovna." I took her tiny, brittle hand and, God help me, made a little curtsy. I was always a stylish curtsier, even with the baby in the sling and the gun strapped to my hip and the bundle and the boots. It was everything I could do not to laugh and give the whole thing away. I was light-headed from exhaustion. "This is his daughter, Antonina." Bless Praskovia for having given her a traditional name. I didn't have to invent that part.

"Please, come in, come in." She kept looking over her shoulder at the baby in her sling as I followed the tiny old party into the parlor. "My goodness! Our own Nikolai Stepanovich... Why, I was just saying to him the other day, *Nikolai Stepanovich, you should find a nice girl and settle down*— really, though, thinking of one of our young ladies, but— Oh, here's Emilia Ivanovna."

The parlor was just as I'd left it, almost a year ago. The rich dark walls, the plush furniture, even shabbier now in daylight. It felt good that it had changed so little. It was chilly, but not too cold, a bit of fire in the *bourgeoika*, the card players with shawls around their shoulders, afghans on their laps, but now it was some semblance of breakfast, and the reading of newspapers. The same flabby old lady, the two old gents, as if they'd been preserved on a daguerreotype. "Viktor Sergeevich Golovin, Pavel Alexandrovich Naryshkin. May I present Marina Dmitrievna—Shurova. Our Nikolai Stepanovich's bride!" She clasped her hands to her breast. "That little beast. What a secret to keep from us, eh? She's just been a month coming in from the Urals, poor dear! Sit down, sit down. You must be exhausted. Aglaya! Aglaya!"

We went through the whole routine, as I was greeted by the old people. Emilia Ivanovna Golovina, a distant relative surely, and more desiccated than the last time—the folds of skin hung on her like drapes. And the two old men: her husband, Golovin, white side-whiskered, ramrod straight—I could imagine his chest emblazoned with medals given in service to the tsar—and Naryshkin, tall and stooped, streaks of white hair across this mottled dome, coat frayed at collar and cuffs, and yet, beautifully groomed for all that. The old gents actually stood and kissed my hand, properly, the symbolic kiss hovering in the air just above the wrist. The old people beamed with pleasure that one of their reactionary own had managed to wed and beget a child in the midst of the enemy's camp. I wondered again how they had not managed to get themselves out of Russia back when the other nobility had fled. Had they seriously thought this would all "blow over"? Were they conspirators? I wondered how many more nests of the gentry like this still remained in revolutionary Petrograd.

I sat on one of the tufted settees under a gilded mirror and had the strangest feeling of being back at my own Golovin grandparents' flat on the Moika Embankment. How had all this not yet been seized? A million questions sprung to mind that passion had blinded me to the last time I'd entered this flat. But mostly, I was interested in Kolya's whereabouts. "So when did you see my husband last?"

"Oh, when was it?" Elizaveta the white mouse asked old Golovin. "July, I think, around the time Yudenich almost made it to liberate Petrograd…*akh*. He came this close." She showed me about half an inch between thumb and clawed forefinger. "The English even sank two Red battleships. Did you hear about that? Sank them like bathtub toys, one after the other, half an hour apart."

"When the English strike, they strike hard," said Golovin. "Our Red masters should think about that."

"It won't be much longer," said the white mouse. "That's

what dear Nikolai Stepanovich told us. To hold fast. So that's what we do."

That battle was back in July. Now it was almost October. When she'd said Kolya was here, I thought she meant now. But I supposed when you were older than the stones, a month, two months, six. What difference did it make to them? When these days you could live three different lives in as many months.

Aglaya served tea—real tea, with a little bit of hoarded sugar—in my honor. They all closed their eyes like cats, sipping, as did I, tasting it with pure pleasure, knowing that it had to have been Kolya's doing. Without his intervention these old people would no doubt be eating the paint off the walls. Up to his old tricks. But that was beside the point. He had been here, that was the thing. I could almost smell his cigar, his Floris Limes. He would return. *Hold fast...*

A middle-aged man and woman joined us from the back of the flat. We were introduced. This was the Naryshkin daughter and her husband—Countess Ekaterina Pavlovna and Count Rudolf Platonovich Sobietsky. Ah, this was how the princess had managed to hang on to the flat—she'd brought in a platoon of friends. The comtesse was a tall gray-haired woman in a rusty black dress, with spectacles on a chain, and he a slighter man with elegant longish silver hair wearing a worn but neatly brushed suit. Sobietsky, seating himself on the settee opposite me, evaluated me with a smirk. "So you're our little Kolya's wife," he said, one eyebrow arched in a gesture that must have slayed them at the balls. "I don't believe it for a minute."

"Why Rudolf Platonovich!" The white mouse gasped, mortally offended that he would think the same thing she had just accused me of ten minutes earlier.

"Excuse my husband, Marina Dmitrievna," said the wife. She was as homely as a raw-boned horse, but a Naryshkin, so Sobietsky must have had a title but no money.

What a shrewd little peasant I'd become.

"Look at her," said the husband. Yes, I could see myself here in their Alexander III parlor, my baby strapped onto me, my bundle, my sheepskin. "Could you really see him marrying her? What would be the advantage? Our man would never do anything that he couldn't turn to advantage."

Of course, he was talking about himself, not Kolya. Kolya was a red-blooded Russian man. He could act upon passion, he didn't have toilet water in his veins like this inbred, aging Petersburg fop. He might have rutted with Faina, but it wasn't because he couldn't feel passion for a woman—the only advantage there was the obvious one.

"Whatever you might think of my appearance," I said, trying for a haughtiness my mother once possessed in boatloads, though I was too exhausted to achieve just the right icy edge, "Nikolai Stepanovich is a man of many facets, and venality is not one of them." Sipping my tea with a straight back, holding my saucer just so.

Sobietsky's father-in-law chuckled. "Got you there, dear Count."

But Sobietsky continued his scrutiny, unconvinced that a ragged urchin like myself would be wed to the Delightful Man. But I had to stay here, this is where he would return.

I tried to make conversation—they were eager to chat—but my head kept dropping, my eyes closing. My body cried out for sleep. On my lap, cradled in her sling, Iskra was already out cold, golden lashes against her soft cheeks, lips parted as she slept.

"So he's nearby?" I asked. "He said he'd be back soon?"

"He's a mysterious one, that husband of yours," said old Naryshkin. "We think he might be in Pskov, in communication with the Northwestern Army." Yudenich, that is. Estonia. It was all achingly familiar.

"But who knows..." Elizaveta Vladimirovna began, and stopped. They all looked guiltily at one another.

"Oh, it can't be a secret, this is the man's own wife," he said.

"Anyway, it's just a conjecture," said Naryshkin.

"He'll be along. He comes and goes," said Pavel Alexandrovich. "He takes good care of us, that lad." The old people nodded. "And as we're speaking, I should say, I disagree heartily with our Rudolf Platonovich. If, as you say, son, he only wants to cultivate advantage, what would be the advantage in our acquaintance? Where's the advantage of propping up a household of old museum pieces like ourselves? If he really wanted an advantage, he'd do better to turn us over to the Cheka."

The white mouse crossed herself. "Don't say that, Pavel Alexandrovich. Not even in fun. He never would do such a thing, never. That boy is a pillar of strength to us. What hasn't he done for us? A godsend, I tell you, a saint!"

Count Rudolf and I shared a laugh at that one. There was no question that I knew Kolya intimately, whether or not we were legitimately wed.

"How long has it been since *you* last saw our Nikolai Stepanovich?" he asked me keenly.

I was too worn out to think up much of a story. "Just before the baby came. He had to return to Petrograd, some sort of emergency."

They nodded. It seemed to mean something to them. Perhaps they believed him involved with Yudenich's try at Petrograd, when the English sank those battleships. Oh, what a nest of counterrevolutionaries. I was exhausted. Would they ever stop talking and invite me to stay?

"I don't like it. If I might speak frankly, the fellow's a well-known smuggler, speculator, and counterfeiter," said Platonovich, "not to mention opportunist, womanizer—pardon me, Madame—and scoundrel. He might have all of you hypnotized"—he pointed around the gloomy room—"but I must call a spade a spade."

"He's Stepan Shurov's son," said old Naryshkin, shuffling the cards. "A wild one, but *ours*."

Nash, ours. Other languages had no cognate to the Russian *nash*. For us, *ours* were relatives, dear friends, one's class, one's race, one's blood. The people we cared about, whose sins we always pardoned, and the hell with everyone else. And the Bolsheviks were as Russian as anyone—they had their own *nash*. *With us or against us*.

"No doubt. But still, I count my fingers every time I shake his hand," said the count. "I'm talking about character, now, not politics."

Although the man was probably right, no one likes to hear one's lover disparaged by those who don't love him—even if correctly assessed. He was our own *nash,* Iskra's and mine. I set my teacup and saucer down on the gateleg table. "Whatever my husband's activities and business affairs, you can rest assured he would not need your fingers."

Old Naryshkin laughed. I imagined he had been quite something in his time. You could see traces of it still, in his sly laughter, his quick blue eyes.

I yawned as they chattered back and forth like so many parrots in a South American jungle, my head drooping, then jerking upright before I fell off the couch.

"Oh, but we've been keeping you awake. Forgive me, how neglectful of us!" At last, the white mouse recognized my situation. "And you've traveled so far. It's just so rare that we have a chance to talk to a new person—one does have to be so careful nowadays, and we've lost so many..." The old people said nothing. Only the sound of the clock's soft chime broke the silence. "Let's not speak of that. Better days, *da?* Come, we have an empty room. Please do us the honor. It's a pleasure to have you with us. No, don't say no. I know you think we're just so many old fools, but it would be lovely, really. Aglaya, Aglaya!"

The next thing I knew I was back in that same empty room next to the kitchen, Aglaya making up the bed, moving the familiar heaps of furniture. Here Kolya and I made love that last night in October. How we burned. Like two pieces of paper in a hot stove.

19 *Night Shift*

Thus, despite Sobietsky's suspicion that I was what I actually was—an interloper, improvident, a libertine—I became part of the commune of intransigent reactionaries, the most likely spot in which to wait for Kolya's return. Most importantly, I was awarded the job at Orphanage No. 6 over Pancake Makeup's friend's claims. In the daytime, I slept, queued, and cared for Iskra in the small room next to Aglaya's. I did my best to skirt the parlor, mainly to avoid confrontations with the young ladies of the household, Darya and Anastasia Sobietskaya. Darya, a few years older, was tolerable, a tall, long-nosed girl, patient like her mother, inclined to melancholy—a real Chekhovian dreamer. She would surely have been married off by now had the Russian nobility not been residing in Paris this season. Instead, she gave piano lessons, and French, though it wasn't in her nature to teach. She didn't have the gift. She was nervous and overly solicitous, didn't know how to correct someone who was paying her. *"Très bien,"* I overheard her telling a commissar's well-fed girlfriend, who came for French twice a week. "Although, really, it's *trop* without the *p*, not *troppe*." She was the one I'd pegged for a potential babysitter.

The other one, Stassya, a student at the university—smaller and more feminine than Darya, clever and waspish like her father—took an instant dislike to me. I wondered if Kolya had made love to her, a smoldering, smoky-eyed blonde about my age, if she was the one the princess had in mind for his future wife. Perhaps she had thought so too. Or perhaps she hoped life would always be aesthetically lovely, without noise and the pressing needs of others. "I can't breathe in here," she told her parents, loudly enough to be overheard. "Why don't you just bring in the yardman and his twelve screaming brats and have done with it."

Of course, Iskra cried when she needed a change, or was hungry, but generally she was a good baby. I knew how lucky I was. I hung the diapers in my own room to avoid the smell that Stassya insisted was *stinking up the house*. I tried to make peace with her early in my stay, complimenting her on a hat that was clearly Parisian—though a little shabby, it still bore the mark of couture—as she arranged it in the hallway mirror.

"Don't talk to me," she said, tucking stray strands of her long hair into her simple coiffure. "Never speak to me. I don't know you, I don't want to know you."

Still, I nursed the possibility that I might be able to leave Iskra with these people from time to time. I asked Alla Denisovna if she could requisition a baby bottle for me, and the next night, I found it waiting for me under the counter. At home, I boiled it for ten minutes, then heated some of my precious Drops of Milk ration, and took Iskra back into our room to practice with it. I thought it would be easy—of course my brilliant daughter would know what to do. It never occurred to me that she would rebel. It was as if she knew I was trying to cheat her out of her birthright, her beloved breast, as if she knew that I was planning to leave her—and she gazed at me with such despair. But it was dangerous to have her only able to feed from my body. *We have to be prepared, Iskra—for everything.* Her eyes welled. "Iskra, please, just a little. Try it, *ma petite*. For Mama?" I teased her mouth with the rubber teat, traced the little bow, squirted milk onto her lips, but she shoved it away and began to wail. I steeled my heart against her sorrow. "Don't be a silly girl. It's yummy!" I pretended to drink. "Mmmm," but she was howling loud enough to be heard in San Francisco, or at least by the oldsters in the parlor, and certainly by the Sobietskys, who already hated us. I was weeping and then my milk let down. In the end, it was not Iskra who surrendered. And in truth, nursing her was bliss, the quiet, her dreamy eyes gazing up into mine, while she still hiccupped from her last fit, her tiny hand reaching up to touch my face. We just could not be separated, and that was that.

And even if I'd been successful, it wouldn't have mattered. One afternoon I floated the suggestion to Darya of looking after Iskra for an hour. The elder sister turned as pale as her music sheets. "I wouldn't know what to do with an infant. Please don't ask." I knew enough not to ask Stassya, who would rather have dropped her out the window, and I was too obligated to the old princess to ask her or the other card players. The countess Sobietskaya was far too busy helping the count with his memoir. I tried Aglaya but she shrank back as if the baby might explode. "Don't I have enough to do with all of them and their fussing? What if she choked?"

Until Kolya showed up, it looked like it would be me and Iskra in our country of two in the servant's room with the diapers hanging.

I liberated an old basket from the flat's junk room, set Iskra up in it on the Europa's famous marble counter, where, safe behind the cage, I addressed myself to the tidal wave of case files. Night after night, I moved grains of sand from one pile to the other. I had stopped reading the details, for the most part, except for the worst, the most heartbreaking. These I felt a duty to read, as if it somehow kept those children company, to witness what had become of them. *Gonchalovsky, Efraim. Age 11.* Drank shoe polish. *Bitov, Sergei. Age 8.* Hung himself in the janitor's closet among the brooms. The result of the endless bullying, beatings, or simply haunted memories of being lost in a train station as parents pushed onto a train, or watching them die of typhus or cholera.

Bit by bit, the mountain melted as I filed the accursed children away into alphabetical ranks, taking their sorrows into my own heart. The cleaner the counter, the darker and more stained my soul. The latrine of revolution, Orphanage No. 6.

One night I arrived for work to discover another girl sitting behind the amber counter, reading *Pravda* on my newly cleaned desk. From the satisfied look on her flaccid face, I surmised that Pancake Makeup's friend had finally found her way to my job. She pointed to the assignment board. There was my name, *Kuriakina*, written in a firm blocky hand, moved from *Administrative* to *Infant Department*. *Well*, I told myself as I climbed to the second-floor rear, carrying Iskra in her basket, *how bad could it be?* Babies I understood. They wouldn't beat each other up, or bring men back to service under the noses of the others. They wouldn't drink shoe polish or hang themselves in the janitor's closet.

I found the room, spacious and reasonably clean, lit by kerosene lamps. The din was tremendous. Twenty babies, crying at once. They didn't notice what a fine view they had onto Arts Square, where a crowd collected outside the Mikhailovsky Theater in anticipation of a concert. This had been one of the best suites, plaster grapes and angels on its coped ceiling, the fancy inlaid parquet. None but the best for our orphans. Strangely, none of the babies exhibited much gratitude for such luxury accommodations. Iskra joined the chorus of wails. A stolid-faced, broad-nosed woman with a creased brow in a nurse's uniform was changing a baby. "I'm Nonna," she said over her shoulder. "They said they were sending someone. About time. Is that your kid?"

I put Iskra over my shoulder, patted her, trying to quiet her, but she was already joining the collective, a good Soviet citizen. "I had to bring her, there's nowhere to leave her."

"There's an empty crib if you want it," she said, nodding toward the wall, a mesh cage on legs.

I didn't want to put Iskra in a crib recently vacated by a baby who may have died of smallpox or cholera or God knew what. "That's okay, I brought a basket." I put the willow basket, which had once held Emilia Ivanovna's balls of yarn, onto the floor near the stove—it was wonderfully warm—and tucked Iskra inside it. I hated to let her just cry. She wasn't used to being treated so foully, but I had our bread to earn. I hung up my coat and put on an apron that hung from a hook, the white nurses' kerchief.

The room smelled of milk, baby shit, and carbolic. "How can you stand it?" I shouted over the noise, then thought of Stassya Sobietskaya.

"Stand what?" Nonna replied, efficiently changing the diaper of one of her screaming charges.

In the Infant Department, we were on a three-hour rotation. Change, feed, sleep. She approached them with all the tenderness of a worker on an assembly line. I began at the far end. The first one had awful diaper rash. "What do I do about these sores?"

She shrugged. "Clean him up, best you can. We used to have fish oil but somebody stole it." To cook with, no doubt. "Keep going, we gotta feed 'em too. Then it starts again."

It was a night of poor, sad diapers, nothing like Iskra's solid,

compact masses. These were watery, greenish, diarrheic—that reminded me all too vividly of my cholera patients at Pulkovo
Observatory. I kept washing my hands in the hot water we left on
the stove, washed them until they were raw, trying to sanitize between each infant's diaper change, as Nonna clucked and shook
her head. I was only midway through my babies when my milk let
down. Now I had to stop and nurse Iskra—terrified I would in-
fect her with whatever was plaguing the orphan babies. I thought I
was going to lose my mind with that screaming. I gave Iskra a quick
feed—her eyes widened in outrage when I pulled her off me. The
look in her eyes was precisely the sorrow of a lover who suddenly
finds her man becoming cold and efficient with her. She screamed
when I put her back in her basket. "Forgive me," I kept saying. I
shut my ears and returned to the diapers.

"Take these down to the laundry." Nonna nodded at the great pile
of them in the wheeled cart. "And bring us up some more water."
She began filling bottles from a pot of milk on the stove—this
precious milk, how far had it come? I only prayed she'd washed ad-
equately.

After we had them all changed and fed, we sat on the windowsill
for a smoke. I could hear people in front of the Mikhailovsky at the
interval, talking in the frosty air. "How can you do this? How can
you bear it?" I asked her.

She shrugged. "They've got food, they've got blankets. More
than what some of them's got out there, *da*? You'll get used to it. It's
these next ones do it to me." She nodded toward another door. "Go
in there if you want to stab yourself in the heart."

I didn't want to stab myself in the heart, but I was unable not
to see for myself. I rose and pushed open the door. In the dim
light of the nurse's kerosene lamp—toddlers, in little corrals of
cribs that had been lashed together, one against the other, to keep
them from rattling, I supposed. Most were asleep, but several stood
and rhythmically rocked, staring at me with big glassy eyes, like so
many piglets in pens, or lay listlessly, looking through the peeling
bars. Two to a pen, they pulled each other's hair and sucked their

fists. Turning to each other for a scrap of comfort. These tiny children had no idea how horrifying they were. Accusing me in their innocence— *Why have you put us here? Do something. We need you.*

Their abandonment made them absolutely terrifying. I could so easily see myself looking out through their staring eyes. If our infants survived our care, mine and Nonna's, they would only end up here, staring and banging the crib. And the silence was worse than the screaming. At least our babies knew enough to howl. These children had already given up. I couldn't stay in here another moment. *Please, God, don't assign me to toddlers.* As it was, I would dream about them, vast rooms of abandoned, tiny, sentient creatures in metal pens, like a stockyard.

Late in the night, a timid woman entered the Infant Department, a bundle in her arms. We were in the middle of the second cycle, up to our elbows in baby shit, but I washed my hands and came to her. The bundle was crying, but weakly. The woman was a worker, not young, wearing a tattered skirt, a wet, felted scarf. Her long, thin face was nearly blue, her hands long and bony. "I can't feed him," she said softly, holding the baby in its poor blanket. She didn't weep, she didn't have enough liquid left in her. A dried-out shell of a woman, speaking in a monotone. "He's a good baby, but I'm fed out." She was missing several teeth, her lips serrated with lines. I had never seen real despair before, despair like that. "I got two older kids," she said quietly. "I need to think of them."

"Don't you get the milk ration?" I asked.

"I have to think of the others," she said in that same monotone, as if it were her last instruction in the world, as she held out the shredded gray blanket that contained the baby. "I give Auntie the milk. She takes a third of my pay. I have to work. But it's not enough." I took the infant from her. It was about three weeks old. It clearly wasn't going to make it, blue faced and thin. She just couldn't bear to see it die. I put it in an empty crib and took the woman in my arms. She didn't embrace me back, didn't weep, just rested her head on my shoulder, weary, weary of living, weary of trying to keep things alive.

* * *

After a week in the Infant Department, not one but two dead babies later, including the one the woman brought in—they just didn't wake up for their shift, swaddled small and inert, like small sacks of oats—I came to work to find my name moved, transferred again—this time, *Kuriakina, Girls 6–9.*

I wept with relief.

In a small room on the third floor, with six bunk beds, two of which were unoccupied, ten little girls gathered in ragged shifts and shaved heads. For the first time, I wondered why there were so few girls, when the halls were full of boys. Was it that they were better beggars, and didn't feel the need to seek the shelter of the orphanage? Or was it that their parents struggled harder not to abandon them, feeling that they wouldn't be able to scratch a living on the street, while their sons could be turned out-of-doors with better chances of survival? Maybe they ran off less. Or worse. Someone else might be finding them before we did.

"I'm Comrade Marina," I said, pulling a stool up to their little stove. They pressed in around me, trying to peer into the sling where my daughter was playing with her fingers. "This is Iskra."

"Can we see her?" asked a small girl, dried snot all over her face.

"She's so pretty," said a tall girl.

"She's ready for bed," I lied. "We're just going to put her in her basket now." But she wouldn't cooperate, started to cry as soon as I put her down, made me pick her up again.

A girl clung to my skirt, dangerously close to my concealed gun, looking up at me with such adoring eyes it was terrifying. "Comrade Marina...will you stay with us now?"

"All night."

"You smell good. Comrade Zoya's mean. She hits."

They were all over me, patting me, hanging on to me. It frightened me how ravenous for affection they were. I hated to be cold, hold them at arm's length, but I had to. They wanted so much—to touch my hair, my dress, my breasts, my legs, sit on my lap, get under my skirt. I had to watch Iskra like a pawnbroker. They loved her, but it all had an edge of hysteria. They demanded to hold her, fighting among themselves for the privilege. I didn't trust their enthusiasm. They were frenetic and full of sudden tempers. One minute it was giggles and kisses, the next a fury of hair pulling and weeping. Hugging my legs, burrowing into my clothing. They would make wonderful pickpockets. I couldn't allow myself to be mobbed. Yet they were only small children, and their desire for closeness was genuine. They were so unused to experiencing affection from adults. If I didn't get control of them, I would be eaten alive.

That first night, out of my depth, I fell back on the classic announcement of bedtime.

"It is not," said the tall girl, with a swagger.

They were so dirty. Didn't anyone even try to keep them halfway clean? "We'll have a wash first." I made it sound like I was giving in. "Get a partner and line up."

"We don't have to." The tall girl was going to be trouble, with her dark eyes, her stubble of dark hair, chin tilted up.

"Only if you want a story," I said.

"What kind of story?" I could see her wavering, sensing a ruse.

"You'll see," I said.

"Alyona, quit." Another girl, sharp nosed, grabbed her and pulled her into line. "There, Comrade."

And with Iskra in the sling, we paraded down to the washroom, the two oldest girls carrying the pot of boiling water from the stove between them. It was dangerous, but carrying it myself and the baby was more so, and them carrying her was out of the question. In the dank tiled room, I mixed our hot water with cold from the tap and, with a bar of harsh brown soap, washed their faces and hands, getting to know them as I handled them, washing necks and ears, elbows and arms. I even used the corner of my apron to clean their teeth with boiled water. I inspected their heads for lice, caressing, careful of scabs. I felt like an English nanny, like I should have been wearing an enormous starched apron and white cap.

I made up a silly song for the procedure. *"Give meeeeeee, those grubby little hands..."*

Such a difference from the Infant Department. Less heartbreaking, and yet, I had a great deal to learn. What to do about pinching, tattling, the furious tears, the incessant stealing from one another? It was hardly a Dickensian regime—Orphanage No. 6 was a progressive Soviet institution and forbade any kind of coercion or physical punishment, withholding of food or isolation. One had to be clever to earn compliance—though most of the matrons just threw up their hands and allowed anarchy to reign.

I relied on the girls' instinctive desire to be tended, even if there was nothing I could do for their hunger. Who didn't want to be cared for? To be recognized as human and worthy of tenderness? Unlike many of the women on the late shift who spent their time in the staff room, I stayed in the dormitory all night, writing as they slept, soothing if they woke, changing wet sheets, feeding the stove, sometimes taking a sobbing child on my lap and singing "Fais Dodo..." Most of all, they loved their stories. Then they would forget to slap and pinch each other, and I could make demands. They had to be washed and in their beds, tucked in, if they wanted me to tell them the tale. If someone was acting up, no story. Ah, the might of the collective.

They wanted to hear about Iskra's father. I made up stories about him, fantastic enough that even six-year-old Olya, who barely spoke, could understand they were stories, and we could change them if we liked. They loved that power, that I could change whole lives any time I wanted to. I turned Kolya into a mountain man, a hunter and tamer of horses, who could ride his shaggy pony standing straight up on its broad back. How a white witch once stole Iskra away and took her to live in the far, far mountains, and my adventures in trying to get her back. They lay in their cots and sucked their thumbs, imagining it all.

Girls 6–9 was exhausting but in a different way from Infant Department. Anything could happen in a split second. I had to be on my toes. Their emotional outbursts could be downright dangerous.

I caught sight of normally placid Matya about to throw a pot of boiling water at Anoushka because of some slight I could barely understand. Adoration of Iskra could easily flip into envious harm. The girls themselves didn't know what they would do next. They were riding their own tigers at all times.

The season deepened. Autumn turned to frost. Now the windows coated over in their miraculous patterns, and my girls shivered, two to a bed, Olya and Alyona, Mashka, scabby Shushka. Their gaunt blue faces, their runny noses. I dragged my stool up among their bunks and recited the verses I composed in the night for them—working in their names, which they adored, and also those of my coworkers, which made them laugh in bubbling skeins. I gazed at them with the eyes of someone leaving. Iskra, awake in her sling, recited along with me in her private language, which I had yet to translate.

> *In the land beyond the seas*
> *Live ten maidens fair*
> *Olya, Alyona, Mashka, Shushka,*
> *Lena, Zoya, Rada the bear,*
>
> *Katya, Matya, Anoushka there.*
> *Into the frost and the swirling snow,*
> *Into the forest to cut some wood,*
> *Into the forest to cut some wood*
> *with saws and little axe they go.*

One night, Comrade Tanya of the pancake makeup lingered in the doorway. She usually abandoned her own post with Girls 9–12 to pursue some sort of personal activity like stealing the children's milk or smoking cigarettes with her Communist friend down in the lobby. But now she just waited, arms crossed, a sour look on her face. She still hadn't forgiven me for being hired before her illiterate friend. She believed her party membership instantly awarded her the status of commissar, and sneered at us and our lowly status as mere "citizens."

"I don't know why you bother with this," she interrupted me, mid-stanza. "Lalala, the dancing deer and the prancing mice. You're not doing them any favors. Softening 'em up, telling your stupid stories, tucking 'em in nighty night."

The girls stared at her with loathing, knowing they were being robbed of their poem. "Shut up," our bold Alyona said. "What do you know?"

"I know you kids're gonna have to fight for what you get when you go to the *detsky dom*." The permanent children's homes, to which they would be transferred after Orphanage No. 6. "There ain't no magic deer and golden fishes there. Better get used to it here, or you're gonna take it all the worse when the other brats are beatin' you up and eatin' your food. Trust me, you're doin' them no favors, Miss Wash Your Hands, Nighty Night."

The girls swiveled with their big eyes to me, frightened and wanting me to defend them, to tell them this wasn't their future. What kind of monster would say something like this in front of children? Scaring them about the *detskie doma*—when they were already afraid. What was the point of it?

"Isn't it better to be warm for a while before you have to go out in the cold again?" I countered. "Or would you just rather stand in the cold because it'd be worse to have to leave a warm shelter to go back outside?" Two could play this game. I let my gaze run over my anxious charges, feisty Alyona and her poor cropped head, little baby Olya, fingers in mouth, leaning on Matya's shoulder. "I say, grab a little warmth when you can. That's a skill too."

Tanya came the rest of the way into the room, and when she spoke, she was speaking in earnest. "Look, Marina, I know you think you're doin' 'em all a favor with your hugs and pretties, but seriously, now. Seriously. It doesn't help 'em. These ain't gonna be just regular kids, they're orphans and they're gonna have to tough it out, and they got a long way to go."

I ran my eyes over my pitiful, scabby charges, human beings so desperate to be loved. "But they *are* regular kids. How can you take this one little scrap of childhood away from them?" I knew I shouldn't be getting into a debate with her in front of them, but she was the one who had called me out—I needed the children to hear the other side. That I didn't agree with her, that her point was not the only one.

"I seen kids who come from your soft homes in here, haven't I? We all have. They're the ones we have to fish out of the canals. I'm tellin' you, you got to let 'em take their lumps, straight out. Harden 'em up for what's ahead."

I was probably holding her too tight, but Iskra started to cry, and then Mashka did, and Olya. Comrade Tanya left, tail twitching, happy she'd put a wet blanket over our shred of contentment. I had to quiet them all down, which I did by telling a silly story about Comrade Tanya sitting outside her house in the snow, and her neighbors asking why she didn't come in, and she said it was because she'd have to come out the next day anyway—she would be colder if she went inside.

Once I got them to sleep, I nursed Iskra, looking down into her uptilted eyes, and hummed "When Irish Eyes Are Smiling." I took care not to nurse her in front of the girls, not out of modesty but respecting the intensity of their yearning. I couldn't help thinking about what Comrade Tanya had said. I knew most of the women here thought as she did. But how hard did a child have to be to live in this terrible life? I considered my time with them as a little vaccination against the hardship ahead. It was their childhood itself I was trying to rescue. My dimmed lantern barely illuminated their little shaved heads covered with knitted caps, two to a pillow. Even if for a few minutes a day, I wanted to give them something sweet to remember, a story at bedtime, the sense that someone was watching over you as you slept and noticed your tears, your snotty nose, your shivering. Would it really make their lives in the *detsky dom* harder when it was gone, or would it give them a little fire to carry inside them, to warm themselves in the long cold nights?

I tried to imagine the ache of having been well treated, and then thrown to the wolves. What if Tanya was right? Maybe living with wolves from the start would be better. Perhaps it was my bourgeois upbringing, wanting to give them a bit of that sweetness without considering its ramification. Was it harder having a childhood snatched from you, or never having one at all? I wanted them to have something to remember, Olya, Anoushka, little Mashka, during the years of nights to come, at least one poem they might recite to themselves under the snow.

Two days after my confrontation with Comrade Tanya, I was transferred to *Boys 9–12, Room III*.

Someone was making a point.

20 *Chieftains and Untouchables*

I now worked with Comrade Nadezhda of the beauty mark, in a big dormitory formed by breaking through a wall in a hotel suite, warmed by stoves at both ends. My new charges, Boys 9–12, needed no organizing; they'd already created their own organization, their own secretive culture, even their own lingo, which they used in front of adults—though to be sure, languages were my strong suit. Theirs was the law of the horde, and no mercy was in evidence, anywhere. I thought I understood about orphans from the little girls, but that had been a mere outpost of the country I'd entered. Now I'd arrived in its central districts. The boys had chieftains and chargés d'affaires, poets and traders, whipping boys and untouchables. Their brutal mistreatment of one another was the law, rarely contradicted by child or adult.

The first night, I caught Makar, a slight but furious boy, systematically kicking a bigger but meek one they called Cross-Eyes, in the clear space between the bunks. The bigger boy lay on the floor protecting his head cradled in his arms, gasping with each blow.

"Stop that!" I yanked Makar off by his collar.

He glowered at me with all the hatred his ten-year-old soul could muster, but said nothing.

"What's the problem?"

"None of your business is what," he said boldly.

I helped Cross-Eyes up. He bent to the side he'd been kicked on, wiped his eyes and his snotty nose on his sleeve. "Are you all right? What was going on here?"

He sniffled and shrugged. "We was just playing." I examined the other boys who'd been watching it all, but not one spoke up for the victim, expressions so blank you could post a handbill. So. Nothing left to be done.

A minute later, a solemn boy with big dark eyes, Maxim, leaned over to examine Iskra in her basket. "He owes him money, see?" he said under his breath. "And can't pay. So Cross-Eyes gives Makar ten kicks." Then he walked away, as if he'd said nothing. *Gives him ten kicks.* In lieu of payment, the opportunity to kick him ten times. But payment for what? They had nothing.

I asked Nadezhda about it, after the boys were asleep.

"Best to turn a blind eye," she said, turning a page of her newspaper. "They'll do it their way in the end, believe me. Why work yourself up?" Natural self-government. It was enough to make Kropotkin renounce anarchism.

I soon learned that the central concern of Room III was gambling, and payment was extracted in all sorts of ways. You had to let them do it too. There was nothing else they cared about, and they had no toys or other games. They made their cards from pieces of cardboard, and woe to the boy caught cheating. When they lived on the streets, they had money, but in here, beatings were the rate of exchange. Or clothes. Sometimes a child suddenly had no shoes. Hair snatching was the most disgusting of their trade items—there were always a few boys who looked like they had the mange. It was all about cheating and debts.

And how they stole from one another! No child ever possessed anything of his own. There was one boy, Sosha, a sad-eyed blond who barely spoke and had no friends. He seemed impossibly lonely.

I sewed him a little horse made of rags and brought it one night, gave it to him. He called it Dima and seized on it like a box of sweets, ran off to a corner to play. But in a few minutes he brought it back to me, pressed it into my apron pocket.

"No, Sosha, it's for you." I tried to give the little horse back to the boy, but he refused to take it.

"You keep him." He gazed down at the little horse, and a tear rolled down his face. "They'll take him away from me." How little it took to make them happy, but how vulnerable that little was. He would rather not have the horse and have him, than have him and lose him.

The boys were wild and wary. Like the girls, they wanted to be near me, but unlike the girls, they didn't dare touch me. It was as if I were a fire, they craved the closeness, but not the burn. I could understand that—people hated the *besprizorniki*, the parentless waifs. They pricked at adult consciences, and people didn't respond well to guilt. The shame people felt to see these ragged urchins—skin blue in flashes under their terrible rags—was quickly translated into an armoring anger, as if it were the children's own fault they were abandoned. *Bad blood*, people said, chasing them off as if they were rats. Assumed they were all thieves, which in truth, some were, but not all. They spit at them in the street, struck them with impunity. No wonder the children feared adults. They all hated going to school, which, in the progressive wisdom of the Commissariat, they attended with the local district children, where they were treated as if being an orphan were a bacillus.

It still surprised me how many of my charges were interested in Iskra, how tender they were to her, that a young boy would want to hold a baby, and although I was afraid of disease, I would allow it as a special privilege—after a boy had washed his hands and scrubbed the nails so that the blue-white of his skin would break your heart—I would let him have her basket on his bed, let him hold her hand and touch her soft cheek. "I love you," I heard more than one of them whisper in her ear.

And they, too, liked their stories and verses. I made up little *chastushki* couplets to make them laugh while I washed their hands and faces and scrubbed their teeth, inspected for lice. They were coming to trust me, and I was beginning to understand their organization—who had to be left alone, who could be cajoled, who longed for attention, and who had to be approached like a wild animal, never looked at straight on. But the routine was a great leveler, and all but the most rebellious were happy to submit to it.

I began to tell them the story of the orphan Vanka Manka.

"He lived in a city under the sun and the stars," I chanted as I walked between the rows of their beds, Iskra on my shoulder. "It was called Pashapashol, and it grew up rich and beautiful on the banks of a wide river that said its name all day long—*Pashapashol, Pashapashol.* The city looked into the mirror of its waters, smiling at its own beauty and goodness.

"The city was built on forty-eight islands, each island perched on a pillar of ice, and the ice itself was as clear as glass. Inside the pillars, bright fish lay suspended, orange and blue and red. And there lived the orphan Vanka Manka, and his sister, Snezhana, the snow child, whose freshness the sorcerer Shinshen craved for his own. One day, he bid his army of shadows to steal her away."

I made it good and scary, night after night, with plenty of plunder and sword fights and untold riches, which they loved hearing me describe in detail, amid many interruptions.

One night I had Vanka Manka up on the rooftops, slipping between the chimney pots, looking for his stolen sister. Even Comrade Nadezhda was awake, listening, when the door to the Room III dormitory opened. In walked a big, wide, terrifying woman, solid, with a chin like an ironing board, and an unsmiling face. She looked like a Roman Caesar, Julius or Augustus. *Matron.* I could feel the same force emanating from this formidable woman as from the heavy writing that made my assignment on the board, that had seen fit to move me from Infant Department to Girls 6–9 and now to Room III. I'd been waving my hands in an extravagant gesture, describing Vanka Manka and the magical Book of Signs, when she'd come in. Was I about to be fired? Her face betrayed nothing but I sensed a heaviness that reeked disapproval. Was it Iskra, some other crime? Or—just perhaps—was Matron's presence here purely a random occurrence? Then, in shuffled a group of serious-looking men and women in dark clothing who arrayed themselves inside the doorway.

Matron introduced Comrade Nadezhda and me to the group, but not them to us.

"You bring your baby with you?" a tiny woman asked in a ridiculously high voice straight from the Komedii theater.

"Yes, Comrade. I have no other place to leave her."

"You can still perform your duties with one hand?" asked Matron.

"Yes, Matron. I have a basket for her when I need both hands."

"Actually, I think it's good," said one of the men, a stooped one with a sensitive face. "It could be a humanizing influence. A bit of family atmosphere." He obviously hadn't heard the policy on the hardening of orphans.

"There should be a crèche," said another woman comrade, young, brash. "When you think of it."

"Do the children seem to have enough to eat?" an older, motherly woman asked me directly.

Perhaps this was an inspection of the orphanage, and not of me at all. I glanced at Matron for a clue as to how she wanted me to respond, but she gave no indication of preference. Of course there wasn't enough to eat. What was I supposed to say? I knew there was tremendous pilferage by the staff—understandable, as nobody had food—but the children were always the losers. If I told them, though, my job would likely be over. But maybe they could do something. "No," I said. "They could use more milk, and meat if you can find it."

Matron blinked, once, slowly, and they all left. Was I in trouble? Would I arrive tomorrow night to discover my new assignment, Toddlers? Or, God help me, Girls 13–16? Or no assignment at all? I sat down by the stove, Iskra in my lap.

"Hey, what about Vanka Manka?" the room's chieftain, Nikita, said from his choice bottom bunk near the stove, his arms under his head like a Mongol potentate. "He was on the rooftop."

They were still waiting. The interruption of the adults meant nothing to them. The artist in me was pleased. It was an achievement indeed if you were able to capture the boys' attention—to create a world in their heads so that even a thug like Nikita wanted to hear more.

"So Vanka Manka gazed through the window," I began, walking Iskra as she grabbed at my mouth. "And there, on the table, was the Book of Signs, with its spine of silver and hasp of pearl, the magic symbols embedded in its cover. Here was the Eye of Horus, which could see across the world, and the Mandrake Root, that could change you into a tree or a hawk. The most wondrous book in the world."

"How much is it worth?" asked Makar, the cardsharp.

I could see my favorite boy, Maxim, in the depths of his upper bunk, the light shining in his dark, dreaming eyes.

"Half a million," I said. "The last time it was at auction, in the reign of Ivan the Terrible." They didn't know a thing about history, but anyone called *Grozny* must be someone special.

"So, is he going in?" Their chieftain closed the door on financial speculation.

"It was very slippery up there, and Vanka Manka felt the wing of a raven brush his cheek, and suddenly he started to fall." I wondered how many of these boys had run along a rooftop themselves, broken in through a window, like those hoodlums that long-ago night on the Strelka. "And as he fell, he smelled the sickening sweet scent of hyacinths."

They shuddered and their eyes grew brighter. Hyacinths, they knew, were Shinshen's favorite flower. The Black Palace was surrounded by them, huge fields, all of the people he had bewitched and turned to flowers. If you walked through it, you could hear their sighs, their whispers, *Alas, alas.*

"And there he was—Shinshen." Seven feet tall in his stockings, and his mad blue eyes could see in the dark, and his hair was made of spiderweb. "He had come to read the Book of Signs, and heard the clatter, but when he looked up, the boy was gone, already landing in a lilac bush in the courtyard below."

I could see the younger boys fighting sleep as if it were a bear as they struggled to hear more of the story. It was time to say good night. They groaned, called me unfair, but I promised them I would tell them more tomorrow. After that, I went around and checked every boy, tugging up a thin blanket, patting a shaved head. I could give them very little but that small contact. I hoped it would help. Who didn't need a human touch? It was true of babies, and of boys who thought they were beyond all tenderness. And of me as well, though that would have to wait until I found Kolya again.

I pulled Maxim's blanket up around his neck. I wasn't supposed to have favorites, but he was a special boy, so unlike the others, solemn and tender and observant. His eyes shone in the light of the kerosene lamp, huge and full of sorrow. "You know, there is someone like that," he whispered.

"Like who?" I asked.

"Shinshen. He's here, in Petrograd." His lips were chapped. Maybe he was a little feverish. I felt his forehead. He seemed hot and clammy. "Kids work for him. He cuts their throats if they do anything wrong. The cops take their bodies away and nobody ever sees it."

I stroked his cheek as if soothing him, but really, I'd have preferred to press it over his mouth. I glanced over at Iskra in her basket by the stove, playing with her hands. I could see them dancing above the lip. "Sounds like the kind of thing kids make up to scare each other with."

He gazed at me with his waxy skin and the shiny darkness of his eyes in the low light. "But it's real. I know kids who've seen them."

"I'm sure you're right." I put my hand on his shoulder to steady him. "But you're safe here, with us, *da*?"

He sighed. His sad smile, the skeptical look in his eyes, told me that at ten years old he already knew better. Even after I finished checking on the rest of the boys, I could feel him watching, begging me to believe him. I couldn't tell him that I didn't have to be convinced. I couldn't tell him, *Hush. Speak the devil's name, and he's sure to appear.*

21 *The Devil's Name*

Meanwhile, General Yudenich burst out from his position behind Lake Peipus, on the border between Estonia and Russia. Within the week, he had taken Luga, one hundred miles away. He led German Freikorps troops, the very ones the German leftists had described on the train, the ones that had crushed the Munich Soviet. We'd beaten the Germans back last winter, and here they were again, under the Whites. But this year was different—in the depopulated city, people were listless, depressed, there was no fervor of resistance as there had been against the Germans. No one flooded out to build trenches, no rallies were called, no speeches. Where was the government, where was Trotsky to inspire us? Rykov, Zinoviev?

Only in the Shpalernaya apartment did excitement bubble like a forest spring. The aristocrats reacted as if they'd received a gilt-edged invitation to the grand duke's ball, delivered by footmen in livery. Oh, happy days! Oh, the talk of what they would do when the general arrived, the revenge they might take upon the Bolsheviks. While in the bread queues, the women stood silent, backs bent in defeat. They didn't even bother exchanging rumors. "Who's going to want us?" said one old man, attempting to joke. "Whoever gets us has to feed us. Lenin's probably begging them right now, *Nikolai Nikolaevich, please, Petrograd's so beautiful this time of year.*"

I held Iskra closer. I could have stayed in Izhevsk. Or done as their factory committee had requested and toured the revolutionary cities talking about the *Red October*. But no, like a dove, I was driven to return here. I couldn't resist seeking my native soil, Petersburg with its mirrors and passages, the smell of water and the cries of gulls. The trees knew me here. My footfalls echoed the city's eternal name.

"We should be preparing, not sitting on our hands," I said in the orphanage canteen before my shift, eating with the other caretakers. In the old tearoom the electric lights shone harshly on the women's faces, each suffused with its own aura of expectation or dread. I let Iskra taste a little of the sweetened tea off my forefinger. "Why aren't they mobilizing us? What's wrong with the Petrograd Soviet? Are they so depressed that the capital moved?"

"They're going to throw us to the dogs," said Alla Denisovna, studying the glowing tip of her cigarette.

I would go to the district soviet and sign up for the defense myself if it weren't for Iskra. But the weight of her, the fact of her here in my lap, happy to be with the women, free from her carrying cloth, reminded me that if anything happened to me, it would be *second floor, in the back* for my little redheaded jewel. I wouldn't risk that, not for anything. Ironic—people thought mothers were the bearers of all virtue, when mothers were the most selfish, the most venal people on earth. Naturally bourgeois. We didn't care what happened to anyone but our own flesh and blood. *Children are everyone's responsibility*, in theory. But in practice? As a category, mothers were endemically counterrevolutionary. My love was reserved for one little baby, a candle barely flickering. And yet, we could not divorce our future from the future of the country. What of the revolution? What of the city? What of this hell of abandoned children, guarding their food from one another at their benches under the absurd, bucolic-painted ceiling of the Europa Tea Room. Their accumulated sorrows should weigh so much it should sink this city back into the Finnish mud.

Comrade Nadezhda and I put the boys to bed. At least half of them were missing. This was happening regularly, now that Yudenich had begun his march. They were too restless, preferring to be out prowling, listening to rumors, poking around corners.

My story—Snezhana's imprisonment in the magical palace of Shinshen—evidently paled in comparison to the story unfolding outside the orphanage walls. The boys wanted to talk about nothing but Yudenich, and why our Red troops kept falling back, and what would happen if the Whites took Petrograd. "Will they kill us?" asked Grisha, an outcast who ate his boogers if not closely watched. "Nikita says they'll throw us out the windows."

Stolid Nadezhda cleaned the corner of her lips with a fingernail, gazing at her pretty mouth in a little mirror. "Nobody's going to kill *besprizorniki*. Who would bother?"

"If they gave us guns, we'd be the best guerrillas," said Ilyusha, as I snugged the blanket around him. "We're everywhere."

"Comrade Tanya's a Communist," said Cross-Eyes. "She's the one better watch out. They'll be stringing 'em up."

"One good thing about being orphans," said Nazar from an upper bunk, "is that you can't be an orphan twice."

The rest trickled back after lights out in twos and threes, laying their coats on their blankets, bringing their boots to bed. I'd tried to discourage that practice but Maxim explained that in the *detsky dom* the staff took the orphans' shoes away, so if they ran away they'd have to do it barefoot, even in the snow. It made me recall Comrade Tanya's advice.

"I heard the soldiers talking," said Makar, the cardsharp, sitting down on his bunk. Boys stirred around him. "They said this is the end. The Whites gonna take Petrograd by the end of the week and you might as well kiss your little asses goodbye."

Squatting by the stove, warming his hands like a grown man, Nikita was not to be topped. "I have a friend who knows this guy in the Cheka. And he told my friend they're gonna blow up the power plant and sink all the ships at Kronstadt so Yudenich doesn't get 'em."

Normally I'd think he was lying, but it sounded about right. A twelve-year-old wouldn't think about blowing up the city's power plant, let alone sinking the fleet. But no electricity? Just when I thought things couldn't get any more grim. With a mixture of dread and admiration, I watched the late arrivals getting into bed with their dirty boots tucked under their arms. Such swagger, all that brave talk, at ten, twelve years old. What did life mean to them? Ilyusha was right, Lenin should arm them. They wouldn't mind dying in a hail of clean, hot gunfire. There was manhood in that.

Iskra was restless, fretful. The temper of the city had infected her as well. I paced the floor, trying to soothe her and reassuring the boys as well as I could. "They won't let them take Petrograd," I said. "The Germans couldn't do it last year, and these ones won't either." Big talk from a girl who couldn't even quiet her baby. "We'll fight them on Nevsky if we have to. You'll see."

The long shadows from the lamp licked the bunks, the bare floors, some of the smaller boys two to a bunk, the flotsam of revolution. And this was just a tiny slice of the millions of children set adrift in this starving, disease-riddled, army-cursed Russia of October 1919. The flame and its shadows jiddered across the silent rows of beds, each boy thinking his own gloomy or heroic thoughts.

Maxim's bunk lay conspicuously empty. I was worried. It was unlike him to stay out wandering after everyone else had come in. I paced with Iskra on my shoulder, calming her, hoping to get her to fall asleep, sat for a while sewing rips in the boys' laundry by lantern light until her fretfulness had me on my feet again. When he finally appeared after midnight, I wanted to embrace him and scold him all at once, but he marched up to me, and his face stopped the words in my mouth. It was white, as if carved in snow. "They found one, Comrade Marina. Come on." Plucking my sleeve, his teeth audibly chattering. "Come see for yourself."

"See what?" I said, resisting his urgency.

He sneezed, wiped his nose on his frozen hand. "I'll show you. Hurry." Pulling at me. "Before they get rid of him."

"Who?" Oh God, oh Christ. "I can't, I'm on duty. And what about Iskra..."

He glared at me. He could see my cowardice as plainly as if it were a yellow-dyed sheet. "Leave her with Hopeless." *Nadezhda*, it meant *hope*. "It's just across the street." He was begging me to join him in his nightmares.

I saw no way to avoid it. I was the one who had called the devil out of the darkness with my stories. Maxim trusted me. I couldn't pretend his fears were just the product of an overactive imagination, couldn't leave him alone with his truth. I owed him this. So I snugged Iskra into her basket, ignoring her squalls, and planted her next to Comrade Nadezhda, who was reading a pamphlet, curling a lock of hair around her finger. "I'll be right back."

"Then I get a break. Fair's fair."

I threw on my sheepskin and hat and shawl, followed Maxim down through the dimly lit lobby, past the blind eye of the desk comrade and out into the night, my hand through the pocket in my sheepskin, touching the gun that I always brought with me, though I knew it was dangerous. If the boys ever found it, Nikita or Makar, someone was sure to get shot, and there would be one more death on my head. But I walked too often through these dark streets, home to Shpalernaya up by the Tauride Palace.

Nevsky lay wrapped in an ice fog. Scarf across my nose and mouth, my eyes in slits, I crossed the wide boulevard, pulled along by my determined charge. Shadows grew in the thin illumination of widely spaced streetlights. The statue of the great Catherine rose like a bell before the ghost of the Imperial Alexandrinsky Theater, and a cluster of dark figures huddled in the faint light of a streetlamp. Maxim shoved his way to the front, dragging me along. I clutched the gun. All around us ranged prostitutes and drunks and the elbow-high faces of the *besprizorniki,* frozen in postures of morbid curiosity as they gazed down at a form slumped against the statue's base.

Someone lit a match, and in the flickering moment I saw the thing they were staring at. A small boy lolled against the base of the statue, legs spread like a discarded doll's, legs ending in bare blue feet. But that was not what they were looking at. At the end of each arm, where hands should have been, a white patch of bone. A cigarette was lit, the flame died.

"What happened?" I asked, or thought I asked, though I could not be sure.

A boy took a drag on his *chinar*—as the kids called their foul butts collected off the streets and out of gutters—and replied out of the side of his mouth. "The Archangel."

I was falling backward into the black void of a dream that I'd kept at bay for so long. The wolf, the colonnade...the rising waters. The hyacinths. He was here. *Run, run,* but there was no place to run. I was glad the light had gone out. I wouldn't have wanted anyone to see my face, my terror. "Anybody know him?"

"It's Eel. One of *his* crew," said the smoker, glancing nervously toward Nevsky, then up in the other direction, toward Znamenskaya Square.

"Probably stole somethin'," the boys ventured, shivering. "Maybe he didn't want to do a job." "Or ratted on him." "Stupid runt." "It's a sign." "He wants us to know."

What was Arkady doing with the *besprizorniki*? Using them—as foot soldiers? As burglars? As anything he wanted. In a sober light, you had to admit, it made perfect sense. They were everywhere, and no one was protecting them. They could easily be swept into criminal life. They lived halfway in the world of myth already, and they had less morality than the most hardened criminal. "Let's go," I told Maxim. If Arkady was here, he would be excited to see this crowd trembling with fear and in awe of his audacity, leaving that child right out on Nevsky Prospect. I knew the man. Perhaps even now he stood among the pillars on the Alexandrinsky porch watching us, smiling that awful ghoul's smile. I made sure my head was completely covered, the scarf leaving my face in shadow as I took Maxim away, his cold, small hand in mine, tight, as together we returned to the orphanage.

"What will they do with him?" he whispered.

He meant the orphan, what would they do with his body. "Bury him."

He put his arm around my waist, leaned into me as if he could draw some of my warmth. "I told you so, didn't I? I wasn't making it up."

I gave him a squeeze. This sweet, anxious, intelligent boy—how could I put a barrier between him and this horror? "We'll be all right. Just stay away from those kids, okay? Don't get mixed up in this."

I could *feel* him out there. The wolf who was always hungry. I was afraid to even think of him. As I walked home with Iskra through the dark of early morning streets, I could feel him, circling out in the trees, slinking along doorways, watching. But how to stop thinking, how to keep him from my door? I could not stop seeing the way the dead boy had been leaned up against Catherine's skirts, as if he'd sought refuge there, but too far below the notice of Mother Russia to be protected. I'd been so rattled when I returned that Nadezhda had offered me a sip of *samogon* from a perfume bottle in her purse. But I wouldn't start drinking. I couldn't afford that luxury. When I saw Arkady's dead body, that's when I would get good and drunk. I would sit on his grave and drink to his health. In the meantime, I would keep watch. I would rub evergreens along the windowsills.

In the queue the next morning, I took my place with the others, the sleeping Iskra warm and smelling faintly of gingerbread under my sheepskin. "Did you hear, they found a dead boy last night," I said to the woman ahead of me. "Near the Catherine statue. An orphan boy."

She shrugged. As if it had nothing to do with her. As if her own children weren't one disaster away.

I wanted to upset her. I wanted to upset someone. "He had no hands," I said. "They'd cut off his hands."

She closed her face like a door. "Well, I didn't do it." And turned away.

Day had broken a dull, heavy gray by the time I arrived home. The worn cards lay on the table in the parlor, the air warm and smelling of old people. They would sleep for another few hours. I rescued my pail from our little room and drained the samovar, changed Iskra, lingering over her little legs. Her perfect hands made me weep. Her rubbery body, slight—the milky skin that summer would cover with freckles like my own. *O blessed Mother, keep and protect her.* Why did we have to live in such a world? I washed her laundry, nursed her, then fell into a black sleep curled around her in our narrow bed.

I was back at the Europa, larger, honeycombed with stairways and halls, passages I'd never seen, corridors and small doors within doors. I stumbled into a room that was Gruzinskaya's parlor. I hadn't realized the two were connected. But instead of the old nobles playing whist, a group of men had assembled to play American poker. And it was the conspirators from the dacha in the woods, the last time I'd seen the Archangel, the last time I'd seen Father, when he'd sent me to my death. Here was Karlinsky, and the spy Konstantin. Father wasn't there, but his Englishman was...and Kolya! He'd been there all along. "One more hand," he said. But he had no hands.

The sight of those stumps wouldn't leave me. It took the pleasure out of playing "Magpie, magpie" with my baby, touching each of her tiny fingers, knowing how easily there could be none. Everywhere I saw dead blue eyes and hair of spiderweb, and his child army, an army of shadows. I choked on the suffocating helplessness of it all, the resurfacing of Arkady, coupled with the relentless approach of Yudenich and his Freikorps. I was mired, and could do nothing but sink deeper into the horror.

News of the murder spread through the dormitories of the orphanage like a bloodstain. The lie was given to the orphans' swaggering and tough talk by their shouts in the night, tears and wet beds. I ended the Shinshen story—Vanka Manka found the egg of Shinshen's soul inside the chest and cracked it open, exposing its rotten contents to the sun and killing the sorcerer once and for all. Quickly I moved to what I could remember of *Treasure Island,* Stevenson's pirates and stowaways. These boys in their rough bunks, the dim light of the lanterns, became the crew of a great ship creaking its way through the night, each alone on his own voyage, together only for a time. Even Maxim would leave eventually. There was no way I could keep him with me, keep him safe. I just hoped it wouldn't be soon.

Our limited time made the small triumphs more poignant. One evening in the canteen, after they'd devoured their meager dinner of fish soup and coarse bread, Maxim came to my chair and thrust a shabby notebook into my hands. "I wrote a poem. In school." I could see him struggling not to smile. The other boys were watching our interaction, so I could not betray any favoritism or it would go the worse for him. But this was the first time I'd heard any of *ours* mention school with anything other than loathing. The older ones mostly skipped that dreaded institution in favor of the far more useful lessons of the street, while the younger ones feigned illness. Maxim opened the tattered book to a scrawl of pencil on the cheap newsprint page.

> *Vadik was a village runt*
> *His nose ran cold and his eyes ran hot*
> *He lived in the corner of a railway den*
> *He rode under boxcars and sang an orphan song.*
>
> *One day he met a sailor Red*
> *He left the rails for a Kronstadt bunk*
> *He once was an orphan, now he belongs*
> *To the Kronstadt fleet and the Kronstadt song.*

"Teacher said it wasn't bad." He shrugged, examining the torn top of his huge old boot, twelve sizes too big for him, he must have stolen them off a drunk. Such hope, such pride in his big, sensitive eyes. Wanting my praise and terrified of it, like a mother protecting her baby from the Evil Eye. Like Sosha, not wanting to lose his little horse. "I can sing it too. Want to hear?" He sang the poem in a minor key, a sweet, true voice.

And I could feel the tentacles of his love reaching through the shattered plates of my armor, searching out my heart.

* * *

Yudenich took Iamburg, less than eighty miles away. You could practically hear their boots on the road. The Petrograd Party seized the moment to announce a "Party Week" — special offer to the citizens of Petrograd to join the Bolshevik Party in this time of greatest danger. Comrade Tanya showed us the announcement in *Pravda*. "No questions asked!" she said. She was working on me and Comrade Nadezhda. "You wouldn't need anyone to recommend you or even to study. It's perfect for you *burzhui*, a time to prove your solidarity. There'll never be a moment like this again. You'll be sitting pretty, better rations, get the housing you want..."

Anyone joining now would certainly be proven in solidarity, that was a fact. But the offer also underscored the party's desperation.

Walking home after my shift in the morning darkness, my bread under my arm, I kept my eyes down, my head and my baby wrapped in the disguise of a heavy scarf, and considered the offer to join the party. It would certainly make life easier for Iskra if I became eligible for other work... But these musings didn't last long. I was too busy watching *besprizorniki* slinking along the house entryways, disappearing into dark arches like feral cats. Shinshen's army of shadows. It was only when I was finally inside the building on Shpalernaya, climbing its toothless stairs, that I felt released from the weight of that ghostly presence, free to consider a warm wash and bed. I hitched Iskra over my shoulder and fished out my key, turned it in the lock.

But something was wrong. The key, rather than opening the door, dropped the lock into place.

It was unlike them — they always fully secured the door, even when the entire Assembly of Nobility was present.

I dropped the key into my pocket, switched Iskra to the other side — away from the pistol — and turned the knob. The door swung open freely. Something was terribly wrong. The firewood was piled high in the doorway as always. The flat was silent, as it always was in the early morning. The samovar stood by on the sideboard—cold to my touch. Discarded hands of whist lay on the green baize. The hair quivered on my neck.

I moved down the main hall, the pistol in my hand concealed in my coat. All the doors stood open. They were gone—the white mouse, old Naryshkin, the Golovins, the Sobietskys, the young ladies. I wandered through the rooms, trying to piece a picture together. The Sobietskys' bedroom had been evacuated in a hurry, books scattered, the wardrobe open, the big manuscript, Count Sobietsky's all-encompassing memoir, gone. Their messy dressing table, powder strewn. Signs of a struggle, or haste? Old Naryshkin's room, as small as my own, neat and dignified, like a retired sea captain's. The Golovins', fussy with bibelots, a squeaky brass bed. I'd never entered any of these rooms. Here was the *young ladies'* boudoir, the flocked wallpaper, the odd wooden beds of differing heights, their mismatched quilts piled high. The icon presided in the red corner, a Vladimirskaya. Forgotten in a hasty departure? Or was it arrest? By Stassya's bed stood a framed pencil drawing of her in profile, no doubt done by some young admirer.

The likely possibility—the Cheka decided at last to end the rule of the nobility on Shpalernaya Street. Perhaps they'd vowed to do a little housecleaning before Yudenich arrived. Matvei on the *Red October* said that whenever an occupying army was forced to retreat, that's when you'd see massacres. That's when pogroms would come, or in our case, Red Terror. Did that mean the Bolsheviks were sure Yudenich was going to win? Were they getting ready to blow up the power plant and sink the ships at Kronstadt? I picked up Stassya Sobietskaya's navy-blue hat with the soft plume and put it on my own head. Very nice, my red hair and the blue…Would she have left it behind? If it was a Cheka raid, they'd be back to clean out the inventory. I had no use for such a hat, and put it back.

Perhaps the families had fled. Maybe Kolya had come back and told them, *Pack up, it's your last chance, don't take anything.* Perhaps they were joining Yudenich, taking flight behind White lines, heading for Estonia, the best chance for escape. No matter how cold the Sobietskys had been to me, I hoped they weren't sitting right now in a Cheka cell, waiting for their fate to descend. Gruzinskaya had taken me in, after all, which was more than Mina Katzeva had done. And old Naryshkin, ever polite, a truly noble man. I wouldn't want to see him in that bloody cellar, or struck by the butt of a Red rifle.

If it had not been for Orphanage No. 6, I would have been here when the Cheka arrived. I might have been swept in with the pack, though I was registered independently with the *domkom*. I held my fingers hard on my temples, trying to suppress the panic.

I had no reason to stay in my cubbyhole while we waited for Yudenich. I chose to occupy the princess's room with its needlepoint hangings and enormous Nicholas I wardrobe. When the house was collectivized—as it certainly would be—one could live quite comfortably inside her yawning armoire. I changed Iskra and washed her diaper in cold water, too tired to boil any. I stoked Elizaveta Vladimirovna's *bourgeoika* and lay down with Iskra in the middle of the aristocratic bed that smelled of powdered wigs and quadrilles and medicinal drops. I wondered how many generations back you could go before you found a woman who had nursed a child here. We curled up in the dusty bedding like rats in a drawer under the gigantic eiderdown, and fell down the rabbit hole of a dreamless sleep.

22 *A Night Journey*

Now the orphanage was my sanctuary from the dark chaos of the city, while I feared returning to the empty flat, dreaded the echoing walk home in the stone prison of the streets. The flat seemed to accuse me when I entered. *How did you avoid their fate?* Guilty, I returned to my servant's room. Just as well in case we had a return visit from the Cheka—this was the room to which I was registered with the *domkom*. And who was I? A stray cat, kitten at my side, shrinking at each noise, flinching at shadows.

The revolution was on the run. There was the sense of life on the edge of oblivion. I paced the boys' dormitory between the double file of bunks, walking Iskra, jiggling her too energetically, and she bawled, upset by my stiffening hands. There was no soothing her. But I was grateful even for my thieving coworkers, for the boys and their excitement at the coming attack. I appreciated their information, what they could glean from the streets. True or not, they knew more than any adult around here, more than the newspapers, that was for sure.

Maxim's bed was empty. I didn't like it when he went out after supper. Nadezhda teased me about my *little boyfriend,* but he worried me. He should have been back by now, most likely with some bit of grotesque news. I wished he would stay inside, wrap himself in the thin blanket of my comfort, but he needed to hear the worst, set it at my feet like a spaniel I couldn't keep home. The Archangel was selling *marafet,* a word I didn't know.

Nikita had sniffed the back of his hand. *"Kalinka,"* he said. *Snowball flower.*

"They sell it to the soldiers," Maxim explained, "so they don't feel afraid."

"The Cheka's all on it," Nikita added. He didn't like being topped by the younger boy. "Makes it easy for them, when they pull your teeth out. They don't care about anything. Where have you been, Grandma? Tahiti?" Teasing me with my *Treasure Island.*

How casually they took it, that the people who had power over our lives were insensate to suffering.

"I've taken it. A lot of us do," said a new boy, Kostya, from a top bunk. He'd been wary of the orphanage's matrons in our aprons and white kerchiefs but now saw others competing to impress me. "On the street, you get cold, and hungry. But you get some *marafet,* you don't care."

I wondered how many of my boys had used it. I'd read about the child addicts in those horrible files behind the amber desk. There were thousands of them. They had their own *detsky dom. Marafet* was cocaine. Stolen from the army, from the field hospitals of the war.

"The Archangel sells it—he sells girls too," said Nikita. "Not for the night but outright, like a rug."

"Let's not talk about this before bed," I kept telling them. "Try to get some sleep now."

But tonight Maxim hadn't returned. Nobody'd seen him. The baby finally fell asleep on my shoulder as I paced the quiet hall from stove to stove, listening to the boys gamble and talk. I could smell *chinar*. The last thing we needed was a fire in here. Then a girl I knew only by sight, a skinny one with a gap in her teeth, stuck her head around the doorway. She saw Nadezhda, then me. She waved me out into the hall, finger to her lips. I gently lowered Iskra into her basket and carried it over to Hopeless. "Back in a moment." She nodded, not even looking up from the battered book she was reading.

In the dim corridor, the girl was dancing from foot to foot with terror, with panic. She clutched my hands. "It's Maxim, he's downstairs, you've got to come!" She flapped her hands with urgency, as if she were drying them.

"What is it? Is he all right?" But she was already running, and I flew after her, down the stairs to the gloomy lobby, the usual loitering boys, veered toward the porte cochere, and there he was, standing with a boy I didn't know, not one of ours. Something was wrong with him. As I neared the entrance I saw he'd been beaten, a black eye, a split lip. He was terrified, his eyes white all the way around like a frightened horse's. "What's happened?" I said as I ran toward him.

Too late. They were all over me. *Besprizorniki*, six, eight of them. I screamed but nobody moved to help, not the dumbfounded Bolshevik behind the front desk, or the oldest boys observing quite coldly, watching these strange children pull me outside by my hair, my arms, dragging me out into the night. Maxim was the only one trying to stop them. He went wild, sobbing, screaming, jumping onto my assailants' backs, trying to pry them away as I grabbed the doorjamb and clung to it. A big redheaded girl kicked my hands away. Then I was moving, out to Mikhailovskaya Street, where a running car waited. A Benz Söhne with a surrey top, another redheaded girl at the wheel.

Seeing that car, I fought like a cat, trying to reach the gun at my thigh, but there were too many of them. I was Gulliver in Lilliput. The first girl worked a rough burlap bag over my head and down around my arms, wrapping it with rope. If only I could get my arms free, I didn't care if they were just little children, I'd kill them all. I kicked someone hard as they shoved me into the Benz. They snatched my boots off, tied my legs.

Now we were driving. The girl at the wheel turned a hard left onto Nevsky, and stepped on the gas. The icy wind filled the open car—it sliced through me like a scimitar.

I pleaded through the rough burlap. "I have money. *Marafet*. I'll pay you. Whatever you like."

Their laughter. "You got *marafet*?" "She's got nothin' but shit-pants." "Oh, look, your boyfriend's following us." The runts jeered and taunted. "Awww, 'e just fell down." "Oww. Oh, 'es cryin'. Boo hoo..." "Slow down, Klavdia, let's see if he can catch us." "Come on, kid, run!"

Poor Maxim! I couldn't imagine what he was thinking. That this was his fault? That he had betrayed me? Ten years old, no matter how tough, was no match for the Antichrist.

I fought to work my hands free of the burlap, get these kids off me. But the crazy motion of the car sent me rolling. The girl at the wheel could barely keep it on the road. We swerved and I hit my head on the car door. She struck something—a curb?—throwing me off the seat onto the floor, the children landing on top of me, screaming with laughter. I roared and cursed. The last time I'd been in this car, little Gurin had been at the wheel. How had I ended up back here, when I had sworn I would fly fast and far? The bag smelled horribly of apples. I'd never eat an apple again.

"Still awake, Comrade?" The sharp point of a knife jabbed me in the shoulder, another in the ass. They laughed as I shrieked curses. Picturing Iskra, sleeping so sweetly in Room III, no idea that Mama was racing away from her, into the night. I knew I had to stay hard for this. At least Iskra was safe, and the farther we went from the Europa, the safer she'd be.

* * *

We were flying in a straight line, southeast toward Znamenskaya Square. I pushed down my panic and imagined us as a moving dot on the map of the city. I listened, *feeling* as hard as I could. Over the roar of the wind and the excited chatter of these infants, the big engine of the Benz Söhne, I reached out to feel the city, hold its design on the page of my mind. I knew its shape like that of my own body, streets crossing canals, bridges. *Concentrate.* But my teeth were chattering hard enough to break, fear and cold redoubling each other's effects, impossible to know which was which.

A change in the sound—the echo of the car's powerful engine dropped away for a moment. It must be the bridge. Anichkov. The Fontanka. I reached out with all my energy to *feel* the width of the river, the openness, and then, the echo returning. Still going east.

"So what's he want with her anyway?"

"Shut your face is what." A girl's voice, commanding.

Now shouts. Harsh, low. Sentries? "Help!" I screamed from the floor of the car. "Shut up, bitch!" The kids kicked me in the head and the stomach as the driver sped on. Two shots rang out—the children shrieked and laughed and cursed in the floridly foul argot of the street. *Put a bullet into us, a hail of them, the more the better,* I prayed. But we careened forward, a crazed hilarity blazing through the quiet.

A different echo—vast. A big sweeping right-hand arc. *Znamenskaya Square.* Alexander III again. I imagined him looking out at this child-filled car racing through the Bolshevik night, and being glad he was already dead. I listened for the shrill of a train whistle, anything to confirm my guess. *Please, O Holy Mother, make this not be happening.* I swore I could taste cinders on the air, the smell of coal smoke.

I twisted on the car floor, desperate to get out of the sack. I'd forgotten nothing of my week in captivity on Tauride Street, I couldn't survive another encounter like that, and this would be worse. Hadn't the Kirghiz said as much? *You should have flown fast and . . . Take care, little hawk. There are bigger hawks than you. Their wings will darken the sky.* I couldn't stop shivering. I knew I should be planning something, but all I could do was think how foolish I'd been to return to Petrograd like it was a game of hide-and-seek. With my redheaded baby, thinking I could avoid being caught…forgetting the depth of the danger. I shouldn't have come back for all the Kolyas in heaven.

I tried to inch the sack up my body, to free my hands. Another series of kicks. "Forget it, shitbrains. Might as well relax." A few more pricks and blows just to make sure I understood that I was completely in their power.

Different paving. Thrumming. I screamed, in case there was another roadblock. "Can't you keep her quiet back there?" Hard little boots, kicking me in the back, head, and stomach. I put my arms around my head inside the burlap.

Rough paving. The crunch of tires. The car stopped. We hadn't turned once since we left Mikhailovskaya. I was bruised from head to toe, my head ached, my breasts ached. This was the end of the road—it had to be the Alexander Nevsky Monastery, where my family was buried in the grand Tikhvin Cemetery. *Please, Dyedushka, Grandmère, help me!* Yes, the Archangel liked a quiet, out-of-the-way spot to set up shop. And this one was cemetery-convenient. The monks must be gone now. Lots of room for his gang of murderous tots.

They hauled me out onto the pavement, dropping me like an old rug. I curled as much as I could not to hit my head. They hauled me to my feet, my soles clad only in stockings on the wet and freezing stone. Untying my legs so I could walk, they shoved me along with kicks and jabs from their knives, talking excitedly, calling me every name in the book, telling me how the Archangel would cut my nose off, my tits, and each of my fingers in turn. Then a creaky door swung open and I stumbled over some sort of threshold. Smooth stone, dry. Still icy, but interior. Another door. Stairs—wood, warmer through my stockings. *One, two, three, four, five…* Then forward. A wooden floor. Warmer now. A long hall.

"Watch your step." A bony little leg caught my shin and I found myself felled, wrenching my shoulder and bashing my nose on the floor. I swore I would kill that urchin. They laughed and mocked me. "Let me go, please oh please oh please," "I'll give you big money," "I'll give you *marafet*," "I'll let you fuck my sister," "Let you fuck Lenin up the ass!" Oh, they were having a grand time. The bubbling laughter of children would never sound the same to me after this.

They dragged and pushed me, again, into a wall. The slam of a door. The dropped bolt.

I explored the space, reaching out inside my bag as much as I could. Small—a closet. They'd locked me in a goddamn closet. The stink of mops, yes. Silence. No footsteps, no whispers, no giggles. They were gone. Terror, wordless and ancient and as absolute as the distance between stars, descended on me now. If only I could reach the gun that I'd lugged around since Kambarka, but I was trapped in his spiderweb, the burlap sack my shroud. Out there, a giant arachnid waited to pull me in on its sticky threads. All that learning, all those aspirations, my hopes for Iskra—for nothing. I would never see my baby again. Oh God, oh God, she would grow up never knowing me, without even someone to tell her who I was and how I loved her. A Soviet orphan, if she was lucky enough to grow up at all. I had played this game like a sucker, a rube. And now I would die.

I couldn't stop my tears.

I thought of Dostoyevsky in his room in Dom 13, on his long walk. I would walk to Siberia too, rather than face Arkady von Princip as a prisoner once more, his human toy. They would hold me down—like in my dream, where the people caught me with their little knives and skinned me in the courtyard, leaving me to walk around Petrograd with no skin. How would he start? With a deer, you hung it upside down, and started at the rear legs, pulled off its skin like a sweater.

Stop it.

I focused on Iskra, picturing her sleeping, snug in her basket next to Nadezhda. She would wake for her next feeding at two, and if I wasn't there, they'd take her to the Infant Department, for Nonna to feed. Maybe Arkady's shadows wouldn't think to look there. And there she would remain, safe. I cursed myself for not teaching her to drink from a bottle, as if I'd always be there to feed her. Would she be stubborn? Would she go on refusing? Wanting what she wanted and only that? Like her mama, the strength of her personality would prove her undoing. Comrade Tanya, you were right, damn you. But she was healthy, she could go without eating for a day or two. If only they didn't think to look for her there.

I thought of Akhmatova, her cool dignity, but she melded into the image of the dark Theotokos, the Virgin of Death. *Have pity on me, a poor sinner.* But I didn't need pity. Dignity was beyond me. I just had to survive.

Suddenly I got the strongest image of Ukashin, as he'd been the day I shot the stag, the Master in his Mongolian robe and astrakhan hat, his energy flowing through his hand into my shoulder, filling me with it, steadying me. Those waves of heat flowing. I knew how to do this. I pulled my life force, or what was left of it, into a pin-point, a red ball, and shot it through the artery of Nevsky Prospect, back to the Europa, back to the baby still sleeping in Room III, Boys 9–12. *I'll always love you, Iskra, whether I'm there or here or nowhere. You'll never be alone.*

But thoughts of death and pain kept flooding in. I was nineteen years old and had taken every wrong road, wasted my talent, burned every friend. Had given birth to a golden child, whose life I'd put in jeopardy just for wanting to return to this cursed place. Would I live to see her run after butterflies, hands reaching to the bright scraps of wing just out of range, the sun kissing her face, leaving its freckled traces? What would happen to her if I died tonight?

Concentrate. Concentrate on the now.

But Ukashin was a fake. Fakir, fraud, usurper.

But not completely.

No, not completely.

A dark, defeated part of myself wished I was already dead, so I wouldn't have to live through these next hours. *The good thing about being orphans is that you can't be an orphan twice.* But I had to live to return to Iskra. I would allow no other thought to come through. If I could just reach my gun, but these ropes, this bag! I twisted and yanked, rubbing my fingertips raw. My stockinged feet ached—the old frostbite had returned like burning flames. *At the detsky dom, they take their boots away, so if they run, they have to run barefoot.* And they did it too. Some of my own charges had done it. In the snow. They'd ridden under boxcars until they'd lost their hearing. They'd done what they had to, far younger than me, weak and malnourished, six, seven years old.

I wasn't dead yet, I told myself. Nothing had yet happened to me but a few kicks and bruises. *You're battling shadows,* Ukashin whispered. *Concentrate. Breathe.* I took big shuddering breaths, in-breathing energy through my skin, *inflowing.* Whether it was real or not, it calmed me enough to think about this bag, and the ropes that held it around my hips and waist. I thought of Volodya's fat pony Carlyle, who took a big breath when you saddled him, so he could exhale later and loosen the girth, making the saddle slide sideways when you mounted—his idea of a joke. I wished I'd had the sense of that fat horse, but I hadn't had the presence of mind.

I exhaled and twisted against the bag, hoping to loosen the ropes. I pushed upward, pulled my shoulders tightly together. After several minutes, I had enough room inside the sack to move my arms. I pushed with my elbows, centimeter by centimeter. I clawed the burlap until I found an imperfection, a little hole in the cloth, probably from one of the brats stabbing me. I stuck a finger through and started working on it. Two fingers, three! I got all four fingers through. It was old and rotten, and after a few tries, it gave way with a satisfying rip. I worked my arm out and went for the gun under my skirt in its makeshift holster.

Gone.

I sat back against the wall. *Breathe.* Of course it was gone. All those hands, they'd probably found it in the car. *Ha ha.* Handed it up to the girl in the front seat, the driver with her red hair. The joke was on me. All this time, carrying that thing around so long I hardly felt it. For just this day. So prepared. Just a joke. So like my life.

I tore the bag off and got my head and shoulders free. It was something anyway, to have that thing off my face, breathe the moldy air, untie the ropes. They'd been secured with a simple square knot. It was my own struggling that had tightened it so. I just had to push an end back through and it fell away.

Although the situation hadn't changed much, at least I was free of that bag. I could think, move my arms. I felt around on the floor for something I could use, something sharp, but there were only mops and brooms. I stood and examined them for the one whose handle seemed heaviest. A mop. The splintered wood bit my palms, but I tried jabbing with it, feeling its weight. It was hardly a spear, but it was something. I would dash it into the face of the first human to walk through that door, child or Archangel. I would not hesitate.

I sat on my heels, resisting the urge to curl on the floor and sleep. I had to be ready. Where I'd dreaded the opening of that door, now I couldn't wait—it was my one chance to fight my way free. I pushed all other thoughts aside—my child, my future. *I was the hunter.* Concentrated only on the door, the hall outside, the rooms on this floor, this wing of the great monastery. I *felt* my way out into the complex, room after room. A great silence. Either they'd killed the monks or the monks had fled. The place was empty like a derelict palace. Full and empty. Empty of monks but full of ghosts, the shadow world of orphans and criminals.

I practiced concentrating energy and radiating it—warming my feet, warming the room—and whether or not it really worked, I felt warmer and more confident. I'd brought my child back to life with that energy, when she lay like a stone in my arms. Now I would be a bogatyr at the crossroads, surrounded by skulls and ravens. I would be the Tsar-Maiden.

I *felt* them coming. Light feet, dragging, all out of step with one another. Disorganized. I felt them in their ragtag enthusiasm, their giggles, their brave whispers. The door was unbolted, dimness illuminated by lantern light. I uncoiled from my closet floor like a spring, leading with the mop handle. I caught one of the girls on the jaw. She staggered back, shocked, while the smaller boys made attempts to attack with their pocketknives. I jabbed the putrid mophead into their bluish faces, pushing them back, feeling like Gulliver. I swung the handle to clear a wider space around me, forcing them back toward the stairs, when the skinny girl with the sharp teeth of a ferret pointed my own gun at me.

Had they not had it, I would have made the stairs, could have run for it, I knew I could outrun these runts or beat them with the mop. I was the one who had brought the gun into the equation. I had stacked the balance against me. "Drop it," she said.

I did as I was told.

"The Archangel wants to see you. Get going."

Would she know enough to pull the safety off? I grabbed one of the children and twisted his arm, feeling like a monster as he started to shriek, but I would not be skinned alive as Arkady drank in my terror like milk. I had my own child waiting for me. I held the boy between me and the gun as I moved toward the stairs, the boy kicking me with his heels, clawing at my arm, swiping at me with his little knife. He turned it backward, the little shit, and stabbed me in the leg.

The girl fired.

The boy sagged against me. His blood was warm, soaking the front of my dress, my stockings. Hot, sticky. I was covered in it. I was holding a corpse. I dropped the boy, who had just been alive. Dead, because of me. A child about eight. Not so much younger than Maxim. "You shot Snotty!" another boy shouted.

The hot gun barrel pressed against my nose. The girl's eyes were old and dry.

The blood spreading out on the floor, soaking my stockinged feet.

"He said not to let her get away. Come on, you." She grabbed me and shoved me, stumbling, over the body, toward a thick door. "The Archangel's waiting."

23 *The Sandman*

They knocked at the wide oak panel. I could smell the child's blood, clinging to my dress, still warm. Blood and death, and I had arrived in the heart of it. The murderous children opened the latch and shoved me in ahead. "We brought her, *Gospodar.*"

Gospodar. Lord. It was how we once addressed the tsar.

The cavernous room was lit by fire in an open hearth, and a tall candelabra dripping with fat candles. Incense, the smell of beeswax. An animal stink. They stood around me, anticipating reward, avid with the hope of my punishment.

He stepped into the trembling light, their Lord. Taller than ever, his spiderweb hair flowing over his shoulders, the long Scandinavian face glowing white in the gloom. The Baron Arkady von Princip. My captor, my lover, my nightmare. It was I who had called him out of the darkness. It seemed the everyday world was the dream, a rickety theater set, while beneath it ran a black river, this monstrous world of myth, which was the true world.

He'd fitted himself out in a black monk's cassock secured by a wide belt, a heavy gold cross dangling over it. On the forefinger of his hand, a huge ring. *Gospodar.* His holiness, the Archangel.

"Klavdia shot Snotty," blurted the dish-faced boy. "He's dead."

"It wasn't my fault, *Gospodar,*" pleaded the ferret-faced girl. "She made me do it."

"I told you she was dangerous." A smile played about his wide mouth with its thin lips. He stretched out a bony bejeweled hand. The girl approached him with my pistol on her upturned palms, like an offering to a god. He took the gun, sniffed it—newly fired—hefted it, and then laid it carelessly on the table among the books and papers. Taunting me.

"Now leave us." He dismissed them with a wave, as if clearing the air. His wine-colored slippers were worn out at the toes. I met his blue gaze, the white wolf that had been stalking me in my dreams all this time, waiting in the shadows of the column-forest. *The Archangel isn't himself...* Was it true, Arkady? *Perhaps,* they said.

"What should we do about Snotty, *Gospodar?*" The second, stocky girl insisted. She would not forget her fallen brother.

"Take care of it," he snapped. "And don't disturb us."

They quickly retreated, like courtiers not daring to turn their backs on their lord.

Once they were gone, he smiled his lipless smile. "Hello, Makarova. It's been a long time." That gravelly rasp I knew so well.

I should never have come back to this cursed city. It was his city, his labyrinth. And not with Iskra—God! What was happening to her back at the orphanage, my baby, my Spark? My mouth went dry, my throat, as if all the liquid in my body had turned to sand. He came closer, his hands tucked into his sleeves. What did he have in there, a knife? Garrote?

He circled me, examining me like a dealer to whom a piece of art had been returned, his mouth in its coquette's moue—my blood-spattered stockings, my dress, my hair wild from my fight with the burlap bag. The air was thick and fatty, and my ribs throbbed where the kids had kicked me, the stab wounds from their little knives ripe with tetanus, I was sure. I swallowed, hoping not to vomit, hoping not to choke on the acid of my own fear.

"You've aged," he said finally. "Another year or two, and no one will ever guess you'd been a beauty."

I would be happy to have two years. Ecstatic! It was all I could do to strangle the whimper forcing itself into my throat, resist the urge to fall on my knees and beg for my life, clinging to his cassock's skirts. I had forgotten the force of his physical presence. But I could not give way to hysteria. I had learned the hard way that a display of weakness brought out his cruelty, his lust to hurt you further. All I could feel was my shuddering breath, my heart seizing like a fist as he circled around me. The creak of his belt, the cross rasping the rough fabric of his cassock. His smell, wormwood and damp earth. Sweat trickled down my forehead, stinging my eyes, running down my neck into my collar. His face, peering into mine—marred by sores and dark spots. He didn't look well. He breathed in my ear. "Eighteen months. Had you forgotten me?"

Yes, I had forgotten, pretending it was just a bad dream. Just a mistake. Imagining that it was over, that he had gone on to other things. It was I who had forgotten exactly who this man was. This was always here, waiting for me.

"You've been clever. Brushing your scent away like a little fox." That rumbling voice I knew so well—low, gravelly, insistent, hypnotic. His hands inside his cloak. "Even when Shurov was here, I kept wondering—where was the girl? Sometimes I wondered if I'd killed you after all."

Kolya had been here! Or was this just a ploy? You could never be sure with Arkady. *Look down, look at nothing, think nothing.* I was not here. I was in a different thread of time, where there is no Arkady von Princip.

"Why did you return, Makarova?" he said into my ear. "Had you heard that I was…incapacitated? That I was drooling, being fed kasha with a bib on my chest?"

"It was hardly my choice. Your brats dragged me here, remember?" Choking out the words, my bravery thin as air.

"You're disappointing me." He frowned. "Of course it was your choice. You'd hidden yourself away, like a little rabbit in a black velvet bag. And suddenly—out you pop. Walking around, brushing your hair, tucking in the kiddies. Why, if not to be found?"

I met his eyes. All pupil. No longer that piercing, clever gaze, no—a jittering, wild stare.

He reached out and ran his fingers through my disheveled hair. I shuddered at his touch. Sweat pooled in my armpits, the backs of my knees. He liked a room hot enough for orchids. The stab wound in my leg throbbed, the dead boy's final act.

"But now you're home."

Alone with the minotaur, surrounded by bones, I stifled the cry that was exploding upward, it tore in my throat like a sharp-toothed rat.

He poured wine from a ceramic carafe, the liquid almost black as it splashed into the glass. That mocking smile as he held it out to me. "Blood of Christ?"

The relief to smell grape and not the earthy copper of blood as I lifted it to my lips. He'd probably broken into the monastery's wine cellar. I drained it fast, hoping he wouldn't see my hand shake. Too fast. A thin stream escaped and trickled down my chin. He took the vessel from me, and wiped my face with his finger. He lifted his own glass and drank. Now he opened a leather-covered book with his scabrous hand, hands that had always been so well kept but were now as mottled as his face, and his nails were long and dirty.

He smoothed the parchment pages. "So many centuries of human thought devoted to devils, revelations, wonders. Look at this."

It was a book of martyrdoms. Saint Catherine on her wheel. Then, Saint Bartholomew, flayed alive. My nightmare. He stopped at the martyrdom of Saint Agatha, her breasts displayed before her on a tray, like pears in wine. My shivering increased. Would this be my fate? Parted from the breasts with which I'd fed my child? I found myself missing the old Arkady, a man merely running a gang of criminals. Not *Gospodar* in a cassock and cross.

"You have to appreciate the imagination," he said, cocking his head to one side, considering the ways in which a human body could be harrowed. "I'm surprised the Cheka didn't take these when they came for the rugs and the priests."

He poured himself another glass. What I would have given for just a drink of water. *Stop it.* I had to listen now, I had to think. Find a way out of this room. I could twist that chain around his neck until his eyes popped out of his head. Knock the candles onto the table, ignite the papers, grab the gun...

He cleared off a spot among the books, the pistol seemingly forgotten. But I knew him. He had not forgotten it. I, who had once tried to cut his throat. And the scar on my palm was a daily reminder of my failure. From inside the breast of his cassock, he produced a squat metal tin, opened the lid. Inside, a powder, very white, like icing sugar.

"Know what this is, Makarova?"

"Cocaine. *Marafet*," I said. "Stolen from operating rooms at the front."

"From both sides. Red, White, it's all the same." He scooped up a pile with a long pinkie fingernail, set it on the back of his hand, divided the pile into two, then snuffed them up his long aristocratic nostrils, one, then the other. He tapped out more, held out his hand to me. I thought of our child addicts—whole *detskie doma* set aside for them. Orphans would do without food, without shelter, just to have this.

But I would not give myself over to him until I had to. He would have to win me inch by inch. I would not make it easy. I turned my head away.

He paused. I knew what he was thinking. *Never say no to me.*

But then he shrugged. A small victory. "It's your loss." He called over his shoulder, "Olimpia?"

A chain scraped against the parquet. My heart jolted upward as if it would leap from my mouth. What was there, a wolf on a chain? A bear?

To my astonishment, from the shadows emerged a naked girl, limbs glowing by reflected firelight, maybe fourteen years old, slight as a deer. Small breasts, pronounced ribs—and her hair was red. Like the other two girls. *They all had red hair.*

And I had hoped he'd forgotten me.

His eyes met mine over her head as he held out his hand for her. This was in tribute to me. In my honor.

She snuffed up what was offered, straightened, wiped her powdery nostrils. Her dark eyes glittered. And then I saw—she was covered with scars. An intricate web of lines and dots like an engraving on a ten-thousand-ruble note. My wounds were nothing compared to this. It must have taken him months. Did he numb her with cocaine? She kissed his hand—for what? Scarring her like that? Chaining her like a wild animal? For I saw, he had a leather collar on her neck, a chain through the loop. I sweated through my woolen dress, my hair was damp. I could smell my fear, like dirty metal, like the dankness in drains.

The girl pressed into him, half hiding. The Kirghiz had said the Archangel was not himself, but as he watched, seeing I fully appreciated his masterpiece, I knew that in fact he *was* very much himself. This had been in him all along.

The scarred girl peered out at me, a pale streak behind his black form. *Olimpia.* It meant something. *Who was Olimpia?* It itched, like a rash. Poor girl, he'd scarred even her face. She stared out at me through a forest of arabesques like a panther through jungle grass, her eyes dilated with the drug. Her blood-red hair merged with the scars as if to continue the pattern.

"Olimpia doesn't speak," he said, stroking her tangled hair. "The perfect confidante."

Had he cut her? But once I too had been a silent girl after my time with this man. Sometimes words just fail. Sometimes what has happened to you is so terrible, your mind can't hold it. Her chain told me she'd tried to escape, maybe more than once, before he put that collar on her. He'd never done that to me.

Then I remembered—*Olimpia.* The mechanical doll in Offenbach's *Tales of Hoffmann.* You wound her up and she danced. The very symbol of captivity.

"And you're the Sandman." I had to resist him as long as I was able, before he did this to me. I had to show I knew him, was not intimidated. I still had a mind, a voice, a self. If only for a few more hours.

He smiled. That wide mouth, like a toad before swiping a fly. "You always were quick, Makarova. I never have to explain myself to you. You don't know how I've missed you, really. You have no idea."

It was something I could do for him that his children could not. He could talk to Olimpia and the others all he wanted, bathe in their adoration, but none of them could hope to understand him. They couldn't satisfy his craving to be known. *Ask me a question.* An Olimpia couldn't soothe his vanity, appreciate his wit. Not one of them could fathom his loneliness, to which their slavish, absolute devotion ironically sentenced him.

Olimpia whined. Had she seen that she, who had endured so

much, was only a facsimile, and I the original, in whose image she'd been created? Yes, she had. And she was jealous. Ridiculous, and yet I could imagine myself after six months with him, chained and tormented, praised and petted, utterly dependent. You could come to something resembling love. Lost between hatred and gratitude, fear and admiration, erotic pleasure and humiliation—anything was possible. He could become the world for you. And what would you have without him?

But I gave him a taste of another mind at work. I could enter the loneliness of his labyrinth—at least partway. "So how long have you been the Orphan King?"

He ran his hand down her back, her hip—gazing at her with affection, as if it had been someone else who had cut her, chained her, kept her stinking.

"It was a gradual transition. The robbery business had grown out of date. All the rubies in the Peter and Paul Fortress might buy you a tin of *marafet*. Whereas a side of beef could buy you an army." He sighed, returning to his hideous book.

"And your men?"

He shrugged. "A man learns one thing, and that's what he wants to do until the day he falls into the grave."

Had he killed his gang? I wouldn't care if he had. All except for the Kirghiz. What had they done for me? Listened and joked while I was locked in that room on Tauride Street. Played cards. I hoped he'd killed them all. "Did they object to your new business? Cocaine, young girls?"

"You like the idea of gunfights and daring daylight robberies. You think drugs and young girls are beneath me. But drugs and young girls are the very staples of civilization." He turned to the girl, squeezed her shoulder. "*This is the rock upon which I will build my church.* There's an endless supply, and you can use what you can't sell." He grazed a line from her mouth with a long dirty fingernail. "And children are so loyal. It doesn't matter what you do. They defend the brute father, the hysterical mother. Tell me, what do children want?"

I thought of my baby, sleeping peacefully in Room III, having no idea Mama was gone, Mama the Archangel's prisoner, on her way to death or worse. "A family," I said.

"No, no." He brought his face close to mine, fire in his mad blue eyes, my small figure there in the reflection of the candles. "They want a lord. Someone into whose power they can give themselves absolutely. And I am the Lord of Lords. If I am on their side, what have they to fear from God or Man?"

He picked up the gun and tucked it into his belt. "Come. I want to hear everything. Tell me where you've been, who you've been fucking. Bring the wine." The tin disappeared inside his cassock.

He picked up the candelabra and, impervious to the hot wax dripping over his skin, he carried the flame into the shadows. The gun winked at me in his belt. "You're thinking again," he said, not turning. "I advise against it. One step outside this room, my tots will fillet you like a salmon."

I could already feel this girl's collar coming around my own neck. He set the candelabra down on a low table. A broad divan swam from the darkness. It spewed stuffing as if from multiple stab wounds. He sat on it and patted the cushion next to him, but I'd shared one too many divans with the Archangel. I knew what it was to serve our Lord. I took a rush-bottomed chair, across from him.

"Oh, don't be like that." He pouted. "After all we've meant to each other..." He removed my gun from the belt and stuck it behind the cushions. Daring me to try to take it. Olimpia knelt right on top of it. Her arm around his neck. *Get the gun, Olimpia!* I could smell that divan—it stank of bodies, turned earth, sex, bad dreams. He must sleep there at night. Probably with the girl. Maybe with all of them, piled onto him like sled dogs.

He was humming. *Sollst sanft in meinen Armen schlafen. Death and the Maiden.* His love song. *Softly shall you sleep in my arms...* as he poured another glass of black wine. "Give this to your new mistress, Olimpia." It trembled in her hands. She would rather throw it in my face. "Nicely... You don't want to displease her. She's a very dangerous person." He encouraged her with a nod, as you would coax a bashful three-year-old.

The girl came around and held out the glass, her dark eyes sullen with banked resentment. She stank like a beast. I remembered how lovingly he'd washed me in *levkoi* soap—my hand still on fire where he'd seared it on the stove. His soaping of my body, my ruined hand, the smell of dooryard stocks...

I drank. The goblet now in my scarred right hand. It was all starting again.

When I lifted my eyes, a sight cut across them, like the lash of a whip.

On the wall over the divan, lifelike in the flickering flames, hung a large icon, a life-sized crucifixion. And affixed to the Christ's painted arms—the small hands of the orphan. Like purple flowers, with nails through the palms.

Was killing and dismembering of the orphan boy not enough? He had to do this? Yes, to remind his flock just how far he would go. In case anyone forgot. And he lived with it every day, as another man would grow plants on the windowsill.

"You like my painting?" the Antichrist asked. His eyes alight with fun. *The Archangel is not himself*...But he was. He'd only been restrained before, by the world, by the men he worked with. Now there was no one to stop him.

I was never going to get out of here alive.

He glanced up at the wall above him. "Do you find it too baroque? But Christians are literal, with their relics and stigmata. *The body and the blood.*"

On the wall alongside it hung a Vladimirskaya Theotokos clutching her child. Was that to be next? A real-life mother and child?

Iskra!

I must not think it. He could read my mind, and he must never know of that redheaded infant waiting for me back at Orphanage No. 6.

"Imagine how it feels to be a city's nightmare," he said in a voice that pressed onward, hypnotic, rumbling, drawing you forward. "The power of that. Like this story you've been telling. Shinshen—isn't that his name? Shinshen the Immortal. Not original, but compelling."

I felt a thousand knives pop open inside my skin, piercing me from the inside out. That cursed story. Why had I even begun to tell it? I had forgotten the power of words. They shaped the world. Naming, they called forth the thing you named. That story was the Ariadne thread that led him out of his labyrinth. He'd followed it through the streets and canals until he'd found me. I'd been telling Arkady a bedtime story every night—a tale starring himself. It had landed me here more surely than the train from Vyatka.

"You've only added to my legend." He stretched his arm along the back of the divan under that horrible Christ, stroking the girl's hair. "When I heard it, I knew you hadn't forgotten me. However far you'd fled, Bukhara or Samarkand, you hadn't been able to stop thinking about me, the Sandman. Shinshen the Immortal."

And it was true. He lived in my brain, squatting there like a poisonous toad. So careless of me, to have thought he would have forgotten me. When perhaps my hands would become the Vladimirskaya Theotokos's, and the Child—oh God. The Child...

"Ask me a question, Makarova."

"Why would you do that?" I spluttered. "Kill that boy. Cut off his hands, and do *that* with them?" I pointed with my chin. "How can you sit there with *that* over your head and talk to me as if it's nothing?"

He stroked Olimpia's cheek, tracing a whorl from her nostril around her cheekbone. "What good is a lord unless he is terrifying? My children would have been disappointed if I'd simply given him a stern lecture—such as I'm sure your liberal papa would have done with your pathetic brother Sergei. That's no way to run a kingdom."

Had the girl seen it? Had she heard the screams? How could she twine herself around him that way, just under the hands of a murdered child, and kiss that repulsive mouth? Though some dark part of myself knew exactly how. Life had trapdoors, and once you fell, the water swirled in the opposite direction. Up was down, down was up. You came to accept the laws of your new universe, its boundaries exactly the shape of your lord. You submitted. I'd been halfway there myself when he'd made the mistake of taking me to the dacha that night. I'd always thought that was the worst night of my life, but it had been a moment of grace.

What a fool, to have come back here. To have thought the nightmare was over. When it was just waiting for me.

I would never be free of him. Not when we both were above ground. One of us had to die. I remembered when Varvara had said she would capture him and kill him for me. And I said I wanted to do it myself.

Now I had only Iskra to weep for me. *Alas.*

The fire crackled and spit into the black gloom. Its flickering light revealing the holes in the ceiling where the plaster had fallen through, the stains on the walls. Arkady's sordid, tawdry magnificence. Yet he was all the more dangerous for being half lost in a dream. I felt the madness calling, like a guitar string that resonates to the one beside it. Persephone had eaten only six pomegranate seeds in hell, and I had eaten far weirder fruit than that.

The Archangel applied another helping of cocaine to his long nose. The girl came for her share, but he elbowed her aside and offered the next application to me. It gave the soldiers bravery, they said. But I didn't trust it. I had to keep my wits about me. I would not end up on that chain. Or on that icon of the Vladimirskaya Theotokos with my child.

"You might as well," he said, lifting his hand again. "You aren't going anywhere."

We'd see about that.

Olimpia whimpered, but he sniffed it himself and put the tin out of her reach on the low table. Sulking, she curled into herself at the far end of the divan, picking at the shredded upholstery arm over which her chain dangled.

"This is all your doing," he said, wiping his nostrils. "After you, I saw what a bore my life was, squeezing the last ruble out of the city of Petrograd—what kind of a life was that? The luster was gone, the pleasure. You'd left me hungry for poetry. Look at this. Olimpia, show her."

But she pretended she hadn't heard him.

Never say no to me. He grabbed her by the chain, fast as a mongoose, swept her out of her seat and down onto her knees. Her eyes glittered tears of humiliation and rage, as she lifted her arm so I could more closely examine the lines, the whorls, and the dots of her flesh.

"Now, tell me that's not beautiful."

It was. Fine work done on a living canvas, no less monstrous than the tiny hands of Christ. He would do this and probably fuck her while the blood dried. If this was what he'd done to her, what did he have in store for me? I wasn't going to wait to find out. I'd rather die all at once.

"When I gave you my poem—it was so crude. I regret it, I do..." Apologizing? For carving into my back like a cook scoring a ham? Like a boy gouging his name into a birch tree? Those letters I had to explain every time I removed my clothes, in every bathhouse, at the shore, with every lover. If I ever had another lover. Or saw the shore, or stepped again outside this room.

"After you left, I met a doctor in need of cash," he said, licking his finger and rubbing it in the leftover powder, tracing his lips with it. "I bought his entire medical bag, quinine to forceps, including a perfect set of German steel scalpels. Straight blades and curved ones, some sharp on the inside and some on the outside. I could take out your gallbladder if I wanted to." He smiled coyly.

A wave of hot nausea passed over me. I remembered dissecting a cat in biology class, or rather, Mina doing it. The pins, the glistening organs. Saint Agatha.

Olimpia crawled to him, her scored buttocks catching the light, like some big tailless cat. How long would it take to become Olimpia—destroyed mentally and physically, unselfconscious as a chimpanzee, incised intricately as a Byzantine plot? Even if she could escape, how would she live? She'd have to join a circus and display herself next to the lizard boy and the bearded lady. Or become a brothel's specialty item, *for the discerning client.* She could run to some savage land, live among the Berbers...

I just prayed they'd had the sense to hide Iskra. That red hair, all of the orphans knew her. Would they know enough to put a cap on? Hide her among the babies of the Infant Ward?

"What are you thinking, Makarova?" The Baron's fingers fluttered at his lips. "Plot, plot, plot. Remember the night you thought you could get the best of me? Your failed little rebellion. Let me see it."

Other men might recall a sleigh ride, a certain small hotel. But our romantic reminiscences consisted of attempted escapes and strange sexual encounters deep in the labyrinth, upon heaps of bleaching bones.

"I don't know what you're talking about."

He raised a snowy eyebrow. I could feel the collar around my neck. The candles oozed, drowning themselves in wax, guttering out one by one. I turned the palm out to him and held it so the candlelight illuminated the shiny surface of the burn.

"Come closer. My eyes aren't what they'd once been..."

Said the blue-eyed wolf, *"Granny, why are your eyes so big?"*

He brushed the scar with his fingertips. My flesh tingled. He kissed the palm. The girl whimpered and tried to pull him away.

"Is the thing jealous? Here." He took off an amethyst ring and pressed it into her hand. She put it on her forefinger, like a golf ball on a willow twig, and scuttled off to play with it. Over our heads, the crucified hands begged me, *Do something!* The air was making sparks in the darkness, and the smell of decay and chamber pots lingered under the fatty candles, and a cloying sweetness. The unmistakable smell—why had I not noticed it before?

On the windowsills, he was forcing hyacinths into bloom. Phallic columns rose from the cups. That pure life in this foul lair with the leaking roof and ruined plaster and hacked-up furniture. The flashing splinters of purple light distracted me, and the smell of the blooms—the thousands of humans Shinshen had enchanted, a field of sorrow. *And if you walked through it, you could hear their whispers, Alas, alas.*

The girl held the ring up to the firelight, her tangled red hair streaming onto her shoulders and down her back.

"So what happened to your men? Borya, Gurin." Trying to remind him there was a time where he hadn't decorated his walls with the relics of murdered orphans, when he'd still had some human qualities.

"Gone. Fled, departed. *Auf Wiedersehen.*" He held up his cross to the three directions.

Had they objected to working alongside children, thinking it beneath them to hang around barracks selling *marafet* and young girls? Or had they balked at his increasingly bizarre state of mind? Even the most evil of them could have recognized the madness of the *object* on the wall above his head.

"I prefer *besprizorniki.* They don't haggle over percentages, they demand nothing but to serve me." He watched the girl with the ring. "A sniff of cocaine from time to time and they're as happy as rats in a wall. What could be better? The perfect operatives." She burrowed her way under his arm. "People go out of their way *not* to notice them. Plus, if something happens to them, well..." He shrugged.

"Poor Snotty."

He chuckled. "Yes, poor little waif."

Were you listening, Olimpia? Did you understand you were as expendable as that boy? Just because Arkady fucked you and spent hours cutting you, didn't mean you were any more valuable to him than any of the others.

But she was too busy playing with the big amethyst ring—holding it up to the light, trying it on her fingers, threading it into her hair.

The blood in my dress had crusted over in the heat. Snotty had never had a chance. I would have to account for that someday, among my many crimes. But today, I could be as savage as I needed to be to get back to my redheaded baby.

"Ask me something, Makarova. Something you're just dying to know." His arm resting on the girl's shoulder.

I reached out and poured myself some wine. "Why did you let me go that night at the dacha?"

He pursed his mouth into that ridiculous moue, mocking the naiveté of my question. "To see what it felt like, of course." He crossed his legs, balancing his worn slipper on the toe of his old sock. "I had already tasted the lord's vengeance. I wanted to know how his mercy felt. What would it be to let you go, to give up something rare and beautiful. It pained me to see you fly across the frosted fields, disappearing in the moonlight. If you only knew what I gave up for you, my lovely, treacherous Makarova."

He has not forgotten you.

The child's hands pleaded with me. *No! Don't walk down that road!*

Softly shall you sleep in my arms...

But how many roads were there? He'd narrowed them all. And that child couldn't know what had transpired in that room on Tauride Street. He didn't know what I knew about this man. Those weird moments of connection amid the outrages, the bizarre playfulness along with the pain, the sexual intensity along with the domination. Confessions, and not only mine. I saw a crack of light in the darkness.

But then my breasts tingled. And back at Orphanage No. 6, an infant was waking. My milk let down. Within moments, my dress was soaked. My body, wanting only to feed, to nurture, had betrayed me. And Iskra. I quickly sat back, away from the candlelight, hoping he could see only my silhouette. I crossed my arms to staunch the flow. I had to distract him, get him talking. "Did Akim tell you he saw me? On Kamenny Island?"

"Long afterward. That's exactly what I meant. Men think first of themselves, even the loyal ones. Akim was too quiet. It's the quiet ones you have to watch. *Cassius has a lean and hungry look.*"

Akim had salved and bandaged me, tended me like a mother, when this man had carved his poem into me. Yet the Kirgiz hadn't sympathized with me overmuch. *If you don't like wolves, stay out of the woods.* He could have freed me, but never did.

My bodice was drenched in milk. My poor ignorant body—all it knew was that it was time to feed the baby. It didn't know what danger it put us in. And that girl sitting right where I'd seen him shove my pistol, oblivious at the chance of freedom.

"Why did you come back, Makarova? When you were warned not to return. You knew the price. And yet, here you are."

I put my chips on *noir*. "I didn't want to," I said. "But it was eighteen months—I thought perhaps you might have forgiven me." *My treacherous Makarova.* Yes, Baron, it was my specialty.

"Bored, I imagine. In whatever outpost you'd gone to ground. You're a passionate woman, you're like a fire in the snow. You didn't belong out there in the straw with the hicks. So you took your chances. Knowing what you needed was a consort, a king. A lord." He recited from the Greek. "Recognize it?"

"Homer?"

"He lifted her up into his golden chariot and bore her away lamenting."

The abduction of Persephone by the Dark Lord. To be his consort in the Underworld.

Alas, alas.

The girl tried turning his face toward her, the way a child tries to get the mother's attention, hands on his long gaunt cheeks, but he swatted her away. "Stop it, Olimpia. The grown-ups are talking now." He poured more wine.

What I wanted was water, but didn't dare draw any more attention to myself than I had to. I wanted him caught up in his words and to forget to look at me, let him be lost in a dream where we were king and queen, ruling the dark kingdom side by side as jaguars prowled and flowers wept.

"Tell me how you've missed me. Tell me about Shinshen. But first, why don't you get out of that wet dress?"

24 *Death and the Maiden*

The reflection of candlelight in the black windows drew my desperate gaze. I could break one, climb out, jump. It was only the second floor. I could survive the fall, run home barefoot. The orphans did it, escaping the *detsky dom*. Find Iskra, and run. I'd have to get out of town, even if it meant on foot. But I hadn't saved my girl from the Virgin of Death just to give her to the Archangel.

"Take it off. It's all right. Don't be shy, it's just us."

"I don't want her watching," I said, stalling for time.

"Olimpia likes to watch," he said.

In other words, *he* liked Olimpia to watch him. I wondered how many women he'd brought here and made her watch him fuck them. Or maybe it was just his orphans. He came to where I sat on the rush-bottomed chair, pressed up behind me, lowered his voice, speaking in my ear. "I smelled it on you when you first came in. *La maternité*." He ran his hands over my shoulders, my neck, sniffing me.

I was in danger of vomiting.

The girl hissed, her upper lip drawn back over her teeth. I swear she was growling. She was going to be worse than useless in any plan to escape. She would attack me herself if she could, so jealous was she of her place in this hell.

He unbuttoned my buttons one by one, patient even when they stuck. Tormenting the girl while indulging himself and terrifying me—what could be more delightful? Except to call in all his foot soldiers and let them watch too. "I've thought of your body so often in these long months." His rumbling voice still held its erotic charge. "That scent, your hair. Are your nipples still pale? Are you wet, Makarova?"

He unlaced my camisole, woven by women I actually knew, and pulled it off over my head, freeing my breasts, hot, full, sticky, aching. I'd never missed a feeding before. He groaned. "No, they're dark. Enormous." He squeezed one, and the milk spurted out like a statue in an Italian fountain. He leaned over and licked me. "Sweet." He lowered his face to my breast, and fed where Iskra's sweet lips took their nourishment. To my shame, it felt good, the full breast releasing. My innocent body, my culpable soul. Feeling a desire, with Iskra in danger. Tears slid down my face, as I stretched my head back, the better to let the milk flow.

How long had he been watching me come and go at Orphanage No. 6? Like Hades watching Persephone picking flowers. Enjoying his power. All those nights I'd felt him there in the dark. I again prayed that Nonna had the sense to cover Iskra's ginger hair. They could be looking for her right now. Perhaps he wanted a redheaded Holy Family to accompany his bizarre Christ. *Don't. Don't think. There was no Iskra.*

He pulled me to my feet, one arm around my waist—how strong he was, still. I could feel him inside the wool of his cassock, bumping against me as he caressed me. The girl crouched, bleating, trying to get his attention. Staring at me, my body big and earthy compared to her small, scarred self—a woman's body, heavy boned, full grown, and his hands on me, the tentlike protuberance.

"It's Shurov's, isn't it?" he murmured into my neck. "You wouldn't have dropped a litter for just any Ivan."

"No. It's my husband's." He was still obsessed with Kolya. Even now.

"Kuriakin? That oversized baby?" He laughed. "No. I can't imagine him packing the ammunition. No, it's Shurov's. *The Circassian cavalier.*" He knew that story too, the one I'd told the little girls about Iskra's father. Maybe he knew when I'd gotten off the train. Maybe he lived in my head.

"So how did it feel? The alien presence inside your body. Sucking your lifeblood like a tumor. And then the birth—all those hands and feet? The enormous head." He shivered, imagining the sordidness of my delivery. "Descending, tearing your flesh, squalling its way out. Was it terribly, horribly painful?"

"It's Nature, Arkady. We're all in her hands. Even you."

He stopped kissing me, pulled away. The look on his face, one of disgust. As if I'd shat in the wine. "Nature? That giant sow with hairless piglets burrowing in at its bristly teats, squealing and rooting? I despise her. If there's death, I want to do the killing. If there's pain, I want to inflict it." He grimaced, showing his yellow teeth. "Nature, the termite queen. White and blind, enormous, the abdomen extended, eating, living, ejaculating offspring. I won't be used by that."

How he loathed what he could not control—the animal self, over which he had no say.

He was now pacing the room, agitated, distracted. I had to keep him talking. Yes, yes, the terrible termite queen…"But Nature uses you with every heartbeat. Your cells divide, living and dying without your permission."

"I won't be used by her! My will is my own, my pleasure—my own. Not like you, spawning, gushing fluids." He stopped at the table to look at his horrible book.

"Our pleasure exists because Nature uses us." I began to inch toward the couch. "Time moves on, and we can't do a thing about it." How fast would I have to be to reach that pistol? Would the girl side with me or with him? Would she cry out, warn him?

"What can we do? There's the Roman solution, of course." He turned the page, glanced up, and caught me in a half crouch, moving toward the cushion. The next moment, he was beside me.

Instead of the gun, I picked up the tin of *marafet,* sat down in the seat he'd abandoned. "I think I'd like to try it after all."

Makes it easy for them, when they pull your teeth out. They don't care about anything. That's what I needed. Not to care about anything but putting a wrench in the inevitable.

"You'll like it. Everyone does." He seated himself next to me, took the tin from me and scooped out some of the powder with his nail, depositing it onto the back of his hand, dividing it in two. I lowered my head and sniffed as they had done.

It burned. And a bitter taste descended the back of my throat.

Then numbness. I glanced up. *So?* Was this it? He lifted his hand, indicated I still had more to ingest. I took the other one, which burned even worse, making my eyes water. But suddenly the room brightened. Darkness that had seemed impenetrable now showed me its secrets. It seemed less sordid, and facing this way, I no longer had to look at the terrible Christ. My heart churned, missing beats.

"There, that's not so bad," he said. Like a nanny, having given you your castor oil.

But this was more than not bad. I felt my alertness expand, my terror stepped back to give it more room. The air shimmered. My headache vanished, the stab wound, my bruised ribs where the children had kicked me. No wonder the orphans liked this—no wonder. You stepped aside from all the damage to body and spirit. I felt reckless and savage. The room around me illuminated as if lights had been turned on—the fire, reflections off the bookcase doors, the mirror, the jewels.

The girl tugged his arm—she wanted more—but he brushed her off. When she became more insistent, he cuffed her, shoved her. "I'm talking to Makarova now."

The girl coiled, drawing her knees up to her breasts, keening. *Yes, Olimpia, this is your master. This is your lord. I'm taking your place and he's going to put you out with the cat.*

The drug plashed inside my brain like a snowball crashing against a window. All hail Queen Persephone.

I wondered when they had last slept.

Arkady snaked his long arm around my waist and drew me to him, bending me back in his embrace, biting me, gripping my haunches, licking my hot leaking breasts, and I was amazed how it felt. I wanted him in my own disgusting way. He aroused me. I could see the termite queen, fat and blind and working her monstrous jaws below the earth, expelling her thousands of nymphs, so pale they were transparent. It was a sexual image. I found it grotesquely compelling.

"Tell me how you couldn't stay away," he growled in my ear. He was stroking himself under his cassock. "Tell me I'm the only one who was ever enough for you. That's why you're here. You don't have to be embarrassed about it. The others couldn't satisfy you. Eunuchs, imbeciles, that preening poppet Shurov." That gravelly voice, urgent—he was talking to me and to himself. He grabbed my hand and wrapped it around his member, that monstrosity, and worked it up and down. I remembered it all, but my fear stood to one side and let this crazy desire well up. "I terrify you, but who else can give you this? Who knows you like I do? I know you've missed me. I forgive you. You can't imagine how many people have waited for my forgiveness in vain. But I give it to you, my bride, my queen."

The girl on her knees flashed her teeth from behind the forest of her scars like a monkey in a Rousseau painting. Like a William Blake tiger. I was taking her place. Yes, he was mine, Olimpia, he always had been. I had returned to take my seat on the black throne. Maybe I could drive her mad, and she would light the drapes on fire.

"Tell me no one excites you the way I do," he said. "Tell me what you were doing in Samarkand or Arkhangelsk, waiting for me."

"I was here the whole time," I said. "Watching you. I stalked you through the streets—did you sense it was me? I wanted you, but I was afraid, so I watched. You felt me, didn't you? When you fucked her, you imagined it was me. You never wanted to fuck children. You were waiting for me to return to you. Remember how we'd made love? Like gods. You don't need this girl. Tell her to go away."

The girl whined and leapt between us, trying to separate us, grabbing for his cock. He took her by the collar. "See this?" he said to her, her chain doubled in his fist, his face twisted with desire. "This is a woman. This is your queen. Apologize!"

She spat in my face.

He slapped her backhanded, flung her into the corner of the divan—her mouth a mute square, her eyes brimming alive with wounded fury.

"I thought I could never love a woman." He was groaning, stroking himself while running his hand over my body, my thighs, my buttocks. "I thought all women were disgusting bags of fluids,

tears, monthly blood, *milk*—but look, I don't find you repulsive.
There's no one like you..." His voice, that compulsive rumble, that
obsessive flood. He shoved me back onto the divan, fumbling his
cassock aside. His organ rose whitely from its root. He held himself out so I could admire it. "I remember that night, your flesh so
inspired me, I wrote you my love letter." His blue eyes black with
the drug and his own desire, the darkness of the world coalesced in
them. "Let me see your pussy. Let me smell your flowers."

I was two people now, Iskra's mother and this thing, Arkady's
black queen. Both at the same time. No one was watching, no one
was keeping score except our audience of one. And then he was on
me, in me, and I was glad for the cocaine, which both urged me on
and let me step away, to watch myself, out where it was crisp and
clear and horror could not reach me.

"Tell me how you've waited for me...how you dreamed of me.
Makarova, there's no one like you..."

As he thrust into me, I plunged my hand into the cushions. There
was nothing behind them but loose stuffing. It was all a joke. A cosmic joke. Queen Persephone, the queen of this filthy prison, this
freakish dungeon. With Hades, her Dark Lord, plowing her fields.

A sound rose above Arkady's groans, a sound like the wind keening. Behind him, she stood, holding my pistol in both hands. She was
not so far gone as all that. She was terrifying, magnificent. Pointing
it at us. Was this how I would die, killed by this tormented girl? If it
would be so, I was ready to stop this nighmare. But Arkady looked
up, panting, following my gaze. Disengaging, his organ springing
free as he moved toward her. "Put that down, Olimpia."

In that moment, I *saw*. The last human part of her remembered
the tortures she'd suffered at his hands, the abasement. She laughed
or growled, baring her teeth.

"Obey me!"

She fired.

The bullet caught him in the chest. His mouth opened in surprise.
And he toppled onto me. I shoved him away and he fell on the table,
overturning it, and from there to the floor, where he lay gasping,

the blood bubbling from the wound, spreading black under him. She fired again, squeaking, like a rabbit's scream, but there was nothing left in the cylinder. The gun had told its six lives.

His gaze flew from her to me, above him on the couch. "Makarova..." He gestured for me to come closer. His erection, I noted, still rose from his monk's skirts, as if word of his shooting hadn't arrived yet. He reached out for me. "Marina..." Why was he still alive? Would I have to kill him myself, the way I'd once killed animals still alive in their traps?

"I thought you said...Shinshen...was immortal." And he laughed, coughing up blood, turning his head to breathe. A last joke.

Banging, shouts in the hall.

Don't hesitate.

"Alas," I said.

And stepped down onto his neck, cracking it under my heel.

25 *The Annunciation*

Crows cawed, pecking through the tatters of the night. A thick, icy fog had settled on the monastery during the night, and rising out of the whiteness, I could see the vague outlines of Holy Trinity, featureless and abandoned, and the Church of the Annunciation.

The Annunciation...The Archangel Gabriel came to the Virgin with the prospect of the divine, but he was also the Angel of Death. Yet the Archangel had died and I had lived. I was free. I was on my way.

Here was the Benz Söhne, parked halfway up on the curb. I'd taken my boots back from Klavdia, and her coat, but hadn't thought about the car. My pockets jingled, heavy with the boys' pocket-knives, though my skin still lay on my body, intact. And someone was waiting for me. Someone precious.

I had lived. I was going home.

I passed under the arch and through the broken gates, turning onto

Nevsky Prospect. How bright it seemed in the milk-white mist. The sights of early morning began to appear and their ordinariness moved me. I'd been locked in the no-time of Arkady von Princip, the halls of the Dark Lord, only to find myself returned like Orpheus to the Soviet dawn: orphans selling newspapers, people leaving for work, lighting cigarettes, rubbing their eyes. Fortunate humans, who'd never seen a crucifix adorned with real hands, or a girl etched like an illustration in a book of woodcuts. I had cut her collar, but she only went to him and knelt in his blood, washing herself in it, covering her face and limbs as he gazed up into nothingness. Shinshen the immortal had met his soul, and died.

How beautiful everything was to me. A skinny horse and driver emerged from the fog, rattling by me, *clippity clop*. A man pushed a baby pram full of firewood. A boy called out, *"Yudenich takes Gatchina!* Pravda*'s got it, four kopeks, right here! Lines to Moscow still free! Petrograd holds firm!"* There was still a world, where news went on and armies marched and mothers took children to school. And soon that would be me, taking Iskra in her little pinafore, a bow in her fox-red hair. I didn't care anymore if Kolya came home. This was the important thing — these people, queuing at a bakery. People in leather jackets and old overcoats crowding into a government office. Soldiers loitering outside their Red Army club. It was all still going on. I had a job, a place on this earth, and a child waiting for me. Here was the train station, that cathedral of hope and despair, millions on the move, train-deafened orphans... But my child wouldn't be among them. Not her, the flower of my life, my tiny sun.

I hurried onward. Above me, the horses of the Anichkov Bridge reared and struggled with their grooms — never free, never subdued. The human condition. I sped past the old roller rink where I'd once skated with Volodya and Seryozha, now a movie theater, and past the Hercules club, still closed at this hour, and Mina's building at Liteiny, where she'd locked her heart against me. I did not feel that grief now. It was nothing to me, compared with rejoining Iskra. I redoubled my pace, a stitch in my side, but grateful I didn't have to run barefoot, as many an orphan had done before me.

I rushed past Alexandrinsky Square and its terrible statue of Empress Catherine atop her bell. Never again would the Archangel haunt the dreams of the city's orphans. They'd have only the cold to fear, hunger and ordinary death. No monsters or myths.

Now the Europa's huge blocky form took shape—its roofline, the dark facade. I began to run, my boots flapping on my feet. Strange, a crowd had gathered on the corner. There was never a crowd in Petrograd now. But people stood shoulder to shoulder, their backs in overcoats, their breath like steam from a manhole. "What's going on?"

"A jumper." "Some kid." "They do this all the time."

My mouth went dry. I pushed my way through the onlookers. The matrons were all here: Nadezhda. Alla. Polya. Tanya. Who was tending the children? They turned to me, their expressions equal parts horror and guilt. The way they tried to catch at my arms. Now I was fighting my way to the front. "Marina." "Marina, don't." "It's nobody's fault."

Clusters of children. Cross-Eyes, tearful. "He kept saying *I didn't mean to.*" Nikita was wearing my sheepskin. "We thought you was dead." Makar, hollow eyed. "He's been cryin' all night."

> *I didn't mean to.*
> A jumper.
>
> Oh God.
> *Maxim.*

The solid bulk of Matron blocked my way. Her firm grip on my arm. "Don't. The ambulance is on its way—"

I broke from her and shoved into the center of the crowd. Two policemen stood over a body.

Patched pants,

298

the too-large boots.
　　　the son of my dreams.
He thought he had betrayed me, that he had killed me.

I wrestled myself clear, knelt at his side.
And then, I saw.
　　　Tight in his arms,
　　　　in the curl of his body,
　　　　　a smaller form.

Her face
　　　beneath his chin

　　　　　Their blood interlaced.

Why

Did he think he was saving her?

　　　So she would not be

　　　　　orphaned
　　　　　　　like him?

I released her from his arms.
　　　Held her close.
　　　　Someone wrapped my sheepskin around my
shoulders.
　　　　　Her blood leaked
　　　　　　onto the pavers

　　　　　but no flowers bloomed.

As if in sleep
　　　long-lashed eyes

the bow of lips
> the tiny hands

Oh Maxim…
> *couldn't you have waited?*

The panic
> in his ten-year-old mind

Iskra!
> that perfection

Iskra!
> the wheel broken.

Iskra!

> my spark.
> my little fox

Was this the way our tale ended?

The ambulance came. Men lifted Maxim onto a stretcher, carried him to the wagon. I didn't want to leave him alone, but he was too big—how could I carry them both? I kissed his dear face, watered it in my tears as I held Iskra bleeding to my chest. His poor face—even in death, so worried. *Where do they bury the orphans?*

They tried to pry Iskra away from me. I bit the man's thick hand. They would not take her. *May lightning strike and thunder roar, and the world drown in my tears.* Arms reached, hands clutched. "You're making it worse." "Come, let them do their jobs." "She's gone now, Marina."

"No!" They could not have her. "She's not an orphan!" She would not go into the ground where the orphans go, their arms small comfort around each other's necks.

The ambulance men tried to *talk sense.* "You've got to give her to us, *devushka.*" "We can't stay here all day." They had other bodies to gather, other deaths to reap.

"She can't be alone, she's only a baby. I'll bury her myself! Please, I have a plot. For the love of God!"

They gazed at each other, at Matron. I backed up into the fog, let its nothingness slide closed behind me.

Once, death had been just a rumor, romantic, veiled in poems. Now it had a name, a color, a weight. Her body was as light as a rabbit's. I sat on the steps at Gostinny Dvor, in the empty arcade, my child wrapped in a kerchief someone had handed me. The Fates had waited for this moment to take the single thing I could not bear to lose. My baby, the broken weight of her, her blood seeping into the soft sheepskin. Where such life had been — nothing.

I sat there gasping, as if I'd swum a great distance, as if the air had thinned, there was no oxygen left. *Iskra, my love, my heart.*

Buildings appeared and disappeared as I wandered, eyeless, with my daughter in my arms. Stopped finally on the Chernyshevsky Bridge, wrapped in fog. The water below flowed green-black, gelid with coming ice. Once I'd stood right here with Genya, gazing out on a moonlight-painted expanse in dead winter, the Germans on their way. So many futures written on this river's empty page. And now I saw nothing.

> *I could part the waters today. Green-black*
> $\qquad$ *down*
> $\qquad\qquad\qquad$ *down*
> $\qquad\qquad$ *down*

Yes, this was the day. The day of all deaths. But how to put her down to climb the balustrade? I could not put her down, and I couldn't climb it holding her, and I would not drop her in alone. I just stood, holding her, my empty lungs, my broken life.

A man stepped out of the fog to smoke a cigarette. He eyed me as if he knew what I had in mind.

I moved on, wrapping the fog around myself.

Foot after leaden foot, I drifted. Perhaps I would wander the fog forever with my dead infant in my arms, haunting the city, listening for the chimes of lost cathedrals. Heavy carts trundled into view and vanished. Factories. Barracks. Poor people, speaking softly. Soldiers.

Which god had I slighted? Had I forgotten a burnt offering? Neglected to paint my doorpost with the blood of the lamb? What kind of a cursed thing was I?

> *Iskra.*
> *Of all the mothers to have been born to.*
> *You, a perfect child, otherwise.*

I recognized the canal—I had marched here once, dug trenches. How could the earth bear so much weeping? How was it that there was still dry land?

I asked a faceless man, "The Novodevichy Cemetery, is it far?"

"Keep on straight, little mother."

Her tiny body, tinier than I could imagine, she had seemed so much bigger in life. She who had been more alive than anyone. The wonder in her eyes, her baby laughter. The way she'd grab my lips, blow bubbles. Where did you go, Iskra?

From the depths of the white, church bells rang dolefully. My legs, heavy as anchors, followed the sound of their chimes to Novodevichy Convent. They still had a bell ringer.

I stood in the back of the church with my baby in my arms, my dead baby, dumbly watching the candles burning in their stand. But it was too late for intercession, Iskra Antonina needed only the earth now, Mother Blackearth, the roots, the darkness. A coffin was being carried out of the chapel. A family walked behind. I followed them into the old cemetery. I had no one to walk with me. I wished Kolya had seen her, I wished he were here. But what difference did it make in the end whether you mourned together or alone? In death, you're always alone.

The family stopped at a grave new-opened, a lone priest. The gravediggers took off their caps. Small candles were lit. I listened out of sight. The family had to lower the casket themselves.

Vechnaya pamyat'
Vechnaya pamyat'
Vechnaya pamyat'

Eternal memory...

Standing in the frosty whiteness, I was grateful she'd been born in summertime, that she'd seen trees and green fields, and the pure Blokian blue of the sky. I would find a place to bury her where the boughs would overarch her in summer, deep in Mother Blackearth, who does not need our pleas or flattery, who knows what's needed without being asked.

I wandered the unkempt graveyard, and found a four-sided plinth near a bank of shrubs under some big bare trees. It would be easy to spot in the spring—if there was ever a spring. I set her on the frosted leaves in her blood-seeped blanket and began to dig, hacking at the heavy clay with Arkady's hatchet. But in the end, I could not dig a hole deep enough. I sat like a child with a shovel at the shore, and wept.

The shock on the gravediggers' faces when I emerged from the fog told me what I looked like, with the bloody sheepskin and Iskra in my arms. "Please," I begged. "Help us."

It took them just a few minutes. I tried to snip a piece of her hair with a penknife, but my trembling fingers couldn't make the cut. I'd never cut her hair before. It was so shiny, so fine. I could not do the smallest thing. The shorter man mercifully took the knife from me and quickly cut off a small ginger lock, rolled it into a piece of newspaper he was using for cigarettes, folded the ends.

I laid her in the grave myself. Tucked her in at the breast of the earth.

Good night, Iskra.
good night, sweet girl.
Mama will come as soon as she can.
We sang, *"Vechnaya pamyat'."*
Or they did.
I gave each man a penknife in payment.

How was it I did not go mad?
How long must I go on?
The strong must suffer everything.

Madness would be a blessing.

I wished I were stone.
If I were stone
I could make of myself a headstone.

The sun had gone out. I lay curled on her grave, smelling the new-turned earth, seeing those hands dancing over the edge of the basket by the fire. The button nose, her impish eyes, her smile, her swoon as she suckled…my arms so empty, my breasts so full. I would stay here and die like a dog, I would howl from loneliness, I would stay until it crushed me. I took the gun out from Klavdia's coat pocket under my sheepskin. Each cylinder, empty. Empty. Just when I needed the release.

I had worried about all the wrong things.

So much fate coiled in those round metal nests. If just one chamber had been occupied, I could put an end to this unbearable tale. A caesura, midsentence.

"I worried about something like this." The short gravedigger standing above me. His good kind face, a wide moustache like Maxim Gorky's. He took the gun from me, that useless thing. "Come with me. I'll take you to my wife. She'll give you some tea. It's not far." His hand as rough as shoe leather as he pulled me to my feet. He smelled of earth. Blessed silent Mother.

A rutted little road. The gravedigger's ground-floor room. His tiny wife at the stove, boiling cabbage soup, a somber little woman in a patched apron, hair like ashes. A thin-faced child tugged at her apron. So there was a child. That's why he was being so kind. A child, thin, but not in the ground. The wife said nothing. The gravedigger dragged a stool to the table. "The girl just buried her baby. She was gonna shoot herself." He put my gun on the table. The woman crossed herself. "It's a sin," she admonished me. The child gazed at me with flat gray eyes. *But what about God's sin against me? Letting Maxim jump off the roof with my Iskra? Why don't you ask me if I forgive God?*

She put a crust of bread before me. I could only imagine what a gravedigger made. "Keep the gun," I said. "You can sell it." She exchanged a glance with her husband, who nodded. She took it and put it high up in the red corner. No Chekists would come to visit this hovel. I gnawed the bread. She lit the samovar for tea. My ignorant breasts yearned for my baby. They didn't understand there would be no baby, ever again. We drank the carrot tea in silence.

"I still have milk," I whispered. "I could feed your son."

She lifted him onto my lap. I opened my coat, my dress, held my breast out to him. At first he shrank from it, but she pinched it expertly, and the milk came squirting out onto his lips. He tasted and drank greedily. He had teeth. I never saw Iskra's first tooth cut that smooth gum. Her child was hurting me—my nipple still sore from the Archangel—but I didn't pull away. A small blessing—Iskra never did have to drink from the breast he had touched.

"Was it your first baby?" the gray woman asked.

I nodded.

She sat next to me, stroked her child's curls. "This is my third. God took the others."

God took them. How simply she said it. As if God had reached into a fruit bowl and selected a juicy apple. If I believed in God so completely, there would be nothing to do but submit. A mysterious God who gives and takes for his own reasons, far too deep for mortals to understand. But I didn't live in that universe. I lived in a universe of chaos and sudden catastrophe.

"You'll have to stop the milk," she said.

Standing on the bench, she took a bundle of dried herbs from a beam she was too short to reach, though I would have been able to unhook the bundle without even straining. She gave it to me, a powdery silver-leafed plant. "It's sage," she said. "Chew on it or make a tea, until the milk stops. If you get lumps, rub them with your fingertips. Like this." She illustrated with her fingertips, little circles. "You're young. There will be others."

"No. No more."

The gravedigger was cleaning his nails with his new penknife. "You have a husband?"

I nodded. My two husbands. Neither of whom had seen their daughter, the perfection of her, the force of her personality. Nor would they ever.

"You'll have more children, then. A houseful of them."

No. No house. No houseful. No children. I shook my head, dripping tears into the child's hair, like raindrops.

"You have so much love in you still," the wife said, her hand on my shoulder. "Look, you love my son. God has filled your heart with love. How could you go on without someone to give it to?"

I had no idea.

After a while, she took him off me. He stood, gazing at us both. He was so short, standing there, like a tiny man in his cut-down clothes. Iskra never got a chance to stand. Not even crawl.

The wife made sage tea for me. After I was done, she embraced me, kissed me three times. "Go home." She patted my hand, which still bore my daughter's blood. "Live, and God bless you. Make a confession. Tell Theotokos of your sorrows. Only the Virgin can console you."

I passed a church by the Obvodny Canal, a narrow little church with a single eave over the door, and obediently, hopelessly, I entered. Inside, a couple of old women lit candles. The icon of the Virgin gazed out of her frame with her son on her lap, so helpless. His death foretold before his birth. As Iskra's had been. I kissed the icon, made the sign of the cross, lit a stub of candle. A priest watched me, but I had confessed enough. *Now you know,* said the Virgin. I was not consoled.

26 *The Petrograd Card*

It seems we are tied to life by bureaucracy. My papers were too precious to abandon. Even with feet like pilings in the shore, I was forced to return to Orphanage No. 6 and recover my bag, my labor book, my ration cards. So awful to understand that I would still have to eat, and sleep somewhere, and continue to draw breath. I kept my eyes averted as I walked past *the place* ... and entered the amber foyer. I shut my ears to the children's clamor. I saw nothing. Alla Denisovna rose from behind her overfull desk. "Marina—" But I walked right past her, down the hall, past the clattering typewriters, into Matron's office. No one stopped me. I was terrifying—like a Gorgon, I would turn their flesh to stone.

Matron was writing something at her desk, a heavy woman with a heavy glance and a heavy job to do. "Close the door," she said, not looking up. "They brought me your things." My bag was there, Iskra's basket. My hat and gloves.

She examined me with a cool brown gaze. "Do you want to tell me what went on here last night?"

It was only last night? I was as mute as Olimpia. My breath froze in my throat. If I spoke, a monster would come out, something murderous with a thousand razor-sharp teeth. My breath tasted of sage and earth.

"All right," she said, folding her thick hands. "What do you want to do? Do you want to come back to work?"

I shook my head. I didn't want to see human beings ever again. I wanted to put screws into metal, sew shoes. I wanted a job in a telephone exchange.

"Do you have anyone you can stay with, friends or family?" The empty apartment on Shpalernaya yawned like a tomb. I shook my head again, staring at my feet, the worn toes of my boots—a surprise to see them on my feet. I thought of Maxim's oversized ones. Had anyone saved them? "You'll come stay with me, then." She lowered her eyes to her paperwork. It had been decided. "Just for a few days. Until all this settles out."

People came and went, ignoring me as I lay on the bench in the corner of Matron's office, my face to the wall. They talked about evacuating the orphanage. Worried about the food supply. I wrapped myself around my grief, pressing it to my aching womb. I thought I would raise my child like a little gift in a ginger-colored box, to present to her bright-eyed father. Not realizing how I would love her, how important she would become to me. Bigger than life. Each eyelash weighed more on the scale of my heart than this whole building. The arrogance, thinking I could just wheel into Petrograd as I had Izhevsk and Tikhvin. I didn't know yet if she was left- or right-handed. Whether she liked to paint, or sing. She'd never have a first kiss, a first love. No doggies, no skating, no picture books in bed. No summer days swimming in a river under the trees.

It won't live, Mother had said.

That curse. She was right, but certain news you should keep to yourself.

I lay on the bench, staring at the same crack in the green wall that looked like Italy. I picked at it. This room, green walls to six feet, then the white of old teeth. The smell of the children's dinner cooking. My breasts ached. *Time to feed the baby,* they said. Time to feed a baby that didn't exist. My breasts were so ignorant, so hopeful. I could go upstairs and feed the infants, but instead I chewed sage leaves. I was a mother no more. The taste of my milk would be as bitter as wormwood, all my grief distilled.

I ate dinner in the canteen with Matron, and nobody spoke to us. Then I followed her home through the dark sleety streets to a good-sized room on nearby Millionnaya Street. All her own, nicer than most. There were books in cabinets, a diploma from the Bestuzhev Institute for Women. Photographs of broad-jawed, broad-shouldered ancestors. *Intelligenty*. She didn't try to talk to me. She didn't tell me she was sorry. She just handed me tea and read the papers. I lay on the divan and followed the fancy molding around the ceiling, oak leaves and acorns—around and around.

What do you call a child without a mother? An orphan.
What do you call a mother without a child? A mother.

The next day, Matron let me stay in her flat alone. "You won't do anything to yourself?" she asked. "I'm trusting you." Her normally impassive face was even heavier. I lay on the divan and watched light move across the room, which faced south. A warm light, kindly as it touched the walls, fingered the books, whitened the glass of the photographs, traveling all day, and then disappearing into the blue of dusk. It was dark when Matron came home again and turned on the lamps. There was a hunk of bread for me, a piece of hard sausage, but I wasn't hungry. I didn't care if I never ate again.

The next day the same.

After that, I returned to the orphanage with her, ate in the canteen, my mouth making the right movements, but things catching in my throat. Matron deposited her bulk between me and the others, to give me some privacy. I could feel my coworkers wanting to deliver kind words, regrets, but there was no reason to talk, nothing they could say would make any difference. The children were staring, I could feel their eyes burning into my skin. I didn't want to love them anymore, my boys, my girls. People died too easily in this world. *They had been there. When she was alive. When he jumped. Any of them could have stopped it.*

At night, we walked the few blocks home in the freezing rain, careful not to twist an ankle where missing street pavers filled with water, passersby shuffling along listlessly. The White advance was coming. Any moment now. Yudenich was in Gatchina, he was in Tsarskoe Selo, a half day's walk away. And nobody was doing

anything about it. We had given up. We were just waiting for someone to end it. Someone handed me a pamphlet and disappeared into
the dark.

PEOPLE OF PETROGRAD, THE BOLSHEVIKS HAVE ABANDONED YOU!
EVEN NOW YOUR LEADERS ARE EVACUATING,
LEAVING YOU TO YOUR FATE——

I crumpled it, threw it into the street. The end was coming, and
no one had the energy to lift a hand to save himself. Exhausted, ap-
athetic, despairing. Waiting for death.

I wondered if this pamphlet was from my father's group, planning
for the arrival of the Whites. In a different time stream, he would
have seen Iskra, his brilliant granddaughter, Iskra Antonina Nikolaevna Gennadievna Shurova Kuriakina. Would he have dangled
his gold Breguet for her baby hands to reach for, let her hear the
hour's chime? His wedding present from the woman who was once
my mother. Where were they now? Alive or dead? The watch I
imagined lay now in the pocket of some English diplomat. The little
chime, exchanged for the White cause.

In her sweater, which she wore like a cape, knees covered with
a knitted shawl, Matron read the newspapers. The progress of
Yudenich, the retreat of the Red forces. Poor Petrograd, this cursed
city. Cursed from its birth, born alive over the bones of forty thousand. Now about to be crushed. As my child was crushed. The party
had jumped off a building with the city in its arms.

Would I prefer that it had never been built? Would I prefer that
Iskra had never been born, so I wouldn't love her? So I wouldn't
have to mourn her?

One morning something had changed. People walked urgently—
they'd stopped dragging their feet. They carried shovels and picks.
During breakfast at the canteen, forcing kasha down my throat,
which fought the groats—my morning contest—a short, grim-
faced woman, one of the typists of the day shift, marched up to

Matron. "We've called a meeting," she said. "The orphanage committee's waiting for you."

We followed her to the office, Matron walking briskly but unhurriedly, rolling stiffly like an old sailor. And I trailed behind, no one. A shadow, a smudge on the wall.

In the large room, the workers' representatives had gathered. Kitchen staff, laundry, maintenance, administrative, matrons. My coworkers, that collection of shirkers, bureaucrats, absentees, and petty thieves all talking at once. Nobody noticed me on the bench in the corner. Comrade Tanya rapped on Matron's desk with her knuckles. "I've just been at the district soviet," she called out as the others quieted. Her normally made-up face was pale and shone with an unfamiliar fervor. "I want to report to you—Comrade Trotsky has returned to Petrograd. He's going to lead the defense of the city."

Trotsky was here. Comrade Trotsky, who'd turned the tide of the war. I turned over to listen.

"As the elected representative for Orphanage No. 6, I've been asked to read Comrade Trotsky's words." Tanya opened a folded pamphlet, cleared her throat, and began to read in her halting voice: *"Petrograd, wounded but still strong, is in danger. Comrades, we took too much from you. Now we are trying, with feverish in-ten-sity, to give back..."* Her singsong voice, the stumbling mispronunciations, nothing like his force, his energy. But it didn't matter. I knew what he sounded like, had heard him speak at the Cirque Moderne. And now he had returned, to save us.

"If Petrograd were to be taken... Soviet power would still stand. But in the last few days, when the fall of Petrograd began to seem a real possibility... an electric shock ran through the country... and all said, 'No!'"

He'd come to shake us from our torpor.

Tanya described the Red successes in the east, chasing Kolchak, the battles for Tambov and Kozlov. *"There may be retreats and advances in this struggle, but there is one retreat, Comrades, which we will never permit ourselves, and that is a retreat eastwards from Petrograd."*

I surprised myself by sitting up.

"We are at present going through a critical period on the Petrograd front. The new re-in-force-ments have not yet been con-cen-tra-ted and de-ployed...Every day and hour now has co-los-sal im-por-tance for you. On other fronts we could withdraw weak-ened di-vi-sions fifteen or twenty versts to the rear and re-form them...but here, on the Petrograd front, we cannot allow ourselves the luxury of withdrawing."

Fifteen or twenty versts—they'd have to withdraw to Finland.

"We realize, of course, that they will not take Petrograd. A city of a million people cannot be carried off in the clutches of a gang of a few thousand men. But they can inflict damage, cause cruel loss of blood."

I remembered Izhevsk. The gibbets standing in the square, ropes still attached, where the Whites had killed a thousand people just three weeks prior to our arrival. I could still see that bloody wall outside the munitions plant. How sick I'd been...my enormous belly. The beginning of my labor. Iskra and I, we had never been apart from this war, not really.

"We will not hide from the broad masses of the people the dangers, the blunders and me-na-ces, that lie in wait for us. Our Petrograd card, which is in-fin-ite-ly dear and important to us, is in danger of being covered. We must defend ourselves not only along the nearby line of Detskoe Selo but here, in the very heart of Petrograd."

Petrograd like an ace in the green baize center of the gaming table. How I'd struggled to bring her here, so she could grow up a Petersburger. Was I a fool? Should I have jumped into a hole and pulled a lid over us? Would she have been safe then? I was too exhausted to think of it. We lived inside a war. There were no safe corners, not in Kambarka or at Smolny itself.

"Comrades, those who are perhaps pre-par-ing to de-scend on Petrograd in a night raid, so as to cut the throats of sleeping workers, their wives and children, must know that...Petrograd is already work-ing fev-er-ish-ly...to make of its districts a series of im-preg-na-ble forts..."

Now I understood this morning's shovels. There might be graves, but first there would be trenches.

"This is a huge la-by-rinth of a city, which covers a hundred square versts, a city with a million in-ha-bi-tants, in whose hands there are mighty means of defense..."

The cotton that had stuffed my ears since Iskra's death had loosened, and I saw his strategy. He was going to use what he had—streets, canals, buildings, and people. Petrograd itself.

"Comrades, in these days, these hours, you must mobilize for internal defense. Everyone who is not capable of, or cannot be taken away for, par-ti-ci-pa-tion in ex-ter-nal defense...working women—wives and mothers able to wield rifles, revolvers, and hand grenades no less well than men—will defend in the streets, squares, and buildings of Petrograd, the future of the working class of Russia and of the world."

Glances caromed off the faces of the staff—the red-faced laundress, the sour typist. Nadezhda, in her white apron and kerchief. Matron herself, as square and firm as a fieldstone. And me, my useless, childless, hollowed-out self.

"Last night we proved that when the alarm has been sounded, the proletariat of Petrograd is able to respond...and if circumstances require this, it will remain at the ready tonight and tomorrow night, in double and even treble strength..."

Could I put my grief aside for two days, to protect my native city, this precious scrap of stone and water? Would Iskra want me to lie on a bench and turn my face to the wall? Was that why I had called her *Iskra?* It would dishonor her to do nothing but weep and wait for the bayonets.

"In these gloomy, cold, hungry, anxious October days of bad autumn weather, Petrograd is showing us once again a ma-jes-tic picture of élan, self-confidence, en-thu-si-asm and heroism. The city, which has suffered so much, which has so often been sub-jec-ted to dangers...is still what it was, the torchbearer of the revolution. And, backed by the combined forces of the whole country, we shall surrender this Petrograd to no one."

I didn't wait for the meeting to break up. I put on my coat and gloves and, before the committee had even discussed the defense, I was out the door. I knew where I was heading. Yudenich would not drive his tanks over my daughter's grave.

27 *Vintovka*

A crowd of gray-faced workers gathered in the sleet outside the Moskovsky District Soviet. I joined a group of women who said they were from the shoe factory Skorokhod. A comrade directed us to a supply center on the Obvodny Canal, where they handed out shovels and burlap sandbags. Our crew leader, a woman with a short, sturdy nose and slightly crossed eyes under thick brows like a man, grabbed my arm. "Who are you? Are you Skorokhod? I never saw you before."

I wrenched my arm away. Who was I? An unanswerable question. But I had no time for philosophy. "I'm a matron at Orphanage No. 6, up on Nevsky."

"So what are you doing down here?" She squinted nastily. What, did she think I was a White spy, down here to steal sandbags for Yudenich? That I would leak the location of the shoe factory?

"This is where Yudenich is coming," I said. "And this is where we should stop him. Not wait until he checks into the Astoria."

A woman to my left laughed out loud. The crew boss shot her a frosty look, shoved my arm away as if it were a dead thing, and went off to stick her nose into somebody else's business. "Don't mind Elizaveta," the woman said. Her blue eyes bulged slightly under her brown woolen scarf. "She's always like that. Constipated. Though with that bread, who isn't?" The snow was starting to stick to her scarf and shoulders. "I like that *shapka*." She pointed to my fox-fur hat. "Did you kill it yourself?"

She was a witty one. Alive, at least compared to me. "As a matter of fact."

"*Vot* fashion plate." She used the English.

Our crew was assigned to the power plant on the south bank of the Obvodny Canal. *They're gonna blow the power plant . . .* Iskra had been alive when Nikita said it.

Iskra. I tucked her into a pocket under my heart with the ginger lock of her hair and thought of my hands, my shovel. Shoulder to shoulder, women and men from the southern factories dug and filled sandbags. The Skorokhod woman and I made a good team, same height, same energy level. We dug the half-frozen earth, and then one shoveled while the other held the bag open. Soon we were both covered in dirt, I could feel the fine particles coating my face, dirt in my eyes and nose and teeth, my snot black with it. I didn't care that the raw wood of the spade's handle blistered my gloveless hands, and that the cold made it hard to grip anything. I warmed my hands under my armpits, grateful for the work, grateful for the heaviness and the sweatiness of it. It was a drug against grief.

My partner's name was Anya. She sewed boot uppers. The workers in her factory were hoping for a bonus ration of a pair of boots per family—they'd gone on strike over it earlier in the year, she told me. "We're the shoemaker's children, it's ridiculous. How do they expect you to sew boots month after month when your own are falling apart?" We kept up a good rhythm as she talked, digging and filling and carrying the bag slung between us crabwise over the rough stones to where men tossed them with a grunt to the top of the growing wall. Other men caught them and ranged them into place. Each bag had to weigh at least sixty pounds. How light my baby had been by comparison. Yet the absence of her was heavier than this whole fortification.

We toiled all day, until the light began to fade. I knew they would blow this plant up rather than let it fall into the hands of the Whites, just as we'd done with Napoleon—but it would leave us to fight in the dark and the snow.

Coordinating our work was an old agitator from the soviet, a white-haired codger in overcoat and cap, red face and white moustache. "Look at our Soviet women! Worth a hundred bourgeoises in silk stockings!" he called out whenever we brought a fresh bag.

"Yeah, I'd rather have a hundred silk stockings than a shovel and a bag of dirt," Anya called back.

The old man had *Krasnaya Gazeta* folded in his hands. He alternately read it and used it as a baton. "The paper says the Whites have already declared victory! They're already popping champagne corks in London, telling everybody that Petrograd's laid down and died. Well, Comrades, look around. They better drink that champagne quick 'cause that's all they're gonna get!"

"That's the truth, brother."

Our next delivery found him reading about a White conspiracy that had just been uncovered in the city. "Just waitin' for the moment old Yudenich walks in. Keeping records on all the Bolsheviks and trade unionists—so they can finger us when their friends show up. Paid for by the English. Well, I hope they'll like it in the Peter and Paul Fortress. Hope they'll be nice and comfy."

The English? Was Father's group involved? Or just another rumor?

I liked working with Anya. She and I labored at a slow, steady pace all day long, while some of the other women started too fast, stopped, started again, and wearied as the day wore on. But working those weeks in the village, the round-the-clock harvest, had taught me to watch my back, let gravity do much of the work, use the weight of the shovel and the swing of the bag. There wasn't much I could do about my hands—I had lost my gloves, and they were a mess of blisters and cuts. But I was grateful for the work—I didn't think about Iskra for whole minutes at a time.

Round-faced Anya gazed at me pityingly. "You can borrow my gloves. We can share." But I embraced the pain as punishment. I didn't deserve anyone's sacrifice.

Past us, rumbling over the Obvodny Canal, moving south, flowed lines of our troops, newly *reconfigured*, purged of *unsound elements*—infantry with their bayonets and bandoliers, cavalrymen. "Oooh look, it's the Bashkirs," said Anya. Leather-faced men from central Asia on their little shaggy horses. The revolution had turned the country over, shook it like marbles in a box. I could imagine these fierce riders from the steppe with falcons on their wrists. Some even wore skullcaps in the sleet. "Trotsky told the Finns he'd send 'em over if they kept supporting the Whites," she said, watching them ride. "I heard they're tearing up the town, beating the whores."

Trucks roared by, crammed with sailors. Handsome and hearty, they called out to us. "Hi, darling! Wait up for me, I'll be home by midnight!" One of the sailors was a big blond like Slava from the agit-train. How kind he'd been when I was having Iskra, when everyone else was so useless. He'd remembered my sheepskin...Let me ride on top of the train, pregnant as I was. I wondered if he'd come home. All these men, streaming out to meet Yudenich somewhere between here and Gatchina—many would not return. "Good luck, brothers!" Anya shouted back. "Keep your shoes tied!"

What would they find when they entered the towns of the White advance? Hangings, mass executions? I thought of the steel spine of Trotsky's armored train. The old agitator said that when Trotsky heard a division was dissolving before the Whites, he grabbed a horse and rode out himself, turned the troops back to the fight. "Drivin' 'em like cattle. Just like he said he was going to."

By three in the afternoon, we'd enclosed the power plant in a sandbag fortress nine feet high, just in time for the arrival of a detachment of Red cadets looking pale and heartbreakingly young, armed with bayonets and two machine guns. Tender, afraid, and afraid of looking afraid—that bravado, each some mother's son, someone's precious jewel, the light of someone's heart. Each could be snuffed out like a candle.

When it became apparent I had nowhere else to go, Anya invited me home with her, to a second-story room in a house on a muddy, snow-dusted lane near Skorokhod, where she lived with her mother and three children. Children, everywhere. I couldn't stand to look at them. They looked like accidents waiting to happen. Her husband was in the army, like all the husbands except mine. She and I shared our defense rations with her mother and the children, accompanied by tea and saccharine. The ration provided was heartier than expected. Perhaps supplies were getting through from Moscow—for some reason Yudenich hadn't cut the railway line. Was Vikzhel up to its clever tricks?

Anya's mother made a great fuss over my torn hands, cleaning and bandaging them. She gave me a pair of old mittens she had clearly knitted herself. I didn't want to take them, they could well be her only pair, but she insisted. "If the Whites get through, what good will gloves be to me?" After our small supper, the mother bustled about, packing for evacuation. Soon the family would move up inside the ring of fortified canals. Anya's older sister lived in Kolomna, by the wharves, near where I'd once mooned under Blok's windows. And once delivered a package for Arkady.

"Come with us," Anya said. "You don't take up much room."

But I would stay down here as long as I could.

Everyone was anxious, we jumped at noises in the street, a bit of gunfire. "When do you think they'll get here?" her mother asked. "Will they come tonight? That's what the papers are saying. And they'll slit our throats in our sleep."

The boys played at shooting out the window.

I sipped tea. My breasts were hard and hot, I chewed the last stems of sage and hoped for relief. I could nurse one of the boys, but then I would just keep producing more milk. I had to get past this—the readiness to nourish someone who was no longer able to be fed. The body was such an idiot. The way it bravely persisted. It didn't know she was gone. I didn't tell Anya about Iskra. I washed my face and hands in cold water—they had no soap—and crawled into bed with the two older boys. I fell into sleep like a cut pine.

For three days we labored along the Obvodny Canal, the first ring of defense, sandbagging the bridges, the only approach to the city from the south. In certain places we rolled sections of giant pipe from the water system, taller than our heads, into place, barring passage over the bridges. Hair-raising, twenty women on a section, everyone knowing that if one of these pipes rolled back on us, it would smash us flat like bits of butter under a rolling pin. In most places, though, we filled sandbags sewn that very night in the district artels. Men with sledgehammers broke up paving, and we filled barrows with rubble, made waist-high piles of it across the streets, shoving bits of siding onto it, fences, broken carts, barbed wire, anything we could get our hands on. Three days we worked in the wet falling snow, shoveling, carrying the bags, which grew heavier by the hour, and every minute I blessed Anya's mother for the mittens. Three nights running, I slept with her boys and dreamed of dirt. Sometimes I was burying Iskra. Other times, digging her up. Or looking for her in the graveyard. I had to move her, the Whites were coming, but I couldn't find the monument. One night I dug a ditch six feet down, a trap for the Whites, only to be buried myself in a collapsing wall of mud.

On the fourth day, the fighting was so close we could hear the guns. We finished the last barricade, and as dusk fell, they told us that if we knew people living north of Obvodny, to go there now. Anya and I kissed one another goodbye. "Come with us," she said, holding my hands in their ragged wool mitts. But the district soviet was looking for volunteers to man rifle outposts, and it sounded like something I could do.

Four of us followed a leather-clad girl through the dusk and wet falling snow to a building at Moskovsky Prospect and Detskoselsky Prospect, a middling kind of building that had had a pharmacy on the ground floor, a tailor, and a bakery, but now all were empty. My comrades—a dark-eyed man with sallow skin, a bandy-legged codger, and a woman factory worker a few years my senior—and I struggled under the weight of small sandbags we'd been given while the girl from the soviet shouldered a long burlap sack and led us up a rickety, banister-robbed staircase, opening the door of a modest room on the top floor. Two windows overlooked the intersection. About twelve feet square, board flooring, peeling pink wallpaper. It still had its flowered curtains, its tables and chairs, a child's iron cot. Requisitioned, and recently. Where had the family gone? The girl comrade just shrugged.

She showed us how to pile the sandbags onto the windowsills, creating squared openings through which we could fire. The girl explained the tactic. "See, there's a barricade up ahead on Moskovsky. So your White tanks, your White cavalry, they see the barricade and turn up here, thinking they can get around it—and then we give it to 'em. POW. Look, there's another installation across the street." She waved, and we saw a white hand in a third-story window wave back.

From her sack, like a magician, she produced a dazzling array of grenades, boxes of shells, two rifles and two revolvers, a package tied in string, bottles of water, and piled them on the scarred table like gifts at Christmastime. The sour metallic scent of guns was becoming familiar. The rifles looked new—I wondered why they weren't up at the front. The revolvers, on the other hand, were old and dirty, their grips worn—I doubted they would even work when the time came. Now I wished I hadn't given mine to the gravedigger. It would have been better. At least I knew it worked.

I picked up one of the rifles, and both men stared in surprise—as if I'd sat at the head of the table in a peasant izba. Just plunked myself down in the master's seat. I ignored their reactionary disapproval. "Show me how to load it," I said to the comrade.

The girl cocked the bolt, slid it back, clicked five shells into the magazine, locked the bolt back down again, and rammed it into place. "That's loaded." She handed it to me. "If it jams, empty it—and make sure the one in the barrel comes out too. Then go ahead and reload."

The ammunition boxes were marked IZHEVSK.

The solemn, dark-eyed man picked out the other rifle, and the woman in her patched coat and the old man had to settle for revolvers, the old man sulky with wounded pride. The girl showed the woman how to handle her gun, where the safety was, how to cock the hammer, suggesting she use both hands, resting her forearms on the sandbags to shoot, so the recoil wouldn't spoil the shot. "It won't be long now." The girl put her own rifle over her shoulder. "No one's going to leave, not till it's over, understand?" She gazed into each of our faces. "Anybody leaves, shoot him. I'm serious. No runnin' down to the drugstore. The rest of you, assume he's on his way to tell the Whites where we've set our traps."

We peered uneasily at one another. Would I be able to shoot that old man if he decided to go home? That patched-coated woman? I'm sure they were thinking the same of me. Which of us might be a White spy. I was the most likely candidate—from the wrong district, no family, no story. My diction too mannered. "Reinforcements are on their way, but Yudenich may get here first. I'll be back tomorrow or the day after. Good luck."

We sat around the scarred table on the cheap rickety chairs. Night fell quickly. We started a fire in the little stove. We could hear the shelling outside, it sounded louder now, maybe because we were high up and facing south, or perhaps it was just the quiet of the evening. "They're already at Pulkovo," said the old man, lines like seams in his weathered face. "They're fighting on the heights. They could be here in three hours." He looked into our eyes craftily, as if scaring us made him more important. "And they got tanks, those sons of whores. To a tank, what's a barricade? They can crawl right over those piles of sticks and stones like kids over a stile."

That's all we needed, a defeatist in our ranks. Why had he bothered to come, then? He should have stayed in his rocking chair and waited for the Whites with a plate of cookies. So they'd made it to Pulkovo. I wondered how my Ancients were—my stargazers, those Five precious heads. I prayed they'd been allowed to return to the observatory, that they'd found a safe spot to ride this out as the war was fought around them. How many lives ago was that? The astronomer's son, buried in his grave up there in the shadow of the observatory. Had the grass grown over it? So many graves now, so many ghosts, you couldn't turn around without bumping into one. There were more dead than living in Petrograd now. I prayed for the safety of those snowy heads. Let them pursue the stars in peace. But nobody would be left in peace, and the observatory was high ground, it would be a coveted artillery position.

"Tikhonov," said the old man to the dark-eyed one, holding his hand out. "Skorokhod."

"Slansky," said the dark-eyed man. "Dinamo." The electronics plant. They shook hands.

"I'm Irina. Chizhova," said the woman in the tattered coat, her hair in a worker's scarf, her large gray eyes. "From the tanning factory."

"Kuriakina," I said, unbolting the rifle. "Orphanage No. 6." Pulled out the shells, loaded them again.

They began to chat, politely at first, then more intimately, as people do in a queue, exploring the packages, which proved to be rations of bread and salt herring. They wondered how long it would last us, how many tanks the Whites had. They discussed the rumors that Zinoviev and the Bolshevik big shots had already packed up when Trotsky arrived. All the heads nodding like wooden toys. More rumors—someone's sister knew someone somewhere who worked in one of the commissariats...so on and so on. The same talk that took place in every canteen and queue, at every kitchen table in Petrograd. The old man had to urinate. It was a problem. Chizhova solved it with a pitcher that we christened the latrine, and stuck in the next room. We'd worry about disposal later.

I carried my chair over to the window, where I could see down into the intersection and along Moskovsky Prospect toward the cemetery, the Moscow Gate, and Yudenich. I was just glad I had somewhere to be, something useful to do, and living, breathing bodies around me. Now that I was no longer carrying sandbags, my body felt as stiff as a woman's of eighty, and I had nothing to keep my mind off my dead redheaded girl, my sweet green-eyed baby, and my own powerlessness in the face of the cruelest fate, the worst cards turning over on the green baize of my life.

Yet some part of me still couldn't fully take in what had happened, that she was really gone. It remained as stupid as a mule. As loyal as a dog that sits at the door after the master is buried, waiting for him to come out in the morning. I didn't believe in her death. Even though I had buried her myself, even though a paper containing her curls weighed down my heart, a part of me could not accept that it was forever. I felt wrong. Without her in my arms, I was too light. I had too much time. She'd always been with me, right on me—in her cloth, or in my lap. It was like losing an arm. Digging, filling sandbags, with Anya in her small crowded flat, there had been something to keep my mind occupied, but now, staring down into the dark street, it hit me like a blizzard—No, a blizzard was too dense, too absorbing, it obscured vision. This was the opposite, a great shock of consciousness. I could hardly bear to sit in this chair. To listen to their chatter.

Flashes of gunfire twinkled through the big flakes of wet autumn snow—they were close. I could feel Petrograd holding its breath. Our fate, the fate of a city, was being decided. Wagered on a round of cards. I stared down the empty boulevard. The building across the way, on Detskoselsky, was dark except for a scattering of windows lit behind curtains. I listened to my comrades the way one listens to birds, their voices filling the air with basic sounds—*hello, hello hello, I'm here I'm here. Danger, danger, pretty bird, come love me.* Humans tell stories about themselves, where they're from, what they do in their work, what they're doing here instead of home with their families. Everyone has some sort of story. Each human being walks around with an epic poem of himself, just waiting to stand up after dinner and recite it, poor bards that we are. Something about humans, we want to be known. We think we're a story: beginning, middle, and end—*and this is how it ended up.* But of course, our stories have no sense, no rhythm, no meaning—an unfolded fan made more sense than a human life. In any case, I didn't want to tell my story. It was as bitter as uncured olives.

The old man, Tikhonov, was with the union at Skorokhod, and one of the founders of the factory committee. "I'll be the first they line up against the wall," he said proudly.

Dinamo—Slansky—built radios, he was studying to become an engineer. He'd joined the party just last year, a real go-getter.

"Why aren't you in the army, a fine young man like yourself?" Tikhonov asked, thinking he was so clever, like a prosecutor.

Dinamo turned around and pulled up his jacket, his shirt. Terrible scars boiled the skin, like a wet cloth that had been balled up and left to dry that way in the sun. "Took it in the back on the Dvina," he said. "My kidneys are shot. I can't march for shit. But people need radios, the trains and the troops."

Chizhova was Petrograd born and bred, her mother a laundress, her father a tanner. She had a boyfriend in the army, Vitya. "I know he's gonna come back and talk about all the battles he's won and where he went, and what am I going to say for myself? That I stayed home and dyed leather? That that was my civil war? At least now I can say I did something."

"What about you?" Tikhonov called over from the table. "Comrade Rifle. What do you have to say for yourself?"

"You can see the shooting from Pulkovo," I said.

"I mean who are you? Come on, be friendly. We're going to be here for a while, we might as well get to know each other." He tipped his chair back, folded his hands behind his head.

I told my story, plain as boiled water. "My baby died in an accident, nine days ago. She's buried down there at Novodevichy Convent." My lungs hurt, from all the dirt I'd breathed. I lifted the rifle to my shoulder, sighted down Moskovsky. "I don't give a damn what happens to me, so I thought I'd do the revolution some good. That's my story. Like it?"

They looked like people in a painting, sitting at that table, the flickering candlelight caressing their faces. Their eyes averted. Yes, I could feel them recoiling, the way you recoil from someone with smallpox, cholera. How they leaned away. No one wanted to be around a bad-luck person. Someone who didn't want to live. Especially with a rifle.

"How horrible. In the middle of all this," said Chizhova. "Such a shame."

"Yeah, sorry," said Tikhonov. "I didn't know."

"No time to even mourn," chimed in Dinamo. "Tough luck."

"Where's your family?" Chizhova asked, her gray eyes big with pity.

I shook my head. "No family." I wouldn't cry. Not in front of these people. When it was all over, maybe then, when I could seal myself into a room by myself, maybe then I could. I went back to staring out the window, into the empty street. So empty, so strange, that broad boulevard in the sifting snow. Waiting for the end.

They started up chattering again, trying to air the dread that lapped at the baseboards of the room with its bit of plasterwork and its empty child's cot. The guns from Pulkovo sounded like thunder. I tried counting between the flash and the rumble, but it was too fast. At one point, I noticed, the men got up from the table and quietly carried the child's cot into the other room. Nice of them. Kindness and death all mixed together.

We slept in rotation, two awake and two down, on the commissar system—someone to keep watch and someone else to keep that person watching. Dinamo and I took the first watch. He had a pencil and notebook, he was sketching something. I gazed out at the curtain of falling snow. Iskra never lived to see her first snowfall. Not even that long. Summer and autumn were all she ever knew. What if she were right here, just on the other side, like Ukashin thought. Would she still be a baby, just a baby, floating, drifting, alone? Or would she have returned to that undifferentiated consciousness? Would she understand? But really, what was there to understand? The accident that life on earth was? Not fate. Just a random hand of cards. We stumbled in and we stumbled out, like a drunk opening doors in a strange apartment.

Tonight, or tomorrow, I would put my own death to some purpose.

I kept thinking of Maxim. His agony, his guilt. I hoped maybe they were together, keeping each other company. I wondered if you were met by those who'd gone before, or were accompanied by those you died with. I looked around the room. I would not want to die with these people. Especially Tikhonov.

I shouldn't have taken that job at the orphanage. It gave me the false sense that I could handle Iskra alone. I shouldn't have left Mina's building. I should have slept in the hall outside their door until I shamed them into taking me in. Like a beggar exposing her wounds. But I'd been too proud, wanted to go my own way. So proud. Damn Mina for her own stiff-necked certitudes—and yet, it hadn't been she who had turned our friendship to vinegar. I'd ruined it myself, not once but twice.

I thought again of that note someone had pressed into my hand on Millionnaya Street. It was astonishing to me that after two years of Cheka searching and spying, there was still White conspiracy in Petrograd. The Cheka cells were packed with supposed conspirators—just ordinary people—and yet, at the hour of the White advance, suddenly a real counterrevolutionary organization had sprung to life like an animated doll. Who would have believed it? Even now I would have been skeptical, but for that pamphlet.

And Papa? Perhaps he'd sneaked off to England after this summer's attack. But I doubted it. He was more like me than I would have been able to see before. Stubborn to the end. No, he would be printing pamphlets and slipping messages to the front. Or sitting in a Cheka cell himself—beaten, bloody, bearded as he'd been that night. Disguised as a worker, but unable to disguise his air of superiority and absolute confidence in his own cause. I remembered what they'd said about defeated armies being the most brutal. The Cheka would shoot everyone in their cells when the Whites arrived, right before we blew up the bridges and the power plants. Yet, even now, I didn't want him dead.

I wish he'd seen her. But we were a nation of orphans, childless parents, parentless children. Civil war had cut the thread. There was no *then*. *Then* was outlawed for people like me. I hadn't realized how important the past would be, family, those connections. I'd thought nothing of breaking them myself. And now it was a dead end. There were no family jokes I would pass down to her—how her Uncle

Volodya had once sprinkled pepper into our *dyedushka*'s mouth on the porch at Maryino when he was enjoying his after-lunch nap, and he chased him around the yard trying to hit him with his cane. The time Grandmère bought a white marten scarf complete with head and eyes, and Tulku would not stop barking at her. Iskra never got to ride the rocking horse in the nursery on Furshtatskaya Street, never held Avdokia's soft, gnarled hand, never played with the hand-painted Columbine and Harlequin in Seryozha's little theater. She didn't know our favorite childhood game—Cossacks and Robbers. She hadn't shared her own *dyedushka*'s English butterscotch, ordered all the way from London. She'd never heard our love story, mine and Kolya's, how we kissed in the coatroom on St. Basil's Eve, or that he smelled of honey and cigars and Floris limes. She'd never smelled white lilacs in December. She never saw December.

"You okay, Vintovka?" Dinamo whispered from the other window, not to wake the others. *Vintovka, rifle.* He was my commissar.

I nodded, swiped at my telltale tears.

"Scared?"

"Not of dying," I said.

He laid his rifle across his knees. "What does scare you?" he said.

"Living." It made my eyes sting.

He swallowed. I could see the Adam's apple jump in his throat under the black, unshaven chin. "Can I tell you something?"

I braced to hear what he might have waited until now to confess. I hoped it was not anything sexual.

"When I was lying out in that field on the Dvina, dying like a piece of meat"—he felt in his pockets, produced a bag of tobacco—"all I wanted was for a moment to live like a man. My comrades to bury me with a few words, knowing who I was. I didn't mind dying, I just didn't want to die like a dog." He rolled a cigarette in a bit of *Pravda*.

"In those days, there was a third enemy—wolves. Whole nations of wolves, starving for game. They started attacking the men in the trenches, both sides the same to them. Sometimes we'd declare a cease-fire to beat them back. They felt like darkness itself, closing in." He smoked, turning away from me, lifting the curtain to see down the street, the falling snow was thickening. "We were afraid of everything. The wolves. Gas. We had no masks, we had nothing. With gas, you don't feel anything until it starts to burn, it burns your eyes away, your lungs." The snow drifting down, the smoke drifting up.

I could imagine him, wounded. I could smell the dirt, the mud, feel those wolves prowling. "So they got you out?"

"Yeah. I was in the hospital a year. Do you know what those places were like?"

All those brave men, groaning, sweating, in their unchanged bandages. Talk about dying like a dog. I nodded.

"I lay in that bed for a year. With those pigs of nurses, changing the bandages every three days if you were lucky. No morphine, not even water sometimes. No piece of it that wasn't hell. You know what I dreamed of?"

I couldn't imagine. Murder? Lakes? Women?

"I wanted a moment, just one moment, that wasn't about the flesh. No bodies, no screaming, no eating, no clawing for this and that. All I wanted was a moment to be a man. You know? A human being. Something with a little dignity, something that didn't stink, that didn't hurt. Just to have a thought, one simple thought. Like, where does electricity come from?"

He was wounded in a bed in some hideous military hospital, and that's what he wanted to think about. Electricity.

"Crazy, I know. But I was a good student back in school, if you can believe it. But who asks a poor boy, son of a *muzhik, You want to go into the Engineers, Mitya?* No. I left home at fourteen to go to work. Up at the Nobel factory. Then the war came. Who cares what Mitya Slansky wants? Into the infantry with him." His bitterness, the hollowness of his eyes, his cheeks.

"Let me tell you, Vintovka, lying in that bed, I decided I was going to be a man. I wouldn't wait until I'd healed, I might die instead, but meantime, I would try to be a man. I forced myself— *Think thoughts, Mitya.* How does a plant drink the sun? What does a fish think about, under the ice? I thought about people on other planets, and if we went there, would they look like people to us? We might walk right by them, thinking they were rocks. Like the bourgeoisie used to walk past us."

In the street, a single man was walking through the falling snow, down the center of Moskovsky Prospect. Where was he going? To report to the Whites? Was he mad? I sighted my rifle on him. Then I saw the sled. Now I understood—he was going to the barricade to pull firewood off it. Didn't he know there were snipers up in these buildings, that we'd turned Petrograd into a fortress?

"I thought about people from long ago," Dinamo was saying, the smoke coiling over his head like a halo. "Egyptians. Greeks. Or Africans. Are they like us, do they think like us, or are there ways of being a man that are so different from us—maybe better too?"

I lowered my rifle. I was a merciful god. Dinamo's eyes burned in the light of the flickering candle. He wanted a question that had nothing to do with the belly, or the nerves, but that came from the soul of a man, doing the one thing a man could do. Think, wonder. "Then the revolution happened, and it was like Easter, remember?"

"Everybody kissed each other in the street." How happy we were then, everyone alive, the country all together.

"The whole country, dreaming of being treated as human beings. Of living like men." He brought his chair closer to mine. His brown eyes, his long nose in his narrow face—in this light he looked like a tormented monk, something El Greco might have painted, Zurbarán.

"And yet, as things went along, it was still the same old thing, wasn't it? The boss, the owners, the generals, the war. The Constituent Assembly, run by the lawyers and the landlords. *No*, we said. *We want the soviet! We want to make our own decisions. We're sick of living like dogs, eating the scraps from the table!*"

The old man on the divan startled awake. "The devil take you," he grumbled. "People are trying to sleep here!"

"Go back to sleep, old man," I said. "Yudenich isn't here yet."

Dinamo rubbed his face in his hand. He looked a little abashed, but still, he had to keep talking. The steady flood of words—had he never shared this with anyone before? "So, here we are," he said, keeping his voice down. "We have our soviet, we have our revolution, we're our own masters, and what has changed? What has changed? It's still the same. Meat."

"Or no meat," I said.

"Rations, production—this is all a dog's life. Is this our fate on earth? Food, work, have a little fun, back to work?"

"I thought you were a Communist," I said. "You sound like a Christian."

"Not God and incense and *holy holy holy, kiss the picture,* and all that. But *something.* I mean, we need to improve material conditions, but that's not what we're talking about either. We're talking about, where is there for a man to go in this world? In *this* world. That's what scares me. That there's material conditions and nothing else." His face was like a Greek saint's, hollow-eyed from his sufferings. How alone he was, in that chair, only five feet from me. How alone we all were in our mortal terror.

I recited from Tyutchev:

> Soft the dove-hued shadows mingle,
> Color fades, sound droops to sleep...
> Life and motion melt to darkness
> Swaying murmurs far and deep.

"What is that?" Dinamo asked.

"A poem," I said.

"Is there more?" he asked.

> But the night moth's languid flitting
> Stirs the air invisibly:
> Oh, the hour of wordless longing;
> I in all, and all in me.

"That's good, isn't it?" he said. "*The hour of wordless longing...* That's just the kind of thing I meant. Sometimes I think I'm going crazy. But you, you don't think I'm crazy, do you? Did you make that up?"

"No. It's Tyutchev. A poet. He's buried in Novodevichy, right down the road."

"What's it called? Say it again." I did, and he wrote it into his engineer's notebook.

"It's called 'Twilight.'"

> *Every sense in dark and cooling*
> *Self-forgetfulness immerse, —*
> *Grant that I may taste extinction*
> *In the dreaming universe.*

Tyutchev, cooling my burning brain. Yes, let me lose myself.

Dinamo's dark eyes shone, a secular monk's, burning, burning. "I wish I knew some poems. I've just got a few *chastushki*."

Ukashin used to say that the soul was earth and spirit violently intermingled. That's what Dinamo was like. Of course he was tired of earth, earth, earth, material conditions, rations, meetings—while God and angels were no substance, worse than our thin fish soup. Soul was what he was after, robust, nourishing. That's what fed a man. Not spirit—pure, eternal, cold, and vaporous. Soul was a different matter. You couldn't have soul without earth and spirit, mixed together uneasily, muddied, restless, animated. Soul was never pure, that was its very nature. That's why my mother was soulless, why she could say, *It won't live.* She *saw,* but soullessly. Purely, remorselessly. And the Bolsheviks, the spacemen, that same purity. That refusal to tolerate the muddiness. Only a soulful man could suffer in this certain way, like Dinamo here. To even recognize this hunger. That was a man.

"Do you know any more?"

And I did. I recited Baratynsky's poem:

> *My talent is pitiful, my voice not loud,*
> *But I am alive. And on this earth*
> *My presence is a friend to someone…*

How a great poet could reach out with words, across the years, and take you in his arms, some unknown reader, whether it be a weary matron in her soiled apron or a grown man with a rifle on the Dvina. He would hold you close, lift you up, comfort you as only another human could.

I understood Dinamo's dilemma. We wanted food for the people, justice for the people, freedom for the people, but then what? Material conditions. The body, the flesh. Sex, food, warmth. Essential, but for what purpose? So that we could live as human beings. So we could feed our own souls. Not just for better and more.

I gazed down into the sifting snow in the street lit by a single streetlamp, and realized I had devalued too quickly my time at Ionia, thrown it out on the trash heap of my short and wasted life. Perhaps Ukashin had been a fake, but some of his teachings came back to me now. It was not any future hell that bothered me but the way through this one. Oh, Iskra, my sweet one. What had become of that little flame? Had she a soul yet? Or only the depths she drilled into mine? What were those green eyes that had looked up into the trees and marked their motion, that had gazed into my face as a thirsty man gazes into a spring?

After two days, our vigil was over. No gun battle ever erupted on Moskovsky Prospect. The Whites had been pushed off Pulkovo Heights, and the Red troops were on the offensive, just as Trotsky had said would happen. The girl from the soviet came and took back our guns. We were free to go. It was the one thing I hadn't been ready for, that I would not die in this room. I shook Dinamo's hand.

"Could I see you again?" he asked. "You could teach me some more poetry."

I saw the look in his eyes. Like Genya's. Like the one-armed man's. I could take him up and put him down, and he would never recover from the blow. For once, I spared his lonely heart. "I've got no address."

He tore a page from his notebook and wrote his own on it. "If you ever want to...it's just around the corner. I'm usually home

Tuesday and Thursday nights..." He handed me the shred of paper. "I'll remember you, Vintovka. *'And on this earth / My presence is a friend to someone'*..."

I put the paper in my sheepskin pocket. We both knew I wouldn't use it. I would have to find that tiny light inside myself, that bit of humanity, and walk a dark stretch of unknown miles with it cupped in my hands. If I wasn't careful, the least wind would blow me out.

Part III
The House of Arts

(Winter 1919–January 1921)

28 Number, Please

CLACKCKCKCKALLLAAACCCKKK
clatterCHATTER
click click click clack
clack CLACK CrACKEtty CrACK

That furious hail, like a universe of pebbles bouncing down a galaxy of stairways, the frozen, echoing hall of the Petrograd Telephone Exchange. Hundreds of girls connecting thousands of calls on Bolshaya Morskaya Street.

Number, please. Number, please.

The telephone exchange needed nothing but my hands, ears, mouth. One more Soviet young lady.

Number, please.

That wall of sound, like a waterfall of kopek coins on a metal roof, as metal plug sought metal nest times ten thousand. Connecting whom to what, and why? In a city of frozen toilets and crumbling houses, rotten herring and carrying water from a pump up four stories, when right on Bolshaya Morskaya the carcass of a dead horse had lain since summer, bones picked clean, first by knives, then crows. The dogs were all dead.

But commissars talked to Smolny. They talked to their girl-friends. They talked to their wives. Narkompros was tracking down a trainload of fuel. Sometimes the girls listened in.

I dreamed of the sound, even at night, a steady rain of pebbles on an icy slab. To me it was astonishing that people still had working numbers and someone to call. The city making calls from beyond the grave, important appointments in this village of ghosts.

Girls listened in. Cheap theater. Hoping to hear something dirty.

Clacketty clack

Number, please.

The blessing of numbers. Of plugs in holes. I was lucky, I could not have returned to the orphanage. Could not bear living children, their terrible eyes, their fragile lives. I didn't want to love anyone. I couldn't hurt anyone here.

Number, please. I'll connect you.

The great hall of technology was colder than a morgue. We wore our coats and hats. My headphones snugged under my fox-fur *shapka,* the mouthpiece on my chest under my dirty sheepskin coat. Some cut the tips off their gloves but I didn't have a pair to ruin. Such was my life.

They never teach you that there will be life after death. That's the worst part. That you will have to go on putting one foot in front of the other. Go to work. Sleep. Just the burden of carting the body around. Keeping it warm. Putting things in the mouth. A half-hearted attempt at staying clean. I gave it a try. You spent your meager calories walking to work to earn ration cards to stand in queues to buy the bread that let you walk to work.

I returned from my rifle nest to find families packed into the Shpalernaya flat's two parlors, Golovin's study, and the old lady's boudoir. Collectivized. I shouldn't have been surprised. Everything had disappeared from my little room on the servant's hall—linens, books, blankets, my one summer dress, my pail from Izhevsk. I had nothing. I stood in the hall and waited. "My daughter just died," I said. "I've been out defending Petrograd. She died ten days ago." The pail reappeared. Some sticks of wood. Blankets and books. The neighbors were cold and hungry, but not without shame.

But the days of aristocracy soon came to an end. The building's old pipes groaned, shuddered, and burst. Now we descended the gap-toothed stairs to draw water from the pump, like everyone else, and shat in the second courtyard. The Ice Age had begun. It was like that all over the city—people took their trousers down right on the sidewalk, squatted. Men pissed off the side of a cart without even stopping, as one might urinate from a sailboat. It was a zoo with no keeper. We didn't need one. There was no outside to run to.

And yet there were telephones.

In the canteen, I sat next to a girl I recognized from the Tagantsev Academy. We'd once shared a desk in Madame Buliova's elocution class. Yelena Rumakhverina. She looked into my face and spoke to me as a stranger. I wasn't even in disguise. I descended to the icy washroom and looked into my own eyes. The person in the mirror was not me. Not merely older, thinner, hollow-eyed, rough-haired, dogged by bad luck. Someone else. A hand not my own put on my headset, a mouth not my own spoke into the receiver amid the clatter of steel plugs against the rims of ten thousand steel sockets.

Number, please.

One of a thousand girls, each in her place, wearing the headset, connected by snaking cables that snapped back into the shelf— multiplied by hundreds, thousands, hundreds of thousands.

Home life was a hunt for food and fuel, the need to keep the body alive, conserve calories, warmth, maximize the little strength we had, we denizens of the new Ice Age. Ice froze in the pitchers overnight. We attacked fences, siding, anything wooden. I took surreptitious trips down to the wharves on the Neva to gouge out wood from Petrograd's fine fleet of rotting barges. It was dangerous, counterrevolutionary—stealing wood from the People. A secret war waged each night between the soviet and the cold, hungry ants of its citizenry. Whole buildings tumbled, eviscerated. People chopped up scaffoldings around buildings under repair. They hacked up the balustrades and stair rails—every stairway became a death trap. I bought a child's sled and, with Arkady's hatchet, stole wood viciously, a small ravenous weasel hacking up an exposed wall, running off before arrest. There were too many of us to catch us all and I was by no means the slowest.

I did my living in dreams. I dreamed of trains, trying to get on, pushing and grappling only to be heaved off at the last moment, butted with rakes and brooms. I hung on the doors, clung to the roofs with bare hands, slid away on the turns. I rode inside cars so crowded they became a tank of flesh. There were dreams of suffocation, clawing for breath. There were dreams of riding on the tops of the cars, and being pushed off, or seeing the impossibly low tunnel coming at me. Or else I was back in the orphanage, losing my way in the corridors. The stairs were all wrong. I had to find Maxim before he did something bad. I dreamed I was back on Furshtatskaya Street in my mother's last room. Bad men pounding on the door. *Don't open it,* I always yelled. But my mother never listened, she always wanted to see who was there.

Yet my one prayer, to see Iskra again, was always withheld.

I dreamed of the telephone exchange. It wasn't enough to work there all day, I also had to labor all night. The cords snarled, the plugs too big for the sockets. I hung up on Lenin. I dreamed of water filling the great hall, and operating the switchboard ankle-deep in water, knee-deep, water rising. The plugs were a million shrieking mouths. One night, bees flew in and out, and the holes dripped with honey.

In the rooms of the collectivized flat, people regularly sickened and died. Some died quietly, freezing to death, starving, others noisily, vomiting, groaning, crying out. Eventually you stopped pitying them. It was just part of life. Their loved ones carried the bodies out in rented coffins. I hated how I eyed those scarred boxes, estimating how long a coffin like that would burn—close to a week if you kept the flame small.

Yet unbelievably, we were winning the war. Gatchina fell, and Iamburg in the west. In the east, we rolled into Omsk, Kolchak's capital. The Tula card had stood fast. But would victory come soon enough? Or would we all be dead by the time it came?

St. Basil's Eve, the women of the flat cast the wax, huddled over a scarred kitchen table. *A sun, a seal, a wedding ring...* They offered to cast mine, but I refused. There was no point in predicting one lone person's fate when the world itself was riding an out-of-control horse. And frankly, if the ship with sails came into the Neva this very night, I didn't know if I would have the energy to climb aboard.

That night, I dreamed of a ship caught in the ice. The sound of its hull cracking, crushed in the growing pack ice. We'd set out too late and winter overtook us. We had to abandon the ship, move out on foot across the frozen waste. A group of city people, dressed in street clothes, arguing which way to go.

In February, amid the hunger and cold, death a part of daily life, I reached my twentieth birthday. No child, no husband, no friends, I was as hollow as a gourd, but still here. No one celebrated. I left work early to buy a slice of horsemeat—happy birthday to me.

It wasn't yet dark. If it had been, I wouldn't have seen him, walking up Bolshaya Morskaya Street. Tall and long legged, in a blue overcoat and gray hat. The poet of poets—Alexander Blok.

Your name—a bird in the mouth, Tsvetaeva wrote.

No one else seemed to notice him as he made his way along the gloom of a dim street—exactly his climate. He seemed haunted and worn, as though he'd lived through some terrible disease. Honestly, I had thought he was dead. A ghost among so many. I supposed I'd been thinking of Andrei, the *intelligent*.

"Alexander Alexandrovich!" I called out, astonished at my own boldness.

He turned. The snow sifted down over his shoulders, his hat of curly lamb. He squinted as he cast his glance around him, looking for someone he knew. But it was just me. My stony eyes suddenly found their tears.

"I have a premonition of you. The years in silence pass . . . " I recited.

"Dear girl," he said.

Heartened, I continued:

"And as the image, solitary, I have that premonition of you again . . ."

We stood there on Bolshaya Morskaya near the corpse of the felled horse for a long moment. The snow fell between us, rubbing out his form like chalk. He came to me. Put his hand on my shoulder. His voice was very soft, his smile sad. He didn't wear his own face anymore either.

"Are you a poet?" he asked, peering under my fox hat.

I was dreaming. I must have fallen asleep. I was talking to Blok next to a dead horse on Bolshaya Morskaya Street!

Was I a poet? I once had been. Though that was when I'd had a face. Not this blank automaton.

I nodded. It was easier to agree than to explain.

"Come, walk with me. I'm going to the House of Arts. I have a meeting in a few minutes." He sighed and together we started off. "But tell me one of your poems."

I recited:

> *I slept just fine*
> *on your floor.*
> *Like a baby.*

> *Who doesn't love concrete?*

My poem about my Cheka imprisonment, "Alice in the Year One." He walked slower, nodding, laughing quietly at some of the lines as I kept pace at his elbow. I was not a short girl, but Blok towered over me.

> *Tell me, where does the Future sleep at night?*
> *Can you see it from here?*

He listened closely, bending his head not to miss my words, and when I was done, I saw that his face had darkened, covered with clouds. "Be careful who you tell that one to," he said. "Write anything, but be careful of your audience. What's your name, dear girl?"

"Makarova. Marina. Dmitrievna. Though it's not what's on my papers," I confided.

"And where do you come from, Marina Dmitrievna?"

"From Petersburg," I said.

He smiled. "And I as well."

We knew what that meant. We were *from Petersburg*. Not *Petrograd*, this hungry, jargon-speaking town where you tore your firewood off a barge rotting in the river, but *Petersburg*, that state of mind. The chimes and bells, silver and lilac. Where there could still be beauty, and poetry, that lost world.

We came to Nevsky, and he turned right. I hesitated a moment, not knowing whether to continue to follow him like a stray dog or have a shred of dignity and bid him good night. I kept walking alongside him.

"Do you know what building this is?" he asked me. The three-story one on our right had high arched windows that extended all the way down from Bolshaya Morskaya to the Moika Canal.

"It's the Eliseevs' house." The very name could flood any hungry Former with near pornographic associations. The Eliseevs had purveyed luxury foods to the upper stratum of the capital. I could see Mama in her big hat pointing to cases full of caviar, tins of Seville marmalade. The pyramids of pineapples! Horrible pungent cheeses, Chinese tea and French pâté, Papa's English clotted cream. Surely the Eliseevs were no longer in Petrograd, fallen to selling horsemeat and frozen potatoes on surreptitious back stairs and in second courtyards.

"It's the House of Arts," said Blok. "Haven't you heard of it?"

But I had heard nothing but the waterfall of the telephone exchange.

"You should come. We have readings and studios—Gumilev teaches one that's very popular. Though I disagree with everything he does, you might enjoy the young people."

Gumilev, the poet! Once married to Akhmatova.

"And Chukovsky's teaching a translation studio—have you read his Whitman? I imagine you'd like it."

"I sing the body electric," I recited in my heavily accented English. *"The armies of those I love engirt me."* Though the armies of those I loved were gone, slipped through my fingers and under Whitman's grass.

People entered and exited the street door at 59 Moika Embankment, stopping to glance at Alexander Alexandrovich talking to this girl without a face. He shook my hand in its ragged mitten. "It was so good to meet you, Marina Dmitrievna. Come tomorrow night, won't you? Bely is reading. One should never miss that opportunity. I hope we'll speak again."

A young woman held the door for him.

The gossips said Bely had once tried to take Blok's wife from him. Such a close-knit mountaintop, our Olympus. "Thank you, Alexander Alexandrovich. I'll be there," I called out as he slipped inside the door to the House of Arts. "What time?"

"At five," he said.

29 *From Petersburg*

I could feel the ice in my soul beginning to crack, as if he were the sun. *I hope we'll speak again.* Nothing but death would keep me from showing up tomorrow night. Blok and I would speak, and he would save me, like a passing freighter plucking a drowning stoker from an icy sea.

I had given him my true name.

I slipped into a courtyard off Basseynaya Street where a furtive, flat-eyed man sold horsemeat at forty-five rubles a pound. I traded him a good Izhevsk brass rifle shell from the box I'd had the presence to forget to turn in when we returned our rifles. He examined it, weighed it in his hand, and sliced a chunk from a bloody package with a dirty knife, wrapped it in *Pravda*. I could smell the raw meat, half enticing, half nauseating, as I carried the dripping package home, its blood dotting the snow.

There was simply no way to keep meat private in a communal apartment. Or anything else for that matter. As the perfume of cooking meat filled the kitchen, I could hear the stomachs of my comrade tenants growl as they tried not to stare. The power of sizzling flesh was primal, magnetic.

A neighbor, Olga Viktorievna, followed the scent, sniffing like a bloodhound. "Our stove is smoking again, Marina Dmitrievna," she wheedled. "Could you come fix it?" Saccharine sweet. A Red Army wife, she lived next to the kitchen with her children, and was a tremendous thief. Everyone knew it. You had to watch your food like a bank auditor. She spent her day gossiping with the wife of a Soviet clerk, whose child was wasting of some unknown disease.

"I'll be there as soon as I'm done," I said.

She eyed my dinner enviously.

I took my meal in my room, as everyone did—we beasts didn't want to be watched while eating. I remembered when dining in public was considered a pleasant thing. Now we hid ourselves away. The pleasure was too intense, almost sexual, shrouded by guilt. My dining table was the nightstand, my chair the cot, my candelabra a smoky candle stuck in a dish. My window looked out onto a mean little courtyard. In the flats opposite, the curtains were drawn. You could only see strips of light in the inhabited ones.

But I had something to celebrate tonight beyond my entry into this world. A new entry, a rebirth. What had given me the nerve to call out to Alexander Alexandrovich? Like a ghost, he'd appeared from the destroyed city where I'd dwelled since Iskra's death. Perhaps he was an apparition from another dimension, some impossible world up four rounds of the spiral, where I'd been granted a wish I'd not even expressed. How else to explain how he'd arrived at just that hour, and had spoken to *me*. Impossible, and yet—his verse welled up in my throat. And I'd recited my own poem, written when I'd still had a self, when I still could take joy in the mustering of words...

I chewed the tough horsemeat, savoring each atom. Oh, it was so good! Thank God I had sunflower oil, not castor or fish liver. The meat and fat raced through my bloodstream like trains through a city. When had I last felt even in the slightest bit lucky? I imagined a table full of silver and crystal. Why not—who could judge my counterrevolutionary thoughts? I wore black velvet gloves. A vase of roses rested on the table, dark red wine, and the tall poet with blue eyes lifted his glass to me! And I thought, like the woman in his poem, said to be Akhmatova: *That one's in love with me too.*

Tonight I was twenty and the poet raised his glass to me—

The knock on the door. "Marina Dmitrievna?" That horrible wheedling sound.

"One minute!" I finished my luxurious repast, licked the plate as clean as a *barynya*'s pinafore. Then locked the door, slipped the key in my pocket, and went to help Olga with her stove.

Somehow I'd become resident *bourgeoika* doctor. It was just as well to have good relations with the neighbors—you never knew when you'd need their help. We had these temperamental stoves, but no one seemed able to make them work without smoking themselves half to death. With a soldering iron, I could have been king of this building. A *bourgeoika* is basically a tin box with a few lengths of pipe venting out the window, and required the gentlest adjustments to make it draw. Usually it was a case of the pipes being misaligned, so that smoke leaked out—people tended to dry their clothes there—or else the stuff being burned was too wet, or the owner had failed to heat the air in the chimney sufficiently, so a plug of cold air walled off the rising smoke.

Olga Viktorievna's room was larger than mine, but crammed to impassability with beds, trunks, boxes, piles of rags, an indescribable puzzle of broken things. It smelled of vinegar. Her son and daughter looked at me as if they were drugged, as if I were a moving shadow on a wall. The boy, about thirteen, coughed, wiped his nose on his coat sleeve. Their little stove emitted clouds of gray smoke. I squatted before it, opened the door. Inside lay a half-burned book, the pages smoldering. *A Hero of Our Time* by Mikhail Lermontov. The sight trampled the good feelings I'd gingerly assembled. This great book had survived almost a century only to be consumed for the worth of its paper.

I showed her, sadly, how to properly burn a book. "You can't just throw it in there, you have to take the pages apart. Look." I made small dense coals, rolling each individual page and then twisting a knot, wondering if Olga Viktorievna or one of her blank kids had burned my youthful poetry, had immolated Genya's fiery verse. Someone had. This sad, hard little woman, like a knot herself. And I was not so naive as to think I would be above burning my books someday. Even people who knew their value were burning their libraries for heat. But it didn't take away the sharpness of the sacrifice. The worst of it was that books burned quickly and gave little warmth. Their heat was all in the mind. *No, I'm not Byron, I'm unknown,* Lermontov wrote,

I am like him, a chosen one,
an exile hounded by this world—
only I bear a Russian soul.
An early start, an early end
little indeed will I complete;
within my heart, as in a sea,
lie shattered hopes—a sunken load…

I went back to my room, my mood soured and my clothes stinking of smoke and the death of poetry. After securing the door behind me, I pulled out the nightstand's drawer. Hidden behind it, wrapped in a folded vellum page, lay Arkady's *marafet*. If this wasn't the occasion, I didn't know what would be better. I shook it onto the back of my hand, divided it with the tip of my knife. *"An early start, an early end,"* I toasted myself. And sniffed it up.

The first nostril burned, and then suffused me with a warmth that had nothing to do with fire. I inhaled the other. Suddenly I had to defecate, urgently, something that didn't occur more than once a week. I was already in my coat and hat, took the scrap of paper—that picture of Saint Agatha—and in Anya's mittens, went down the back stairs into the courtyard, where I relieved myself in the dark, politely ignoring others doing the same. We would pay the price come spring, when the water table rose, and cholera struck us down like ants.

But all that seemed so far away now. In this moment, I felt free.

Shimmering with health and beauty, untouched by grief and the brittle cold. A strange sensation. These days you braced yourself whether indoors or out, as tight as a fist. Suddenly I could stand up straight, breathe deep the frosty air. No wonder the orphans liked their *marafet*. No wonder they froze to death wearing next to nothing, having failed to find shelter. Starving, buying cocaine instead of food. No wonder.

I walked out onto Shpalernaya Street, feeling light, feeling immortal. I wasn't even sure people could see me, I was so beautiful. Perhaps I would look to them like a fish gazing up at the sun through water. Though no one was looking at me—who would be out tonight walking in the dark and snow? The street unrolled between elegant buildings, crisp and precise. All down the block one could discern the living apartments, dark between the silvery dead ones. I felt I could *see* through the walls to people curled in their beds, nose to tail like foxes, preparing to live through yet another cold night. Like bedbugs, we retired at seven. Bedbugs, that's what we were now. But not me.

What freedom! To walk through the streets unchilled, alone, as snow drifted past the streetlights on Shpalernaya, globes like great South Sea pearls, heavy and far apart. *I sing the body electric!* I didn't want to stand in the light, it was more beautiful to stand in the darkness and watch them burning in their crowns of snow. Like giants, like stars. I pictured them as Pushkin, and Lermontov—still smoky from the fire—as Blok and Akhmatova, Tsvetaeva dancing by campfire light, Tolstoy and Whitman keeping pace with one another, their hands behind their backs. They lit our darkness, and I was the only one who could walk among them.

The weight of Iskra's death slid from my shoulders. It had been cracking my back in two. *Iskra, just for this one night...* I let the syllables rise like bubbles into the air. I pictured her eyes, fingers wrapped in mine, and for once it didn't make me want to die. I recalled the soft, compact weight of her, her adorable limbs, her ginger curls, and yet the twisted blade of my grief remained in my hand. The snow fell with such tenderness, forgiving me.

Tomorrow I would pick up my burden—but tonight I was

twenty. Tonight I was a poet. I'd met Blok. *You'll come, won't you?* I walked out to greet the great frozen Neva, ice covering its secret life where water still flowed and fish whispered into the darkness. The important thing was this—the life within the ice, the water flowing. I could feel it, Kitezh—the city inside the waters. I could hear its bells. I laughed out loud. I'd met Blok! That silver stag among cattle. *Your name—a bird in the mouth*...What fate had dropped him in my path, what undeserved charity? I had been silent for so long, crushed by the weight of Iskra's death—what had inspired me to call out to him? Was it madness, or did he seem as grateful as I? Snow fell on my eyelashes, making stars of the streetlights. My breath a white cloud. How I loved this city, loved it still.

> *Petersburg!*
> > *I love you!*

> *Your frozen poetry*
> > *your bridges and facades*

> *Neglected and abandoned,*
> > *mirage amid the northern swamps.*
> *The young queen wanders*
> > *mad, staring into windows.*

> *No wonder politicians scramble*
> > *behind Moscow's ancient walls.*

> *Here we need no walls.*
> > *Our ghosts protect us, our illustrious dead.*

> *The echoes of music in our frozen air—*
> > *waltzes and tangos.*
> *The thrum of balalaikas never suited us,*
> > *never suited the lap of our waters,*
> > > *the sweep of our skirts.*

May we be forgiven our decadence,
our snobbery,
our pitiless exploitation—
the ancient curse.

But our modernity was glorious, wasn't it?
Though it bloomed and died
like a great unnatural mushroom.

We exploded
and cast our spores
to the earth's four corners.

What a death we are dying,
Petersburg, my brother.

How long did I wander, touching the stones and railings? Only the dead accompanied me. Yet the city shimmered, alive, alive, this miracle at the edge of the world. Like legendary Kitezh, safe beneath the waters. I heard its bells tonight, I heard them! We who were *from Petersburg* knew how, we kept its melody sewn inside our skins. They rang in Blok's smile and would never disappear. Even in death, we'd gather together with our poems in a circle and watch the buildings brush their hair in the mirror of the waters.

Tomorrow a thousand shivering Soviet citizens would rise and shovel fresh white from the walks, snow duty noted in their labor books. But tonight it was as sumptuous as ermine, like a clean white featherbed covering the sins of the city. All mine. The abandoned buildings silvered with frost. For a moment, freed from hunger and insensate to cold, I felt like an angel. *I sing the bodiless, ecstatic.* I had not known how heavy Iskra's death had been until it slipped from my shoulders. Now I floated untethered along the stately streets, remembering carriages and duels, the echo of a waltz and harness bells.

Furshtatskaya Street. The most beautiful of all, with its parkway and netted streetlamps. I stood in the dark and gazed up at the flat in which I'd had parents, and brothers, lived all my young life. Most of our old building was already dead, but our flat remained dark, inhabited. I had hoped to show it to Iskra when the trees came into leaf again. Not to be. I understood in that moment that we were all prisoners of time—and I too had my fate awaiting.

I breathed out great plumes of white vapor and stamped like a horse, the cold was beginning to creep in, but I was not ready to go back. I wanted this night to go on and on. Perhaps we were still up there, the Makarovs. It was only dinnertime, nine o'clock at most, glasses chiming as we shared our daily triumphs and sorrows over the fragrant dishes, the white-clothed table, Seryozha imitating a schoolmaster, making fun of his pretentious gestures, Volodya as he'd been when he left for the war, a man—the clinking of his spurs, his dark glossy eyes, the rich moustache, his laughter. Mama, her skirts trailing behind her, playing Scarlatti. I in my room, preparing for bed in a pressed nightgown, combing my hair in the round mirror, taking from my shelf a volume of poems. What should I read tonight? Blok, of course! Those perfect rhymes, as effortless as snow. I imagined I might stay here in the freezing parkway until I became another statue, a Galatea in reverse. But Blok had reached down from a passing ship called life, called art, called memory, and offered me his hand.

30 *59 Moika Embankment*

Snow wet my hat, blew sharp flakes into my eyes. People lingered in my way, people walked into me. I shoved back, bristly as a hedgehog. The whole day had been like this, gritty and coarse. I felt feverish, but I didn't want to be late for Bely's reading. When I finally stood before the door at the corner of Nevsky and the Moika Canal, I grew suddenly shy. What if they didn't let me in? I waited for at least three people to enter before I gathered the nerve, rehearsing my lines: *Blok invited me. Alexander Alexandrovich said I should come.*

I pushed open the anteroom door, and found a girl sitting behind a rickety table. "You're here for Bely? Ten rubles."

Admission, I hadn't considered that. But of course, the writers had nothing, of course they would take up a donation. That was probably the point of the evening. Tolstoy would have had to sell his beard if he lived in Petrograd now. I handed over the ten rubles, the entire contents of my purse—made from a chair's cushion, after I'd hacked up the rest into kindling.

Inside, the splendid hall was filling with people young and old, their faces familiar—not that I knew them, but their curiosity marked them, the light in their eyes. *Intelligence.* Tall windows framed the snowy vista outside, magical in the glow of streetlamps, and between them, where a painting had once hung—I could detect its ghost on the wall—stood the lectern. The view framed dark, boarded-up shops and ragged, huddled passersby, but it was easy to imagine what it had been—bright with signs, the chicest pedestrians, new automobiles, the Eliseevs sitting here enjoying an aperitif before the theater. I *saw* it. Otherworldly, when everyone in the room was gaunt and still wore their coats and hats in the unheated hall. All except for one tall man in a suit and white shirt with a high stiff collar. Without having to be told, I knew this was Gumilev, Akhmatova's ex-husband.

> *Three things in this world brought him joy:*
> *white peacocks, the singing of vespers,*
> *and faded maps of America.*
> *He hated to hear children cry,*
> *hated tea with raspberries*
> *and women acting hysterical*
> *...Me? I was his wife.*

No cringing for him, cold or no cold. He was as proud as an officer. I marveled at his cleanliness—his linen, his face. You had to admire his strength of will to shave in icy water, somehow wash that shirt. Gumilev was surrounded by young people, each one speaking, hoping for his approval. What I would give to be that young again, competing for the teacher's attention. But I wouldn't know how to do it anymore, idolize someone like that, hang on his every word. I'd grown as wary as a trap-wise fox.

I'd have thought Akhmatova would prefer someone ethereal, deep and full of music, more like Blok. *His eyes are so serene, one could be lost in them*...And where was he? I stood at the back of the crowd, watching for him as the audience found seats. I felt as I had that night at the Stray Dog, waiting to be thrown out. How could I possibly be here, watching my heroes at play? I recognized the poet Kuzmin with his heavy, sleepy eyes, and Khodasevich, tall and lanky, with round spectacles.

"Well, look what came in on the storm," said a man to my right.

Standing next to me in a worn-out overcoat stood the ultimate anti-Gumilev. Long-nosed, badly shaven Anton Chernikov. Just when I thought my life was a series of rooms, where the doors slammed firmly shut behind me. But here he was, still sneering, this angular bony figure. Smoking his cheap *makhorka*. I would have hugged him if his expression—that permanent ironic scowl—hadn't warned me off. He'd shaved his dark hair, as most men did now, and glowered like a convict. "Still living with your mother and that old *baba*?" His cigarette dangling from his lip. Tough guy. But I remembered those sweet days when he and my mother had labored together translating Apollinaire.

"I was in the countryside," I said. I wanted to touch him but knew he would flinch. "You?"

He shrugged. "As you see."

"*Okno?*" Our literary journal.

He shook his head. "No journals. No paper."

"I had a baby," I said, my eyes on the crowd, still coming in. "She died. In the fall." A fact. The fact of my life. "Her name was Antonina." I hadn't even thought about the echo.

Anton confronted by human tragedy was always several levels

out of his element. That hadn't changed either. He scratched the back of his neck. He took off his cap and rubbed his head. "A baby. That's rough," he said. "Does Genya know?" Anton and Genya, inseparable.

"He knew I was pregnant." More people passed before us, in various stages of starvation. But what faces! So clever, so awake. I was struck by a wave of pure love. I could die here, with these people, and die happy.

"He didn't say anything. Not a word."

We stood together, as awkward as children. "Did you ever publish the Apollinaire? *Alcools*?"

He brightened. "No, but I'm trying to get Gorky to take it for Universal Literature—have you heard about that? He's publishing translations—but it's all those old warhorses. *Dee-kens, Shaks-peer. Gyu-go.*" The eloquence of his sneer.

"You think the worker would rather have *Alcools*?" said an older woman standing with us, with wild gray hair and bright brown eyes. "You think that's what he's clamoring for after a hard day's work? Gorky's got to justify those titles."

O Holy Theotokos, they were arguing about Apollinaire! I felt as giddy as a prisoner broken out of a dark police cell walking into the sunshine.

"Inna's translating *Gyu-go*," Anton said, and I understood he'd exaggerated Victor Hugo's name on purpose, to tweak her.

"Jealous. It'll keep me in work for years. Thank God for Universal Literature," she said, her hand on my arm. "Gorky's single-handedly saving the Russian intelligentsia, translation by translation. He's gotten us rations and labor books. But he has to publish titles useful to the common people."

"What about useful to me?" Anton said. "What about my needs?" I noticed the people around us eavesdropping. "Am I not also a worker?" Appealing to his audience. "A literary worker? A miner of verse? There's more to literature than what the worker wants to read of an evening, you cow. Mayakovsky said there was literature for the consumer and literature for the producer. And the

producer needs advanced literature. Otherwise, we'll keep on cutting the same old shoes, year after year."

"I could use a pair of shoes," said the older woman. She studied
me with her friendly dark eyes. "So who's your friend, Chernikov?
I didn't know you had any."

"Marina Makarova, this untidy female is Inna Gants."

I'd heard of Inna Gants! She'd written short fiction, ghost stories,
and a popular detective novel.

She took a hand from the pocket of her capacious sweater to shake
mine. "I'm a neighbor. Third floor. When the moon is full, we hear
the howling." She pulled me closer, lowered her voice theatrically.
"But no one has actually seen the transformation."

"A bald exaggeration," Anton said. "Only a slight growl. I keep
it quiet."

They were living here? All these writers? How could all this have
been going on, and me know nothing of it? Because I'd been in the
grave, that's why. I hadn't looked up from my shoes since Iskra's
death. "They rent rooms here?"

"*Rent* being a relative term," said the older woman.

"Like bats, clinging to cliffs. And literature is our guano." Anton
obscured his head in a cloud of smoke.

"A pretty image," Inna said. "But of course, you're the poet."

When was the last time I'd witnessed a witty conversation? I felt
the fizzy intoxication of last night's *marafet* rising in me again.

"And I will survive these frozen caves as I survived the Poverty
Artel with the lot of you sleeping on my head."

"You lived with Chernikov?" Inna Gants took a step back. "My
God."

"She's Genya Kuriakin's wife," Anton said.

Now Inna's expression changed, became less warm but more curious. She examined me as if we hadn't just been chatting away like
old friends, her silence an awkward contrast to her volubility a moment before. Clearly Genya did not feature as a universal favorite at
the House of Arts.

I pretended a terrific interest in the beautifully carved plasterwork of the reception hall ceiling, the gilded mirrors still fitted to the paneling. "I've never been here before," I said. "I met Blok on Bolshaya Morskaya and he invited me to come tonight." Was I boasting, or justifying my presence?

"I just saw him," Anton said, scanning the crowd. "There. Sans streetlamp and pharmacy." *The night, the street, the streetlamp, the pharmacy*—one of my favorite Blok poems. Blok stood directly opposite us in the back of the room, hat in hand, blue coat slung across his shoulders. The famous curls shorn, no longer the masculine angel of my childhood, the face that had once made me debate whether it would be better to be a poet's Beautiful Lady or the poet oneself. He was in deep conversation with a tall, stooped man with a broad moustache and the heavy-boned face of a peasant. It was Maxim Gorky, whom I recognized from the frontispiece of a collection my parents had had in their library. A long-time socialist, he was supposed to be personal friends with Lenin. I'd read his poem "The Song of the Stormy Petrel" when I was six, and wanted to be like the courageous Petrel, unafraid of any storm. So strange to see him talking to Blok—the proletarian realist and the symbolist stag of the Silver Age. The revolution certainly made strange bedfellows. The light from a dusty electrolier lay upon the proletarian writer badly, accentuating his rough skin, and hair that bristled in every direction without a parting. He was taller than I'd imagined, and almost as weary as Blok.

Around these giants, the buzz of the assembly increased its volume, the way people always grow excited in the presence of the famous—pretending they didn't notice them. That had not changed with the revolution. A pretty, plump woman with wavy dark hair and a clever face stood at Gorky's elbow. "That's Gorky's mistress," whispered Inna Gants. "Moura Budberg. An Estonian baroness, they say. His *secretary*. Or was that *translator*? They say they're all living together over on Kronverksky Prospect, the wife and the secretary, plus Khodasevich's niece, two cousins from Rostov, and a Negro opera singer—so close they all have to turn over in bed as one."

A Negro opera singer! She was still here? I glanced around to see if I'd missed her, but no, there was no such jewel in attendance. I didn't know if my poor dry soul could absorb any more. And to think, if I had not left the telephone exchange early last night, sneaking out for horsemeat, I would have just gone on in my death-in-life, never knowing all this existed a few blocks away at 59 Moika Embankment.

"So when did you last see Genya?" The ash from Anton's *makhorka* was now at full length. It was dizzying to watch. At least he wasn't spitting sunflower seeds on the floor.

"Last summer," I said. I took his cigarette, flicked the ash, and took an awful puff, stuck it back between his lips. "On an agit-train heading for Perm."

"The *Red October*? You saw the *Red October*?" His smirk for a moment dropped into genuine surprise.

I thought again of that poem Genya had left for me before departing for the Urals, his supposed suicide note for his own soul. He never saw the infant who had borne his name. "He left me behind when I went into labor." Was that unfair of me? I softened my tone. "The battle lines were changing. He had to move on. I assume he made it."

"He's back in Moscow." Anton pulled me to him to make room for another man on my left, then realized what he had done—touched me—and quickly dropped my arm. "He's got a new collection coming out."

Inna Gants made a disgusted *kh*. "The rest of us are reciting in unheated halls, but Kuriakin gets a nice shiny collection."

Yes, I could imagine if the government had any paper at all, they would make it available for Genya.

"I'm editing it for him, actually," Anton said. "It's called *On the Red October*."

I had written nothing, and he had a new collection. Iskra had died and Genya's star had rocketed into the heavens. Well, good for him.

"Come up to my belfry after the reading, I'll show it to you," Anton said.

Against the far wall, Blok spoke urgently to Gorky, who kept shaking his head. Perhaps he didn't want to take Blok's translation either. The plump mistress Moura said something amusing, breaking the tension between them. Then Gorky and the woman took their seats, while Blok remained standing against the wall near the door. I wished he would stay out of that draft, he looked like he would catch pneumonia if he didn't have it already.

"I'm thinking of taking Gumilev's studio class," I said, watching a bald man swat the snow from his shoulders. "Blok thought I might like it."

"You can't work with Gumilev." Anton was outraged. "He's a monarchist. And a womanizer. Plus, he hates vers libre. Plus, he thinks he's God."

"Blok is God," I said.

"No, *Shklovsky* is God," said Anton.

"I think Gorky's got the title locked," Inna said.

I imagined the House of Arts must have ferocious politics. Like a cave in a snowstorm, all the animals had gathered here. I gazed around at faces I didn't recognize but they all had that air of belonging to *someone*. Ah, the luxury to still have a face. *Litso, Lichnost'*. *Personality, Identity*. To be one recognizable thing, and continue to be that, put your name to it, your signature. Like Gumilev's starched collar.

But maybe I was wrong about having no face. Anton had recognized me. I tucked my arm into his, and felt his shocked stiffness. But I was half in love with him tonight. Despite his tough pose, *he knew me*. And I'd introduced myself to Blok with my true name. Maybe this was the start of a restoration. I would pick up the shards, glue them together once more. I didn't know how they would fit, but there must be some motif that would encompass all the half-truths, the eighth notes. I wanted to live in the whole house for a change, not just the legal nine square meters. I'd been pretending that it was safer, to take up the least possible room, but it wasn't. It was dangerous in a very private way, like dry rot, like termites.

A cheerful blue-eyed man mounted the podium. He had the round bald head of an egg.

"*That's* Shklovsky," Anton whispered proudly. As if we'd come to the point of this whole excursion. "He lives here, right on my hall. We speak every day."

The critic made a few announcements: about an upcoming lecture by Eikhenbaum about the Young Tolstoy, a Dobuzhinsky exhibition opening next week in the front gallery—Dobuzhinsky! He was still here?—and a reminder that the Poets' Guild had moved to the Muruzi house. Then he introduced Bely.

Every cultured Russian had encountered Bely's novel *Petersburg* in installments before the war. The risk of it, the intricate jokes, his portrayal of the city! The work delighted us as it had shocked others, the absurdity of its presentation of deadly serious issues—a bomb-throwing son assigned to assassinate his own father with a sardine-can bomb. It was hard to really know what Bely's politics were. There was a big dose of Gogol—even I had tried a bit of fantastical prose under its influence.

And here was the man himself. All of them were here, in this icy heaven: Blok, Gorky, Gumilev, Bely. All that was missing was Akhmatova.

Bely was balder than his photographs, and what hair he had was white and uncut. But it was his eyes you remembered, their mad blue flame. Bely took the stage to applause that seemed faint compared to the thunder that had once met Genya when he alit from the *Red October* to address the agitprop crowds. But these lucky eighty or hundred souls weren't just any crowd. They were the remaining intelligentsia of Petersburg. And, of course, most of us still wore our gloves.

Bely explained that his new work, *Notes of an Eccentric,* was a memoir, very direct and simple. He had repudiated skill and craft forever! I was sorely disappointed—that's not what we'd loved about Bely. Had he surrendered so utterly to our spartan times? But when he began to read, I realized he either had been joking or really didn't understand how strange his own language was, his native mode of thought. The made-up words, the cadences of imagistic prose. His skill, his craft, *was* his face. He could no more write without creating new language and sounds and strange encounters than breathe without lungs.

The phantasmagorical tale, this supposed memoir, was populated by dreams and doppelgangers, a gentleman in a bowler hat, a mysterious brunet spy. And of course, bureaucrats. The section he read concerned a train trip from Switzerland to London on the eve of the war. It felt like a novel, except its hero was no longer the hapless son of *Petersburg* carrying a sardine-can time bomb. Bely himself had become the bomb. I supposed that's what he meant by memoir.

As he read, I had the strange sensation that the House of Arts was moving, that the whole building had swung out from its berth on the Moika Embankment and set out to sea. We were on a journey together, setting forth to some port as yet unknown, with Bely as our captain. He described the beginning of the war, and in his mind the war and his own inner conflicts had become fused. In fact, the war was the result of that internal turmoil. It reminded me of Andrei Ionian, who had believed that the civil war was a result of a struggle in the upper dimensions, manifesting itself here below. But this was an even stranger expression of the idea, more personal, more terrifying: *"Explosions in me thus became explosions of the world; war crawled out of me—circled me."* This was true horror. His own contradictions had *caused the war.*

"They know everything, they know that I am not me, but the bearer of an enormous 'I' stuffed with the global crisis; I am a bomb, flying off to explode; and exploding, explode everything there is; this they would not allow, of course; to restrain us with hugs... They know that the nurseries were warm and bright: the baby in me lowered into the thunder of the world's speech."

Oh that beautiful thunder!

"I hear distinct whispering all around:—It's—Him!" A momentous thing, to be so greeted into the world. What would it be to feel that you mattered so much? No ordinary human being, but a symbol, a mythic figure—*It's Her!* That would never be me.

The crowd blended into one, following this astonishing invention, the language, the philosophical position. Blok, standing across the room, watched his old friend the way you'd watch a tightrope walker crossing an abyss—admiring and terrified. I could see, he loved him still. I was less worried for Bely than Blok. He seemed exhausted—so the opposite of his friend, whose blue eyes held the crackling intensity of a downed electrical line. Who dared to walk out onto thin air, supported only by the force of this language. Stroking his bald head, sweating, stammering, as if his words could even now explode the Eliseev parlor.

He moved into imagining his birth, birth as the soul falling into the Void, into the disgusting, robotic abyss of the body. No, I would not agree with him there. The body was no Void. I had seen the Void—and it lay on a sidewalk on Mikhailovskaya Street. It lived in the barrel of a Mauser pointed at your head, in the greased eyes of a provincial Chekist unbuttoning his pants. The Void coiled in a cellar's bloody drain. And it hung between the fingers of a dangerous man simply playing with a string. Not in the waiting flesh of an infant body.

It was wonder I had seen in Iskra's eyes, wonder at the things of this world. I tried to imagine it Bely's way, entering this heavy, confused thing—incarnation—this peculiar fragment of spirit being shoehorned into the swollen fleshy form. But I found it repugnant. Certainly an infant might be frightened, but what of wonder? To me, all this revealed a generalized horror of life. No matter what had happened to me, I still pitched my tent on the side of the living. I had seen those green trees in Iskra's eyes.

Perhaps my brain had been blunted by all I'd been through these last months, but I had to apply the greatest concentration to follow Bely through the symbols and figures of his story, like translating from a language half learned—Hungarian, or Greek. I couldn't be sure I understood him or the very opposite of what he'd intended. The shattered form, the tricks with language, the invented words. Was I fatally damaged? I had been more clever at fifteen. Anton was in his element, needless to say, standing next to his hero

Shklovsky. Khodasevich tapped his foot in time to the rhythmic beats. I wove in and out of the story, returning when the images grew more concrete—the brunet man and terrorist bombs on the train, and a delicious series of scenes as Bely arrived in England. His humor as his alter ego scurried around to the various subdepartments of the English bureaucracy, trying to get stamps on his papers to declare he was

> —*In London*
> —*In London*
> —*In London*
> —*In London*
> —*In London.*

The sweet music of stamps being pounded onto one's documents was a sound that everyone in the audience could recognize. The man was a poet, more a poet in prose than a novelist. Certainly it was the strangest memoir one could image. Anton chewed on his cuticles, his arms folded in front of him, making comments under his breath. Moura Budberg whispered to a woman in a black coat and a hat with a broken feather, who became increasingly animated. Gorky scrawled something on a notepad.

Finally, Bely read a section describing his return to Russia, where he found that our very souls had been blown out of the tops of our heads with the explosion of war, leaving us so many empty grotesques. *"Like a corpse—the only thing that remained as before: arms, an abdomen, I seemed to myself to be an abdomen irresponsibly propped up on legs: the rest—a chest, throat, brain—I felt just emptiness. I monstrously shot all this from the split darkness into the sky. 'That' was . . . a nonliving, dull, deaf abdomen of a body.*

"And so—I saw that picture of myself multiplied into millions of darting bodies in greatcoats everywhere: deaf, dumb, abdomen bodies moved all over, shooting into space, like nuclei, their human I's; these I's flew out of the bodies; and the body, unloving and mindless, walked

everywhere:——Has Russia not shot its 'I' into the great void? Did the shot of the world war not leave a totally dull 'It'...?"

We'd been deafened by war, the war had shot us from our souls. Grief washed over me. Yes, we had not been killed——we lived on in a city of ruin and aftermath that was "nothing" and extended over the whole earth. People reduced to legs and stomachs. I looked for Blok across the room. Surely he was no abdomen on legs. How sad he looked. I saw, Blok felt this too. That he had shot his *I* out into the void, and what stood here was a shadow. Dying.

No, not dying——dead. Literally, I was looking at a dead man. All at once, I saw it. *Oh God, please not Blok.*

But I saw it as clearly as Bely had seen the brunet man on the train, as my mother had seen me in the forest. I *saw* that Blok had died. Hollowed out. I clapped my hand over my mouth. Carrying the weight of my own dead child was heavy enough, but to see Blok staggering under the weight of his own corpse, it was like watching a horse falling in the street, struggling to get up, but not having the strength. What terrible bravery dwelled in that tall gray figure! How horrible to still have to walk around in public, as if one hadn't passed away. Didn't anyone else see it?

I looked around at the others of his generation, Kuzmin, and Bely and Gorky. All of them, hanging on by a thread. *Come back! Who can take your place?* We were ants by comparison, Genya, Anton, me. Though there was still Mandelstam, I told myself. And Tsvetaeva, Pasternak in Moscow. Mayakovsky. Maybe this sniffly girl with the handkerchief would be the next Blok, or the young man with the broken nose.

I would not accept that our souls were gone forever. It could not be. If it was so, what would you call *this,* this House of Arts, and these intelligent, cultured people who'd come to listen to Bely in this freezing hall, who had stood for nearly two hours, listening to his shattered, difficult story? Had their souls blown out, leaving them only their stomachs on legs? No, they were fighting for their souls day after day, fighting for the soul of Russia as I'd once fought for Iskra in a village bathhouse.

At last the reading was done. I felt as though I'd run a marathon in a lightning storm. My head still buzzed. The heroic audience rose from their seats, or stretched in the back, lit cigarettes, and the hall rang out with their talk as they greeted one another and congratulated Bely, who seemed if anything more animated than when he began. Most of all, I wanted to talk to Blok, to tell him what he meant to me, tell him not to die.

But already a young woman was at his side, speaking quickly, animatedly. Blok was listening but with such weariness—he hadn't the energy to fly from the leaden circle of her chatter. I stopped where I was. I didn't want to approach him, one more person who wanted to bathe in the last glow, like light from a dead star. What need did he have of my pleasantries? He needed the very angels to come and take him home, to pick him up and wrap him in his broken wings, and lift him into a sky of immortal blue.

He looked up and saw me, where I stood halfway across the hall, and smiled at me. And death slipped away from his features, and he became himself again. *Not quite dead,* his smile seemed to say.

I found Anton in a hallway off the dining room where a number of young people had taken refuge. It was warmer there than the formal rooms, where the Eliseev servants were passing out cups of weak tea. Here were the other members of Anton's literary circle, some who lived here, some who had come to hear Bely. The boxer, Tereshenko, I recognized, and Nikita Nikulin from our old days as the Transrational Interlocutors of the Terrestrial Now.

I had to be at work tomorrow at nine, but I was shimmering, dazzled by the company, and could not imagine leaving to slog through the blizzard that was now hurling down snow out the windows. "I'd love to see that manuscript," I said to Anton.

And I let him lead me deeper into the House of Arts.

31 *The Towers of Ilium*

What a vast beehive it was, a warren of art, an ark, an ocean liner. I would never be able to find my way out again. Anton opened his door, a narrow door someone had marked with the letter *ZH* in chalk—for *Zhenshchiny, Women*. Cold poured out as if he'd opened a sluice. He stumbled in and lit a lamp with the skritch of a match. The room proved cluttered, with a strange window that began at floor level and ended around chest height, where one could presumably sit cross-legged and gaze down Nevsky, were it not for the frost flowers blooming on the panes.

I smoothed out the blankets on the unmade bed as Anton fiddled with the lamp. Its wobbly flame cast its light on the mess of his table, the untidy piles of letters and manuscripts, books. Books—a good sign. They'd not yet been forced to burn them. Perhaps they received firewood from the House as well as their daily bread. It was cold enough in the room to see our breaths curl whitely into the air. Anton moved to the stove and attempted to light it, but these temperamental little goddesses didn't favor brusque treatment, and the smoke of its disgust immediately began to spill into the room.

Sometimes I really did feel like a peasant, watching urbanites struggle against their sullen material objects. I squatted next to him. Shutting the *bourgeoika* door against further pollution, I rolled some paper nuggets from pages of an old "thick journal" he was using—*Russkaya Mysl'. Russian Thought*. A Chekhov story, alas. I didn't have my hatchet but used one of the orphans' penknives to peel a shard of wood from a rough plank that looked like it had been torn off a fence. The revolution's forbidden fuel. I lit the end of the stick and shoved it up into the pipe to warm the freezing air. In a few minutes, the little goddess was happily humming.

"How do you *do* that?" Anton frowned, rubbing his badly shaved jaw like he had a toothache. He threw himself into the one chair. Always the good host.

"Witchcraft," I said, dusting the soot from my hands. "I sold my soul to a man on a staircase."

"Hope you got a good price," said Anton. "I'm going to put you forward for membership immediately—no one can get these stoves to do anything but stink."

"Nice to have something to offer. 'She writes a certain *incendiary* line.'"

He laughed. "Yes, that was always your way. Leaving a swath of smoking rubble in your wake. Our own little Helen, toppling our towers of Ilium." Was that how he saw me? The femme fatale? And what did he mean *our*? But he was digging through the papers on his little table.

"Here it is." He handed me a stack of typewritten pages. *On the Red October* by Gennady Yurievich Kuriakin. Moscow, 1920. Government Press.

As I sat on the hard little bed, I saw he was nervous. Meeting my eyes by accident, he quickly busied himself with his books and papers. He'd seemed happy enough a moment ago. I took off my dirty mittens and blew onto my hands. The room was warming. I couldn't see my breath anymore. I began to read.

It was a long *poema* about the journey of the *Red October*, pencil-marked in the margins in Anton's small neat hand. I could hear Genya's voice—of course he would write an epic. A train demanded it, one car linked to the next. Here were the sailors and the crowds and the stupefied peasants, the steppe nomads, the leather-clad commissars, Gaida and Kolchak out in the distance. Matvei the journalist, Yermilova, even Trotsky was there. Everyone made an appearance but a long-lost beloved found in Tikhvin living with a one-armed man, a woman pregnant with another man's child. She who had to be put off the train in the middle of nowhere to give birth to her only child. "Funeral for Myself on the Tracks at Kambarka" didn't make the cut.

It was strong, beautiful, and thunderous, immense and iron

wheeled. What place could the fate of one confused woman and her infant have on a stage so grand? I'd left no trace. Gone was the man who wrote *Who would have dreamed / I would / drop / my own heart / from the gallows / pull the rope myself*. It was as if he had scraped off half of his face—the tender one, the lover, the boy who couldn't bear the sight of cruelty. He'd erased that self, chopped him up and fed him into the boiler of the *Red October*. He'd cut out his own heart for his enormous beloved, Russia, as she rolled out before the train hurtling along the vast steel cables of its tracks.

I caught Anton watching me again, his intelligent hazel eyes, the pugnacious mouth. I wouldn't cry. Life was as it was. And we would all be erased soon enough—except Genya. It was sad that he'd erased me, but I would do my own remembering. I would have to cut my mind into the stone of the world just as he had done, if I wanted to leave some trace.

"It's good, but hard," I said, handing the pages back. "When did he get so hard?" Anton the faithful, Anton the believer. "I miss the old Genya."

I heard someone moving around on the other side of the wall, the scrape of a chair. I'm sure he or she was surprised to hear a woman in Anton's cell. I examined his oddly shaped room, his piles of books and solitary bed, the one strange window. Perhaps it had once been a passage between two other rooms. On the walls, grease-pencil drawings had been applied directly to the plaster—cubo-futurist objects and portraits and letterforms. Yes, here was Anton scowling, and other people—Nikita Nikulin, the broken angles of his body; Galina Krestovskaya: hair, one eye, music. I recognized the style. "Is this Sasha's? Do you still see him?" The handsome blond painter who was so in love with Dunya Katzeva.

"He was in the army for a while. Got wounded in the Ukraine. Also in the ass." He was smiling, a Mona Lisa hint, and yet I saw it. "They shipped him home. He's living down the hall. Shall we get him? He's teaching at Svomas, living with that girl—the Katzev girl..."

Dunya! They were here! But I thought of that terrible day when

Mina threw me out with my child in my arms. How could I face her? I didn't want to have to tell her what had happened to my girl, that I had not kept her safe. "No, let them be. It's good to see you, Anton. Really good."

He seemed uneasy to be alone with me, without other people to throw between us. He shuffled nervously, touching his papers, leaning on the window, scratching at the frost flowers. He rubbed his cropped hair, as abashed as a small boy, and irritated at his own awkwardness as only Anton could be. He sat back down at his scarred table, edged in cigarette burns—desk, dressing stand, dining table all in one—his long legs crossed before him. Our feet almost touched. He fished through the papers, looking for something, putting some aside, collecting others. I wondered what he'd been doing for female companionship—still going to the whores? Or maybe Galina Krestovskaya had taken him up now that her husband had been shot. She might need some sort of anchor, and Anton had always appealed to her for some reason.

He read some poems aloud by people in his circle, some I knew, some I didn't. Most had a strong element of the sound poetry he loved. Arseny Grodetsky was still around—I remembered him from our evenings at Galina's, the sixteen-year-old radical who still lived at home with Mama. But such wonderful sounds. *Ou ou ou, aya, kaya, kataya.* There seemed to be room for everyone at the House of Arts. Perhaps even me.

We talked on, joyously, seriously, on an infinity of subjects, I felt as though I hadn't spoken for years. We talked until it was far too late to try to get home, not in that snowstorm, and my head drooped like a dandelion. I must have fallen asleep at some point. I dreamed I was on the *Red October*, and I kept trying to jump off, but it was moving much too fast.

Eight inches of snow fell during the night, snow without blemish, calf deep as I left the House of Arts. A sleepy, mystic snowfall, it needed a Blok to sing it—a real prewar snow. It begged for a fast sleigh, a fat coachman, gray horses with dark noses and intellectual eyes. What I would have given for a sleigh ride—rushing behind a feathery-hoofed horse with bells on its harness, snow encasing my collar and dusting my hat, face tingling with pleasure.

Citizens on the day's snow detail were emerging from the courtyards, preparing to take up their Soviet shovels.

Take your time, Comrades. Don't be so quick to strip us of our ermine.

I practically waltzed down Bolshaya Morskaya to the telephone exchange, but forgot where the dead horse was and tripped over it. It sent me sprawling, face-first, hands outstretched, into the new snow. Like landing on a featherbed.

Entering the vast exchange, I let the monstrous, oceanic wave of noise pour over me like waves turning stones over on a thousand beaches. Last night, Anton had said that Blok stopped writing poetry after "The Scythians," because there were no more sounds. He should come here, then—there was nothing but sound, clatter of metal on metal like a hailstorm. But no fine long Blokian *ah*s and *ou*s and *oh*s—modern sounds were all consonants, *cktcktkttkkkk*...I thought that Arseny Grodetsky and his *ou*s and *aya*s and *kaya*s and *kataya*s would enjoy a class trip to the telephone exchange.

How paltry and inhuman it seemed now, my refuge of these last dry months. I sat down at my station and donned the mouthpiece that rested on my chest, the headset, one of a chorus—*Number, please. Number, please.* The open mouths of the switchboard sockets—like souls frozen in hell, screaming in the Dantean symphony. Clamoring, all these people, hungry for connection.

> *Voices echoed along the nerves...*
> *Snakelike twined, in cables cased*
> *Orders, whispers, sighs,*
> *linking leaders to their bureaucrats*
> *Lover to beloved.*

"One moment, please. Sorry, yes. Number, please."

Sonya, my switchboard stall mate, cast sidelong looks in my direction. "What's wrong with you?"

We were supposed to be as much a part of the switchboard as the switches and sockets, with skins of steel, the wires our nerves and blood vessels, connecting the city through the strings of ourselves.

But the more I listened to the poetry of the telephone exchange, the worse my performance grew. I disconnected calls that were not yet ready to terminate, or forgot about them when the light signaled that the call had ended. I accidentally connected people who had never met—and laughed out loud at the mischief of my hands, capable of introducing perfect strangers. Well, there was too much disconnection in our city.

> *Who's to say the connection's wrong?*
> *Perhaps he was someone*
> *you should know.*
> *Or one to whom you haven't*
> *spoken for years—*
> *"Milashkov,*
> *From Kirochnaya Street?*
> *Gerasim Milashkov?"*
> *"It's he."*
> *"My God! It's Dmitry Grushin!"*
> *"Dima? With the pretty big sister?"*
> *"Well, yes! Though*
> *she's as big as a horse now,*
> *God bless her."*

Sonya stared at me, walleyed. Why on earth could I be laughing? What could there possibly be to laugh at nowadays, in this kingdom of cold and hunger? I was not doing my job and I was laughing. I clearly must be drunk, or mad.

Yes, I was. Drunk to be back in the world where people knew things, had ideas. What didn't we talk about last night in that odd little room? About sound, I recalled, and the elimination of the hard sign. About *Notes of an Eccentric*, and Blok's "Retribution," and the *Red October*. The sound of it—Genya on top of that train, the wind in his ears, all of Russia rolling out before him. The poem matched that scale, gigantic. It straddled the world, hurtling the times ahead like a giant relay from stop to stop. All uncertainty and loneliness left behind with the miles. In the end, I forgave him the absence of "Funeral for Myself." That's what happened in life. You held funerals for parts of yourself.

Number, please.

Anton had railed against the Gumilevs and Khodaseviches, sure they would dismiss Genya's epic out of hand as mere agitprop. "They're worried that he'll show them up, that's all. Genya doesn't have time for their minuets."

But I was *from Petersburg* as well as Petrograd and had time for minuets as well as locomotives. Was tenderness only a side dish? Perhaps it would return when this was all over, when the souls that had been shot from our heads had found us again.

Number, please.

I should write a poem about the switchboard: "Who's to Say the Connection's Wrong?" All these Soviet young ladies with wires coming out of their heads. I'd recited poems for Anton last night, but they were old, and so much had happened since then—the Five. Ionia. I had not written yet about my father. I had not written about Iskra, or the orphanage that was Russia.

"I wasn't joking about your joining us," Anton had said. "We need you. A woman writing stuff that's not about love and Mama and the time a Red Guard smashed my doll. They need to hear you." He rubbed his face, embarrassed to have let such a personal statement escape his lips. "You should be here, not working in some telephone exchange. Putting wires in holes when we're making the literature of the future."

"You just want someone to take care of your stove," I teased him.

"You have that book. You're Genya Kuriakin's wife—"

"I haven't seen him for a year."

He'd rubbed his forehead, like a schoolboy over a mathematics problem. "But you're still married, *da?* Everything is political. We can't afford to be naive. Plus my recommendation, your publications in *Okno*...and Blok's on the board. We'll get Shklovsky, that's three, surely there will be two more..."

Would they ever consider me as a member of that august league? Gumilev lived there, Shklovsky. Who was I? The biggest nobody.

The switchboard's lights blazed, everybody with such important calls to make. Astoria to Smolny. Second City Soviet, a commissar looking for a lost load of fuel. *Number, please. Number, please.*

> *Honey oozing from the boards*
> *paints the arms*
> *of the Soviet Young Ladies*
> *stickysweet.*

Evidently our group's literary output had not vanished from the earth. Rooting in his boxes, Anton had produced miracles. A copy of Genya's *Red Horses*. Also the first one, *Chronicles of a Misspent Youth*. Here was Anton's finished Apollinaire, and eight issues of *Okno*. He still had his copy of Khlebnikov's poems, hand-lettered by Guro. And, the most startling revelation—a little bound volume, the sky-blue cloth cover, my name on the spine. *This Transparent Hour* by M. D. Makarova.

The delicate pages, slightly edged in mold. I turned them with such tenderness, as if this was my very self, my youth. So outspoken! So fiery, so in love with the idea of greatness. One page had been turned in—a poem in imitation of Pushkin by way of Akhmatova, about a man walking through a field, still in love with a girl of his youth. How he regretted their separation! Wondering what had become of her, how she'd marked him forever.

> *Where is she, those eyes of liquid night,*
> *the thick red hair that curls upon her dress?*
> *My heart, circling, cries like a gull for her caress*
> *On her lost shoulders the map of my hopelessness.*

And Anton had read and reread it.

Anton the futurist, the soulless beast, had carried this along with him all this time, this bit of retrograde romance. And here I'd always thought he considered women merely annoying, especially me—an unfortunate appendage of Genya's. Yet how pleased he'd been to show it to me, despite his nonchalance, as if it were proof of something he could not say.

Our own little Helen.

I had to be careful. I wanted no more toppled towers, I had witnessed enough destruction.

32 *The Golden Fleece*

The temperature dropped down, down into the sarcophagus of negative numbers. Minus 30, minus 40, minus 50 degrees. On Shpalernaya Street, all the tenants dragged their mattresses into the front parlor, where we slept pressed together for warmth, pooling our wood, breathing each other's breaths, sharing each other's lice. When the wood was gone we tore up floorboards at the back of the apartment. A dying city eats itself alive the way a starving body consumes its own flesh. Every day, people died in the street, just dropped as they walked along, or fell in the queues. Nothing could be done.

Queuing was brutal. Like everybody else, I did it during the day when I was supposed to be working. Come nightfall, no one remained outdoors. No more evenings at the House of Arts. Only mandatory street-sweeping duty and a house-sentry shift could force me outside of this packed hellish room. I wished I still had a little of that confiscated *marafet* to steel myself for the horrific obligatory night shift stuck inside the *dvornik*'s shack, watching the gate, holding a rusty pistol I was sure dated from the Crimean War. I would never forget being forced to let the Cheka in to search in the building, and watching them drag a fellow tenant away after midnight, an older man, his wife trailing him in 30 degrees below zero, keening like a pietà.

Otherwise I sat on my mattress in the airless room with the other tenants, chockablock, wrapped in all my bedding and every shred of clothing I owned, even my boots, a brand-new notepad open on my knee and a shaved pencil in my hand. I worked in the wavering light of my small lamp, which I would not turn off until I was ready, no matter how the neighbors complained. I fixed their stoves, they could give me this much. I smoothed the page of my precious notebook, my prize.

I'd gone to the registrar to see if I could trade Wednesdays for Sundays, as Anton's studio met on Wednesday afternoons. The registrar was an original employee left over from before the revolution. Most of them had refused to abet the Bolsheviks in any way, and struck—but there were a few old girls like this one for whom the telephone exchange was a sacred trust. This was her Temple, and she, loyal Vestal, would not leave it in its hour of need, no matter who ruled the city—the tsar, the Bolsheviks, the Germans, or Bannik the bathhouse devil. I couldn't imagine what she had been like before the revolution, but her Soviet role had shriveled her into a bitter, brittle leaf blowing down the center of a vast, deserted square. Just opening the big work schedule book for me seemed a violation of its sanctity.

She gazed at me through her pince-nez, outraged that I would put my own needs before the needs of the exchange. In that, she fit in with the Bolshevik project perfectly. "You think this is all just for your convenience? That I can just switch Wednesday for Sunday at every girl's whim? You lot take off whenever you like it anyway—there's only half of you here on any one day, the rest are ghosts. But you all come to work when we hand out the ration cards, oh yes, you can count on that."

It was the same with every workplace in Petrograd. We all had to eat. Too bad we couldn't all live on self-pity and propriety like this old bag. "I need Wednesday afternoons."

She glared at me. Who was I? Only an insect in this great swamp, a clicking cicada in the vast hall of the switchboard, the merest gnat. On and on she went, flatly refusing my request and heaping invective on every Soviet worker, every girl with a bit of a flush in her cheek. The old bat. I would take both, then, Wednesdays and Sundays. Some provisioned their bodies, I would provision my mind, and bureaucrats be damned. When she finally did turn away, I personally provisioned myself of the pad of paper lying unguarded by her telephone. It was the least she could do for literature.

Now, propped up with my pillow against the wall, covered with my featherbed and my sheepskin, my fox hat on my head, surrounded by my fellow coughers, farters, yammerers, shiverers, and snorers, and someone quietly weeping, I tested the ice of my imagination. Would it hold me? I felt the sharp tip of my pencil, which I'd shepherded since the orphanage, carefully shaving only so much from its precious lead. Lord knew when I'd ever get another.

An unholy scream shattered the normal quiet talk. The man in the next room had typhus. His wife was nursing him in his awful fever. "Leave me alone, Devil!"

A few of the neighbors shouted back, "Keep him quiet in there!" "Take him to the hospital already!" "Let the devil take him!"

You had to admire his wife's determination—most of them packed their relatives off to the typhus hospital as fast as you'd turn a pancake. But she refused to move him, and we quarantined them in their own arctic room so as not to spread it to the rest of us. Typhus was a monster, and the epidemic had finally found its way into our flat. I was terrified. If I got typhus now, who would fight for me, nurse me, keep me from jumping out the window? We were all so close to death here, I could see its black veiled form walking among the mattresses. It was a terrible thing to say, but I was lucky that Iskra had died when you could still dig a grave. So many succumbing in the city now, you couldn't get a burial. We ourselves had bodies stacked in an empty room—the daughter of this one, husband of that. There was no one to collect them. How much worse it would have been to have Iskra frozen in the next room. And yet people stood it. It was hideous how much a human being could get used to.

I took off my mitten, blew on my hand, rubbed it against my face and returned it to its sheath, concentrating my attention on that little stub of a pencil. I breathed through the pores of my skin as we used to do at Ionia—otherwise, the stench in the room was unbelievable. Old stale clothing, dirty hair, flatulence, the horrible tainted breath of people who cooked their dinners with linseed and cod liver oil, added to the smokiness of the little stove, which my neighbors had placed under my care. Oh, for a moment out of the fug and the horrible togetherness! But it was beyond unthinkable to attempt the outside air.

I would have gone out of my mind, except for this, the notebook, the pencil, the sounds alive in my head. Despite the cold, the deep nausea of hunger, and the higher nausea of half-rotten potatoes fried in cod liver oil, I was alive again, and poetry was like a reed I could breathe through, connecting me from this premature burial to the fresh outer air of my imaginative life. Meanwhile the man next door screamed and pleaded with his monsters. I imagined his wife, perhaps sick herself, mopping his brow. Perhaps they would both die. Sometimes being with someone was more terrible than being alone. At least if I died, no one would mourn me. It was cleaner that way, simpler. My exit would leave an unblemished surface on the waters.

The flickering of the lamps gave life to exhausted, anxious faces. A family installed closer to the door was arguing about the division of their rations. The father kept shorting one of the daughters. She shrieked and swore. "You're trying to starve me. Why do you hate me?"

"Because you're a noisy bitch," someone shouted.

"Mind your own business!" she shouted back.

The one thing nobody could do, however much we wished it.

I lowered the flaps of my fox hat, and thought of that long-ago night on St. Basil's Eve, the night we had cast the wax. Mina got the key, Varvara the broom, and I the sailing ship. I tried to remember sailing. The feeling of giddiness on a summer's day. The freshness of the wind off the gulf, all heaven before us. Sailing in a little boat with the big boys, Kolya and Volodya in the sun, Kolya saying he was taking us to Spain. Seryozha left behind on shore with Avdokia and his paints and little easel. Oh, the speed of it, the sun on the water.

But I couldn't write about that. *Mama and the time a Red Guard smashed my doll.*

All the foreign shores were out of reach now. All the sails furled. The world had retreated from us, behind the blockade, leaving us to stand or fall, indifferent to our fate. The sight of the empty Neva this silent autumn had filled me with melancholy. No freighters, no fishing boats, just ruined barges. The river had never glittered so, people could actually fish it again after the centuries of heavy shipping. This Petersburg, built for sailing, built for the world, dying alone.

> *Petersburg the seafaring,*
> *You opened your arms to the world.*
> *Sailed out, nose to the great earth's winds, to . . .*

To do what? *Adventure, explore, buccaneer?* Nothing was quite right. Come back to it.

> *But now the world's retreated*

What could be quieter than the Neva stripped of commerce, more naked, more neglected, more forgotten? The city was returning to that miserable Finnish marsh that Pushkin had described so well. Just another provincial outpost, crumbling away on this misty shore, this mausoleum of ice, this dead city where citizens crowded themselves into a single room like animals in a pen. Cave dwellers.

> *and Petrograd lies dying*

How does Petrograd lie dying?

> *like an old sailor in a bed by a window,*

Yes, I could do something with that.

> *legs black with gangrene,*
> > *no nurse to bathe him tenderly,*
> > > *Yet despite the stench of death*
> *he still smells the brine.*

Yes, let's give ourselves that much.

> *No longer does your ship leap beneath you.*
> > *Dolphins doubling in the wake.*
> > > *Once the silver line of any distant shore*
> *under gull-winged, light blue skies*

My Blok—light blue, gull-winged.

> > *was your*
> > > *homeland.*

My true homeland. Not Russia, not Red or White, not passports and *propuski*, but anywhere the mind could take you.

> *Oh, for those windward wild days,*
> > *a brazen long-limbed crew*
> > > *dazzling white-toothed Argonauts.*

> *Yes, yes, old man.*
> > *I too have stolen golden fleece*
> > > *and tasted the oxen of the sun.*

33 *The Thaw*

Like Yudenich, winter sounded retreat. Snow grudgingly gave way to the first rains, pelting the window of my little room, where I worked in the nest of my bed, rereading my poems. I already had them memorized, but I wanted to be sure, for tonight was my first public reading. Anton had managed to convince our elders that our group, the Squared Circle, was ready for a Living Almanac. These had taken the place of printed publications in this paperless year. Would I be able to make my words sing for strangers, as they sang for me in my head? Or would I just stare out at a crowd of stones? At least I would know if I belonged to the fraternity of poets, or whether I was simply fooling myself. I had been happy with my poems, but now that the reading approached, I was less sure.

Even if it was a disaster, it was still thrilling to see our fliers posted in windows and on fences, boldly drawn and lettered in cubo-futurist style by Sasha Orlovsky. The little cultural newspaper *Literary Herald* carried an advertisement. This was no mere salon reading. Living Almanacs were treated as publications and would be duly reviewed and criticized. I'd been working like a peasant in harvest time to finish the poems Anton had picked for my part of the offerings, cutting and replacing and adding and reordering. The audience would include the city's best poets and literary figures—by no means supportive of our aims. Knives would be sharpened. We were known as having futurist sympathies. Anton was a protégé of Shklovsky's, an avant-gardist and upstart. They would be out for blood—radicals and conservatives both.

I rose and tipped some water into my pail—you didn't even have to break the ice anymore—when a smart knock came. It was Olga Viktorievna, that busybody. "Marina Dmitrievna, they're here for your sanitation duty."

Oh, it couldn't be. Today? Of all days?

"They're out in the hall, waiting for you."

On the day of my grand debut, it seemed I would have to serve as part of a mandatory sanitation squad. I could have pretended I wasn't here, taken the chance...but Olga Viktorievna was on the job, dedicated to being wherever she was not wanted, hoping to find an unguarded door. I locked my door firmly behind me and descended to the street.

The spring thaw had revealed all our sins. As the frost retreated, human waste tidily frozen all winter was beginning to melt in the apartments and courtyards. It was up to the sanitation squads to clean the rooms that had been used as latrines and remove the evidence from the courtyards before it washed into the groundwater, cursing us with cholera again. Much as I disliked this duty, I had seen what cholera could do. I wouldn't want to see its effect on the capital of Once-Had-Been.

There were eight in my squad. We handed around cotton wool soaked in menthol to stuff up our nostrils and picked up our shovels. In our party were old bourgeoises who did nothing but complain, plus five real workers—two men and three women. We started with the top floor and worked down. One of the men became our crew leader. His name was Sinyakov, an old-style SR with nothing but abuse to heap on the Bolsheviks as we shoveled and carried the result in buckets down long flights of stairs to the wagon. We consoled ourselves that it wasn't as bad as the first crew, who'd had to clean the courtyard in the rain. Nobody envied them—though the stairs made this a harder job. It made my heart sink to see the devastation the winter had wrought. The occupants avoided meeting our eyes, the shame of people who three years ago would not have thought themselves capable of such filth.

"What do they know about how to run a city? We knew how to run a city," said the SR, "but they kicked us all out. That's the thing about the Bolsheviks. Anybody who knows how to do anything—a bullet in the back of the head. They don't care how it all falls apart, as long as they're kings of the shit heap."

What a day.

I preferred working with a housewife, Agnessa, who joked about the state of gastric health of the tenants as we scraped down the boards. "Look at this—my God, a wolfhound! I'm lucky if I shit once a fortnight."

We went from apartment to apartment, knocking on doors, always the same—the tenants avoiding meeting our eyes, someone showing us down a hall to the next site of the terrible and the repulsive. Some were beyond help, they'd torn out the floorboards for firewood and then shit between floors. It would soon seep down into the next apartment, rendering those rooms uninhabitable as well. Some flats had only two livable rooms left. No flat was any better than ours and most were worse. At least ours didn't have the water damage of the upper floors—not yet anyway. My throat and eyes stung with carbolic. I shoveled and scraped and carried and retched, and recited my poems to myself, imagining the audience, then trying not to imagine them.

I wondered if Blok would be there. He was the only one I really cared about. Terrifying, but essential. In a moment of madness, I had taken a flier to his home on Ofitserskaya, third floor, that window I'd once gazed upon as another might gaze upon a star. His name was still on a strip of paper over the doorbell. BLOK. I touched it for luck and rang.

His wife answered, a big, tall, academic-looking woman—it had to be she, Lyubov Mendeleeva, the daughter of the eminent scientist. A pretty hall, red-and-white-striped wallpaper. Was it still a private flat? She was taller than I'd imagined, with graying hair in a fringe. Was this woman really the inspiration for the Beautiful Lady? They had once all lived together in a shocking ménage, Bely and Blok and Lyubov and Soloviev...now she was just a rather stolid old woman. I had to remind myself, this would happen to us all. No matter how scandalous we had been, some young person would look at us and think, *How conventional, how dull.*

I'd pressed the flier into her hand. "I'm Makarova—" I pointed to my name. "I hope Alexander Alexandrovich will come. He was the one who introduced me to the House of Arts. He's been so very kind..."

She took the flier, shaking her head. "You poets. Isn't there a sane person in all of Petrograd?" Sighing, closing the door.

We worked all day in the sleety rain until the wagon was full, then turned in our shovels and had the *domkom* sign off on our labor books that we had accomplished our citizenly duty. Oh, for a real bath. I could only dream of the old bathhouse at Maryino, the oceans of hot water, the steam and fragrant branches. I had to make do with what was in the flat, carefully cleaning my boots with newspaper and water and ashes, then scrubbing myself in my pail with boiled water, but the reek of carbolic and human waste clung to me. Or maybe it was just my imagination. I dressed and stopped to comb my hair in the hall mirror. Olga Viktorievna squeezed out of her room, an obsequious smile on her awful face. "Date tonight? A boyfriend?"

I didn't let anyone in the flat know about my other life. To them I was just the little scribbler, the Soviet young lady who spent an unusual amount of time in her room and could sometimes be heard talking to herself, who was so good with their stoves.

I swept my hair, cropped to the jaw, back off my face. Honest, straightforward. *Comrade.* Then tried it forward in waves. Prettier. More *Soviet young lady* than *comrade.* Who did I want to be for my first reading? I wished I were like Akhmatova. She knew how she wanted to look, the famous fringe, the long hair twisted up, the beads, the shawl. But who did I want to be? From now on, this was how people would know me—*Marina Makarova.*

So stupid to worry about such a thing. Still, a decision had to be made. Side part, a single wave. There it was. A scarf instead of the fox-fur hat...but I had only Klavdia's tattered coat, or my peasant sheepskin. The coat. I could take it off as soon as I got there, showing my Ionian patchwork, or leave it on. All of my clothes were outlandish, but everyone had seen them before. We couldn't all be Nikolai Gumilev.

A bite of dry herring, a drink of hot water with saccharine, then the dash down through the sad, wet streets—it was still light out, but far from gladdening. You could see every half-ruined building, every dead horse surfacing like a drowned body cast up by the sea.

Down at the House of Arts, light shone from the windows like a liner on a dark ocean. Inside, I quickly found the others in the little room to the side of the main hall with its gilded mirrors and bare floors, each preparing for what was to come. This night might clinch my acceptance into the House of Arts, maybe I'd secure housing. God, to be rid of Shpalernaya! I watched my comrades' faces to see if they could smell me, the reek of carbolic and shit. This would not be an audience of tired workers coming out of a factory; this would be a gathering of educated, opinionated people judging us against the best. People would listen, they would *remember*.

In the anteroom, we prepared, each in our own way. Everyone responded differently to the pressure—Arseny Grodetsky, the eighteen-year-old futurist, was showing Anton a whole new set of poems he wanted to read instead of what he'd so carefully planned. Dmitry Tereshenko, with his sturdy build and beat-up boxer's face, relaxed and joked with Nikita Nikulin, our senior member, perched on the back of a divan. Nikita had been in a terrible accident as a young man, he'd fallen from a tram, and his body was as cubist as his poetry, offering angles and asymmetrical forms that suggested nobility in the face of terrible suffering. And Oksana Linichuk, from our old Transrational Interlocutors circle, she who had brought flowers to my wedding, geraniums raining red petals onto the grimy floor. Still gray-eyed, frizzy-haired, she sat calmly on the worn cushions, legs crossed at the ankles, her notes neatly in her lap. Her poems were exact, calm, contained, and very clear, just like the poet. While Anton ran around like a cat watching six mouseholes.

Galina Krestovskaya came back to kiss us all and wish us good luck, showering her loveliness around herself like a scent around roses. She still wanted to write, took Anton's abuse in his Wednesday afternoon studio, but what she was doing now had become clear at various House of Arts evenings when she'd bring her new lover, a commissar in finance and member of the Petrograd Soviet with a car of his own. Always politics, even among us.

I peered out from behind the folding doors to see a full house. Gumilev, Khodasevich, Kuzmin, and—yes! Blok! He came. But my God, he looked tired, standing by the door—most likely to make it easier to escape in case we were terrible. And here was Gorky, and, walking in on the arm of Moura Budberg like some great plumed bird, garbed in emerald green, the exotic figure of Aura Cady Sands. Did she know it was me? Did she remember the girl with the baby in Mina's apartment? No, it was impossible. She must be simply taking in the offerings of the wet spring evening with the Gorky contingent.

Anton grasped my arm. "Ready?"

We walked in together, sat in the front in a semicircle on the little spindly formal chairs in the blue mirrored room. Friends and students from Anton's studio had settled eagerly in the front rows, as it was our night. Here were Galina Krestovskaya, with her commissar, and behind them Gumilev leaned forward, saying something amusing, flirting with pretty Galina right under the nose of the soviet. What confidence! Kuzmin and kind round-nosed Chukovksy, who had translated Whitman into Russian. And Sasha Orlovsky, with a familiar dark-haired girl, braids crossed over her head—Dunya Katzeva.

Anton rose and introduced our group, the younger poets at the House of Arts, the Squared Circle, *embracing an array of styles and ideas,* so on and so on. He was nervous, he spoke too quickly...

We began with Nikita Nikulin, the grandson of the great poet Nekrasov—chosen as most likely to still our elders' fears about the offerings of the younger generation and our worthiness of their consideration. Nikita read three poems in his cubist style. I liked the way he stacked his poems around a central spine of a syllable, as if twisting his way down a spiral staircase. It was more for the eye than the ear, but he paused after each iteration, making sure the reader descended the staircase with him. He was a good performer of his work, though his voice was on the nasal side. A man with a face like a monk took notes. The blue eye, the pointed nose with its long slot of nostril—it must be the critic Tomilin.

I thought Nikita did well. Then came our little bomb—Arseny. Ear to Nikita's eye, explosive, a barrage of sound. He was the cannon. His poems were unfathomable, you had to just give yourself over to him, the sound of him, the energy. In the circle, Anton didn't like us to talk about what poems *meant*. Only the recurrence of sounds, the structure, I learned a great deal from listening to him, though he never left meaning behind. I was the proletarian of the group, worried about emotional clarity. Arseny was our Red Rimbaud.

Oksana cut through the smoke, etching her precise visions: the cooling relationships between a husband and wife, the hopes of a young girl, a soldier home from the front—poems about the residents of her collective apartment. The critic stuck out his lower lip, he sucked his teeth. But many people sighed, nodding in recognition—finally, something they understood.

I was next. I wished Oksana would go on forever, that I could sit here watching the back of her blessed head, the halo around her light frizzy hair from the electrolier. I couldn't look into the faces of the audience—the audience! Not people on the street corners hurtling to and from work who had to be captured by a simple clever line. Literary Petrograd. I had wanted this, I had wanted to be a part of this—I would have to show them that I belonged here. It was not politics. Politics could not get you a seat on Olympus. For that, you had to sing.

It was my turn. I walked to the little lectern behind which we declaimed. Here they all were, Eikhenbaum and Chukovsky, Zamyatin, Grin, Gumilev with his students, Kuzmin. Was my hair ridiculous? Should I have tried to be prettier? Or more serious? *Breathe, don't smile, don't trip...Don't rush!*

Taking a breath, I recited the poem I had not wanted to write, had never wanted to write, but had to, if I were to keep on living:

Janet Fitch

Under the Trees at Kambarka

She slept all the winter
covered with white eiderdown
curled at the foot of a hard gray bed.

Now it is spring.
Rain waters the earth.

The spark that glowed between my two cupped
hands
*   Didn't last the night.*
*   The wind blew it out and*
*   the world went dark as the devil's armpit.*

Oh, give me the trees at Kambarka
Soft-lipped summer green.
And golden the fields
*   And the scythe's ancient song.*

Yes, I know, that future is past,
*   the leaves fallen*
*   from the family tree.*
*   Sweep them, sweep them away.*

But leave me the green trees of Kambarka
*   The gold of the fields*
*   The long dusty road*
*   The midwife's shack*
*   The slow river's turning*
*   The pattern of leaves*
*   In her dazzled eyes.*

I could feel my words move out into the room. The stoniness of
the crowd. *Free verse.* Why couldn't they hear, there was music even

386

if there wasn't the pattern they wanted? There was rhyme, just not where they were listening for it. But then, I saw my words enter the chests of a few—a woman here, a man there, Galina. Inna. *Listen,* I said, and they said, *Tell us, then. Tell us how it was, make us shiver with your song.*

They took me in, they rose, they fell. Even Blok looked less haunted, riding on the sound of my voice. I was so afraid people could no longer feel these things, that their souls were gone, that they'd had enough of death, I'd feared they were so hardened that you couldn't vibrate them anymore with feeling and sound. But they were still able. *Lift us up,* their hearts whispered. *Make us live.* Even these poets, these artists of song. And I did.

I recited the other two poems Anton had chosen—"The Five," and one about the telephone exchange, "Listen to Me," where honey poured from the sockets, and it became a honeycomb full of bees. I recited, feeling them with me, like making love to them, whispering to them in the darkness, when I saw a familiar face appear at the back of the hall. Standing behind a broad-shouldered sailor, the sharp face and frizzy black hair of Varvara Razrushenskaya. I stumbled, recovered. Paused. There was no way to escape. I gathered my courage and finished strongly. If I was going to be arrested by my Chekist friend—lover, enemy—if I was going to be shot, I would go standing at full height and not cringing.

Then she was gone.

I sat down. I could hardly see for my confusion, my pride, my mortification, my shock at seeing Varvara again. The thing I should have considered and had not. Arkady was dead, Iskra—wasn't it enough? I had taken a chance to use my real name on the fliers, thinking who but other poets would trouble to look in the literary papers? I tried to gauge the applause—polite? No. Genuine. And I had so enjoyed being myself—Makarova, not Kuriakina, but me. I had done nothing illegal. My crimes were personal. I was unable to listen to Dmitry Tereshenko, who followed me. My thoughts were thundering, cascading in my head.

Afterward, the old Eliseev servants, who had stayed on for the housing and the rations, handed around tea and even a few stale cookies. I was suddenly shy, as if these people had seen me in my torn underwear. I stood with Anton and Oksana, Inna Gants, the people I knew. I should go over and speak to Aura Cady Sands, but she was with Gorky—and I literally smelled like shit. Was it a success? Just to be here was a success, I told myself. To be among these people. I wasn't torturing citizens for a living, interrogating them, imprisoning aristocratic old ladies and wizened peasants selling frozen potatoes. I was creating worlds.

I didn't see Blok—had he left? I probably should vanish too, before Varvara caught up to me. I knew she would still be furious—*Did you think I would forget?* I could sneak out through the interior courtyard on Bolshaya Morskaya Street. But I didn't want to leave. This was my night. It might happen only once if I disappeared into the cells of the Cheka. People would think, *Whatever happened to that poet, Makarova?* I was someone. I would not vanish without a trace.

I began to move toward Aura Sands, my songbird, my hope, when Kuzmin joined us—fin de siècle sulfur rising from his slight figure. "A very interesting evening," he said to us, slowly raising his heavy-lidded eyes, his hair combed up over his bald pate. "I'm especially looking forward to hearing more from *you*," he said to me in particular, shaking my hand. His touch was light, moist, cold. "I don't care for vers libre, but this was quite musical, very much like contemporary music, that horizontality—like Debussy, and Brahms. And I liked the odd rhymes, like little explosions."

I was burning with joy. Kuzmin was a classicist if anybody was, but he was also a well-known musician. He'd understood my work musically—how generous of him! "Thank you, Mikhail Alexeevich." Kuzmin! Another legend. He had lived with Olga Sudeikina, Akhmatova's beautiful friend from the Stray Dog Café, and her husband—until Sudeikina found out he was having an affair with her husband! What a generation—like the Blok ménage. It made me happy to know that I wasn't the only one with two husbands.

He took his handkerchief and pressed it to his nose. Did I stink? Oh God.

Terrifyingly, the tall, erect, correct figure of Gumilev approached. I shrank back into myself. He could crush me with a word. Before I knew what he was going to do, he took my hand and kissed it. If it reeked of carbolic and Shpalernaya shit, he gave no indication. His long thin hand was as dry as paper. "May I ask you, why did God create the Russian language with its potential for rhyme and meter, like no other language in the world, if not to create verse?"

Oh God, was Gumilev going to make me argue the case for free verse? I was no theorist. I left that to Anton. Gumilev was one of our greats. Also, he wouldn't let go of my hand. He was standing embarrassingly close. "I have nothing against established poetic forms, Nikolai Stepanovich," I said, trying to defend myself while stealthily attempting to recover my hand. "It's just not what spoke to me when I was writing these poems."

Not only did he not relinquish my hand, he tucked it under his arm and began walking away with me, leading me somewhere. Where? Away from Anton, most likely, who scowled after us. Away from my well-wishers. I had the feeling of being led to the headmistress's office for some disciplinary offense. He guided me to some chairs under the gilded mirrors. The lights would be coming on down the street in Orphanage No. 6 now, the orphans settling in to dinner. And I was sitting with Nikolai Gumilev, in the anteroom of the hall where I'd just given a reading.

"They're really not poems," he said. "They're just images set in rhythmic prose. Sometimes you're just a fraction away from the lip of the pool, the very edge of poetry, but then you sidle away. It's terrifically frustrating to listen to. Chernikov is doing you no favors, my dear."

What an ugly man he was, walleyed, like a goldfish, but interesting, commanding. He had a clipped, military way of speaking. Yet he kept taking my hand, gazing at my mouth, my breasts in this old patched dress that had seen me through so much. Wasn't he remarried to a beautiful doe-eyed woman who lived in this very house?

"You mustn't waste your talent," he said. "You had some wonderful lines tonight." He stared out toward the others, milling and smoking and talking—or at least one eye looked in that direction, the other lingered on me. "*'Soft-lipped summer green. / And golden the fields / And the scythe's ancient song.'*"

He remembered my lines. Nikolai Gumilev. But he kept ogling me too, an interest that was by no means literary. "I'm glad you liked that."

"But it's still not poetry. Yet." He held up a clean, bony finger. He leaned closer, this man at the very heart of literary Petrograd. "I could teach you to write poetry, Marina Dmitrievna. That first piece, your elegy—that should be an ode. Then people would remember it forever. They could recite it in their sleep. Have you ever recited a poem to save your life, Marina?"

I nodded.

"It wasn't vers libre, was it?" He gazed at me from under his neat eyebrows. "What was it?"

I would not tell him it had been Pushkin, under the snow halfway to Alekhovshchina. Or the Tyutchev I recited to Dinamo that night in our sniper's nest on Moskovsky Prospect. I said the thing I hoped would stop this conversation. "Whitman."

"*Whitman?* Are you now an American? Are you writing in English? Do you have the blood of Shakespeare running through your veins?" he said decisively. "No, I suspect that Mayakovsky's the stronger influence, and Chernikov. First see what our treasury has to offer. The Onegin sonnet. Alexandrines, iambic tetrameter, terza rima. Once you're a master of prosody, write all the vers libre you like. Write in Chinese if you prefer. But learn to handle the palette you were born to, make its brushes dance for you. You must work with me. Chernikov can teach you nothing. I made Akhmatova, I made Mandelstam, and if you would put yourself in my hands, I would make you a poet."

It was lucky I was sitting down. No wonder Blok had been hesitant about my attending Gumilev's studio. I could not imagine anything less Blokian than his saying he'd *made* another poet. Like God, like Pygmalion. What arrogance! Yet... wasn't that secretly what I had been hoping for? Someone to anoint me? To bring me in, to "make" me? No. Not anymore. This might work on the doting girls I'd seen following him around at the House of Arts, but I was too old for masters.

"Honestly, I could never put myself entirely in anybody's hands, Nikolai Stepanovich."

"Come, come. Every woman wants to put herself into someone's hands, my dear." The light from the electrolier fingered the side of his elongated head. He looked like he'd been extruded through a tube.

I could only imagine what Varvara would say to that. Me, I'd already known the Archangel, had seen Ukashin at work. I didn't need a father, a master, or an elderly, overbearing lover, only colleagues and friends. I saw people eyeing us, but no one would approach me as long as the Maître had me to himself. And there was Blok! He had his coat on. He looked like he was leaving. I had to speak to him before he left. I rose and offered my hand to Gumilev, smiling coolly, just as my mother would have done to break a conversation with a wearisome guest. "Thank you. I'll think about that ode."

He rose as well, and I could see he was irritated that I'd eluded his little seduction—as a teacher and God knew what else. I hoped he wasn't a vengeful man. I had enough enemies.

I located Blok in the foyer, putting on his galoshes. "Alexander Alexandrovich!" I had to catch my breath. "Remember me, from that day on Bolshaya Morskaya? Marina Makarova?"

He glanced up, those light blue eyes. "Yes, of course," he said. His face was very still. He stood, picked up his briefcase and umbrella. "You didn't work with Gumilev after all, did you?"

"No," I said.

"Quite right. I so disagree with the man. Poets aren't made," he said. Softly but clearly. "They *are*. A poet can hear or he can't.

What's important is listening. The sound, the harmony. Trust the sound. Not classes and critics."

"Do you think I'm a poet, Alexander Alexandrovich?" I blurted it out. I knew how ridiculous it sounded, but I needed to know, once and for all, and Blok would not lie.

He stopped in the doorway and put his heavy briefcase down next to his galoshed foot, wrapped his scarf tighter around his neck. "A poet isn't a person who writes in verse, Marina Makarova. A poet is a person who writes in verse because he *hears* verse—the harmony, the rhythm, the chimes and water. He takes the sounds he hears and makes them heard in the world."

I could see why Blok didn't teach poetry. He was a genius, and geniuses never knew how they did what they did. Even if they wanted to, they couldn't explain it to mere mortals. I just needed to know: Was I a poet at all? Or only someone who loved poetry, loved it so much she wanted to be one of the elect, prayed for the Muse to kiss her lips? I needed him to tell me, he who had for so long been the Muse's favorite.

He put his hand gently on my arm. So light. Like a snowflake. "When I hear poetry—so-called poetry—for the most part, it's so boring and unnecessary it makes me wonder whether I shouldn't stop writing altogether. It makes me think that I really don't even like poetry. That poetry is a worthless occupation. It makes me want to curse it from the rooftops. Tonight, when you read your poems, I felt that I do love poetry. That it's not nonsense, that there's joy there, the sound of leaves, skies, and weeping. I envied you those sounds. Really envied you."

He didn't take my hand, he didn't kiss me three times, but it felt as if he had done both, and more.

"Write," he said. "Write while you can." And went out into the early spring rain.

I walked back into the gathering and found Aura Cady Sands coming my way, her dark skin and green dress so vivid in this wren-brown gathering that she looked like a bird of paradise. She was accompanied by Gorky and his mistress Moura Budberg and others in their party—a small neat man in his fifties, a tall boy with pale skin and dark hair, a grizzled man in his sixties. The mistress was the one to speak. "Marina Dmitrievna, may I introduce Alexei Maximovich Gorky?"

He was a warm and appealing man, tall, with a low, broad forehead and dished face, a good face, a *muzhik*'s face, short-nosed, his cropped hair not even gray—sporting his full shoe-brush moustache. Here was the man single-handedly keeping the Russian intelligentsia alive. The living link between our world and that of Gogol and Dostoyevsky. "Congratulations," he said, shaking my hand with his right one, patting it with the other. "A fine debut. Marvelous work—substantive, emotional, wonderfully controlled. You make us feel your purpose while we soar on your song. How old are you, child?"

"Twenty, Alexei Maximovich." Luckily, the mistress had introduced him or I wouldn't have known how to address him, *Maxim Gorky* being a pseudonym and pseudonyms had no patronymic. I couldn't just call him *Gorky* like a fireman on a locomotive. *Eh, Gorky, pass me that jug.*

"Twenty." He chuckled—a bit ruefully. "Poets and mathematicians start so young, don't they? A young poet is like a string of fireworks, exploding in the summer sky. We novelists are so shamefully slow, it takes us forever just to learn to put our pants on."

Moura translated for Aura Cady Sands. The singer was dazzling. We all disappeared compared to this marvel. "We say that about our *blues*," said the American in Russian—she had made progress since I had last seen her. "The blues takes a whole lifetime to sing."

"May I introduce the famed American soprano Aura Cady Sands?" said Gorky's mistress.

Sands praised my poem. "Very strong." The compliment sweet to my ears. Though she could not have understood it, she heard its song.

I shook her firm, fleshy hand. "We've met before," I said in English.

I had startled her. It was my face she didn't recognize, my new face. "We have?"

"At the Katzev photography studio. Last fall." It would be understandable if she didn't remember. Sometimes an encounter can be hugely important to one person, even change his life, and yet make no mark on another's. Just like love. "You invited me to visit you at the Astoria."

Her smile widened. "Yes! With that adorable baby. Irish Eyes. How is she?"

Oh, she remembered Iskra. My eyes smarted. I had to tell her, before my throat closed entirely. "She died this winter. That's what the poem was about."

"Oh, baby...no." She cupped my face in her hand. "This awful life."

She wore L'Origan, the only person in Petrograd these days who wore a scent. Perhaps it was just a memory of fragrance on her clothing, but I wanted to stand next to her and breathe it in forever, listening to her rich voice. If only I had found her before it was too late, before I'd marched off to Orphanage No. 6. If only this moment had come in the fall. But I had to be grateful it was happening at all. She knew us. Moura was translating for Gorky now.

"So you're a poet." She brushed at my hair, tenderly. "Of course I couldn't understand most of it, but the music! Glorious! Why didn't you ever come see me?"

I didn't want it to sound like I was blaming her. "You needed a *propusk*. I had no way to reach you."

"*Propuski,*" she said, her mobile face contorting with disgust. "I never saw such a country for red tape."

I laughed. "Yes, that's our color. The Astoria's the First House of the Soviet. They can't let the riffraff wander about—some ragged, raving poet who might read free verse and bring down the government." I didn't want to clutch at her arm with my sad story, like a beggar.

Moura laughed and translated for the others.

"Well, I'm not there anymore," Aura said. "I'm at Gorky's and you must visit me. You won't need a passport and twelve official stamps. You will come, won't you? You must." She turned to Moura. "Tell her she must."

Moura Budberg seconded the invitation. Her English was plummy, British—even her Russian was accented. I wondered what her story was as she leaned toward Gorky. "She must come to visit, we're going to adopt her—is that all right, Alexei Maximovich?"

"It would give me great pleasure." A jolly man, a man who I could see liked bustle around him. I wished he would take care of that cough. He was smoking too.

"Come, then. Sunday. At four?" said Moura. She told me the address—Kronverksky Prospect 23, flat number 5.

Aura kissed me on both cheeks. "I'm so glad we've found you at last."

"I look forward to following your career," said Gorky as they moved off. "I hope to see you on Sunday, if they haven't killed me first."

"Thank you, I'll be there," I called after them. If I wasn't in a Cheka cell by then.

We continued celebrating up in Anton's room, comparing notes, who had said what to whom, who had been there, whether Tomilin or Eikhenbaum would review us, Anton analyzing our performances, Arseny careening off the walls with the adrenaline of his own success. "We did it, we pulled it off! Did you see those stinkers, Gumilev et al.? Gnashing their teeth. Ha! Let them go off and knit their antimacassars."

Tereshenko had found a little bit of vodka, God knows where—we passed around the perfume bottle he kept it in. We even persuaded Oksana to stay a few minutes. She and Petya Simkin, part of the Squared Circle, sat next to me on the crowded bed. How far we'd come since our days at the Krestovskys'. Everybody but Tereshenko had been there when we'd celebrated the end of the war—just before the White advance. "Just think," I said, rosy on a few drops of alcohol, taking Oksana's hand. "We will always be connected in people's minds, 'The Women of the Squared Circle.' Someday we'll be old ladies drinking tea with our cats in our laps, remembering that horrible Anton Chernikov."

"Who made your fortunes," Anton added.

"What a time this has been," Oksana's hand squeezing mine. "I already feel like I'm fifty, don't you?"

"I still remember those geraniums," I said. The ones she'd brought to my Red wedding. We would share each other's futures and disgraces.

"It looks like Galina's done well for herself."

"Some cats always fall on their feet," said Tereshenko, always happy to be nasty.

"I hate to go but I teach in the morning." Oksana brushed her fair hair back from her amused gray eyes, stood. A philology student at Petrograd University, she was already teaching at the Third University, the Workers' Faculty—Rabfak. Petya rose to accompany her—reluctantly. It was a wild walk back to Vasilievsky in the dark.

I watched them go with a twinge of envy. If my father hadn't ruined my chances to enter the university, I too would be leaving now, getting ready to teach in the morning, instead of facing another day plugging cords into sockets at the infernal telephone exchange. But that was a horse dead for too many years, there were only a few scattered bones left to trip me.

More and more people crammed into Anton's tiny, messy room, spilling out into the hall. Nikita sat down in Oksana's seat, told me that Eikhenbaum was going to write up the evening. Such a heady time, I could hardly sit still, as bad as Arseny ricocheting off the walls. Was I not dreaming? And so what if Varvara knew I was in town? I'd face that when I had to. Surely she understood the poems, could see I had not survived unscarred. But would it be enough to pacify her? Pity was not her strong suit.

Here was big blond handsome Sasha, leaning over, kissing me. He always smelled of linseed oil and turps. "Look who's here!"

From behind his broad back, holding his hand, was Dunya Katzeva.

"Marina," she said.

I wanted to bolt, like a convict leaping from a train. Her brown hair in crisscrossed braids the way Mina used to wear it. She crouched down in front of me. "Marina, I didn't know. Not until tonight." Her face was pale, her dark eyes large and wet. "I'm so sorry. You don't know, we had a huge fight after you left. I moved out." She knelt on the floor, holding my hands. "Everyone hates her. Mama hardly speaks to her. It's just her and that horrible *Roman* now. I kept thinking you'd come back, and we could make it right, but you never did. Forgive me, forgive me!"

Oh, why did she have to show up tonight? I just wanted to have my little scrap of pleasure that had nothing to do with losing my green-eyed baby.

"Was it typhus? Forgive me, it doesn't matter..."

I would not cry in front of these people, please, God! *Dunya, why are you doing this?* I explained tersely the bare bones of what had happened.

She clutched at my hand, covered it with her tears. Did I have to comfort her? I could see Inna Gants eagerly watching this little drama from the corner of the room. The House of Arts was a fishbowl, as bad as the collective apartment on Shpalernaya Street. Living here must be like being on stage. I had to end this ghastly scene. She'd been wrong, I'd been wrong, we'd all been wrong, and not a scrap of it would bring Iskra back.

She gazed up at me from the floor with her big wet eyes...sweet and kind, she'd always been this way, even as a child...and there was no virtue in salting the wound. Suddenly I hated it here, all these people in the crowded, smoky room, everyone half performing. I wanted to get outside and breathe, be alone with my jumbled thoughts. "We were all idiots," I said. I put my hand on her shoulder. I'd known her before she lost her first tooth. "None of us is a fortune-teller. I'm sorry, I have to go too, it's a long walk and I work in the morning. Night, Comrades," I called out to the poets.

"Sasha, we're walking Marina home," Dunya announced, rising from the dirty floor.

Anton glanced up from Arseny and his beloved Shklovsky. I was surprised he'd heard anything. "You can't go, it's still early."

"It's late," I said, and kissed him three times. "Thanks for including me tonight." For saving me, for bringing me in. He looked stricken to see me go, as if I were taking the party with me. "I'll see you next Wednesday." The others shouted their congratulations.

There was no shaking my escorts. But outside in the quiet hissing of the rain, I felt less oppressed by Dunya and her sorrow. After all, I loved her better than all the other people in that room put together. She was the only one with an umbrella, and none of us had galoshes—what an ill-prepared trio. Huddled together, splashing down the dark streets of Petrograd in our sad boots, like the fools we were. Now that I could see how it was with Dunya and Sasha, it softened my heart. Still together through everything. They had their mythology, kisses and misunderstandings, the old days when the Transrational Interlocutors had taken advantage of the Katzevs' generosity, like stray cats being fed by the back fence. Dunya had had such a crush on the big painter, and Sasha unsure what to do about the love of such a young girl. The city map of their courtship. Well, something good had come of all that. Why shouldn't life work out at least for some?

And me? I might always be alone, as my mother had foretold, but still there would be friendship. And my verses were becoming known. There was no longer Arkady to fear, and Varvara would do what she would. Whose fault was life? I didn't know, only that I was glad for the companionship of these lovers and the freshness of the rain. We chatted the whole way back to Shpalernaya Street. And when I lay down to sleep, I was happy, safe for tonight in my little room, soothed by the whisper of rain on the window. I fell asleep smelling L'Origan, clutching my future in the palm of my hand.

34 *The Flea*

It was a clear, fresh April day, the wind driving the white clouds down toward the gulf against the blue silk of the sky. Blue reflected in a million puddles. The ice on the River Neva broke all at once. In two or three days it went from a white solid mass to violently cracking towers of slabs that heralded the onset of spring. I expected to see whales breaking through, leaping into the air, as I crossed the Troitsky Bridge over to the Petrograd side. The sun on my face, the shush and slap of the water, freed from the paralysis of ice. The wind tore at my hair. Fortunately my fur hat was non-aerodynamic. Someone else was not so lucky, her hat flew off her head—how joyous, a loose hat!—as if it were tired of its responsibilities and decided to take off for a new perspective.

I felt like I could fly, just like that, tumbling into the sky. I was going to tea at Maxim Gorky's—*Alexei Maximovich's*—in my patched woolen stockings and sheepskin coat. I laughed out loud. How alive the day was. New shoots on trees, plants coming up right in the middle of Palace Square, no horses to eat them—the restoration of Nature's green after her long imprisonment in the halls of the Frost King. Then, miracle of miracles, I heard the tram coming—screeching and groaning, passengers hanging from its doors like clusters of grapes. I jumped onto the fender and rode, though truthfully I could have walked it faster.

As we shuddered and groaned, the Peter and Paul Fortress rose up on its small island in the Neva, the crown-shaped embankments, the very first structure that Peter the Great built here—a fortress, a cathedral, a mint, and a prison, all in one. Gorky had been jailed there after the 1905 Revolution. How strange that he would want to live so close by, have to pass it every day. I watched its great yellow-gray walls coming closer, the Dutch-style needle of its cathedral glinting gold, communing with its brother across the river at the

Admiralty. I remembered the night it fired on the Winter Palace. Long the dungeon of the autocracy, its cells now held hostages and enemies of the revolution.

Swaying and clinging and trying to avoid being hit in the eye by the man to my left, whose elbow curved just above my face, I gazed back at the fortress, so familiar, so grim.

I still had not heard from Varvara. She wasn't stupid. She had to know everything by now, where I lived, where I worked, that I was using *Kuriakina* on all my papers. It was more a matter of *when* than *if*. Well, it would come when it would come. I would not run from my fate. *Write while you can,* Blok had said. My life had started to take root and bloom, and I would enjoy these moments of springtime, no matter how short they might prove.

Now came the sweep of the Kronverksky Embankment with its trees, blue sky reflected in the bow-shaped canal behind the fortress—the way to the zoo, as every St. Petersburg child knew. But today I would not be seeing mere lions and elephants. Today was for opera singers and great authors. At Kronverksky Prospect, I swung down, stumbling a bit on the stones. I began to walk—not fast; no one liked an early guest—into the afternoon sunshine.

Kronverksky Prospect, 23, was a big five-story bourgeois building facing the park. I could smell the fresh grass, the new leaves—and could not help thinking, *Iskra would have loved this park.* This was my life from now on. I would always look at green and think of her. "Irish Eyes." The building was in far better shape than any I'd seen in some time—the hall lights worked, the carpet lay intact, muffling the sound of my boots. The banister practically boasted its solidity. They even had a concierge, although all she wanted to know was where I was going. "Flat five. Madame Budberg invited me." That seemed to be sufficient for the stolid *dezhurnaya.* I wished she was more rigorous—I could have been an assassin, I could have been anyone. For us, Alexei Maximovich was the most important man in Petrograd, far more important than Zinoviev, chairman of the Northern Commune, and anyone could walk in and shoot him at any time.

I ran up to the second floor, rang the doorbell of the flat opposite the staircase, heard the buzz resonate deep inside.

Aura herself answered the door. Today she was glorious in a sky-blue suit, her hair pinned in a simple chignon. She could have been wearing a robe and a diadem, so queenly did she appear. It was like Nefertiti landing on our cold Neva shores. "Marina, you made it at last." She kissed me on both cheeks, *à la française*, her perfume tinting the air. "They're all in the dining room."

I followed her clicking heels and solid hips into the depths of the large private flat, decorated with heavy, old-fashioned furniture, plates, and dark paintings. The size of it! It just went on and on. I eagerly peered into every open doorway—a study, a sitting room...Alas, most of the doors were closed. A big old intelligentsia household. I could smell food. My stomach growled.

"You haven't eaten, have you?" she asked.

You never had to ask whether someone had eaten. These days, one could eat a Petrograd dinner and then another one five minutes later, and one after that, and still have room for a feast.

We entered a large dining room in which a number of others were chatting, though no Gorky, no Moura. Were they not going to join us? Aura introduced me in her wobbly Russian. Evidently I was a completely beautiful writer. It was something I'd noticed about her—nothing was just okay. Everything was superlative, the *most* marvelous, beautiful, spectacular. Stupendous! No Russian could be so enthusiastic, even on *marafet*. She introduced Lajos something, the most *marvelous* Hungarian mathematician, and his son Tamás, and the poet Khodasevich's *darling* niece Valentina, and a set of *the sweetest* visiting Gorky cousins, a man and a woman, and *this most distinguished* Eugene Harris from the British Trade Union delegation. I marveled at how many people Gorky could afford to feed.

Aura seated me between herself and Harris at the far corner of the table—a little enclave of English speakers among the Russians. The British comrade's ears stuck out, his moustache was small and bristly. "So when will the revolution come to England, Comrade?" I said, half teasing.

He sighed. "Lenin asked me that when I was in Moscow. All I can say is that it's heating up. But more like a Petrograd tram than the Zurich Express."

"Lenin asked me too," said Aura, settling into the seat next to mine, her arm across my chair. " 'When will we see red flags fly over Wall Street, Comrade Sands?' I told him, 'Vladimir Ilyich, if there's a revolution in America, I'll be the first one going back. But it's the only way you'll get me on that boat.' "

"Do you hate America so much?" I asked, thinking of our wonderful trip to New York, my father giving a talk at Columbia University. My nine-year-old impression was of terrifying skyscrapers, crowds, the Brooklyn Bridge. I remember dining with my mother's brother Vadim and his glamorous lady friend, and especially her hat, more vertical than horizontal, pinned to the side of her dark hair. White straw, faced in black taffeta. The most elegant thing I ever saw.

"When your country's against you, it's not hate." Aura's lips curled inward. "It's more of a love that's been trampled. Like being rejected by your own mother. Like being turned out onto the street by your family." She couldn't know how familiar I was with that feeling. Yes, it wasn't hate. It was pain. "I'm a Negro," she said. "This doesn't wash off." She licked a finger and rubbed the back of her hand to stress the point. "I can sing at La Scala, dine at Maxim's, I can have a million dollars in the bank, but I still can't stay in a decent hotel in New York. Not only can I not sing at the Metropolitan Opera, I can't appear onstage with a fourth-rate white tenor in a tenth-rate hall in a two-horse town anywhere in the U.S. of A. Tell me, how could a sane person live in a country like that?"

Yes, it must be enough to drive a person mad. "But you could live in France," I said. "Drink aperitifs on the terrace at La Rotonde." As I would love to be doing. "Why get involved in our problems?"

"Because I believe in the revolution," she said, her golden-brown eyes flashing. "This is for all of us, not just you. So my father doesn't have to step off the curb when a white man walks past. So the people who do the work are the ones who profit. Who wouldn't want to be part of it? You'd have to be dead not to want to be here."

For the first time in quite a while, I remembered the revolution as more than deprivation, suspicion, and terror. She made me remember the other side of it, what we'd already accomplished in only three years—and we were almost done with the civil war, the Whites had clearly lost. Maybe the West would soon recognize the fact of us and drop the blockade. A few years of peace to mend and feed ourselves, repair our factories and railroads, and we'd see what Communism really could do.

But I'd been ignoring Harris too long, and turned back to the trade unionist. "Are you the whole delegation?"

"Oh no, there's a whole gang of us," he said. "I just wanted to get away from the minders and do a little poking about on my own. Gorky's been very accommodating. A great friend to the trade union movement."

A servant in a white apron brought in a tureen of soup, placed it on the sideboard. Spices, meat, cabbage. *Solyanka,* my favorite. I had the nose of an animal these days. She left, and we passed around plates and cutlery, family style. She brought out a platter of *piroshky,* and we passed it from hand to hand as she doled out the soup with a keen eye to portions, everyone receiving a potato and one ladle of the precious liquid, bits of plump sausage floating. And crusty *piroshky.* I had not dreamed of such largesse.

Just as we began to tuck in, Gorky emerged through a door with Moura and another woman of middle age. "Please, sit over here." Moura steered the woman past the Gorky cousins into the seat on Harris's far side, facing me across the corner. Evidently the woman and Harris already knew each other. "Emma," she introduced herself, smiling, holding out her small hand—uncalloused, with little sharp nails.

"This is the poet, Marina Makarova." Gorky introduced me himself, in Russian, from the head of the table. I almost fell from my chair. *Maxim Gorky knew me!* It was like being known by Blok—not the same; Gorky was a good writer, while Blok was one whom the angels had chosen for their own. But Gorky was our greatest prose writer, and he ruled the life of intellectual Petrograd. If something happened to me, I would not disappear. He would re-member the young poet—*we had her to tea.* "And this is Emma Goldman, American troublemaker."

Goldman laughed. Her Russian was obviously excellent. "Some-body has to do it, Alexei Maximovich."

Aura explained to us in English, "Emma came in on the *Buford.*"

I had no idea what that meant.

"You didn't hear? People have been talking about it all winter," said Aura, putting another *piroshok* on my plate. "In America, they decided to silence every leftist who wasn't born there, threw them on an old rusty tub—the USS *Buford*—and sent them off to Petrograd."

"I'm sure they hoped it would sink." Under her tangled topknot, Emma Goldman had a soft, kind face and piercing hazel eyes. Some-thing about her, the animation, the intensity, reminded me of the Left SRs I'd met during my imprisonment in Gorokhovaya 2. *Who doesn't love concrete?* "Two thousand Americans, arrested without cause and deported without trial," she said, taking a plate passed to her. "*Well, at least I'll see the revolution,* I thought. *Do something useful.* But the Bolsheviks have stymied us at every turn. The Com-munists were all right, but the anarchists? Once they saw we weren't going to pledge allegiance to Lenin, *pfft.*" She snapped her fingers. "Red tape, red tape, red tape. I thought something else was going to be red besides tape."

All the Russian speakers laughed but Moura, at Gorky's elbow, and Gorky himself.

"Emma and I first met in America in 1906," said our host from the other end of the table, trying to lighten the mood. "Remember that trip, Emma?" I translated for Aura and Harris. "Quite the ex-perience. I got two books out of it. Have you been in New York, Harris?"

"Twice," said the Englishman in Russian.

"Monstrous place," said Gorky. "The most interesting people in

America were the Indians and the Negroes. The rest were as ignorant as mud. Completely caught up in the pursuit of Mammon. Like
livestock raised to feed the great mouth of Capital. Such a scandal,
when they discovered Maria Andreeva and I weren't married!" He
laughed merrily, which devolved into that heavy cough. "It made
the front pages of all the daily papers. We were turned out of our
hotel—and this wasn't some little provincial capital; this was the
Holy Babylon herself. Mark Twain refused to introduce me at a dinner held in my honor, I was thought to be such a scandal. Emma
here had to come to my defense."

I translated as best I could. When had all this happened? I must
have been a child, unaware that the author of the "Stormy Petrel"
was causing such an uproar.

"Imagine," Emma drawled. "Me, coming to Gorky's rescue. I
only hope that you won't have to return the favor before too long."

"I hope not as well," Gorky said. Not smiling now, and there was
a warning in his face. I got the feeling that their meeting had not
gone well.

Above a sideboard, in the red corner, a series of small icons
gleamed. They confused me. Was Gorky a believer? Or had he
just rescued them, as he'd rescued so much else in our times? The
mirror over the sideboard reflected our images: glorious Aura;
Emma Goldman, intense and messy; Harris; and this scrawny
corpse—who was that? My pale face, my hair, it seemed darker,
drabber than it used to be, my patchwork dress. I was so used
to thinking of myself as possessing a hint of beauty. Always an
unpleasant shock to see how vanished it was. What would Kolya
think if he saw me now? Would he feel even a shred of his former
ardor?

The hell with him. I may have lost my charm but I was gaining
something far better—the right to sit at the table with Gorky and
Aura Cady Sands and this Emma Goldman. To be *someone*. To have
a face.

"We saw you last week at the House of Arts," said the mathematician's son, a young man with black longish hair and green eyes

behind spectacles, his Russian clear but accented. "I liked the one about the telephone and the bees." He switched to English for Aura. "The poem of the bees."

"Do it for us — could you?" Aura asked. In that electric light, her skin shone like polished walnut. Though her profile was stern and fierce, her dazzling smile exuded ten thousand volts of joie de vivre.

I couldn't think of anything more embarrassing. Like a drunk standing on the table and doing a clumsy dance amid the plates and glasses. "No, really, I can't."

"No, you must," said Moura at Gorky's elbow.

The Gorky cousins and Khodasevich's niece concurred.

"It would be so kind of you," Gorky said.

Well, it was Gorky's table, Gorky's *solyanka*. How could I refuse him? I took a sip of tea and decided against rising — it seemed too awful — and I began to recite in a soft, conversational voice, letting the rhythm, the chant of it rise, looking mostly at Gorky's cousins, the Hungarian boy, and Khodasevich's niece, and purposefully avoiding the scarecrow in the mirror. The way the girls at the switchboard became part of the machine, the signals whirring in our hair, the dream of bees, the honey. When I finished, a round of applause greeted me. I hoped I hadn't seemed a fool, but the response appeared genuine and not merely the expression of relief that the clumsy child had performed her last pirouette without upsetting the glasses.

"Is that where you work, the telephone exchange?" Emma Goldman asked. "Do you have a union?"

"We have a committee," I said.

She frowned. "Do you really think it's the same thing? How do you redress grievances?"

"Through the committee, to the Commissariat," I said.

"The Commissariat's your boss. You should organize. You'll need that union sooner or later."

I thought of the Soviet young ladies, my fellow telephonists. A few were studying to become Communists — ironically the last ones interested in collective action on the shop floor. They were interested in currying favor from those above them and lording it over the rest. And most were Formers who wanted as little to do with the collective as possible. I told the American as much.

"This is what I worry about," said Goldman in Russian to the British trade unionist, and to Gorky. "The way the party is taking over the unions. This so-called militarization of labor. I've visited factories where workers are literally chained to their machines. Soldiers with bayonets guarding factories against their own workers. In the so-called workers' state."

"Absenteeism is crippling industry," said Gorky. "It's an unenviable position, but we have to do something."

I wished she wouldn't fight with him, he was clearly not feeling well. Me, I just wanted to enjoy my *solyanka* and not listen to people argue. I wanted to talk more to Aura, find out what she was doing, where she was performing, what she thought of us. I wanted to talk to Gorky about the House of Arts. Or to the mathematician's son, or the cousins, about Nizhny Novgorod. Khodasevich's niece was a painter. I wanted to enjoy the life of these cultured people. But the politicals wouldn't quit.

"I worry when they take us to tour factories, and we see plenty of fuel and materiel," said Harris. "It doesn't seem possible the country would be in such straits if what we are being shown is the true state of things."

Emma leaned forward over her soup and gestured at the Englishman with her spoon. "Go to Putilov. No one would tell me a thing until they found out who I was—an American anarchist, not a Bolshevik flunky. Then I got an earful. They're not getting their rations, and they've got soldiers breathing down their necks. One old man said there's only two thousand working there now, and another five thousand watching them. We've all seen it. The Bolsheviks have created this monstrous bureaucracy that's sitting on the backs of the worker. It's slavery that wouldn't be tolerated in a Ford plant. The workers would have struck months ago."

What a firebrand this Emma Goldman was! To talk like this at Gorky's table? I translated some of it for Aura. It might be true, but it was awfully insensitive to rail against the Bolsheviks, who were, after all, her hosts in Russia. Then I thought of myself in the days when I lived under my parents' roof, the dinner conversations so much like this, where I would speak out just as heatedly against their bourgeois smugness, and I was ashamed of myself. How cowed we all were these days, myself included, how politically nervous. No Russian would speak out against the Bolsheviks so plainly without wondering when the axe would fall. Even Gumilev the monarchist stopped short of criticizing the Bolsheviks directly. I wondered what Emma Goldman's status was here in Petrograd, what the Bolshevik policy on anarchism was these days. I wasn't following politics so closely since I'd had Iskra. I only knew that the White threat had subsided, and I was writing, and that was enough.

Gorky's face looked waxen as he rubbed it in the palm of his large hand.

"What do you think, Harris?" Goldman demanded. "What are they saying in trade union circles?"

"Well, it's unfair to say what we in the West would or wouldn't put up with, Comrade," said Harris, leaning away from her on one elbow. "The situation here is so different. Think of what they've had to bear, and how long. I think the Bolsheviks are doing as well as they can with what they've got—"

She slapped the table. "The full Punch and Judy show," she said.

"I'm not here to take in a show!" Now Harris was losing his temper. "I've talked to Shatov—"

They started quarrelling about Shatov, who I gathered had been some colleague of Goldman's in America, now here working for the Bolsheviks, who'd "swallowed the Bolshevik line, hook and sinker," as Goldman snorted contemptuously, while Harris argued that the labor situation here couldn't be compared with that of England or America. "It's a workers' state," he stated. "If strikes cripple the country, who pays the tab? The worker. It's a much different situation." They got into the militarization of labor and Trotsky's call to overcome "trade union prejudices" in favor of labor armies.

The mathematician's son whispered something to his father, who laughed and ruffled his son's hair, kissed his temple. Khodasevich's niece Valentina rounded her eyes at me. *Good poem,* she mouthed. *Thanks,* I mouthed back.

"You watch. The unions will be completely suppressed before long. *Unnecessary in the workers' dictatorship,*" Goldman continued. "Already they've become adjuncts of the state. Unless their independence is secured, they'll just be absorbed. What happened to the 'disappearance of the state and centralized power'? The factories aren't being run by the workers, the worker is no more than a gear now. All the shots are called by Moscow. And from what I can see, the trade unions are enabling them."

Gorky looked so painfully tired. What a crossroads this household was, not only for literary Russia but politically as well. His was the only independent voice in the country—of course, everyone would be scrambling for his attention. I wished the wind could pick him up and blow him into the blue, like that escaped hat. He saw me gazing at him, and smiled. "Lenin thinks Trotsky goes too far, saying that the unions are no longer necessary," he said finally, steepling his sensitive fingers. "The workers need to defend themselves against the state whenever necessary. Also to *defend* their state, when that's necessary. But let's ask someone of the younger generation. Marina Dmitrievna, what do you think of all this?"

Everyone was looking at me—to decide the fate of the Russian worker! I must have turned pale, because Aura patted my hand. Hers was solid and meaty, her nails unpolished like everyone else's but well manicured, and she wore a large ring with an odd-shaped, unpolished green stone. "I think everyone's looking forward to the end of the war," I began. "So we can take a breath and repair and rebuild. Maybe the blockade will end by then." Then I realized that, yes, I did have an opinion. I wasn't as dead as all that. "During the White invasion, I worked on fortifications with women from Skorokhod, our shoe factory. They'd gone out on strike because they had no boots. I think the state is thinking on the big scale, and I suppose it has to...but the worker as an individual will be overlooked if he can't strike and remind the state of his existence."

"Well said," said Goldman. Moura nodded her approval, and it was clear Gorky was relieved at the slight lessening of the militancy of the discussion.

Now Moura was able to turn the talk toward Aura Cady Sands, who had sat for so long with the Russian political talk swirling around her, to ask about her recent trip to Moscow. "You met Lenin in Moscow. What was your impression of him?"

"Well, you'd never guess he was the leader of all of Russia," Aura said. "He's very unassuming. Maybe he'd come by to sweep up or something. Yet—you look in his eyes, and oh. There's that focus, that *will*, that *plan*. You know he's very capable of ruling."

"We met him too," Goldman said, in English. "He told us there were no ideological anarchists in jail. *Only bandits and Makhnoists.* Madame Ravich was kind enough to help us get two of them—two little girls, fifteen and seventeen—out of that nonexistent jail last week."

Clearly Moura had had enough of Goldman, and the anti-Bolshevik line of her conversation. She wanted Aura to talk. "Did you sing for him?"

"I sang Isolde," said Aura. "He speaks German. I don't think he liked it much—but he admitted he's conservative in matters of art." She sipped her tea. "I was surprised. You'd think revolutionaries would be revolutionaries of art as well as life."

Moura translated for her end of the table.

"It's just as well they're not," said Gorky, his amusement masked by his big moustache, but blooming in his eyes. "Preserving culture is a good project for the state. Let the artists be the ones to swing the axe."

Valentina took the view that modernity required the base of rooted culture. "If we destroy culture for the sake of modernism, I mean really destroy it, there won't be anything for the next generation to root themselves in. Nothing to react to, to advance or reject. You won't have modern men, you'll have ignorant ones who'll think there's never been anything worthwhile except for the few pitiful scraps they themselves have been able to assemble." She sounded very much like her uncle. That must be quite a family. She made me want to talk more with Khodasevich when I saw him next.

It was a heady afternoon, and Aura promised me tickets to *Aleko*, the new Rachmaninoff opera she was singing with Chaliapin at the Mikhailovsky Theater on May Day. I recalled watching the crowds emerging from the Mikhailovsky through the windows of the Infant Department at Orphanage No. 6. It put a crimp in my pleasure, to think that Iskra had been alive then, howling with the others. I thought their fate was the worst it could get. How simple I had been. And how I had yearned to be in that intermission audience. "You sang there last fall."

"Did you see me?" Her smile, her smooth gleaming cheeks.

"Oh, I didn't go. I just thought it might be you."

"Well, you'll absolutely adore *Aleko*. Very modern. I play the gypsy, Zemfira. Chaliapin kills me in the end, of course — marvelous. The Russian hero claims to love me as a free woman, but in the end he is not liberated enough to live his ideals. So strong, so passionate!"

Aleko was Pushkin's "The Gypsies." I knew I would love it.

"The next time you visit, I'll sing you some of it," she said. "And you will come again, now that we've found you? Moura, she must come, yes?"

"Of course she must." Moura smiled, a feline smile. She said something to Gorky.

"Anytime," he said. "We'd be honored."

"Do you believe in destiny, Marina?" Aura asked, gazing into my eyes with her own, large ones not a solid brown but flecked with gold. I wondered how old she was. Twenty-eight? Thirty? "When's your birthday, honey?"

"February third." What did that have to do with anything?

"That's Aquarius. I love Aquarians! So avant-garde, so daring."

Oh no. A spiritualist.

She patted my knee. "And your name is Marina. Appropriate, don't you think? Do you believe in astrology?"

I didn't want to hurt her feelings. She wanted to include me in her life, wrap it around my shoulders like a cape. Cautiously, I

411

responded, "I hope we have the power to shape our own destiny. If we have the courage to do so." Though Iskra's death hadn't been shaped by me. There had been a black fate waiting for her. But I wanted to believe our will still mattered.

"What about Marx?" she teased. "Aren't you a Marxist?"

I could hear the Hungarian mathematician eating his soup. The muddy truth—I did believe in fate, though I didn't want to. I could not take the spaceman's view of human life, it was capitulating to helplessness. "Economics shapes our lives, but what's the virtue in fatalism? We should act as if we had free will, even if we don't. A Negro American classical singer comes to Soviet Russia—that must have taken a fair bit of free will." Emma was listening, as was Moura across the table. "Say that parts of life are predetermined—say that most of it is. There will always be areas in which our actions matter. And we'll never know which ones they are. So I'd rather concentrate on that, whether I'm being compelled by destiny or history or economics." That wasn't very Marxist of me. "I can't accept that I'm just an automaton run by blind forces." An abdomen on legs. Yet, certainly, I was compelled by all sorts of forces. Freud's as well as Marx's.

"The individual can either help or hinder development," said the British labor man, dabbing at his salt-and-pepper moustache. "But the control of the means of production drives history. You're mad if you think you're free. Here at least you're in possession of the means. On the side of the working man, you're making progress."

"I'm with you, Marina Dmitrievna," said Goldman. "You're an anarchist, even if you don't know it."

Moura translating.

"Lajos, what does the mathematician think?" Gorky asked.

"No free will," said the Hungarian. "The structure of the universe is discoverable, we're born into it, and it works through us. What we think of as will is just another aspect of the predetermined structure."

"So why teach anybody anything?" asked Valentina. "Either way we're just enacting the predeterminancy."

The Hungarian's eyes smiled while the rest of his face remained mournful. "Intriguing, yes?"

I translated for Aura, who began talking about an idea she had for a school—for orphans. *Orphans*...I didn't know whether to laugh or cry. "You see them everywhere, the poor things, you know?" Oh, I did know, Aura. Alas. "I want to do something for them. Give them their voices. Teach singing. And dance! Languages. Music and theater arts. Maria Andreeva says she'll help me once she's done with the May Day spectacle. She's head of the entire Theater Department now, you know. Right up there under Lunacharsky." What a nest Aura had found her way into. Maria Andreeva wasn't just Gorky's wife but a power of her own. "Perhaps you'll help me with it," she said.

My throat closed. I was trying not to see orphans at all—their needy faces, their cunning, the horror of their lives. *Write while you can.* If she had asked me in the fall, I would have thought myself lifted right up to heaven. Now I felt myself dangling over an abyss. But what were the chances she'd actually get something like this done?

"All I can say is good luck," Emma Goldman concurred. "Every time we've tried to get anything going here, they cheered us on to begin with, promising every ounce of help, but nothing ever comes of it. Hospital work, a rest home on the islands, labor exchange for the *Buford* refugees. Nothing comes to anything here, unless it's Cheka business, and that's on a different set of rails."

"If Maria Andreeva says she'll help, she will," said Gorky, clearly irritated.

After a while, the party broke up. I thanked Gorky and he invited me to come back again, and soon.

"Tuesday evening, we're having guests, you must come," Moura told me, pointedly not inviting the anarchist.

Goldman and I walked out together. She was much shorter than I'd imagined. "You think me rude, don't you?" she said as we descended the stairs.

"I think he was hoping for a little more fun at tea," I said. "A break from the political threshing floor."

She sighed. "I'm sure you're right." I held the door for her, let her out before me.

The sunset had gathered on Kronverksky. The smell of new grass lifted us up out of the gloom of the apartment, lifted us up into spring. I just wanted to stand on the sidewalk and breathe, breathe in the headiness of the conversation in the quiet of the canal and the trees, but Goldman was still worrying her argument, like a dog with a bone. "It makes me so mad," she said. "Do you really think the Bolsheviks are going to loosen the reins once the Whites are defeated? This has all played right into their hands. They'll keep coming up with enemies and emergencies, whatever it takes to deflect blame from themselves. You just watch."

"I assume we all will," I said, a little stiffly, not wanting to start her up again.

"Oh, don't be like that," she said, shoving me with her shoulder like a schoolgirl. "I'm not just some boor, trying to vex our Alexei Maximovich. The system needs fleas to keep it honest. Everyone's being shackled by their dread and fear of reprisal. In the hospitals, the workplace. And it gets worse every day. We have to speak out. Never stop letting people know what you think. Once there's silence, no one will want to be first to break it."

A flea indeed. I prayed for her safety, that no one would squash such a flea. She'd given me much to think about. "*Bonne chance*, Emma Goldman." I shook her hand, and prayed she would not be assassinated like Rosa Luxemburg. A woman like that had a calendar over her head and a target painted on her fiery breast.

35 *A Visit*

I stopped halfway across the Troitsky Bridge in the beautiful dusk, shadows blue against the silvery blue, pausing to glory in my new life. It was beginning again, dangerous and volatile, as heady as champagne. Gulls screamed overhead, fighting over something. That's when I saw the unmistakable lanky form, my brunet, the Void in a leather jacket. There was no point in running. She knew where I was registered, where I worked. If she wanted to talk to me, she would. I prayed she would walk on, showing herself as a warning, as she had at the House of Arts. But there was no safe place—the shifting depth of the river was the only place she could not follow.

The figure grew larger on the long bridge, crossing from the Palace side. The wind tugged at her narrow skirt. The glossy leather of her jacket gave her an insect look, like the carapace of an ant, a slender black wasp.

If I jumped in, could I swim to shore? I was a strong swimmer, but the current was mighty, few people survived it. No, I would meet her, get it over with. I would walk away a free woman, or under arrest, but I would not play the mouse again. She kept coming, her stride confident, hands at her sides. I couldn't see the square Mauser at her hip but knew it was there. I gazed west, toward Kronstadt and the open sea, a lick of gold still at the horizon.

Petersburg the seafaring,
You opened your arms to the world
And sailed out, nose to the great earth's winds . . .

At last, Varvara leaned on the railing of the bridge next to me. She looked older than she had when she'd rescued me from the Cheka prison at Gorokhovaya 2, stronger than she had in the flat I'd shared with her off the Fontanka, more severe, less kinetic. We said nothing, just watched the water pass under the bridge in the unfrozen center—green-black waves heading for the open gulf. Sheets of ice traveled past from time to time. How many desperate people had jumped from this bridge in the last few years? I avoided looking back at the Peter and Paul Fortress, the enormous silent fact of it.

"You're back," she said.

I nodded. Everything had caught up with me eventually—Arkady, and now Varvara.

"I heard your reading," she said. "It sounded pretty good." She leaned forward, her hands clasped, the Mauser at her hip. "Though I'm no critic."

What was she after? Varvara couldn't have cared less about echoes of sound or the movement of the human soul.

"I didn't know you had a baby." Gazing upriver, not meeting my eyes. "Was it Genya's?"

Why should I help her? If she wanted information, she would have to ask the right questions.

"Shurov's?"

Just beyond the rail, a gull hovered on the freshening wind. She put her hand on my arm, and I flinched.

"I'm not the enemy, Marina."

I had used my own name, that was my mistake. My hubris. Ever my weakness. To feel confident that now I was safe. That's how she'd found me. I could have used a pseudonym, created a new self for the next life. But I wanted to stand whole, with all my mistakes, to be everything I had ever been.

"Where did you go?" she asked.

"Daleko," I said. *Far away.* I knew her, she would never forgive my having abandoned her for Kolya, for humiliating her. She had offered me her love, and I had left her.

"Von Princip's dead," she said. Pretending to be casual—ah, she was an operator, our young Chekist. She turned, resting her back against the railing, a silhouette against the western gold. "He was running a gang of orphans out of the Alexander Nevsky Monastery. He was half eaten when we found him."

The starving children...I could feel her black eyes, probing. "What's this got to do with me?"

"Seems to be a theme, don't you think?"

"What theme? Dinner?"

"Orphans," she said.

"It's our major industry," I said. "Orphans and corpses. If only we could build tractors and rail stock so bountifully."

The Kamennoostrovsky tram trundled slowly onto the bridge, groaning and screeching, the bell clanging, people hanging from the sides like bags off a donkey.

"Why did you come back?"

"The baby," I said. "I didn't want her growing up a hick."

She turned her face to the wind. "I never understood the attraction of the countryside. *Fresh air. Trees, fields!* What's so special about a bunch of trees?"

As we stood together in the lowering dusk, I waited for the axe to fall. I could see the edge glinting. I knew her better than anyone on earth.

"That was Emma Goldman you were talking to," she said.

The flea. So that was it.

"You came from Gorky's."

Yes, an interrogation. I gazed downriver, toward the other bridges—Palace, Nikolaevsky. And Kronstadt, unseen on the horizon. West. Where one could breathe. "I was visiting a friend who's staying with them."

Her black cropped hair whirled in the sea breeze, flying up like a wing. "What was Goldman doing there?" she asked.

A man pushed a large bundle on an old bicycle past us, as if we were just a couple of girlfriends standing on a bridge, taking in the view. Or did he see her Mauser? "I don't know," I said. "I was there for tea. Probably wanted something from him. Most people do."

"Any idea what?" She leaned toward me.

I shook my head.

"What did they talk about?" Not *what did* she *talk about*. I had to be careful. "The other guests."

"Typical political things, trade unions, what Lenin said about art. I was visiting my friend, an opera singer. She came to my reading."

"The American, Aura Sands."

I once might have teased her about keyhole peeping, but I had seen her in her element, an interrogation room at Gorokhovaya 2. My mouth went dry. She was getting closer to her purpose and I waited with dread to see what it would be. She seemed compressed within herself, steely, her rangy shoulders braced, her thin hands spread beside her along the rail. The fingers seemed too delicate for what she did with them. I wanted to swallow, but I knew she would notice.

"How well do you know her?" Was this about Aura, being an American?

"We met at the reading, she invited me to visit." I made no show of resisting. I imagined myself a clear pool, hiding nothing. I knew to resist her was like tugging at a rag when you played with a dog. If you wanted the dog to lose interest, you had to stop tugging.

We began to walk again, south along the wide bridge with its art deco stanchions for the tram wires, toward the Palace Embankment. The farther we got from the fortress, the better I liked it. I told myself if we made it as far as the Palace Embankment without incident, everything would be fine. She might still be hurt by my abandonment, but nothing would happen to me. But, oh Lord, if we turned back...

She took my arm, startling me. "This is me, remember?" Leaning in. She smelled sour, of dirty hair, and pencil shavings. "I know you. You remember exactly what they said. Who said what, and how they said it. You remember how many buttons Gorky had on his shirt and whether he cut himself shaving. Who do you think you're talking to, some provincial strawhead?"

Yes, I knew who I was talking to. The girl who'd asked me to spy on my father in the days before October. Who had revealed all his secrets and tore my family apart. The young woman who'd pulled me out of a blood-soaked cellar at Gorokhovaya 2, who had released me, but only in exchange for more betrayal. I'd made love to her, and then left her without a word. "He had a waistcoat on," I said. "Two buttons showing. He hadn't cut himself." The leather jacket. I could hear it, creaking.

"That's better. And what did they talk about?"

"Varvara. I'm sorry I didn't tell you I was leaving—"

Her sallow face darkened. She stopped, wrenching me around by the arm. "You think I give a damn about that? You think what happened with us, that's what this is about? Do you think we matter in the least, our so-called feelings? The safety of the workers' state, that's what this is about." She let me go with a *tcha* of disgust. "I don't give a damn that you ran off with that speculator, that saboteur, and had your sordid little baby and that it died. I have counterrevolution up to my elbows and I want to know who was there." Her eyes crackled like a frayed cord, sparking.

She could squash me like a fly. And yet, to say something like that about Iskra... "No," I said.

"No?" She laughed out of sheer amazement. "You're telling me no?"

Never say no to me. Well, no to him and no to her. "You can't use me anymore," I said. "I spied for you twice. I think I've done enough."

Suddenly she was twisting my arm up behind me, like a cop. Right out in the open on the Troitsky Bridge. Forcing me onto the railing. "I say what's enough," she hissed through clenched teeth.

"You're hurting me." I said it as a matter of fact. I would not cry.

"I say what's enough." She leaned over and repeated it in my ear, as I tried to escape the pressure on my shoulder. "I could shoot you right here and no one would say a thing."

"Do it," I said, my vision fogged with tears. "Because I'm not going to inform for you. I've got nothing to lose anymore."

"So you think," she said, but she let me go.

Passersby, a woman with a child by the hand, a man carrying rations, two old ladies arm in arm, turned their gazes pointedly riverward, left and right, and I knew it was true. She could shoot me and nobody would say a thing. People would make a point of not remembering this encounter on the Troitsky Bridge. "I think you're going to change your mind about that."

I hunched my shoulder, rotated the arm. I didn't like the crooked smile on her face, the air of withheld knowledge. I couldn't tell if she was bluffing. She was a professional, she could make me think anything. But what did she know that I didn't? What exactly could she hold over me now, when I had nothing? "I don't think I will."

"Come with me," she said, and nodded back the way we had come. "I want to show you something."

36 *The Fortress*

The fortress loomed ahead of us in the dusk. It was still daytime in London. In New York, people were bustling in the streets, reading the newspapers, the ships thick in their harbor. And in California, where Uncle Vadim slept, the sun had just come up. I would give anything to be there. "Am I under arrest?"

"Have you done anything wrong?" Varvara asked. As if the Cheka needed a reason.

We turned off the wide Troitsky onto St. John's Bridge, then passed into the fortress, entering a dark weedy forecourt bounded in stone walls. It was terrifying to see the golden steeple of the Peter and Paul Cathedral so high above me, an angle at which I'd never seen it before. Like a sword threatening the peace of the evening sky. All the warmth and gaiety of the afternoon at Gorky's had dissolved like wet tissue. I was glad I was wearing my sheepskin. It hadn't been strictly necessary, but if I were imprisoned, I would be happy to have it.

Avoiding the puddles, we approached a stout and heavily guarded inner gate.

"It's called St. Peter's Gate," Varvara told me as she swaggered up to the guard on duty. He looked like an ant in the arch of the enormous wall. The post was reinforced with a machine gun. St. Peter's, but you'd be lucky to be refused entry. Varvara passed the guard her credentials. He made a telephone call. A raw patch of brick showed where they had torn down the imperial eagle over the gate, where red flags now flew. He came back and opened the second gate.

I would have given anything for a drink of water. My mouth had gone stone dry. But I refused to show her how frightened I was. The blue sky tinged with gold—it could be the last time I ever saw it. This horrible place was like a person you had known all your life, a frightening, powerful figure you recognized on sight, maybe even nodded to in the street, whose carriage or motorcar sometimes passed by you, but now the black door opened and he was beckoning you to go for a ride. "You want to tell me where you're taking me?"

"Isn't it obvious?" Now we were in the inner court, pavement and water and big avenues of bare trees, eighteenth-century administrative buildings and barracks and those inescapable walls of stone. Before there was anything else in Petersburg, there had been this—a church, a barracks, and a prison. The crude basis of a state. Power in all its forms. Reluctantly, I followed Varvara past the Dutch-style cathedral of Peter and Paul with its spire, and a brick-and-stone building on the left. I needed time to gather my wits, to think of a plan. Some way to stop this. "Can we go into the church?" I asked.

"It's closed," she said. "What, have you become religious in your old age?"

"I've always wondered what it's like inside." Pretending I was merely sightseeing.

"You slay me, you really do. Do you even know where you are?"

I knew very well, as every Petersburg child did. Each alcove at the six corners of the wall had its own name. Behind us, the Menshikov and Peter the First Bastions. To the left, the Naryshkin Bastion, where the noon cannon used to sound across the Neva each day, the very cannon that had landed blows the night of the Bolshevik uprising, tearing chunks from the Winter Palace. And somewhere beyond the cathedral, the Troubetskoy Bastion, prison of the tsars, where the regime kept its most famous inmates. Here, Peter the Great had held his son, Tsarevich Alexei, invited him home like a prodigal son and had him beaten to death. Trotsky had done his time in the Troubetskoy Bastion, and the anarchist Kropotkin. Dostoyevsky spent eight months there before his mock execution changed the course of Russian literature.

"Do you want to see where we shot the four grand dukes?" she asked with a smirk.

Something else I'd missed. "No," I said.

I didn't dare breathe. The yellow-red stone was a nothing color in the gloom as we crossed the large yard. Varvara, long-strided in black leather, seemed as tall as the spire of the cathedral. We passed the Neva Gate, where the prisoners were brought by river, its classical pillars and lintel so at odds with its grim purpose. Our steps echoed on the cobbles, splashed in standing water. To our right, a detachment of soldiers marched. I could not pretend I was that brave girl she'd once known. "Varvara, tell me you're not going to leave me here."

She gave an arrogant snort. "Oh, you poor dear. Yes, you'll sleep in your own bed tonight, with the storeroom on one side and the old Jews on the other."

She knew everything. "Swear to me?"

Tch, she exhaled in disgust. "Have I ever lied to you? Ever?" She walked on faster. "That's your specialty."

It was true. Varvara didn't lie. With her, it was what she neglected to tell you that you had to worry about. What she conveniently omitted, and then later dropped on your head like a slab of masonry.

We got to the end of the lane, and entered the last bastion.

Troubetskoy.

Again, she showed her papers. A Chekist in riding breeches and leather jacket, graying hair, a small tight mouth, clicked down the low-ceilinged hall, painted yellow to shoulder height and a dingy white above. Varvara took him aside. They were both looking at me, but speaking too quietly for me to hear.

I breathed as we breathed at Ionia. I stepped out of my body, stood alongside myself. *I am not my body. My spirit is eternal. I have lived many times before, and will live many times again.* Not that I believed it, but I took comfort in the idea, the ritual. I counted the lightbulbs in the ceiling. Seven. I heard voices, but the walls must be ten feet thick. It was cold and damp and smelled of the river. I would live through this day. I would live through it, and sleep in my own bed. Gorky had lived through this, Trotsky, Dostoyevsky—but I was shaking. The Cheka tortured people, knocked out their teeth, cut off their fingers and toes—they could get you to confess to anything. I kept seeing that drain in the cellar of Gorokhovaya 2, filled with blood.

Varvara and the elegant Chekist in his jodhpurs escorted me into an icy room furnished with a table and four chairs, two on each side, where Varvara searched me thoroughly, though not roughly, as my teeth knocked together in terror. Her mouth was set and she didn't look into my eyes, which I kept on the portraits of Lenin, Zinoviev, and Dzerzhinsky on the yellowed walls. I thought of how many Lenins I'd seen since the revolution. Every office and canteen and bakery had one. Some were smiling and warm and grandfatherly, like in the Women's Club of Tikhvin, others noble and intelligent, like the portrait in the main hall of the telephone exchange. But this one was severe and unflinching, the spaceman himself, flanked by the soulless vanity of our Petrograd boss and the thin, cruel, fanatical face of the Chekist, like a medieval inquisitor.

It gave me small comfort to note that my friend left me my labor book, but she did confiscate the three penknives I'd been carrying, which she pocketed without comment. "Comrade Mstinsky will take you from here. I'll see you when you're done."

"Let's go, sister," Mstinsky said, shoving me in front of him.

We turned at the bottom of a set of narrow stairs. *A good omen.* Even in the Troubetskoy Bastion, up had to be better than down. The bristlecone of keys chained to his belt jangled with each step. His boots were fine, well polished. Did he get them with the jodhpurs, or had he commandeered them from a well-shod prisoner? Was he taking bribes? I tried to think of the boots, rather than where we were going. I could feel the weight of a hundred feet of heavy stone above us, pressing down on me, the narrowness of the staircase. The light was harsh, electric, bulbs in simple cages. There was not room for two people to walk abreast. It was stuffy and held that smell I recognized from Gorokhovaya 2. Fear. It smelled acrid and dirty and electrical.

A small landing, another door, metal this time, with great metal bands and studded hasps. Mstinsky knocked and the grate opened. A man with deeply set eyes and a prominent brow bone appeared.

"Number thirty-two," said my Virgil.

The guard opened the door and Mstinsky walked me through. It swung shut behind us with a bang, and I found myself in a low-ceilinged hall, a wide brick arch dotted with bare light fixtures. Doors punctuated the hall on either side. The whole thing was terrifyingly medieval. So many doors, it could easily be a monastery, but for the fact that each door had a slit in it at waist level, and a peephole with a disk over it. The guard stopped before one door cut into the stone, swung the little cover open and peered in, nodded to my guide, and unlocked it. The door opened and Mstinsky shoved me inside. I heard the bolt run home.

There was a man in the cell, in torn trousers and a dirty singlet, a bloody bandage on his head covering one eye. He rose to his feet.

My father. Dmitry Ivanovich Makarov.

He looked nothing like he had the last time I'd seen him in that cabin in the snow, when he told his friends I was a Bolshevik spy. Now he was a starved, beaten prisoner—long, ragged beard, his feet bare on the cold stone. They were absolutely blue, with heavy uncut nails. He had no coat, no jacket, in this ice chest of a cell. His blanket lay crumpled on the bed, I imagine he'd been wearing it as a shawl but had dropped it when he stood. I noted—he had all ten toes.

"Marina." His voice, a harsh whisper from between his cracked lips.

I took off my sheepskin and put it around his shoulders. I knew the warmth from my body would feel good to him. I didn't know what else to do—hug him? Too much had transpired between us. It was unbearable. I sat on his bed. He came to me, limping, stiff,

and favoring his right leg, gingerly lowering himself down. The
bucket in the corner stank. I told myself I didn't smell it, didn't
smell him. He smelled like the grave. I took his thin hand. It didn't
feel like his. It was an old man's hand, nothing but bone. How
many times I had held that hand, walking across the street with
him, my whole hand wrapped around a single finger? *Papa*...I
didn't know where to begin. There was nowhere to get a foothold.
He had been willing to suffer my death for his cause—and I
had betrayed him to the Bolsheviks when still a schoolgirl. I had
named his mistress to the Cheka. Seryozha was dead, and he had
caused it. Maryino was gone. My mother, his wife—abandoned,
now unrecognizable. His country was lost. His cause was over. He
was a prisoner. Which of us had suffered more? We had both lost
children. But I was free, and my country was in the future. I was
young, an artist. I had work and friends. He had only a past.

And me.

He patted my hand, covered it with his own. He had terrible sores
and bruises. "Marina." His voice was a grated whisper, like a rusty
hinge.

I let my tears fall. I was surprised to find that I didn't hate him
anymore. We'd both been caught in this terrible trap.

"Papa..."

He searched my face with brown eyes that were the same as mine,
but haunted, uncertain, yellow with jaundice. "Are you really here?"
He touched my cheek, so gently with his horny split fingernails. "Is
this real?"

I nodded, making no attempt to conceal tears. I let them water his
hand. His dear sweet hands.

"I dream of you. About that night—" he began, but I didn't let
him go on.

"It's a long time ago. Don't think about it."

"No. It isn't." He shook his head, as if shaking the vagueness
from it. He lifted my hand to his lips. He was weeping like an
old woman. "I was a fool. Mad, vain...The things I've done...
Forgive me."

"Let's not talk. Let's just sit together." I wished I could have brought him some cherry tobacco, a pipe. Maybe Gorky could help me. Maybe they would let me bring him food, some clothes...

He put my coat around the two of us, around both our shoulders, and we sat that way for the longest time. He kissed my hair. "Still red. Where did you get that red?" It's what he always used to say. *Where'd you get that red, Little Red Riding Hood?*

I wanted to tell him about Iskra, but I couldn't. One more tragedy—how would that help him now? "Guess what—I'm a poet now. I had a reading at the House of Arts. Blok was there. He said it made him like poetry again." I heard my babbling. It sounded ridiculous. "What happened to your eye, Papa?"

He rested his head on my hair. "I've got another." A joke. He could still joke.

"How did they catch you?"

"It was last summer. At Krasnaya Gorka." The mouth of the Gulf of Finland. The British sank a Soviet battleship there before they were routed. "The sailors mutinied, Marina," he whispered. "Your sailors. They came over to us. They're sick of the Bolsheviks. The Reds are going to have their hands full soon." He broke off in a fit of coughing, the coat sliding from his shoulders. I wrapped it around him again. "What I didn't understand..."—he resumed his former voice—"was why they didn't shoot me when they shot everybody else." His brown eyes with their yellowed whites, reddened from lack of sleep. "Then your horrible friend came to call."

I still remember the two of them, facing off in the parlor at Furshtatskaya Street when she told him I'd been spying for the Bolsheviks. And he sent me into the night, the gunfire and the storm. But he wasn't the same, and neither was I.

I tried not to stare at the sores on his hands as he held the coat around him. "She said the only reason I was still alive was because of her friendship with you. Said she was keeping me alive in your honor."

Could that be true? "I thought you'd gone east, after Kolchak fell."

"I did. It was hideous there. Worse than anything the Bolsheviks could have done." He drooped, gazing down at the floor, down at his toes, the long, yellow, broken nails. Next time I came, if I could, I'd bring scissors and cut them. He couldn't have worn a pair of boots if he'd had them. "Do you ever see your mother?"

I had to stop looking at his feet. "She was out at Maryino." How could he stand to be in this cell? You could reach out and touch both walls at the same time. Their surfaces oozed water. How was it he hadn't gone mad? "She found a spiritual leader, a man named Ukashin. They turned Maryino into a commune. She thinks she's Sophia, Mother of the World. But they're gone. My guess is they headed for Persia."

"When was that?"

"A year ago March."

He rubbed his forehead, and I realized he was having trouble taking in so much information after sitting alone in this cell since Krasnaya Gorka. There was no way to note the passing of time—though I assumed they must turn off the lights at night. Or he could have noted the changing of shifts. He was not a stupid man. I wanted to say something that would be worthy of the occasion. Any second that door could open and end this precious visit. But all I could do was say, "Papa...I'm so sorry. About everything."

He sighed and kissed my temple, his arm around me. "Are you still with...that boy? That big clodhopper?"

"He's a famous poet now. We married in 1918. We're separated, but I use his name for my papers. Kuriakina." He nodded. It never would have occurred to him that marrying that big clodhopper might have been the only thing that saved his bourgeois daughter. "But I'm writing under my own name."

"That's how she found you."

I nodded. "I got tired of being someone else."

"What does she want from us?" he asked. "Your so-called friend."

Of course, this wouldn't come free of charge. She would extract her pound. The thick stone walls, the high window, the tiny cot.

"She wants to know what's going on inside Gorky's flat. He's befriended me. She wants to know who comes there, what they say. Foreigners visit him. I just met Emma Goldman."

"Don't do it," he said. "She'll hold it over your head forever. You know she will."

"But maybe I can come see you. Help you." I took his hand, but too hard—the pressure made him wince. I brought my head closer to his. I could smell him, unwashed, he who was always so fastidious. "I could bring you food. Maybe even medicine. Get you out of here—who knows?"

He looked at me so sadly, ran his palm over his stubbly hair. So much gray, and in his beard. "They're not going to let me out, Marina. She's only keeping me alive so she has something to hold over you. It's all very clear to me now." His wrists were so thin, I could see all the veins and sinews, bruises.

I didn't want to argue about Varvara. I would deal with her in my own way. "Did you see Kolya? In his cloak-and-dagger for the English?"

"*With* the English," he corrected me, and his hand came away from mine. "*For* Russia, Marina. Always for Russia. Kolya helped set up that meeting at Pulkovo." That debacle in the woods. Conspiring to bankroll the Czech Legions against Red Russia.

We both heard something in the hall rattling and fell silent, waiting to see if it was the guard coming to fetch me, but the sound moved on.

"He's established a reputation for a certain sort of business venture. Comings and goings, so to speak."

Smuggling. "In the West? Finland? Estonia?"

He nodded.

That meant he came to Petrograd, or at least close enough. I had not been expecting to hear good news! So the fox was still trotting across the ice, doubling back on his tracks. The clever fox was yet at large. "Moving...livestock?" *People.*

"All sorts of...commodities. But it's been a while—I haven't spoken to anyone but your friend and Marley's Ghost out there for a very long time." He smiled and attempted a laugh. The saddest laugh I'd heard.

"Did she ask about him?"

Now he examined my face closely. He was never that observant before. He was someone for whom information generally went one way—from him to you. But experience had made him aware of other people. "Is that how it is? You and—?"

"We had a child. He doesn't know."

"Had?"

I nodded.

"God, this life." Fingering the back of my hand, tracing the veins, then lacing his fingers into mine. "Yes, she asked about him. I said I'd seen him in Estonia, didn't know his associates." The trace of a smile, his old intelligence, keenness. Then his face grew bright. "Oh! And I heard from Volodya! He got a letter through before they closed the Estonian border. He's in the Kuban with Denikin."

That was a year ago. "It's Wrangel now. Denikin's out of the picture. They've evacuated to Odessa."

The air left him in a rush. I shouldn't have told him. "It's almost over, then."

"We've just been attacked by Poland. They're marching on Kiev."

"The Poles? What's next, Brazilians? Hottentots?" He pressed the bandage to his eye, as if it was hurting him. "So tell me something else. You became a poet. Recite me a poem." I recited "The Argonaut," and "The Trees at Kambarka," and "Alice in the Year One," very quietly. He knew that concrete floor. After a while, we just sat together, holding hands, until Marley's Ghost came to collect me.

He handed me my sheepskin, but I wouldn't take it. "It's spring. Anyway, I'm an important poet now, I can't run around looking like the village shepherd."

He kissed me three times, ceremonially, and held me as long as he could before the guard took me out, delivering me to Mstinsky in the hall, who returned me to Varvara.

We walked out in silence into a beautiful night, Venus rising over St. Peter's Gate.

"Well?"

I thought about what I could ask in exchange for what she wanted me to do. "I have three conditions," I said. "First, I want to see him every week."

She nodded impatiently.

"Second, I want him to have food. Shoes, linen, soap. Paper, books."

"It can be done," she said.

"Third, he needs medical treatment. His feet. His eye. If I see him well taken care of, I'll tell you about the goings on at the Gorky tea table." I knew my father would be angry with me, but I had to try to help him. I could figure out what to do about Gorky later. Surely I could find some bits and pieces that wouldn't be too incriminating. I was a tightrope walker, wasn't I?

We walked in the dark back to St. Peter's Gate, avoiding the puddles now shining with moonlight. Yet even in the quiet, I could still hear the sound of keys and slamming doors in the Troubetskoy Bastion. I shuddered. The evening had turned cold, and certainly Varvara would have noticed that I'd left without my coat. "Thank you," I said. "For saving him."

"I thought you'd appreciate it," she said. "It'll be like old times."

No, it wouldn't be. But I would let her think so.

37 *The Spy*

A couple of lovers, tattered, half-starved, passed us on the street, arm in arm, their heads pressed together. Soon it would be May, and June, the White Nights. But no romance for me. Only betrayal. It was at that moment I understood how completely the trap had snapped shut on me. Varvara walked me as far as Shpalernaya Street, offering to let me wear her Chekist's leather coat. I was horrified at the idea of wearing such a thing, preferring to huddle against the wind as she enumerated the information she wanted about the Gorky milieu. His contacts with people from opposition parties. Anyone from the trade unions, anyone espousing anti-Bolshevik statements. Emma Goldman particularly.

"And keep an eye on Moura Budberg," she said. "That one's a British spy, I'll give you twenty to one." She wanted to know about visiting foreigners, foreign writers. "Even if you've heard of them. The Brits love to use their writers as spies. They've done it for a hundred years. I want to know who they meet, where they go. Make yourself useful. Foreigners need guides and translators. Especially a pretty girl, and a poet—"

"I already have a job." Who had the time to play Mata Hari? It was hard enough to sneak out for Anton's Wednesday poetry studio.

"Not anymore. You're working for us now."

O Holy Theotokos, help me, a poor sinner. "How will I get my rations?" Grasping at straws.

"They'll keep you on the books at the telephone exchange. Or maybe old Gorky can cough up a job. We'll think of something."

And I had thought myself safe after Arkady's death. I hadn't realized who my true enemy was going to be. Varvara was building a case against Gorky—why? *Because he was there,* the only independent voice in Russia. The Bolsheviks couldn't tolerate a man who was still respected, Lenin's close friend, the one man in the country who was allowed to go his own way.

Having sold my soul, suddenly I found myself free. I woke in the mornings, and the day was mine. My rations prepaid, I was a ghost at the telephone exchange. Anyone not knowing the price would have envied me. But Father was in the Troubeskoy Bastion, and what I'd agreed to do was a filthy rag stuffed in my mouth. I couldn't write, I couldn't sleep. I paced, I stared out the window. A dim light glowed in the one window across the courtyard... *Another soul lies restless there. / I will not put out my light.* I could only imagine the horror my sixteen-year-old self would feel at the predicament I'd been put in.

The very idea that Varvara wanted me to be a rat in the walls at Gorky's, listening at doors, riffling through his papers and Moura's dressing table. I turned the problem around in my head like a nanny turning the facets of a thermometer, trying to get another reading, but I could see no other outcome. If I wanted to help my father, there was no way out, only ahead, into the next turn of the labyrinth.

I had the time to write, but all I heard was the roaring silence. Blok had stopped writing poetry after "The Scythians," because there were no more sounds. This was what he meant. You couldn't say anything real or true when there was an immense lie sucking up all the air. Instead, I turned to the streets of my beautiful, crumbling city, walking, hour after hour. Here was the garbage, the dead horses, the broken pavers, the sins of winter exposed in all their horror—as I might be exposed for the hideous thing I would soon become.

Everything around me—the familiar buildings with their pilasters and caryatids, the ice sheeting off the canals—seemed heavy, hiding malevolence, danger, and betrayal. The sky itself untrustworthy. No forgiveness, no hiding place. The flowing water just a good place to dump a body. Everyone I passed seemed to be watching me. I could feel the wolfpack moving silently through the trees. Only the vaulted sky was untouched by it. It would see our deaths with the same vast unconcern as it would see a scythe cutting through a bird's nest hidden in the wheat. Each building stared defensively out at all the others. There could be a murder in every flat.

She'd planned this for a year. Narrowed the paths, hung the snares—while I was still in Udmurtia. Worse than mad Arkady and his drugged children, for this was cold calculation. Her love had turned to hatred, her joy was only the chess player's joy, seeing her opponent beaten long before the fatal move. It was my fault, for thinking I could live out in the open like other people, and possess my own face. For thinking I had nothing to lose.

Thank you for saving him, I'd said to her. I cringed to remember it. And now I was to be a tool of the Cheka, to bring down Maxim Gorky, that heroic, generous soul. I clung to the idea that I could feed her garbage, but even as I grasped at that straw, I knew she would not be satisfied. She was clever and ambitious. And if I didn't cooperate...

I lay on my narrow cot on the kitchen hall on Shpalernaya Street, watching the lit window across the yard, imagining him in his cell—*Papa, I'm sorry. But what would you have me do?* This old room might be small, but I could still open the window. I could go out into the street. But if I didn't give her what she wanted, she would kill him, and I would be the one in the cell. Even thinking of it made me feel as if I were suffocating. Or she'd send me to a camp in the north, where I would starve to death or freeze. And I'd given my father my sheepskin...

At eight o'clock that Tuesday night, I presented myself at the Gorky flat, my woolen scarf wrapped about me like a shawl, Klavdia's tattered jacket in place of my sheepskin, my fur hat back on my head. How happy Aura was to see me, hugging me, engulfing me in her strength and warmth. I drank in the golden spicy smell of her.

"What happened to your warm coat?" she asked.

"Stolen," I said. Lies already streaming behind me.

"Poor kid," she said, her big hand on my arm. "You can't be without a coat. Wait, I'll find you something."

As she led me down the corridor, I was busy memorizing things, things I hadn't paid attention to before. The number of doors on the corridor. The first door was open—the old front parlor, a room facing the street, where a commanding woman stood with a group of people around a table, going over notes and sketches. "Andreeva?" I asked.

"That's right."

Maria Andreeva's office—the old parlor. "She still lives here? With Moura?"

Aura laughed, her laughter rich and full of music. What glorious teeth she had. Big and square and even. No one had such teeth in all of Petrograd, not even before the war. "They don't step on each other's toes as much as you'd think." She led me toward the dining room, *eight doors, four and four.* "Andreeva's the queen, she's got her own life, her own *assistant.*" She arched an expressive eyebrow. "Moura organizes the cook, types Gorky's letters, does the fussing. Andreeva's not doing any of that. She's got the May Day extravaganza to worry about, not what kind of soup we're having for supper."

At the L of the large flat, the dining room—the arena where the lions would be loosed and the Christians torn to pieces—was already full of people. I could feel my face hot with shame as they greeted me warmly. A girl called Molecule, a friend of the ménage. The artists Didi and Valentina. Moura's greeting was cool, as if she already suspected me, but Gorky was pleased to see me. He seemed tired, overburdened, as if every care in the world lay on those stooped shoulders—it tore my heart to shreds.

"Somebody stole her coat," Aura told him.

"Call me Akaky Akakievich," I joked. Gogol's pathetic hero in "The Overcoat."

"We'll find you one," he said. "Moura?"

"Of course we will," she purred, patting him on the shoulder.

There were some new faces at the table, the two publishing colleagues of Gorky's from Universal Literature and a middle-aged man in rugged good health with a sharp narrow face and bushy eyebrows. He wore a broad beard like a man of the last century—the English playwright Clyde Emory. *Spy?* Even I knew who he was. I'd been taken to one of his plays in Drury Lane when we were living at Oxford. He was also a famous socialist, scandalous in England for supporting Irish nationhood and female suffrage. He sat next to Harris, the British union man. *Anyone from the trade unions*... They seemed to know each other. I wished I could tell my father that I was sitting here at a table with Clyde Emory! While spying for the Cheka. To meet great men only to betray them... My blood turned to vinegar as Gorky introduced me as "our most promising young poet." I might have been, before Varvara stuffed clay down my throat.

"Tell her she should come to England," Emory said to Moura, while gazing at me with frank interest—not strictly literary. "We've got a crop of the most marvelous new poets."

"Marina Dmitrievna speaks perfect English, Mr. Emory." Moura gestured to me with her chin. *Talk to him.*

Those piercing blue eyes, the pale face with the red cheeks. A still-handsome man. "And do you read our English poets, Miss Markova?" he asked me.

"Ma-KAR-ova," I corrected him. "Like a car. Yes, though we have been out of touch since the war." Hearing my poor pronunciation. *Vor.* My father hated that. *Ouar.* "But what is happening in poetry now, Mr. Emory? Before, we read Yeats, and your imagists—Pound, Aldington. Rather like our Acmeists, Akhmatova and Mandelstam."

"Pound and Aldington? Not Masefield and Gibson?"

Masefield and Gibson? Awful, sentimental poets who took working-class life as their subject matter. I tried to think of some diplomatic reply. "I think sentimentality about the working class is as bad as any other sentimentality." Down the table, Moura was translating our conversation for Gorky. He smiled and sucked on the black holder of his cigarette. "For the English workingman, I prefer Hardy, or Lawrence." I didn't want to insult him, but God!

"You're not one of those *art for art's sake* types, are you? Now? Here in Soviet Russia?" Emory lowered those expressive eyebrows with their quizzical points. "It seems you have an aesthete at your table," he said to Gorky.

Gorky stroked his great moustache, waiting to see how I would respond.

This was not the way the evening was supposed to play out. I thought I would be able to sit quietly and let the others reveal their opinions and secrets. Not be under the spotlight and cross-examined by this nettlesome Englishman. "I don't think there's ever purely art for art's sake," I said, and waited for Moura to translate for the Russian speakers. "I don't think it exists. We always create in the real world. We speak of this world. Our art comes from somewhere. On the other hand, whatever audience you imagine, and whatever your intent, you still have to create art. You can't falsify that."

But then what did that say about me? This liar, this thief of lives, this spy who had been somehow tracked in on Aura's shoe. What was I doing right now? Falsifying. In the worst way. Pretending I was a friend to these people. Pretending I cared about truth. Polluting everything.

Emory made a cage of his fingers, small and thin and sensitive, tapping their tips together. "Since the war, a whole new literature's emerged. This Irishman, James Joyce, has changed everything. And Eliot—he's one of Pound's boys, remarkable, really remarkable. It's a whole new world out there."

So many writers I'd never heard of. Time had moved on in the world outside our borders—without us. "Unfortunately, we've been cut off—by the British blockade."

Gorky was amused. Emory's blue eyes glittered. Oh, he was a provocateur, and seemed to relish the provocative in others.

"That's changing as we speak," said the English writer. "That's what I'm doing here. Investigating the current conditions. I'm planning a series of articles. People are very interested in Soviet Russia, Miss Ma-KAR-ova. Very interested indeed." He was full of confidence. He reminded me of my father somehow. If this had been one of my parents' soirees, he would be the man whose opinions mattered. Everyone stopped talking to listen when he spoke. "In the meantime, I've brought some books with me. I hope you might accept them as a bit of literary diplomacy."

The cook brought in the soup and the maid the *piroshky*, clearly the only dishes she knew how to make. The cook spooned up the borscht—it smelled ravishing—while we handed round the bowls, passed the platter of pies. It was a grand soup. I didn't begrudge the old girl's lack of culinary variety.

I learned a number of things that night. The garrulous Englander spoke to the assembled company as if addressing a hall, working his eyebrows like oars. His mother had been a singer. His father was

Irish, Aura explained, which was like being a Negro in America. During the war, Emory had been jailed for his pacifist views. How rightly proud he was of himself, I thought, to have been so strong, so determined, to have stood up against even his nation's patriotic fervor. *He* would never have informed for the Cheka. Nor would Gorky, or the British trade union man, or even Aura Cady Sands. Moura was the only one at the table capable of understanding my predicament, if Varvara's suspicions about her were even partially true. Yes, there was something about her—that wariness of someone who had been forced into things not to her liking, a cat on ice.

Gorky looked exhausted. What on earth had they been talking about in his office off the dining room? Was it his publishing partners who made him look like that, or Mr. Emory, or something else entirely? He smoked and coughed and even suggested he might leave Russia, go to Switzerland or Italy for a rest. "Vladimir Ilyich is urging me. But I think he just wants to be rid of me." *Oh, you don't know, Alexei Maximovich. Someone certainly wants it.* I translated for Emory and the British labor man.

"Well, perhaps it's something to consider," said Moura. "They all think that he has inexhaustible powers—*Alexei Maximovich, I need ration cards. A pair of boots, a winter coat.*" Was that a subtle jab? "*A job. My mother's in jail, my husband, my son. Talk to Vladimir Ilyich, he'll listen to you.*" How much did she know?

"They don't realize, sometimes it's worse for them if I intervene," Gorky said. "I'm no sorcerer. I'm not even much of a politician." He held out his glass to his publishing partner, Grzhebin, a sturdy fellow with broad shoulders and round spectacles—he looked like a stevedore who'd been to university. Grzhebin refilled Gorky's glass with wine that had somehow appeared at the table—maybe Clyde Emory had supplied it.

"Zinoviev wants to sink us. That's the plain fact," said Grzhebin. "He personally closed our paper." *Novaya Zhizn*, Gorky's newspaper, shuttered during the Terror after the assassination of Uritsky and the attempt on Lenin. "We were no opposition, unless you call simply having the gall to speak up *opposition.*"

As I began to translate, Moura sent me out a telegraphed message with a glance and slight shake of her head. *Don't.* I caught the words in my mouth. But the pale, lively girl called Molecule, studying medicine at the university, a distant family relation from Nizhny, tried to explain. Luckily, her English was abominable. "Zinoviev, he don't like how friendship close with Alexei Maximovich to Vladimir Ilyich? Like little boy, Papa like brother better."

"Abel and Cain," said Emory.

"Yes, he want only one close to Ilyich. Poison to his mind." She gave up and continued in Russian, and I let it go. It was clear Moura didn't want this discussed at the table, but Gorky kept nodding, *Yes, it's the truth, sad to say.* Looking at the burning tip of his cigarette. "He's trying to poison Vladimir Ilyich's mind against us," Molecule went on. "He even dared order a Cheka search. In Gorky's own apartment! They were here for hours, went through his papers, my medical books. Moura's room was a disaster. Purposely humiliating him. Of course, they found nothing. They knew they wouldn't. Zinoviev's just trying to harass him."

"Oh, we don't know that it's…the person of whom you speak," Moura said. The name that should not be spoken.

But Gorky had clearly had enough of *the person of whom you speak.* Whatever had happened in the office before supper had lifted his normal reticence about revealing his personal opinions on such matters. "It's a campaign, I have to say. Against the intelligentsia as a whole and me in particular. For example"—he leaned forward on the table, his hand wrapped around his wine glass, his cigarette curling smoke into the borscht-fragrant air, eyes fixed on Emory—"last winter I campaigned to get warm clothing for the scholars. You can't believe how cold it was, and no firewood. It's forbidden to cut it oneself. Here we're surrounded by forest and we're freezing!" He nodded for Moura to translate. "Well, after much negotiation—you can imagine, you've been here long enough—I win a firewood distribution for the scholars, and warm clothing." He waited for Moura to catch up. "Then, just as we had everything cleared and on its way—at the last moment, *our friend* had it all commandeered. Diverted, redistributed. Just to spite me. He'd rather fling it on the railroad tracks than let it go to anyone on whose behalf I've appealed."

Now I understood the gray face, the exhaustion. He was being foiled at every attempt to respond to the needs of desperate people who had no one to turn to. He was one man fighting for the intellectual sector Zinoviev had long ago proclaimed should be annihilated. I heard it so often at the House of Arts: *We'll ask Gorky. Gorky can get it. Gorky can do it.*

"People come to me day and night, asking for my help. It breaks my heart. They think I'm a sorcerer, that I can make one phone call and prison gates swing wide. Galoshes fall from the sky. I do my best, but frankly, I think it goes the worse for them when my name appears on their papers. That son of a whore goes out of his way to foul it up."

Moura stood up, ostensibly to speak to the maid, but obviously to avoid having to convey such damning thoughts to the foreigners.

Gorky turned to me. His color was up. "I've known Emory a long time. No need to mince words." I translated succinctly, taking a bit of the bitterness from his speech as he continued. "I think our friends in the Extraordinary Commission go out of their way to bury people I've tried to help. And now Vladimir Ilyich keeps suggesting I go abroad—for my health." He said it with a heavy layer of irony.

It wasn't a bad idea, though. He was coughing wetly, and he smoked like a stove with a bad flue. Clearly he wasn't well. He shouldn't be drinking. "It would certainly simplify *his* life," he said. He tossed down the contents of his glass and held it out again to Grzhebin. "I'm his conscience. He knows me, knows I've been there from the start. It gives me the right to speak. With me gone, all he'll have is that little dictator of the Northern Commune. A sorry day when he picked that weakling to head the region. Well, I'm not about to give him a clear field, sitting in a deck chair in Zurich while he plays out his ambitions over the bodies of the Russian intelligentsia." He drew on his cigarette, flicked ash toward the ashtray, though it fell short, dusting the tabletop.

I translated, wishing that he would keep his thoughts to himself. For his own sake.

He leaned forward again, pressing his fist to his temple. "If you had been here last November, you'd understand. When the Whites attacked Petrograd, a city of a million souls under his command, *our friend* lay curled on his couch at Smolny like a Victorian missy. Everyone knows it. He'd already surrendered. People were in a panic. If Trotsky hadn't arrived, we'd have been hanged from the tram wires on the Troitsky Bridge. *Our friend* is brave when the road is open and the footing's fair, but God forbid there's a whiff of danger, the man's utterly paralyzed."

There it was. What I could give Varvara. Gorky's verbal attack on the most powerful man in Petrograd. If what Molecule said was true, Zinoviev was using the Cheka to torment Gorky and perhaps worse. To convey what Gorky said in private could be essential ammunition for the Zinoviev camp, building their case against him. I was starting to see the larger game being played—not just the one Varvara set for me but the one being played against Gorky, the greater game.

I stayed late, later than I'd planned, drank some vodka someone had hidden away, and heard much too much about things I should never know anything about. Gorky and Moura finally retired, but the younger people, and Clyde Emory, stayed up. Records were produced, a gramophone, and we danced, a regular party! I danced with Emory—the tango. He was a surprisingly good dancer, and I could forget that Varvara was probably waiting for me on Kronverksky, ready to leap on me the moment I walked outside. As long as I stayed, everyone would be safe. So I stayed, later and later, playing charades. Aura sang a number of Russian songs she'd learned, including "Oh, Moroz, Moroz!"—a famous drinking song. She got it perfectly, just the right loping pace. Emory—*Call me Clyde*—sat with his arm casually across the back of my chair. "I could use a translator," he said. "I'm hopeless. And I need to see the real Red

Russia, not just the model factories and Potemkin villages. Will you do that for me?"

Foreigners need guides and translators...the walls closing in. "I suppose it's possible."

Eventually, the party broke up. It couldn't last forever. Emory kept trying to kiss me, lure me into his room with promises of the poet Eliot. Was I also to whore myself to the English, was that next? Aura noticed my hesitation, the reluctance with which I wrapped my shawl around Klavdia's shredded jacket. "You're not leaving! Lord, it's two in the morning. Absolutely not. There's a divan in my room. One mugging's enough, don't you think?"

She didn't have to convince me.

38 *Gorky*

I woke up very early, Aura still sound asleep in the dark across the squarish room that smelled of her clothes, her perfume, the menthol she sprayed on her throat. A crack of dim light showed between heavy drapes. I was beyond exhausted, but my dreams would not let me rest. No way to know the time. Could Varvara still be standing down there, waiting to descend upon me like an owl on a mouse? If she was, I hoped she was cold and miserable. She would have to wait a little longer to crunch my bones and vomit my remains, a clump of fur and teeth.

I'd been dreaming of an abandoned factory, the floor full of water that lay in stinking puddles between the rotting boards. I was waiting for a guide to get me out of there, out of the city, with other people who were gathering there too, but we were afraid to speak to one another, all hiding in the shadows. Then someone tried the doors and found we were locked inside. It was a trap. There were no guides. We had been lured there to die.

I lay on the divan, and couldn't help thinking that if I died now, I wouldn't have to go through with this. It would be a relief. Who would care about someone like me? Why didn't I just jump out that window? She couldn't hold that against Father. Perhaps she would be ashamed of what she'd driven me to and leave him alone. I went to the window, heavy velvet drapes cutting the light for our opera singer. No early riser, she wore a silk mask over her eyes. I peered through the slit. Out on Kronverksky, the sun was just straggling up, the Troitsky Bridge looked newly polished with its tram stantions, from which we would have hung... The river shone like a new bride.

I heard a toilet flush. Clearly someone else was up. I dressed and stole down the corridor toward the dining room. The samovar was hot, and the door to Gorky's office lay open. I could see him at his desk—just him, no Moura. I knocked quietly and he looked up. "Couldn't sleep?"

"Can I talk to you, Alexei Maximovich?"

Although he carried the fate of every intellectual in Petrograd on his shoulders, he smiled and waved me in. "Close the door."

I did, took a great breath, and sat down in one of the chairs facing his desk, my hands shaking so violently I had to sit on them. He was writing something, a letter, maybe a new short story. What was I going to do? I did not know how to proceed past this moment. "I want to tell you about myself," I began. "May I?"

His face brightened, and he leaned back in his chair, a man who clearly loved to hear someone's story. "Yes, please do. You're a bit of a mystery around here, you know. No one can figure you out."

I told him everything. Who we were. Who my father had been. What had happened to us. Varvara, Kolya, Genya, my mother, my brothers. Arkady, Pulkovo, and Gorokhovaya 2. My wanderings in the countryside, the death of Iskra. And the meeting on the bridge. What I'd found in the cell at the Peter and Paul Fortress. My deal with the devil. He didn't interrupt, didn't ask questions, didn't say a word. But his pleasure at hearing my story faded as I spoke, when he began to see the shape of things, the great storm gathering.

I didn't know how it would feel to finally unburden myself as I'd never been able to do. I held nothing back, didn't try to paint myself a victim or a hero. I was exposed, without a skin, like Arkady's book of saints. "I'm in the trap and don't know how to gnaw my leg free. I've seen foxes do it. Tell me how. You know I'd rather die than inform on you."

He sighed, shook his head. "It's a terrible time."

"I just don't know what to do." I lifted my ugly, teary, snotty face. "I know her. She's not going to let me feed her a bunch of straw. But I can't be a tool. Hurt other people, send them into the trap. I'm going mad."

He rose and went out. Was he going to wake Moura? I waited, without hope, grateful that there was finally someone to whom I could confess. I felt shaky, emptied, like finally vomiting after being nauseated all night, and ashamed of seeing it in a puddle on a figured rug right in the middle of Gorky's study, in the middle of his heroic life.

He shuffled back to his office, tea glasses in hand, and shut the door with his heel. He wore a pair of old felt slippers. They made such a homey sound, the soft scuffle. He sat at his desk, rubbed his face in one downward gesture, lit another cigarette, sipped his tea, nodded toward the other glass. "What have you told her already? Only about Emma Goldman?"

I picked up the tea, held it between my hands. "She said I needed to make friends with Goldman. She's interested in knowing more about the movements and plans of the anarchists. Also she wants me to get close to the foreigners—tell her where they go, who they see. She's sure they're all spies."

He coughed deep and wet into a large handkerchief.

"It's Zinoviev, isn't it?" I said. "Behind all this."

He leaned back in his chair, which groaned with his weight, the hand holding the cigarette shading his eyes. "I would never have said all that. But someone I know, a commissar and an old friend, was recently arrested. A completely trumped-up charge. I was trying to get him out, but they'd already shot him. *Before* they heard from Moscow. He was to be released, but they shot him first." He sighed, a long shuddering breath.

I sat as meekly as a prisoner with her head in the cradle of the guillotine.

He got up and turned to the window, opened the drapes onto a shining new day. "I have terrible insomnia," he said. "I can't sleep past dawn." He gazed down at the park, the greening trees. "It used to be I could hear animals at the zoo from here. But they're all gone. The deer, the camels, the elephants. Do you like animals, Marina Dmitrievna?"

Who didn't like animals? But there were none left, not even rats. Only the birds that children tried to trap and sell.

Still gazing down at the park, hearing the cries of animals long dead. "I've been a Bolshevik since 1903. I turned over my earnings from my writings to fund their operations. But they're like a child who grows up so differently than you'd imagined. So headstrong, so violent. But good. Basically good. Right now, I'm just trying to neutralize some of their worst aspects."

His eyes followed something down below, someone passing by in the park perhaps. Light filled his tired face. The study smelled of stale cigarettes. "I'll tell you a secret—I don't like reality all that much. We artists, we want to dream a new world into being. But someone has to protect this—it's the only way advances can ever happen. Enlightenment, culture. Science. Man—as he is—will continue to wreak chaos. I have no illusions about the masses." He touched the old velvet drapes with a loving hand. "Blok despises the intelligentsia, as only a real *intelligent* can. Me, I worship them. I joined them only by the skin of my teeth. Alexander Alexandrovich doesn't know how the village respects the schoolmaster. A literate man's a magician to them. Only enlightened men will produce an enlightened world. Not the dictatorship of the proletariat. The transformation of the proletariat into *men*."

That was the reason for Universal Literature, and the House of Arts, the House of Scholars. Why he woke up before dawn, to smoke and worry in this room.

He opened the *fortochka,* stood breathing in the freshness of the morning. After a time, he tore himself from the scene of the awakening city and sank back down into his big worn chair. "So now you find your leg in a trap." He took a pencil in his broad hand, turned it end over end, thoughtfully, like a baton. "It might make you feel better if I tell you you're probably not the first person who has taken notes at my dinner table for the sake of our friends at Cheka headquarters. You're just the first to have confessed it."

I felt the house shift under us, the fragility of what he had built here. "Tell me what I should do."

"I can't do that," he said. "But as a writer, I can help you consider the various ways the story could go." He sat back in his big chair, as if thinking of a novel's plot. "What happens, for example, if you go ahead with the plan and tell your friend everything you heard last night?"

I knew that answer immediately. "My father will be fed and clothed, and receive medical care. And the authorities will be more sure you are in opposition to them."

"And what happens to you?"

A question not so easily answered. I gazed into his kind, snub-nosed face, the pale eyes. "I get to live."

"Go further."

I thought of the next room of the nightmare. "She'll want more."

"Exactly. You'll dig yourself in deeper. You'll have to put yourself in a false position with everyone and everything, knowing you're a fraud. A dangerous fraud. It leaves you alone, except for your friend." The house was so silent, I could hear the tick of the clock on the bookcase behind me. "She took away your job. You'll depend more and more on her. There's no escape."

Claustrophobia descended. I had hoped he could see a way out, not confirm what I already knew.

"Either you'll find a way to rationalize it or you'll take your own life. And your father's still in prison." His face, so sad, so gentle. "I've been in that cell, I know what I'm talking about. I don't say this cavalierly. In these times, the scarcest commodity is not bread but courage. The way you've described him, it seems that your father is a courageous man, a man of principle. You might not like his principles, but he chose his path. The question is, what are you going to do with your own life? Where are your principles?"

My principles. Did anybody have the luxury of principles these days? But Gorky had been in that cell, maybe the same one my father now occupied. Gorky's principles were no luxury. We all depended upon them to shield us from the roaring furnace of Bolshevik power. What were my principles? Not Genya's, with his perfect faith in the future, his poems about blood and fire, the Red Dawn. Certainly not Varvara's and the other spacemen's: the forcible perfection of mankind through ideology, regimentation, and terror. What then?

I knew that I believed in more than just saving my own skin, myself and my family's. I was not Mina—I could not slam the door in the face of a friend. There was Gorky, there was the House of Arts, all those scholars and artists. There was the truth. I was no Kolya, just seeing what he could get away with, no sense of how his choices reverberated in the world around him. I was uncomfortably stretched between many realities, but if a poet had no compulsion toward truth, he should go drive a tram.

"And if I decide not to go along, then what?"

Gorky screwed another cigarette into the black holder. "It would be a very grave thing." He lit it and sank back into the chair again. Into himself. His voice was very low. "Your father goes to his fate. Which I imagine he is prepared to do." He met my gaze. "He told you so himself. He doesn't want you to cooperate. He knows what that means. Imagine his agony if he discovered you'd become a tool of the Cheka because of him. Of all the terrible reversals of fortune. The very thing he falsely accused you of that night, in that snowy cabin, becomes true because of him."

Of course. I had only felt such pity for him in his wretched condition. That cell. Torture and cold. I hadn't thought of that other agony, the moral one.

Well, that was the question, wasn't it? Was I a moral person? Or was this a ridiculous time to think of morality? It must not be or I would have blithely run to Varvara with my newfound treasure, and the hell with Gorky.

"So what do I do? Try to find my way to Finland?"

Gorky examined the burning tip of his cigarette. "You go and live your life. And wait for the knock on the door. It might come, it might not. Write your poetry, give your readings. I can talk to Korney Chukovsky about a translation job for you at Universal Literature. Maybe you teach poetry, a literacy class. It's no small thing to teach a man to read. You have courage. You'll live in the sunshine, though you might pay for it with your life."

I tried to force air into my lungs. "But what if she has me arrested? What if she has me shot?"

"You go to prison. You go to the camp. But you won't have fed the monster. You won't have become a puppet. What is this life, Marina? We don't live forever. We're here to use our time, not simply exist."

"Just...live my life?" That was not something I'd considered. Walk out of here and say no, and continue.

"Look at Gumilev," Gorky said. "Much as I despise the man, you have to admit, he doesn't bow his head. He doesn't stuff his mouth with dirt. He lives like a man. And if necessary, he'll die like a man. His courage gives courage to others. You should study him."

I heard a door close. The house was awakening. I would have to leave soon. Suddenly I was filled with terror again. As if nothing had been decided. It was still up to me. It was still in my hands.

He smiled and came around the desk. He put his hands on my shoulders. "And if anything happens, you know I'll do what I can," he said. "The important thing is to live honestly and leave something behind. Not to disappear without a trace. How brave are you, Marina?"

I didn't know. But I had a feeling I would soon find out.

39 *This Transparent Hour*

No one loitered outside the house on Kronverksky in the early morning light. Walking toward the Neva in slow, measured steps, wearing Aura's green coat, I felt as exposed as Andromeda on her rock. The grim fortress loomed on my right, its gold spire a lance, cruelly gleaming. The river ran fresh and swift, dotted with white-caps and floes of ice. I could smell salt on the air. If only there was a ship, its white sails filling... Behind those cold stone walls, my father would be just waking up, or perhaps he didn't sleep and had been up all night. He'd hear the clang of doors, a shift change. Light would filter into his small window, illuminating the narrow cell's grim solitude. They would bring him food, maybe allow him to shave, surprising him with a basin of hot water, a change of clothes. I hoped he enjoyed the privilege of these last hours, these last few pleasures, before Varvara learned that I would not ransom him. Most likely, he would be too brokenhearted to enjoy them anyway, if he knew that they'd come at the cost of my moral freedom.

Yet I knew too that he had been glad to find I was alive, that his outcry hadn't put a bullet into my skull that night in the woods at Pulkovo. Oh, those few precious minutes when we'd sat side by side, when he'd held my hand, together at last. When the fine treatment stopped, he would know I had not betrayed him. Would he be happy, though it would mean his death? I would live with the decision of this morning for the rest of my life.

White gulls sailed upriver in the light blue morning, flicking wings bright in the stillness, shrieking their plaintive calls. Could he see them through his tiny window, sunlight on white wings, could he hear their windswept cries? I stepped onto the Troitsky Bridge, that immense span, the end just a point, vanishing. The tram stanchions like so many gibbets. Beneath, the clean flow of icy water, inexorably seeking the sea. A figure in black stood at the opposite end. *How brave are you, Marina?* I didn't slow down or speed up, just kept walking, step after step, toward my fate, as the river flowed toward the Gulf of Finland.

Halfway across, our paths met. "You spent the night," Varvara said. Her black eyes sparkled with excitement.

My old friend, who used to clash with schoolmistresses. Who had brought me to the Stray Dog Café that night, made me walk down those stairs. *In Petrograd, you go down into heaven*... The nights I had slept with her in her sagging bed on Rubinshteyna, her face in my nape, her arms around me. If I hadn't known her, I might be in England now, with all my family, studying at Oxford. If I hadn't known her, I might already be dead. Our braided fates, mine and hers, twisted and bloody.

"Well?" she prompted me, blowing on her hands, rubbing them.

I forced myself to look at her, shook my head.

The excitement drained, the smile died. "Don't tell me you're backing out. Out of some misguided liberal conscience, after all this time?"

I let her examine my face, feature by feature. "I can't do it."

"You can't." Small angry patches of red appeared on her sallow cheeks. "That wasn't the tune you were singing the other night. You couldn't thank me enough. Now, suddenly, you *can't?* What if I just throw him into the Neva, is that all right? Tie his hands and feet and throw him in? I could make you watch."

"Varvara." I reached out for her, an old reflex, and she flinched as if I would burn her. "In your world, it's everything for the cause. That's not my world."

She laughed, and then snatched a fistful of my hair, making me bend back my head, baring my throat, my eyes watering. "Where do you think you're living, Marina? It's everybody's world now," she hissed in my ear. "Everybody's a part of it, even weaselly little poets like you. Don't try to be a hero."

I didn't try to free myself. "I've done enough," I said, though my tears were flowing. "I sat up in a sniper's nest the week I buried my baby. I've written slogans, filled sandbags. I was on the *Red October*. What more do I have to do to prove my loyalty?"

"Give me what I want. That's what we need, not your bourgeois adventurism—riding the *Red October* like a parade float. You think I'll give you a pass, because we...used to know each other?" *Because of my feelings for you.* "You think you don't live in this world?" She yanked my hair. "You think for a second I'll spare him? I'll turn him on a spit, all Petrograd will hear the screaming." Her face, narrow and sharp chinned, glittered like a bayonet. She turned to glare at a man who dared glance in our direction. He stumbled as if from a blow, immediately turned his gaze to the river. She finally let go. Her hands opened and closed with frustration, her face burning with humiliation that she couldn't control me as she wanted to.

She stood gripping the rail of the bridge, gazing downriver toward Kronstadt, as if there was an answer there. Somehow I had made an unthinkable move—sacrificing the king. She could pretend to be as cold-blooded a spaceman as she liked, all theory and ideology and black leather, but this was not about ideology. This was the dark cave of what she didn't know about herself. Her hatred of her father, her mother, her class, families, men, tenderness, anyone who had ever rejected her, judged her, belittled her. Those early years had forged her as proud and savage as Achilles.

I turned away and continued walking toward the Palace Embankment. What would she do, shoot me in the back?

"Marina!" she barked.

Overhead, the gulls screamed, wheeling. Lost, like me, like her, like all of us. My back itched as I waited for a bullet to pierce me like a letter on a spindle. I walked past the third tram stanchion without a shot. Then the second. I could feel her fury like a house burning. The heat of it singed the back of my hair. She could never stand losing. I knew I would pay, if not today, two days from now or next month or next year.

But for now, I walked across the Troitsky Bridge, and down the Swan Canal, along the Field of Mars, a lonely procession of one.

40 *The Spacemen*

I sat cross-legged on my bed, the window open to the warming day, translating *The Valley of the Moon* by Jack London. How good to have something to do besides chew on my own raw nerves. It came through Anton, the same afternoon I'd refused Varvara her devil's due. A note inside from Korney Chukovsky said: *I've heard your English is good. Universal Literature is publishing all of London's work. See what you can do with this. KC.* I knew it was Gorky's apology. If it met with Chukovsky's satisfaction I would get more translation work. It would be a way out from under Varvara's thumb. I'd returned to the telephone exchange for my ration cards and received them. They must not have been informed of my defection. But if I persisted, I knew my rations would stop. Chukovsky was giving me a lifeline. Clearly news of my misfortune had spread among the upper echelons of the house. I wondered who else knew about me.

The Valley of the Moon was a story of love and proletarian struggle. A laundress, specializing in *fancy starch,* meets her young man, a teamster, at a village dance in rural California, and in the midst of labor unrest, they decide to go find their own land and grow their own Paradise. It wasn't Shakespeare, God knows, but the simple language was vivid—*sizzle, swinging, whitewashed, a tremor of money loss*—and I was happy to be in Jack London's world of agrarian California instead of 1920 Petrograd with my father in the Troubetskoy Bastion. But I would need to locate an English dictionary soon.

A soft knock on the door.

"Who is it?"

No answer. I set my book down and went to see who it was. Someone had left a small package, brown paper bound up with twine. I untied it. The oily paper unfolded by itself.

Inside lay an ear, crusted with blood.

Mole on the outside rim. The breath froze in my lungs.

She had done this.

The ear like a lotus, like a lily. *So you can hear the screams across the Neva.*

I folded the ear back into the paper and put it in the pocket of my summer dress. I had to get out of here. I put on my boots and Aura's coat and locked my room. Outside, I was barely aware of where I wandered. I bumped into a woman carrying a cuckoo clock. Suddenly I was on the Field of Mars. A brisk wind swept the empty space. The Field of Mars, where I had watched Volodya's regiment disappear into the sun. Grass shivered between the stones. I remembered my father's tears. *Papa, tell me what you want me to do.*

I heard his voice so clear in my head, *Don't fall for the trap. It will never stop.*

I was trying to be brave—but what might be next? His thumbs? His eyes, his hands? Would he be nailed to a crucifix? I could hear him begging me not to succumb.

How brave are you, Marina?

I tried to breathe, and pictured the Five in their precincts on the hill. I thought about the universe, how vast it was, how old. From the point of view of the stars, how little any of this mattered. A boy had died in the grass of cholera. A man's ear was cut off. A girl might slide into the river from the Troitsky Bridge and it was all the same.

I walked up to the Neva and watched the river flow, sparkling and swift, waiting for me to join it. *Are you sure you want to refuse us?* I imagined the drop, the water closing over my head, the deep cold, my breath leaving, water coming in. The fortress across the river stood waiting. *Are you going to submit now?* said the fortress. *We'll never let you go. You will be nothing. There will be no pity for either of you.*

In the river's depths, Varvara could not follow me. I would have peace among the fishes, and the spires of drowned cathedrals. Without guilt, suffering, or responsibility.

But in the end, I did not climb the parapet, did not offer myself to the young queen, grown mad and staring into windows, her purple raiment in tatters. I had not done it when I held Iskra's broken body in my arms, which had been a far greater shock, a far purer sorrow. If I had not done it then, I would not do it now. *Just go about your business,* he had said. If I died today they would kill my father anyway. Then there would be nothing left of either of us. The important thing was to live, not long perhaps, but as honestly as one could, *and leave something behind.* Not to disappear and let the waters erase us from the story of time.

I took out the package with his ear, and let it fall between my fingers into the water, where it could listen to the chimes.

I stayed away from Gorky's flat on Kronverksky. I didn't blame him for what had befallen me, but I didn't want to see him, his broad pocked face, his drooping moustache. The sight of him would be a painful reminder that I'd chosen to protect him, and everything he did, at the price of my father's suffering.

Alexei Maximovich pitied me, but he could not carry my burden. There would be no solace in his company.

On May Day, that traditional day of proletarian celebration, Molecule came to my room to fetch me for Andreeva's theatrical spectacular, *The Mystery of Liberated Labor*, which had been in the works for almost a year.

"He sent me to collect you," she said. Her kind eyes studied my tiny room, all the papers spread out. "We miss you." Gorky once again extending his hand. I was in no mood for celebration, but what other family did I have? If I stayed it would not help my father grow another ear. Jack London's young idealists could wait. Molecule broke into a smile when I pulled on my boots and donned Aura's green coat. She held out my red kerchief, which I had knotted to my bedframe. That too? I sighed and tied it carelessly around my unbrushed hair.

The Gorky contingent had gathered on the bleachers set aside for the elite on the Palace Embankment. What irony, on a workers' holiday to be seated among commissars and their families in comfort, separated from the sea of Petrograd's gaunt, hungry workers filling the riverfront in anticipation of the performance. Maria Andreeva sat up front next to Lunacharsky, Commissar of Enlightenment, whose Scottie-dog looks I recognized from the first anniversary of the revolution. The day I left with Kolya, and soured my relationship with Mina, the day I fled Varvara. And here was Ravich, Varvara's heroine, and Zinoviev shaking hands and pretending he wasn't playing his treacherous game with Gorky, chatting just a few steps away. I felt an urge to protect Gorky, even now, with my father's ear listening from the bottom of the river, and him bleeding, right there, in the Peter and Paul Fortress. I didn't know how long I could sit here and pretend to have a good time.

Molecule and I sat with Aura and Clyde Emory, Aura the brightest thing on the embankment in a yellow suit and red turban. My American friend flung her arms around me, kissing me, tucked my windswept hair inside my kerchief. "Marina, honey, where have you been? You just disappeared. Have you been ill?"

"A little cold, I think." We took our seats on a bleacher bench, and Molecule squeezed my hand. I suspected she'd been informed as to what I was enduring, and I was grateful for it. Out on the Strelka in the middle of the Neva, a giant assembly of tiny human beings moved into position. *The Mystery of Liberated Labor* was about to begin.

"I'm singing Zemfira tonight," Aura said under her breath. "Chaliapin's singing too. You have to come. Clyde'll bring you, won't you, baby?"

"It would be my pleasure," said the Englishman, his untamed eyebrows shading his bright blue eyes.

Aura took my hand in her warm one. Who was I to say no to her? I was wearing her coat.

Now the play began. Thousands of actors swarmed the Strelka, and from this distance, I could see they represented the toiling masses. Slaves being whipped by overseers, peasants at the plow. You had to give it to Andreeva, it was a vast, astonishing tableau. The actors moved through their paces like an army on maneuvers. Lunacharsky, in the front row, beamed as if the performance was the finest thing he'd ever seen. Clyde Emory took a few notes in a small book he kept in his breast pocket. The extravaganza unfolded beneath the Rostral Columns, from which I'd watched the first anniversary naval parade with two hooligans. I couldn't help comparing the genuine joy of that day to this lumbering spectacle. Though I tried to keep in mind that it represented work for thousands of actors, artists, designers, writers and directors, carpenters and painters and dancers, how could I keep my anger to myself? It was a bloated piece of collective absurdity, a stilted, simplistic tableau that wasn't so much performed as occupied. No scrap of dialogue could possibly carry across the river to the packed embankments, so the whole thing depended on shouted choruses, with music and drums. Witnessing the movement of all that humanity was like watching ants building a dam. First, moaning slaves toiled about the base of the Stock Exchange. Then the gentry and clerics and demimonde arrived to ascend its broad steps to the "Paradise" of its neoclassical porch, where they commenced the requisite feasting and showered themselves in coins.

As the hours dragged on, the history of the proletarian struggle was illustrated, epoch by epoch—billed the Pageant of Labor. Subsequent waves of uprisings showed the downtrodden assaulting the stairs—you could tell them apart by their costumes and banners, the music. Spartacus: short togas. Stenka Razin: Cossack dress. Pugachov: serfs. Jacobins: red, white, and blue, "La Marseillaise" reaching us over the water. Aura burst into applause each time they attempted to rush Paradise, and groaned when they were forced back. Emory scribbled and sketched. I thought of my father, having to hear all this through his one ear.

As we endured the extravaganza out in the river, the actual workers around us shifted, squinted, sullen—women standing on swollen legs and aching feet. It made me suspect this was an obligatory appearance, like a food brigade or sanitation detail. They probably would have preferred the day off. So this was what Lunacharsky's Revolutionary Carnival had come to—another aspect of forced labor. Death by theatricals.

Out on the point of the Strelka, real soldiers and real sailors were playing soldiers and sailors in this extravaganza, their guns real guns, and probably loaded. It suited the literality of our times, the death of poetry. What would come next? Would a play's villains actually have to be slain onstage, run through with bayonets? Would we enact the execution of Marie Antoinette with a real guillotine? What happened to the imagination? There was no fun here, no wordplay, nothing clever, nothing stirring to the soul. It was all too big—vast and elephantine and as earnest as a piece of agricultural machinery. As art, Genya's little play at the Miniature Theater had done it so much better, and he'd said it all with a handful of actors and some scaffolding.

I tried to keep a pleasant look on my face, tried not to groan, or yawn, or weep, while time stalled and the revolts continued, and the Peter and Paul Fortress waited on the far side of the Troitsky Bridge, the ultimate literalism. At some point, Emory passed me a flask, tapping it against my knee. I gratefully took sips and concentrated on the meditative flow of the river.

At last, the final onslaught. With a thunder of drums and the Red Army songs, led by actual Kronstadt sailors, the masses finally stormed Paradise. Even I stood and applauded.

But then a new configuration of actors assembled on the Strelka, dressed in bright clothing. Oh, I'd forgotten. We must have the Utopia to come. My bitterness knew no bounds. "Let's get out of here," whispered Clyde Emory, shifting on the bench for the hundredth time. But it was impossible, we were jammed in too tightly and our departure would reflect poorly on Gorky. We remained through a choral Dance of All Nations, the soldiers and sailors laying down their arms and picking up hammers and scythes, and the Mounting of the Tree of Freedom.

At last, the mass singing of "The Internationale" marked our own freedom. The sound reverberated from our side to the crowds on Vasilievsky Island. I thought of the millions who'd sung this song, what we had given, what we had lost. It was plain to see that the People's Revolution had become a prisoner of the state. I felt like my heart was being cut from my chest and held aloft before being eaten, still pumping blood.

"Quite the spectacle," said Emory, helping me to my feet. I could barely feel them. "Sure there's not time for a fourth act?"

We edged down toward the crowd around Maria Andreeva where she was accepting bouquets and congratulations, Gorky shaking hands, embracing friends. Poor Gorky, he must know this Brobdingnagian event was an utter disgrace. Our eyes met. He smiled, sadly, but appeared relieved that I was still free and among the living. Moura, standing faithfully on his right, followed his gaze, and sent me a brief nod. They knew—it did make me feel better. Aura stood out in the crowd like a sunflower in a field of poppies as she made her way to Andreeva. "Remember, tonight at eight," she called back.

"I'll be there." Then to Emory, under my breath, "Get me out of here."

The streets were impassible for a good long time. Emory did his best to be amusing, though the effort of smiling was too much for me. "You're being awfully mysterious today..." He reached to tuck a strand of my hair behind my ear. "The inscrutable Miss Makarova. Come to the Astoria, I'll buy you some tea."

We pushed our way along the embankment. Why shouldn't I have tea with the Englishman? Maybe I could pump him about his trade union connections or what he thought of Zinoviev. I would be happy to report on him. The worst they could do to him was kick him out. I was halfway to laughter and half to tears. He was talking about Shaw when we were interrupted by shouts from a gang of sailors. "Kuriakina!" I heard. "Hey! Comrade Marina!" A sailor was lifting his rifle over his head—Slava from the *Red October*! Slava, who'd pulled me onto the train's roof when I asked, who'd cared for me better than my own husband had. I could still see him, lowering my things into the wagon as I went off with the midwife. His grinning, weathered face brought it all back. "Slava!" I waved.

"I'm an actor now!" he shouted, his hands cupped around his mouth. "Did you see me?"

He had been in *The Mystery of Liberated Labor*. What would happen to the actors in this new world—would they have to become soldiers? Yet it made me happy to see how proud he was, glad that all surprises weren't pure horror. "I'm Uncle Vanya! *Kronshtadtsky MacBet*." So full of life. He radiated energy and good health—they fed the fleet well. He fought his way through the crowd, hopping and plowing through the workers the way a bather breaks the waves at the seaside. Emory scowled, jealous that I was more interested in this chance meeting with a sailor than in his analysis of contemporary British theater.

"Kuriakina, you look great!" Slava reached me at last, grabbing my arm, looking down at my belly. "Where's the baby?"

A needle in the heart. I'd maintained my demeanor up to now, but my nerves were as thin as Bible pages. I shook my head.

"Oh, poor kid." He patted my shoulder as if I were a big dog. "But you're still here. Better days, eh? Where's Kuriakin? Who's this clown?" He gestured with a big thumb toward Clyde Emory.

"Englishman. A writer. Genya and I aren't together anymore. Look, it's good to see you." I thought of that girl, bright on the roof of the *Red October,* roaring into the future, rotund with hope. And now, lost on my own Sargasso Sea. "Who's guarding Kronstadt if you're all here, Uncle Vanya?"

"We're going back tonight—I'm on the *Petropavlovsk.* Come out for a visit!" he shouted as his group bore him off, a man caught in a tide. "I'll let you fire the cannon!" And then he was gone. I stared after him as one stares at a ship as it vanishes over the horizon.

That night, Emory and I went to see Aura in Rachmaninoff's *Aleko*—the adaptation of Pushkin's "The Gypsies," the poem that had once saved my life, letting me climb, hand over hand, out of despair the night I was buried alive under the snow. I hadn't heard Chaliapin in years, but he was in great voice, his expressive basso the perfect foil for Aura's rich mezzo. The staging was simple, a few stools and a wagon, the costumes slapdash, the musicians' formal suits ragged with age, their faces gaunt, but with those voices, these artists at the height of their powers, this *Aleko* could have been staged in a cowshed and still rivaled La Scala. In the anonymous dark, I wept unabashedly. Oh, the luxury of that! For my family, for myself, for beauty, for the ruin of everything. But they couldn't kill this music. Not tsars, not Bolsheviks, not Varvara, not the rampant mediocrity of *The Mystery of Liberated Labor.*

Emory's tweedy arm came around me, an attempt to console me perhaps, or the first sortie in a seduction. I pretended to search in my bag for a handkerchief, and managed to shrug him off. I didn't want to be soothed or handled, I just wanted to weep in peace.

Tonight, the old gypsy's lines after Aleko slayed Zemfira and her new lover seemed a direct rebuke of our Bolshevik masters. Was I the only one who noticed? No, I was far from the only one sneaking glances at Zinoviev, seated with his family, stone-faced and pale in the darkened theater. The political context of Pushkin's verse resonated across the years:

> *We are untamed, we have no laws.*
> *We do not torture, execute —*
> *We have no need of groans or blood —*
> *We cannot live with murderers . . .*

And the last line hung in the air

> *Oh anguish, oh gloom*
> *Again alone, alone . . .*

echoing my own emptiness as the curtain slowly fell.

As we filtered out through the foyer, I saw Varvara, leaning against the doorway. Nonchalant, as if she were just waiting for someone. I could have hung back, I could have hunted for Gorky or someone else to hide behind. But I didn't. I chose the other door, but I didn't crouch, I didn't run. I took one look at her and she at me. She was giving me a last chance. *Change your mind?* said her naked stare. *Ready to play the game?*

I didn't lower my face like a woman walking into a storm. I stared at her over Emory's shoulder. He saw her too. "Friend of yours?"

"No," I said. And we walked out into the waning rays of a very long day.

41 *Music, When Soft Voices Die*

The White Nights came upon us. The barely setting sun skimmed the horizon, sank, and then popped up immediately like a restless child refusing bed. A fuss in the corridor of the flat roused me from a pit of awful dreams. It couldn't have been later than five or six in the morning, yet voices could be clearly heard. I threw a shawl over my nightdress and cracked the door. Other neighbors peered out from their own rooms. "What's happening?" whispered Tatiana Glebovna, the clerk's wife across the hall, the edge of her scarf stuffed in her mouth. As the voices grew louder, tenants slipped out of their rooms in their nightshirts and robes to see what the trouble was. I could see Olga Viktorievna waiting to see who would leave his room unattended, and locked my door behind me.

The noise was coming from the front rooms, murmurs and cries. By the entry door, a crowd of tenants had gathered. Russakova was holding her children. "Somebody dumped a body out there."

"Rang the bell and left it," said the postman, Vrachkov. "I was just on my way to work."

I clawed my way through the crush out to the stairway landing, and knelt. My father lay on his side on the filthy floor—bearded, barefoot, hair streaked with gray. There was a clean bandage around his head covering the wound where his ear had been. I wished I could faint, but my body remained stubbornly attached to this waking nightmare. Denied even the mercy of unconsciousness.

I took his hand in mine, pressed it to my forehead. Cold, stiff. People hovered nervously in the doorway. It was clear to them that this was a dangerous death, an official death, the death of a person one should not admit knowing. Such a death had a way of attaching to the living. *Yes, stay away,* I thought, *and the devil take you.*

Dmitry Ivanovich Makarov. Famed jurist, author, member of the Provisional Government, liberal counterrevolutionary. This was how it ended, on this broken tile, a stair landing in a broken building in a city that had lost its name, in a country that had lost its soul. His poor face, the chestnut hair frosted white. The last of his kind. Every hope for Russia was embodied here, in this broken body, this discarded bundle. Misguided, foolish, and faithful. Papa…Even now I'd half believed Varvara might relent, her fury spent, that she might have been satisfied with the mutilation. But she'd waited, holding the blow until it could be delivered with maximum cruelty.

Why did they say *inhuman* when they talked about monstrous acts? When cruelty was every bit as human as mercy, this human instinct for revenge, hatred, envy. The hot, smoky taste of power.

His beard had been trimmed and his feet were clean. She must have believed I would relent eventually. Believed I would come bearing betrayal like a great leaking basket of heads to lay at her feet. My hand pressed to my face as if to erase my mouth. She'd kept her side of the bargain—got him a doctor, cleaned him and fed him. He had a new eye patch instead of that dirty bandage. How angry she must have been that I had refused her deal. "Papa," I whispered into the bandage. Pressed my forehead to his stiff, cold hand again, watering the knuckles. To be so erased from this world, wiped out like a badly cleaned chalkboard. And so it ended—a man of courage and energy, his biography closed with murder. Never again the downward tilt of his chin when he prepared to say something weighty, which could also be contradicted by the laughter in his eyes. Eyes I would never see again, rich brown, with little lines at the corners and underneath etched deeply now. He and he alone had made me. Everything I was, and did, and thought, I could trace to him. *Why did we have to be at war, Papa?* What had cursed us so, to be born at this time, what evil fate had decided that our paths would be separated, and what furies came together to make them cross again?

"I got the morgue. The cart's coming," said the Communist from the Sobietskys' room who could never get his stove to draw. He always sent his wife to fetch me. A kindness, as it was clear this was a dubious death, full of meaning. The tenants got tired of the show and went back into the flat to prepare their meager breakfasts and ready themselves for the day, feed their babies, draw water, get laundry started. But I stayed where I was on the floor next to my father. Like a dog on a grave, I would not be moved.

I examined him tenderly, lifting his head, ever so gently. Blood on the floor. He had been shot, a small bullet wound to the base of the skull. So, they'd made him kneel. No exit wound. Had she done this herself? Made him kneel in the basement or in the yard. *You did this,* I could hear her saying. No. I had just refused to stop it.

Eventually, men arrived with a stretcher. They brought a coffin they'd rent me for one hundred rubles. Was it the same cart that had come for Maxim, for Iskra? I wished I could pick him up and bear him away as I had my daughter, but he was too big to shoulder and there was no fog in which to vanish with him. It was a bright May morning. And he was not mine the way Iskra was, not mine alone. He belonged to this city and it would be an insult to bury him anonymously. He deserved his name, his rightful place. He had given everything he had for his Russia, his idea of it. He deserved to be buried amid the illustrious dead.

"Take him to Tikhvin Cemetery."

The carter gazed at me skeptically under eyebrows like black caterpillars. Tikhvin Cemetery at the Alexander Nevsky Monastery was for Petersburg notables. He didn't budge, folding his arms across his chest. His partner, with the stretcher, waited patiently for our negotiations to complete themselves. "Who's gonna pay for it?"

"You'll get your money, Comrade." Capitalist vampire. "It's the Makarov plot. I'll show you where."

A doctor on the second floor had a working telephone, the only one in the building still in service. His wife hated the tenants continually asking to use it, but they were bourgeois and vulnerable to complaints, and as this was an emergency, I pushed myself on her. "Number, please?" the girl on the line asked. I had the uncanny experience of speaking to myself. My father was murdered and I was speaking to myself. I gave her the number. When she put me through, Moura answered. "Marina?" I didn't identify myself, just asked for Gorky, my voice as flat as an overcast day. When he came on the line, I said, "He's dead. They dumped him in the hallway. The carters are here. I'll need to pay them, and the gravediggers. We'll be at Tikhvin Cemetery."

A pause. "Courage, my dear. I'll meet you there."

We stood at the Makarov graveside, just me and Alexei Maximovich under the new green of the ancient trees. We watched the laborers down in the friable earth, making the deep furrow for planting my bitter crop. Thank God Gorky made no move toward conversation as we watched them dig. It was a beautiful, tender day. A breeze rippled the boughs overhead as the shovels bit the damp earth. All around us waited my silent family, Makarov grandparents and parents, aunts and uncles, babies dead in infancy. *Alexei 1841–1842, aged nine months. Tamara, one and a half years.* But no Iskra. No *Antonina Nikolaevna Shurova, July–October 1919.* But now they would be together on the other side, all my loves, Papa and Seryozha and Iskra. And someday I would join them, perhaps very soon. Perhaps today.

A flight of swallows darted and wheeled as the gravediggers took my father out of the rented coffin. I kissed him, let them lower him into the grave. In the absence of a priest, I recited the Shelley poem he'd loved most:

> *Music, when soft voices die*
> *Vibrates in the memory—*
> *Odours, when sweet violets sicken,*
> *Live within the sense they quicken.*
>
> *Rose leaves, when the rose is dead,*
> *Are heaped for the belovèd's bed;*
> *And so thy thoughts, when thou art gone,*
> *Love itself shall slumber on.*

He'd given me everything, and I had given him this, a miserable Bolshevik death. I could not bring myself to weep, for him or myself, or the tender leaves that too must die.

42 *The ABC of Communism*

When I returned from the monastery, Russakova, whose large family occupied the front salon, handed me a bulky package, my name on the brown paper. She averted her eyes. I could only imagine who had brought it. The tenants watched me as I carried it through the flat under my arm. I knew what they were thinking. *It won't be long before that room comes open. Maybe our Masha...* Safely locked away, I tore the brown paper open. The same paper that wrapped our bread rations, and the ear. Inside, rolled leather side out, rested my sheepskin. She'd sent it back, a gesture of what? Regret? Pity? A coup de grâce? I sat down on my bed and pressed my face to the leather, the wool, to see if I could smell him. Maybe, I thought, *maybe...* There was blood on the collar. They'd shot him in it. I unrolled the coat and out fell a pair of slippers and Bukharin's *The ABC of Communism*. I threw the latter across the room. It hit the baseboard with a satisfying *thwack,* losing a few pages from its cheap binding.

Curled on my side under the sheepskin from which I could imagine I smelled cherry tobacco, I shivered, clutching the slippers he had worn. She'd given him slippers. Rocking myself, I tried to remember what Gorky had said—that my abandonment of him had let him know I had not abandoned him. But compared to these slippers...*Look,* she was saying. *I kept all my promises. You let him die, you asked for it.*

A conversation was taking place just outside my door. An argument in lowered voices. A rap. Not commanding. Muted, apologetic. "Marina Dmitrievna? It's Korbatinsky." The *domkom.* I hauled myself out of bed, opened the door.

"I'm sorry, but I've been informed that your room..." He twisted, he chewed on the ends of his moustache. The house committee must have decided—no, there hadn't been time for a meeting. He'd been *informed*. "A couple is coming in... You understand? It's not my doing..."

I was to be removed. First she'd taken my job, now it was my lodging, for which I was legitimately registered. "How long do I have?"

"Tomorrow," he said. "Really, I argued with them..." His eyes pleaded for understanding.

I closed the door and locked it, sat on my bed. Even this little room, where I had lived with my baby, was to be denied me. I looked at the pipe that stretched across the ceiling. How hard was it to hang oneself? How long would it take to die? It was what she wanted. To force me to take my own life, the thing she didn't have the nerve to do. In the corner sat the broken book, *The ABC of Communism*. I picked it up. Perhaps they had given it to him as an attempt at reeducation, or just to torment him. It was divided into neat sections and subsections like an algebra book: "Capitalism Leads to Revolution," "The Dictatorship of the Proletariat," "Communism and Education," "The Organization of Industry," "Subdivision 5: The Scientific Character of Our Program," "...*the marvelous leniency of the workers' courts in comparison with the executioners of bourgeois justice*..." A catechism, a handbook for spacemen who could not see the difference between words and reality. Once I might have read this and thought, *Yes, yes, of course. This is how it is. This is what must be done.* How reasonable, how self-evident.

I tore out the first page, used it to light the lamp. I held it until it burned my fingers, dropped it into the ashtray. Then one by one, I tore the pages out and lit them, letting them burn. *I renounce thee, I renounce thee.* All the spaceman theories, the little tables of declining production, Bukharin's theories of agriculture. *I renounce thee.* No more spacemen. No more bibles. No more ideologies, no more programs. No more pointing to cruelty and calling it justice. I believed no more in this bastard, this Smerdyakov our revolution had become. I would believe only in pity and compassion, poetry and weakness, and the truth as I saw it through my own two eyes.

Then I packed up my few things in my carpetbag, my books, my knives, my hatchet, then rolled my winter clothes, the sheepskin, my blanket, up into my bedsheet, tied it in twine. I stuffed *The Valley of the Moon* and my translation into my Izhevsk pail.

There was still one place in Russia where a human being might be allowed to stand. And I went there.

43 *House of Arts*

Anton took one look at my face and asked no questions. I set my things down, the bundle on the bed, the bag and pail on the floor. "I buried my father today," I said. "It was a rented coffin. They dumped him in the grave and took it for the next guest."

"You can have the bed if you want," he said.

He accepted my presence as one accepts rain.

The Valley of the Moon stalled midtranslation. I couldn't imagine a circumstance under which that book would be worth the paper it was printed on. I lay on Anton's bed under my sheepskin, listening to him write—he was lecturing on formalism—reading sections to me, pacing the small room. Poems circled in my head... *Music, when soft voices die*... and Tennyson's *Idylls of the King*:

> And indeed He seems to me
> Scarce other than my king's ideal knight,
> "Who reverenced his conscience as his king..."

Days passed, bright without notice. Anton slept on the floor and brought me food, ate what I did not. *Who reverenced his conscience as his king*... Conscience was no meadow, pierced with shining streams and ripe with birdsong. It was a trench-filled battleground strung with wire, an iron mountain against a starless sky. Conscience was the hardest master of them all. There was no rest, no congratulations, only a long march from dawn to dawn.

One afternoon he came in, excited despite his attempt at casual nonchalance. He tossed a letter onto the bed. "You're in. Chukovsky, Gorky, Blok, Shklovsky, all signed for you. And guess who the fifth was? *Gumilev*. Can you believe it?"

Five signatures, officially admitting me to the House of Arts. How kind of our elders to have taken such pity on this wretched flotsam. They knew the price of conscience in today's market. I was by no means their equal. Nevertheless they'd offered me shelter, a place to root in the gale of my life.

As a member of Dom Iskusstv—the House of Arts, which the inhabitants simply called Disk in revolutionary preference for acronyms in all things—I was entitled to receive a scholar's rations and a room if one turned up. The most important part: I was officially in residence. I had a place in this world. I could hear the music of official stamps. And I received my first assignment, to teach a women's poetry circle down at the Skorokhod factory. "They want a woman," said Ksenya Alexandrovna, a sort of house secretary who handled such requests. She held out a ticket between her fingers.

"I've never taught poetry," I admitted, nevertheless taking the ticket. I was afraid. I didn't want to leave the house on the Moika Embankment. The only safety was here.

Her kind, young face. "Perfect. You'll learn together. Don't count on much in the way of extra rations. They're as poor as gravediggers down there."

I sat at the table in Anton's room, turning over the ticket. Who was I to teach anyone? I was afraid to even look people in the eye these days. I could feel the demons circling my head like smoke. "Blok doesn't think poetry can be taught." I sipped my carrot-peel tea.

"He means you can't teach sheep to be lions," Anton said, paring a pencil with a penknife, letting the shavings drop where they would, table, floor, manuscripts. "But of course you can *teach* poetry, at least enough so these shoe women will know it when it hits them in the face. And if it's a disaster, so what? You have to go outside eventually."

And I thought I was the one who hated walls.

* * *

What a great, ugly place it was, Skorokhod, where all those women I'd dug with made their living. Down on the Obvodny Canal in the ugliness and stink, the heat of summer making it worse, chemicals pouring straight into the water. The factory was cavernous, half empty, the bulk of its workers gone—drafted, dead, or out scouring the countryside for a bit of grain. It took me a while, hunting through the dusty rooms, the silent tables, the assembly lines, to find the committee room, where twelve women waited for a poet to show them some beauty, to pull back the curtain on Poetry, catch her naked in the bath. Twelve ragged women. But no Anya. I supposed she had better things to think about.

They had no books, so I recited for them—Pushkin, Tyutchev, Tsvetaeva. Taught them the essentials, the simple rhymes and meters. We clapped hands to beat out the metric feet. They knew few poems but scores of songs. "Songs are poems set to music," I explained, "and poems are songs without music." And taught them the balladic form, *abab*.

This committee room, surrounded by chain-link, was the true revolution. Not the bloody, airless cells of the Cheka, not *The Mystery of Liberated Labor*. These women, these human skeletons with hands like leather, their own boots in shreds, for the first time discovering the flexibility of their own language. I set them to write a poem about shoes, or the factory, but most couldn't do much with it. I feared the class would be a dead loss—when a black-haired girl with pale blue eyes brought a shoe to life, delighting us all with its tongue flapping saucy talk at a male supervisor.

> *Comrade, how'd you get so many hands?*
> *Did your mother marry an octopus?*

After that, the chains fell. Though few could emulate the girl's humor—the women mostly wrote poems about roses and Grandma's sweet smile, poems homesick for distant villages, for Mama's weaving, for husbands lost to the war. Babies and drunks.

And love of all kinds: young love, unrequited love, a meaningful glance at a factory dance. Girls drowned themselves in the Obvodny Canal or drank solvents for love. Solvents—I hadn't thought of that. They wrote about youth, and growing older. And paid me with precious bread from their own children's mouths. I loved them all, even the barely literate ones who could only rhyme *June* and *moon*. Maybe them most of all. There was no need to defend literature here. I had only to earn my bread and give them the feeling of belonging to the world, of creating something that had never existed before—and maybe a glimpse of something within themselves.

A few weeks later, I picked up a second class at the Vikzhel club. Vikzhel—what a tangled past we had. An experienced poet, Vasily Sabitov, had been teaching them but he'd recently quit, unable to *teach those idiots*. They liked simple ballads, *chastushki*, a good laugh and a churning rhythm, and I let them stick to it. Poems about trains and parodies of officialese. Their clubroom was tucked into the ground floor of a house off Znamenskaya Square near the Nikolaevsky station. They paid with a whole pound of bread, and promised coal in the winter.

"Little comrade, what's another rhyme for *zhit'* besides *pit'*?" *To live, to drink.*

"How about *kurit'*?" *To smoke a cigarette.*

I was surprised how attached I became to them—my shoe ladies, my railwaymen. And I fell in love with that moment of magic, when a poem was born into those humble hands. With them I had no expectations, anything they produced was a God-given miracle. There was no way to disappoint me unless someone's seat was empty—gone on a food detachment, or ill, or just mysteriously vanished. I rejoiced that there were still humans who wanted to learn something more soulful than *The ABC of Communism*.

And I resumed work on *The Valley of the Moon*. Work, the great solace.

Though I still jumped when anyone knocked on the door.

* * *

My students' pleasure in the word brought back my own, and I began to craft new poems in our stuffy, hot little room. I wrote one about the Vladimirka, the bitter lane that crossed all of Russia, the long road to Siberia. I took the point of view of a Decembrist wife following her husband into exile, walking the five thousand miles behind the convicted men. These days a poem like that could be read ambiguously, for who was the tsar and who the convict?

A bang on our door. We both leaped out of our chairs, Anton spilling carrot tea over his lecture. "It's open, you idiot!" he shouted, mopping up pale gold tea with the tail of his shirt.

The door opened slowly, and in the passage stood Gumilev. Very straight, very cool, and clearly offended at being so rudely addressed. "Marina Dmitrievna, may I speak to you a moment?" He considered our room with his fishy gaze, taking in our domestic arrangement. I could see him making assumptions. There was only one bed. Though what I did with Anton was none of his business, I was grateful to him for being the fifth signatory necessary for acceptance into the house. He pushed the door open farther—and gestured that he wanted to speak to me in the hall. What could he want of me that couldn't be said in front of Anton?

I joined him in the hallway. He was erect and correct, parted and shaved, wearing a clean shirt, brushed jacket, and tie—but he stood too close for my liking. "It's the sailors' club on the Admiralty Embankment. Thursday evening." He was holding out a ticket. "I would do it myself, but I'm at the Poets' Guild." His night holding court at our sister organization. He was doing me a favor—the fleet received category 1 rations, and Anton and I needed every scrap of bread we could forage. Yet why me, and not someone more established? Because he felt sorry for me? Because he wanted me to join his circle? I felt I was jumping the queue.

His walleye stared up the hall, the other fixed me with purpose, flicking the ticket. "A bit of advice—these won't be your factory women. Don't let them lead you around by the nose. You have to let them know you're boss, or they'll wipe the decks with you. No *chas-*

tushki or nursery rhymes. They're bright boys. Put them through their paces."

I tried to imagine why I'd been singled out for such an honor, why he trusted me to represent the House of Arts there, but I could understand nothing. "I'll do my best, Nikolai Stepanovich. Thank you." *Nikolai Stepanovich*, just like Kolya. But could two men be any less like one another? I didn't think so.

Early evening but still bright as noon in July, the wide Neva lay fresh and empty. Boats clattered gently against the wharf of the Admiralty Embankment. In the clubhouse on the shore, thirty men, the pride of the Red Fleet, well fed, impatient, awaited me in their classroom, their caps printed with the names of their ships across the bands. I felt like a rusty old scow pulling up among white-sailed yachts. The weight of their stares brought blood to my face. This underfed scrap of a girl with dark circles staining her eyes, her ragged dress, this was what the House of Arts decided to send them? What an insult! They could break me in two. It reminded me of Gorky's famed story "Twenty-Six Men and a Girl."

The protests began. "Where's Gumilev?" "We sent for a real poet, not a schoolgirl." "Though if you want a date, stick around." What a handsome breed they were, as pampered as racehorses, the proud Red heart of this red, red land, aware of their power and my powerlessness. I decided to decline the blindfold, the last cigarette.

I stood at the head of their clubroom and, using all the rhetorical tricks I'd learned at the House of Arts, all the experience of street-corner readings and Genya's spellbinding recitations on the *Red October*, gave them three of my own poems: "The Oxen of the Sun," the old seaman in his bed; "The Trees at Kambarka," for Iskra; and the new one, "Vladimirka," which no one had heard yet. They'd either toss me out into the Admiralty Canal or accept me as I was. *Be careful*... I heard Blok's warning. But I was through being careful. Courage was the tenor of the day.

By the time I'd finished the third poem—*and the road bore no more trace of us than the sky*—there were no more catcalls. I might have

471

been twenty, skinny and ragged, but I was a poet and they were just sailors. Was this what Gumilev wanted to give me? Restoring a bit of myself to myself?

They took a simple vote, show of hands, whether to keep me or throw me back to the sea, and it was done. We negotiated in Soviet fashion, as the students told me what and how they wanted to be taught. Each week I would read a few poems, which they would discuss, me pointing out nuances they might not have caught. Then they'd read in a circle, *the way poets do,* and discuss their work.

While it was hard to find even scratch paper and stubs of pencils for the Skorokhod women, all of the sailors came with notebooks and pens, and books of poetry they had of their own. I pushed them. I took them through binary meters and ternary meters, the five-foot trochaic line, Pushkin's iambic tetrameter—the Onegin stanza, with examples. I showed them Blok's accentual verse. Their poems were full of sea and sky, foreign lands, great storms and guns and brotherhood under the smokestacks. The women they'd left and their own weeping mothers, the winds of the revolution. Realistic deaths—so many deaths. They admired Mayakovsky and Gumilev—strange bedfellows—and, surprisingly, me.

They didn't care about: Tyutchev, Lermontov, Akhmatova. They wanted only the most modern with

> *EX:P:LOSIONS!!!*   *and great unfurling*
>   *B A N N E R S*
> *like the sails*
>   *on four-masted ships*
> *RiSING AND pLUNging*
>   *in heavy seas.*

One evening I sent greetings to Slava through a sailor from the *Petropavlovsk.* "Tell him Kuriakina hopes his acting goes well."

"Kuriakina? As in Gennady Kuriakin?" They all knew his poetry, had already memorized verses from *On the Red October.* How impressed they were that we were married, that I had ridden on the agit-train. Now I was not just Marina Makarova, the scarecrow poet, but *Kuriakina*. The name drenched me with a glamour I hadn't had before. "Why aren't you with him?" they asked, imagining some awful betrayal. "Did he dump you?"

Glamour is best maintained by silence.

After classes, my students insisted on walking me back from the Admiralty Canal along the sparkling Neva in the twilight of ten p.m., a brace of handsome young men, white blouses glowing in a night bright enough to read the names of their ships on their hatbands. Their precious bread was tucked into my carpetbag, as well as a new notebook, courtesy of the Red Navy. Each time we passed the yellow mansion on the English Embankment, I recalled Kolya, and how he'd left me there. I could still sense our ghosts watching from an upper window. Wondering at the girl walking with all these beautiful men. Petrograd, Petersburg, city and dream, past and present folded together, into each other, like a map.

The men talked at once, trying to entertain me. Oh, the battles they'd fought, the Whites they'd killed, shipwrecks and snowstorms and fifty-foot seas. None of them willing to let any of the others have more of a chance with me, they laughed at each other's exaggerations and disputed the facts. One in particular could have easily been at home among the Argonauts, with his blue-green Aegean eyes and blond cropped hair. Another boy, a sensitive one with liquid brown eyes, was like a seafaring Maxim. But they were killers all. I had to remember that. Killers. I'd seen them with their machine guns on the agit-train. They had fought against Yudenich and the English, against Gaida and Wrangel, against the Poles. They might have been the ones to capture my father. They were without guilt. They still believed in the ABCs.

The evening smelled of the sea, or maybe it was they who did. Light glowed from them, as if they were the source of it, like certain fish. I admired their confidence, the depth when they laughed, their guiltlessness and pride — while I still walked on nails, glancing over my shoulder. No demons whispered into their ears. They sauntered with a rolling sailor's walk, as if still on deck. While I could see shadows scurrying around us, the whispery rustle of disaster in the blue passageways. But nothing could touch the gods of the Soviet Fleet.

I lay on my sheepskin by the odd window that came down to meet the floor, looking out. Nevsky Prospect was still illuminated by the milky midnight of summer and stirred with its secret life. I could see it all from here. The scene resembled the way I'd always imagined death: that strange half-light, a starless Blokian shadow world. Down in the street, a girl and a man kissed in a boarded-up doorway they had no idea was once the entry to Pushkin's Literary Café, where the poets of his day would gather and trade gossip and insults, and challenge one another to duels. The Stray Dog had been that for the last generation. And now, in our impoverished time, it was the House of Arts.

Ghosts, I thought, watching the figures pass. We were all ghosts, sowing our ectoplasm, creating shimmering memories with which we too would haunt the world.

We would die and drift along the streets of our youth, this whole city was nothing but a necropolis. I thanked God for Anton, just across the room in his bed, which I'd relinquished for the month of July. "You asleep?"

I heard the bedsprings creak. "Yes," he said. "You?"

Down in the street, a woman and a man turned the corner, she in white, he in black. Who in the world wore white now? How could you resist wiping your hands on her?

I returned to the young people in the doorway. I remembered desire like that, my lips throbbing, my breasts reaching, my thighs. But my blood had jelled in my veins, I was as sexless as a piece of waterlogged wood, a mourner sewn into her shroud. "Anton, do you ever think you're going to start screaming and never stop?"

He lit a cigarette, the scratch, the flare. "People think I'm crazy as it is," he said, exhaling a cloud. "When I'm just sensitive."

I laughed. When I was younger I couldn't have imagined how I would come to appreciate Anton. "So sensitive. But it's getting to be a problem. I'm afraid to sit in lectures. The other night when Dobuzhinsky was talking about contemporary Petrograd art, I thought I was going to start screaming." I traced along the window the curb, the Police Bridge, the cupola of the Dutch church.

"I think we're all about there," he said. "It's a good start for something. *I'm about to scream...*"

"*Inside the sweltering hall...*"

"*A straitened silence stains us all...*But you should go ahead and scream if you like. It won't bother me."

"I feel like a character in Bely's book."

"Everyone feels like that," he said.

"Not Gumilev." In his clean white shirt, the picture of self-restraint.

"Especially Gumilev," Anton said. "If anybody was sitting on a scream the size of Russia, it's Nikolai Stepanovich. His scream would blow down St. Isaac's. The statues would take wing like sparrows."

It made me feel better to think of Gumilev screaming, fists tight to his sides like an enraged five-year-old. I thought of Blok:

> *Suddenly the clown twists in the lights*
> *Screaming...*
> *And the merry circus slams its doors.*

The weight we were living under, we humans. I had to let go of that scream somehow.

44 *Zapad*

By summer's end my nerves were failing. I was given a room of my own in the House of Arts, on a newly opened corridor they called the Monkey House, though I still crept back at night to the safety of Anton's room. Things had started moving along the edges of my vision, like a cat brushing your leg. The feeling was like the night terrors of children, but this was worse—it could occur in the flat banal light of noon. My classes gave me some relief, the Skorokhod women, the sailors. But I found myself panic-stricken at the least convenient times. During a student reading at the Poets' Guild. In the canteen at the House of Arts, having a glass of tea with Inna Gants. During a recital at the House of the People, near the Gorky apartment, to which I had been invited by Molecule. Just as Aura lifted that glorious voice into "Un Bel Dí Vedremo"—the fear descended. I felt like my mother before Red Terror. Something awful was about to happen and I had to get out before it did—the ceiling falling, fire breaking out—or I would start screaming. I climbed over scores of people to walk outside the old wooden theater. I stood trembling in the autumn afternoon, smoking—hanging on to a cigarette like it was a railing, my new habit—until I calmed enough to return to the hall.

I remained standing in the back in case another spell overcame me, and I wept for this impossible loveliness and for myself at the end of my rope. For I was clearly going mad. Before too long, I too would be one of those poor creatures wandering around Petrograd, arguing with invisible entities, shrinking from devils, spitting and crossing myself.

Soon they emerged from the hall, the whole Gorky entourage—Molecule and Didi and Valentina, Moura and Gorky and their friends, even Maria Andreeva and her assistant. We walked together the short two blocks under the white sky of early autumn. Moura joined me, took my arm. "Are you all right, dear?" I nodded, afraid to speak, afraid it would happen again. Crows cawed in the trees. A relief to enter their homey apartment, solid as it always was. I prayed that the devils pursuing me wouldn't find me here.

I ate the little meat pies, but they tasted like dust to me. Aura entered to applause a half hour later, holding a bouquet of monstrous yellow chrysanthemums, accepting everyone's congratulations and praise. I was afraid to go to her, afraid I would burst out weeping or babbling nonsense and be forever after remembered that way. But she saw me, exhausted and tremulous by the windows, and came to me, pulling me aside. She led me down to her room.

Another shock. Big trunks stood open in the center of the room, and clothes were strewn on the bed and the armchair, over the silk screen.

She was leaving. For the West. *Na zapad*. In five days. Leaving Russia for good. *West*—that word, sweeter than honey on the tongue. The world was emptying out, and I would be left alone. "You can't do this," I said. The shaking had started again.

"I can't stand another winter, baby." She sat down on the edge of her bed and kicked off her shoes. "It's just not what I thought it would be."

I sat next to her.

"I thought I'd be free, you know? But it's like I'm a prisoner here. You understand me, don't you?"

More than she could ever know. But a real prisoner can't just decide to leave, throw a few things in a suitcase, and be off. "The war will be over soon," I said, taking her big hand, the rough-cut stone in the big ring. My fingers looked like birch twigs twined with hers. "Everyone says so. They say it'll get better then." But I didn't believe it. I drank in the warmth of her sensuous perfume. The war with Poland was dragging to a close. The last battles with Wrangel in the Crimea. Maybe the revolution would finally prove itself, at last unfold its luminous wings.

But Aura wasn't waiting. She'd secured her permissions. She glanced at the piles of clothes on the bed, the nightgowns, the dresses. She could leave, and I couldn't. "Will you go to Finland?"

"I'll drive to Estonia, then take the ship to Stockholm." In Sweden she would give some concerts before making her way to Berlin, Prague. "Paris by Christmas." The war was over, but not for us. She stroked my cheek. "You always said I should go to Paris."

Christmas in Paris. We sat on her bed, holding hands as I fought for my equilibrium, fought for a smile. She gazed into my eyes—I could see the flecks of gold, flecks of green, like a forest floor. "If you ever come west..." she began, but let it trail off. Now she was crying. We both knew I wasn't coming west. She was going to leave and I would be trapped, my foot caught in the snare of my country. She straightened the collar of my dress. Her hands were big and dry. "You won't always be here. Look me up. I'm never hard to find."

"Do me one favor," I said.

"Just name it," she said.

My last hope, a message in a bottle thrown into the sea. Into the West. But how to address it, and to whom? I could ask Moura. She was Estonian, but I thought she'd discourage it. *If you were trying to contact a White speculator and saboteur, smuggler and traitor, said to be working out of Estonia, how would you go about finding him? Where would you look?* She was kind, but first and foremost protective of Gorky. She already didn't trust the extra measure of peril I represented, I didn't think she would do anything to advance my cause. Whereas I believed in this woman, Aura Cady Sands, a woman who had renounced her own country in search of freedom. I knew she would do what she could. "Could you get something into the newspaper at Reval for me? The biggest one they have."

"You know I will. There's some paper over there in my desk."

I pushed aside perfumes and knickknacks, dishes with jewelry, and composed my note as she went back to the party. After working a while, I got this:

> *The river's so empty nowadays.*
> *All the gray horses are gone.*
> *I try to remember the tango.*
> *But one can't dance it alone.*

> *Regret is a bell, a secret,*
> *An island carved in the mind.*
> *Brave words once said in a station.*
> *Their chimes never have ceased.*

I sat at the desk, looking at the clothes she'd already packed, gowns and day dresses, crammed in every which way. In Paris she would have a maid for such things. In Paris, there would be flowers and hairdressers, rooms with heat and a private bath. I should be ashamed to envy such trivial things. I lived in the most modern country in the world, didn't I? This broken wreck of a land, this prison, this torment. Clyde Emory was already gone, returned to England to print his analysis of the triumphs of Bolshevism, the Buddhalike wisdom of Vladimir Ilyich. I'd seen him off at the docks. How startling it had been to see a ship there, flying a foreign flag.

You'll always have a friend in me, Emory had said, and kissed me on the lips. I stood on the wharfside as he carried his suitcase up the plank, and wondered how long *always* might be.

I came out to the parlor, handed Aura the page. "Put it in the Lost and Found section. Or in Missing Persons." Or perhaps I was the one who was lost. I was the missing person.

She folded the poem into her bosom. "What if they ask me what it says? Or if there's no Russian paper?"

"They've been Russian for five hundred years," I said. But she was right. With independence, who knew about national feeling. Kolya didn't speak German, and neither of us had a scrap of Estonian. Even if they printed it, I imagined there would be rafts of spies sniffing around Reval. Well, good luck to anyone tracing me through Aura. I returned to her room and wrote it out again in French, just in case. It wasn't half bad.

"It's the baby's daddy, isn't it?" she said from the doorway. "You think he's in Reval."

"It's possible."

"Want me to stay on, try to find him?"

I embraced her. The woman who had opened her throat and spilled out that gold onto the vast stage of the House of the People. One of the few who had known Iskra. "If he doesn't contact you, leave a Paris address. He doesn't speak much English but his French is perfect."

She gave me a wool dress, books, underwear, a pair of her boots. I put the boots on then and there. They were too big, but, like a heart, better too big than too small.

On the way home, I paused on the Troitsky Bridge, my arms full of undeserved gifts, gazing out at the ruffled mirror of the Neva, watching the gulls skim the empty river. Imagining sails here again, smokestacks. Barges laden with grain. That vanished maritime world. Oh, for a Finnish skiff with a single sail like the ones Uncle Vadim once piloted around the islands with us, even Seryozha and Tulku on board, landing us somewhere for a picnic, a bit of a swim. Papa usually stayed in the city, but one time, he was the one sailing the boat, in shirtsleeves rolled up, his pipe clamped between his teeth. Mama laughing. I leaned on the rail, pressed my face into the bundle of clothes, smelling Aura, and let myself weep.

Gazing west under the blank eye of heaven — how lonely it was. The empty palaces, the silent river, all that was left of Peter's great dream. Like our lives, crumbling facades with God knows what festering rubbish curled inside. I wanted to sail away with her so badly I could taste it, soar toward that gleaming horizon. *Zapad*. Beautiful and melancholy, as the end of summer always is in the north. The tides pulled at me, reaching right into my blood. The moon, as faint as chalk, had risen, barely visible in the east. Was this the winter I would go mad for good, locked away in my head, jabbering about monsters and demons? I had a terrible feeling of something unseen on its way, as horses sense a coming storm.

The morning Aura was to leave for Reval, I hurried to the Kronverksky apartment, terrified I'd miss her, carrying a package wrapped in *Pravda*. I could see the big Lessner motorcar waiting in front of the building, men already loading her trunks onto its roof. By noon she would have crossed over, she'd be on the other side, unreachable. The entire Gorky ménage had come down to see her off with flowers and promises to write. I embraced her and thrust my burden into her hands. "Could you mail this for me, when you get to Sweden?" A manuscript, tied with twine. I'd been translating it myself for the last five days. I'd written the address on top of the first page, *Mr. Clyde Emory, 29 Fitzroy Square*. My poems, in English. In case I perished this winter, or went completely mad, something should remain. Something had to.

I stood with the others as the big sedan pulled away. Aura leaned from the window in her gray traveling outfit, gray hat, waving a white handkerchief. I could still see the handkerchief as the car turned the corner and headed across the Troitsky Bridge.

45 *On the Embankment*

Autumn washed summer away, replacing warmth and dust with rain and the dankness of drains. The worst time of year, even worse than winter, the sky like a weeping wound. For the first time I could see no future. Just dread. Like waking up and finding the windowpanes painted over. It was a world drawn in watered ink and charcoal dust, where shadow people lived shadow lives in the sooty dampness, ate and slept, made their shadow love. I moved in a city under the city, through catacombs invisible to the naked eye.

Zapad. If only I could flee this melancholy place, to where the sun still shone. I imagined Kolya in Reval, sitting in a café, reading my message, *Kolya, come — it's so close . . .* But why would he return? It would never be anything but this, struggle, poverty, and the implacable, leather-clad arm. A jungle of *propuski* and queues and iron nights. My Skorokhod students grumbled about labor militarization. Henceforth, Trotsky vowed, the workforce would be run like the army. They would shoot deserters, people absent without leave. The dictatorship of the proletariat was rapidly dropping its prepositional phrase. How could one breathe? Where was our revolution, how had we lost it just as we were winning, the end almost in sight?

I could hardly bear to teach, to stand before my students' trusting eyes and read their little poems — for what? Meaning drained from everything, no matter how hard I tried to stop the flow. It was like sugar dissolving in the rain. Was poetry merely a toy to distract the starving? Everything felt so heavy, I could hardly stand up.

I rose early one morning after a night of grim wakefulness—Anton still in a dead sleep, wedged against the wall. I dressed in the sheepskin in which my father had been murdered, a woolen scarf over my hat, and walked in the rain down to the roiling Neva. I followed the river past the Admiralty and St. Isaac's, past the yellow mansion on the English Embankment. Children materialized out of the gloom, following me at a distance. Or maybe they weren't children at all, only ghosts, wet and forsaken. Child ghosts. More huddled on the porch of the Stock Exchange. *The Mystery of Liberated Labor.*

I stood in the driving rain under a red pillar, by the statues of river gods, the column's prows overhead full of water. Unbelievable that I'd once climbed this. These days I could barely lift my knees. I leaned against the railing, watching the watery tons arrive. I was so tired.

Once I'd strolled these banks with Genya, and he'd given me Saturn as a wedding ring. But the Cirque Moderne was closed now. No more discussions, no more arguing deep into the night, the excitement of those days. Now it was all gone, everyone leaving, or dead, or transparent with hunger. Ink running down a page. *Say goodbye . . .*

Beyond the point of the Strelka, the rivers massively converged in a surge of gray waters. I could barely see the blurry outline of the mansion from here, yellow gray in the rain. I walked down the little circular road right to the water's edge. The river's current sucked at me. I felt its desire. I moved along the very point, thinking, *What if I just fell in?* What if my foot just slipped? How fast would I sink and be carried out to Kronstadt, out to the West? To the West, at last. The relief to stop struggling and give myself over to the power of the tides. I had reached the end of my faith.

The water mesmerized me, liquid ton on ton. *Leave this place, this time.* Perhaps we returned, perhaps we didn't. Perhaps I would find the city under the waves. On and on the river came and opened its terrible mouth. I tried to recall what Gorky had said that morning when I told him my shameful story, confessed the awful choice I'd been handed. And he told me why it was important to live. But I couldn't remember...

God separated the land and the waters but the rain erased the line, and now I couldn't tell my tears from the rain, the rain from the river. *West,* with all the great river's rushing might. It felt inevitable, the pull of the water, the slant of the ground, this was what everything had been leading to from that night we'd read our fortunes in the wax. And here my story would end. It was as if the divine bard had wearied of it. It wasn't death I wanted, stately and plumed, it was only death's forgetting. There was nothing I knew that I would not want to unknow. Iskra's unconscionable death. Father's body, crumpled in the hall on Shpalernaya Street. Seryozha's senseless passing. My own mother's curse.

What had Gorky said? I tried to remember but the river was too loud, water streamed down my face, soaked my scarf, my sheepskin so full of water I would sink without stones. Once I could see the future, but now I saw no way out of a present that would just go on and on.

How brave are you?

The water swirled over the curbing. Just one more step...

The question is, what are you going to do with your own life? Where are your principles?

My father was dead, that was where my principles went. My revolution was dead. My brother was dead, my daughter was dead.

I came closer again, trying the freezing water with my boot's toe. The sudden shock of the cold and the power of the river forced me to take a step back.

But life was unbearable. I couldn't stand one more hour of it. How long would it take to drown, a minute or two?

Unbearable?

You can't live one more hour? A half hour?

But then there would be another, and another after that. And there I'd be, back chained to the rock of existence. I was ready now.

Marina! Someone called my name. Was it the storm, the river? The devils in my head?

If I could only forget. Forget burying my baby. Erase the picture of her on the pavement in Maxim's arms. If I died, I would never again see an ear wrapped in brown paper. I would not have to know what became of all our beautiful dreams.

If you die, who will remember?

I stepped down into the river. Water immediately filled my boots. The swiftness threatened to pull me out into the current. It was deathly cold. I cried out and struggled back without thinking.

Marina!

Who was calling me? Mother? At this late date? "Mama?"

Reaching across space and time, was she seeing me from wherever she was, as she'd seen me in the forest that night on the way to Alekhovshchina? "She died, Mama. Just like you said she would. Papa's dead too."

You must remember.

And I wept, my hand clapped against my mouth. Iskra in her basket, her hands dancing above the edge, moving to her own music. What would happen to Iskra if I took that memory into the Neva with me? And Papa as he'd been when I was small, taking my hand, tying my skates. The way he'd looked that St. Basil's Eve, standing next to my pile of books?

Perhaps I was brave enough to live another hour. Perhaps I did not need to die. I backed away from the water. Tomorrow was a buoy bell, so quiet, but I could hear it, and I let it guide me away from the river, off the Strelka, onto the Petrograd side.

The maid let me in, her soft wrinkled face a haven, a lighthouse. The hall smelled reassuringly of Gorky, cabbage and cigarettes. The woman helped me shed my wet sheepskin and scarf, my soaked boots, and put me into a pair of oversized felt slippers. The clock in the hall chimed noon. I stared at it as if I'd never seen one before. Everything resonated with significance. The hidden had become visible. Signs were everywhere. The maid, the guardian of the entry, led the way, deep, deep inside to the beating heart of the flat. My teeth chattered violently, I tried to stop them, clamping my jaws together in the effort, but to no avail. I could hear the clatter of the typewriter. The maid knocked, opened the door. "It's Marina Dmitrievna," she whispered and backed away.

Inside, Gorky and Moura were companionably at work, as they were every day—Gorky at his desk, the inevitable cigarette in its black holder between his fingers, Moura typing at a little side table. Before them lay petitions for imprisoned *intelligenty*, correspondence with writers all over the world, maybe a new book or play. The room was hot and close, the electric lamps were lit. Water wept down the windowpanes.

"Marina," he said, standing, reaching out his hands to me, I could tell he was alarmed to see me standing there, teeth chattering, as wet and sordid as a canal rat. His hands, so large around mine, warm. I wept just to see him, as real as a bale of hay, tall and stooped with that snub nose and enormous moustache, the rumpled wool suit. Like seeing land after a shipwreck, a streetlamp on a dark night.

Moura cast me a penetrating look as she handed me a folded blanket draped over the back of a chair. I wrapped it around my shoulders, tried to keep my teeth from breaking. "Please, sit down," Gorky said. "We were about to take a break." I caught the glance he exchanged with Moura. Like an old couple—she understood him perfectly. Without saying anything, she stood and stacked her pages, placing them on top of the typewriter. She put a finger on Gorky's desk. "Don't forget you have an appointment at Smolny, quarter after one." Her accented Russian. She always addressed him as *vy*, the formal way, as my own grandparents once had done. But to her credit she didn't sneer or frown at my soggy appearance or my interruption of their workday. A small nod and a smile let me know her departure wasn't from unfriendliness. She closed the door behind her.

"Please, sit down."

But I could not sit. Still shivering, I went to the window where I could gaze down into the park and the bare treetops, half erased by the rain. It struck me that this was how the world would look just before it drowned. Someday the river would rise and cover the treetops. Shouldn't we be building an ark? Find animals that had not been eaten and put them on board? Who among us would be righteous enough to be saved? Not I. Gorky, certainly. Blok. Akhmatova. And where was she now? Out there in the rain? Dead? Had she left? *Na zapad?* Nobody talked about her anymore, except to say she was over, that the personal was out of step with the times. I never saw her at the House of Arts, or the Poets' Guild. "Whatever happened to Akhmatova? Is she still here?"

Gorky glanced up from his writing, laughed softly. "You came here in this storm to ask after Anna Andreevna?" He flicked ash toward his ashtray.

"You never hear about her. Did she die?"

"She's still here," he said, resting his face on his hand, his green eyes watching me. He saw everything. "Larisa Reisner was over there the other day. They were completely out of food. She brought a bag of rice—which our Akhmatova promptly gave to the neighbors." Larisa Reisner, a leading Bolshevik, married to the commissar of the Baltic Fleet, ironically called Raskolnikov. For some reason it surprised me that she knew Akhmatova. I thought the poet had refused to have anything to do with the revolution. But perhaps even Akhmatova had her Varvara—though evidently a less vindictive one than mine.

"She's not writing anymore. Her new husband doesn't like her poetry. He's forbidden it, evidently."

A husband forbidding the High Priestess her throne? *My* Akhmatova would never allow anyone to stop her writing. "She permits that?"

"Why women put up with men, I have no idea," he chuckled. "He's not even attractive, though he's a forceful personality, let's say. Shileiko. Translated the *Gilgamesh* into Russian." He studied me, smoothing his big moustache. "Our Anna Andreeva is a great poet, but if you ask me she's a martyr looking for a cross. You'd think there would be enough to choose from, she wouldn't have to go out and find this particular one." The skritching of his pen. "At least Gumilev understood her."

He loved three things ... "He once told me he *made* her as a poet."

Gorky snorted. "What makes you think of Anna Andreeva?"

Down in the little park across from Gorky's building, I watched a man alone walking among the bare trees, his hands in his pockets. I wished he had a dog. A black dog, who could run around sniffing. He looked so terribly alone. "It makes you think of her poem, '*The dark road twisted / the rain was drizzling / someone asked / to walk with me a little way.*'" The weight of time seemed so heavy, so thick with the dead. "I have this awful feeling that something terrible's about to happen. It's like that all the time." I was shaking again, my teeth clattering like a child's tin windup toy. And what exactly did I think Gorky could do about it? But here I was laying my burdens on his shoulders like everybody else did. When he was just a writer. Just a friend.

He put his pen down and came away from the desk, put his arm around my shoulder, the plaid blanket wrapped about me. "Sit down for a moment." He led me to the old leather armchair in the corner. A miracle, nobody had yet cut it up for shoes. He settled me there, pulled Moura's stenographer's chair out from her little table and sat down before me, knee to knee, his dear pockmarked face, his clear eyes. "Tell me, what are you afraid of, Marina? Hasn't the worst already happened?"

"Maybe being the one left behind is worse. I was standing on the Strelka just now, looking down into the water. I just wanted to slip and fall in."

He sighed, crossed his long legs, bumping my knees. "I once tried to shoot myself, did you know that? When I was nineteen. I'd been denied admission to university. And my grandmother had died. The one who raised me, the only one who'd been good to me. Of course, I botched it, shot myself in the lung. The despair you're feeling is not unfamiliar to me."

Gorky had felt this. I should not have been surprised. He'd been through more in his long life than any ten men. He had written an entire book just about his childhood. "Is it ever going to get any better?" I asked through my chattering teeth. "I can't see the future anymore. I'm afraid that it's just going to be like this from now on, only worse."

"You can see the future?" he joked.

"Once I could." I wiped at my tears.

"You mean your own future?" He wasn't joking anymore. "Or ours?"

"Both," I whispered. I didn't dare say it out loud. I could feel the awful panic rising, just speaking of it. "What if this is all for nothing? What if we're all riding in the dark, toward a cliff?"

"You're not crazy to be afraid," he said. "Anybody in his right mind would be."

I was shocked. Gorky, who'd been a Bolshevik since the beginning. Gorky, who basically funded the party in the early days on the sales of his work. Yet, he'd never been one to put his head in the sand. I'd read his stories—he told the bitter truth. *Gorky*—the name he'd chosen for himself—meant *bitter*. "You thought this would be easy?" he said. "That revolution would be something that happened, like a great earthquake, or a lightning storm? And then the clouds would clear and the sun would come out?" He patted his pockets, looking for something. "And now you see what it is. A dangerous beast. An opportunistic leadership riding the vengeance of the underclass—disorganized, dangerously ideological."

How could he be so supportive of the revolution if he felt that way?

He touched my blanket-clad arm. "Have I shocked you?"

"But you're a Bolshevik..."

"I'm a writer first. We must see things clearly, and never lie to ourselves about what we see."

I thought so too. I'd thought so since Grivtsova Alley.

He leaned over his desk to extract a fresh handkerchief from the drawer, handed it to me. He plucked his smoldering cigarette from the ashtray. "Think of the work you're doing. You're teaching at the shoe factory, aren't you?"

I wiped my face with the clean cloth. The heat of the room was causing my dress to steam, but my teeth stopped chattering so badly.

He leaned forward, speaking calmingly, the way you talked to a panicked dog. "It's mostly women, isn't it? Can you picture your students?"

It wasn't hard to do. Young women's faces already lined, teeth falling out—they covered their mouths with their hands when they laughed. Older women, their nails split from the work. Their swollen ankles. I thought of the way they shuffled into my class after work—like cabmen covered with snow, shaking themselves off and coming to life over food and drink.

"Imagine them five years ago. In the same factory." Smoke wreathed his head, wove its patterns into the lamp's light. Water beaded on the windows, trickled down like tears. "Imagine going in and telling them that in the year 1920, they'd be studying poetry. That they'd have a workers' committee, a voice in the shoe factory. That there would be no more owner, no landlord, no tsar." He rose and opened the *fortochka,* gazing out. "Imagine telling them that in five years they'd have won themselves domestic rights. Birth control. Free housing. That they'd be taken seriously by the courts, and their children could attend university. What do you think they would have told you?"

"That I was dreaming." Even now I could see their pride, a little bewilderment even, that all this had changed in so short a time.

"It's easy to forget that when the bread runs out. When there's no firewood and they forbid you to cut it yourself." He sat back down into his worn desk chair, leaned back, launching into a coughing fit. Rumor had it that he had tuberculosis, but it was that damaged lung. "The revolution's not an event, Marina. It's a creature. A young, proud boy, say, who fights with everyone, breaking the windows, shoving his father, realizing his strength. He thinks he knows everything. But he knows nothing, and it's up to us—me and you, the artists, the scholars—to humanize him before he breaks up the house. So something good can come of all that raw energy."

"You think poetry can do that?"

He smiled. "Think about your women at the shoe factory. Like flowers, drinking you in. The mere fact of you is some kind of proof to them."

I thought of the way one of my women might close a book and give the cover an affectionate pat—my gesture, my father's gesture when he had finished reading. And the way they laughed and clapped their hands when someone wrote a good line, an apt metaphor. I had touched their lives. I, me, this nothing.

"For them, *you* are the future." He leaned forward, his cigarette in its black holder sending up a wending plume of smoke. "You remind them that there will be a time when they'll write poetry and speak proper Russian and notice the color of the sky. We need that more than bread now. You're the emissary from the future."

The plants on the windowsill peered out from the steamy panes, but there would be little light for them today. I unwrapped my blanket, finally warm enough.

"Rousseau once said, 'Civilization is a hopeless race to discover remedies for the evils it produces.'" He flicked his ashes toward the ashtray, a dented brass bowl with a monkey on the rim. "I'm convinced it's just the opposite. I think natural man is a terrified brute." He took another draw and crushed it out. "Have you ever seen a pogrom, Marina?"

I had not but had heard plenty about its terrors from Matvei on the *Red October*.

"I saw one in Nizhny when I was a young man, and it's something you never forget. It's why art is my religion. Science. Knowledge. I have no illusions about the common man, because I am the common man and it's repulsive what he's capable of. I want him to get a glimpse of what it would be like to be fully human. What you do with those shoe factory women, that's the most important thing. We can't have you trying to fall into the Neva."

"But there's got to be more than just being useful," I said. "What becomes of us—you and me—our art? They keep saying *Akhmatova's dead, with her mourning and her lovers*. We're all supposed to write about drumbeats and bayonets now, *Onward brothers!*

I don't mind being useful, but is that the poet's only job?" The debate had raged from the Krestovsky apartment in 1918 to the halls of the House of Arts and all its detractors. The question of whether the personal had any place in a revolution.

"Mourning and lovers are as important as bayonets," Gorky said. "More so, because they're human and universal. We don't need more bayonets. Getting people to listen, to think, to feel something, that's where the work is. I'll tell you something. The poetry of Anna Andreevna will never disappear. Whatever trash Mayakovsky and your husband, forgive me for saying so, espouse, all of their drumbeats will not supplant one tear, the petal of one Akhmatovian rose." He screwed another cigarette into the black holder and lit it with a match—*skritch*—from the match stand, coughed.

As he spoke, I felt the panic ebbing. Maybe he was right. Maybe I still had a place in the world, a reason for being. I wished I'd known him in the months after Iskra died. He had somehow given me a moment of sanity, or at least shared his with me, like sharing a warm coat on a cold night.

"Don't lose heart, Marina Dmitrievna. If you lose heart, all is lost. We don't need any more revolutionaries, we've had our revolution. Now we need human beings. The river will wait. It will always be there if you change your mind."

I wanted to stay here forever, but I could hear lunch being prepared, and I couldn't very well lie under Gorky's desk like a dog and have him feed me by hand like Ukashin did his pets. I had to preserve this feeling of carrying something essential, and learn it like a poem, condensed and easily memorized, to recite in the dead of night when the ghosts came thick and fast.

I forced myself to rise. My hands no longer trembled, my clothes were drying. I was ready to face the rain and the city, bearing this precious gift like a basket of eggs. "Thank you." I shook his big hand.

"And be careful on the embankments," he said.

46 *The Argonaut*

It took the great Neva a long time to put itself to sleep. I stayed off its wide bridges and away from its icy embankments, kept to the interior streets and peaceful canals hardening, filling with the white breath of winter. I wrote, taught my dwindling classes, and no longer ran from the phantoms sidling after me along the streets, lingering in doorways of broken facades, moving past empty windows. The ghosts were more at home in the city than the living—why shouldn't they walk as freely? I no longer startled if something moved in the corner of my eye with the liquid motion of a cat. Perhaps it wasn't madness but simple starvation. If it weren't for the bread my students gave me, I wouldn't have the strength to walk as far as the bakery to redeem my own ration cards. Up ahead on the Moika Embankment, I spied a little girl, about four, in a hand-knitted cap and green coat. Not in line but obviously with someone—she couldn't be alone, could she? That green coat...Hadn't I had a coat like that? She gazed at me directly, her green eyes...

Iskra!

But then a woman got in the way, and when she'd passed, the girl had vanished.

People walked past me on the pavement as if I were a lamppost. Just another hungry citizen, holding her pitiful quarter pound of bread, gazing at nothing. The ghosts were on parade. I'd seen Avdokia this week, even spied Arkady ducking into the loggia at Gostinny Dvor. It made a certain sense, the dead were the permanent residents. The empty houses gawped with their busted eyes. Perhaps they would come to life once this endless war was over, their windows reglazed, their floors rebuilt, their plumbing restored to working order. I liked to picture that. Furniture carried in, the rugs we'd cut into shoes replaced. On the other hand, perhaps the city would empty out completely and sail on in legend, into the mist, leaving behind only the swamp from which it came.

My Red Fleet escort flotilla had thinned somewhat over the autumn, the men drifting off in search of likelier objects for romance. There was no end of available women in the hungry city. But one sailor stood out among the others. A bit of a troublemaker, blond and wiry, in his early twenties. I'd dubbed him the Argonaut. Everything about him spoke of warmer climes and white sails. At rest, his face wore a quizzical look, his sandy eyebrows curling over his narrow blue-green Aegean eyes in a permanent squint, but he broke into a quick smile if anything interesting was going on, flashing his good white teeth. As he did now, when I asked him to walk me home.

"You have a home?" he teased. "I thought you slept on the wing, like a gull."

We walked from the Pryazhka wharf past spooky, deserted New Holland—Peter the Great's brick shipyards. I took his arm. I could feel his muscles through his heavy coat. Who could blame me for craving the touch of the living? He was so animated and lively in his wool coat and sailor's cap. I was used to the writers' melancholia. His sailor's good cheer and physical ease were a balm. His blond cropped hair was coarse and dense—I wondered if it would curl if it were longer. His name was Pasha Kislov.

I could well imagine him on the *Argo,* having just killed the oxen of the sun...Pasha wouldn't have cared which gods he'd offended. *Pashol,* the men called him. I'd accidentally given him that nickname. It meant *He went.* I'd come back from a break one night and noticed his empty chair, asked the men where he'd gone. *Pashol,* they'd said, and then realized how funny they'd been, after which he was baptized.

We meandered along, talking lightly about rations, poets, conditions in the city. I talked about the knitting artel, and the telephone exchange. He grabbed the metalwork of a lamppost and pulled himself up, like a boy showing off. He jumped onto one of the granite posts on the Moika Embankment, and posed like a cupid, and then flipped himself into the air, landing on his feet, making me laugh. Why hadn't we met long ago, when I still had that kind of energy? I would have walked atop the balustrade and performed ronds de jambe, pirouettes.

Standing before the door of the House of Arts, with its fancy plasterwork and fanlight, he grew suddenly shy. His eyes were a question mark. *What am I doing here? Do you really want me?* This was unexpected. He was normally the brashest one of an entitled lot, full of confidence in his role in the national destiny. For my part, I didn't know what the others would think of me bringing a sailor home. But I knew enough about the world to know that such things were best done with elegant confidence.

There were a few stares as we moved through the gallery, past buzzing participants leaving Chukovsky's translation studio. I met no one's eye, but looked past them, as normal as could be. And who wouldn't stare, seeing the wiry beauty of my Argonaut? Surely not Inna Gants, whom we met coming down the stairs from Anton's floor. She practically missed her step. Alla Tvorcheskaya, a painter on my hall, looked at him carefully from boots to cap. Pasha was touchingly intimidated. He tucked himself behind me, as if my starveling self in sheepskin coat and fox hat could conceal the pride of the Red Navy.

Seeing the decaying halls through his eyes lent them a glamour I'd forgotten—the mystery of all those doors, the brotherhood of literature—though the double line of close-set rooms must have seemed very familiar, like a third-class ocean liner. My room, narrow and tall, with its touches of ornate plasterwork at the ceiling, my cobbled-together *bourgeoika*, the nudes on the walls, a red scarf on a hook. It all must've seemed very strange to a military man. Feminine. He picked up my hairbrush, he touched my books. I started a fire, feeding the stove as one fed a sick child, trying to tempt it.

"And you all live here together?" he asked. "Gumilev? And Blok?" He'd taken off his cap but he couldn't quite figure out what to do with the rest of himself.

"Blok lives near your club. But Gumilev lives upstairs, in the Eliseevs' personal bathroom. It's supposed to be amazing."

"He lives in a bathroom?"

"With his wife, of course."

He'd assumed we lived in monarchial splendor. I hated to disabuse him of the notion. But our splendor lay not in the lavishness of our surroundings but in the company we kept.

"Sit down," I said, indicating the bed. There was that or the desk with its one chair. Gingerly, he sat on the sagging springs, as if afraid he would break it. He kept spinning his cap. Although I was only twenty, I felt like the elder—his teacher, and a poet. His nervousness gave me confidence.

I set some water on the boil for carrot tea. The room seemed less frosty with two of us in it. When I glanced across Bolshaya Morskaya at the house opposite, a man's face appeared in the window, just for a moment—a tall man with a stoop, and white hair. He seemed to be saying something, but what? A message from the future? *Go back.* I wished I had curtains, but there were none, the last tenant had used them—for a new skirt most likely, or a shirt, or to pad an old jacket. Who had cloth to spare? Soon the panes would frost over and I wouldn't have to see out at all.

Voices traveled from the hall and the other rooms, just the normal sounds of the building. My left-hand neighbor, Shafranskaya, was talking to someone in her famous reading voice, and old Petrovsky on the other side coughed up a lung.

"Are you still married to Kuriakin?" he asked, flipping his cap in his calloused hands. He tossed it up, tried to catch it on his head and failed.

Talking about Genya could lead nowhere good. I wasn't going to display the tattered rags of my life like some saint's relics. "Listen. I like you, Pasha, don't take this the wrong way," I said. "But don't ask me anything, all right? Let's just be together."

"Never?" He raised his bushy eyebrows and his forehead wrinkled.

"No," I said. "Tell me something about yourself instead." I dumped carrot scraps into the hot water, set out two cups.

Around and around went the flat sailor's cap. Was he regretting having come? "What do you want to know? About girls? The old folks at home? The war?"

"God no. Tell me about the sea."

He gave a startled half laugh, the sound of someone who can't quite believe something unfamiliar but pleasant was being done to him. I doffed my fur hat, plumped it on the desk like a cat, combed out my hair with my fingers in a scrap of mirror. It was still too cold to take off my coat. He watched me primp, fascinated, as if he'd never seen a girl comb her hair before. "How did you get to be a sailor?" I asked.

"Well"—the hat must be getting dizzy by now—"I come from a village near Yaroslavl, Mologa it's called. My father was a bargeman. I dropped out of school to work on the boats. It's a big port—not big like this, but a big one."

"I've only been to Nizhny."

"The Volga's beautiful but it's not the sea. Anyway, when the war came, I joined the navy. I told them I was eighteen, but I barely shaved." He rubbed his fingers over his square chin. Few of the sailors grew beards, unlike most of the men in Petrograd. "Nobody cared. I took the training. A lot of the boys had never been on a boat before. I was posted to the *Petropavlovsk*. We were part of the insurrection." He glanced over at me to see if I was impressed. His eyes, turquoise in a bright light, seemed more gray in my sad, cold room.

No, not so sad. Not with Pasha in it. "I think a lot about the sea." I poured water into a small metal teapot with the carrot shavings, moving the manuscript of *The Valley of the Moon* to one side. "We have our origins there," I said. "And it lives on in us, like blood. The smell sometimes makes me cry, I want it so badly." I stopped, avoiding the topic of sailing, and my brothers, which would require mentioning a lieutenant in the White Army, perhaps even a captain by now, and a cadet dead by the Kremlin wall. No brothers. No fathers. No mothers. No past. Only now, these few living moments.

"I've sailed my whole life," he said, elbows on his muscular legs. "Out at Kronstadt, of course it's all battleships and gunboats. But we've got a basin of schooners, they teach everybody to sail under canvas—canvas, that's what I like. No engine, no noise, no stink. Maybe this spring I'll take you out. Would you like that?"

"I would." I would like it better than chocolate, or silk stockings, or jewels. I handed him his cup of chipped porcelain, filled my own, made of tin.

I waited to see what came next, half expecting him to throw himself onto me like a beast. But he was surprisingly talkative. Maybe he'd had a woman more recently than I'd imagined, his desire wasn't as urgent as I'd supposed. "It's fantastic. Out there, all by yourself, the ropes in your hands. Don't you ever feel there's just too many people?"

I could smell the ocean spray on him, the salt air, seaweed. I ran my hand through his short wooly hair. "I wish we were there now."

"Winter's the worst." He picked up my foot and pulled my boot off. "Everything's all locked down, there's nothing to do but polish brass." He removed the other one. "I hear they're going to send us to work in the factories, now that the war's ending. *The Labor Army*." He snorted, massaging my feet. His hands were strong and felt good. "That's not going to sit too well with the boys. It may be fine for the army, but not for us."

I lowered my feet, put my fingertips to his lips to quiet him, raised my mouth to his. He tasted of tobacco and hemp. All of us, Peter's children. Our blood was salty and turned with the tides. I kissed his rough cheek, and the wave of desire rose. The tide turned. I pressed my mouth to his, and sat on his lap. My body reminded me there was more to flesh than simply the hollowness of one's gut and one's sore bloated feet and standing in queues and wolfing down inedible scraps of food, all of the indignities of slow starvation. My body sparked and ignited like a neglected brush pile, like an abandoned house.

I unbuttoned the bodice of my dress, pulled it off over my head. I knew how dirty and unkempt I was. You got one bath a month in the Eliseev bathroom downstairs. I took off my slip and my underpants—though it was freezing, I wanted to let him see me before we made love. My body altered by childbirth, the white marks, my breasts larger and lower than they had been. I was a bit ashamed—sailors were cleaner than poets now, but Pashol didn't seem to notice or care. I couldn't wait to see his skin—oh, so white! He pulled off his shirt and struggled to loosen his pants in the cold. Lean—but not starving, just hard and flat muscled like a coil of rope. Like a big cat that could take you by the neck and kill you with a shake if it wanted to, but it didn't want to.

He took handfuls of my hair, ran his fingers through it, smelled it, I was sorry it was so dirty. He felt the scars on my back, and his blue eyes glanced at me with their intelligent wryness, his forehead wrinkling into a series of parallel breakers. But true to his promise, he asked me no questions. Our bodies were not even bodies, the body was simply the tinder, the precious wood, and the fire we raised sought more fire. I flamed with his touch. His hands were rough but brushed me lightly—teasing, in no hurry.

I don't know how long we made love. Until I was too sore to go on. And how we laughed. God knows what Shafranskaya and Petrovsky thought. I'd been as quiet as a nun since I'd moved in—surely they couldn't have expected that to last. I tried to keep my voice down, but it was such a joy to shout, and I had always been noisy in bed. I tried to stifle my cries, planting a hand over my mouth. But sometimes I was not quick enough. I imagined a sea as green-blue as his eyes, with blue and white villages on islands breaking straight upward on craggy islands blazing in the sun. I heard the sails crack overhead, the halyard clanging against the mast, felt the bed unmooring.

Afterward, he brought out a bar of chocolate and shared it with me. "You have to keep up your strength," he said.

I dragged my quilt up over us, and we lay, my head on his outstretched arm, dancing my hands above us in their own joyous semaphore. I should write an aubade. How long had it been? I felt beautiful again, desirable, young. *And if I became pregnant?* It was unlikely. I had not bled since Iskra was born. A child from Pashol would smell of tang and brine and foreign lands. It would have those eyes.

But there would be no child.

We slept a little, the stove went out. I yawned and stretched. He sat up. "I have to go."

I watched him clothe that whiplike body. Oh the Gods...I couldn't wait to hear the gossip tomorrow. My presence already an anomaly, the only girl among the younger poets living here in my own right. Would they kick me out? Oh, I'd worry about that if it happened. Tonight I was alive again—I'd recovered part of myself. I felt like a pirate on the deck of a ship, knife in my teeth, face to the wind. I wouldn't give this resurrection up for all the disapproving fogeys in Petrograd. Even literary ones.

Man does not live by *vobla* alone.

47 *The Guest*

Something must have shown of my pleasure. People scented it like a perfume. Colors seemed brighter, I laughed more, felt warmer, even in cold rooms. I took more care to wash and launder my underthings, even when it required staying in my room until two pairs of bloomers had dried. Or going without on occasion—a bit naughty, to stand in the drafty hall talking to Anton or Khodasevich with the December wind blowing up my skirt. Men attempted to be charming. They wanted to stand close—Tereshenko, Nikita, and even Shklovsky—to warm themselves at my hearth. Guests wanted to meet me. I could feel myself returning to life, thanks to my sailor.

The House of Arts assembled a dinner for the English writer H. G. Wells when he came to visit that winter. Such a flurry! I knew his works well—my father had been a devoted fan. An important leftist in England, Wells knew Gorky from before the war, he was staying with them on Kronverksky Prospect. None of the younger members were invited to this dinner, only those in the inner circle. So we hung about in the salon, hoping to catch a look at the great man. We watched our elders arrive and enter the icebox of the dining room in their coats and gloves, all but Gumilev, who wore a dinner jacket and a flower in his lapel—which would keep as if in a florist's refrigerator. Talk about fortitude! There was a smattering of applause, and Gumilev bowed, ironically.

Now the Gorky party arrived, Moura leading Wells through the public rooms, introducing him to the uninvited. A well-fed man with drooping eyebrows, he seemed personable, and Moura clearly thought so too. She was in her glory, animated, plump, laughing, laying on the charm. Wasn't Gorky jealous? I watched Alexei Maximovich across the room talking with Kuzmin, seemingly indifferent to his mistress's flirtation with the foreigner. Didn't he notice the way she bared her white throat as she laughed? The way she leaned in, taking his arm. But perhaps it was part of a wider plan to get something out of him. Who knew what was going on behind the scenes? Inna Gants said that Wells was quite the womanizer, had children by any number of women, but it was hard to picture this portly, avuncular fellow as a figure of romance.

Moura saw me and said something to the author, pointing me out. They came right over. "Marina Dmitrievna Makarova, this is Herbert Wells. He wanted to meet you." He shook my hand. His eyes were a transparent green, like sea glass, and his touch was warm and he smelled like leather. His smile endeared. Yes, perhaps there was something to the rumor at that.

"How lovely to meet you, Miss Makarova. I've been looking forward to this—but hadn't expected such a lovely young lady. I might have known." He put his other hand on top of our joined ones. There was something to him. Like Kolya. Yes, I recognized that warmth, the intimacy, the charm. "I believe I knew your father. Dmitry Makarov—the lawyer, yes?" Moura's face went white, as I imagined my own did. "Knew him in London. Brilliant man. Could talk about anything. How is he these days?" Moura shot me a look of alarm.

"He passed away," I said. "This summer." My throat closed. I didn't trust myself to say more. I composed my face as if his death were a solemn but not dangerous event, as if it had been from some sort of disease. Which it was, of course. Not typhus, but a virulent strain of retribution.

"So sorry to hear." Patting my hand. "He was devilishly witty too. A wonderful man. My condolences." I nodded, as Moura exhaled. What did she think I would do? Discuss my father's political murder in the salon of the House of Arts?

"Marina Dmitrievna is one of our most promising young poets," she said.

An understanding smile from the Englishman. Oh, another Charming Man. I could tell he would be a fountain of trouble for the next unfortunate woman. "Well, I happen to be carrying a letter for you, Miss Makarova. From London." He patted his pockets, handed it to me. *Marina Makarova, House of Arts, Petrograd.* But Moura was already tugging him away. "I'd love to hear more," he said over his shoulder. "Maybe afterward, if there's time." And she led him toward the icy dining room, where the long table had been set with the Eliseev china. We'd all had a peek, a sight enough to stop all our mouths. They went in, and the doors closed.

I tore open the envelope, glanced down at the signature. It was from Clyde Emory.

Dearest Marina, it began. *I hope this winter is finding you well. I worry — the news about Russia is grim. I cannot bear the thought of you cold and hungry. I sent some things with Wells. I hope they will make your winter a little more bearable. I hate to think of you suffering.*

A package? Hallelujah! Food rations had been cut again, worse than they'd ever been — half a pound of bread a day for the intelligentsia, and the bakeries regularly ran out. Without my students, I would have already boiled my sheepskin and eaten it. I was half out-of-body, and no longer had the trick of *inflowing* that Ukashin had taught. I skimmed the rest of the letter, typewritten and single-spaced. He had pressed so hard, the o's had punched through.

I want you to know that I've submitted one of your poems to Clarion *and they want more. I've sent another two to* The Dial. *I don't necessarily think they'll publish, but they should know you. Send more stuff via H. G.*

They were publishing one of my poems? I wondered which one. *Clarion* was at Cambridge University, showcasing new poets like Amy Lowell and H.D. Emory had left me copies of the journal in his attempts to court me.

So my poems had arrived in the West. That message in a bottle I'd sent with Aura had found landfall. No news from Kolya, but instead—this. Life never gave you the thing you asked for, but sometimes something else. Like Pasha, and *Clarion*.

Please don't fall in love with anyone until I can come again. I should have put you in a suitcase and taken you as cargo. Will you forgive me? Just enough of a joke to cover his dignity, in case I chose to be offended.

I see fox fur on women everywhere here, and the hairdressers are mad for henna. It's enough to drive a fellow bonkers. I bought a recording of Aleko. *It fills me with memories.*

Then, he returned to the impersonal. *Write to me, tell me how things are.* As if one could get that news past the censors. *The situation in England is galvanizing in support of Soviet Russia. The British longshoremen won't allow arms to be sent to the enemies of Russia's people. The workers are with you. And I, most of all.*

Your servant, Clyde.

Thank God, not *love.* I could hardly still my racing heartbeat. I was going to be published in the West.

"Borscht," Alla Tvorcheskaya hissed, spying on the supper through a gap in the dining room doors.

We uninvited guests crowded the hallway, trying not to drool as she whispered descriptions of the courses emerging from the kitchen, borne by the ancient Eliseev servants, who thought little of the writers and artists but preferred to stay on at the House of Arts rather than try their luck in the city at large. The repast was the finest we could offer—borscht, blini, fish in aspic, stuffed cabbage with meat—probably horsemeat. Not so impressive, compared to what that pudgy Wells probably ate for an average Thursday lunch, but the best we'd seen in years. Anton, standing behind me, craned his neck, trying to read the letter over my shoulder. "An English admirer?" he asked, a sarcastic edge to his voice.

"Someone I met at Gorky's." I quickly folded it away. "It's nothing."

"Then why are you hiding it?"

"Why are you reading over my shoulder?"

"Shh!" We were irritating the eavesdroppers.

Evidently things started to get ugly over the fish course. Some of our more intransigent anti-Bolsheviks were harassing Wells over his political sympathies. We could hear far better than we could see, and they made no attempt to keep their voices down, growing louder and angrier as they piled on: "Kid-glove treatment." "Potemkin villages, that's all they are." "You've got to ditch your minders." "Don't believe a thing." We couldn't hear Wells, he spoke too reasonably, but the others were unmistakable.

Here was Shklovsky. I recognized his voice, clear, wry, cutting socialist Wells for being "an unwitting toady for British capitalism." Anton laughed out loud, and ruined the cigarette he was rolling. I could only cringe, imagining how mortified Gorky must be at this disgraceful performance. He was always embarrassed by bad manners. And Gumilev, in his dinner jacket, attempting to show some elegance to our foreign guest—Nikolai Stepanovich would be rigid with shame.

"Poliatnikov is taking his jacket off," said Alla, peering through a crack in the door. A resident gadfly. The others crowded around. "Are they going to fight?"

"He's showing Wells his shirt. It's pretty bad, just collar and cuffs. Well, what makes him so different? Nikolai Stepanovich looks ready to explode." *Gumilev*.

We heard his response clearly: *"Parlez pour vous!" Speak for yourself!*

What a horror show. The others were as thrilled as children when someone else behaves badly. But I felt shame, and pity for Wells, who'd come to do his best, to listen and learn.

I retreated to the hall to read Emory's letter again.

"You're missing the fun." Tereshenko braced his arm against the wall next to my head. "Don't you want to see the coup de grâce? See Gumilev punch out Poliatnikov?"

"Wells isn't stupid, he doesn't need to be shown our laundry."

"Bourgeois," he said. "He deserves it, looking at us like worms under a microscope. Telling us what to do. Like he knows what's best for Russia. He should have stayed in England and just sent his money." He was standing too close to me, as he often did, trying to push himself on me. He was attractive enough, with his boxer's build, funny in a rough way. And a good poet. But I didn't need another lover.

"*Parlez pour vous,*" I said, and ducked out from under his arm.

The dinner broke up in disorder. People were yelling. Gorky and Moura left grim faced, steering Wells out from the House. There was no chance to speak further, or inquire about my package. Damn Poliatnikov! I imagined what it could have been, a sweater? Tinned salmon? I'd have to go to the Kronverksky apartment to collect it. The poets continued to argue long after their victim had left, with pro- and anti-Wells factions hurling abuse at one another. Anton was as happy as a bear in honey, reveling in the controversy. He didn't give a damn about Wells, or the Soviet's image in the world. He just liked to see people fighting.

I pulled him aside, into an alcove off the salon—I didn't want the others to overhear, for who was I to be published when Akhmatova was silent, when Blok no longer heard the sounds of life? "Anton, I'm being published in England. I sent my poems off with Aura Sands, and she gave them to Clyde Emory—"

He snorted. "That mediocrity."

"Listen to me! He sent them to an English magazine, and they took one." I shook him by the shoulder. "Be happy for me."

"Which magazine?" He needed to sniff around it, see if it met with his approval.

"*Clarion.*"

He shrugged. "Never heard of it."

"It's out of Cambridge. Emory showed me a copy. It's very good."

"Sounds like a schoolboy rag."

He was trying to take the wind out of my sails, so I could be as sour as him. "Schoolboys grow up," I snapped. "If you weren't so pigheaded you'd see that you might get a translation yourself. We could send it through Wells."

"Clyde Emory's not going to do anything for me." Anton scowled. "Are you really that dense? He's not in love with *me*. He doesn't want to get in *my* pants. Or Arseny's, or Oksana's."

"Well, thank you for that," I said. Of course it was why he was doing it, but not the only reason. "If something's not your idea, it can't possibly be any good." Just when I'd thought he was my friend, my best friend. "Damn you. Just—leave me alone."

Tereshenko was still hovering, so I took him by the arm and pulled him away with me, leaving Anton to stew in his bitterness and envy. The boxer and I sat on the stairs of the Monkey Hall and drank sweet plum wine from a flask—he'd bought it from some old woman on Sadovaya Street. We got drunk immediately. He was rougher than he needed to be, grabbing me, our teeth clinking together. I couldn't stop thinking how different he was from Pasha. Ironic, that he was the poet and Pasha the sailor. I had considered taking him back to my room for a moment, but I really didn't want Tereshenko, I only wanted Anton to stop being such a shithead. The burly poet was angry when I sent him away, but I owed him nothing. I was going to be published in *Clarion* and I didn't give a damn what anybody thought.

48 *Moscow*

The winter twilight already fading at four o'clock, my breath billowing in great white clouds, I hurried along past desolate New Holland, rushing to make my class on the Admiralty docks. I couldn't wait to see Pasha, tell him about *Clarion*. I ducked into the warmth of the sailors' clubhouse, the welcome light. The men were already waiting in the second-floor classroom, but where was the compact, sinewy form that always sat four seats down on the left? Others were missing as well, but I saw only that one vanished form.

"They got summoned back yesterday," said Barsky, Pasha's friend. *"Return to base."* He shrugged and passed me a note. "It was bound to happen."

The handwriting was simple, regular and childlike.

> *Sorry, sweet Marina,*
> *Duty is ringing her bell*
> *and back I go.*
> *I belong to the People*
> *And can't say where or when*
> *the bell will sound*
> *but when it rings*
> *We go. And so — Pashol.*
>
> *Yours, P.*

I didn't remember getting through the class, what I taught, what they wrote. That week was a blur. I taught at Skorokhod and Vikzhel, stood in queues, ate my scholar's ration of bread which was by now mostly sawdust, studded with little rocks. I sat before the frost-fingered window that looked out onto Bolshaya Morskaya. No more would Pasha escort me home, or surprise me by waiting in the House canteen playing cards with Kuzmin — who naturally adored him, having a penchant for sailors. No more would I lie in his embrace, as alive as waves. But he'd healed something inside me — not quite my heart, but that life that had been swirling down the drain. He'd managed to plug the leak. I should be grateful instead of resentful and bereft.

Tonight, the electricity was off again, I wrote by kerosene lamplight. Outside, snow sifted past the lighted gape of the window across the street, where someone else was squandering their lamp oil. I'd had a dream. A man was pouring blackbirds into an intricate chain-driven machine with swinging compartments like the cars of a Ferris wheel, climbing and falling. Men came carrying bushel baskets of blackbirds, and the worker fed them into the hoppers. *Don't!* I begged the feeder, an ordinary worker, potato-nosed in a corduroy cap. All these blackbirds, killing them for what? He wouldn't listen. He fed the blackbirds in, and the machine froze them, one to a compartment. All those blackbirds, each in its block of pink ice. Then someone came and took the blocks to the shore, where the sun melted them. And to my amazement, the birds thawed and came back to life, walking around on the grass with their black bead eyes.

> *They feed the machine on—blackbirds*
> *Bushels of glossy breasts,*
> *Handfuls, baskets*
> *That terrible fodder.*

> *Poor birds.*

> *The poem's a machine*
> *for the processing of*
> *—blackbirds.*

> *Freezing us solid.*

> *Later*
> *Frozen chunks of us*
> *Thaw in the sun*

> *We walk around alive*
> *Squawking*
> *good as new.*

That *good as new* was off. Tsvetaeva wouldn't be caught dead in the same room with it. But how to capture the horror, then the surprise of the resurrection. And who was the workman feeding the machine? The Muse? God? I could see his baggy corduroys, his bulbish nose, his cap. *He* was more accurate than *they,* but that might bring the figure into too much prominence. You might begin to think more of *him* than of the terrible feeding. And I hated *good as new,* but what to replace it with…

A rap on the door interrupted my struggle.

Tereshenko. He'd begun to drop by late at night. News must have gotten around that Pasha was out of the picture. I waited for him to go away—what a pest. But he kept on knocking. The venerable Shafranskaya was deaf enough, but Petrovsky on the other side was ill. Irritated, I threw down my pen and unlocked the door, a voyage of a single step.

To my surprise, waiting in the doorway wasn't the pugnacious Tereshenko but Anton Chernikov in all his tall and awkward angularity, unshaven and haggard, his overcoat draped around his shoulders like Oscar Wilde. What was he doing down here visiting such a mediocrity whose poems were going to be published in a schoolboy rag? "Stove still not working?"

He stared at me as if it was I who had interrupted him. What did he want now? Though I was still irritated, I stepped aside and let him in. He'd never been down here in the Monkey House before. He gazed at Sasha's sketches pinned to the walls, my boots by my sagging bed, the desk cluttered with papers. The lamp, the window, the small pile of damp firewood on the grimy parquet. What was he looking for, Apollinaire?

He picked up my poem, began to read it. "Garbage," he pronounced. He sat in my desk chair and bent over the page, pulling a pencil from his pocket, and began circling and crossing out, adding words. "I can't believe they're publishing you. They must have assumed something was lost in translation. At least use *hard* instead of *solid,*" he said. "The abstraction undercuts." His brow knotted as if ropes were being tied, painfully, behind his forehead. "And cut some of these blackbirds. *Poor birds*—Christ, you want to write for the women's section of *Pravda? Frozen chunks thaw* is all you need."

What on earth was he so agitated about? "Is this what you came to tell me?"

He kept reading, flicking the pencil against his teeth. "*Squawking good as new?* Unbelievable." He circled *good as new*. He could always see what wasn't working, but I wasn't ready for him to critique my newborn.

"Why are you trying to strangle my poem?" I tried to take it from him but he pushed my hand away.

"Because it's crap. Who is this *they* anyway?"

"It's a first draft. I was just trying to get at the feeling—"

He threw the notebook on the floor. "Get the language, get it on the page. Who cares about *feelings?* Do something interesting with the line."

I snatched up my notebook and pressed it to my chest. I had not been prepared for an assault. Now I wished it had been Tereshenko. "Why are you being such a *govnyuk?*" *Shithead.* "Is this what you came to talk about, my poem?"

He looked around at everything but me, as if indeed he'd forgotten what he'd come for. With a shuddering sigh, like a man throwing himself into a well, he said to the calendar, "I thought you might like to know. I'm moving to Moscow."

That stopped me cold. Had he lost his mind? Anton hated Moscow. He hated everything about it, its antiquity, its forty times forty churches, its *housewifery*. He examined the dusty plasterwork on the ceiling. "I've applied for my travel *propusk*. Glavlit can damn well pay for the ticket." The administration for literary affairs. "Petrograd's over. It's done for. You can't take a breath for all the old farts here—Gumilev and so on. It's getting to be that I don't dare light a match, the place might explode for all the loose gas." He took out his *makhorka*, and a piece of what looked like a letter, and began to roll himself a cigarette, messily, spilling tobacco.

"What are you talking about? Are you crazy?" I said.

He tore the paper trying to roll it, tried again, snorting with frustration, his hands shaking. I could feel the scent of electrical smoke, like a burning cord, coming off him as he struggled. I would have helped him but was afraid he might strike me.

"This place is dying—don't you feel it? We're clinging to the shreds of our culture. In Moscow, things are coming to life again. There are poets' cafés, a real scene."

What did Anton care about cafés and scenes? "What about the Squared Circle? What about your studio?" Was this about my being published in *Clarion*? Was he that envious?

"I'm sick of it all. We're just parading around to ourselves here, telling ourselves that we matter. But we don't. We're dead. This whole place is one walking mausoleum." He couldn't get that cigarette rolled, just kept crushing half-made ones and scattering tobacco everywhere.

It was insane. He loved it here at the House of Arts, as much as Anton was capable of happiness. He had his own literary studio. His hero, Shklovsky, lived right down the hall—he saw him five times a day! There were twenty people he could talk to about the things that mattered to him. Was this Genya's doing, denigrating Petrograd? Mayakovsky's? Anton was pale and sweating. Maybe he had a fever. Typhus. I'd never seen him in such a state. He was the one who looked down on the rest of us for our dramas and passions.

Finally, he got that cigarette rolled, put it in his mouth, and turned to me. His mouth twitched, his hazel eyes were full of tears. He tried to light his hard-won cigarette, but he broke the match, then a second.

I took the box from him and lit it for him. "What is it, Anton? Is it Genya? The studio? Is someone pressuring you?"

He turned away, filling the room with smoke. He laughed, wild, almost a sob. "You really don't know."

"How could I?" I made the mistake of putting my hand on his shoulder.

"Don't touch me!" he roared. I moved away as if from a hot stove. Then he groaned, leaning with both elbows on the desk, grabbing his dark messy hair, rocking back and forth like a religious hysteric.

I sat on the bed behind him. Something terrible was happening, and I wanted to soothe him like a child, but he seemed so beside himself I was afraid to try. "Anton, just tell me. Give me a hint."

He shook his head. "I have to get out of here. Tomorrow. I'm going to Moscow. Or Vladivostok—or Peru! I don't give a damn! I'm going to ship out on the first rotten scow that'll take me."

Anton Chernikov, man of the sea. If he was in any other mood I might have teased him about it. But this was no time for a joke.

He bent over, gasping, choking. "Don't you see? You've ruined my life." He smacked his forehead on the table, was about to do it again, but I put my hand over his forehead. He struggled, shaking me free of him. "Ruined it! I can't stand it anymore!" His tear-stained face was unrecognizable. "First it's the sailor—all right, I understand. I'm sure he's very good at knots. But *Tereshenko*? His knuckles drag on the ground! How could you? You whore! You look right through me. Just like that. Like I'm a hat rack. I am not a hat rack! I AM NOT A HAT RACK!" he roared, his eyes so full of suffering I could barely look at him. "Am I just a place to hang your coat? A useful bit of furniture?"

His explosion was so unexpected, words abandoned me. His eyes were bloodshot and ringed with shadow. I thought of the months I'd slept in his room, and he never once tried to touch me, kiss me, watch me undress, nothing. I thought back to the night I came to hear Bely. *Our own little Helen.* Oh no. Exactly as if he were a hat rack.

My one friend in the world, my comrade, my editor. How awful. What a disaster. I could hear Petrovsky coughing through the wall. Love was a cosmic eagle, raking us with talons and beak as we lay helpless in our chains.

He started laughing, the most painful laughter, as if it was tearing his throat. "No. The idea is abominable to you. Repellent. Look at you! You can't help me. Nobody can help me. I'm a joke, a clown!"

Petrovsky banged on the wall with his cane.

I knelt next to my suffering friend. "No, you're not a joke. Look at my face. Am I laughing?"

He wept, tears streaming down his lean stubbled cheeks. "You don't think of me as a man. I'm just the fellow who reads your poems. Just answer me one thing, though. Why Tereshenko? For God's sake, why him and not me?"

I couldn't stand it anymore. I drew him to me and held him, his head against my shoulder. He didn't fight me. I rocked him like a child as he sobbed. *Why him and not me?*—a question man has asked since love began. "I never slept with Tereshenko. Is that what you want to know?" Anton was a difficult man, cutting and angular, ironic, biting, desperate. But he wasn't a hat rack. "I do what I want. But I'm not a whore."

"I'm sorry...I didn't mean it." Rubbing his face into my coat, drying his tears. "I was never going to say anything, I swear. I just can't stand it anymore. It was one thing when you were with Genya, or when it was just you. But—Tereshenko is telling people you're his girl. It's too much."

I sat back. We were knee to knee. I cupped his cheek in my palm, and kissed his wet eyes, wiped his tears with my thumb. Those hazel eyes, the rumpled black hair, the sharp nose red from weeping, the petulant mouth, the argumentative chin. All those contradictions. "You want me so badly? Just as I am?"

He nodded, the downward U of his mouth quivering.

"There will always be other men."

"I don't care."

Maybe this was what I really feared, being loved so completely by someone I cared for, someone made vulnerable by his love. Genya had the party, he had his ideals, he was handsome and well liked. He had somewhere to go with his pain. If I'd been made of sterner stuff, I would let Anton go to Moscow and be rid of me. Or have him right now, cruelly, hot enough to burn, as Arkady had once burned my hand on the stove. But I did love him in my way. And cared how he felt, and what happened to him. I would be bereft if he left for Moscow or Peru. His presence was like the good steady bass of an orchestra, or maybe the bassoons—the music of my life would sound paltry and thin without him. That too was love. Perhaps a greater love than passion.

I kept thinking of the blocks of ice where the blackbirds froze, and how they somehow came out alive. "I'm willing to try," I said.

"Maybe you'll fall in love with me," he whispered, his face pressed to mine. "Stranger things have happened."

He wasn't much of a lover. He came very quickly. I supposed he'd spent too much time with prostitutes to even notice my lack of satisfaction. There was a lot I would have to teach him if we were to go on. "I never thought this would happen," he told me afterward, stroking my hair. "Really, I just came to say goodbye."

What an odd creature to have come for shelter in my arms. I'd known him so long—I'd seen his displays of peevishness, rage, his sulks, the moments of high wit and even thoughtfulness, but never had I seen him in such a naked state of desire. It made other things so clear. How he'd argued with Genya the night he threw my mother and me out into the storm. The way we'd been before Genya returned. Why he'd been so uneasy with me at the Poverty Artel whenever we were alone—he was at his best with a third person in the room. I recalled his outrage when I returned from the yellow mansion to the Poverty Artel—*the more you hurt us, the sweeter we sing*. Us. I should have heard him better.

"Remember when I first came to the flat?" I said. "I thought you hated me. You couldn't have been nastier."

His pale face, his burning eyes. "You were like a sunset. Everything suddenly looked shabby by comparison, and I saw my life as it was, moldy as an unaired closet." He touched my face tentatively, tracing my profile with the tip of a finger—forehead, nose, lip, lower lip, chin, the length of my throat. "The room was too small with you in it, I had to go out in the hall. I had to go somewhere to get away from your happiness." He lay gazing at me as if I were an unfamiliar poem, his head propped on his hand. "Of course I was nasty. Who wouldn't be?"

Perhaps we would save each other, Anton and I. Stranger things had happened.

49 *Masquerade*

Despite the absence of firewood, the breath-pluming cold, the thin-ness of our rations, the desperate state of our clothes and our shoes—or perhaps because of it—the House of Arts came alive that winter with lectures, talks, demonstrations, exhibitions, theatri-cals, concerts, something happening every night, and if not with us, then at the House of Scholars, or the Poets' Guild, or the IZO, the Department of Visual Arts. In the midst of this excitement, Mayakovsky arrived from Moscow.

"It's because Chukovsky told him you had a billiard table," said Oksana during our literary circle.

"What do you have against billiards?" Anton said.

The poet, staying in the House library, took pleasure in being dif-ficult, jabbing the members for their politics, joking that in Moscow we were known as the House of Slime. He saw us as a nest of bourgeois aesthetes and backsliders, accused us of not having fully embraced the revolution. Yet he couldn't completely dismiss us either, not with Shklovsky living here, and Anton Chernikov, as futurist as anyone in Moscow. Yet I saw too that Mayakovsky still wanted the approval of his peers here, while at the same time be-littling them. A more complex man than he appeared. Anton spent much time with him, and therefore, so did I.

We gathered one December afternoon in the library of the House, surrounded by those red-painted bookcases dotted sparsely with books, to hear him read from his new long *poema, 150 Million*. He seemed nervous, loud and aggressive, glancing over at his girl-friend, the elegant Lilya Brik, for reassurance or disapproval, it was hard to tell which.

I couldn't help but examine her, the famous muse. The night I'd heard him read "A Cloud in Trousers" at the Stray Dog Café, I had wondered what kind of woman would be capable of withstanding such a volcano. Brik was rather cool, very modern looking, with red hair and dark, savage eyes. She and Mayakovsky and her husband, Osip Brik, the critic, all lived together à trois, and had for years. As I watched her, listening, I wondered if we too would be remembered for our romantic geometry. Genya and Anton and me. Was this where we would be in ten years, in the hall of mirrors called love? Still be in the same room, stepping on each other's shoes? Or would there be a fourth and a fifth in the crystal formation of love, sex, politics, boredom, and other unnamable ties? This red room, the glass bookcase, Anton by my side, the afternoon light the only warmth. We junior members arranged ourselves against the walls, Anton on my left, the hyperkinetic Arseny Grodetsky on my right, bouncing on his toes with the excitement of standing in the presence of the glowering genius.

The *poema* began leadenly. It was Mayakovsky's most thunderous mode, heroic without a scrap of levity. Most absurdly, it claimed to be anonymous. Though who else would write:

> *150,000,000 is the name of this poem's creator.*
> *Its rhythm — a bullet.*
> *Its rhymes — a spreading fire.*
>
> ...
>
> *Who can name the earth's brilliant designer?*
> *And so*
> *it is*
> *with my*
> *poem —*
> *work of no single writer.*

As if that voice could belong to anyone else. The first selection was sheer bombast, but the mood lightened in the second. Mayakovsky in the end could not resist his own laughter, couldn't help it even in propaganda. His urge to tip over into comedic hyperbole was deeply a part of him. Here he'd portrayed a mythic battle between an electrified Woodrow Wilson as a top-hatted giant of Chicago, and the colossal, Neva-armed peasant Ivan with his 150,000,000 heads wading across the Atlantic to meet him—the folk gigantism was irresistible. Well, it was never the job of propaganda to tell the truth, to discern and make exceptions. Propaganda was a peasant *lubok* print—its outlines bold, its colors crude, and cheap to make.

But I found myself missing the other Mayakovsky, the cloud in trousers. I knew he was there somewhere. I could only hope that other poet would reassert himself someday. The civil war was over—the forces of Denikin had finally evacuated from the Crimea, Wrangel defeated. This kind of broad caricature would soon be a museum piece.

I wondered mostly at the relationship between Mayakovsky and Lilya Brik. I saw him watching her as she flirted with the Petrograd poets, and her watching him watching her. *You torment us, so we sing all the sweeter.*

The next night the tables were turned, and we read for Vladimir Vladimirovich. Ballads were the order of the day. Gumilev read "The Lost Tram," which I thought was the best thing he'd ever written. Zamyatin and his group read short prose pieces. But most of the elders—Khodasevich and Blok and Kuzmin—declined to read, so it was up to us, the younger members of the House, to shine. Anton recited one of his own and one from Genya's new collection. I'd been tempted to do "Alice in the Year One"—as defiant as any Mayakovsky poem—but instead, I did "The Trees at Kambarka."

Mayakovsky sat with his arm draped around Lilya Brik's chair, his face heavy as always with the potential for storms, like a line of thunderheads. I couldn't tell if he understood it was a message for him. That our lives weren't lived on the plane of *150 Million*. A reminder to remember the human scale.

Anton came to me in the crush afterward. "He wants to meet you." A little nervous, but also proud, he led me over to Mayakovsky, who was drinking tea with Shklovsky and Kuzmin, Lilya and, yes, her husband, Osip. Anton introduced me as one of the Squared Circle, and I noticed that he didn't mention my connection with Genya, whom Mayakovsky knew in Moscow. We had our own relationship now.

Mayakovsky took my hand in his enormous paw and gazed at me with depth and understanding. Then I knew he still had his man's heart in there among the 150 million heads and Neva-long arms. His soulfulness, alas, was something my new lover could never know. Anton stood with us, stiff and aggressive as a tall, skinny cock, pleased that Mayakovsky had recognized one of his protégés, but not much liking the way the poet was still holding my hand. It was Lilya Brik who waltzed him away from me, flashing a smile— *You still have much to learn about men, little fox.* I would never know as much as that woman, not if I lived seven lifetimes.

I wrote a poem for Mayakovsky that night, just for him, and managed to slip it into his pocket before he left for Moscow.

The Buried Miner

To VM

The mine collapsed.
    The great timbers could no longer hold
        against the weight of the whole earth
Crushing the hundreds who dug there
    In the soft seam of Donbass coal.

And yet by a miracle
    one miner still lives.
        Down the black miles
            his leg caught in the rock
            he lives
                and lives.
Is it a miracle?
    Or hell?

The lone miner sings

to keep himself company.
He recites a prayer he once knew,
but doesn't believe.
Then remembers an old poem
from schooldays.
He whispers it over and over.
Sometimes a man must be alone.
Sometimes no comrades soften his days.
Sometimes there is only despair.
I have been that lone miner.

Love is not enough.
When the weight of the earth falls,
there is only you, and a poem.
And sometimes, only the poem.

Gorky had missed Mayakovsky's visit. I wondered if it had been intentional, to avoid any more embarrassing brawls like the one during Wells's stay. Universal Literature was his main concern. But he appeared one evening at the House of Arts before a lecture by Zamyatin, to give us all a report on developments in Moscow. From the gossip, we knew that Narkompros—the Commissariat of Enlightenment—was being reorganized, and why, and by whom. It wasn't good news.

Gorky spoke about his ongoing battle to defend his institutions—Universal Literature, the House of Arts, and the House of Scholars—against the "elements of the Left" who wanted to take over the future of Russian literature. He looked terrible, smoking and coughing and drumming the lectern with his restless fingers, stroking his drooping moustache.

"Russian literature has always been judged by its politics," he said to the crowd. "It's the reason we've endured such terrible work and are enduring it now. Literature should be judged only by literary standards." A spontaneous round of applause. This was also a criticism of Mayakovsky. "Insistence on political conformity will be a disaster for literature and for the development of the Russian proletariat as well. These days, we hear that a writer must be a Communist, first and foremost. If he is, then he must be good. If not, he must be bad. That's no standard for literature. Why must it be that only the panderers, the Smerdyakovs, are being encouraged today?"

It was dangerous stuff, to attack the programmatic Left, the Proletcult faction—the organization calling for proletarian art, created by proletarians to the exclusion of all else—in a public venue. But I still remembered what Alexei Maximovich had told me when my father was in the Peter and Paul Fortress. All you could do when you were in a trap was continue on as honestly as you could and let the blow fall if it would. Moura shifted nervously beside me. Gumilev sat with his legs crossed elegantly, nodding, whispering to the pretty student next to him. I wondered if there was anyone here from *Krasnaya Gazeta,* taking this down. Or perhaps one of Zinoviev's spies. The blockade had at last been lifted, but now it was the House of Arts under siege, we could feel it. Every mention of us in the popular press included slurs like *snobbism* and *elitist*—pointedly ignoring all we were doing for the city, the public events we offered, the classes we taught, the open evenings like this.

Everything that kept a roof over our heads was in danger. I approached Moura afterward. "How did Moscow go?"

"Lenin's begging him to leave," she said, "for his health's sake. But there's more than one kind of health, as you well know." *Think of your father,* she didn't have to say. Lenin wanted to protect Gorky from political typhus. Yes, I well knew the consequences of having the revolution turn on you. But Gorky, leaving? Everything he had achieved would crumble without him. He was the only one who had Lenin's ear.

"Will he go?" I watched him talking to Zamyatin and Chukovsky. He looked grim. My skin prickled, my throat felt as if someone had gripped it in one hand. How fast would the Bolsheviks close us down and throw the writers into the street? My last home in the world. "He's not considering it, is he?"

Just knowing Gorky was in the world was an anchor I could not imagine living without.

"I don't know. His health really is awful. Look at him."

He leaned against the wall, sweating, his breathing labored.

"You haven't met my friend Anton." I waved him over, but he clung to the far wall like a barnacle. His pride was so convoluted, he would not even deign to meet Gorky, who had saved my life, my soul, put a roof over all our heads. He considered it kowtowing. Love had done nothing to disentangle his twisted heart. He was just Anton with a wound, it hurt him no matter what I did.

In January our rations were cut again. The writers went out all day, scrambling for food. I stood in line at the Petro-Soviet with Korney Chukovsky to try to get a saw to cut firewood for the House. The city was allowing the destruction of another fifty houses for wood. Soon Petrograd would be nothing but rubble. "I've heard the House of Scholars has gloves. Do you think I have any chance of getting over there before they're gone?" he asked me. "My wife's gloves are in tatters." His own were out at the thumb.

Thus was literature produced in the winter of 1921.

The elders—Kuzmin and Blok, Gants and Shklovsky, Gorky, Gumilev and Zamyatin, Chukovsky and so on—met again and again, trying to find a solution to the ongoing political threat to the House. You could feel the tension in the hallways. I kept my head down, taught my classes, collected my mouse-sized rations at the House of Scholars and tried to bring the *The Valley of the Moon* to a close. If the House of Arts died, where would I go? How would I live?

Yet despite the grim conditions—cold and malnutrition, worse among the old people, who were dying before our eyes—there was also great camaraderie, a defiant gaiety that winter. Masked balls were the craze—most of the arts organizations threw one, giving us a moment to step outside fear and shabbiness to ascend into an imaginary world of our own delight. It reminded me of the Ionians and the Great Feast of the Golden Egg.

What would we wear? dominated conversations the week beforehand—a shallow concern, but better than worrying about the fate of the House. I took Anton to Gorky's to select costumes from Maria Andreeva's extensive theatrical wardrobe. Moura and Valentina Khodasevich were there, and Anton grudgingly allowed himself to be introduced. Moura's eyes flashed in amusement. *So this is your new lover? Is he always like this?* I nodded. She didn't even understand—this was him on good behavior.

We thumbed through the rack of wizards and princesses, clowns and devils, and I assembled an outfit from a *kokoshnik* crown with blond braids attached, a gypsy skirt and jacket with bells, a pair of red ballet slippers that nearly fit. After much cajoling by Valentina and me, Anton eventually accepted a false beard with a curled moustache, a crown of thorns, an eye patch, and a long Spanish cape. "I'm Western literature," he said. "A half-blind courtier with a Christ complex, wrapped in darkness."

The House of Arts ball, though sparse in food and heat, was a success in every way. It was a less formal affair than some, as it was sponsored by the younger members—our leaders had weightier problems on their minds. It wasn't as elegant as the one at the Zubov Institute, but we had the old Eliseev lackeys in their wigs and white gloves to hand out the pastries and sausage rolls, the saccharine tea. We opened the ballroom, and poets from all over the city came, young people and artists in their constructivist costumes. Sasha painted all our faces cubo-futuristically. I had a large letter *M* over one eye, and Anton a red square set at an angle under his eye patch.

The men outnumbered the women, and I had no shortage of partners for dancing. I danced with everyone but Anton, who held up the wall, scowling, as if it were all beneath him. I danced with translators and poets, scholars and painters, studio students, the old and the young, even Bely, dressed as a holy fool in rags. He was a very jazzy foxtrotter. Who would have guessed? *It's Him!* I kept thinking, making myself laugh, and ignored Anton's glare whenever I happened to look in his direction. What did he think, I'd hold up the wall with him all night?

I found myself having a glass of tea with Bely—Bely! Telling him of Ukashin and Ionia. I was giddy enough to make light of it, and I knew he would be interested—when a tall Harlequin joined us, embracing the fool. It was Blok. As Harlequin! What could be more appropriate? Bely turned to introduce me, but he had forgotten my name. "Have you met our...Columbine?"

If Bely had forgotten my name, Blok had not. "So good to see you again, Marina Dmitrievna." He shook my hand as the band struck up a waltz. "Would you care to dance?" I turned to Bely but he gestured, *Go on.* I may have been mistaken, but I thought I saw a smile exchanged between the old friends. As Bely had once courted Blok's wife... We moved onto the dance floor as if heralded by trumpets, my hand on his forearm—both of us the product of childhood dancing lessons. *I'm from Petersburg...*

If I ever had grandchildren, I would tell them that on the evening of January 23, 1921, I danced with both Andrei Bely and Alexander Blok. *Yes, me. Your old babushka, milaya...*

It was exquisite to move in his arms. His touch was light, and he possessed a perfect sense of rhythm and motion—just as you would expect from his poetry. He towered over me, yet unlike many tall men, he knew exactly where all his limbs were at any moment. The absurd complement of musicians—oboe, guitar, piano, and accordion—somehow pulled together in unexpected harmony. Everything around Blok was like that. "I've heard excellent reports about your factory class," he said, swirling me around, as natural as breathing. "They say your students love you. What is it that you do with them?"

I felt drunk, though I had imbibed nothing stronger than roasted oat tea. Blok had heard about me! I knew that Blok didn't believe poetry could be taught, so his curiosity was thrilling. "I try to imagine what it would be like to be a gluer," I said, flying in his arms. "Doing the same thing all day. I ask myself, what would I look forward to at the end of my shift? I'd want to enjoy myself, surprise myself. Use my mind instead of just my hands." I thought of Dinamo, of his longing to be more than the flesh.

"But is it poetry?"

"Mostly not." I thought of my women, their leathery stained hands, their toothaches, their worries. Not waltzing with Blok tonight. "One of the Skorokhod women is fairly talented. But that's not the point. It's something that doesn't require ration cards, a *propusk*. It makes them value themselves more."

How bewildered he looked. For him, for us, poetry was vital, its seriousness absolute. The idea of poetry for the untalented simply for the pleasure of making it was nothing short of blasphemy. Like a musician watching you use a flute to pound a nail. Then, a tiny smile formed on his wide mouth. "You must be a remarkable teacher. Look, even I understand you. Maybe I'll take your class."

It was ludicrous, and lovely. "It's Tuesday afternoons. The committee room at Skorokhod. On the Obvodny Canal."

He laughed. "You just might see me there."

Magical Blok. How lucky I was to have crossed his path on the street near the telephone exchange. He'd given me my life back—no, not my life. A new life. He bowed when we were done, the reflex of a lifetime's habit. I imagined the scent of his genius clung to my hands as he returned me to Anton. A smell of raw silk and geraniums.

I was in the clouds, standing with bearded Anton and round-faced Nikolai Chukovsky, the translator's son, bravely dressed in lederhosen in the unheated ballroom, and Valentina Khodasevich as a playing-card queen, as they discussed the season's offerings, Anton's ideas for the Squared Circle, when we were joined by a slight, intense man of about thirty, dark haired, with a high forehead and deep, clever dark eyes. It was the poet Osip Mandelstam. He'd just moved to the House of Arts. And the weather changed in our little group, a slight realignment of atoms, like air before a lightning storm. How strange it must be to have people know so much about you, while you know nothing of them. To have this effect on people everywhere you go. Of course I'd read his collection, *Stone*. I was dying to talk to him about it. I also knew he'd been Tsvetaeva's lover before the revolution, and tried not to scrutinize him. He wore an open shirt and a jabot made of a napkin under a burgundy bathrobe that looked like he'd borrowed it from Gumilev—who else at the House of Arts would own such a thing? "And who are you supposed to be?" I asked. Flirting—yes, I was.

"I was trying for Schiller," he said, striking a pose. He recited, *"Lebe mit deinem Jahrhundert..."* The German sounded like music from his lips. I could see Anton roll his one visible eye.

"Live with your century," I said, *"but don't be its...*something..." German was my worst language, but I remembered this much from German class.

"Live with your century, but don't be its creature," he said. *"Give your contemporaries what they need, not what they praise."* And he was taking Schiller's advice to heart, this little man with his curling hair and elfin ears and receding hairline, who looked nothing like Schiller and yet was his very incarnation. Mandelstam, who had written, *Brothers, let us celebrate liberty's twilight, / The great and gloomy year...*

"Dance?" he asked, offering me his hand. I would not look at Anton as I let him lead me away but caught a glimpse of my self-mortifying lover burning holes in the back of Mandelstam's precious head. This was the man about whom Tsvetaeva had said, *Where does this tenderness come from? / And what shall I do with it, young / sly singer, just passing by? / Your lashes are—longer than anyone's.*

And they were.

We stepped out into a polka, a brisk gallop. "I've seen you before," I said over the music. "But you wouldn't remember."

"I remember everything," he said. His eyes were as bright as a blackbird's.

"It was in 1915, at the Stray Dog Café. You were with Akhmatova and Kuzmin."

He laughed, scrutinized me again. Such a merry soul, a surprise after reading his poetry. He was shorter than I but sure of himself, not in an arrogant way but simply knowing what he knew, knowing his value. I liked the way he led me, securely, his steps as nimble as his mind. "And where were you, in your pram?"

"With my brother and my girlfriends...We hid behind the coats. I was trying to get a look at Akhmatova."

"The cult of Anna the Great." He took me galloping, my cottony braids whirling about my shoulders. "Come to think of it, I do remember something like that. Schoolgirls. But I don't remember the plaits." He nodded toward the yellow yarn skeins attached to my crown.

"You don't remember any such thing." Flirting with him quite baldly. As we whirled, I could feel Anton's one-eyed glare, accusing me, tugging at me. God, what did he want me to do, join a nunnery? I had told him who I was. This was my life, and I would do as I pleased. Pushkin said that a poet's freedom was accountable to no man.

"I remember you quite well. Big dark eyes under a fringe of chestnut red. Like the future, peering out from the coats of the past. You had a tall friend, a brunette, and a plump blonde. And a beautiful boy who spent the whole time drawing."

"My brother Seryozha."

Mandelstam smiled, triumphant. "And a very young Gennady Kuriakin, dying for a chance to impress us."

I was a little afraid of him. He wasn't just brilliant, he was uncanny. "Do you know him?" I asked warily.

"We've met a few times. The golden mouthpiece of the Left. I believe he's nipping at Mayakovsky's heels. He should be careful. He's a decent poet, but someone should tell him, once you've sold your soul to the devil, he never lets you have it back."

The maniacal orchestra sped up by degrees, the wheezing accordion, the sinister oboe. "By the way, I appreciated your poem, 'The Trees at Kambarka.' Always a relief to hear a single voice and not a hundred and fifty million. I don't even want to hear fifty, speaking quietly." He danced me past Anton, an unkind thing to do, before he swept me away again. "So you're with Chernikov. How did that happen?" The glance he gave me was a mixture of amusement and puzzlement. "He's staring at us right now. Hoping I'll trip over my own feet."

"We lived together for a while in 1917. The Transrational Interlocutors of the Terrestrial Now. Genya Kuriakin, and Anton and me. Zina Ostrovskaya, Gigo Gelashvili, some others." Should I tell him about my husband? Some mischief was afoot tonight. I bit my tongue.

"Sounds like fun," he said. "Look, there's Gumilev." He turned me so I could see. "Some people don't even try to live in this century."

It beat all the rest. Gumilev made his grand entrance in a tuxedo he'd somehow managed to preserve, and snow-white linen, as if it were 1910. I could only imagine the hours of labor it must have taken him to wash and iron that shirt, clean and mend and press the formal suit. And on his arm came one of his students in a bare-shouldered gown of blue satin that someone must have lent her. Given that the only heat in the ballroom was in our minds, it was a triumph of will.

The polka ended, the orchestra took a break. Mandelstam kissed my hand—not at all properly, on the knuckles. And left me to join some friends. "Don't leave without me," he said over his shoulder. "And don't hide behind the coats."

I chatted with Sasha and Dunya, dressed in elaborate papier-mâché masks, he a cubo-futurist Janus, she the moon in its phases. We were joined by others from the Squared Circle—Oksana and Petya, Nikita and Arseny. I didn't listen very hard, my heart still romping from my dance with Osip Emilevich. Anton joined us a few minutes later, scowling, refusing to look at me. He was mounting a boycott, smoking fiendishly, and I could smell the scorched hair of his fake moustache. "I hate these things," he snarled. "Yackety yack. As if music drained the human mind of the least function." He drank off his tea in a gulp. "What's the point of dancing, I ask you? This strange pointless movement, using up valuable calories and turning sensible people into idiots. I wonder how it came into being. Maybe someone stepped on a coal."

When the musicians returned from their break, they struck up a tango. It cut me. The tango was Kolya, the music of that first night, St. Basil's Eve...and the song of that lost afternoon on the Catherine Canal. The olive and gold apartment, my hairpins falling, snowflakes twirling above the ice on the canal like little fish in a reef. I didn't want to dance it with anyone else. I wandered away to stand by myself at a frozen window, where I scratched a circle with my thumbnail. The music went on and on. God, would they never stop? *Kolya, where are you?* Loving somebody else. Making love. Oh, this was crazy—hadn't I just danced with Osip Mandelstam? And Blok and Bely? Would he always be there, the music in the very back of my mind? "Mi Noche Triste"?

Mandelstam found me there, my forehead to the glass. He'd brought me some tea, and I shoved Kolya back into the box where he lived, down deep in the waters of my silent self, and turned to the pleasure of the moment, talking to the poet with the long eyelashes. We spoke about Akhmatova, who he said was writing again, and Tsvetaeva...I had to ask very gingerly, I didn't know him well, didn't know how he would react if I mentioned her, I only knew the poems in which they'd said their farewells. "Do you see her anymore?"

"No," he said. "Not for a long time." He dusted something off my face, showed it to me. An eyelash on the tip of his finger. I made a wish, the one I always made—inspiration. And blew it away.

We talked about Clyde Emory, about whom Osip was in agreement with Anton—*that mediocrity*—talked about the poet H.D., and her Greek verses so much like ones Osip Emilevich would write if he were a woman. We both liked her. And this new writer Eliot whose book Emory had sent along with the dozen tins of sardines in oil and ten of sweetened condensed milk that I'd finally collected from Moura. I'd stuffed myself on them both.

Mandelstam was dying to see the Eliot, and I was dying to see more of Mandelstam. So we slipped away from the party together.

Did I think of Anton? Yes, I did, but Mandelstam stirred me in a way not even Pasha had. He made me feel alive, not just as a woman but as a poet. Someone like him could see you entire. I felt exciting and smart and real. His bright eyes, his lashes *longer than anyone's*. I was dying to ask more about that other Marina. *What was it like to enter a relationship with someone so incandescent? Why did you abandon her after such an affair?*

"She feeds you to her fire," he said. "She prefers to burn on the page. I didn't wait until she'd eaten me."

We sat on my sagging bed and I showed him *Prufrock and Other Observations* by T. S. Eliot. He kicked off his shoes and lay down, his hands folded on his chest under the ruffled jabot. "Read it to me," he said, and closed his eyes. I began to read the first poem to him, "The Love Song of J. Alfred Prufrock," doing my best with the Italian epigraph, which, to my astonishment, Osip Emilevich recited without even looking. "It's Dante. The *Comedy*. Don't be so impressed, or we won't be able to be friends."

I read the poem through, slowly, finding the cadence of the English, and Mandelstam listened with his eyelids fluttering, his long lashes against his cheeks. When I got to the end—*wake us, and we drown*—I let the sound drift and fade. "Read it again," he said.

Some of the stanzas he now recited along with me. His English pronunciation better than mine. He was already memorizing it.

I read it two more times, until it had settled into our bones. Then I wanted to make love. "Let us go, then, you and I," I said, removing my crown and braids.

Osip Emilevich had had innumerable women, and I was sure every one of them found him as delightful as I. He was playful and passionate, understood the music of love. I hadn't had a lover like that since Kolya. And I had the strangest sensation I was also Tsvetaeva, as if I kissed him with her lips, held him with her arms.

Afterward, we lay together in my narrow bed and he asked if I would recite some of my own poems. He liked the new one about blackbirds—it had become much better. I'd never forgive Anton for being such a shit about it. Osip liked them all, had some interesting critiques. He recited portions of a new poem of his for me: *"Who can know this word called separation / What kind of parting the coming days mean..."* Sometime during the recitation, I heard footsteps in the hall, but no knock on the door, only the sound of their retreat. I felt a pang of guilt, but I was tired of guilt. I would never have another night like this. Whatever happened in life, this would be mine forever.

The day the slanderous poem appeared in *Krasnaya Gazeta,* Gorky was still in Moscow. A nasty little ditty penned by an unnamed poet, Browning No. 215,745—an obvious reference to *150 Million.* It was called "The Masquerade on the Garbage Dump." A little joke. *Pomoika,* the garbage dump, was also *po Moike,* along the Moika—a reference to the location of the House of Arts.

> *House of high art, fat with rations,*
> *Dinner jackets adorned with asters, amazing pants…*

And so he characterized our ragged masque. Whoever the poet was, he had clearly waited until Gorky was gone, retaliating for that Smerdyakov remark Gorky had made about the ultra-Left poets. Once again, we were cast as the last sanctuary of the bourgeoisie, holding our fancy soiree at the expense of the masses, as if we were Marie Antoinette's courtiers. Just because some of us had clean hair. We were hardly well fed—even the slandering poet had cast us as dining on rations instead of market beef. Any commissar's girlfriend or Soviet young lady ate better than we did. Our ball was one of any number of amateur theatricals occurring all over the city—though the people who read *Krasnaya Gazeta* would hardly be expected to know that. Who could have penned this? Who would have it out for us like that? The poets analyzed the work, trying to detect the Judas. The poem was a little too good. It had to be one of the Proletcultists, perhaps even Mayakovsky himself.

Anton was as worried as anyone. Though he had little guilt in the fiddling-while-Rome-burned category, he knew the charge went deeper. As a formalist—someone who valued form above content—his glass house was more exposed than most. To his credit, he never once mentioned my night with Mandelstam, or how he had suffered.

He felt such shame about his love for me, such anguish that he needed something from another person, and had it and yet not. He hated and loved me both. And the more he loved, the more he hated. The closer he got to what he wanted, the more sharply he felt what he could never have.

Part IV
The Kronstadt Revolt

(February–March 1921)

50 *Soviets Without Communists*

Like a patient having endured a long siege of illness, growing ever weaker, Petrograd was finally dying. It was undeniable. Its death was not surprising, but no less terrible for its prolongation. The factories closed—those giants that had made it through the war, the ones we'd thought were ironclad—Dinamo, Putilov, Ericsson. Gone. Their workers—stranded—struck. The misery in the city had never been so bad. Our rations were cut by a third again, and we poets at the House of Arts existed on the lowest rung, hanging on to our right to a scholar's pittance by our fingernails. I prayed my classes wouldn't be cancelled as so many had been—the little donations my students made, an extra chunk of bread or small piece of leathery fish, made the difference between producing new poems or just staring at words moving around on a piece of paper as my stomach digested itself. At the House of Arts, our oldsters stayed in bed all day, living on thin soup and hot water. I saw an elderly woman go mad in front of an abandoned butcher shop on Sadovaya Street. A small crowd gathered to watch her try to claw the pictures of sausages off the shutters, her mouth up against the wood.

I tried to pry her away—"Babushka, please, let it alone"—but she fought me off. "I want that sausage. Don't you take it from me!" Some of the onlookers jeered, as stupid as oxen, while others squinted with pity, knowing we were all just a few missed scraps of food short of the same condition. We would all be poets eventually, and try to eat the symbol for the thing itself. The distinction between reality and poetry was already terrifyingly blurred, as when the anonymous Browning No. 215,745 mistook our pitiful masquerade for an embassy ball. What a fever dream. Gumilev had captured the unreal feeling of the times perfectly in his poem "The Lost Tram."

I was walking down an unfamiliar street
And suddenly I heard the caw of crows,
And distant thunder, and a ringing lute;
A tram flew by before my eyes.

Just how I ran onto its running board
remains a mystery.
The tail it trailed, even in daylight,
was firebird-fiery.

Anything could happen now, clocks might talk, trams leap their rails and whirl off to the Neva or the Nile or the land of the dead. We were all edging closer to the cliff's precipice.

A sign...It announces in blood-swollen letters:
"Greengrocer." I know that instead
of cabbage heads, swedes, and rutabagas
They sell the heads of the dead.

The executioner, with a face like an udder,
red-shirted, stout as an ox,
has chopped off my head...

As hunger rippled through our vision of the city, it grew as weird and distorted as any poem, insubstantial, full of grotesquerie. My hands shook, my legs wobbled. The cold was especially piercing as I trudged through the gloom to my class at Skorokhod, hoping that the women would still be there, that the factory wouldn't have vanished and in its place, a mountain of imaginary sausages or four-headed hedgehogs singing "Fais Dodo, Colin." Was this the future? Had we arrived? It was more a lunatic asylum where the keepers had simply abandoned the patients to their fate. I slogged through the uncleared snow past the deserted buildings, the frost furring their facades. The war had ended, Kolchak had fallen, Denikin was gone, Wrangel had sailed off to Paris. All our enemies melted away. Even the blockade had lifted. But the last six years had broken the back of the Future. We were futurists and yet there wasn't a scrap of future left, not even its bones. We'd eaten them all. What was left—today. This hour, the next meal, the condition of our boots and our coats, the price of oil, the scarcity of firewood. Surrounded by forests, we were tearing up the dead houses with our bare hands.

Every week the House lost another irreplaceable writer to starvation. Each death seemed like one more door to the future slamming shut, the key turning in the lock. *Why are writers and scholars more important than any working man?* I could hear Varvara say. But to see these ancients fall—what they knew, what they were, could never be recovered, like giant trees that would never grow to that size again. The Bolsheviks couldn't plaster that over with anonymous Browning poems and Proletcult. Who could create a Blok out of this poverty? In these poets and writers were the seeds—a whole world could be sown anew from their depth of culture, just as Gorky envisioned. Their deaths were the deaths of worlds. Maria Andreeva was taking our Russian art treasures to sell off in the West, but what about our real treasures, starving under their blankets at the House of Arts, just trying to make it through until spring? I couldn't help thinking of the package of tinned sardines and condensed milk that blessed Clyde Emory had sent from England at Christmastime. That sweet, thick ambrosia, the salty, oily sardines. I gave a can of milk to each of my elderly neighbors, and two to Chukovsky for his children. The tears in his round dark eyes… The rest we drank ourselves, me and Anton and the Squared Circle. I still dreamed of punching a hole in the lid of a can with a nail and drinking that heady, thick sweetness, gulp after gulp. I'd had a hard time stopping, though I knew it would make me sick, which it did. But so glorious. Someday I imagined bathing in condensed milk.

On my way down Moskovsky Prospect toward Skorokhod, I encountered a crowd of unemployed workers protesting before a closed factory. As I grew closer, I read their signs. BOLSHEVIKS— ANSWER BEFORE THE REPRESENTATIVES OF THE PEOPLE FOR YOUR CRIMES! and SOVIETS WITHOUT COMMUNISTS!

Soviets Without Communists! I trembled with the boldness of it. After years of hardship, of Red Terror, of incompetence and arrogance and spacemen, Bukharin's ABCs, *Krasnaya Gazeta*'s baying for blood, shuttered factories, and dead buildings, a tiny crack of hope bloomed in the crusty snow of the Moskovsky District. My eyes bulged from their sockets. *Soviets Without Communists!* Proletarians daring to protest the so-called Proletarian Dictatorship. A year ago that would have been unimaginable. It reminded me of that day in March 1917, in Znamenskaya Square, when we'd watched the Volynsky guards arrive on their blooded horses. These brave, desperate workers—they had had enough. They were going to be arrested. They were going to be executed. Yet they stood up with their signs.

Thank God Skorokhod's ugly brick building was still open. "I didn't know if you'd still be here," I said to my students, putting down the books I'd brought for them.

"You should have been here yesterday," said my young poet, Yeva. "We stopped work. Demanded category one rations, and a pair of boots for every family."

"Our own kids don't have boots. I gotta keep 'em home from school," said outspoken Irina. "We go from one office to the next, begging to get a boot ration for our own kids. For what we make with our own two hands!" She wiped at her eyes with the back of her dye-stained hand. "What Communist have you ever seen without boots?"

"They get a galoshes ration," agreed Galya. "Every year."

I wasn't sure that was precisely true, but the inequality rankled more than the sheer scarcity.

Irina leaned over her poems in the freezing committee room. "They sit up there, faces plastered with makeup, telling you no, your kids aren't good enough to get boots, get back to work. She closed the counter right in my face!"

"It wasn't this bad under the emperor," said Polya, a believer whose poems were about a village called Pocha. "We never starved like this before. The Bolsheviks just want us to go off and die so they don't have to feed us."

Her comment weighed on me. *Not this bad under the emperor.* All that had happened, all our hopes, our hard work, had brought us to this? A starving worker wishing for the return of the tsar. But there was another way: *Soviets Without Communists!* I once thought that only the Bolsheviks had the will to bring us this far. But now we'd reached the end of that road. The Bolsheviks had revealed themselves for what they were, vicious opportunists who were single-mindedly interested in gathering all power into their own hands. For their own benefit. The greengrocer with our heads on sale. I had the women write poems about their own aching, wise hands.

The Vikzhel club buzzed with angry men. There wasn't an empty seat in the low-ceilinged rooms. Everyone shouted at once, the air grown unbreathably smoky. An old man, Rodzevich, greeted me. "Welcome to the 'school for Communism'" he sneered, his teeth splayed in his lined mouth. "Like it?"

"A school for Communism?"

"That's what they're calling us in the papers. That's what they're saying a union's for. So we can dust off the chair for some fat Bolshevik to sit down and tell us what to do."

"It's Bukharin—you tell a snake by its bite."

The ABC of Communism. I remembered it well. I would remember it until the day I died.

The men showed me the article in *Petrogradskaya Pravda,* a piece on the usefulness of unions—to help teach the worker about Communism. That was the official line now. I knew the argument—if the proletarian state was already the true voice of the proletariat, the worker had no need of protection from their own state. It was a clear threat to the independent power of the unions, and Vikzhel, the railway union, was the most prominent, the last one with any real power. Lobachevsky, a fitter and one of the worst poets, a Vikzhel organizer, called out from his chair. "Don't kid yourself. This isn't Bukharin. This is coming right from the top. You think Lenin's not behind every word? Not a goddamn sparrow falls, brother."

I put my books down on the table at the head of the room. I had a feeling there wouldn't be much poetry written here tonight. One of the younger men and a sharp rhymester, Markel, put a cup of hot tea into my hands. "Bukharin's saying the union's role is to 'educate the worker, pass along party policy,' and make goddamn sure he knows his place. The hell with what we want." He pulled a pamphlet from his jacket pocket and tapped the headline: *The Workers' Opposition,* by Alexandra Kollontai. It called for worker control in the factory and in the party. "We're gearing up for the Tenth Party Congress. We're going to fight this."

What the Vikzhel men were so angry about was a new tactic by Trotsky to weaken the unions. He'd called for further labor militarization, the strict discipline of the army transferred into the factories, to revitalize production and restore our broken economy. I'd agree, that things were desperate. Trotsky had brought back discipline in the army, abandoning early principles of soldier democracy and returning to the old model of ranks and capital punishment. It had won us the civil war, why not the economy? But there was infinitely more at stake here than simple efficiency. After all, what was a Soviet government without worker control? Slavery. Without their unions, the workers would have no voice except outright revolt.

"What does Trotsky know about how to run a train, just because he rode on one? How does he know how to run a factory?" Lobachevsky bellowed. "The Bolsheviks got a lot of theories but they can't run a corner grog shop."

"They can kiss my Red ass," said the old man.

I remembered the left opposition, *Kommunist,* back in the old days. That was Bukharin. Now he was the status quo and Kollontai was forming some kind of worker resistance group. This one the Bolsheviks couldn't blame on the Whites. The civil war was over, and now the Workers' Opposition wanted the party to make good on its promises for worker control and Soviet democracy.

Lobachevsky leaned to one side and spit a mouthful of sunflower-seed shells onto the debris-strewn floor. "I've been a Bolshevik since '09, but I'm about ready to tear up my party card. That little dictator's got something coming if this union has anything to say about it. Wait until that armored train of his ends up on a spur at Gatchina."

That got a laugh. Everyone remembered when Vikzhel shunted the tsar's train around the countryside when he'd tried to get back to Petrograd and stop the unfolding revolution. But Trotsky's train had won the civil war. I couldn't reconcile my love of the revolution and certain of its leaders with my disgust with what they, and we, had become.

"Ever seen convict labor, Comrade?" said Lobachevsky. "Go into the factories. That's your so-called militarization of labor. How it works is this: they close down the factory, get rid of the 'troublemakers'—meaning union men—then they reopen and march the workers in, under guard. Special factory committees, only nobody elected 'em. They watch the benches all day long. Poor bastards too hungry to lift a hammer? They'll call it a stoppage and shoot 'em."

I thought of my women at Skorokhod. They'd already had a stoppage. "Nobody got shot at Skorokhod."

"Guess they haven't reorganized it yet," said Markel. "Metal first, electrical. They shot a guy this week at Dinamo."

Dinamo!

"It's that little yid," said Lobachevsky. "He's gotten so used to running the army, he thinks he can run labor the same way."

"I'm a Jew," said Markel.

"I'm not talking about Jews," said the organizer. "I'm talking about Trotsky." He threw a handful of sunflower seeds into his mouth, crunched on them angrily. "'If you ain't got bosses, whaddya need unions for?' Except we do have bosses. We got the whole goddamn Communist Party sitting on our necks. I'm going to the Tenth Congress, and if they vote against us, I'm going to tear up my party card in their faces."

The country was turning against the Bolsheviks. Not furtive reactionary fliers in the street, not poems about heads and rutabagas, but workingmen moving into open rebellion. I felt dizzy, excited, and terrified all at once. The Workers' Opposition had revealed a fundamental flaw in the Communist ABCs. If the party and the advanced proletariat weren't identical, if the workers were ready to throw the Communist Party overboard from the ship of socialism, then the theory was incorrect. We didn't need the Bolsheviks to build our socialist state.

But what would the party do? They would never allow the workers to dictate to them. They would do something—demonize the unions, break their backs. Shoot the leaders, and turn the workers into virtual slaves.

Yet—though I wouldn't say so in this angry hall—I could see the other side of the argument as well. The country was broken. Jesus Christ couldn't make it run at this point. I could see the dilemma Trotsky found himself in. The Bolsheviks had to get our factories running somehow, and worker control was fractious and time-consuming. It could never be as nakedly efficient as it would be with specialists running it, and soldiers to stand over the worker with rifles. Democracy was never the most efficient way to run things. It took time, and people could be wrong too. But it was just as Mandelstam had said—once you sold your soul to the devil, just try getting it back again.

"Comrade Marina, we want you to help us write a poem," Lobachevsky declared. "About all this." He pounded his table and shouted, "Shut up! We're writing now."

They got out paper and licked their pencils, and waited. Was this happening to Gumilev in his groups? The Vikzhel men were in revolt, and they were asking me to help them write slogans. What if there were a Cheka agent here? What if Lobachevsky himself was an agent provocateur? I had been in that cell at Gorokhovaya 2. I knew what was waiting for those who opposed the regime.

And yet, if this unrest could turn the revolution back to what it was supposed to be, if it could restore Soviet democracy, it wasn't counterrevolution, it *was* the revolution. The one we had fought for. During the civil war, every voice in Russia that didn't belong to the party—and the upper party at that—had been silenced one by one.

These men were entering dangerous territory, and they were asking me to help them.

How Varvara would love to see me back in Cheka hands. Smearing the House of Arts in the process, she would probably win some award. If I were arrested, there would be no one to rescue me. An agitator, daughter of a well-known Kadet executed for treason? Fomenting counterrevolution among the disgruntled workers? She would stamp me out like a lit match. What could the House poets do for me then? Hold a poets' stoppage? Put their pens down? They didn't have the massive reach of the railway union. I wished I could talk to Gorky, to Gumilev, but it was too late to ask for advice. The Vikzhel men wanted me now.

How could I refuse? I had to put my trust, not for the first time, in them.

> The prolet's chained to the fact'ry bench
> The union's got the gag
> The ration's down to begging scraps
> The country's dressed in rags.

> But your commissar, he rides in cars,
> His girlfriend's dressed in minks,
> They tell you now the union's dead,
> It ain't the streets that stink.

51 *Pushkin Days*

Pressure was building, not just in the factories but in our refuge, our beleaguered ark. After the poem by Browning No. 215,745 appeared in *Krasnaya Gazeta*, the newly reorganized Petrograd Narkompros—Commissariat of Enlightenment—threw the hammer at us. It found the House of Arts lacking in public zeal, pointed out what we did not yet have—no music course, no art workshop, only a hundred students actually attending classes out of the three hundred on the books. Never mind the impossible conditions, the brutal weather that might have discouraged participants. They questioned our financial affairs, the art auctions—wasn't that akin to private trade? I just had to pray no one discovered my collusion with Vikzhel's defiant rhymesters. As it was, *Krasnaya Gazeta* made our art sales out to be almost a black market—never mind that we used the money for events and books. Our House manager came under special scrutiny—they recommended the Cheka examine the dealings of our canteen. Luckily for him, the turmoil of the streets delayed action in our direction. Zinoviev evidently had his hands full with industrial havoc and worker demonstrations. *Soviets Without Communists!*—it felt like it had just before the February Revolution. And it was February again—the significance escaped no one.

Meanwhile, I turned twenty-one, and was touched by a small celebration in the House canteen, hatched by my friends. How could I have forgotten, that day by the river, how many people considered me part of their lives? There was a potato-peel cake and the stub of a candle Sasha had carved into the shape of a cone on a sphere on a cube. He gave me an ink drawing—of me, bent over my desk, writing by lamplight, clutching my hair. Dunya embroidered a handkerchief with a willow tree. Anton even wrote me a poem, full of jokes and inside references. The first initials of the lines spelled out *Marina My Madness*.

A far more significant occasion was the Pushkin anniversary, February 23, 1921, when literary Petrograd turned out during a snowstorm for its celebration of the anniversary of the poet's death. It wasn't a major milestone, the eighty-fourth, but it was a time of anniversaries—the winter was thick with them, like mushrooms in soggy loam. We needed something right now to connect our past with our present, some justification of the continuance of culture.

Pushkin was not a neutral choice. Yes, he was our greatest artist, but more importantly, his name in particular resonated with overtones of freedom of thought and expression. His genius was both our shield and our sword. Most of the institutions took part, seizing the chance to close ranks against the snapping dogs of the Left.

Our House of Arts elders were on the presidium that night: Kuzmin, Sologub, Blok, Gumilev. Even Akhmatova came out of hiding, marking the gravity of the event. She was very erect, gaunt, thin cheeked—she had been starving as much as the rest of us, but she bore it with greater dignity. I saw her speaking with Gumilev—it was uncanny, a moment in history. I wish Solomon Moiseivich had been there to capture it. He took her hand. Although they probably had once fought like wildcats, that night they sat side by side, the very picture of nobility.

There were other speakers, but the only one anyone remembered was Alexander Alexandrovich Blok. The hall at the House of Writers wasn't large, but it was larger than ours, and packed like a tin of smelts. I stood in the back with Anton and Oksana and Arseny and Tereshenko—we'd been lucky to squeeze in—and could just see Blok's suffering head and cropped curls as he began his speech, listed in the program as "The Mission of the Poet." Innocuous enough.

But within the first paragraph, I saw that he was skating right for the patch where the ice was thinnest. Freedom against tyranny, freedom of the artist. He posed the name of Pushkin against all the other names that history preserved—"the somber names of emperors, generals, inventors of instruments of murder, names of torturers and martyrs of life, and together with them, the radiant name Pushkin."

No one failed to understand the message. I could see people in the audience nodding, or clutching each other's arms in shock. No one blinked. No one coughed. How far would he go?

He was not an orator of the Mayakovsky type, he was a poet whose foot barely made a print in snow. But his words held thunder enough. He began to explain that it was often painful just thinking about Pushkin, because the poet's course had been that of an artist whose endeavor, an inward endeavor—culture—"was all too often disrupted by the interference of people for whom a stove pot is more precious than God."

Even the angels held their breaths. He began speaking about the "rabble." We knew he was referring to the Pushkin poem "The Poet and the Mob," but would the Proletcultists know that? Blok was playing a dangerous game. His revolutionary poem "The Twelve" had been misunderstood by readers on the right and on the left—but like Pushkin, Blok had had to keep his inner freedom and pursue his inward task.

He did his best to explain. The rabble didn't mean the common people, who simply didn't have the education—that wasn't what Pushkin was referring to—but those who claimed to serve culture. Critics, censors, boors who believed poetry could be used for some outer purpose, who tried to insert themselves between the poet and his inner freedom.

I clapped my hand to my mouth so I would not cry out. I must not gasp. He was putting his head in the guillotine.

Luckily, he began to elucidate his theories of poetry in a labyrinthine way, which lost many of the journalists, for who besides the poets could follow what Blok meant about chaos and cosmos and sound? They were all waiting for more comments on Pushkin and his relationship to the bureaucrats who censored his work and played such havoc with his life, with the thinly veiled comparison to our own increasing unfreedom.

I could hear the old wall clock tick whenever he paused in that crowded room. No one so much as shifted; though his voice wasn't loud, no one even exhaled for the twenty minutes during which he spoke. I believed Blok didn't think he was talking about politics but about vulgarity, and the poet's inner freedom, which had nothing to do with politics. But he was not a naive man. *Be careful where you read that.* He had been dealing with the Soviet bureaucracy for years, and had been pummeled by the ignorant reactions on both the right and the left to "The Twelve," his poem about the Red Guardsmen patrolling the snowy streets of revolutionary Petrograd—with the invisible Christ leading the way.

He looked like Petrograd itself—dying but still mustering the strength to discuss Pushkin's inner freedom and the stifling effects of the new bureaucracy. Yes, he was saying it right out, that the literary bureaucrats and the hounds of Proletcult were our rabble, no different than in Pushkin's time, wanting to use poetry for outer ends, rather than allowing the poet the inner freedom he required. They demanded he be useful, that he enlighten the hearts of his fellow men. "As Pushkin simply puts it: they demand the poet sweep garbage off the street."

You could hear the grumbling from certain sections of the audience.

The rabble didn't understand the poet's gift, he explained, and were thus unable to enjoy the fruits of his labor. They demanded that the poet serve the same thing they served—the outside world. In fact, they felt threatened by his inner freedom. Felt that somehow it diminished them. They instinctively sensed that the testing of hearts by poetry had no bearing on the achievement of goals in the outside world.

Were they following his argument? Part of me hoped he'd lost them, but another part wanted to cheer. My heart was beating wildly. I could hardly stand to watch him up on that high wire.

The poet's job was not to get through to every blockhead, he explained. Poetry would choose, because it called to those who could hear it. And no censorship in the world could stop this election. *Elitist, anachronistic*...I could see the Proletcultists taking notes, scribbling objections. But great art called to what was great in men.

He argued that the poet had been sapped by all the boorish attempts to use him, to censor him, to make him sweep the streets, so to speak, and the culture was crippled along with it. "Pushkin died not from D'Anthès's bullet but from suffocation...The poet dies because he is stifled; life has lost its meaning." Now he was speaking in the present tense—not of Pushkin but of the poet. Him. Us. At this very moment these things were being decided by people also in this room. The poets and the rabble alike—propagandists, cultural bureaucrats, the insensible hand of the state. "Let those bureaucrats who plan to direct poetry through their own channels, violating its secret freedom and hindering it in fulfilling its mysterious mission, beware of an even worse name." Dictator. Murderer. Assassin. Plague.

The audience applauded a long time. Each one of us applauded in order to recapture our own inner freedom, our own courage. In applauding Blok, we were signing our names to his speech. The silence of the Proletcult faction and the leftists underscored the power of what had just occurred. No one had died, no troops stormed down the aisles of the House of Writers. But a line had been drawn. And the vulgarians found themselves in a tiny minority. Some of them, abashed, even clapped softly. Although I overheard two disapproving leather-clad writers muttering. "The author of 'The Twelve.' I'm amazed to see him turn around like this."

But "The Twelve" was the *sound* of the revolution, not a political tract. Blok was a poet, not a tool or mouthpiece. He was saying there was no air, that people like these apparatchiks were taking it all. It wasn't just the workers who were getting tired of the airlessness.

Kuzmin also spoke that night, and Eikhenbaum, but it was hard to think of anything but Blok. Akhmatova seemed to take strength with every word, her transparence becoming corporeal. Perhaps she would come back to us, perhaps she too was finding her inner freedom and would begin to sing again.

Back at the House of Arts, Anton and I lay in bed, huddling for warmth, snow piling up on the windows, going over Blok's speech point by point, committing it to memory. My face against his dirty neck, I thought about the secret freedom of creation. Not to corral an opinion and express it with subservient words, but just as Anton had once said about my blackbird poem, how the language itself gave birth to it all. I kept wondering whether I could be included in *rabble*. I had too easily agreed with Gorky, art being *for* the elevation of the people. Here was the core of the disagreement between Gorky and Blok. Now I understood how dismayed Blok must have been with my description of teaching the workers to write, his kind offer to enroll in my class notwithstanding. But clearly Blok had confessed his own sin, all our sin, against the spirit of poetry's inner freedom. To think—Anton was closer to Blok than I was. Poetry was a mystery, with its own purpose that had nothing to do with the outside world. You either believed in it or you didn't.

Following Blok's astonishing speech, the House of Arts' new journal, *Dom Iskusstv*, published an essay by Zamyatin called "I Am Afraid" that was even more direct. Zamyatin, a prose writer, addressed the question of art's value and the role of cultural establishments in the revolution. He bluntly argued a clear link between the absence of quality literature and the lack of a free press, the difficulties of life and the meddling of the regime. He concluded that the regime's tendency to orthodoxy was giving birth to a new generation of court poets and toadies, which would stifle the dreamer and heretic who created art. He lamented that writers of genuine literature were being hounded into silence.

The elders were standing up to the firing squad with everything they had: dignity, intellect, the last bit of defiance left in their starving bodies.

Three days later, a cheer ran through the House when we read that Lunacharsky, head of the Commissariat of Enlightenment, seeing which way the wind was blowing, had given in on the issue of control in the publishing houses, allowing for a measure of independent action in the press. The government would not be telling us what to publish. Were the independent newspapers going to come back? A crack was growing. We could see daylight.

Oksana was the last to arrive for the morning editorial meeting of our own new journal, *Anvil*. We ran it like a conventional journal. Perhaps someday, when there was paper again—if there ever was paper again—it would be a printed journal. There was still snow on her coat. She removed her scarf, shook it out, sat down on the bed. Six of us already sat crowded into Anton's odd-shaped room with its floor-level window: Arseny Grodetsky, bright-eyed, his fair hair still showing the tracks of a comb wielded by his doting mother, with whom he still lived—though he spent so much time in the House of Arts he qualified as an unofficial member. Sasha

Orlovsky, representing the visual arts, reviews of shows and upcoming events. Oksana, Nikita Nikulin, Petya. Dmitry Tereshenko, unshaven, rumpled and barely awake, wearing a turtleneck and felt slippers. Shklovsky had volunteered to be on our board, as had Bely, though neither of them came to the meetings.

Oksana's cheeks were tipped with frost, she rubbed them and they turned fiery red. "There's a huge protest happening on Vasilievsky Island. I'd say there were a thousand people."

"Where?" Petya and I both asked.

"I think it's the docks," she said.

Everything the Vikzhel men had said came swimming into my mind. A demonstration, a thousand workers! The structure was shaking, listing. Something important was unfolding out there, and we would not read about it in *Pravda*. I stood, buttoned my sheepskin.

Anton looked up at me, as if huge demonstrations were just another kind of weather. "Where are you going?"

"I need to see what's going on."

"This is what's going on." He slapped our sheaf of poems with the back of his hand. "This"—he waved the pages at me—"is a fight to the death, for the future of the mind. What was all that about the mission of the poet? The inner freedom you've been on about since Blok spoke? The poet who has no interest in the affairs of the world, *lya lya fa fa?*"

Did it make me rabble? Less than a poet, because I wanted to know what was happening on Vasilievsky? A thousand people were demonstrating. Knowing the severity with which the Cheka could put it down—this could be the beginning of another revolution. The outer world would always exist, and would affect all of us, poets and citizens alike. I wasn't about to ignore it, even if Blok made a speech. Anton was a man of limitless opinions, but he went rigid whenever he was called upon to interact with concrete reality. Was that inner freedom or just plain cowardice? "I'm going. Anyone wants to come with me, they're welcome."

"I'm not getting arrested over rations at the pipe factory." He held up the sheaf of pages that would be our first *Anvil*. "This is my revolution."

Oksana's gray eyes grew worried, the circles under them were deep charcoal smudges. "There's going to be trouble, you can just feel it. What are you going to do, give a speech?"

"Petya?" He lived on Vasilievsky. He was in his third year at university.

"I just got here, I didn't see anything. Anyway I've got Chukovsky's studio after this."

I looked over at Tereshenko. "How about you?"

He yawned, scratched his head over his ear. "Sorry. Committee meeting over at the Poets' Guild."

No one wanted to know what would become of a thousand workers demonstrating against the Bolsheviks? "Well, the hell with all of you." I wrapped my scarf around my neck and fitted the fox-fur hat to my head.

Arseny piped up. "Hey, I'll go. I was just a kid in '17. I missed everything."

Now Anton scowled, twitched, crossed his legs and recrossed them. Somehow the idea that Arseny Grodetsky would have the nerve to go with me roused his competitive nature. "Oh, all right," he said angrily. "Damn you both. Somebody's got to look after you." He dumped the pages into Tereshenko's lap and unfolded his long legs. "But I'm warning you, if there's any shooting, I'm not waiting around to see if we're among the casualties. Agreed?"

"*Ladno,* " I said. *Agreed.*

We struggled against the heavy wind and blowing snow, Anton cursing the whole way, onto the Nikolaevsky Bridge—now known as the Lieutenant Schmidt. I couldn't resist looking back at the yellow mansion where Kolya and I had made love so long ago. Its yellow walls only a slight creamy blur through the scrim of swirling snow. Here I'd stood that day, watching the Cheka search the house, the diamond stickpin in my coat. It must be a busy time for them now, strikes were unfolding all over town. What would they do with the demonstrators? Who was it who told me *An army is at its most dangerous in retreat?* I knew we wouldn't see anything in the papers, except blame laid at the feet of the usual suspects, the SRs and Mensheviks, anarchists, counterrevolutionary agitators.

The half-mile bridge with its icy panels of arched-necked sea-horses gave way to the familiar embankment. We walked toward the shabby end of the island, past the Seventeenth Line, where Varvara had lived, and into the factory quarter. Up on Bolshoy Prospect, we saw an enormous gathering, mostly women, protesting in the falling snow. Signs read BREAD AND BOOTS, TROUBETSKOY STRIKE COMMITTEE, DOWN WITH THE BOSSES, LEATHERWORKERS' UNION, SO-VIETS WITHOUT COMMUNISTS, and even ALL POWER TO THE SOVIETS, NOT TO POLITICAL PARTIES, along with a couple of less-progressive notes, like DOWN WITH COMMUNISTS AND JEWS.

"So much for your egalitarians." Anton's nose was red with cold. He sniffled, wiped his nose on his sleeve. "Is that supposed to excite us about their demands?"

We got closer to hear a speaker, a man in a brimmed hat shouting to the crowd, telling them to hold firm, that this was their country and they had a right to express their demands. On the border of the crowd, I saw a squat figure of a woman among a group of somber workingmen, wrapped in an old fur. Something about her was familiar... Then I recognized—the Flea! I pushed my way over to her—"Comrade Goldman! Comrade Goldman!" I jumped and waved.

She squinted at me from behind her little round glasses, trying to remember who I was. I came closer. "It's Marina!" I caught myself before I shouted *We met at Gorky's!* Who knew who was watching us now. "Aura Sands's friend, remember?" The steam of my breath clouded my view of her, but I'd seen a face no longer ardent, not the woman I'd met over tea at the Kronverksky apartment. All the fire seemed to have gone out of her. The air around her was dense with worry. She looked ten years older. "Oh yes, the poet." Now her expression sweetened. Her round glasses were frosting over. She took my gloved hand, patting it as if it were a small dog. "I remember your poem. About bees—honey coming out of the holes in the switchboard. I think of it every time I make a telephone call. Seems like a lifetime ago, doesn't it?"

"At least one." My father's, to be exact.

I introduced her to Anton and Arseny. Neither of them had any idea who she was, but Anton seemed relieved that this middle-aged woman was here. If she thought it was safe, how dangerous could it be? I didn't want to tell him that Red Emma, the famous anarchist, was more dangerous than fifty union organizers.

"The Troubetskoy Works is on strike," she explained under the shouting of the speaker, leaning close. "All they want is an increase in rations and a pair of boots. There was a shipment of shoes in the shops this morning—but for party members only. It was clearly a provocation. The Petro-Soviet refuses to negotiate until they go back to work. Now they've got the leather factory out, and the Laferm Cigarette women. It's getting bigger by the minute."

I stamped my boots to keep the blood in my feet—even Aura's good boots could not prevent them from turning to stone. The size of the crowd! A bold assembly of the determined and the desperate, bundled in their ragged black and brown coats and scarves and caps. "Now the Bolsheviks will have to listen."

"They don't have to do anything," Anton said.

"You're the anarchist." It was just occurring to Arseny whom we were talking to. "The American. *Emma Goldman.* Goldman and Berkman." He glowed with the contact with revolutionary royalty. The revolution he'd missed was giving way to one he was going to witness.

"We just got back from Moscow," Emma said, her frizzy gray hair sticking out from her oversized tam. "Me and Sasha. The Democratic Center and the Workers' Opposition have been crushed."

I felt it like a punch in the gut.

"Lenin's never going to let the workers dictate to the party." She sighed, hopeless. So different from the peppery rebel I'd met that day in Gorky's apartment. "They've put themselves in a corner now, bungling everything from top to bottom. So arrogant, they just keep making it worse. We're trying to help negotiate with the strike committees." Her comrades were watching us. They looked just as worried as she did. "Trying to keep people from getting hurt. But it's going from bad to worse and of course the party doesn't need any help from us." The anarchists. She indicated the crowd, a sign: ALL POWER TO THE SOVIETS, NOT TO POLITICAL PARTIES.

Anton shivered in his old coat and cap. "Seen enough? I'm not going to stand here all day. I have things to do."

"Are you going to speak?" I asked Goldman. We had to stay for that.

"An American anarchist speaking out against the Bolsheviks?" She snorted, shook her head. "They'd just blame us, say it was us inciting the workers. They wouldn't even let us print a funeral pamphlet for Peter Kropotkin."

Kropotkin, the famous Russian anarchist, formerly a prince. "He died? I didn't hear anything about it."

"He was like a father to me," she said. "The kindest man."

Like a father. Just a phrase people used, but that specific order of ordinary words had the power of a blow. They struck me in the throat, tears welled, only to freeze in my eyes.

"In Moscow, five thousand people came for his funeral. We laid him out in the Trade Union Hall. But they're terrified of anything becoming a nexus for protest."

Something was happening in the crowd. People were shouting. We were shoved this way and that. "Here they come!" Arseny said, pointing back to the river.

We turned and saw the companies of gray-uniformed *kursanty,* Bolshevik cadets, marching up from the bridge, rifles over their shoulders, bayonets attached. Women approached them, trying to speak to them. "Join us, boys. We're your mothers, your sisters." "All we want is boots, and bread." "Join us."

The boys were on edge, clearly terrified at the size of the crowd. They shouted at people to disperse. Boys seventeen, eighteen years old telling starving workers what to do. Didn't they know what the revolution had been about? I remembered the soldiers who fired on the workers at Znamenskaya Square—it was starting all over

again. "By order of the Petro-Soviet, we command you all to return to work." Brandishing their rifles. The workers yelled at them
to go back to school, blow their noses, run back to Moscow. The
demonstrators began to push them, throwing snowballs, then rocks.
Women even grabbed for their rifles. The boys fought back, one
shot over the heads of the crowd, up into the swirling snow.

"There it is. We're going," Anton said, grabbing my arm. Yes, I
could not live through Znamenskaya Square again. I saw that dead student on the ground, his blood in the snow. I had no more lives to spare.

Part of me wanted to stay and see the outcome regardless of the
danger, but Anton had my arm and was pulling me through the
crowd. I took hold of Arseny, who kept turning to watch the boys no
older than he in cadets' uniforms. Shouts of "Disperse!" and "Down
with the Communists!" filled the air, and shots. We ran, arm in arm.
The people swirled around us like snow.

We reached the embankment on the Vasilievsky side and began
moving back in the direction of the bridge as workers pushed the
other way, toward the sound of the rifle fire.

"Can't go that way." It was Emma, at my elbow, her face red and
sweaty from running. She pointed toward the bridge. Soldiers coming across—Red troops with rifles on their shoulders. It was crazy,
unthinkable. Red troops coming to put down a workers' protest.
I would not have believed it had I not seen it with my own eyes.
We could hear them, faintly, through the snow, their commissars
haranguing them. "Get a good look," she said. "This isn't about
Communism, or the good of the people. This is a state protecting itself against the people, as it always does. Power protects itself." We
climbed down onto the ice, and began crossing the Neva, passing
longshoremen coming toward us from the Admiralty docks.

"Did they shoot anybody?" the men called out.

"Not yet. Over their heads," she shouted back. "But they've got
troops coming. Be careful, *bratya*!"

That day, the Petrograd Soviet declared martial law. Proclamations
were posted everywhere, on every wall, every door. No public

meetings, strict nightly curfew, the workers ordered back to their factories on pain of losing their rations. They were going to starve the workers into submission. True to form, they placed the blame on anarchist, Menshevik, and SR counterrevolutionary plots. It couldn't be the actual workers, with actual grievances and a right to voice them. After three years, you'd think they could have found something better.

All night, I kept thinking of my Skorokhod women, keeping Anton awake as I tossed and turned. Would they go back to work? Would they ignore the *prikazy*? I couldn't stop thinking about the soldiers crossing the bridge, and the terrified, determined faces of the *kursanty*, and of my little brother—how panicked he must have felt, facing the Red Guard in '17. I longed to lie down on Iskra's small grave. I wanted to talk to her. It was the one thing that would never change. She would always be there, just off Moskovsky Prospect, like a lodestone, my Polaris.

In the morning, I wrapped my scarf up high on my face, squashed the hat down as low as I could, and with just those slits for my eyes, like a bedouin in a sandstorm, I headed out into the wild weather, south, toward the Obvodny Canal and the Novodevichy Convent. In my mind, I could see that big granite four-sided tomb, the side closest to the church where she rested, my redheaded child. I wanted to tuck her in, if only in my mind, to tell her *I'm still here.*

But as I neared the canal, I saw troops stationed on the New Moscow Bridge—the exact spot where we'd built fortifications during the Yudenich advance. They looked cold and unhappy. One of the soldiers, bundled to the eyes, stepped forward as I neared the bridge. He pulled down his scarf. "It's closed," he said.

"Has there been trouble?" Had the soldiers forced the workers back to the bench, the way Lobachevsky had described? Or had the workers held out? Then it occurred to me—obviously they'd held out, or the Bolsheviks wouldn't have sealed off the district. "I'm going to the cemetery. My baby is buried there."

"You'll have to visit some other time," said the soldier, stamping his feet. "We've got our orders."

"Has there been shooting?" I asked.

"Just the usual," he said. "They go back to the bench and then pop out again, like a bad nail in your shoe. Wah wah, rations and boots, rations and boots. What if everybody did that? I'd like some boots too—who wouldn't? They need to get back to work so we can all go home." He replaced his scarf and waved his rifle, indicating I should clear off.

So the workers were fighting regardless of the threat to withhold rations. What a brave thing. It was clear to anyone that the Bolsheviks weren't listening. *The Workers' Opposition has been crushed.* Not exactly. I gazed across the canal and prayed for my Skorokhod ladies, for Dinamo, the railwaymen, all of them. The workers' government was preparing to starve the workers into submission. I remembered Anton, sitting at the Katzevs' table all those years ago, saying, *Whoever gets power will find a way to keep it.* Sitting on a footstool at the end of the table, wedged between Dunya and Shusha, chain-smoking. *Bolshevik, Menshevik, the Committee for the Preservation of Wigs—they'll set up a nice system of privilege for themselves and their friends... Once you have a concentration of power, you're screwed no matter who's in charge.*

Anton had been more prescient than anyone.

"Would you shoot them, if you were ordered to?" I asked the soldier, his unhappy hard eyes, the frost growing on his scarf from the dampness of his breath.

"You want me to shoot you, just to see if I can? Get out of here before we both find out."

There was no other choice but to return the way I had come, up empty Moskovsky Prospect, passing the sniper's nest I'd inhabited those days and nights after Iskra's death. What if someone had told me back then that this was in our future, that after we'd fought back our enemies, there would be worker protests against the government in the very streets of Petrograd. Strikes and *kursanty,* sentries on the bridges. Would the mothers of those *kursanty* someday have to receive the kind of letter my parents had, notifying them that their boys had died in a mistaken cause?

Three years now. I liked to think of Seryozha with Iskra, and Maxim, waiting for me on the other side of a fast, cold river full of ice. I never saw my father with them, though. I only pictured him as he'd been the last time I'd seen him—a corpse, dumped on my doorstep. Or a prisoner in the Troubetskoy Bastion—hungry, beaten. I wanted to remember him in a dinner jacket as he'd been that New Year's Eve, laughing with his guests, the dimples underneath his beard. Or at home nights in his smoking jacket and Persian cap, pipe clamped between his teeth, consulting his enormous dictionary on its stand, or playing a masters' chess game out of the paper, studying both sides.

What a dream this life was. Perhaps Blok was right—we should just listen to the sounds, and write what we could still hear, let the world attend to the things of the world. Anton's fatalism was his bulwark against the chaos. But my poetic spirit rose up against fate. Fatalism was ignoble. Blok wasn't talking about fatalism—he said the poet must resonate with every sound, whether he liked it or not. He had to be free to hear it, to absorb it and express it. He was talking about freedom, not fate.

It was hard work tramping through the uncleared snow, avoiding the holes in the wooden pavement, and I was so weak. Hunger was a paradox—the lighter I became physically, the heavier I felt. The snow whirled around me like a living being. What had been so clear the day of Blok's speech now was lost in the swirling snow, like his mysterious Christ—*tenderly treading through snow-swirls, / hung with threads of snow-pearls, / crowned with snowflake roses*...Was caring about the outer world a waste of my consciousness as a poet? Did I hear the sounds? I stopped in the street and heard—nothing. The wind had stopped. I heard only my breath, coming short, and the pounding of my heart. Would Blok be disappointed in me, that I cared so much about the events taking place in our world?

There had to be something between the rhythms and music of elemental poetry and following my soul's inner freedom, the hell with stove pots—and being a self-serving careerist, a boor, a fashionable weathervane, to whom a stove pot would always be more important than the divine. I needed both the stove pot and the divine. I was a poet, but I was also a human being who lived the life of her time, a woman who had lost her child, her father, her family. A woman who loved men, who cared about the future of her country, who had to worry about stove pots. I needed both the inner and the outer life. Perhaps it was a muddle, no doubt it was—whereas Blok, the eagle, preferred the purity of the icy heights—but it was an authentic expression of my own being, as elemental to me as fog and mist and clods of dirt. I was my own bargeman-Keats, finding my own way.

52 *The Third Revolution*

We sat over tea in the House of Arts canteen. Viktor Shklovsky and Anton were talking very animatedly about something said in an Opoiaz meeting—the Society for the Study of Poetic Language—a formalist hotbed. I'd sat in on some of those events, where the newest criticism was being forged. But I couldn't concentrate when at this very moment the workers in their forbidden districts—Narva, Moskovsky, Vasilievsky, Petrogradsky, Vyborg—were starving. For food, and shoes, and the right to speak for themselves. The ridiculousness of that anonymous Browning poem didn't seem so ridiculous to me now.

Anton did his best to include me in their conversation, speaking of *Anvil* and our Living Almanac coming around again, while Shklovsky spread out his amusing anecdotes, what he'd said to Punin at IZO, his agent provocateur role. My attention kept drifting. Power fought for its existence like a living creature, while there was nothing I could do besides control the terrain I had—the continent of a piece of paper, the country of one word after the next.

I saw Anton's eyes jerk, his face drain of color. "The Baltic Fleet's in," he said dryly, and went back to his conversation.

Behind me, a face poked through the canteen doorway. A rugged face with a dimple in its chin, sailor's cap with a ship's name on the hatband, eyes the color of the sea. I downed the rest of my tea in two gulps, crammed my uneaten bread into my pocket, and ran into the hall. This was my inner freedom.

"I've got to talk to you," Pasha whispered, holding my hands. "Can we go somewhere?"

I didn't want to talk. I wanted to kiss him, hold his ropelike form against me. I wanted to parade before him like the long line of daughters in the underwater kingdom of Sadko the Bogatyr. He could choose any one of me. I led him down to the Monkey House. My dark room smelled of mold, old paper, and pine needle tea. "I didn't think I'd see you again."

He grinned his goofy little smile. "We sailors get around."

"Is that why you're here, to take me sailing?" I wrapped myself around his neck like an Orenburg scarf, as soft as a cloud.

Surprisingly, he gently unwrapped me. "Sit down." He sat on my bed, and I next to him, and his face was still easy, a smile even behind the serious look he put on. "I don't know if you heard," he said. "The workers are rising against the Bolsheviks."

I told him about the demonstration on Vasilievsky Island, the *kursanty*, the troops on the bridge. The approach to the Moskovsky District was under guard. No rations until the workers went back to their factories. I told him about the Vikzhel club, and their poem. He reached up under his shirt and pulled out a tin, a wide brush like housepainters use, and a sheaf of papers. No, *posters*. Handbills.

I took one and began reading, slowly.

KRONSTADTSKIYE IZVESTIA 2 MARCH 1921
PETROPAVLOVSK RESOLUTION
Having heard the report of the representatives sent by the general meeting of ships' crews to Petrograd to investigate the situation there,

We resolve:
1. In view of the fact that the present Soviets do not express the will of the workers and peasants . . .

It listed fifteen points, each more incendiary than the next. The sailors were demanding new elections by secret ballot, to be held immediately, with freedom to agitate among the workers beforehand. Freedom of assembly for trade unions and peasant organizations. A *nonparty* conference of workers, soldiers, and sailors to be held no later than March 10. In eight days! My head was swimming. "Can you possibly think they'll agree to this?"

"Keep going."

The liberation of political prisoners of socialist parties, and those imprisoned due to labor unrest and peasant resistance. A commission to review the cases of those held in prisons and camps. The abolishment of political departments *since no party should be given special privileges in the propagation of its ideas*...

I bit my lip. "It's a third revolution."

He rose from the bed and perched on my desk. "It's the rest of the revolution."

Cultural commissions should be locally elected, financed by the state. It called for the removal of the roadblocks for food arriving into the city, and equal rations for all working people. Abolition of Communist detachments in the army, Communist guards in factories—or if they were found necessary, to be appointed from the ranks and factories *at the discretion of the workers.*

The sailors had not forgotten the peasants, either. Their resolution demanded freedom of action on the land and the right to keep cattle, as long as the peasants didn't hire labor.

They requested that all branches of the army as well as cadets endorse their demands. It was signed, *Petrichenko, chairman of the squadron meeting, and Perepelkin, secretary.*

My eyes went back to the top: *In view of the fact that the present Soviets do not express the will of the workers and peasants*... "You agreed to this?"

"We all did."

It was mutiny. "Are you going to present it to the Petro-Soviet?"

He screwed up his face, exasperated that I would even think such a thing. "What, are we schoolboys? It's already in force." He sat down next to me, took my hand, pressed it to his chest. "We voted on it two days ago in Anchor Square." Kronstadt's central square, where its domed cathedral rose. "Sixteen thousand ayes, three nays, and no abstentions. We're electing a new soviet." His smile grew broad, his blue eyes turquoise again.

"Who were the nays?"

"The commissar of the Baltic Fleet, the chairman of the Kronstadt Soviet, and Papa Kalinin of the Central Committee."

I tried to imagine the scene. The nerve in each of those nays, you had to admire it. The *Petropavlovsk Resolution*...like the MRC—the Military Revolutionary Committee—in February 1917. It had gone beyond the point of no return.

"The Bolsheviks sent Kalinin up to try to change our minds," Pavel said. "We let him leave, to carry our demands back to his masters. We put the other two under arrest, by order of the Kronstadt Provisional Revolutionary Committee."

His blue-green eyes held the question *Do you understand?* I did. I sat with the handbill in my lap, trying to breathe. They'd *arrested* the commissar of the Baltic Fleet! And the chairman of their own soviet. Two days ago. This was really happening. And not a word in the papers, not a squeak! How had the government managed to keep something like this quiet? How did we not know?

He smiled, and touched my nose with his rough forefinger. *"I too have stolen the golden fleece,"* he recited. *"And tasted the oxen of the sun."*

Kronstadt had stolen the golden fleece. Sixteen thousand sailors, soldiers, and assorted citizens had voted to free their island from the Bolshevik yoke. The Free Republic of Kronstadt. And now they were inviting the country to join them. They had tasted the oxen of the sun, and now the sun was going to be very, very unhappy. Did the Bolsheviks know about this, I wondered, staring down at the paper. But of course they knew. They would have known when Kalinin returned. What were they doing about it? We hadn't heard a thing, not from *Pravda,* not from *Krasnaya Gazeta.* "Who's Petrichenko, he's your leader? An SR?"

"There is no leader. That's the whole point. He's just a sailor. We wrote it on the ship, voted on it, brought it to the people of Kronstadt. They approved it. No parties, no leaders." His eyes were bright, his teeth flashed for a moment in the light from my little lamp, his lean face with its sandy brows. "We sent sailors to investigate what's been going on here. They were on Vasilievsky Island. They went to the factories. We heard the demands of the people of Petrograd and seconded their motion."

I gazed at him for a long time. That good brave face. They would call him a traitor. A mutineer. This was how revolutions began. This was not a street protest. The Bolsheviks couldn't put it down with a few truckloads of *kursanty*. *Watch the soldiers,* Kolya had once said. And these weren't just any soldiers, this was Kronstadt, the pride of the revolution. They had escorted it in on the *Aurora*. They had been its very first support. They were our heroes—even Maxim had dreamed of becoming a Kronstadt sailor. And now the island had declared Russian independence from the Bolshevik straitjacket. They had raised their own red flag. My hands sweated, softening the paper of the declaration. No wonder the soviet had proclaimed martial law.

"It's not about us," Pasha said earnestly. "This is the voice of the people. We're just putting some teeth in it. The Bolsheviks might be able to ride over the workers, but let them try us." This list—an end to the grain requisitioning, the thing the peasants had demanded for so long. An end to the roadblocks—preventing workers and peasants from bringing food into the starving cities. The end of Bolshevik privilege, the end of the suppression of speech and the press. "We get letters from our own parents asking why we're supporting the oppressor. It stops here. The workers have been asking for these things, we're demanding them. We're *claiming* them."

Taking the revolution back to what it was supposed to be all along. Not to my father's cronies getting ready to divide Russia up like a slab of beef. I couldn't think of one thing they had missed. Freedom of parties. Freedom of the press.

I was shaking like a braking tram. For him. For all of us. This had moved beyond factory stoppages and protests over rations and boots. Another revolution was beginning.

Pasha leaned forward, taking my cold hands in his. "I've killed good men—better men than me probably—and for what? So Bolsheviks could climb to the top and stay there? We went along with what they said—it was war. But the war's over. This"—he rested his hand on the page lying on my lap as a father rests his hand on his child's pretty curls—"is the start of the peace."

I tried to look brave, but tears spilled down my cheeks. I thought of us at the House of Arts, our terror when Blok had spoken out. And all he had done was argue against bureaucratic vulgarity. Not against the whole Communist regime.

"We've fought on ice. In sandals, because there were no boots," he said, quietly. "I've fought on a quarter pound of rye and two moldy potatoes. There won't be any more boots until the workers believe in their leaders again. Those skinny bastards aren't going to repair the trains and grow food if they don't believe. And they don't. Not anymore."

He took the sheaf of posters and put them behind him on the chair.

"They're going to arrest you," I said. "They're going to paint you as counterrevolutionaries." I wondered if Varvara knew—of course she did. They would be preparing their reprisal. And it would be terrifying when it came.

"Who would believe them? No one." He stroked my hair, letting his fingers linger in the strands. "Who was on the front lines in February 1917? In October? We were. Who won the civil war? We did. Who fought alongside Trotsky's troops in the very worst days? We did. Nobody's going to paint us as counterrevolutionaries."

"And if they refuse your demands?"

He picked up the comb from my desk, flipped it in his hands. "The Bolsheviks are not the revolution. They've taken it somewhere and hidden it under a haystack. We're sick of Bolsheviks. The worker is sick of them. How is this country going to repair itself when the people don't trust their own government?"

I pressed my cheek to his, drinking in his scent, the salty decks of the rebellious ships. *Freedom.*

"It's not just us." He put his arm around me, spoke into my ear. "It's everybody. The workers. The peasants. You know the peasants have to turn over more out of this year's harvest than they planted? It can't go on. It's time for them to listen. We're just making sure they can hear."

He tried running my comb through my hair, but it snagged in the tangles. I took it away from him and combed his own crinkly blond hair, so cropped it was impossible to snag, and marveled at the daring of Pasha and his men, men and women like him. Not just to join their voices with the millions—that would be easy, it had a momentum of its own. But to be among the few, to let their voices sound out as a collection of individuals, with individual faces, minds, and hearts. He would be so easy to kill, my Argonaut, sitting here holding the black print of the future in his salt-toughened hands. Would they succeed? Could they really do it? I could just as easily see his vulnerable body hanging from the tram wires on the Troitsky Bridge, or crumpled before a firing squad. Or worse. I didn't want to imagine what they would do to these men.

But who was to say history stopped with us? Who was to say this too would not pass away—the Bolshevik stranglehold on the soviet—as the Provisional Government had, and the tsar. "They'll have to negotiate with you. How can they not?"

He thumbed my cheek. Rope, seaweed, ice. "They might, they might not. They want the respect of the people. But if they decide not to listen... You know how big a 350 millimeter gun is? The shells weigh a ton apiece. They reload three a minute. We can hit a target thirty kilometers away. Each ship has twelve, and that's just the ships. Think the Bolsheviks are up for a fight like that? Over open ice, with no cover? Against us? Our Red brothers, whom we've defended in battle, who fought alongside us for three long years? They know what we're made of. Do you think they'd willingly fight us—we, who died for them?" He pressed his forehead to mine, blue-green eyeball to brown.

"This is it, Marina. I had to come tell you. I know my poems stink, but this is my poem."

We clung to each other, foreheads together, as the gravity of the moment sank in. Kronstadt, the flower of the Red Navy, had challenged the Bolsheviks to a high-stakes game. Its price was blood and its prize was Russia. Something banged in the next room, Shafranskaya moving around. She probably heard every word we said. Pasha was in danger here. People had seen him downstairs, they knew he was in my room. Were there informers at the House of Arts? I let my inner eye run over the faces in the canteen, in the halls. None stood out. Anton was jealous, sulky and resentful, but not treacherous. Anyone else? Did I have enemies? I didn't take as much care as I might... If anyone found these posters at the House, we all could be accused of treason.

Pasha's hand moved under my coat, inside my dress, sought my breast. He kissed my neck, my mouth. His blue-green gaze grayed in seriousness. "I wish we had more time."

We kissed, like sea creatures, not needing to breathe, twining our tentacles around one another. Not even time to make love. "I have to go." He gently extricated himself from my arms, collecting himself before battle. Now I felt the other side of him. That unknown language of him—the man of blood, the fighter. Fist of the revolution.

"Can I help you post the bills?" I was no soldier, only a poet, and I had no 350 millimeter poems. It would mean death to be caught with such papers. I touched his face like a blind girl, memorizing the hard bones. He kissed the palm of my hand. There were worse fates than to die with such a man. Now I understood how a wife could follow a husband to prison or exile. "I could hold them for you. I could keep a lookout."

He patted my face, roughly, between both his palms, as if catching and releasing me, as a child pats his mother's cheeks. "I'm not the only one in town. You just keep the lantern lit. Write a poem about me, your heroic Kronstadt sailor. I'll be back before morning. You can read it to me."

* * *

The light guttered in the lamp, I had the wick turned down as far as I could to save the kerosene, and waited for him to appear out of the black night, my mouth dry with the fear that he wouldn't. I'd remember his courage, whether he was killed tonight or not. I wished I'd asked him about the joke he told himself about life and kept behind his eyes, the laughter that never went out. I prayed it wouldn't be tortured from him. I would imagine it living within him until the very end.

I sipped pine-needle tea—it was bitter, but we'd heard that drinking it kept scurvy at bay. Since then we'd all switched to pine needles. The corridor smelled like the forest at Maryino. I imagined Pasha with his resolutions and a glue pot nestled under his shirt to keep it warm, out in the dark and the swirling snow. Finding a wall, somewhere the resolution would be seen but not torn down too quickly—a courtyard, a corner in a workingman's district, the opening of a passageway. Brushing snow off the stone. As he held the poster up by a forearm, the brush went into the pot and *slap slap*, up onto the wall. Watching for patrols, and on to the next spot. How diligent would patrols be on a night like this? Normally I'd say not very, but it was martial law—they must know the rebels were in town, or why impose a curfew?

I hadn't even thought about that. The patrols, the sentries on the bridges, weren't only to keep the workers *in* but also the sailors *out*. If they spotted him, they wouldn't even wait to see what he was doing. They'd shoot him before he had a chance to run, because he was out, and the night belonged to the Bolsheviks, and also the day. I saw his flawless body facedown in the snow, and the falling flakes erasing him. By morning he'd be buried, along with the secret joke. He said he'd go toward the Admiralty docks and Kolomna—the neighborhood of the sailors' club, which had been recently closed. Now I knew why. The spot where we were going to launch our sailboat this spring, when all this was over. If he could only live through this night.

I listened as a dog listens, for the smallest sound. All sounds were suspect. Anything at all could mean danger, anything could lead to death. No gunshots, that was good, silence was sweet on a night like this, but snow muffled sounds. Would I hear a shot? No boot steps in the hall or on the stairs—that was important too. No visitors and no shots. Here was where Blok's sounds had gone.

I thought of Pasha's smile. How could he still smile like that? I wished I were a sculptor, to capture forever the ropy square shoulders, his chiseled leanness, that grace. How I wanted to see him on the deck of a boat, sailing between islands in an azure sea, leaning into the wind. I knew how he'd squint, take our bearings. He was so straightforward, never really raised his voice—that easy manner, like a man showing open hands to a dog: *I'm not making problems.* Yet he was a battle-hardened fighter, a killer, and now he and his brothers were out in the night, raising their old red banners against Bolshevik power.

I kept the flame as low as I could, so it would last the night. He must be able to find my window in the dark.

It was almost morning when I heard a stone tossed against my windowpane. I took off my boots and ran—flew—down to the Bolshaya Morskaya courtyard gate, that discreet entry Pashol was accustomed to leaving by so as not to disturb the house. He was hiding in an arch, ran for the door when I opened it. I shut it behind him and locked it. I pointed down to my feet, *Take off your boots.* He saw and took off his own—cold on the feet but no one must know he was here. It would be dangerous not just for me but for the entire house. Even Gumilev would not have sheltered a Kronstadt sailor now.

In my room, in my tiny bed, we made love as silently as starfishes. You wouldn't think two such weary, half-starved human beings could find such tenderness. That irrepressible smile, the private joke behind his eyes, the sound of the breakers I could hear in his chest when I pressed my ear to it as if to a shell. He slept deeply, instantly.

Too soon, Petrograd's weak, despondent dawn smudged the window, and then the inevitable, dangerous day. We shared some tea and a bit of bread and a sausage he'd brought, and when it was safe for him to reappear on the streets, he went. *Pashol.*

53 *A Visit from Moscow*

As could have been predicted, the soviet lashed back with accusations and flat-out lies. The Kronstadters had beaten their commissar hostages. The Kronstadt sailors were counterrevolutionary traitors in the pay of foreign powers. They were following a White general. It was absurd, horrific. Could anybody believe this, having read the Kronstadt Declaration? Who could entertain the notion that such loyal sailors were following some White general? I wanted to share what I knew with someone, but didn't dare speak of it, not even with Anton. My knowledge was too intimately tied to my sailor lover.

Within the beehive of the House of Arts, the buzz was about *Dom Iskusstv,* not the declaration. They talked about who would be in it, who would be excluded. They worried about attacks on us by the Left at IZO, the House of Arts' frequent rival. They talked about rations—the bread situation was dire. But most of them hadn't seen the declaration, and those who had, considered it a symptom of the generalized chaos, just another part of the great storm. Whereas it was all I could think about. What was going on out there, across the ice in the fortress of sea and salt and might?

There was one person I could ask—the man who had placed me at the sailors' club to begin with. Gumilev had been born on Kronstadt, his father was a naval doctor there. He still had ties to the island. Surely he had some information. I climbed the stairs to where he lived in the Eliseevs' famous private bathroom and knocked on the door—making sure no one was watching. He answered, wearing a jacket and scarf, felt slippers and a fur hat. "I'm sorry to disturb you, Nikolai Stepanovich. Can I speak to you privately?"

He smiled his little smile. "Of course."

I'd never been inside the Eliseevs' personal bathroom, only the big one in the basement where I got a shower every month. This was glorious, tiled with glazed Tiffany fish, three windows and a bathtub, a tiled vanity with a big round mirror. Gumilev's bed was just a cot, but it was made up with military precision, taut enough to bounce a gold ruble. He'd been writing at a desk that faced Nevsky. The snow drifted past from one window to the next. He took my hand.

"Sit down." He indicated the cot. "What can I do for you, Marina Dmitrievna?"

God, did he think I was accepting his pass? I perched uncomfortably on the edge, wondered where his wife was. She'd been sent out of the city, somewhere with their child, leaving him to play Don Juan, the scourge of the studio girls. "I wanted to ask if you knew what's happening out at Kronstadt."

His friendliness soured like milk. It curdled on his face, you could smell it. "I have no idea," he said stiffly. "What made you think that I would?"

Now I was confused. "It was you who sent me to the sailors' club. You have classes out there on the island. You grew up there! Surely you still have contacts—"

His froggy green eyes grew as hard as glass. "I have no contact with them. No one does. They've been outlawed, or haven't you heard."

"But surely someone must know…" I could feel myself starting to cry, giving in to the strain.

His manner became more and more clipped. "Gorky probably knows something. But I wouldn't bother him now. There's nothing to do but wait, and I highly advise you do just that. Go back to work, and for God's sake keep your concerns to yourself, which is what I'm doing." Indicating his desk, he was working on a new poem. "And will continue to do. Thank you for coming by. Now, if you'll excuse me…" He led me to the door, opened it for me. "Goodbye, Marina Dmitrievna." A slight bow.

And so I was dismissed from the presence of Count Gumilev. As if he'd never heard of Kronstadt.

Well, I was certainly not going to sit in the House of Arts and wait for the list of the executed, as Nikolai Gumilev suggested. I buttoned up and walked through the bitter wind to Znamenskaya Square and the Vikzhel club. They would know everything. But when I got to their club, I saw that the door was thickly padlocked. I shook the icy chain. No Skorokhod, and now no Vikzhel. I imagined the same fate had befallen the sailors' club. No classes, no rations. Life was going to get very tough indeed. But I was not in the danger my union men and women were, not to mention Pasha and the sailors. I only prayed that the Bolsheviks would see sense and give in, that the third revolution would come soon. Four days had brought down the tsar. And October went even faster than that.

I made my way home in the worsening storm. I could barely see through the snow, it was falling so fast. I stumbled upon a group of workers marching ahead of a cadre of soldiers with fixed bayonets. How weak the protesters looked, their heads bowed against the blowing snow, the fight gone out of them. They appeared, then were erased by the swirling snow. Like the Twelve. How would this all turn out? I thought of Mina, just overhead, in her father's studio, the bay windows on the fifth floor from which we had watched the last revolution take place. If only I had that small camera again, I would take a picture of those strikers. I wished Mina and I were still friends. Those had been good times. We'd had no idea how it would end. We'd believed in the promise of the revolution, believed our time was coming.

I sat at my desk, writing a poem about Pasha and the Kronstadt sailors. *Pravda* said the government had dropped leaflets on Kronstadt. That they'd arrested the families of the mutineers, were holding them as hostages. They warned that the sailors must either end the rebellion, hand over the ringleaders, and return the commissar and the chairman of their soviet, or the hostages would pay with their lives. The demand came from Trotsky himself: *unconditional surrender*. These the sailors who had supported him most courageously in 1917, who had cheered him at the Cirque Moderne, had marched to his defense against the Provisional Government, who had closed the Constituent Assembly, and had fought under him to turn the tide of the war. And now this. Unconditional surrender.

The Defense Committee for the Northern Region one-upped Trotsky with its own ultimatum—of course Zinoviev had to have the last word—reminding the Red Fleet of what had happened to Wrangel's White forces in the Crimea. The Whites that hadn't already succumbed to Bolshevik arms and Cheka retribution had died by the thousands from hunger and disease. "The same fate awaits the Kronstadt mutineers unless you surrender within twenty-four hours. If you do, you'll be pardoned. If you resist, you'll be shot like partridges."

Shot like partridges. Zinoviev, who fell to pieces any time danger approached. Who did he think he was talking to? Even Trotsky was not so dismissive of the bravest, truest of the Red fighters.

I could only imagine the response on Kronstadt.

I waited for a massive reply from the people, an outpouring of outrage. Demonstrations on Nevsky, clamor, clashes. But there was nothing. The Kronstadt men were risking everything for us—their honor, their arms, their ships, their very lives! Where were the workers? Where were the people, the strikes in support?

I learned the answer the following day in the bread queue at the House of Scholars. Wagonloads of food had been delivered to the workers' districts, with promises that Bolshevik privilege would be ended, the roadblocks eliminated. All items from Kronstadt's list of demands were being addressed. The soviet was undercutting the sailors by acquiescing to their demands without acknowledging that that's what they were doing. The question was, would the Petrograd workers be so easily bought off?

Ships creak in their coats of ice
The stony fortress groans
Winter seals the sea in its tomb
The sea-bell's clapper
cleaves in its mouth

No way to toll its warning.
The sea heaves against its chains
The icebound ships lie dreaming
of swift currents and dawns,
quickening sails before a bright wind.
While the land bears its terrible weight
of roads and laws, plows and fields.
Cold casts the sea in its likeness.
Come, spring, and break winter's spell!
Shatter it like mirrorglass
Restore the sea to its shifting
And the sailors to the shores.
Those with tidal hair
will be masters here
The rearing horse fights the rein
While the spring floods
carry the wakening ships.

Since Pasha's brief reappearance, Anton had been nothing but considerate. He saw my fear and refrained from any commentary. He must have guessed what Pasha's visit meant. "Don't worry. They'll agree in the end," he consoled me. "Right now they're beating their breasts and spouting ultimatums, but you watch, at the very brink, somebody will come to his senses and they'll all back down—*for the sake of the revolution, lya lya fa fa.*"

He never directly referred to Pasha, always to the "situation." Nevertheless I could tell he was secretly relieved that Pasha was out of the way. That my sailor might end up at the wrong end of a Bolshevik bayonet didn't trouble him except for my sake. I couldn't fault him for it. He was doing the best he could with his jealousy, and perhaps there was even a measure of grudging admiration.

I brought my poem to show him. As I turned into his corridor, I could hear laughter and chatter. Anton's door halfway down the hall lay open. Light spilled out and people stood talking in the hall, Mandelstam chatting with one of Zamyatin's circle, Alla Tvorcheskaya laughing. Was it a party? Alla stared at me in the strangest way. I reached the door. The room was thick with poets, hazy with smoke. How did so many people cram themselves in there? Someone was telling a story, and I recognized the voice. There, looming in the center of the crowd, a foot taller than anyone else, broad arms extended to emphasize a point—Genya Kuriakin. His tawny hair had grown out—and why not? After all, the war was over. He wore a tweedy suit with a vest. A real grown-up, an important man. He looked well, fleshed out in this time of starvation. Perhaps things really were better in Moscow—at least for some. Curtailing Bolshevik privilege? I thought not. He was talking about someone reading in a café, a fight that had broken out. I tried to back away, but he saw me. He stopped in midgesture.

My heart was leaping around in my chest. I thought I was going to have a heart attack. "Why is it so smoky in here?" I said. The *bourgeoika*, as usual, was leaking. I pretended that was why I'd come, and picked my way through the people, hardly noticing where I was or who was there, what I was doing. Genya, Anton, and Mandelstam in one room—like the Ghosts of Christmas Past, Present, and Future.

"Marina!" Genya shouted. "Are you real? What are you doing with this nest of reprobates?"

I struggled for breath. "I live here. Didn't you know?"

"No one told me."

We both turned to Anton, sitting on a box next to Shklovsky, his lap full of papers, trying not to catch our eyes. His face was white with guilt. He hadn't told Genya anything, all these months? Not about my arrival at the House, our love affair, none of it? People were staring. Our fellow members of the House of Arts always had a nose for a good drama brewing, a story that might be shared for days, or years.

"Please. Not now," I said, under my breath. "Finish your story. We'll talk later." I would not cry in front of these people, make a scene. I was already a two-headed calf here. "Please."

He gave me a wounded look and turned to Anton, who was busying himself stacking pages—sweating and pale, his expression like a cornered fugitive's. Had he been betting I wouldn't come see him tonight? That I was too wrapped up with my sailor's fate to venture out of my room? Or perhaps Genya's visit had been a surprise to him as well.

"Tell us about Moscow," I said to Genya as I squatted by the stove, peeling off bits of kindling with my pocketknife. "You look good. It suits you."

But right now, Genya looked more like a man riding in a cart that had just overturned, leaving him sitting in the road among the rutabagas and cabbages. I opened the door of the belching *bourgeoika* and started tending to its needs—like old times—while Anton pretended to read the manuscript. I could tell he wasn't even seeing the pages, his cigarette clamped between his lips. How long did he think he could hide our affair? Pretend he didn't see me every day, read my verse, make love with me on that very bed?

I poked at the fire. True to form, Anton had thrown an account book in there without wadding it up. We'd found a whole cache of them behind a wall at the far end of the Monkey House. Everyone was writing on them, burning them, wiping themselves—it was quite a treasure trove. I plucked out what I could and began twisting sheets into burnable form, returning them to their little queen, coaxing the flames.

"Mayakovsky was here. He read *150 Million*," Tereshenko told Genya. "What a piece of pompous shit." Seeing if he could start a fight. He envied Genya, with three collections behind him now, and his boxer's aggressiveness tended to surface at times like this. "Lenin said it was posturing twaddle."

"Politicians aren't the best judges of poetry," Genya said, standing up, walking to the bed, squeezing himself between Sasha and Dunya, putting his arms around them. "I wouldn't want Comrade Lenin picking out a girl for me either." Everyone laughed. What was Genya doing here in the first place? *He didn't even know about Iskra.* That she had been born. That she had died.

"You wouldn't trust Vladimir Ilyich to pick out a nice girl for you?" teased Inna Gants, perching on the edge of the desk, flirting. She was fifty if she was a day, but she knew an attractive man when she saw one.

My husband flexed his eyebrows in a filmic pantomime of surprise. "Yes, I told him, 'Ilyich, you run the country and let me take care of the poetry. And my girl.'" He glanced at me again.

My lover became very interested in sharpening his pencil with his little penknife.

"He's actually said as much. He doesn't like futurism, cubism, rayonism, *zaum,* or anything that doesn't have a doily and a vase on it, but thinks the artists should be in charge of the art, no matter his opinion."

I finished with the stove, brushed my hands on my black stockings, and stood.

"The leadership looks at all modern art the same way," said Shklovsky, balanced precariously on a three-legged stool. "Exactly the way a horse looks at a piece of sculpture. As something to scratch itself on." I wondered if he had any idea of the forest fire that was roaring between his two favorite poets, whether he cared. Thank God for theorists. "Or like a housewife—'Where's the handle? Which end sweeps?'"

Sasha wiped his face in his hand. As a founding member of Transrational Interlocutors of the Terrestrial Now, he had been there since I first appeared that horrible night my father had put me out. He and Dunya understood exactly the awfulness of the situation unfolding before them, and did their best to keep the conversational balloon afloat. "I don't know, I wouldn't mind designing brooms," Sasha jumped in. "Popova's designing textiles, even china. It's all culture in the end, isn't it?"

"Or the end of culture," Mandelstam quipped. His brown eyes taking in our details, sorting. I couldn't look at him, he'd read me like a theater's marquee.

Dunya leaned forward across Genya. "I can't wait to see your broom, Sashenka. A cubo-futurist sweeping machine." I wondered if Genya recognized her as Mina's little sister. She'd been just a girl in the days of the Poverty Artel.

"You should give us a poem," said Inna Gants. "From the *Red October*. It sounded thrilling." Did I note a slight edge of sarcasm?

"Oh, I'm sure you'll hear plenty," Genya said.

"Chernikov read one when Mayakovsky was here," she persevered, smelling blood in the water.

I tried to escape. But as I passed, Genya caught my arm. "How long have you been here?"

"Since summer," I said, trying for a noncommittal voice. Anton stacked the pages one more time and abandoned his place by Shklovsky. "What do you think of Petrograd these days? Have we changed much?" Nonchalantly.

"I don't know yet. I just got in," he said. "I've had meetings all morning at ROSTA." The Soviet news agency. "This afternoon, we were up at IZO." All the avant-gardists collected there, ever looking for an opportunity to undermine the House of Arts, questioning our revolutionary credentials, itching to get control of all the arts institutions, tear down the museums. Shklovsky was part of that group, Sasha worked in their studios with the wonderful artist Petrov-Vodkin. How I wished artists could stop dividing into combatants—couldn't we have Petrov-Vodkin *and* Dobuzhinsky? Couldn't we have Genya *and* Mandelstam? How we artists loved to define ourselves in opposition to others, separate into camps.

"And how do they find us at IZO?" Inna Gants asked. "Are we hopeless creaky antiques, becalmed in the wake of the great modernist ship?"

Genya began talking about Petrograd and relations with Narkompros, but he didn't take his eyes off me. I couldn't very well leave now. I found a place to lean against the wall and listened to them talk about the rejection of narrative poetry in Moscow circles, the death of the ballad. I thought of his poem to me as I held my newborn baby, "Funeral for Myself on the Tracks at Kambarka." *Who would have dreamed / I would / drop / my own heart / from the gallows / pull the rope myself.*

Anton was fiddling at his desk. He wouldn't look at either of us. His world was crashing in. Now Genya knew he'd been lying all this time, though my husband still had no idea why. How would Genya react if he knew we were lovers? Had Anton been thinking that if his beloved Genya just stayed in Moscow he could have us both? As long as we didn't meet. I went to the desk, leaned over to him. "I think that pencil's sharp enough." I picked up some of the pages he was pretending to sort. A new manuscript from Gennady Kuriakin.

Anton blew on the pencil, now sharp enough for surgery, tested the point with his thumb. Was he going to jab it into his jugular? Death by graphite? "I didn't know he was coming until yesterday, I swear," he whispered. "It was Shklovsky's idea. I tried to talk him out of it. The curfew...I said that he'd have to sleep on the floor instead of on a swan at the Astoria, but he insisted on coming. Said he wanted to see Gumilev in his dinner jacket."

But Gumilev had been making himself scarce since the Kronstadt "situation" broke loose. Maybe he'd gone off to wherever he'd stuck his wife. Though martial law meant no one in or out of the city...except for certain Bolshevik poets traveling here from Moscow. Perhaps Genya had been sent. Just being in the room with him exhausted me. So much unsaid, and how could I say it now? My head hurt, my eyes hurt. I edged out into the hall, hoping to make a clean getaway.

"Wait. Marina!" Genya called from the doorway. "Where are you going?"

"A stroll in the moonlight?" I said over my shoulder. "Ah, these balmy Petrograd nights..."

"Wait." And I waited, my back to the party and all their wondering eyes.

His hand, so gentle, on my sleeve. His shock of hair like rye hanging down in a forelock, his body solid and strong in his new suit. "I've been thinking about you for so long. I assumed you were still in the country, or...God, what happened to you? I can't believe Anton didn't say anything. Why didn't you write? Why didn't you let me know you were back in Petrograd?"

I could only stare at him, hoping he could read tragedy in my eyes and leave it at that.

"I'm sorry I had to leave you there." He was twisting with guilt. "Did you get my poem?"

I nodded. I didn't dare even speak. I could feel my mouth, trembling.

"Do you blame me?"

I shook my head, bit my lip.

"Where's the baby? I thought about you so much, thinking you'd died in the village."

I led him farther down the hallway, away from our audience hanging in the doorway of Anton's room. "It was a girl. I called her Iskra."

He sighed, leaned against the wall, his eyes closed. A little laugh, and then a shudder. "We were always going to call our child Iskra."

I could feel his great body, warm and familiar, and resisted the urge to melt into him. Life was complicated enough. He was waiting for me to tell him the rest. He gazed at me when I told him, his tender face unmasked, then he turned to the wall, laid his forehead against it. "It was that damned *baba*, wasn't it? With her Christ and her spells. I should never have let you go with her."

"That woman saved my life." What could he know of Praskovia, and his threat to burn her village. "The baby came, and she was so beautiful, Genya." I clutched his sleeve, laid my cheek against the wool, breathing in his scent, so familiar. My feelings for him trickling back. "She had red hair, and green eyes." But they were Kolya's eyes, not his. "I helped bring in the harvest to pay off my debt. It was just as well. All of their men were gone."

He stared at the ceiling. "I never even thought...How could I have been so stupid?"

Yes, we were quite the pair. What we hadn't thought would fill an ocean. He'd sent me a poem, but left me without any money. He was in such a hurry to move on, save his train, slip across the Urals through the opening in the fighting.

"They'd wanted to adopt her. But I brought her back. The comrades in Izhevsk helped us."

He moaned and rolled his head against the wall. "Forgive me, Marina. I didn't know."

How much of this to keep in, what to leave out. Certainly the face of the Chekist on the train, that stinking toilet. The *besprizorniki* helping me get rid of the body. "She was brilliant, Genya. So funny. I never knew a baby could be funny." I was finding it hard to breathe. *Don't look at me, Genya. Let me finish.*

"Do you have a picture of her?"

"No. Just a curl of her hair." Cut from her head just before I buried her.

"I want to see it."

"It'll wait. But I need to tell you, when we got back I found a job in an orphanage, so I could take her to work with me."

He nodded. How to finish this story. Arkady, the black thread running through my life. "There was a man, a criminal. Someone who felt he owned me. I was taking a chance to come back. He found me."

He stood facing the wall like a boy being punished in class.

"I was kidnapped... And one of the orphans jumped off the roof with her."

He winced. "Why would he do a thing like that?"

"He didn't want her to be an orphan. He didn't want that life for her. Can you understand that?"

He pounded his big fist on the wall. "I don't understand anything!" Now he was shouting. I could see people staring from Anton's doorway. "I'm an idiot and I don't understand the simplest thing!"

I turned away, so the poets couldn't see my face. "You don't have to understand. *I* understand. Every day, I think of her. Every day, I see something and think, *Iskra would love this!* I see a redheaded girl and can't stop staring, thinking, *How old would she be now...*"

Suddenly Genya's fury melted and he threw those arms around me. "Come to the Astoria with me," he said. "There's decent food, hot water. You could wash up, wash your clothes."

I didn't give a damn about my comfort, about my clothes. "I

buried her at Novodevichy Cemetery. Next to someone else's grave."

"Come with me to Moscow," he said, taking my hand. "I've never stopped loving you, Marina."

I remembered how Anton had wept in my room. *I'm moving to Moscow.* Anton, who had stayed with me through the terrible nights. Anton, who would not have ridden off on the *Red October.* "I'm living with Anton now," I said. I moved away from him. Such a fantasy, to think that we could be together again. We'd been through too much, both of us.

He laughed, once, then realized I wasn't joking.

I couldn't leave Anton. I had found a home here. I began to recite:

> *She slept all the winter*
> *covered with white eiderdown . . .*

He leaned against the wall listening, hung his head. "Forgive me." I put my hand on his shoulder, to say farewell, and left him there, as I disappeared into the labyrinth of the House.

54 *Sea Ice*

Pung. Pung. The windows shook. The sound rolled through, the echoes lasting until the next shock arrived. A thunder more thunderous than anything I'd heard from Pulkovo Heights that night in the sniper's nest on Moskovsky Prospect. It sounded like dinosaurs pounding the earth. I kept thinking it would stop, but it kept going. *Pung PungpugnpungPUNG.*

The battle for Kronstadt had begun. Anton came down to my room, lay next to me on the bed, and we listened, helpless. Trotsky, my Trotsky, our Trotsky, Flame of the Cirque Moderne, Savior of the Revolution, was bringing a message to revolutionary Kronstadt. *Unconditional surrender.*

And the sailors were answering.

We counted seconds the way Seryozha and I used to count thunderclaps, the seconds between the flash and the rumble. But tonight's awful black blossoms of sound were too close to count. They overlapped like an evil bouquet and would not stop.

All the night long we lay in bed listening to its dreadful music. How could anyone bear this, the force, the power? I tried to picture the battle as Pasha had painted it for me. Downy-faced boy cadets and Red soldiers marching over the ice, no cover except that of night and the storm. Shells the size of pigs weighing a ton apiece let loose from the *Petropavlovsk*, crashing into the ice as they crawled across. The deafening barrage, the crack of sea ice. Their terror as the Red soldiers broke through in the dark, the upturning floes delivering them to their deaths in a sea liquid and voracious under its deceptive crust.

And on the island—the Kronstadt sailors. How alone they would be in the dark, firing on men they had fought beside during these long years, who returned their fire with guns dragged onto the ice, or perhaps firing from the shore. The awful loneliness of the ice-locked ships. Only the men and their guns were free, and free to die, as perhaps all of us would. If only spring would come in time, the ships would be free to move about. They could head to sea, and return for battle. The troops could not get close enough to attempt the island. I prayed for warm weather. It had happened before, in February 1917. How long could they hold out like this—alone, with the full force of the Red Army pitted against them? The land forces could resupply, but Kronstadt had what it had.

Red against Red. It sickened me like a boat in heavy seas, pitching and rolling. I could not lie still. *Pung. Pung pung Pung. POMpompom.* I blew out the lamp. Anton lay curled around me in the small bed. "Are you sleeping?"

"No."

Between percussions, snow sizzled on the glass. A vicious night. I took his hand, laced my fingers into his. I could hear him breathing. *POMpomPOM.*

"What did you say to Genya last night?"

"I said we were together." I rested my head on his shoulder. And that was enough for him.

Pung Pung Pung Pung.

Around five a.m., I sat up on one elbow. Anton had fallen asleep. He was snoring. Something had changed. I jostled him. "Anton, wake up."

"What." He tried to rouse himself, rubbing his eyes.

"Shh. Listen." It was the sound of no sound. The snoring of Shafranskaya next door was the only thing that let me believe what I was not hearing. We waited. Five minutes. Ten.

I lay on my back and gazed out at the streetlight. The storm still howled, but that was all. What had happened? Had the army retreated? I felt the urge to cross myself, but resisted. It would have alarmed Anton. "Trotsky's killed them." I could feel hysteria rise up in me like an uncoiling snake. "Oh God, please let it not be so." Such bravery, these Saint Georges, slashing at the dragon's breast with a hero's short knife, only to be struck by its tail.

Anton held me, tight. "You don't know. All we know is that the shooting's stopped," he whispered into my hair. "They could be reloading. They could be negotiating. Lenin could have radioed in. They might have seen Christ in snowshoes. You just don't know."

But what if they'd lost? All the Argonauts. Their bright summer sails. Everything that was good and clean and strong. The pain sat in my chest like a sharp-toothed rat. Around dawn, I fell into an exhausted sleep. Anton never let go of my hand.

We woke at about noon. Now I thought maybe I'd been wrong. These days, I always expected the worst. It was possible it was just as Anton had said. A cease-fire. Negotiations. I got out of bed and rearranged my clothing, my coat, donned my hat. The blizzard raged. "Someone knows what's happened. Someone's got to." I went out into the corridor. "Anybody know what happened? Did they take Kronstadt?"

Slezin shook his head. Grin, the old eccentric who roamed the corridors to escape the cold of his room, didn't know. Anton appeared, dressed, his hair in every direction, and we went down to the canteen, where the residents looked grim and haggard from the night's bombardment. Here was Gumilev, alone at a table by the wall. He crossed his legs and went on reading a manuscript, making marks in the margins, avoiding looking at me.

"Does anybody know whether they took Kronstadt?" Anton asked.

Kuzmin regarded me pityingly. "Nothing but threats," he said. "But wouldn't there be a parade if the Bolsheviks won? We'd know, I'm sure."

We sat with our mugs of tea. I took my last bread from my pocket, gnawed on the corner, choking on my tears. I smacked the hard heel on the table, trying to crack it. "Somebody's got to know."

Gumilev shot me a warning look.

"We'll go ask Genya," Anton volunteered. "He's got to know something by now."

Ask Genya whether Kronstadt had held? "Why would he tell us? He's working for them."

Anton shrugged. "That's why he'd know."

It was true—Genya was working at ROSTA. And he was living at the Astoria, the First House of the Soviet, the very nostrils of the dragon. Across the room, Gumilev turned the pages of his paper, pretending that the fate of the Kronstadters was nothing to him. That strange man.

55 *ROSTA*

We hurried along Bolshaya Morskaya, steeling ourselves before we were hit by the full force of the blizzard in St. Isaac's Square. I could barely see the lights from the Astoria glowing through the swirling white, fortified by a new machine-gun outpost manned by grim, no doubt miserable sentries. A picture that illustrated better than anything the isolation of the Bolsheviks from the people of Petrograd. As propaganda, it failed completely.

We leaned into the wind, clutching tightly to each other, heaving ourselves forward, fighting for each step. Only the vaguest outline of St. Isaac's vast dome impressed itself through the snowstorm. I *felt* the presence of the *besprizorniki,* huddled even now on the porch of the cathedral. *God help them, or someone.* But today I could do nothing but press on.

It was a relief to enter the relative shelter of narrow Pochtamtskaya Street. So much snow fell you couldn't see the post office arch connecting one building to the next. Here was ROSTA: a three-story stone edifice housing the Bolshevik propaganda machine, the indefatigable supplier of posters that filled the windows of a hundred empty shops with cleverly stenciled figures in folk fashion or futurist boldness, with short *chastushki* couplets telling us to brush our teeth, or showing how Lenin would sweep the globe of capitalists and imperialists.

Now the windows exhorted,

> *Do you want—*
> *To fight cold?*
> *Fight hunger?*
> *You want to eat?*
> *Want to drink?*
> *Hurry, to a strike group of*
> *exemplary labor!*

I could see the delight of starving workers, hurrying to work longer shifts for no extra pay or rations. But I knew the artists who'd screened these posters, week after week, Sasha and his friends. And they did liven up the empty shops, selling revolutionary hopes, though people would have preferred bread. But all the cheerful cartoons in the world wouldn't stir one starving worker to join a strike group of exemplary labor.

ROSTA: Rossiskoye Telegrafnoye Agentstvo. I was tired of

acronyms, which to others seemed the height of modernity. Life was so swift now, no one had time for full words. *Narkompros. Sovnarkom.* We had ours too—*Disk.* But I never used it. The House of Arts seemed the last mountain ridge, representing a geological formation underneath it, so different from a rampant weed like *ROSTA* or a fast-moving train like *Proletcult.* You didn't want a sanctuary with an acronym. You didn't want a lover with a number.

Anton pushed the doors open—outer, inner. The lobby seethed with noise, with purpose, hornets buzzing angrily, the feel of the telephone exchange but even more frenzied, more important, it was half telegraph, half news agency. I could not imagine what it was like in calmer times. But then again, when had there been calmer times? Not since 1914. Typewriters beat out staccato rhythms, telephones jangled, people rushed around with papers in their hands—"people" the way Blok had described them, self-important, impatient, without a moment for humanity, their own or anyone else's. Soviet young ladies, official-looking Bolsheviks, clerks and more clerks. The glances they cast us would have suited horses or lampposts. While our factories were as empty as tombs, the great machinery still, the furnaces cold, tended by a few silent ghosts, a real skeleton crew, the feverish business of Soviet news hummed like the Ford Motor Company.

All I wanted to know was what were they saying about Kronstadt, and, if I could learn it, what was actually happening on that ice-bound island. I mourned the closure of the Vikzhel club. It made me sick to be here, trespassing into the cavern of the dragon and its treasures. I could smell its stink, its sulfurous breath, but I had to know about the silence of the guns. Had the sailors survived? Had they won? I could not read the faces—they only looked sharp and professional. How could we ever find Genya in a hive like this?

Anton walked to a high counter where a long-chinned woman scanned a newspaper, circling with a blue pencil. "Excuse us," he said. "We're looking for the poet Gennady Kuriakin."

She didn't even look up.

"He told us to meet him here."

She glanced at him, reluctantly. Saw him, saw me, and went back to her paper. He bent over the counter like a giraffe over the fence of a zoo. "What do I need to do, send a telegram?" he persevered. Down the counter, two Soviet young ladies giggled, watching him try to engage the newspaper marker. I slid down to my Soviet sisters, one a bleachy blonde, the other a brunette with makeup as thick as a fresco. "You're not hiding him under the counter are you? Big handsome poet, about twenty-three? Just up from Moscow?"

"Sure." The brunette pretended to search under the counter. "Come out, handsome. We need you to rearrange the furniture."

The blonde giggled, hid her mouth. They reminded me of the girls at the telephone exchange. The tragedy of last night seemed not to have touched them. Men fighting for the fate of the revolution were hardly as interesting as the arrival of an attractive man from Moscow. "What floor's he on?" I asked the brunette. She seemed the leader. "Or wouldn't you know, stuck down here with the *babas*?"

Anton was getting nowhere with the supervisor.

The brunette glanced toward the hall on the right. "In the radio room. Tell him to come out when he's done. Valya wants him to move something for her."

"Shut up," said the blonde and they had another giggle.

I linked my arm into Anton's, pulling him away from his unfulfilling negotiations with the sour-faced woman. "He's in the radio room."

"Hey, thanks for the help," he told the woman, and was treated to a sneer worthy of Anton himself.

We asked a comrade copyboy the way, found the stairs, where we had to watch our step, dodging people coming down—so strange, their feverish energy. I imagined Moscow was like this all the time, like a consulate of the future. We passed a vast room of clattering telegraph operators, finally finding the radio room. It was jammed with men and women, standing, arms crossed, faces grim and straining, listening to a crackling broadcast through a tarnished gramophone horn while a radioist with headphones adjusted dials on a wireless.

A tinny voice emerged from the phonograph bell: *"The result, however, was the creation of a still greater enslavement of the human personality. The power of police-gendarme monarchism passed into the hands of usurpers, the Communists, who brought to the laborers, instead of freedom, the fear every minute of falling into the torture chambers of the Cheka..."*

It was Kronstadt, radioing the mainland! Haranguing the Bolsheviks. They'd survived! No wonder these apparatchiks were seething. These "people." Free men were speaking to them in the voice of unconquered Kronstadt! I struggled to keep my face a mask. I wanted to burst out laughing, I wanted to dance a pirouette! They would have torn me to shreds. As it was they shouted taunts and curses at the disembodied voice rising like fragrance from the flower of the bell. *"They have done this for the sake of preserving a calm, unsaddened life—for the new bureaucracy of Communist commissars and bureaucrats! With the aid of bureaucratic trade unions, they have tied the workers to their benches, made labor not a joy but a new serfdom. The protests by peasants, expressed in spontaneous uprisings—"*

"Spontaneous, my wrinkled pants," said a man with cropped gray hair.

"Ask General Kozlovsky, you White swine," shouted a slender woman, mopping her face with a red handkerchief. Flaunting the symbol of revolution without the thing itself. Sausages painted on wood.

"I can't listen to this tripe," said a small bald man. "I need some air."

He left, and two more clerks pressed in, avid to hear. But I was the only one rejoicing. *Free Kronstadt stands firm!* I wanted to shout from the roof. *Wake up, Petrograd! The moment is now!*

Anton glanced about us with barely disguised panic, sweating. We were so much more ragged than the rest of these comrades, surely we would be discovered forthwith. He lifted his eyebrows in a gesture of emergency, indicating the door with his head. But I was savoring every word that emerged from the brass horn of the radio. This was history. I was going to drink it in to the last drop.

I imagined the sailors on their ships, gathered together, writing these words. Pasha and his mates. Laughing, hunching over their papers. I prayed that the people of Petrograd could hear this. Somewhere there must be secret wireless receivers in basements and back rooms. How dangerous it must be for them. If they were caught, the Chekists would say they were transmitting to the Whites, forming a counterrevolutionary cabal inside the city.

"Let's go," Anton said under his breath.

But I was not budging. I wouldn't miss this for a tsar's ransom. I stood mesmerized by the boldness of the broadcast. We hadn't heard anyone speak out like this since October 1917. *"They pretend to make concessions: in Petrograd Province they remove the antiprofiteer roadblock detachment. Assign ten million in gold for purchase of produce abroad."*

I'd heard this rumor, that the Bolsheviks were making concessions to the workers in exchange for a return to work. But ten million rubles? That could purchase a lot of food. Would starving workers hold out, or could they take it and still stand their ground?

"And how much are you getting from the Entente?" a man with bags under his eyes shouted at the speaker. "From the émigrés?"

I couldn't look at him, I might scream in his face. How could anyone think the Kronstadt sailors were on the payroll of the Whites? How could they think this was coming from anyone but the beautiful red heart of the Baltic Fleet? *Krasniy, krasiviy. Red and beautiful,* one and the same. Anton stared at me, his eyes rounded like railway warning lights.

"Who the hell are you?" The man in leather suddenly noticed us. "Do you have permission to be in this room?" He narrowed his piggy eyes. People turned to stare. "I don't know you."

Before I could find words, Anton leapt in. "We're looking for Gennady Kuriakin. Hero of the agit-train *Red October*. For an interview in the *Art of the Commune*. The comrades downstairs told us he was here." He'd always been quick on his feet.

"Moskovsky poet," said one of the intellectual-looking men, thick glasses, frizzy hair. "The big one."

"I know, I know," said the leather-clad man irritably. "But you see him here?"

"He's in Propaganda, working on a broadcast," said the bespectacled apparatchik.

Now a different voice came through the radio's megaphone like a tarnished morning glory, a younger voice, hearty and brash. *"Greetings to the International Women of the World!"*

It was International Women's Day! March 8. Four years to the day from when the revolution began. How could I have forgotten? Because there were no parades, no speeches. They didn't dare, the symbolism was too strong. *"We the people of Kronstadt, under the thunder of cannons, under the explosions of shells sent at us by the enemies of the laboring people—"* I liked that *under the thunder* ... Poetic. Perhaps it was one of my students, or Gumilev's. *"We send our fraternal greetings to you, working women of the world!"*

"Well, the working women say nuts to you, Kronstadt scum!" said a thin woman in a thin sweater.

Kronstadt scum?! It was all I could do not to slap her face. *I killed better men than myself and for what?* Had these people been completely wiped clean of memory? The Kronstadt sailors were the midwives of the revolution, the soul of it. It made my heart swell with pride to hear: *"We send greetings from Red Kronstadt, from the Kingdom of Liberty. We wish you fortune, to all the sooner win freedom from oppression and coercion. Long live the Free Revolutionary Working Woman! Long live the Worldwide Social Revolution!"*

For the first time in four years International Women's Day had not been greeted by celebrations, factory holidays, parades. Kronstadt had shown us what had become of that revolution—their resistance had stripped the skin from the body of the state. Everything but power and the will to survive had been left by the side of the road. Anton was begging me. *Let's go!*

"Go back to your mother, you son of a whore," spat the man in black leather at the grimy brass bell as we slipped toward the door. He turned around just in time to catch us leaving. "Hey! You! *Art of the Commune.* I want to talk to you." But we were already gone.

I was walking on air, following Anton down the long noisy hall. I trotted up and grabbed his arm. "I don't need to find Genya. It's okay, we can just go." Glass-paned doors ranged on both sides of us, from which we heard typing, ringing telephones.

"No, we do need to." He glanced back and I followed his gaze—the man in black leather, like Bely's brunet spy, was watching from the door of the radio room. A woman carrying a stack of papers passed us. "Comrade, we're looking for Propaganda."

She shrugged, her tired eyes sliding from Anton to me in my provincial sheepskin. "This is ROSTA. I guess you've found it. Maybe you were looking for *Pravda*?" Her little joke. *Pravda* meant *truth*. "Keep going, you can smell the brimstone."

I didn't need to see Genya now, but we required an alibi. I already knew what I wanted to know. Kronstadt had held. *Congratulations to the Women Workers of the World*—what cheek!

A few more doors down, we heard someone reading in a deep, clear actor's voice: "*There is complete calm today in Petrograd. Even those factories where attacks on Soviet power occurred earlier are quiet. They've understood what the agents of the Entente and counterrevolution are pushing them to do*—"

Anton opened the door. Cigarette smoke billowed out like steam from a *banya*. A burst of typewriter clatter, then Genya's familiar voice: "Add *isolated attacks*. And make them *small* factories. Microscopic. Manufacturers of flea underwear and galoshes for mice." He emerged from the fug like a train arriving in a station. Head tilted back, picturing the words behind his forehead. Six or seven other writers sat at desks or perched on chairs turned wrong way round, smoking and drinking glasses of tea. A regular strike group of exemplary labor.

An unshaven man at a typewriter was reading: "*—an eight-thousand-person meeting of Petrograd dockworkers unanimously passed a resolution supporting Soviet power. The Petrograd garrison has not wavered...*"

"*The Communist Party and the Workers Are One,*" Genya said, leaning over an artist who was evidently sketching a poster. "No, bigger. *Kronstadt Take Warning!* Yes, like that."

"Demoralization," said a young man whose sweater was unraveling. *"Demoralization grows among the isolated sailors."* He was no older than the *kursanty* they'd sent against the workers. *"The number of those deserting grows by the hour. General Kozlovsky is losing their trust."*

It was as if we'd walked from one world to its mirror opposite. In that other world, the radio broadcasted the triumph of Kronstadt, proof of their survival, their integrity. In this room, they were demoralized and led by some General Kozlovsky, and the party and the workers were one. What was Genya doing here, creating these lies? Safe and warm and sitting around a ROSTA office making up news out of whole cloth, when there were men like Pasha and Slava out defending the revolution with the pledge of their own blood. Men he'd known!

Now he saw us, his eyes dark with purpose. Was he ashamed of being caught at this evil work? Not at all. "Anton! Marina...Sorry but we've only got twenty minutes to finish this broadcast. Have a seat if you'd like. Speak up if you've got any ideas."

A plain little woman read aloud from her typewriter carriage. *"News from abroad shows that, simultaneously with the events in Kronstadt, the enemies of Soviet Russia are spreading the most fantastic fabrications — saying that there are disorders in Russia — "*

"There aren't disorders in Russia?" I asked Genya.

The woman glared at me.

"That's enough," he said sharply.

"They say the Soviet government has supposedly fled to the Crimea. That Moscow is in the hands of the rebels. That blood pours in torrents through the streets of Petrograd. There is no doubt that the actions taking place on the Petropavlovsk are part of a greater plan ... to shatter Soviet international standing at the very moment when a new administration is coming in America, and is considering entering into trade relations with Soviet Russia."

Gospodi bozhe moi. This is what ROSTA was going to say

about the rebellion? "You don't really believe that. This is a joke, right?"

"Who is this, Kuriakin, your anarchist sister?" said the unshaven man at the typewriter. "Get her out of here. We've got work to do."

"Please, Marina," Genya said. "We have fifteen minutes until the broadcast. We'll talk later. I'll explain. Keep going, Raika."

The woman tugged at the hair on the nape of her neck as she read: *"The spread of provocative rumors and rigging of disorders in Kronstadt clearly works toward influencing the new American president, preventing change in American policy relative to Russia."*

"Don't forget the London Conference," said the man at the typewriter.

"I've got SRs manipulating the stock markets, getting ready to dump tsarist stocks," said an older man, looking through his notes. He had the rough skin of one who'd had terrible acne as a boy.

I couldn't move. I couldn't believe what these people were doing, what Genya was allowing. They could hear with their own ears what was really going on, and in response they were fabricating something so bizarre even Lewis Carroll would hesitate. And my husband, my good Genya, was at the heart of it. This was why he was in Petrograd. He'd come up from Moscow just for this bit of dangerous propaganda, yes, like the *kursanty*. And he'd wanted me to come to Moscow with him, be part of this?

The artist was sketching Red soldiers and workers clambering onto a battleship, and the sailors—white outlines, the familiar stripes of their jerseys—fleeing out the other side, climbing into boats labeled ENTENTE and FINLAND.

The boy at the typewriter was pounding away. He rolled the sheet up to read: *"Before us is the provocation work of Entente stockbrokers, and of agents of counterintelligence agencies working by their orders. In Russia, the main figures carrying out these policies are a tsarist general and former officers, whose activities are supported by Mensheviks."*

"That's good," Genya said, "but you've said *work* twice, and *agents* twice. Just *provocation*. Also that last sentence, see if you can straighten the syntax. "Just, *carrying out their sabotage are the tsarist general Kozlovsky and several former officers, supported by Menshe-vik…"* He frowned, trying to think of a good word.

"Treachery," said the boy. Genya considered it, weighing it with his mouth.

I could not stay silent one more moment. "No one in the world will believe this. People will see through you like a pane of glass."

Genya's face turned to stone. I knew that face. It was the face he'd worn when he'd smashed Avdokia's Virgin of Tikhvin. "You'd be surprised who'll believe it," he said through clenched teeth. "You think this is a joke? This is not a joke. This is a war."

The unshaven man pressed on. "We've got ten minutes. What about those stocks?"

"But it's a *lie*," I said. Didn't anybody care about that?

Genya squatted down on his haunches. He took my hands. "Marina, this isn't the House of Arts. This is *war*, you understand? It's got to be done."

"We did agitprop," I whispered, hard and fast through my knuckled throat. "But we never lied! What's happened to you? You used to know the difference."

His face was dark with emotion. Black fury, and what I could only hope was shame. "This is not the time." He stood. Everyone was watching him. "Your overconcern with the 'truth' is petty bourgeois. We don't have that luxury." Playing to the room.

I stood up. *"Now I put on my costume / GREAT RUS."*

I could see his lips tremble. Or maybe it was just that I knew him.

"I'll see you tonight," he said. "We can talk about it then."

The bile in my mouth, the hot tears in my eyes. I wanted to spit. "I understand everything, petit bourgeois though I am. Don't come. You can't justify this."

And we left him there, with his sulfur and his guilt and the hollow clatter of Bolshevik typewriters.

56 *The Kronstadt Card Is Covered!*

The bombardment resumed the following day, continued the day after. A weak sun appeared, trying to break through the clouds, trying to melt the ice and free Kronstadt. Without ice, there would be nothing for the Red Army to cross upon. The fortress would be impregnable, and the ice-locked ships would be able to move out. They could come right up the Neva, shell the Astoria, and all the rats would come streaming out.

Meanwhile the streets teemed with new soldiers. I watched them with increasing dread, flooding in from the train stations, coming from all corners of the country. Not just impassioned *kursanty* from Moscow but provincial soldiers from far-flung regions, Uhlans and Bashkirs, the troops we'd seen in 1919. It was a familiar Bolshevik tactic—to bring in men who'd had little contact with those they were charged to subdue, in this case the fierce fighters of the Baltic Fleet. They were men with no allegiance to Petrograd and little understanding of our revolutionary past, no associations with our workers—all the less likely to be tempted by fraternization.

But they still hadn't won. People went about their business, jumpy from the sound of the guns' steady *pungPUNGpungPUNG*. The sun vanished again, and it began to snow. I headed for a talk at the House of Writers when I passed what had been Levine's dress shop, empty since 1918. In the window, a ROSTA poster, quite attractive. It depicted a playing card, a black spade, with the simplified rendition of a Cossack soldier, knout over one shoulder. And in reverse, connected at the waist, a Kronstadt sailor with a little curly moustache and striped jersey, holding a small SR flag. Boldly stenciled, top and bottom: THE KRONSTADT CARD IS COVERED! And across it all, an enormous red RSFSR—RUSSIAN SOVIET FEDERATED SOCIALIST REPUBLIC. Canceling the card. I slipped on the icy pavement, falling to my knees and hands. Nobody stopped to help me up. Perhaps afraid they would fall themselves.

I got to my feet and, gasping, breathless, scrambled back toward the House of Arts. I couldn't bear the lies. And that Genya was part of it. Those letters should have read *VRKP*—the All-Russian Communist Party. It wasn't the revolution, nor Soviet Russia, but the Bolshevik prison camp. And that was the point they were making, in bright red letters—that Soviet Russia and the Communist Party were now not only inseparable but identical. No God but God.

If I were a simple proletarian, without any information from any other source, would I believe its message? That the sailors were a new iteration of the tsar's guards? The terrible thing was, I might. That's the way it was when public lies were repeated often enough—you crossed to the other side of the looking glass without even knowing it. And there was no other way to know what was happening. What did we have? Either the official channels or the rumor factory of the bread queue. The approaches to the factory districts were still closed. No way for information to spread, even from district to district. No way to know what was happening anywhere.

But until there were official parades down Nevsky Prospect saying the sailors had been defeated, I would not give up hope that Kronstadt could triumph. If they could just hold out until the ice melted—then it would be *our* parade. The final victory of the revolution.

Watch the soldiers, Kolya had said.

I stood on the curb watching a group of new soldiers being herded up Nevsky. How young they were, how confused. *Mutiny*, I prayed. *You're fighting against the will of the workers, against the peasant in the field, against your own brothers.* I itched to know what the workers were doing. The papers said they were going back to their factories—that meat and flour had been distributed among them. Meat, flour! Didn't that tell them something—that the Bolsheviks *could* come up with goods if they wanted to? If they absolutely had to? I missed the newspaper of the breadline, now that I got my rations at the House of Scholars. They knew no more there than I did. Was it working? That's what I wanted to know. The workers' political demands were born of desperation, and there were no parties left to fan the flame of revolt. No mass demonstrations, no organization, only the shrinking of the people back into the mist.

Mutiny was Kronstadt's only hope. If these soldiers refused to fire…if they went over, as had happened in February 1917. Soldiers in the barracks talked. Surely they could make common cause with the strikers and sailors against the Bolsheviks. If only it weren't Trotsky waging war against them. I knew what an orator he was. I'd read in *Pravda* that three hundred delegates attending the All-Russian Tenth Party Congress—experienced commissars—had left Moscow for Petrograd to stiffen the troops.

What did they need stiffening for if they weren't softening? I tried to cheer myself as I watched the soldiers march past. Their faces betrayed a grim and haggard fatalism.

A boy on the street corner hawked the most recent edition of *Pravda*. I recognized him—the little cardsharp from Orphanage No. 6. So he'd become a *biznissman*. "Makar, do you remember me?" Either he didn't or he was too busy selling a paper to a man wearing a woman's coat, a tragic but not uncommon sight. His wife had died, and her coat was warmer than his.

"Makar, it's Comrade Marina. Remember me?" The man moved away with his newspaper tucked under his arm. "With the baby?"

He looked at me now, his shiny eyes like black plums. "Sure. I remember." He glanced away. Guilt. He couldn't look me in the face. As if he had pushed them off that roof, instead of being one of the children gathered on the sidewalk below.

"It's good to see you," I said.

He glanced back at me, unsure. "Yeah?"

"Yeah. You look well." He was a clever boy, quick. I wondered… "Do you ever sell things to the soldiers? *Preservativy?*" Rubbers. "*Marafet? Samogon?*"

He brightened. "Sure. Want something? I can get just about anything if you give me ten minutes." Oh ho, big man!

"What's their spirit, do you think? The soldiers. Think they're going to win?"

It felt odd, asking a child such things, but he'd never been a child really, and probably would never be an adult either, not that you'd recognize. He was something in between, a wild little beast. He looked at me cannily, gauging my intent. "Well. Let's just say they ain't singing, *Lalalala, we get to go fight Kronstadt.* Whaddya think—they're shittin' in their pants! Trade's booming. *Marafet* gets their dicks up."

"Any signs of mutiny?" Thank God there was no way this kid would run off and tell someone I was asking questions like that.

He wagged his head, ear to shoulder, *maybe yes, maybe no.* "Between you and me? I hear some of 'ems refusing to fight. There've been arrests. Keep your eyes open, you'll see 'em marchin' through here."

Let it be true. "So they're siding with the sailors?"

"They don't give a shit about the sailors." He stood up straighter—clearly having his opinion asked made him feel important indeed. "It's the ice. They're scared of the ice. They see their mates go under—the shells break it up, and then it's like a whole raft turning over. Under they go, in the dark, and no one comes up once they're down. *Pffshht.*" He imitated soldiers sliding off the ice into the sea. "Scared off their nuts. That's what they talk about, how they ain't going out there and they don't care who shoots 'em for it. It's so bad, the Cheka troops gotta follow 'em up with machine guns, so if anybody turns around, pow-pow-pow-POW!"

The terror of those troops. I felt pity for them as well. Scylla or Charybdis. I could see why they would take cocaine, drink, whatever might give them the courage. "What about the strikers?"

He screwed his face up, as if he'd eaten something rotten. "They ain't got shit. Maybe they take some *samogon.* Want some? We're making it in the basement of the orphanage. The janitor's in on it."

I could only imagine its contents. "What does Matron think of that?"

"Who's going to tell her?" Now he was smirking. *You?*

"I'll just take a newspaper." Though the *marafet* sounded tempting. I folded his *Pravda* under my arm, broke a bit of bread off my loaf and handed it to him. "Thanks for the insight."

"Any time." He ate like a wolf, not even chewing. "Got any *chinar?*" A butt, tobacco.

"Sorry," I said. "Listen, you hear anything interesting, any real news, come see me. I'm at the House of Arts. You know where that is?"

"On Moika. All the pinheads."

I squeezed him softly on the arm, pipe thin under his ragged coat. "Stay well, Makar." I began walking away.

"Listen!" He called out. "Sorry about the baby. I still think about her. He shouldn't of done that."

He wasn't as hard as he pretended to be. "Let me know if anything happens."

The canteen at the House of Pinheads was warm and smelled of cabbage soup. When I entered, I saw Genya sitting with Shklovsky and Anton and some of the studio participants at a table by the windows. My stomach lurched. I really thought I would vomit. He saw me, but after I got my soup, I selected a seat as far from him as I could get, as if he were a stinking corpse. How could Anton sit there with him after what we had seen at ROSTA? I took a bench over by the wall where we hung the obituaries, next to Alla Tvorcheskaya, the painter. I took out my bread and spoon and ate, trying to ignore their conspicuously noisy conversation.

"That Kuriakin, where do you ever see men like that anymore?" Alla sighed, her chin in her hand.

"Go to ROSTA," I said dryly. "Because that's where he is, writing filthy propaganda."

"Well, I didn't say he was an angel, darling, only that he looked like one." And he did. It was as if a beam of light followed him around, even in this underlit room, even now. "Oh look, Poliatnikov's on the move."

I watched as one of the older, lesser poets, a waspish, balding little terrier of a man, the very one who'd showed off his tattered linen for Wells and embarrassed Gorky so badly, rose to his feet and headed to Genya's table, his face flushed with emotion. Everyone stopped talking to focus on what was sure to be an amusing interlude.

They were not disappointed. "You have a nerve, coming here, showing your face among *real* poets. We don't spend our days supporting the *rabble*. You have gall." Spraying him with saliva. "Bolshevik lackey."

I might have told Poliatnikov he'd picked the wrong person to try to embarrass. This wasn't an Englishman, a foreign dignitary. This was someone who'd spent a year on an agitprop train. Genya grabbed the little provocateur by the collar of his jacket—luckily, as his shirt would have torn—and drew him close. Seated, he was nose to nose with the furious wretch. "Listen, you sniveling shirker," loud enough that everyone in the place could hear. "Where were you during the war? Sitting here safe, hoping for Kolchak and composing sonnets about the violets of yesteryear! If you believe so much in counterrevolution, why don't you go do something about it? Find your local branch of the National Center. I'm sure they're still around."

The man was writhing in his grip, his face red with fury and the hold around his neck. "You call yourself a poet? You're nothing but a thug, like your masters. Where's your rifle? I don't see it. I see a suit and a well-fed Bolshevik lackey. *Rabble*," he spat.

Genya pulled back his fist. Suddenly here was Gumilev, his hand on Genya's arm. "Let him go, Kuriakin," he said in his cool, commanding voice. "You're making a scene."

Genya let the little poet go, shoving him backward. He fell against the next table, as the poets guarded their soup, and sat down hard on a bench.

God. Don't let this be happening. I sipped my tea, trying not to watch, but it was impossible not to, like two automobiles colliding in front of you. Genya had risen from his chair, and now it was him and Gumilev, taking one another's measure. They were the same height, but what two men could be more different? Would my husband actually punch Nikolai Stepanovich, the helmsman of the House of Arts, founder of Acmeism? But when Genya was most in the wrong, that was when he was the most unreasonable, most dangerous. "Well, if it isn't Mister Africa," Genya said, his pose softening. "Gone on safari recently?" Referring to Gumilev's wide travels and his poetry about them. How Genya hated everything Gumilev represented—as a man, as a poet. He despised his class, his erudition, his self-discipline, and his political affiliations.

"Don't underline your reputation as a fatuous boor," said Gumilev.

But Genya was not to be intimidated. He hadn't been by my father, and he wouldn't be now. "If I'd wanted to do that, Violets of Yesteryear would be picking up pieces of his nose." He projected in a clear, deep voice that would have made a Shakespearean actor proud. Yes, it was Poliatnikov's fault, the man was an unbearable gadfly, but Genya should have known where he was and how people would feel about him. "Who called who *rabble*? I just came in for a quiet conversation with my editor and my wife." And to make matters worse, he gestured toward me across the room. The Acmeist's gaze shot to where I sat cringing with Alla Tvorcheskaya, his well-shaven face registering surprise. He hadn't known this little piece of the puzzle. Alla, too, was taking my measure, as if I'd been holding out on her, hoarding a cache of chocolates or tins of condensed milk.

Genya kept on, not even noticing the ellipsis. "Doesn't he know what century this is? I'm not going to ask you, of course. You're still praising the tsar and crossing yourself. Yeah, I know who you are. God knows why you're still even here."

"God does know," Gumilev said and turned on his crisp, monarchist heel.

Anton glowed. There was nothing he loved better than a fight in which he wasn't directly involved, and Shklovsky beamed at the futurist rough justice. The futurist brats settled back down in their chairs. A cloud of laughter rose from their table. I stared down at my soup and my tea and finished quickly. I didn't want to be associated with him. I didn't even know why Genya was here and not with his propagandists and liars back at ROSTA, or feasting on double rations at the Astoria. But I was done. I excused myself and hurried out, not wanting to make eye contact with anyone. Genya Kuriakin and catfights in the canteen—I was embarrassed to be associated with him.

I lay in my bed, wrapped in my sheepskin, trying to read a copy of *Leaves of Grass* that Korney Chukovsky had lent me, while the shell blasts kept up their steady distant percussion. *Pung. Pung. Pung. Pung. Pungpung Pung.* The barrage had resumed after our visit to ROSTA, it had been going on for seven days around the clock. At night you could see the flashes from Kronstadt. The sailors weren't getting a second to sleep. I imagined them on their icebound ships, making their brave pronouncements on the wireless, the last bit of unfiltered truth in all of Russia.

I got up, paced, stared into Bolshaya Morskaya Street—empty. Nestled into the jamb, I watched the snow fall, fall, fall. Would it ever be spring? Would it come soon enough?

A knock on the door. *Fais dodo.* I ignored him.

Again.

"Go away."

But he opened the unlocked door, and the cold came in with him from the hall. His bulky presence filled the small room. He was still wearing that suit, though with a wool turtleneck and a cap now, an overcoat. Anton was tall but skinny, and Pasha lively but compact, a man who could live in the narrow confines of a ship. But Genya was a fact that you could not get around.

"Marina," he said, closing the door. "It wasn't my fault. You saw how he attacked me."

Always so warm, he raised the temperature in the room just standing there. I remembered what it was to lie next to him, skin to skin. But now that I knew his purpose in coming to Petrograd, he was as appealing as rotting garbage. I could never forgive THE KRONSTADT CARD IS COVERED! These weren't cartoons, little sailors with curled moustaches and rosy cheeks—they were lives. Pasha with his crinkly blond hair and his quiet hands. Slava, who had pulled me up atop the *Red October*. The revolutionary sailors, fighting for the future of Russia. I could cut his throat right now. "I'm surprised you'd trouble to announce your association with a petit bourgeois anarchist like me."

"Don't be mad about that," he said, leaning against the door, as if he was going to try to keep me from running out. "What was I supposed to say? You can't just stand in the middle of ROSTA and shout, *Liar, liar, liar.*"

"What should I call you, then? *Savior of the Revolution?*"

He swallowed, came a little closer. "You know what's going on. It's how the game is played. You were on the agit-train."

"But you weren't a liar then." I leaned against the window, looking out at the snow, remembering how it fell after I'd seen the note from Seryozha's commander. "You've gone through the looking glass, Genya." A vicious series of artillery concussions bruised the fading afternoon. "You're disappearing. You're not even here. I can see right through you."

"Don't be like that. We're not on opposite sides here."

The snow changed directions, it began blowing to the west. Was it a sign?

He began sniffing about, examining the pictures, the books, hands behind his back like a man in a museum. How he had changed since 1916. No longer the yearning boy waiting his chance to show Mayakovsky his poems. No longer the hooligan, the dreamer who had given me the rings of Saturn. His awkwardness was gone. He was a statesman now, a politician, a man polished by the approval of others. Looking at him, I could feel how much I'd changed as well. We'd grown up. Layers of experience and beauty and loss had saddened that bright girl I'd once been.

"Remember that boy, who defended the thief in Haymarket Square? That brave boy, unafraid to tell the truth to the mob?" I said. "What would he have thought of the apparatchik wearing his face?"

He picked up the fox-fur hat that sat on my desk, keeping me company as I wrote, like a cat that crouches watching his mistress write a letter. He stroked the soft fur. "I remember this from the train. And that coat. You used to carry a revolver in it. You imagined yourself with crossed bandoliers, riding up on top of the train with the sailors."

That revolver. How human paths intersected, at random, inexorably changing one another's fate. If I'd never met this man, I wouldn't have been so angry at my father, I wouldn't have agreed to spy for Varvara. Papa might not have been so rash. He might have brought us out of Russia. We might be in England now.

He put my hat on, posed like a fashion model, trying to lighten the mood. "It's all the rage in Moscow." It looked like a small animal perched on the roof of a shed.

"Very stylish." I gazed back at the falling snow. I didn't want to be so at odds with Genya. But I could never forgive him for feeding his poetic genius into the ROSTA machine like meat into the grinder.

He continued his inspection of my little room—examined the shelf on which my few possessions lay, a comb, a bottle of kerosene, a sliver of soap from the Skorokhod women. My toothbrush, a gift from the sailors. He broke into a grin. "You still have this?" *Chronicles of a Misspent Youth.* I'd forgotten, I had borrowed it from Anton earlier that summer. The hand-cut wooden letters that Sasha had carved. I could never hate the boy who had written those poems, he was still in there somewhere, drunk with shame, a pillow over his head, knowing what the man was doing with the gift they shared. As Genya opened the yellow covers as if they would crumble to dust in his hands, I saw him again as he still was, under all this Bolshevik bluster. To think, he'd once been my conscience. He flicked through the poems as if playing with his firstborn child. "Pretty good. For a kid."

"You weren't a liar then."

"And you were." A jab, and it hurt. He'd never gotten over my leaving him for Kolya. He licked the corner of his lower lip, picked up the kettle, sloshed it. "Is this boiled? Can I at least have some tea?"

"All right, but then you have to go." I waited for him to move away from my desk, took down two glasses, or more accurately, the porcelain cup I bought from an old lady in Kolomna and a tin one I'd stolen from the canteen.

Then he was studying my clothes, my summer dress on the hook, the wool dress from Aura, and her good wool coat—my entire wardrobe. He pressed his nose to my summer dress. Like a man smelling lilacs. "You hurt me more than I could imagine," he said. "When I found out. About him."

"Imagine how Russia will feel."

He dropped the much-washed printed fabric. "What is it about these mutineers that has you so captivated? You were fine with agitprop on the *Red October*. Those *agitkas*, that wasn't exactly the truth."

I took the can of pine needles, pried open the top. "They were cartoons, but about something true."

"What isn't true? That it's not a mutiny? That these sailors aren't acting against the soviet, opening the door for the Whites?"

"You know that's not what they're doing." I fought to check the treble of frustration sounding in my voice.

I knew the thrust of that stubborn jaw. "Oh, do I? Money's pouring in from the émigrés, the Entente, earmarked for Kronstadt."

"They'd never take White money."

He slapped himself in the forehead. It sounded like a wet fish hitting a dock. "Wake up, Marina. Where else are they going to get it from? Can they turn seawater into cannon shells and Swedish ham? They'll need funds, and that's what's available to them. And it'll come with its own agenda. The sailors won't be able to resist."

He didn't know them. "The people will support them. The strikers. A general strike."

"Oh, really." Genya went over to the window looking out onto

Bolshaya Morskaya, leaned forward, theatrically cupping his hand to his ear as he would have on stage with the Theater of the Future. "What's that I hear? Is it the sound of marching workers? The clamor of thousands for a general strike?"

The only sound was the *pung* of the big guns echoing off the building opposite, the shiver of the old glass in the windows, and Shafranskaya moving around in the next room, reciting a poem she was working on.

"Nobody's coming to save Kronstadt," he said quietly, approaching me, crouching to look into my eyes. I could smell him, his breath, his scent of hay and new wood, the same as ever. How could such a liar smell like that? His warmth, warmer than the *bourgeoika*. "Face it. The workers have hung them out to dry. The sailors'll take the White money, all right. But why this sudden partisanship? Since when do you favor counterrevolutionary mutiny?" He studied me, scratching his underlip where he often found it hard to shave. There was a new opacity in his hazel-green eyes, which used to be as transparent as a sun-shot pool in a forest glade. I didn't know what he was thinking anymore. He'd spent too long in Moscow.

"It's not counterrevolution," I said. "You read the resolution. It's all the things you and I believe."

"What we believed four years ago," he said quietly, steadying himself, his hand on my chair. "That was a dream. *Worker control. Soviet democracy.* People didn't even think the revolution would survive this long. But here we are." He peered into my face with a slight rueful smile. "We've won. All we need is a chance to rebuild. And no, it's not going to be what we'd dreamed. I'm prepared to accept that."

I wanted to claw my own face. I wanted to howl. "Your bosses are counterrevolutionaries. Not the sailors."

"It's the only revolution there is." He stood, shaking out his legs. "This is where it went. We built it ourselves. You did too. You're as much a part of it as anybody."

I struggled against the sense of what he was saying. I felt myself scrambling. I wasn't a part of it, not anymore. Not since that day on the bridge, when I said no to Varvara. "Just be a poet again. You don't need to do this."

He studied me with his new eyes. "Varvara was right about you. You're no revolutionary. You're just a bourgeois girl with enthusiasms."

I didn't want to hear that name, ever again. "And she's a Savonarola. Don't you dare quote her to me." *Pung pung. Pung-pungpung.* I imagined how loud that was out on the gulf. Men were losing their lives on both sides because of him and her, the spacemen and the liars.

"But why the sailors, Marina? Things are always personal with you."

"Yes. I know those men. I don't live at the Astoria, dining with commissars and party dignitaries. I teach poetry to workers. I taught at the sailors' club on the Admiralty docks. Those men are the very soul of the revolution."

"The *sailors'* club..." he repeated as if licking ice cream off a spoon, and I didn't like the expression his broad face was wearing now—as if he had me all figured out. "There wouldn't perhaps be one sailor in particular? Some handsome devil in a striped jersey?"

"That's none of your business," I said.

He burst out laughing. "You're still you, aren't you? Oh, the angelic saviors of the revolution, noble Kronstadt!" He laughed, ugly and harsh.

"Stop it, Genya."

He held his hands up in the air, surrender, mocking me. "*Oh, they're not counterrevolutionaries, they're preparing to die for our sins, they're Blok's goddamned Christ.* Oh! Oh!" His arms outstretched, they almost reached from wall to wall.

Now there was nothing at all attractive about him. I knew which side I was on. Pasha or no Pasha, I would feel the same. "You know them too. How dare you print those signs, saying they're the same as Cossacks, saying it's a White conspiracy. You parrot. You never used to be a mouthpiece."

"You're incredible, you really are." Wiping his eyes. "My God, Marina, is there nothing you wouldn't do? I thought you were having an affair with Anton."

I turned my back to him. Steam was rising from the kettle. I took it off the stove and splashed water on the pine needles. The air filled with the smell of forest. "You didn't think about him when you came up here. How he must be suffering, right now, thinking I'm betraying him with you."

That took the smile off his face.

"And if you must know, I was with the sailor first. It was Anton who came to me. Said that he'd loved me since the beginning, and he was going to leave if I couldn't love him back." Moscow went out of his hazel eyes, as he pictured his best friend back on Grivtsova Alley, when we were living on top of each other.

"You're making this up. He couldn't stand you."

I lingered over the open kettle. The scent of pine would always recall to me that long walk through the snow to Maryino, my night under the snow in a burrow of pine boughs. "I thought so too, but it was just the impossibility of competing with you. It was unbearable to him." A huge explosion rattled the windows. I thought they might break. The snow changed direction again, hammering at the windowpanes, building up on the sills.

"Loving you is a curse I wouldn't wish on my worst enemy." His voice had lost its stentorian ring. "I know. I've tried to kill it, but I can't. No matter how many times I mow the field, cornflowers keep coming back up."

Even now. What a mess, what an unholy mess. I poured the tea into the two mismatched cups. I handed him the tin one.

"Come to Moscow with me. Both of you. We'll get away from this mausoleum, the Gumilevs and Khodaseviches. This will be over soon, and we'll be part of Russian literature—we'll live forever."

"You won't be part of it," I said. "Look what it's done to you. Come to Petrograd and be a poet again. Stop working for ROSTA before it kills what's good about you."

"I can't," he said, stroking his hair back. "You think I'm just a mouthpiece? I've thought about this long and hard. I believe in what I'm doing."

Worse yet. "They've broken you," I said. "You're like a racehorse that's been put to the plow. You'll never be able to run again. Your knees are broken. What's happened to that red horse, the red horse that was you?"

"It doesn't matter about me," he said. "I'll go on. Broken kneed or not."

"It hurts just to look at you."

He held the cup and gingerly took a sip. I knew it was biting, sour. He made a face. "What is this?"

"Pine needles. For scurvy. The Bolsheviks take the real tea for themselves."

He sat on my cot, holding the cup by the rim, and drank, grimacing with every swallow. "Revolutions in the mind are perfect—so long as they stay there. Nobody's selfish, nobody's featherbedding. But real ones have a life of their own. They work through real men, with all their warts and bad breath and selfishness. Now that it's here, we need to see it through."

His good suit, his handsome face. Who was the naive one? "No, we don't. The emperor is naked, Genya. Don't try to convince me about his suit's sumptuous contours."

He held the cup with his fingertips, it looked like a piece of a little girl's tea set in his oversized hand. "Look, say you had a child—"

My eyes watered with the surprising blow.

He blanched. "No, I mean...listen. Say there's a child. And it's playing near the stove. And the mother—the *father*—says, 'Be careful, you're going to get burned.' But the kid doesn't understand *burned*. So the father says, 'There's a devil in the stove. He's going to eat you up.' The kid's afraid of devils, so he stays away from the stove. That's what I'm doing here, Marina. Keeping Russia away from the stove. Is that so bad? I could explain that the country's about to go up in flames. There's a peasant revolt in Tambov going on right now that's going to make the Ukraine under Denikin look like *Swan Lake*. And that's not the only mess on our hands."

There was a revolt in Tambov? This was the first I'd heard about it. I studied him, hunched on the edge of my small bed, his forehead knuckled with care, the hot cup on his knee.

"Let's say you did get your Soviets Without Communists. You know what that's going to look like? Mealymouthed Mensheviks and speechifying SRs. Anarchist dreamers. They're going to wring their hands and talk, talk, talk while the country burns down around them. Then in rides a strongman, some general—Kornilov's still around, Wrangel, maybe Denikin himself. *Urah!* Someone has to restore order. This time there are no Bolsheviks around to do it. Oh, they'll whip us back into line. Dissolve the soviets, massacre the socialists, string up the workers. They've got to keep the bad Bolsheviks from coming back, don't they?"

He set the cup on the desk and came to me where I was standing at the window, put his warm hand on the nape of my neck.

"So, no, these sailors aren't Whites. They're every bit as noble as you think they are. But they're opening the door. They're going to have to take White money, the revolution will be lost, and everything we've done will have been for nothing. It will just be an interlude in a history book, like the Paris Commune. *The four years of the socialist experiment in Russia.*"

No. No, I would not listen. I would put wax in my ears like the sailors on Odysseus's ship. I turned away, but he held my shoulders, turned me back. He would force me to see his point of view.

"I can't let that happen, Marina. People get lost in the niceties. So for now there's got to be a devil in the stove and Whites behind the Kronstadt revolt."

"Don't touch me!" I shoved him off. The Genya I knew would never speak of devils in the stove. I remember how he once smashed an old woman's icon. He hated priests and superstition, anything remotely fabricated. "What happens when your child finds out his father's lied to him? That it's all shit?"

Genya's voice, soft and deep in my ear. "He'll be grateful that his father kept him safe when he was too young to understand. The grown man will understand why the father did it."

"No! He'll wonder what else his father lied to him about." I took his cup and opened the stove door, threw the remnants of the tea into the fire.

"He'll have been kept safe, and life will go on."

He sounded just like an old man. "Is that the son you want? A sheep? A gullible ignoramus? Superstitious, terrified of devils? Don't you want your son to demand a say in his own life?"

He sighed and sat down on the sagging bed, his long legs taking up much of the floor space, cradling his head in his big hands. "The people don't care about politics. They just want to eat. They want boots, and fuel. They'll get concessions too. They'll be able to go out and bring food in. And, trust me, they'll say, *Ah, the Bolsheviks aren't so bad after all.* You better give up hope for your sailor. The days of anarchist communes are over."

How had we ended up on opposite sides of this thing? "Even in America they couldn't get away with this."

How he hated even the name, America. "You don't think capitalists have monopoly power in *America*? You don't think when the workingman comes up against power in *America* they don't crush him like a flea under their fingernails? You and I are living in the first workers' state on earth. It's already a miracle."

"It's not a workers' state. When a shipment of boots comes into the shops, it's set aside for the Bolsheviks. Meat. Butter. Cloth, sugar, all of it. Is this what the civil war was fought for—corruption? Elitism? A new ruling class? They walk around like grand dukes. People hate them. They're not workers. Do you see them at the lathe? Or gluing shoes?"

He grabbed my hand as I passed, stopping me, pulling me to him. He craned his neck to peer into my face, like a child. Those hazel eyes I once loved. "But think what we do have. Yes, I hate their pushiness, too, and I hate what we have to say about the sailors. I know them too, better than you do. They're good, brave, loyal—and wrong. They have no plan, they're not thinking it through. I'm not going to let them play the piper and march the revolution off a cliff."

I yanked my hands away. "Why won't the Bolsheviks listen to the people, then? Why are they surrounding themselves with a wall? They fire off pronouncements—*Makhno and his anarchist troops, our brothers in the Ukraine!* Then, once they've served their purpose, it's *Makhno! Traitor! Counterrevolutionary!* Why can't you be for the revolution and question the people at the top? Why can't there be other voices?" *Pung. Pungpung pung.*

"Why not free ice cream and puppet shows and carriage rides?" he shouted, picking up my chair and slamming it back down again. "Give me your list. I'll see what I can do!"

He turned around in my tiny room like a horse in a stall. There was no room to pace. He threw up his hands like an actor on stage, almost burning himself on the stovepipe. "I don't know, Marina. I'm just a poet. But I'll tell you one thing—Lenin won't be forced by the Kronstadt sailors. Or trade unions or the Entente. Or Blok, or you or me. He's doing what he needs to do to make sure the revolution survives."

Lenin reminded me of Ukashin. The same mysterious philosophy, which somehow covered every situation. I said, "I've seen four years of Lenin, and if you ask me, he's got no more plan than the sailors. He finds a way to justify everything. But his only program I can see is that he'll do what's best for the party, to make sure they come out on top. Just like in 1918 when they left us to the Germans."

Genya toppled back onto my bed with a groan. I thought the whole thing would collapse under him. "This is giving me a headache. Come, sit with me for a while. Don't talk. Just rub my forehead. Then I'll go."

His silky tawny-colored hair, like rye in the sun.

"The next time we meet, we'll meet as strangers," I said.

He turned over and gazed at me, as if he hadn't heard me all along, as if I had said something completely surprising. "It's a lost cause. Can't you accept that?"

"I don't believe in anything anymore. Not in the revolution, and not in you. It ends now." It was as great a shock to me as to him. I suppose I thought we'd always be together in some way. He had kept saying, *Wake up,* and I finally had. Pasha and the sailors, that hope…but I saw that the Bolsheviks had gotten there first. They'd given the people food, but no power. They would never give them power. And the people would be happy with the food. They were starving and beaten down and hypnotized by lies. The people wouldn't rise to save Kronstadt. The sailors, loyalists, idealists, *Victory or Death.* They were doomed.

I sat down next to Genya. This monster we'd created, out roaming the streets. We had done this. We had marched for it, we had spoken out for it. I had given up everything, for this. My family, my country. The enormity of it. We sat together, Genya and I, like people after a funeral. We were burying our best dreams, in separate graves. Two little graves. We sat side by side while the snow fell, covering the raw earth in white.

57 *The Turn of the Tide*

The Squared Circle group huddled in Anton's room, cold enough to freeze fish, but everyone came, all but Oksana and Petya, who were caught on Vasilievsky Island. I was reading the Eliot to them line by line, translating roughly into Russian, which Anton jotted down for later refinement. He'd decided that Eliot could be extremely important for us. I wasn't sure if it was that vital, or whether it was his way to distract me from the horrors of the moment. Eliot had no political perspective that I could see, except for a cynical and depressing one, a poetry of aftermath, which suited my mood perfectly.

The door, already ajar, began to move. "Comrade Marina?" The face that appeared in the crack of the door was somewhat lower than expected—the orphan Makar, in his cap and lice-ridden rags, his bright dark eyes. Makar took in the poets, the books, the scissors on the desk, the typewriting machine, with the quickness of a magpie. His boots didn't match. "You said to come," he said. "If anything changed."

Anton lifted his peaked eyebrow like a boomerang. "How'd you get in here?" The presence of the orphan terrified him. He had no contact with the streets anymore, he didn't know anyone who wasn't familiar with Khlebnikov or Kruchonykh—meaning all of humanity except for the people in this room.

Makar indicated the door with his head, and I followed him.

"They're stopping Communism," he said in the hall. "Come on."

I pulled my scarf up over my face as I tried to keep up with the poorly clad boy scampering ahead. *Let us go then, you and I...* The day was sullen, maybe 10 below, the hairs in my nose froze. My words were a cloud of white as I followed him at a half run. "Where are we going?" Once again I said a prayer of thanks to Aura Cady Sands and her sturdy boots.

"Can't you go any faster?"

I didn't have the strength. I was fighting for air, huffing like a surfacing whale. He must be taking something, cocaine most likely. He turned around and fairly danced in front of me, trotting backward, his eyes glassy black with excitement. "It's over. They told the soldiers this morning. It's Bolsheviks without Communism! You think I'm kidding? They're letting the markets in. Free trade. No more grain seizures. It's all going to be out in the open. No arrests."

I stopped, stooped over, holding my knees like an old woman trying to catch my breath. "Who announced this? Is it in the papers?" Nobody at the House of Arts had heard anything. Free trade in Soviet Russia? What happened to *He who trades in the free market, trades the freedom of the people?* It was on all our ration tickets. It had to be some kind of Bolshevik trick, more propaganda to disarm the workers and defuse support for Kronstadt.

"It was Lenin said it. Old Egghead himself, swear to God. This morning." Makar's skinny bones jerked with excitement, his black cropped orphan's head under his poor cap. "They're going to let everybody buy what they need. The peasants can sell. No more Cheka, no more arrests. I'll be a *biznissman.* Unless the sailors win. They say the sailors are the only ones holding it back."

Ice in my lungs, winter's hand wrapping itself around my chest. How cynical. How brilliant. "But the sailors are supporting the strikers. This is exactly what they called for."

"The strikers are against them now. They want the market. They want the food. The soldiers aren't scared anymore. They're ready to die for the good of the people. You said to watch them. They're leaving. Let's go!"

I followed him in and out the small lanes and snow-filled court-yards. He knew every back way, past Haymarket Square, so huge and bare it could have been a field. Would there be a market here again? If Communism was over, there was no sign of it. Only soldiers marching, a new firmness on their faces. Oh God.

Makar led on, crossing the Fontanka at Moskovsky. We were heading into the soldiers' district, the old Ismailovsky barracks. The garrison of Petrograd.

It was huge, monstrous, ugly, a world unto itself—street after street of long old buildings, stone and brick, a whole quarter boiling with soldiers. Soldiers called after me, laughter followed. "Hey, sweetheart, let's have a quick one." "Hey, Katya, over here!" That one clasping his crotch. *Laugh all you want now, bratya. You won't be laughing when you cross the ice.*

Makar disappeared into the courtyard of an old brick barracks with shutters on the windows like a stable. I held my breath and entered. In the yard, soldiers lounged, assembling bundles, checking rifles, stowing grenades and ammunition, sharpening bayonets, smearing boots with something out of a big bucket. Couldn't be lard, they would have eaten that. Wax? The boots had seen many miles of marching, but their clothes looked warm enough. Soldiers, everywhere you looked. Some knelt in prayer. My God, how many thousands had been assembled in Petrograd for this assault. Twenty? Forty?

I kept close to my young guide, who led me up to a group of soldiers packing provisions into knapsacks. Preparing for battle. Money was exchanged for small packets, *marafet* no doubt, each man scanning the yard with quick eyes. They pulled out tin cups and the boy furtively filled them from an old canteen he had tucked under his coat. The men drank it off in single swallows, coughed, laughed. I could smell the fruity alcohol of the *samogon*. Their accents recalled those I had heard in Izhevsk. They'd brought these troops in from the Urals.

"How much for her, *bratik?*" a reedy-necked redheaded soldier asked, his cheeks flushed with the *samogon*.

"This is my aunt. She's a teacher. She wants to know about the proclamation," said Makar. "The new one, about the peasants."

"A teacher, eh?" said a sturdy man sitting on a crate. "How would this little criminal know you, then?" He held out his cup for another drink.

"He said they're ending the grain seizures. Is that true?" I didn't want to get involved with a lot of chitchat down here.

"You know, little teacher," said the reedy soldier, breathing out a great scroll of white vapor. "I could use a quick fuck. A hand job. I've got five hundred rubles—"

"Shut up," said the sturdy man, a wide face like a wall, with clever small eyes. "She's a teacher. Have respect."

"He says there's going to be a return of capitalism, that Communism is over," I said.

"He said that? Stupid runt," said the soldier, sticking out his foot to try to trip Makar, who was pouring out *samogon*. "The soviet's giving 'em what they been askin' for is all. Lettin' city folk bring in food if they want, a tax in kind for us peasants. I'm a peasant myself. From Okhansk." *Name, region, district, profession.* "We pay the tax, we do what we want with the rest. And the workers can stay home and do something useful instead of crawling all over the countryside stealing our food. I'm happy to sell 'em what they want, if I can set the price. Better they get back to work and make us some boots, eh? Then we'll have real Communism. We just gotta stop these Kronstadt bastards from wrecking it. They want to start the war all over again."

This was wrong in so many ways. "But that's exactly what the sailors want!" I said, trying not to cry. "They made just those demands. The end to the requisitioning, tax in kind, bringing in food, all of it." Lenin was acceding to the sailors' terms. So why was he sending all these men out to crush them? "It's the *Petropavlovsk Resolution*—didn't you see it?"

He screwed his eyes narrower. His affable demeanor melted away. "What are you, some kind of agitator?"

Why hadn't Pasha given me some copies? I could hand them out, show them. "No. I just—"

Makar quickly interrupted me, taking my arm. "She's just trying to understand. We oughta move on, Auntie. They got their work to do."

"Sailors," said another soldier, and spit on the ground. "Sit around on their lazy asses dreaming all day, polishing brass. Fishing. Got too much time on their hands, nothing better to do than hatch up conspiracies and pal around with foreigners."

The others laughed and nodded.

The first soldier's wide face still held its rage. "We ain't gonna let sailors take away everything we fought for. Four years, now they want to piss all over it."

It was terrible, terrible. How could I convince them? But even if I had a copy of the resolution, would they read it? Would they believe me? "They only listened to the strikers. They're trying to support the people. The same thing as you."

The way they were all looking at me now, uneasy. Their leader spoke again. "Hey, we listen to our commissars, not some anarchist school lady who's about this close to getting her ass kicked." He puffed away like a stove. His cheeks were very pink. "Hey, get her out of here. And bring us some real women. Maybe we'll leave a few brats behind before we head out for the ice." He held out his cup one more time, and the other men followed suit. "Get her out of here before I hand her around to the boys."

"How about a kiss, Teach?" the reedy-necked one asked, his face hovering next to mine. "One kiss? I don't want to die without having kissed my last woman."

"You mean your first woman," said a soldier with a beard, who got a round of laughter.

The redhead shrugged, ducked his head, but his eyes pleaded. His politics mattered to him, the approval of his comrades, but his longing mattered more. He might kill Pasha tonight, but he looked so sad, his freckled face, eyes the sludge green of the Volga. All soldiers were the same in the end. They killed, they died. They fought for things they believed, or that others believed, gave their spark to an idea, a flag, a movement, brotherhood, a notion of justice, a leader. Never knowing which board they were being played upon. Maybe I was an anarchist after all. So I kissed him. The taste of the *samogon*, of sour breath, of fear.

Makar tugged at my coat. An official-looking man was striding forcefully toward us in a long greatcoat. We slipped away and ran, through another courtyard, skidding on the ice, into a second yard, all the way back across the Fontanka.

A ferocious battle began that night, like nothing we had heard yet. The rattling of the windows was fierce, even in Anton's room facing Nevsky. Dust filtered down from the bookshelf over my head. I lay on the bed watching reflected flashes of light in the odd floor-level window. I felt sick. I should have stayed in Kambarka. Anything to be away from this. I was going to lose my mind. Everything I had believed, everything beautiful and heroic, was fighting for its life out there on the ice.

Anton brought me a bowl of soup and held it for me while I drank. Sweet Anton—who would have guessed? *They'll never make it.* I kept pushing the thought away, as if my thoughts would make it come true, though I knew my mind had no such powers, or my daughter would still be alive. I was powerless to keep anything from happening. There were too many soldiers, and again they *believed*, convinced they were riding the magical red steed into the golden dawn—not an iron train to an icy destination.

I rolled and sweated and shook. I couldn't help remembering what Genya had said. I heard his words in my head, like bullets fired in a stone room. Kronstadt too was its own red steed. The sailors would end up taking money from somewhere, or lead a peasant revolt of the bloodiest kind, and civil war would begin again.

History was a ravaged plain, no hill, no tree, no hiding place. No quiet forest glade or rocky cove in which you could build a refuge.

A book fell off the shelf, loosened by the continuous thunder of 350 millimeter artillery. Those soldiers, fortified by *marafet* and delusions of the future of Russia, were marching on Kronstadt as the ice cracked beneath them. I wish I'd bought some of that *marafet* myself, or a canteen full of *samogon,* so I could stop imagining those boys from the Urals and men from Astrakhan, converging on the island and the helpless icebound ships. Every blast and shudder told of their fates and that of the sailors. *We shall not hear those bells again...*

Anton lay down with me and recited Apollinaire's *Alcools,* and Khlebnikov's "Rus' You Are but a Kiss in the Frost," and "The Presidents of Planet Earth," while I shivered and moaned, my head on his shoulder.

At ten in the morning, March 18, the rumbling of the guns ceased. I waited for it to begin again, but — nothing. Five minutes. Ten minutes. Twenty. Anton made tea, brought me soup, fed it to me, as I could not hold a spoon, I was shaking so badly. Finally I sent him out into the street to see if he could find out what had happened. He returned two hours later with a *Petrogradskaya Pravda* full of the news of the Tenth Party Congress, the abolition of restrictions on trade, the tax in kind, and more lies about SR manipulation of the world stock markets, framing Kronstadt as a blind.

So the new policies were true, or true enough that the spacemen were willing to put them in black and white, willing to be held to them — at least until the next sharp turn, when we'd all have to hang on to the tram for dear life. I remembered what Varvara had said about Lenin, back when they signed the peace with Germany: *Lenin used to be a revolutionary. But now he's just plugging the dikes like the little Dutch boy. Just another politician.*

The silence continued. I listened until my ears hurt. I listened like an old woman in a darkened house, waiting for footsteps.

* * *

It wasn't until eight that night in the crackling frost that we heard the first troops returning. Oh God, they were singing "The Internationale." I opened the big window, not caring I was letting the heat out, and shouted down into the street as the soldiers marched by, their chins high, their step sure. "What is the fate of Kronstadt?"

A soldier heard me. "Taken," he shouted back.

The revolution was over. On March 18, 1921, it was pronounced dead. All I heard was the hollowness of "The Internationale," with its bold promises. I could hear the devil laughing. How many Kronstadt dead? I couldn't exactly shout that out the window. I closed it, noticing a new crack from the force of the bombardment. I thought of sixteen thousand sailors—would the army have accepted their surrender? Would the sailors have offered it?

Watching the soldiers head back into their districts, squadron after squadron, bursting with their triumph, I felt like a citizen of a defeated nation, watching the victors roll in. I imagined Pasha in a long row, his hands tied behind him. They would have dragged him up out of the hold onto the deck. Lined him and his comrades along the rail. Pasha wouldn't look away. He would try to talk reason to them—they'd make him turn around. Then the signal given, a stream of machine-gun fire like the stitches of a sewing machine. And down they would go, wheat before the scythe. The limp bodies thrown overboard, but first, the soldiers would search them, confiscating weapons, souvenirs, money, boots... *They fought on ice, in sandals...*

I had not given Pasha anything of mine to die with.

Never, never to sail, racing on the blue, wind cooling our bronzed faces, our work-toughened hands. His Aegean eyes, his calloused feet in the rigging, his head in the sky.

The world was a net, a noose, a cell with a judas hole in the door. Nothing would escape it—not a beam of light, not a chime, not a whisper. The door of the world clanged shut that night. I heard the key turn in the lock.

Part V
Little Apple

(Spring–Fall 1921)

58 *Pashli*

A flower shop opened on Liteiny. A beauty parlor in a courtyard off the Fontanka. Like dandelions pushing their way up between the stones of an empty square. On the Neva, the ice was beginning to break. *Too late.* It was all too late. Too late, this shop in Gostinny Dvor, filled with ducks and chickens. Where had they come from, these miraculous fowl, when we hadn't seen meat in years? A bakery appeared on the Moika Embankment—not one of the official ration stations barely able to supply ticket holders with scant ounces of bad bread, no. This one's tantalizing windows attracted us like clouds of ghosts to peer in at rounds of golden-topped breads, flour-dusted white rolls, *rogaliki,* and raisin buns. No one could afford even the scent of them, and yet the shop was busy. Who were these people who had such riches in the spring of 1921? We stood on the broken pavement, gaping at women filling bags from the trays.

On Nevsky Prospect, a former emporium unshuttered itself. The display mesmerized us—pâté, glistening hillocks of butter, stacked tins of goods displayed like the treasures of sultans. A young man leaned forward and kissed the glass. A little Former in black wept silently.

Another wailed, "For this we starved? My old man died this winter, and they've got caviar. White flour! The prices! Who's got that kind of money?"

For this, Kronstadt had been crushed. For this, my father was shot by the Cheka. For this, Seryozha had been buried in Moscow. For this bald-faced inequality. Yet like all the others, I couldn't stop staring. Tins of condensed milk, small bags of real tea. Cones of jaggery. I wanted to plunge my face into that pâté and lick that butter. Bottles of milk. How had they manifested cows from thin air? The world had changed once again, so fast you could break your neck.

A woman with a self-righteous air and a hat à la Monomakh

squeezed in past us as the crowd heckled. Guards shoved us back. Guards, protecting a capitalist food emporium in the cradle of the revolution! Even Lewis Carroll could not have imagined this. How many soldiers had fallen in this war—Red, White, Green, and anarchist Black? How many peasants had been shot for fighting grain seizures? How many families torn apart, how many civilians sent to labor camps in the far north, for selling a photo album or a bolt of lace, for bringing in a wheel of cheese or a *funt* of grain. I would never see my mother again. Maryino was a cinder. And yet there was white bread in the capital of Once-Had-Been.

A moonfaced shopgirl packed a tin of smoked sprats for the customer. I knew those tins. There was a little key in the bottom to roll back the metal lid. My father had eaten them. Now new people would have that same fishy breath my mother had hated. Not proletarians, not Formers, but party officials and businessmen. *The New Soviet Bourgeoisie.* My stomach growled. I wondered if my mother would object to fish breath now, wherever she'd landed, on a chessboard square in Bukhara or in the mountains of Tibet. Eggs and butter and smoked Riga sprats in olive oil. How many writers and scholars could be saved by those tins, how many workers? Two weeks ago, you could have been shot for any of this. The mind simply couldn't take it all in.

We had paid for this with four years of cold and darkness, lice and filth and hard bits of *vobla* and pine-needle tea, bread full of sawdust and rags. Rooms turned into latrines. Apartments ravaged for wood.

The people had allowed themselves to be paid off in lies and flour, leaving Pasha and his comrades to die on the ice of Kronstadt. An entire class of human beings lost, so that Soviet apparatchiks and speculators and criminals could dine on roast chicken and halvah. Like cicadas, crawling forth from burrows in the warming earth.

In *Pravda*, Lenin admitted that the sailors weren't really counterrevolutionaries. They simply didn't want party rule. And so they had had to die.

Genya left for Moscow without returning to the House of Arts. No fanfare, no public evening. Anton the only one who went to the station to see him off. "He said he couldn't bear to look into your eyes."

And rightly so. I tore myself from the spectacle of butter and ham and wandered the thawing streets, trying to feel my way into this new world. My poor city. Grass coming up in the middle of Nevsky Prospect—you could graze goats here. Perhaps I could find some goats and become the Goat Girl of Petrograd. They said a man was keeping bees up on Vasilievsky Island. You could buy honey.

On every street, houses had crumbled under their own rotting roofs, eaten away from within, finally collapsing in defeat. Some blocks had only one house left standing, the rest just rubble, as if they had been bombed. One could imagine them succumbing to the weight of centuries, like ancient Rome. And we, like starving barbarians, living rough among the ruins of the noble ancients, without any notion of who had constructed the walls within which we sheltered. But we'd done it ourselves, termites that we were, the wood disappearing into a million tiny stoves.

The flower shop on Liteiny proved as irresistible as white rolls, and here there were no guards to keep me out. The mingled perfumes of lilac and lily, cherry blossoms, hothouse violets, overpowered me. I stood in the middle of the shop and wept like a child, hands hanging at my sides. An old man arranging cherry branches forced into bloom looked up and smiled, an old-fashioned face, an old-fashioned smile, soft and pitying, the way you hoped God would look, among the pink blooms. "Like old days, a little, yes?" I was Former enough to remember florist shops full of forced branches, forsythia, cherry, lilacs...the white lilacs at New Year's, my mother's signature. Lily of the valley, drooping their small fragrant bells.

I turned a corner in the shop and almost fainted. A handcart held a raft of blue hyacinths, the smell so strong it drowned out all the others. I had to press my hand to my mouth not to cry out. That smell, filling our apartment on Furshtatskaya...

The old man with the eyeglasses watched me curiously, pretending to clip and arrange lilies. Perhaps he'd known the Archangel.

Perhaps he'd lived through these years working in a greenhouse on the Vyborg side, tending plants in their timeless, glass-encased world. "You like hyacinths?"

Ai, ai. Regret, distilled.

They were cheap, but I could not bear it. I bought lilies of the valley with all the money I had. He wrapped the stems in twine and the whole bouquet in an old copy of *Pravda*.

I walked along the Neva Embankment, the air scented with the fresh wind and the melancholy sweetness of the flowers. Out in the river, newly broken flats of ice traveled west. *Na zapad*. If the ice had only melted two weeks earlier, the sailors would have held Kronstadt. But it had not, and they had not, and now the revolution was over.

I walked down to the westernmost bridge, the Nikolaevsky, where the water rushed black to the sea. There was still a possibility that Pasha had escaped, I told myself. Out of sixteen thousand Kronstadters, surely there had been survivors. Some must have escaped, fleeing across the ice, that same treasonous ice that had not melted in time. He could have made it to Finland. Some must have escaped, I knew, because of the rigor with which the Cheka searched every night. But I also knew Pasha. I didn't think *flee* was even in his vocabulary. He wouldn't have run if his mates were still fighting.

I stood on the bridge, facing west, smelling the tidal reach of the sea. The Neva ice was moving below me in the center of the river, and the gulls screamed. Legend said that gulls were the souls of dead sailors. *West*, they screamed.

I unwrapped the bundle from its cloak of *Pravda*, its headlines all threats and lies, unbound the twine and loosened the stems of the tender white blooms. Picking out a sweet-smelling cluster, I called out his name. "Pavel Vladimirovich Kislov. *Vechnaya pamyat'*, dearest." And tossed them into the place where the current showed black. Let the tears roll. Then one for "Iskra Antonina Nikolaevna Shurova." It hit the edge of a floe, but in time, it would find its way to the sea. *Eternal memory*. "Dmitry Ivanovich Makarov." I had had no flowers for him that day. "I love you, Papa." Another bloom, floated, bobbed, sank. "Sergei Dmitrievich Makarov." Seryozha, four years gone. "Avdokia Fomanovna Malykh, be you alive or gone." I continued with the roll of my dead. Maxim the Orphan. Solomon Moiseivich Katzev. Andrei Alexandrovich Petrovin. The family Podharzhevsky. Krestovsky. Viktoria Karlinskaya, God forgive me. Slava, and all the heroes of Kronstadt. Eternal memory. In the bottom, there was one more bloom—a scrap of blue. The old man had put it there. I held it in my hand and thought of that strange twisted soul, mourned by no one. "Arkady von Princip. May you find peace," I whispered, and threw the last trembling sprig into the black water.

I stood on the bridge and sent my regrets to the lands of the dead, west with the setting sun.

59 *Summon the Ravens*

We rose from the winter, from the broken years, as you do when you rise from bed after a grave illness. Shaky, weak, squinting at the sun, glad to be alive, but not yet recovered, not trusting the state of your health. Yet we had lived, and it was spring, and the city managed to find a lilac shawl in her steamer trunk to wrap about her emaciated frame. The light had been well kept under winter's bed, and was around us once again, glamorous and tender, as only Petersburg could wear it. I walked in the light and touched the stones of the mirage. Overhead, the same gulls wheeled. How empty the city had grown.

Trees budded into May, burst forth in summer green. Iskra would have been walking, saying her first words, *Mama, Papa, kitty, doggie.* Avdokia said my first word had been *Opusti! Put me down!* Seryozha had been a silent child, but Iskra was a great chatterer, even at three months. Oh, such stories we would have told...

As the nights grew short, I walked alone in the Summer Garden, the warm breeze ruffling the trees where Genya and I had once embraced under the strict stone eye of Diana and her bow. A young couple walked toward me, in and out of twilight's glow. How old were they, fifteen? She fit perfectly under his arm, her makeup gaudy. Like any other plant unsure of the future, they grew up fast. Fast to grow, fast to seed. There was no time for great oaks now. No Tolstoys would rise up among us. There was no time for giants. To think, when I was the age of these young lovers, I still wore a pinafore, and curtsied when introduced. As they passed, they glanced at me with no more curiosity than if I'd been a tree. I felt ancient. They would live lives I could not even imagine. I was twenty-one, my youth past, my beauty lost. My time was over. I'd become this somber creature, *a survivor,* no longer starving, but changed. Lines already formed on my forehead. Looking in a mirror, I would not have been surprised to see gray hair. I sat on a slatted bench, took out my notebook. *He holds her hand. / Between the stones sprout daisies...*

The time of the poets was passing. We were entering an era of prose. Zoshchenko and Lunts, Nikitin and Slezin, boys from Zamyatin's studio—they called themselves the Serapions—had won this winter's House of Writers prize. A triumph for the House of Arts, but all were writing fiction. Gorky was giving them an annual—*The Year 1921.* The first issue of *Dom Iskusstv* appeared—but it included no younger poets, only the great ones, Mandelstam and Gumilev, Khodasevich and Kuzmin, essays by Blok and Chukovsky. Akhmatova had a new poem:

> *Why is this century worse than all others?*
> *Is it because, dumbstruck with grief,*
> *it touched the blackest of wounds, but couldn't*
> *heal it or offer any relief?*
>
> *The earthly sun still shines in the West*
> *and city rooftops glow in its rays...*
> *While here, the White One marks houses with crosses*
> *and summons ravens—and ravens obey.*

Critics bashed the publication, clamoring for new voices, people who could *speak for our times*. Well, I was alive, writing about our times, as were Tereshenko, Nikita Nikulin, Elizaveta Polonskaya, Irina Odoyevtseva, Anna Radlova, Arseny Grodetsky, and Oksana Linichuk. What about us? But the prose writers had the people's ear. The night of *The Year 1921* reading at the House of Writers, there wasn't an empty seat. Certainly some came to hear Zamyatin, and old Grin, who had finally finished his novel, *Scarlet Sails,* and Inna Gants, but for a change it was the young people they wanted to see. How could I fault their success? People wanted stories to help them make sense of the times, not puzzles to challenge their souls. Solid matter had trumped the fiery spirit of verse.

Yet Akhmatova had emerged from literary exile—all was not lost. And the State Publishing House was releasing a volume of verse by Polonskaya, the lone female Serapion brother. But she was a Marxist, a doctor. She'd distributed leaflets for Lenin in 1908. Her poems admitted the struggle but put a hopeful face on the outcome. They didn't chalk the doors and summon ravens.

I sat very still on the bench in the Summer Garden and kept company with the statues freed from their winter boxes, moldy and crumbling from frost, yet back in the light, pleasing our eyes with their grace. Passersby strolled arm in arm, or trailed children like little ducks, as the statues gazed on benignly. These nymphs and heroes were also survivors; it was no shame.

A black-clad figure came forward. I thought: *Summon the ravens.* She'd left her Chekist leather at home today, had donned a dark blouse, a skirt. No square-handled Mauser decorated her hip. Instead, she carried a cardboard briefcase. Her black hair was unbrushed and matted. It looked like the coat of a dusty black spaniel. She sat next to me, took a cigarette from her skirt pocket, and struggled to light it. Those hands, I'd know them anywhere, long fingered, with sensitive small tips out of place in the life she'd chosen. She still bit her nails, halfway down the nail bed.

"Am I under arrest?" I asked.

She squinted against the smoke, examining the hip of young Aphrodite, mottled with age and moss, and rested her head in her hand.

How dare she come here, and sit next to me? I'd never forget the way Father looked dumped in the hall, wrapped in my bloody sheepskin. The vicious last touch when I had come home from burying him to find my room reassigned. "Look, you won. You've stuffed my throat with dirt. Can't you just enjoy your triumph and leave me in peace now?"

People passed us: boys playing with sticks, girls sharing secrets with their arms around each other's waists, men and women in their patched old clothes, so much more evident in the clear May light than under coats in the winter's darkness. But every so often a new shirt or summer dress appeared. Already the changes were show-ing. And how did we seem to them, Varvara and me? Two harmless women, having a quiet conversation in the shade. If only they knew who we really were, what we'd done for the sake of history. "I don't have to sit with you. You make me sick." I rose but she put her hand on my arm.

"Wait," she said. "Please." Something about the way she clutched her cigarette, as if she was holding on to a stair rail. Did she have some fatal disease?

"What's wrong? Are you dying?"

She flicked ash into the gravel. "Who isn't?" Her lips were cracked, her eyes sunken into bluish rings. "The revolution is over. It lies at the bottom of the sea."

"You should know, you were the ones who sank it. The sailors—"

"The sailors were adventurers. Anybody could have told them they didn't stand a chance... You could have. Surely you didn't think they'd succeed?"

"They had enough of a chance that you Bolsheviks changed all your policies."

The spark in her eyes died. She kicked her heels into the dirt. *Chop chop chop.* "Don't you like your dance halls?" she said.

"Traders doing business right out in the open, to the tune of the soviet's applause?"

Was that what was bothering her? Dance halls and bakeries? "You've crushed the people's last hopes to have a say in their own country. Don't begrudge them a few eggs and dance halls."

She snorted. "You mean the return of capitalism in Soviet Russia? Haven't you heard? They're granting concessions to foreigners, selling off everything that's not nailed down. You don't know the half of it." Her hand trembled so, she had to tuck it under her armpit, bringing her cigarette to her lips with the other. "I thought I could talk to you."

I leaned over her, keeping my voice down. "After what you've done to me? You can talk to that statue. It'll hear you better than I can." I began to walk down the gravel path.

"I saved you more than once," she called out after me. "We both played our hands. Your old man too. You think that was the worst thing I ever did?"

I couldn't yell what I was thinking across the Summer Garden. This was the world she had created, where people disappeared, later to be dumped in apartment hallways. I marched back, stood over her. If I could have picked up a rock and smashed her skull open, I would have. "No one forced you. You could have been anything, but you chose to be Torquemada. You're a blot on the sun."

She looked up at me, hunched over her briefcase, as if she had a terrible cramp. "We were building a new world! And now the whole thing's kaput." She raised her cigarette to her lips again, those bleeding nails. "We should have seen it coming. In 1918 when that *politician* signed the peace with Germany." Lenin. "Gave in to all their demands. First he sold out the German worker and now he's sold out revolution for a tin of herring."

Yes, think what you've done. "The Bolsheviks killed the revolution." I sat back down on the bench so I could speak without being overheard. "You gutted the soviets. You turned workers into units of labor. God forbid that people can buy a tin of herring, a bit of

629

meat. *You* and your people were the ones trading. You traded the revolution for Bolshevik power. *You* did it."

"That tin *is* the death of the revolution," she said.

"If he hadn't changed the policy, Lenin would be ruling over a nation of the dead. But he killed off the voice of the workers. The soviet's a sham. And you're complaining because people can buy and sell a handful of flour? Who are you, Varvara?"

She rubbed her forehead hard with the flat of her hand, as though she could wipe something from her memory, or clear away years of soot and cobwebs. When she began again, her tone had changed. Raspy and listless. "I was a human being when this started. Remember? I liked things. Beethoven. Those little sandwiches your mother used to make. Remember when your family took me to see Chaliapin, at the House of the People?" My friend, my mortal enemy, my sister, lover...hunched over like a dirty crow. She took a last drag on her cigarette and flicked it away. "I remember sleeping over the first time. You gave me your robe—remember that? We all slept in the bed together, you, me, Mina, and the dog." She laughed. It sounded like a sob.

"And now you're sorry, is that what you're trying to say?"

She hung her head so I couldn't see her face, only her nose's sharp outline, her prominent chin, and the dirty hanks of her frizzy black hair. "It's killing me. I see their faces. I hear them, begging." She coughed, and then kept coughing. She sounded like Gorky or old Petrovsky. "I can't go on, Marina. It's a nightmare. It was all for nothing." She covered her eyes, shading them from the sun's accusation. What she had done for her spaceman's dream. That blood did not wash off. What agony she must be in. I knew she'd thought what she was doing was right—but it couldn't save her from the guilt. So the spaceman had finally crashed to earth. That she, the most brilliant, our Ivan Karamazov, had not seen the obvious—that the Bolsheviks were not glittering theorists after all but just power-seeking politicians. What a terrible moment when the truth flooded in. They'd lied, they changed course when it suited them. Power was their true north—and ideologues like Varvara, the ones who couldn't bow and hang on during the sharp turns of state, would fall or be thrown from the ship. Unlike Genya, who was proving himself quite capable of making these transitions, Varvara was dying of shame. She was the worst, but also the best.

"If you were in my shoes, what would you do?" she whispered.

I had never felt further from her in my life. Not angry, or pitying. But as implacable as time itself.

A worker family strolled nearby—mother, father, a little boy about four with the shaved head of summer—taking the air amid the Greek and Roman statues commissioned by emperors. The Summer Garden had only been open to the public since the 1850s, and then just to the well-heeled, the formally dressed—there'd been a strict code. Avdokia had avoided it, preferred taking us to the more relaxed Tauride Gardens. Looking at this family on the gravel path, the woman in her old flowered dress, the man in a Russian shirt, examining the statue of Alexander the Great, I thought, maybe we'd done some good. Perhaps someday, something would remain. The boy rode a stick horse, galloping along the path. He'd probably never seen a live one, though certainly he'd eaten its flesh.

Her hand crept out to hold the fabric of my skirt. "Forgive me, Marina. But there's no one else I can talk to."

"What about your Cheka comrades?"

She laughed, painfully. "That boatload of psychotic freaks?"

"Manya?"

"She's in the Volga, doing famine relief. It's a disaster out there. Kazan, Ufa, Samara. You have no idea." She slumped unhappily on the green slatted bench, her long legs stretched before her. "Meanwhile we're selling off pieces of Russia. You can hear the auctioneer's gavel from here." She pinched her nose at the bridge, trying to compose herself. "When I used to think of the future, I could see it as clearly as I can see that statue's fat ass." She nodded at Aphrodite's derriere. "Now all I see is a wall."

I knew the sensation. I had felt it last autumn as I gazed into the

Neva. Pressure, that made death seem like a rational alternative. While all around us, early summer unfurled, hope juicy in the green leaves, the innocent hope of the natural world.

"Ever think of leaving?" she asked me.

"Sometimes," I said. "You?"

She shook her head the way even a good chess player sometimes does when he looks down at the board to discover that in his pursuit of the adversary, he's closed off every avenue.

Two men walked past, smoking desultorily, looking us over. One said, "Hey, girlies—"

"Keep walking, *bratya*." She had no Mauser but her tone commanded respect.

We watched the men's backs moving away in their frayed shirts, their tattered jackets. "I just came to warn you," she said. "Your name's being mentioned in connection with the mutiny."

I felt the familiar *tzing* of terror in the center of my chest and up my spine. "What did they say?"

"That you taught at the sailors' club. That you'd been regularly seen with one of the instigators. Sleeping with him, of course."

"It's not a crime."

"*Kislov, Pavel Vladimirovich,* of the *Petropavlovsk.* You are in daily contact with the monarchist Nikolai Gumilev, and your father was shot by the Extraordinary Commission. It's starting to look like a picture."

I felt dizzy. My skin prickled in an ugly way. Gumilev never made any secret of his beliefs, and no one had ever bothered him. Who told them about me and Pasha?

She sighed, put her briefcase on the bench between us. "Think about going to Moscow. Hole up with Genya. He's the best defense you've got."

Diana, moon browed, frowned, raising her bow, notching her arrow. "I can't stand the sight of him."

"Better listen to me. I know what I'm talking about."

I nodded. But I would not take any more favors or advice from Varvara. Not after that delivery, wrapped in sheepskin.

"If anything happens this time, I won't be around to save you," she said. She turned to me, her black eyes rimmed with red.

"Where are you going?"

She shook her head and turned away. "Don't remember me like this."

We were caught in a great net. I could feel it scooping us up out of the water, like herring. We struggled and flapped as the net drew closed and dumped us on the deck in a vast heap, gasping.

She took my hands. "See you around," she tried to say, but her voice cracked.

I'd never seen her despair. She gazed into my eyes, hers so familiar, her hair as black as a raven's wing, and, my God, she had strands of white woven in with the black. *"We'll meet again in Petersburg…"* she recited. "Isn't that how it goes?" Mandelstam's poem. Varvara, the least poetic soul in Petrograd. "This is for you." She handed me the cardboard briefcase. "It'll give you a head start."

I opened it, withdrew a gray file folder. *MAKAROVA, Marina Dmitrievna.* Varvara had stolen my Cheka file. It was terrifyingly fat, an inch thick at least. I remembered the files we'd burned on the street when they'd broken into the police station on Liteiny. She'd gone in, while I had stayed outside on the sidewalk, feeding files to the fire. Back when I thought people would be free of such things. My own dossier: my picture, my aliases, addresses, known associates, my number at Gorokhovaya 2. My father. Kolya. Genya. The Krestovskys. *Current residence: House of Arts, 59 Moika.*

Varvara was not planning to return. Not to Petrograd, not anywhere.

We kissed each other formally, three times. She smiled her crooked smile and left me there by the haunch of Aphrodite, the statue's hand shielding its face from the light.

60 *Famine*

In the black-earth belt of central Russia, from Kazan down to the Caspian Sea, the dry hot summer replaced our rye and wheat—our elemental gold—with dust. This wasn't just hunger, where "somewhere" there was food—a problem of distribution, a problem in the city—but famine. Famine in the Volga, starvation in the Don, drought in the Crimea. Kazan, Samara, Izhevsk, Kambarka. The ravens flew in the cruel cloudless skies over the exhausted land. After last year's poor harvest came the blow of drought. The rains in Petrograd belied the searing pitiless sun blanching the agricultural lands of the Volga and the Ukraine. Starvation spread out its ghastly rule, tenfold anything we'd experienced in the city. No one in Petrograd complained about his rations now. The Povolzhye, the great basin of the Volga, was down to its last grains. Unthinkable.

Even from here, I could tell how bad it was, the way hunters read the migration of birds. *Besprizorniki* were pouring into the city, their numbers like locusts emerging from the ground. They arrived by train, thousands each day, begging, mobbing passersby. "Where are you from, sweetheart?" I would ask in the street. Samara, they said. Tambov. Taganrog, Tsaritsyn. Some could only stare. Little children, perhaps they didn't know themselves. Only that the White One had chalked the crosses on their doors, and summoned the ravens, and the ravens obeyed.

Finally, even our lying government stopped trying to cover it up. *Pomogi! Help!* cried the old man from the posters in the windows where the ROSTA campaign against the sailors had made its claim just a few months ago. People who had not been seen in public life since the October Revolution came out of the woodwork, stepping forward to raise money for the starving. The All-Russian Famine Relief Committee consisted of an unprecedented cross section of influential Russians—SRs, old generals, even Tolstoy's daughter—

framed by the usual Bolshevik officials. Of course, Gorky led the way. Benefits for the victims were held all summer long—concerts, art auctions, readings, plays. Citizens parted with their money, the little we had.

But everything conspired against the victims—seven years of war, everyone taking the peasants' grain as they rode through, the Whites and the Reds alike, the food detachments from the city. The Bolshevik policy that everything belonged to the state compounded by the lack of manufactured goods from the cities' exhausted factories, all caused the peasants to plant less. Why should Ivan work so hard when there was nothing to buy and it would all be taken from him anyway? But Ivan hadn't planned on last year's poor harvest, and—fatally—this year's vicious drought to finish him off. His rebellion had backfired, and now temperatures above 100 degrees baked the land to ceramic.

The propaganda, of course, was that it was all the fault of the Entente and the bourgeoisie. Everything had been forced upon us, the war, the civil war, everything but the weather was bourgeois wrecking, and if the Bolsheviks could have figured out a way to blame the weather on "the capitalists," they would have. And yet, who was allowing capitalism into Russia?

A note from Lenin in *Pravda* appealed to the trade unions of the West. He admitted the size of the famine, but blamed it on Russia's backwardness and the war and the civil war, *forced upon the workers and peasants by the landowners and capitalists of all countries.* He asked for the help of the oppressed masses in Europe, who should make common cause with us *whose lot it was to be the first to undertake the hard but gratifying task of overthrowing capitalism,* and then enumerated the ways in which the capitalists of all countries were revenging themselves on the Soviet Republic, preparing new insurgencies and counterrevolution. The hypocrisy took your breath away.

You could see the crosses on every house. The fear was a scent. It smelled dry and parched. It sounded like wind. How terrible the situation must be if the Bolsheviks allowed people like Alexandra Tolstaya; the well-known anti-Bolshevik intellectual Kuskova;

Prokopovich, a Kerensky minister; and Dr. Kishkin, also a figure from the Provisional Government, to sit on an independent famine relief committee that had the right to collect money, publish their own newspaper, start projects that would employ people, and so on. The Bolsheviks said things like "Only they and not the government could get help from abroad." Perhaps it was also intended to show the West that independent voices were still permitted in the Bolshevik state. It was the strangest time, the government grasping at every straw.

I couldn't sit on my hands at such a time, comparatively well fed and well housed and producing my poems while starvation gnawed the raw bone of the Povolzhye. I didn't have much to offer, but I contributed what wages I made, and participated in fundraising readings at the House of Writers. But it wasn't enough. There was something more I could do, and so I did it.

I had never seen Orphanage No. 6 as busy as it was that morning, the first of August. The lobby was as impassable as a train station, the new arrivals baffled and glassy-eyed with hardship from their recent ordeals. Behind the bars of the amber marble front desk, Alla Denisovna shuffled through a mass of files, grown to impossible height. I knocked on the counter. "Any room at this hotel?" I said. "A double, facing the square?"

The shock on her face when she saw me. She laughed, holding her head at the temples with one long hand. "They say there's a drought, but the Volga's flooding—right through the doors. Are you coming in to work or just to marvel?"

"Work," I said. Children clustered around me, gazing up at me with hollow eyes, patting my skirt. *Pomogi!* I smiled down at them. I didn't want my horrified face to be their mirror.

"Thank God," she said. "Start anywhere. The canteen's a nightmare. Tell Matron you're here."

I trailed a flock of tiny starvelings to her office. "Wait here," I said. Knocked and slipped in.

Matron was speaking to someone on the telephone, from what I could gather tracking down a load of rice. "It's here, you devils, just bring it—before you find yourself in the fortress." She lowered the earpiece to the cradle with a smart click, and took in the sight of me. She'd not changed—still a wall against the chaos—calm, heavy, and capable. "Are you back?"

"I want to help. Whatever you need."

She smiled. "I saw you read, Comrade. At the House of Arts."

A sun rose inside me. There were few people whose opinion really mattered to me, and hers was one of them. "I'm sorry I didn't see you."

"I didn't want to disturb you. Sometimes I see you walking. It's good you've come. Not everyone can look at this. Most people turn their heads, and how could they not? A problem without a solution, only grief."

I started in the canteen. Little food, children in rags, scarce water. They were short on everything—chairs, and adults. So many orphans. All I could do was help them sit down, four to a chair, and keep the old-timers from grabbing their food and terrorizing them. Later, I washed them—Boys 6–9, a lesson in horror. What could keep human beings alive with so little flesh on them, their ribs like birdcages made of bamboo. I smiled and washed them as they stared and stared. Sang them a song, "Fais Dodo, Colin."

There were few fights now—mostly they were in shock—but keeping them from being preyed on by the old-timers was no easy task. They'd snatch the food on its way to the new ones' mouths. I put them to bed, told them stories—no sorcerers or magical infants, only funny tales of talking cows and wise ravens and sneaky foxes. They were as hungry for the security of a big person's care as they were for potatoes and *vobla*.

I'd meant to spend only a day or two but ended up staying on through the days and nights, taking up the rhythm of the orphanage, soothing, watching over the children in their sleep, five to a bed, head to tail and more on the floor. Held them when they woke up screaming. What these children had endured to make that journey of thousands of miles—crossing the famine regions on foot, then fleeing by train to the farthest reaches of the country in search of food. I still remembered the children huddled on the carriage's platform that night I shot the Chekist and shoved the body off the train. These children wanted to hear stories about houses of spun sugar where you could eat the doors and windows, about sheep knee-deep in green grass, and wolves valiantly beaten off by brave children with sticks.

One morning I returned to the House of Arts for my ration cards, to find the residents crowding the downstairs corridor outside the canteen. They stared at me as if I'd intruded from another world, as if I'd grown three heads. Anton pushed through the throng, flung his arms around me as if I'd just been saved from a shipwreck. "Where have you been?"

"At the orphanage," I said. "What's going on?"

"They arrested Gumilev," Shafranskaya chimed in, her white hair twisted into a messy chignon, her crumpled floral dress misbuttoned. "Woke up the porter. Forced him to lead them to his room. And then to yours! They tossed it, took your notes, asked me and Alla if we knew where you were. Of course, we'd never heard of you. We didn't even speak Russian."

"Where's Gumilev's wife?" I asked. She'd come back from the country just at the wrong time.

"Still up there. She's in shock."

They'd arrested Gumilev. He always said they'd never arrest him—they had a gentleman's agreement, him and the regime. He would teach, serve the Bolshevik state, and stay out of politics, and they would let him have his opinions, his prayers, his antique beliefs, and go on writing. Evidently not. Varvara had told me as much. *It's starting to look like a picture.* "Has anyone told Gorky?"

No one knew.

I ran. I flew. Down Nevsky, through the General Staff arch, across Palace Square to the Troitsky Bridge. I caught a tram past the fortress, where Nikolai Stepanovich might now be imprisoned in a cold cell. I had missed the Cheka search by just a few hours.

Saved by orphans. It didn't matter that I'd drowned my dossier in the Neva. They had come for me anyway.

Though it was a hot August morning, I could feel the damp, cold walls of the Troubetskoy Bastion, the weight of the low ceiling. I did not turn my eyes from the east as we trundled past the fortress, staring into the sun glinting on the river until I jumped from the tram at Kronverksky Prospect and ran to Gorky's house.

Molecule answered the door, her small face pale and drawn. There were dark circles around her eyes.

"I need to talk to Alexei Maximovich. Did he hear about Gumilev?"

She wore a work apron, her dark hair in a knitted beret. "It's not just Gumilev. It's all the *intelligenty*. Professors. Doctors. The relief committee. They even got Ukhtomsky at the Hermitage." The director of the museum! *Bozhe moi.*

"Everything's coming apart," she said, "while Lenin's got him writing to everybody in the West for famine aid. He's even working with the Patriarch, if you can believe it." Unthinkable. Who hated the church more than Gorky? "He's just back from Moscow. He finally got permission for Blok to leave."

Blok? I grabbed her arm. "Is Blok under suspicion?"

"No, he's just sick. But here's the thing—they won't let his wife go, and he can't go alone." She wiped her eyes.

It was too much to take in. Gumilev, Blok. In the front parlor, the plants were dying, the furniture was dusty, the house felt uninhabited. "Where is everyone?"

"Gone." She stuck her hands in her apron pockets. "Moura's in Estonia. Maria Andreeva's in Germany. She's head of the Petrograd Office of Foreign Trade now—art and antiquities. It's a mass sell-off."

I followed her down the hall toward the heart of the apartment. No sounds came from any of the rooms, no laughter, no one talking on the telephone. How could Moura leave Gorky at a time like this? Everything was coming to an end. Now I could hear Gorky coughing.

"Lenin wants him to go to Germany to put pressure on them for aid. Is he the only person in Russia who can do anything?" she said under her breath.

"They've made sure there isn't anyone else," I said.

I knocked gently on the office door and opened it. Gorky sat in the middle of a fug of smoke, writing by hand. When he saw me, he waved me in with two nicotine-stained fingers. He was gray with exhaustion. And he was on his own now. Why had she decided to leave now, without him? Was she preparing the way? Or had she fallen under suspicion herself and decided to slip away when she could?

He reached forward and pressed my hand, gestured to a chair. His hand was hot. He was sweating, though the window was open and it was not hot in the room.

"Any news about Gumilev?" I took a seat in the leather chair where I'd once sobbed out my confession.

"They haven't charged them yet," he said. He rubbed his gray face with his large square hand. He was still in his dressing gown. "I never thought they'd arrest him."

"They're looking for me too," I said. "They searched my room." I hated to burden him with my problems, but he knew things, knew how a person should act. I would try to be brave, but my instincts were poor. If I was alive with any of my soul still intact, it was this man's doing. In a way, he was my father, the father I never lied to. "I should tell you, I was seeing a Kronstadt sailor. They know that."

When I saw the painful expression on his face, I wished I had kept that to myself. How tired he looked in that worn dressing gown, his seamed face, his hollowed-out chest. He turned his head to cough. He really needed to get out of Russia, every bit as much as Blok did. The phone rang, a relief. God knew from what hidden reserves he summoned the energy to keep his hand in all our lives. I tried not to eavesdrop, but how could I not. It was about Ukhtomsky, the roundup over at the Hermitage. Though it was perfectly calm in the room, I felt the storm raging outside—huge trunks cracking, branches flying in the wind. Would this be the final storm? I could almost hear the house groan.

"You need help," I said after he'd hung up. "Why did Moura go?"

"I wanted her to," he said. "I wanted to get her out of this before it gets any worse." He screwed a cigarette into his black holder, lit it. "So what were you doing with a Kronstadt sailor?"

"A lover."

He nodded. "And how did you meet him?"

"I was teaching at their club on the Admiralty docks. Gumilev gave me the class."

He winced. "And people knew—about the sailor?"

I thought of the eyes watching us as I brought him through the House of Arts. The way he would sit in the canteen with Kuzmin, waiting for me. "It wasn't a secret. But he was from the *Petropavlovsk*. On their committee."

He closed his eyes, massaged his broad forehead with his fingers, along the ridge of his brow. "Luck has not been your friend," he said. "Is there anywhere safe you can go? A school friend in the suburbs? Cousin in the country?"

Cousin in the country.

It's starting to look like a picture.

The air left the room as I realized with a sickening jolt that I could not return to the House of Arts. I was done there. Done as a poet, a member of that blessed fraternity. Just when I'd finally joined their world. Blok knew my name, but Blok was dying. Now it was over. Just like that. I'd had everything, and then it was taken away. What had I thought? That I would tell Gorky about Gumilev and go back to the House, clean up my room, set the furniture to rights, pick up where I'd left off? What a fool.

"Will you be all right?"

I struggling to breathe, to see, bumped my leg on the chair in my hurry to get away, to keen and sob somewhere private. "I'll be fine."

"Marina?"

I stood at the door, my hand on the knob. I rested my forehead against the wood, the intricate grain of the oak.

"I'm sorry. I'd invite you to stay here—we've got nothing but rooms—but it's impossible now. You have some idea of the situation...But come back if you can't find anything. I'll think of something."

His kind face. We never did lie to each other, Alexei Maximovich and I. "Don't worry about me." I tried to smile. "Good luck with Gumilev."

He reached out his big square hand and I shook it. "I wish I could do more for you." He let me go, took out his wallet from the desk drawer, and handed me five hundred rubles. A month's wages for a workingman, or used to be. The sight of it only emphasized the danger he felt me to be in. I waved it away, but he took my hand, pressed the money into my palm. "It won't help much, but for my sake, take it."

I put it in my pocket. I could hardly see for the tears in my eyes. I would never see him again either? It was all ending.

"Who would have guessed we'd have to be so brave in this life, eh? I thought I could just get rich and take it easy." He laughed and started coughing. "Be well, Marina Dmitrievna."

"And you, Alexei Maximovich."

I slipped out of the apartment, down the back stairs, and out into the courtyard, and through the little alleys and the park, the long way home. Home to Orphanage No. 6, where they knew me only as Comrade Marina. With Matron's connivance, I could stay hidden among the children. I had paid my passage on this ship well ahead.

61 *The Poet, Blok*

I cut off all contact with the House of Arts. I only hoped Anton would think to go to my room, get my clothes, the things I'd need this winter, and keep them safe—and for Christ's sake not come looking for me. Orphanage No. 6 was only two blocks away, but it might as well be Irkutsk, and had to be. I set the distance in my mind, already a parallel dimension, unreachable. The House of Arts simply did not exist. Here at the orphanage, my petty literary ambitions were nothing compared to the desperate needs of these starved children, hands as light as paper, eyes so wounded it was hard to return their gaze. What was I compared to this? Longings, friendship, community—dreams.

When I thought the situation could not be more depressing, the last blow arrived. Taking a break in the summer dusk in Arts Square, I glimpsed Makar selling *Pravda* and God knew what else, with a group of older...you couldn't call them *orphans*. At fifteen or sixteen they were men of the city, *biznissmen*. I went over to buy a paper, hoping for news of Gumilev. On the front page, lower right corner, a box edged in black held a simple notice:

Last night the poet Alexander Blok passed away.

I felt as if a giant guillotine had sliced me in two, from the top of my head to my feet. I would split like a log and fall to the stones of Arts Square. My lips formed the words. "Blok is dead." As if saying the words would make it anything less than lunacy.

"Blok, Blok," Makar mocked me. "*Lya lya fa fa.* Who was he, Lenin's brother?"

I leaned on him so that I would not come apart in the middle of Mikhailovskaya Street. Tried to breathe some air but suddenly my lungs seemed glued together.

Although I'd been sleeping with starving children for days, rubbing empty, aching bellies, holding them as they described their villages where people lay on the sidewalk with only the strength to hold one hand outstretched. Although I'd been cast out by poetry, and brave Gumilev languished in prison, and Pasha was dead in the gulf, and Anton was out of reach, this was the thing that I could not bear. I would have thought myself beyond such grief, but this anguish was of a very special sort.

I looked around me at the noble, shabby buildings, the bushes and lawns, the statue of Pushkin, covered with pigeons. Pushkin, hounded by the rabble, and now, Blok was dead. I lowered myself to the bench where I'd once sat with Varvara and Mina as we ate nonpareils out of a paper cone and watched the doorway to the Stray Dog Café. Now I paged through *Pravda*. Surely there would be a paragraph or two devoted to the poet, a famous poem or two, but it was just that one line: *The poet Alexander Blok...passed away...The poet.* You might as well have said that poetry itself had died.

I headed out to Kolomna through the shimmering summer dusk as if pulled by an unearthly hand. Every canal, every square, whispered his name. I remembered the day I went to speak to him about our reading and his wife came to the door. The day we met on Bolshaya Morskaya outside the telephone exchange and he invited me to the Bely reading at the House of Arts. Those afternoons I sat on the Pryazhka Embankment, a young girl, watching his windows. His name trembled in the air like radiograph waves, vibrated along the stones. *The poet Alexander Blok passed away...*A streetcar sailed by me on Kazanskaya Street so close I had to jump. I didn't even hear the screech and bells. Gumilev's lost streetcar. But it wouldn't be suitable to take a tram to Blok's house. One should go on one's knees.

The air grew cooler as I passed the Mariinsky Theater and entered Ofitserskaya Street, wide and commercial. A few shops had opened here—a pastry shop, a cobbler, a pharmacy. How appropriate. *The night, the street, the streetlamp, the pharmacy...*He should have died in wintertime. Summer wasn't his season. Blok needed a frozen canal, a group of poets escorting actresses home from Ivanov's Tower on a frosty midnight. I passed the Komissarzhevskaya Theater, where his famous *Puppet Show* had played. And what about *this* puppet show? *You die—and then relive it all...there is no change. And no escape.*

Was I weeping because I'd never had that beauty? Or because he gave it to me, gave it to everyone who had heard his song. I stumbled down to the Pryazhka River and his tall house on the corner, 57 Ofitserskaya. I stood on the embankment where I'd stood so many times, staring up at those windows. In a world of poets, he'd been *the* poet—who had seduced us all, the angel of light, shadow against blinds, the flicker in the mirror. Blok. *You saved my life. You can't be dead.* He'd taken me—this orphan—from the streets, and breathed life into my lungs, called me *poet.*

I heard singing through the open windows, the Orthodox liturgy. People entered and left by the main street door. Did I dare go up? Who was I? Just another dreamer whose life he'd touched. One of millions. Millions, alone and lost on this earth, and just a few angels. They show us how we must live, breathe life into the mud we are, and give us—beauty. Colors to which we would otherwise be blind. Light blue and silver and lilac. His, the snow falling. His, the fog. His, the masquerade. His Twelve, that blizzard, that mystery, with Christ leading the parade. But for me, he would always be the lover who sends roses to the mysterious woman in a restaurant, a woman with a feather in her hat who nods and says to her friend, "He's in love with me too."

I wasn't planning to go up, and yet, I went. The door was open. After the greenish summer-river smell of the Pryazhka, it was hot and close in the apartment. All was just as I remembered, the door, the stairs, the striped wallpaper in the entry. The flat was full of people, a service going on, the heat and smell of flowers overpowering. A man was leaving. He passed me by, wiping his face with his handkerchief, overcome with heat or emotion. I stopped in the doorway of the dining room, where Blok was the guest of honor as well as the host, on the table in a white coffin and, oh God—in death he looked nothing like himself. I remembered him tall and golden, but the corpse was slight and dark, with a dark stubble of beard and dark hair. Death changed a man. Illness, suffering—though who of us had remained unchanged? An old lady hovered nearby, his mother maybe. And two other women. I recognized his wife, Lyubov Mendeleeva, and a woman I realized with a shock was Lyubov Andreeva-Delmas, his Carmen. He had written an entire cycle of poems about her. Now she was just an ordinary stout middle-aged woman, but the poet had made her immortal, the voice that had driven him mad. His fourth muse, or his tenth. Lyubov *i* Lyubov. Two loves among the many.

And here was Kuzmin, and Inna Gants, and Zamyatin with his sophisticated face, his moustache. People I didn't know, but who knew each other, from his precious life—not long, but long enough to mark a country. The singing went on and on. It lulled me as I listened, just outside the doorway. At one side of the dining room, standing with a woman friend, was Akhmatova. She rolled against the wall, leaned her cheek on it as if it were alive. So much suffering in this world. Enough to go around for the rest of time. Bely arrived, white-haired in a black skullcap. Seeing Blok, his blue eyes grew so wide they were squares. How strange that death admitted all, opened every door. People who had not the sense to gather before had gathered now. Blok, where did you go? We were orphans without you, starving, lost. I'd cut a pine bough across the street. You could see the light green of the new growth. I held it to my nose. Like Blok, it freshened. Like Blok, tall and ever green. I laid it with the flowers. Someone, a girl—I remember having seen her but not who she was—told us the funeral would be tomorrow at ten at Smolensk Cemetery, up on Vasilievsky Island. A breeze blew the curtains. It was still light outside. How could that be?

More people arrived. It was time for me to give up my place. I shook his wife's hand, said something, even curtsied—my God, where did that come from?—and rushed out, back down the stairs, onto the Pryazhka Embankment. The green freshness of the river calmed me. I found a little copse of trees down by the water where I could sit and watch the ripples, the silver and rose of the Petersburg twilight, hear the plash of the water, a flash of fish, and remain with Blok a little longer, in sight of the lit window. No point in walking all the way back to the orphanage. I lay down and fell asleep to the singing on the air and in the mouths of frogs.

I woke in the morning stiff and rumpled, leaves in my hair. Old people and girls with flowers had already gathered on the Pryazhka Embankment above me. A bright, clear day, without a cloud, inappropriately halcyon for a poet whose preferred moods of nature were fog, gloom, and storm. I shook my hair and my dress, tried to smooth myself out, relieved myself behind a bush, washed in the water lapping the embankment, and joined the others who waited on the corner—forty, fifty, a hundred souls. More kept arriving.

I could smell the flowers—lilies—in their hands. Suddenly the sound of singing swelled, loud and full throated as the gates to the courtyard were flung open and the white coffin emerged.

They bore him aloft at shoulder height, so that all could see his profile against the sky, whittled to dark wood like a mannerist Christ. Carrying the coffin seemed surprisingly light work for such as Bely, Zamyatin, others I knew or didn't recognize. In the crowd was every last remaining member of literary Petersburg, all but Gumilev. I wonder if anybody had told him Blok had perished. Here were Delmas and Lyubov holding up Blok's mother as we began our march in the morning sun, and Akhmatova, in a black veil, as if she had been the wife and not Lyubov. But where was Gorky?

The corpse seemed happier in the open air, and the choir's voices swelled as if unloosed from the walls. I tied my white matron's scarf around my hair, peasant style, low on my forehead. I didn't want anyone recognizing me. I only wanted to be close to Blok in these last minutes, as long as he remained above soil. It made me feel like a nun as I followed the procession, several modest lengths behind the notables.

So many women followed that procession! His poetry hadn't been written for women any more than for men, but it spoke of us so passionately. I wondered if he had ever had that rumored affair with Akhmatova. She could barely walk from grief, clinging to her female friends. Here they all were: Benois, Ivanov, Volynsky, Shklovsky's bald head, Anton, saying something to Tereshenko and Arseny. Here were the boys from the second floor, Zamyatin's crew. And Gumilev's studio. We were all here to bury our souls, following the white coffin up Ofitserskaya, turning at the Mariinsky, where more people joined us, singers and actors. Perhaps some had performed in his productions or just wished to pay tribute to the true heart of what had been and would never come again.

By the time we crossed the Nikolaevsky Bridge, the procession had lengthened to a full city block, a thousand people at least. It hadn't been mentioned in the newspaper, and yet the whole city seemed to know. A carriage followed behind, empty, the pallbearers clearly set on carrying the coffin all the way. Gorky's absence troubled me. Was he too ill to come? Had he been arrested? Summoned to Moscow? Was it political? But Blok had done nothing wrong, except talk about inner freedom.

At last, we stood outside the small chapel of the Smolensk Cemetery, a vast, silent crowd, as the choir of the Mariinsky Theater sang the service for the dead—Rachmaninoff, and then Tchaikovsky. One last explosion of sound, like red and gold flames.

Then we followed the coffin through the unkempt little lanes to his family plot. No one spoke. The birds were silent. The wind had ceased its rustling in the birch trees. *No more sounds.* A thousand people bent their heads. Silently, the gravediggers lowered him into his berth in his white ship. And silently, they filled the grave, burying the sun. *Safe journey, Alexander Alexandrovich. May the immortal poets rise to greet you.*

Across the city, Iskra too, lay in her grave. Papa, Pasha. All the dead, welcoming him. Our loss was their gain.

I hid myself in the crowd, not wanting to talk to anyone. The small sun of the poet was a secret still alive inside me. I didn't want him to spill out of my mouth. Luckily Shklovsky was easy to see, and tall Anton with his shock of black hair. I hid until they were gone. Although I hadn't eaten since breakfast the day before, I was in no hurry to return to the clamor and suffocating closeness of Orphanage No. 6. Air and silence were what I needed. Wasn't that what Blok had been complaining about—airlessness? The pillow of the times pressed to his nose and mouth.

Finally alone, I strolled along the cemetery's narrow, shady paths. I liked how unkempt it was, the untidy rows and heavy trees. Perhaps this was how it was going to be—beauty relegated to the hidden places, to tall weeds and mossy corners. I collected blooming weeds, asters and carrot and Queen Anne's lace. I remembered walking with Mother in the yard at Maryino, the Queen Anne's lace waist high. Then I noticed strawberries growing on the graves and along the paths, no bigger than my thumbnail. The longer I looked, the more I saw them. I collected the little heart-shaped berries in my pocket, careful not to bruise them. I wished certain of my charges were with me. I'd already taken a special interest in a few, though it wasn't right to favor one over another. But that's how it was in life—you liked certain people, and didn't we all need to feel singled out by someone as special? Wasn't that a secret gift I could still give? I'd had the idea I would save the berries for them, but in the end, I ate them all myself, sitting against a tree, watching clouds sail overhead. I could collect more before I left.

A man came strolling up the path, well dressed, wearing a light-colored suit and hat—a foreigner? An Englishman? French? And then the hat tipped back, and the grin. My mouth still full of strawberries.

62 *The NEPman*

He squatted down in his beautiful suit, not wanting to get grass stains on his trousers. I held out my hand full of berries. He lowered his mouth to my hand and ate them from my palm. The blood of the berries stained his lips as he chewed. It was my heart he was eating, that graveyard fruit. His mouth in my hand, his eyes closed. He had come for me, my Orpheus, to pluck me from the dead. Was he even alive, in his light summer suit and straw hat, shoes of two colors? His laughing eyes, upturned, oh, just like *hers*.

He took his hat off, his chestnut hair curly, longer than before. Slowly he pulled the scarf from my head, revealing my uncombed locks, which had spent the night in the bushes on the bank of the Pryazhka. His smell, I'd have known it in the last darkness before the grave—honey, and lime. And then we were falling into the grass, the years dissolved like dandelion floss.

A meadowlark *cheeeeeed*, the little flowers bloomed, and holding his face between my hands, I couldn't remember what had ever parted us. His weight pinned me to the earth or I might have spun into the blue air. Kolya. His cheek against my hair. Who was that spoiled girl, throwing herself around in self-dramatizing outrage? Three years lost over a poor peasant woman in a cowshed.

I could hear people from the funeral shifting around us, unseen, the leftover song of that choir still hanging in the air, and this, gold and bright, lime and cigars, this secret of secrets. My love had come for me. The fleshy solidity of him, this was real. He'd put on weight. He'd always had a tendency, a chubby child, but had grown hard in the war years. "You saw my poem."

"One can't dance it alone, " he sang in my ear as he worked the buttons on my dress. That mouth, the top lip thin, the bottom full. His eyes, very blue and turned up at the corners, eyes made for laughter. His mouth on my neck, his hand under my skirt.

I didn't believe in salvation. I knew prayer protected no one. But how else to account for this miracle? I could feel him against me, his knees parting my thighs. Were we going to make love in the cemetery? But what was all lovemaking but love in a graveyard under the sad, envious eyes of the dead.

We heard a gasp and looked up. A woman in patched clothing, accompanied by two children, hissed, "Have you no shame?"

"Have you no shame, Comrade?" I asked Kolya, my irrepressible love.

"Honestly, no." But we stood and brushed ourselves off. I rebuttoned my dress and Kolya retrieved his hat. I retied my kerchief. We began to walk, arms around each other's waists, like skaters. Our footsteps fell in perfect harmony, as they always did. We passed the poor scandalized woman again—she just couldn't get clear of us. My face hurt from smiling. He'd come for me, as he'd said he would. I glanced up and down the paths, making sure no one else was watching. If either of us were arrested, it was hard to say who would be in more danger. But my fear seemed to be missing. I couldn't remember its address. The Cheka would have to catch me on the run. Even they didn't have the manpower.

From Smolensk Cemetery back to the center of the city was a two-mile walk, but it could have been fifty for all I cared. My head against his, my arm around that solid waist, the scent of his body, we could have walked right off the face of the earth, our feet in step. We stopped at the Sphinx on the Neva Embankment to pay our respects, stood, hip to hip, contemplating the statues—ancient, patient in exile, built for the timeless heat of the desert, and forced to endure the damp and the tedious frost of our northern clime. They seemed to be laughing at our clothing of frail flesh. *Stone* being the answer to all riddles.

Egypt made me think *Gumilev*, languishing in the hands of the Cheka, reminding me of the danger—but distantly, like someone shouting from a far shore. No one was paying attention to us, except to eye Kolya in his foreign clothes, glances variously revealing distrust, admiration, or disgust, depending on their outlook on the New Economic Policy, which had spawned a new race of people, the so-called NEPmen—traders and middlemen, gangsters.

But we'd never been able to walk the streets of Petrograd like this before, arm in arm, back when we'd been young and unscarred, when there weren't ghosts fluttering all around us. There'd always been some reason we had to hide. First I was too young, next I was a boy. Then we were peasants. I laid my head on his shoulder. He didn't know about Iskra. He didn't know about Papa. And in the time we'd been apart, what women had he known? Where had he been? Across the river, the yellow blotch of the little mansion's facade stirred in the water's mirror.

We stopped beneath the Rostral Columns, the wind fresh in our faces. I thought of the day I almost gave myself to the river. Not even a year ago. And now he'd returned. His hand found my breast, his lips, my neck. His breath buzzed in my ear. "Don't be sad," he said. "We're together."

We crossed the bridge, the shifting green waters glinting in the summer sun. He glanced up as we passed the yellow mansion, an end and a beginning, and leaned in to rest his cheek on mine. We didn't say anything, we didn't dare. There was broken glass everywhere in the space around the present. In Palace Square, the weeds grew up through the stones, and the sculptures atop the General

Staff arch watched us enviously, the way chessmen would watch two pieces moving across a board of their own volition.

We leaned against the railing where the Moika met the Fontanka at the foot of the Summer Garden, our faces pressed closer as we peered down into the cool shifting blues and greens. A swan floated by, poking at some duckweed. "Still love me?" he asked. I leaned against him as a horse does when you groom it. "I dreamed this," he said. "Standing here with you." Holding his straw hat, he looked like a figure in a French painting. His wristwatch was gold, his necktie soft yellow. There was too much to say. *My father saw you in Estonia. They dumped his body on my doorstep. We had a baby, her name was Iskra. Varvara's dead, I think. There's no one left but us.* He bit me softly where my neck met my shoulder, sending an electric charge through me. I could stay here forever, in the shade of the tossing boughs, an old man painting on a small easel . . . I felt sleepy, as if I were in a trance.

"Don't stop, we're almost there," he said, pulling me to him as if we were dancing.

We crossed into Salt Town, past the heavy facade of the Stieglitz Museum to the ancient St. Panteleimon Church with its domed cupola and square bell tower. "Let's go in," he said, opening the door for me. It was awfully unlike him. But pleasant inside, empty and cool. Our footsteps resounded between ten-foot-thick walls. The iconostasis was still intact. I'd have thought the Bolsheviks would have confiscated it for its gold and silver. A priest conducted a service for three old ladies, who sang like perfect fountains in a convent courtyard, liquid and serene. The fragrance of powdery incense excited long-ago memories. I remembered walking through Gabriel's door and into Arkady's world. And it was Kolya who had sent me there. *If you ever need money.* So much of my fate bound up with this one man, so much pleasure, so much suffering. In the end, I supposed, we were each other's destiny.

The Theotokos watched me. *Was this what you wanted?* Gazing at me with such pity. Kolya put some coins in the offering box, lit a candle that had already been burned, and handed it to me. The simple, symbolic act was like a marriage. We'd never had that, something solemn. With us it was either sneaking or pretending. He took my hand and kissed it. The priest glanced up to see if we'd stay for confession, but either God knew it all or the heavens were as empty as a beggar's pockets. In the one case, there was no need, and in the other, no sense.

Outside I blinked, temporarily blinded. Kolya took my hand. Where was he taking me, back to Furshtatskaya Street? Perhaps we would slip back into ourselves as we had once been, and start again. But no, it was still 1921, and the leafy, elegant houses were as dirty and dilapidated as everywhere else. Here was the Muruzi house, where the Poets' Guild was garrisoned—Gumilev's group. Were they still meeting, now that the Maître was under arrest? Had they too been taken in the sweep?

Mother's old friend, the art dealer Tripov, lived there. Arkady's one-time customer. I wondered if Kolya knew Arkady was dead. He must, or he wouldn't be here, walking around like an English aristocrat. If it wasn't for Kolya, I'd never have known the name Arkady von Princip. On the other hand, Kolya never said, *Go have an affair with the Archangel*. Who could say whose fault it was. Life wasn't a tapestry, it was some sort of felt, formed by water and pressure—primitive, yet stronger than anything woven, impossible to tear.

We entered the square by the Preobrazhensky Church, where Avdokia once bought oil and potatoes while Mother prayed for deliverance. A man smoked in the shade—was he selling something, or watching one of the flats? Over a doorway a flag hung, white with a blue cross. "That's new," I said.

"Finnish consulate," Kolya replied, kissing my cheek. "Things are changing. In six months, you won't recognize your Soviet Russia."

"I already don't recognize it," I said.

We stopped on the south side of the square, in the shade of a maple. How much he looked like Iskra—I couldn't get over it. Grief ripped my throat. How could I tell him about her, how could

I even begin? Not yet. I would savor what the gods had offered one precious moment at a time.

"I used to pass here on the way to your house," he said. "Like the poor country cousin, hat in hand."

The most confident boy in Petersburg. "Poor you."

"Your father was so brilliant, he could cut you with a word. And your *mother*—"

"Let it go. Please." The last thing I wanted was to talk about my parents. Enough to have him back, for however long. He pulled me into an archway, pushed me against the wall, kissing me as if he would devour me. Pressing into me, raising my skirt, anyone could have come by and seen us. But I couldn't have stopped him if I'd wanted to. Were we going to do it up against the wall like some poor soldier and his whore? I twisted, but he held me there, grappling with me, whispering how he adored me, making me laugh.

At last, we passed into the courtyard of a once-stately building, where he led me to a battered door, yanked it open. Then I found myself upside down, heaved over his shoulder, as he stumbled up a flight of dark stairs to another door. Leaning on the wall, he opened it with a key and carried me in, raced me through a hall and into a light-filled room—table, brass bed, where he dumped me like loot after a robbery.

Oh, to make love to Kolya Shurov again. Our lips needed no introductions, our skin no drinks or chitchat. We only managed to get some of our clothes off before we couldn't even be bothered with that. We panted, we clawed as if we were scrambling from a well that was filling underneath us. As if we were running a relay but both of us running at once.

I came to myself with one boot still on, my panties looped around that leg, the sheet torn off the bed exposing the striped mattress. Kolya still wore his socks and his singlet. Sock garters. We lay gasping on the beach, having made it to shore with our pirate's plunder. He brought in a bottle of beer and some glasses, opened it—the fizz, amber, the bitter bright taste. I was so thirsty, I drank mine in three gulps. Where did it come from? Where had any of it come from?

"To our new life, Marina. May all our troubles be memory, and may our memories fade." We drank, watching each other without blinking until we had drained the small, faceted pink *stakany* to the bottom, and then he refilled them. The flat looked out onto the square. From the bed I could see the dome of the church, the tops of the trees through the light curtains.

"Is the man still there?" I asked. "There was a man by the church."

He got up, all rosy, sturdily built, his body hair red-gold. He went to the window, peered down. "Gone now." He opened the windows, let the freshness roll through. The curtain took the wind like sails. "Like it?" He smoothed his unruly hair as he lay down next to me. "The flat, I mean."

"Whose is it?" I asked, pouring the last of the beer into our glasses.

"Yours. If you want it," he said. That mischievous smile. My bright fox. A private flat like this would be the possession of a commissar at least. A telephone hung on the wall. How did he get it? "Whose place is this, really?"

He tapped his nose. For him to know and me to find out. How he loved a secret. He carried a box to the table, opened it. A gramophone! A little gramophone, all in a box: a miniature horn, turntable, everything folded out. He laid a disk on the spindle, cranked it, and lowered the needle. The room filled with music—"Mi Noche Triste." He'd been that sure of me. These sounds contained the worlds we'd lost that day, betrayals and heartaches, but I couldn't remember them now, only the joy, and the possibility that it would resume. What were the chances? Life could turn around as fast as the Bolsheviks.

He plucked the beer glass from my hand, set it onto the table, and pulled me to my feet. I held on to him to remove that one remaining boot, and my underwear, before he placed one warm hand on my back, the other to my palm, and we danced. Five years since that first tango. Five years since the afternoon on the Catherine Canal, my hairpins falling. And here we were again. We danced as if we'd done it every day of our lives. We made famous the space between table and bed, the curtains blowing, nothing between my skin and his, our bodies pieces of a puzzle that we had solved. He ran his hands down my hips, holding on to me, kneeling, pressing his cheek to my pelvis as if listening to my heartbeat there. Whose dream could this possibly be?

Later, I lay on the bed, its linen on the floor, covered with sweat and his unique odor. He brought in a tray with vodka, roasted chicken, fresh summer pickles, black bread, and butter. Together, we made the bed and sat in it. I couldn't stop eating. Licking my fingers. It was a sin when there was famine in Russia, when children were eating dry grass. Yet I stuffed myself shamelessly. He'd made coffee, real coffee, with evaporated milk, fed me pastries—hand pies with apples. My starving orphans just blocks away. And yet I couldn't help it. So easy to be virtuous when you had nothing. In the face of riches, I was as squalid as anyone. Yet if I ended in some Cheka cell when all this came to pieces, who would thank me for not enjoying the pies?

It was fully night when he revealed the flat's final secret. In the back hall, past a tiny kitchen, a door revealed a miracle. A private bath. Toilet, sink, little clawed tub. He turned on the taps, and water ran. But that wasn't the end. In a few moments, hot water splashed into the slipper-shaped tub. "Your bath, madame." He extended his hand, helped me in. I had to suck my teeth as I lowered myself into the steaming tub—the water was that hot, and my body had been thoroughly tenderized. But then, such bliss. Kolya knelt next to me, soaped a washcloth. *Pears soap...* It brought back my childhood, the English herbs, slightly resinous, Avdokia kneeling by the tub, washing me. I should have gone back for her. *Everything could have been different...* which wasn't to say it would have been any better. I had to remember that. There were infinite ways things could go wrong.

But right now, Kolya Shurov was washing my back, the old scars. Shampooing my hair. It was mesmerizing to be so intimately tended, his strong, short fingers rubbing my head, then pouring water through my hair. "It's grown out," he said, squeezing it with the side of his hand.

I was a boy the last time he saw me, leaving him at the Tikhvin station, as he'd wept and begged me to come back. I didn't want to think about that now. Life was giving us another chance. I wouldn't question it, question what he was doing here or how long he would stay. I could feel he was dying to tell me. He was fat with secrets. I had secrets too, but unlike him, there would be no fun in revealing them.

Kolya scrubbed my feet, my knees and elbows, the water in the tub grew as murky as standing water in a Petrograd courtyard. As he laved me, he sang a song. I didn't recognize it at first. And then I realized he was singing in English, and though it was somewhat changed, I knew it. *The river's so empty nowadays. / All the gray horses are gone . . ."* He rinsed out the cloth, hung it on the side of the tub. *"I try to remember the tango, but one can't dance it alone . . .* Some friends set it to music. Like it? The drowned bell is a little obscure, but it was quite the success."

"When did you learn English?" I said.

"One does what one must," he said in English.

I rested my head on the back of the tub. Yes, yes, there was something about him, now it had come up. "That's where you've been, England? Where in England?"

"Different places. *Regret is a bell, a secret, / An island carved in the mind. / Brave words once said in a station . . ."*

My poem had become a song. People in England sang it. "Funny, I pictured you in Paris. At a café, drinking champagne with a flock of attentive mademoiselles."

"Oh, squadrons of them. Battalions," he said. He pulled the plug, helped me out of the filthy water. "Unfortunately, there's not much of a living in drinking champagne, and money doesn't come floating down the Seine. Many other things, but not money. Paris is stinking with émigrés—they're driving cabs, waiting tables. Princes and generals." He wrapped a clean linen towel around me and rubbed my shoulders. "England provided a clearer field. They remember Dmitry Makarov there."

Oh God.

"There were some interesting prospects—better on a number of levels." He lit an Egyptian cigarette, oval-shaped, from a box with a bird goddess on the lid.

As I dried my hair, he sat on the edge of the tub and ran a bath for himself. Hot water gushed. I thought of my poor orphans being washed ten to a pail of cold water. He climbed in, set the ashtray on the rim, and sighed as I combed my hair in the mirror, wiping the steam. "Look how domestic we are," I said to him in the mirror. "Like an old married couple."

"Married couples don't fuck like that," he said.

"How would you know?"

He turned his head to the side to puff on his cigarette. "From keen observation. How is your husband, by the way?"

"Writing propaganda for our masters. How about you? What brings you to our shores? Nostalgia for *vobla*?"

He stuck a foot up in the air, twitched it to the left and the right. A squarish foot, not as long as Anton's nor as shapely as Pashol's. Funny that the sailor had the aristocrat's foot, the aristocrat a peasant's. I picked up the washcloth, knelt and soaped it, scrubbed the wide sole, the sturdy toes.

"England and Russia signed a trade agreement," he said. "At the end of March."

Just after Kronstadt. You could never underestimate the duplicity of our masters. They had to have been negotiating it even before the New Economic Policy. At the very moment they were crushing the rebellion, they knew what was coming.

"British labor unions pushed the trade deal through. They knew that the revolution was going to topple unless Lenin got some help—grain for the harvest shortfall, and the restoration of manufacturing. Now he's offering concessions in exchange for hard currency. Mining, industry. You can't make this kind of thing up—Western trade unions, pushing for a treaty that's going to help bloodsucking capitalists get their hooks into Bolshevik Russia. There's a poem in there somewhere, don't you think? You could call it '*Zholty Dom.*'" *Yellow house*—another way of saying *madhouse*. He turned over in a slosh of water like a fleshy seal so I could wash his back, perching his chin on the tub's rim. "Of course, the capitalists need a little help when it comes to dealing with the Kremlin. Someone with Russian insight, who knows the game. So who happens to be in London just at this very time? Why, our old friend Nikolai Shurov!"

"I've heard of him," I said, smoothing the creamy soap over his shoulders. He still had freckles…like mine. Iskra would have had them too. I kissed them, trying not to think about the new political turn. "Shurov, wasn't he a speculator, an agent of counterrevolutionary émigré groups?"

He laughed, flicking his ash into the ashtray he'd placed on the floor. "*Biznissman.* Old family friend of Dmitry Ivanovich Makarov, Russian liberal and friend to the English."

And shot in a Cheka cell.

I didn't know how I felt about Kolya trading on Father's reputation to find a place for himself in the world. I tried to get over my sense of shock. Of course he would use whatever tool came to hand. He was stateless, a pariah at home, a foreigner abroad. He wasn't doing anything any of us wouldn't have done. Though it looked as if he was doing better than we ever would.

"This Shurov, he meets a friend of your father's, Sir Graham Stanley, owner of coal mines in Wales and a steel factory in Sheffield. Sir Graham is particularly interested in the idea of Russian mineral rights. Oil, specifically. So, they meet with Litvinov and Chicherin, our good Soviet foreign representatives, first in London, then in Moscow, to see what goodies the Bolsheviks might be willing to lease. They even meet with the Great Revolutionary Devil himself."

"You met Lenin?" It was ludicrous, but I believed him.

"Or a brilliant facsimile." He ducked his head back into the water, holding his cigarette aloft. He shook the water off his face and hair like a dog. "No doubt he'd read my Cheka file, but nothing was said about that. Nothing must disturb the deal with Sir Graham.

Suddenly capitalists are back in vogue. The very thing I would have eaten lead for last year. But this year I'm *the honorable Mr. Shurov*, of the What-Can-We-Do-for-You Shurovs of St. Petersburg, Moscow, London, and Nottingham, England. *Yes, Mr. Shurov. No, Mr. Shurov.* Chicherin himself takes my calls. *Mr. Shurov calling on behalf of Sir Graham Stanley. Oh yes, Mr. Shurov, what can we do for you?* Hang around, you'll see."

The very thing Varvara had seen coming, that she could not abide, that had driven her—yes—to the river, or a bullet. *This* should not be happening here. This influence peddling, this selling of the Russian storehouse, exactly what we had fought to rid ourselves from. Yet I also understood—what else could we do? We had to get food to the Povolzhye. At least the government had finally relented, allowing foreign famine relief. It was a maze, a labyrinth over a cesspit. While the Cheka still hunted for the poet Marina Makarova, the lover of sailors.

He got out of his tub, that good sturdy body streaming with water. I gave him a towel and he began vigorously rubbing himself, singing a snatch of "The Internationale." "They're desperate for cash, your masters. I've helped broker purchases of the people's art—and not just your *baba*'s bric-a-brac. The émigrés are throwing a stink, of course. It never occurred to Chicherin that the rightful owners would get wind of the thing and sue. But as a go-between, I can help Sir Graham *and* the heroic Soviet Republic. I'm a most useful fellow."

The Bolsheviks going into business with Western capital, while arresting leading intellectuals right here at home. You would think they couldn't get away with it, that the West would see through their smiling faces. But the business folk didn't want to see the shadows in the corners, the bloodstains on the tile.

Suddenly it was too hot in the bathroom and I wasn't used to drinking. I had to open the door. "What about the famine?"

"Soviet officials are in Riga right now, negotiating with the American Relief Administration."

The Americans?

"They're the ones who know how. They fed Belgium after the war, and Poland. They're the only ones who can handle the scale, and they're surprisingly incorruptible." Americans rescuing Russia from the Bolsheviks' mistakes. The ultimate irony.

"Lenin's worst nightmare."

"He's got no choice."

I thought of my orphans—so many, and they just were the ones with the will to make it to Petrograd. What of the millions too weak to even walk out of their izbas? The stories I'd heard were too awful to be believed, but I believed them. *We had to eat the baby,* my own children had whispered to me.

"Everybody's anted up," Kolya said, examining his chin in the mirror, wondering if he needed to shave. "The émigrés, the laborites, the pious churchgoers. But only the Americans can organize it." He sudsed his face, washed the soap from his hands. "Of course, there's a snag vis-à-vis the Bolsheviks. The Americans are demanding to bring in their own people, hire local help, man their own kitchens, run their own trains." He began to shave with a glinting razor, starting with his neck, washing the foam from the blade with each stroke. "Their man Herbert Hoover's pretty canny. He knows not a bag of grain would be left for the Povolzhye if they left it up to us. Naturally, the Bolsheviks think they should run the show—when they couldn't run so much as a tobacco shop."

The children had told me how they searched the dust along the railway tracks near stations, looking for wheat that might have spilled, staying alive grain by grain. "It wasn't until last month they even admitted there was a famine."

"They wanted the trade agreement to look good. So they'd get better terms."

How I'd missed knowing what was going on. Since I'd stopped going to Gorky's, I was as in the dark as anyone. I read the signs, like a farmer reading clouds or the thickness of fur on caterpillars. We saw arrests, the sudden appearance of flower shops, and guessed at the rest. We combed every article for loose grains of news.

He examined his smooth face in the mirror, stroking his cheeks, rinsed and dried his razor. I pressed myself to his warm, moist back, resting my chin on his shoulder. I should tell him that I was tainted, that the Cheka was looking for me. I could ruin all his hopes for his deal if they found me here. He saw my worried face in the mirror. "Don't be sad," he said. "Things are going to work out. Trust me, this is just the beginning."

I started to cry. How could I let him believe I could be part of this? "Kolya, there's something I need to tell you—"

But he turned and put his fingertips to my mouth. "Talk tomorrow." And replaced his fingers with his lips.

63 *Secrets*

I woke in the morning to find my love on the telephone, speaking low. Then he hung up, asked for another number, a Moscow number. "Yes, hello," he said, in English. It was a shock. He'd never spoken more than two words of that language in his life. "Good to hear you too, Graham." He had trouble with *Graham,* he pronounced it *Gram.* "Yes." He laughed, sipped from the fragrant tea he'd made, stirring with a little spoon, that light chime. He sat on a chair he'd dragged up to the telephone on the wall in the little hallway. "Yes, well, they've been through it. You can't expect—" He laughed again. The sun filled the white curtains, painting them with the boughs of the trees just outside. The warm air sucked the thin fabric, making it billow, then pulling it flat. Kolya perched in his fine underwear, socks and garters, his hairy legs and arms solid. That adorable, maddening man.

And I was happy. Nothing had changed, everything had changed. Beads of sweat clung to my hairline and under my breasts, the fragrance of the sheets. I yawned and turned onto my side, watching him, that mobile mouth, the persuasive sandy voice—and a slow, liquid pleasure rose from my thighs and my hips to spread throughout my body like wine. He was here. He had come for me, plucked me from the sea just as the water closed over my head. I could still feel his lips where he'd eaten the strawberries from my hand. I put my mouth where his had been.

"God, don't let them pull that—" he said. *Pull that*...I had not heard that before. "No. Litvinov assured us— Mmmm. Yes. It's sitting in Amsterdam, all ready to go. I can have it here in five days, maybe less, but don't tell them. We'll just have to watch the docks when it gets here. But I've got good contacts in the railway union. We won't have any trouble with them." He listened, drinking his tea. "A week, two at most. Good. Send her my love. Of course. Easy Street. See you soon." He replaced the handset onto the cradle above him, stood and stretched.

I felt too lazy to get out of that messy bed. I watched him through the curls of shiny brass. "Who was that?"

"My partner, Sir Graham." He slid onto the bed like a boy falling onto a pile of leaves, nuzzled my neck, bit my shoulder, stroked my arm. He didn't seem to care how bony I had become in the time we'd been apart. If he found me attractive, that's all I cared about. I reached under his singlet to feel his chestnut pelt. Ah, I had missed that. Anton had only a few stray hairs, without curl, although Pasha...may he rest in peace. So many men, but only one Kolya. How I loved that good ruddy skin, all the textures of him, his curls growing out, the smoothness of his closely shaved face, though I missed the beard he'd worn as Mechanic Rubashkov and my peasant husband. How many lives we'd lived through together. I knitted my fingers in with his, threw my leg up over his hip. "Why don't you take off your socks?"

He kissed me, but shoved my leg off him, sat up. "Don't you like my socks?" They were an argyle plaid. "I have some errands to do. Eat some food, write me a poem about how much you love to fuck me."

"Send who your love?" I asked, sitting up against the big pillows.

"Lady Stanley," he said. "Lumpy, middle-aged. She grows sheep. They win prizes. Also she paints on plates." He tugged down the sheet, traced the curve of my breast, tickling the nipple, making it

stand up. "Don't be jealous. She wears *gum boots,* probably to bed."
He bit my haunch. "Poor Graham."

"I thought you didn't like the English."

"I like doing business with them." He went to the table in his argyle socks and his erection, buttered some bread, brought it back to eat it—dusting me with crumbs. He offered me a bite. "They don't see the rest of us as quite human. But once you know that, you can work with them. Which is to say, they'd sell out their own mothers, while saluting the Union Jack. Crazy, but..."

The English had brought him here. Also my poem. What were the chances that two such people, loose in a world of chaos, would end up together in this pretty flat, on these crumpled sheets? There was no reason to believe it would go on, but for this moment, I would drink it deep.

"I could see you living in England," he said, running his hand along my flank. "In a big hat. Playing croquet. When I'm done here, maybe you'll come with me."

I opened my mouth to say that I wasn't going to pretend. No fantasy futures, I'd had that burned out of me. The future was unknowable. In trying to imagine it, you were just projecting the present. But he put his fingers across my lips, kissed the crumbs from the corner of my mouth. "Just think about it. How long has it been?"

"Eight years." My father, at Oxford. *Father...* How could I tell him? He'd never understand. "What's sitting in Amsterdam?"

"A ship, loaded with grain, medicine, for the Povolzhye. A *goodwill gesture.*" He said it in English, obviously a Sir Graham phrase. "It's been sitting there a month, we just got clearance from the Bolsheviks. Even with a famine, they sit on their hands. That's your Soviet government."

Those sons of whores. A hard knock on the door broke into my fury, and I flew out of bed, sank to the floor.

"It's only my driver," Kolya said. "What's wrong with you?"

"They're all Cheka." I raced down the hall, shut myself in the bathroom. I heard Kolya answer the door—men's voices, laughter. A minute later, Kolya rapped on the wall. "You can come out now."

I cracked the bathroom door, listened, padded back into the flat, peered out the cutwork curtains. No car. No one standing in the square. "They'll be watching you," I warned him. "Everyone they send to you will be Cheka."

He pulled on his pants, buttoned them. "You're telling me something I don't know?" He found a shirt in the wardrobe, crisp, pressed. "Why are you so jumpy?"

So I told him about Gumilev, the sailors' club, the search of my room at the House of Arts. "If I hadn't been working that night, you wouldn't have found me at Blok's funeral. I'd be with Gumilev in the Peter and Paul Fortress."

"But why would they want you? A girl who writes little poems." To him, there was nothing more innocent.

"Sit down."

Kolya sat at the table, half dressed, and listened to each worsening turn of the story. Father's imprisonment, Varvara's offer to keep him alive in exchange for my service. My conversation with Gorky. The ear. His body dumped on my doorstep. Burying him with only Gorky in attendance.

He wiped his tears. "I've always hated that girl."

"The feeling was mutual."

He took out an Egyptian oval cigarette, lit it with his old lighter. "You wouldn't do it to save his life?"

"Once they have you, they never let you go. Everyone I knew would be in danger."

He turned away. Now I wasn't so beautiful. He sat smoking and watching the curtain breathe.

I pulled on my slip. "He begged me not to work for them. It would have driven him mad if I'd agreed."

Kolya reached out and hooked the curtain with a finger, peered out through the parting of the cloth. The leaves on the trees were fluttering, fingering his face with their shadows. "Is there more?"

"It's enough for now. But you should know, it's Red Terror all over again. The Bolsheviks are telling us, *Don't be fooled by restaurants and flower shops. We're still in charge.*" All the fear that I'd been barely containing since Kronstadt came bubbling up again. "I can't be arrested again."

He came back to our bed, tucked my head under his chin and rocked me. "You're safe now. They won't risk screwing up this deal for some girl poet, even if she's Dmitry Makarov's daughter." He kissed my hair, murmured in my ear. "If I shot Lenin and you fed me the ammunition, they still wouldn't arrest us, that's how much they want this deal." His confidence began to invade me, calm me. "If they haven't arrested me with my record, I promise they won't arrest you. People start getting arrested around Sir Graham, he gets nervous. They won't take that chance."

But why take the chance on attacking the intelligentsia now, with so much at stake?

The answer came quickly: to keep us quiet, while they did their *bizniss.*

We sat like that for the longest time. Like survivors of a shipwreck, in which everyone we knew had drowned. What he said sounded reasonable, but I knew not to trust it entirely. In our looking-glass world, things changed overnight. You could break your neck. Deals fell through, political players changed partners. I didn't think he would intentionally try to deceive me, but he'd been out of the country too long. Before, he'd been a cautious and clever fox. He cheered me as he always did, but worried me as well. I had already seen a fox in a trap. I'd made a hat out of him.

The next day, Kolya bought two large containers of milk from a Finnish peasant at the market in Salt Town, paying for it in fat handfuls of Kerensky currency, newly back in circulation. I had a hard time getting over the look of them. My lover insisted the Finn help us convey our purchases to Orphanage No. 6. He wanted to thank Matron, and see if she'd allow some of the grain Sir Graham was bringing to be delivered for the children. I'd forgotten this side of Kolya, his generosity, his capacity for tenderness, as well as his love of grand gestures.

We picked up a trail of *besprizorniki* as we walked along, this well-dressed foreign gentleman handing out coins and cigarettes through the park at the Mikhailovsky Palace and past the bronze statue of Pushkin, hand outstretched as if he too wanted a tip. The old Stray Dog Café had reopened as a new restaurant for New People, their pockets bulging with new money. More ragged children rushed over to see what was going on. Some wore only shirts, all were barefoot. The Finn set down his cans and wiped his forehead before setting off again. We waded through children like Moses as we made our way up the stairs of the porte cochère. Orphans clutched at our clothes and wouldn't let go. "Comrade!" "Comrade Marina!"

"Merde," Kolya said, as we entered the lobby and he saw for the first time what I'd come to accept as the new reality. Children slept right on the bird's-eye marble without so much as a pallet. They rocked themselves, thumbs in mouths. At the desk, Alla Denisovna and my lover eyed each other like boxers in a ring, assessing each other's reach and condition with wary approval, her eyes flicking to the Finn with the milk cans. We waited as she went to get Matron, children climbing all over Kolya, who was handing out smiles and kopek coins like a pasha. He would have been a good father— indulgent, playful, the kind any child would have adored. I still could not bring myself to tell him about Iskra. I ran my hand over the cold marble and wondered if he'd ever checked in here with some elegant lover in years gone by?

Matron emerged, her solid military air. She evaluated the situation immediately, instructed Alla to take the Finn to the kitchen, and not to take her eyes off that milk until dinnertime. Meanwhile, Matron led us back to her office, where we sat before her desk and Kolya explained that he was involved with a group bringing in aid and wanted to make sure the orphanage had what it needed. The more he talked, the more skeptical she became. He started making assurances, not only about his cargo but about the Americans as well. Finally we rose. I kissed her three times. "Thank you." Then under my breath, "You might see me back here yet."

"It's the baby's father, isn't it?" she said, low. "Does he know yet?"

I shook my head.

"You can come back if you need to," she said. "You always have a place with us."

Me and all the other orphans.

When we emerged, the children surged, clinging to us. "Are you leaving?" the little girl Tinka wept, a bright, sensitive child, clutching my dress. "Are you getting married, Comrade Marina? Please don't leave..." She was making the others cry.

I knelt down. "I'm going for now. Give me a kiss and say *Poka.*" *See you.*

She flung her arms around my neck. I looked up at Kolya—now he could see what I'd been doing here. She kissed me, hiccuping, her lips a ripple of grief. *"Poka,"* she whispered tearfully.

"Poka," I said to the children, who followed us to the lobby door.

By the time we got onto Nevsky, most of them had returned to the porte cochere. Kolya took out his handkerchief, wiped his face. "Poor devils." He kissed me on the forehead. "We'll do something for them, you'll see." He drew me close, his arm around my waist.

That's when I realized where we were standing. I'd been so distracted, so frankly relieved to be away from them, I'd failed to notice. I jerked Kolya away from the spot with a cry. He must not walk there.

He stumbled off the pavement. I started walking fast across wide Nevsky, blindly, then realized I was heading toward the House of Arts. I turned in the other direction, away from my life.

"What's going on? Are you having a seizure?"

There was nowhere to go, no place I could step that was free from my ghosts. The city was a minefield.

Kolya drew me close, made me stop my panicked flight. He held my shoulders, had me gaze down Nevsky, spread out on either side, shining in the sun. "Look. We're here. Together. Look how beautiful it is. Stop running." I took a deep breath. Yes, it was beautiful.

The columned sweep of Kazan Cathedral, the Singer Building with its art nouveau dome, the old red Duma tower, the yellow arcades of Gostinny Dvor. The Catherine Canal, the golden-winged griffins of the Bank Bridge, which had led to our first tryst. "It's coming back to life," he said, "and so are we."

But the weight of that corner, where my baby had died, stained the beauty of the day.

We walked arm in arm, away from the House of Arts, toward the Alexandrinsky Theater. Its park swarmed with *besprizorniki*—ours, turned out of doors to fend for themselves until nightfall, and also the feral ones who avoided the orphanage, they fought like tigers if someone tried to bring them in. I needed to tell him the rest, the last piece of my story. "When we parted in Tikhvin...turns out I was pregnant."

I felt the intake of his breath, the stiffening of his body at my side. "You never sent word."

I shook my head. "I wouldn't have known how anyway." The air had gone out of the day. "She was born in July, in Udmurtia, near a town called Kambarka. She died last October, right on that corner where we were just standing. Just before Yudenich attacked." I tried to keep my voice level, like someone reading a newspaper aloud. "I'd come in from the country, thought I could stay with Mina. But she was mad at me for abandoning her. I got work at the orphanage. It was fine for a while. I lived in the flat with the Golovins and the Naryshkins, worked nights. I could take the baby. It was working out. But Arkady found me there."

I watched the orphans, begging, picking up butts, lolling against the Catherine statue. He tipped his head back, staring up at the white summer sky. "And?"

"He had a new gang by then—Orphans. They found me at work, dragged me out and stuffed me into a car. But the baby was left behind. When I didn't return, one of my boys thought I'd been killed, and he jumped off the roof. With her under his coat."

His eyes closed, his tears dripped back into his hair.

I pitied him. I'd had all year to get used to this. I'd just given him a child, and then taken her away. I slipped my hand into his, brought it to my lips.

"What was her name?"

"Iskra," I said. "Though the midwife baptized her Antonina. She looked just like you. Matron knew it right away when she saw you." I put my arm around him, rested my head on his shoulder.

"Do you have any pictures?"

"No." She'd come and gone, like snow melting in your hands. "Only a lock of her hair. I'll show it to you." We stood, eyes closed, forehead to forehead the way we always did, leaning in for the comfort of one another, like good horses.

"I want to see her," he said. "Can you take me?"

"It's Novodevichy." A good hour's walk.

"We have time." He rubbed his forehead against mine, then his clean-shaven cheek. We walked around the Alexandrinsky Theater and down Carlo Rossi Street out to the Fontanka, across the Chernyshevsky Bridge, where I'd stood on that terrible morning, with her on the balustrade, wondering how to climb it with her in my arms, and jump. Now the water flowed freely, and three houses painted green, pink, and yellow admired their reflections. Like three old friends. So much of my history locked into these stones, the chains, the towers overlooking the river. Varvara's old room where she'd tended me after my release from the Cheka prison was just a few steps away. Had she thrown herself off this bridge? Sometimes I hoped she was on a train to the Povolzhye, to help with the famine. But I knew she wouldn't be, that she would not be able to bear the sight of the starving, knowing what she had done to ensure this disaster. I'd always thought we would be together, like these three houses—Mina, Varvara, and me. Three fates tied together—well, that proved true.

A few boats plied the embankment. Bargemen hoisted boxes onto their decks. Suddenly the waterfront was alive again. Change in the air. Perhaps for me as well.

"I wish I could have seen you pregnant," Kolya said as we walked down the other side, his straw hat pushed to the back of his head, our arms around each other's waists. "Fat, waddling along." He kissed my temple. "Then the child in your arms."

"Everyone loved her. She had red hair, and eyes like yours, only green."

The ripples in the water, following us down. "Maybe we could have another one," he said.

I felt a flash of anger. He was master of the conditional tense. I pulled away from him. He didn't know what he was asking.

"Don't say anything now. Just think about it. We have time. We have our whole lives."

But there was only so much pain a person could endure and I had reached my limit. I watched the boats rocking among the reflections of the stately buildings. Were they fishing boats? Were they moving produce?

"Does she have a stone, the baby? Some kind of marker?"

"She doesn't even have a legal grave." That horrible day came flooding back. Even now, the memory was too fresh, too raw. "The gravediggers took pity on me and buried her. I gave them your gun."

"I should order a stone."

"No," I said, more emphatically than I thought I was going to.

He put his hand in mine. "Why not?"

"We're the only ones she was important to." Skeletons of old barges, torn apart for firewood, bobbed at the river's edge. "When we're gone, there'll be no one else." It seems too sad to leave a monument. "I wrote her a poem... That's my stone."

Gulls flew upriver from the sea, screamed and circled. Lost, lost, lost.

"Those shoes," he said, nodding at my feet. "Are they your only pair?"

Aura's boots, stained and scuffed. "They're almost new."

"You don't have to do without anymore." He cupped the back of my head in his hand. "It's the least I can do. And the apartment, that's yours."

How could he give me an apartment? It wasn't London. People had to be registered, the *domkom* kept records. "I don't understand."

"What's not to understand?" He shrugged, adjusted his boater. "A man gives a woman a flat. You're the only girl in Petrograd who wouldn't understand." The way he was smiling, sweet, I sensed a joke he was having with himself. I'd been on that cart through a thousand muddy villages. I'd learned a thing or two about my clever man.

"And where will you be?" I asked.

He looked like a schoolboy, swinging along. Like Tom Sawyer, chewing on a piece of straw. When he looked the most innocent, that's when Kolya Shurov was sure to be up to something. "Me? I'm the Holy Ghost. Everywhere and nowhere. Decisions are made in Moscow. Coal in the Donbass, mines in the Urals, gold in Siberia. Famines in the Volga. And in Petrograd—my Beautiful Lady." He stopped and bowed, pretending to doff a plumed hat.

"Not so beautiful anymore."

He rubbed his smooth cheek against mine, lime and fresh linen. "Always beautiful." He held my face in his hand. "Don't you see? I've designed this whole business so I could be with you. I could have done a million things. I'm not here because I missed Lenin's borscht." He kissed my eyes, my mouth, softly. "We're no good apart. Look what happens—all hell breaks out."

We walked to Novodevichy, stopping on Moskovsky Prospect for peaches, and flowers. He wanted little white roses, tinged with pink, wrapped in ivy. "Daisies were more her flower," I said. "She was so bright, so gay." He bought both, peeling off banknotes—he didn't even bargain. As we continued to the convent, eating our peaches, holding our flowers, I thought of that girl I'd been in the days after Iskra died—Vintovka up in the corner room overlooking Moskovsky Prospect, waiting for the Whites. Everywhere, ghosts and more ghosts.

Finally, we entered the shady, moist precincts of the convent, moving along the overgrown paths alive with buzzing cicadas. It still bore the feel of abandonment, more melancholy than Smolensk.

Some of the headstones had fallen. I searched for the four-sided plinth that marked the spot, picking my way through the vines and tall grass that knitted the cemetery together in burgeoning green. Finally, I saw it, the gray mossy granite. I led him through. He had to hold on to his hat not to lose it to low-hanging branches. To the right of the tall column marked SVORTSOV, I showed him where I'd buried our child. Her patch of earth, indistinguishable from the rest of the graveyard, the grass starred with tiny flowers. I knelt. "Iskra, it's your papa."

He lowered himself next to me, handkerchief on the grass under his knees. "Hello, sweetness," he said to the earth. "Dearest. I didn't know. Forgive me." Tears rolled down his face. He put his roses on the grass and I scattered my daisies. His grief was unfeigned.

Perhaps we should have another child. Perhaps we could start again.

64 *Spilled Blood and Roses*

My apartment. *My* kitchen, *my* bath. I worked at the gateleg table as the sun filled the room, the pretty windows overlooking the trees and the Preobrazhensky Church, with its eagles and chains. I wondered who had lived here before us. Perhaps someone Kolya had known from before. I imagined a woman—the one he'd brought to the ballet that night when I was still a girl with a bow in my hair. How I had wanted to tear her hair out, or his. The low back on her dress as he led her away. Her perfume, L'Heure Bleue.

I kept thinking people were watching the flat. I couldn't help noticing a bald man in a light-colored jacket. A neighbor? Or something more sinister. And a small man in a straw hat, cigarette holder in his mouth, seemed to be spending an inordinate amount of time waiting for someone across the square.

When I pointed them out to Kolya, he shrugged. "Don't worry. No one's looking for a little girl poet."

The flat had two exits—stairs to the street and back stairs that led to the courtyard. I promised myself that if anyone came up those stairs, I would be out the back like a shot. The lipstick and new shoes were lovely, coffee and butter, the brass bed, the taps that issued hot water just for the asking, but all was a dream, I had to remember that. Reality was still out there, whatever Kolya said. I had to take care not to fall asleep inside this fantasy.

On the other hand, my passion for Kolya hadn't faded a bit. When he returned from his *bizniss,* I never could wait for him to make a leisurely drink, put his feet up, tell me about his day—all that domestic rigmarole. We made love like a hurricane. The top of the mountain blew off and spewed lava, created new islands, new continents. I smelled him on me as I wrote, when I read, as I made my lunch. We couldn't be in that room together for five minutes without our clothes flying. We made love on every piece of furniture, in the bath. We tore the bed to shreds. Only then, exhausted, could we eat and talk.

And how he loved to talk, to share the grand exploits of his day. I privately called these monologues Tales of Brave Ulysses. His glee at receiving two pink marble urns right out of the back of the Hermitage. The tense negotiations for a bauxite concession in Murmansk. A comradely meeting with the commissar for transport. He never asked about the poems I wrote, more interested in whether I went out and spent some of the rubles he'd left me. It hurt that he was not interested in my work, but I had to accept that this was not part of our shared life.

Every night, we made love, bathed, and set out for the evening, to some restaurant or nightclub—a new city was springing to life, full of people I'd never seen before, thuggish men and their girls. How could they have sprung up so quickly? Five months since we'd had the NEP, and the gangsters were already triumphant. I couldn't get used to it. I couldn't get used to any of it. The phone rang at odd hours. I hadn't lived in a flat with a working telephone since before the war. Kolya and I had a special signal—ring twice, ring off, ring again. Otherwise I let it go. Kolya told me to ignore it. "If you start taking messages, I'll have to return them, track people down, blah blah blah. I have better things to do with my day. Best to keep my sense of mystery. I'll call them when I want them."

A flood of presents crossed the threshold. He was always a generous man. Blue satin shoes, a pair of emerald earrings. "For the lovely Esmerelda." A dance dress sewn with silvery beads shimmered and hissed when you shook it. It looked just like water. That color...reminded me that Blok was dead, that silver and lilac world. I was happier with the simple cotton dresses Kolya reluctantly produced, one in green with red chevrons, the other, navy with a white collar. A pair of leather pumps, scarves. But he loved buying me underwear, and silk stockings. I had been wearing my underwear for so long, sewing up the holes, that my body couldn't imagine such luxury. He teased me when I protested about silk underwear. "When did you become practical?"

What a question. So many things we still didn't know about each other. I had no faith in his unreal world, no expectation it would continue. What would I do with a silver dress when the trapdoor gaped and all this disappeared? Yet...a beauty shop opened in a courtyard off Manezhny Lane, and I finally succumbed. Unreal to see myself in the mirror, my hair newly cut, knowing that people still didn't have tea, or shoes, that the Povolzhye was shriveling. I felt ashamed of having the money to have my hair styled. It cost ten thousand rubles—the denominations exploding. How long would a worker at Skorokhod have to labor to see that kind of cash? The Kerensky bills didn't even seem real, nobody had accepted them in years.

I wandered the streets full of uncertain people, ragged and vulnerable. Slightly out of plumb. They didn't walk so much as dart, glancing quickly out from under their eyebrows, startling easily, picking their way like invalids who didn't trust their footing. In the cool of a courtyard, children played under a grandmother's watchful gaze. A woman hung her laundry, a man sat on a box before a cage of rabbits, letting them take the air. He must have been raising them in his apartment. From the windows above, a woman was scolding someone.

An old *babushka* rested her sagging bust on a windowsill. Her gaze met mine. *You will be me tomorrow. In the blink of an eye, all this will be over.* The Catherine Canal flowed green past the Church of the Spilled Blood with its twisted cupolas. I stood at the rail, gazing down toward Nevsky and the Kazan Cathedral with its pillared crescent. So much water had flowed under the bridge since terrorists spilled the blood of Alexander II, ushering in the iron rule of Alexander III. So much water, so much blood. All these islands connected by their pretty bridges and ugly past. The autocracy it supported, vanished forever, the moment of freedom, when the revolution could have saved itself, gone as well, in blood. I studied my city with the nostalgia of an exile, as if these impressions would have to last me a lifetime.

Now I could see the great bow of the House, our ship, the country in which talent was the only passport. Already an outcast. Exiled. Just a woman, like any other woman, stockings and skirt, a hank of hair, lips fattened by kisses. Where once I had been a member of a God-given fraternity. I had been *one of them*. Not somebody's girl, not a hopeful hanger-on hiding behind the coats. I'd been invited there by Blok himself. He still lived on, not in Petrograd, where they buried the sun, but *in Petersburg,* where he lived and always would—in certain sounds, in the color of sky, in the gathering mist. And what of me?

As I pondered, three figures were headed my way. I would know them in the dark: Anton, tall and angular, scowling; Tereshenko, with his boxer's shamble, hunched, aggressive; and Slezin, slight, quick, small shouldered, hands in pockets, listening. The three of them hogged the sidewalk, pale, intent, oblivious, discussing some urgent matter. A woman with a handcart ran into them on purpose to teach them a lesson. I wanted to join them. Kolya didn't understand the communal life of art, the intense involvement in the making of it, the sense of its absolute value. This was where I belonged, not having my hair cut and eating éclairs in the flat on Preobrazhenskaya Square.

Yet it was over for me. I had been associated with Gumilev and the Kronstadt sailors, someone had said something to someone, and it was done. If Anton was ever brought in for questioning, he had to be innocent of my whereabouts. They came closer, and I stepped back into the shadow of a passageway in my chic shoes and green dress, my bright new hair, and let them pass by, close enough to touch. How thin Anton was, how shabby and badly shaved in the bright summer light. I was already growing used to Kolya's fleshiness, his vigor. My friend was pale, but utterly engaged. Talking to the others about some urgent literary matter—the future of futurism, their inclusion or exclusion from some reading or other. The role of Kolya's mistress fit me a bit like the party frock my Golovin grandmother's dressmaker had once constructed for me—sea green with a satin sash, it made me look like an angel, but frankly it itched where the netting was sewn to the waist and left an angry red line on my skin. I loved Kolya, but I was also a poet, and this was my flock, my tribe. Couldn't I have both? Couldn't I have everything? But life was not kind to me, and the sword of arrest hung heavier. I leaned against the grimy stones, my new shoes in dirty water, and waited for the bitterness to subside. I had Kolya again. And no one was keeping me from my verse.

Outside a café on Mokhovaya Street, a whistle greeted me. The orphan Makar, out selling his newspapers. "Hey, Comrade Marina! What's up—rich boyfriend?"

"Something like it." I smiled, pushing back my curls. "How's business?"

He shrugged, hoisting his merchandise higher on his hip. "Getting out of the newspaper racket. *Pravda* stinks." He tugged on my sleeve, lowering his voice. "I got a new line. *Galoshy* is what sells." *Rubbers.* "I know this guy who brings the good stuff in from Finland. Packs 'em in fish. Ha ha ha ha. Fish! Anybody looks, it's just fish. Smells right too. Pre-stunk."

I gave him a ruble and got my *Pravda.* "I'm sure you'll clean up."

"Everybody's looking to have some fun. You want anything, I'm at the Little Brick after midnight." A dance hall for workingmen. "That's where the money is. Your fellow gets an armful, some nice

Katya, and remembers, *Ai! I got no preservativ for Comrade Eel!*" The boy was growing a slight fuzzy moustache. He must be eating better, or perhaps puberty happened to everyone, even orphans. "For you, five hundred rubles."

Well, that certainly would pay better than *Pravda*.

I returned to the flat, took off my new shoes and cleaned them, hung up my dress, and made some tea, and in my new slip with a lace edge sat down with a biscuit and opened the paper.

A counterrevolutionary monarchist group, the *Petrograd Fighting Organization,* had been infiltrated and captured. *Eight hundred people arrested.* Eight hundred monarchists! I couldn't imagine. *Led by Professor Vladimir Nikolaevich Tagantsev.* A jolt of terror shot through me. My gymnasium — the Tagantsev Academy — was founded by Nadezhda Nikolaevna Tagantseva. The same family, it had to be. It said this Fighting Organization had been waiting for the Kronstadt uprising to seize power. I tore through the paper to find the list. There had to be a list — the list of the executed. There it was. Sixty-one names. Sixty-one executions. My eyes flew down the page and stopped at number 30.

> GUMILEV, Nikolai Stepanovich. Former nobleman, philologist, member of the editorial board of Universal Literature, nonparty former officer...
> EXECUTED.

I held my hand over my mouth. *Actively helped create counterrevolutionary content...received money...* He'd thought that they had a gentleman's agreement. That he would serve them faithfully, and in return they'd let him keep his conscience. *Wrong. Wrong wrong.* That they would let him walk around like that, free in his own mind. With an intact spine. *EXECUTED.*

> Prince Sergei Ukhtemsky, sculptor, publisher of *Rech'*.
> EXECUTED

Professor Vladimir Tagantsev, Petrograd University, former landowner. Nadezhda Tagantseva, former headmistress, Tagantsev Academy, his wife. EXECUTED.

A Kerensky minister, Lazarevsky. Gizetti, literary critic, and his wife. Naval officers, geologists, chemists, physicists—*EXECUTED. EXECUTED. EXECUTED.* I didn't know what to do with the paper. I threw it down, I picked it up, I marched about the apartment. None of them had done anything but think for themselves. The Bolsheviks were killing symbols now, like slaughtering real swans because they were a metaphor for the Whites. They knew what they were doing—attacking the symbol because the thing itself was gone. Creating enemies out of nothing, so they could justify their crimes. Like that hungry old woman trying to eat the painting of sausages off the shutters of a shop. It didn't matter that the Bolsheviks had crushed the last real opposition—the revolutionary sailors. Now they would impress upon us, the intellectuals and disgruntled workers, that despite the return of capitalism, and the famine, the Bolsheviks were still firmly in the driver's seat, reins looped double about one hand, the knout in the other.

Out the window, the bells of the Preobrazhensky Church began chiming vespers, then farther off, St. Panteleimon, and the Church of the Spilled Blood. Kazan Cathedral, and St. Isaac's replied. I found the bottle of vodka—prerevolutionary—and poured out a glass and saluted them all. *Nikolai Stepanovich. Vechnaya pamyat'.* I was sure he'd died with valor. He'd lived his freedom openly, and they'd killed him for it. I'd admired him, his quixotic position, but was this really what Gorky had in mind for me when he'd said to go home and live as if I were free?

I refilled my glass and toasted Nadezhda and Vladimir, then Blok, and Pasha. I reread that sickening list and kept stopping at Gumilev. Something was off about it, the way they described him. *Former nobleman, philologist...board of Universal Literature...* So many things could have been said about the man: *Poet. Belle-lettrist.* His foreign connections, positions on the boards of the House of Arts, the Poets'

Guild, the House of Writers. He'd been *born at Kronstadt,* for God's sake. But none of that was mentioned. Only *Universal Literature.* I'd thought at first: that's what happened when your enemy wrote your obituary. But one had to read *Pravda* like a poem. What wasn't said was always as important as what was. That *Universal Literature* was a shiver in the air.

Gorky's crown jewel, his most treasured idea. In saying *Universal Literature,* they meant *Gorky.*

Now I was seeing a second picture. Gorky hadn't especially liked Gumilev, but would never have allowed them to shoot a poet, any poet, without a tremendous fight, and for Gumilev he would have gone all out. For whatever reason, Gorky had not been able to prevent Gumilev's execution.

I saw it.

A case was being assembled against Gorky and all he represented, everyone he protected.

The sound of chimes, dying in the twilight.

I prayed he'd left by now. Yet without Gorky, we were all on the run. What chance did we have if the Bolsheviks terminated the House of Arts and Universal Literature? No protection, no work... We'd be blown to the four directions, to disappear like the last grains in the drought-stricken Volga.

I peered out the curtain into the darkening square. Below, the man in the straw hat smoked in the shadow of a tree. Why did they have to keep watching the flat if Kolya already had a driver who knew his every move? Why wasn't that enough? How I hated this cat-and-mouse game. I couldn't stand to be locked up again. And to think that Papa had stood a year of solitary confinement. That cell, the weight of the walls, the moisture, the dark, I would go mad. It terrified me to consider whom I might implicate under duress. I thought of the list of the executed. Varvara had told me she wouldn't be there to save me.

I thought of Genya waving his red banner like a windup toy. He had thought I was the naive one, explaining that the death of the sailors was inevitable. What did he think of his masters now?

Oh, what were they doing at the House of Arts? I should be there. Were there protests? A defiant evening of Gumilev's poetry? Or would they be hunkered down, speaking in whispers, waiting for the next blow. I had to see Anton. Neither of us had liked Gumilev and yet from now on to say *Gumilev* would mean *literature, culture,* a Russia we'd hoped we could live in. I thought of Anton's agitation today on the street. This must have been what they were talking about.

But how could I contact him? They would certainly be watching the House of Arts today. They might have informers. One of Gumilev's students, perhaps, a wide-eyed hanger-on. No, I couldn't go there, trailing the contagion of my own political cloud, like typhoid. And what about Gorky? With Moura gone, oh Lord.

I heard the automobile outside, the slamming of the car door. Thank God, he was home. But he lingered downstairs, chatting up the driver. He couldn't turn it off for a second, could he? He had to charm any and everyone. Finally, I heard him clambering up the stairs, ran to meet him, pink cheeked and smiling, clutching a bunch of big-headed roses and a bottle of champagne. His flushed, grinning face. "They've offered Sir Graham a copper mine. Near Chelyabinsk. A sure thing. Get dressed, we're celebrating."

"They shot Gumilev," I said.

"Who?" He set his gifts in the kitchen, handed me the roses.

In the future we'd say *roses* when we meant *slaughter,* when we meant *blood.*

"The poet Gumilev. I told you, they arrested him. Right out of the House of Arts. And they searched my room, remember? They shot him."

"Poor devil." He set two pink *coupes* on the counter and was already removing the metal net from the cork, unwinding the foil sleeve. He popped the cork, and the champagne spilled out. "Hand me that glass, quick!" I handed him one, and the bubbling liquid poured in. He handed it to me, licked the spillage off his hand, took the bottle and the other glass out to the table by the windows. I stared at that paper of roses, and left them where they were.

I stood over Kolya where he'd sat down at the table and kicked off his shoes.

"They shot him, Kolya. Sixty-one people!" I picked up the paper and thrust it at him. "I could have been on that list."

"But you weren't. Here's to good timing, and Englishmen."

I simply stood there. Was it Gumilev I was weeping for, or my-self? "They're watching the house. Your driver's Cheka. This isn't a joke."

"Drink." He lifted my glass to my lips. I drank, watching him over the rim. "They're not going to arrest you. What matters to them right now is the restoration of the rail line and copper for Lenin's electrification of Russia." He took off his straw hat and his beautiful pale jacket, smoothed out his chestnut hair. "Listen. You and me, we're not Gumilevs. This is a different game altogether." He toasted himself and drained his glass, caught the hem of my slip and tried to pull me over to him, but I brushed his hand away.

"You're wrong. They can play two games at the same time. Three." I wondered what the man in the street could see of this. I turned off the lamp. "If Sir Graham wanted mining concessions, why would he care about me, some girl poet he never met? He might even be willing to sacrifice Kolya Shurov, and chalk it up to the cost of doing business."

My love smiled that smile that said he had a secret, that he *knew things*. "Trust me," he said. "Sir Graham's interest in this deal in-cludes Kolya Shurov."

"What do you have on him?" I said. "Murder?"

He grabbed my wrist and pulled me onto his lap. "That's top se-cret and classified."

I drank the rest of my glass, let him pour me another. I hooked my arm around his neck, drew him close. His smell made me want to kiss him, to forget all this, but I could not. Was I drunk? Not drunk enough. "Listen to me, Kolya. I want a visa. A passport. Passage to England. Before you sign the deal." My own words sur-prised me. But now that I'd said them, I saw that was exactly what I wanted. To fly, to go somewhere I could take a breath. Where

I could live without looking over my shoulder, where I could use my real name.

"Why before? This deal's a triumph," he said, pouring another glass. "I'm sorry they shot your friend. But this is the future."

I tipped up his chin so he could see how serious I was. "Once it's signed, we're all expendable. Especially me."

He grinned. "Believe me, the only one who cares about you is me. Of course they're watching the flat. I'm acting for an English industrialist. Of course they want to know where I go, who I meet. But they're not going to do anything about it."

"I need to leave, Kolya," I said, my voice rising, an edge of hysteria. "I don't want to be what they have on you."

"There's plenty of time," he murmured, his hand on my neck, sliding down inside my slip.

"Stop it." I grabbed his hand and bit it. "Listen to me. Get me my papers, or I'll find a way, I swear." I didn't realize until now that I could not stay here anymore. I couldn't be a Gumilev, living so nobly among the ruins, proudly, bravely, steadily, while the Cheka pounded on my door. Or an Akhmatova, that tower. I wanted more than to witness the end of all this, and then to be killed myself. "You've spent too much time among the English. You've forgotten what it's like. You haven't seen what we've become." I heard the panic in my voice, but I couldn't help it. "I've been in that cell, Kolya, and you haven't."

His upturned blue eyes, finally serious. "If it makes you feel better, I'll get things going, all right? I can't guarantee it'll happen by the time we sign—we're pushing for a quick resolution. But I'll contact the trade office in London, get things started from that end. 'My assistant requires a visa.'" He nodded at me, as you nod to a child, so that he'll nod in return. "I swear. You'll get your papers, and then if you decide you don't need them, you can put them in a drawer."

I wiped my face, exhausted. Clever Kolya, too clever by half. But as long as I had those papers, it didn't matter what he thought.

* * *

I couldn't sleep, not even after the nightclub, the sex, more champagne. As he slept, I wrote:

> *One by one the poets disappear*
> *Into the dark at the end of the hall.*
> *I turn back*
> > *see the smiths*
> > > *fitting new locks on the doors.*
> *The new tenants come in through the front*
> > *carrying carpets, brass beds,*
> > > *birdcages, gramophones.*
> *We, we don't even have shoes.*
> *And it's a long walk to anywhere.*

He lay on the bed, snoring, spread out like a king, as if no harm could ever come to him. His daughter had slept the same way. God, I loved this man, but we'd both become what we had within us to become — he the businessman, gambler, maker of deals, charmer for a purpose and for no purpose. And I was still me, after these long and difficult years, putting one word against the next, holding up my tiny pocket mirror to the world. We'd grown into our destinies, Kolya and I. Yet after everything, I still felt him like a rush of cocaine. The smell of him all over everything, the bed, my hair. *We could have another child...*

He turned over, making the springs squeak, squinted against the light. "What are you writing? Come back to bed."

"Go back to sleep," I said. "I'll be up for a while."

He stretched like a cat, twisting his solid body clockwise and counter, enjoying each ligament's torsion, poured himself some water, drank it down. "What's it about?"

"Roses," I said.

The time would come when you couldn't even say *Pushkin,* or *Blok.* People wouldn't know what that meant. Russia without her poets...what would that place be like? Poetry replaced by prose — like dance replaced by long-distance marching. Nothing to recite when life turned and flashed its teeth, and you had to retreat inside yourself to the place only poetry could reach.

He got up, nude, shuffled to the toilet, pissed like a fire hose. Then he was back, leaning over me, kissing my neck, loosening the pen from my hand, putting it on the table, screwing the lid back on the ink. There was no question of writing when Kolya was awake. A haze came over me, I got lost, his touch, his spell. But I knew now I would not give him another child, not in Russia. He could have me, body and soul, but not that.

65 *The Call*

I went out the next day to sniff the wind, see if I could learn something more about Gumilev. With a hat, new dress, new shoes, who would recognize me? Still, I went to the House of Scholars, where I was not as well known. I found a handwritten sign on the wall:

Nikolai Stepanovich Gumilev,
Requiem Mass,
Kazan Cathedral, noon.

I stood staring at the note. Noon *today.* The black clock over the entrance showed quarter past eleven. In "The Lost Tram," he had imagined everything, though he'd placed his requiem at St. Isaac's.

The church was cold, the marble dirty, a feeling of neglect, death and more death. There were requiems all day for the fallen. The writers stood together, just as they had with Blok, but far more perilously. His studio students, hundreds of people. Each of them knew he would be watched, his presence noted, but it was the moment to show one's face, albeit silently, with eyes lowered. The choir sang, the ruddy priest grimly swung his censer. No coffins. No bodies. It was a brave thing on the part of the priests as well. I prayed for him, and the Tagantsevs, for all of them, the precious ark of Russian culture, slipping away. What would become of us? Akhmatova stood by the wall. She looked ready to collapse. To have lost not one but two of her great generation, first Blok and now her husband, her friend. She was the only one left. So pale, thin, and tall. Grief personified. I stood near her, not daring to speak. There would be no more services like this. I imagined they'd close the cathedral after these requiems. *"Vechnaya pamyat'..."* we sang. Akhmatova crossed herself.

What we'll be asked to bear, before this is over, her profile seemed to say. *Remember this. We can't save anyone, we can't save ourselves. All we can do is the thing no one wants us to do, live on. And spare ourselves nothing.*

Yes, she would witness, and wait for the executioner. Just as Gumilev had done. These giants. I thought with shame how I'd begged Kolya for that visa. But I remembered too what Gorky had said: *She's a martyr looking for a cross.* And what greater cross than Russia? I recognized her old friend Olga Sudeikina. I saw Anton, standing with Sasha and Dunya, and he saw me, even in this crowd, even in my new finery. I nodded back. *Yes, I'm still here. Still above ground. Don't ask.* He started toward me, but I shook my head, pulled my hat lower, and backed into the shadows.

I returned to the consular district, back to our little flat, missing my friends, feeling my forfeited place in the family of Russian courage. I felt the chill of autumn coming, the anxious calls of birds taking to the air, the honking of geese. Bears in the forests were gorging, preparing for a long sleep. And how long would our sleep be—our Sleeping Beauty castle back under the spell of the sorcerer? How many more centuries before we awakened again?

The phone was ringing as I entered the flat. Not thinking, I answered. "Hello?"

A man spoke in terrible Russian. *"Izvenite. Nikolai Stepanovich tam, pozhalusta?"* An English accent.

"He's not here," I said in English.

"Stanley here," the man said. "Give him a message, will you? Tell him Adela's arrived safely, she's tucked up at the National, safe and sound. And we're looking forward to seeing him."

"I will tell him," I said, and hung the handset onto the cradle.

So Sir Graham Stanley was not a figment of Kolya's imagination after all. He had a certain kind of clipped voice, a regional accent. I wrote down the message. *Sir Graham called. Adela's arrived. Hotel National. Look forward to seeing you.* The National—Moscow's best hotel, it was their equivalent of the Astoria. First House of the Soviet. Obviously open for foreign businessmen of a certain rank.

I lay on the bed, still thinking of Gumilev's requiem mass. Of Akhmatova's mute presence. Such grief, all we could do was hold it, our piece of it. It was too heavy a cloak for any one of us to bear alone. And seeing Anton...

But something about that phone call began to nag. *Tell him Adela's arrived...*

Why would Sir Graham call Kolya to say that Lady Stanley had arrived safely? Kolya often took an interest in old people, I knew. Perhaps they were fond of one another. Yet it didn't feel quite *English.* Sir Graham referring to his wife as *Adela.* He would have said *Lady Stanley.* I wondered...Kolya had said nothing about going to Moscow.

I went back to the telephone on the wall, lifted the receiver. I'd never placed a call from here, only accepted them. *Ring twice, ring again. Don't answer.*

I depressed the cradle a couple of times. "Number, please," said the operator. I could see her at her station surrounded by hundreds of other girls just like her.

I took a breath. "Hotel National, Moscow."

"Connecting. Please stand by."

I waited, listening as the operators on the trunk line forwarded the call, the hailstorm of clicking at phone exchanges from Petrograd to Moscow. How I wished there was something like this that could connect people through layers of time as well as miles. Layers of secrecy and misdirection.

At last, the Moscow operator came on the line. "Hotel National, go ahead."

"Hotel National," said a nasal, official-sounding hotel operator.

"Yes, could I have the room of Adela Stanley, please? Englishwoman. Just arrived."

"No Adela Stanley. Sir Graham Stanley…Oh, here. *Shurova, Adela.* Same suite. I'll connect you now."

Shurova. Of the Knock-Me-Down-with-a-Breath Shurovs of Petersburg, London, Nottingham, Hell, and beyond. *"No, that's all right—"* But the phone was already ringing. I was paralyzed. No! I did not want to hear her voice.

"Allo?" Youthful, high. Just a girl.

"Eto Meesis Adela Shurova?" My strangled voice, it would not cross the hurdle of its last jump.

"Da?" Her voice warbled, a bit impatient. Spoiled.

My arms felt weak, my throat narrowing. "Velcom Moscow Gotel Natsional," I said in the heaviest accent I could muster. "The gotel wish you fine to stay with us." Tears burned my face. "From Petrograd, message to Meester Shurov. Call Petrograd office at earliest convenient? You tell?"

"Yes, I will. *Budu. Ya budu skazat' evo." I will to tell his.* She'd been studying, so she could talk to her Russian husband.

I hung up the handset, my arms so weak I almost dropped it. *Shurova.* I fought to catch my breath. I felt like someone had punched me in the gut. Someone should tell her he wouldn't give a damn if she spoke Russian or Swahili, as long as she was beautiful, as long as she liked a good fuck. What went on in her head mattered not at all. To him a woman was an animal, a glorious one, but anything else about her was simply the difference between a brindled roan and a bay with black socks. Bile filled my throat. *In the same suite.* I saw it all now. Even if she was a cold English fish with eyes on the same side of her nose like a halibut, it wouldn't have mattered. She was related to *Sir Graham.*

Not his wife, his *daughter.*

I collapsed onto the bed, clutched at my head. *Sir Graham's inter-*

est in this deal includes Kolya Shurov. My brain exploded, coated the striped wallpaper in blood and gray goo.

I thought I knew him, knew the shape of his deceptions. But there were dimensions, whole universes I had yet to suspect. And I'd told him everything. About Pasha, and Iskra, and Gorky, and Father. And he'd given me nothing.

Don't answer the phone. I don't want to have to chase my messages.

Married. I should have known something was wrong in all this *bizniss.* He was playing everyone. Why did I think I would be exempt? No, Sir Graham would never trust just any Kolya Shurov riding in on a rented horse...He had probably gotten her pregnant too, to seal the deal.

I had to think fast, but my mind was up circling the pattern of grape leaves around the ceiling light. I could kill him. I could slit his lying throat when he came in the door. I could wait until he was sleeping.

Don't do anything rash.

But *Shurova.* It kept shocking me, like a bad socket on a lamp. I couldn't resist putting my wet finger on it. *We could have another child...* How could he have said such a thing with a secret like this up his sleeve? To think how long I'd waited for him, the way other people wait for the Messiah. When was he planning on telling me, after I'd borne him another little redheaded baby?

I rolled from side to side, trying to find a place to rest. I felt like my ribs were broken. I could do nothing for him, none of the things she could do with her name alone. What could I offer—a poet with one dress and another woman's boots, this restless orphan—besides love him as richly as any man could desire, and remember him, an officer in a sleigh, a fattish boy with a top hat and a pony whip? No wonder he was so sure they wouldn't arrest him. No wonder.

That gap between my ribs, a heart-sized bruise.

I could imagine his reunion with his wife. How he'd make love to her in their room at the Hotel National, Moscow. Maybe not passionately, but with exquisite tenderness. She would probably undress in the bathroom. And he'd be the perfect gentleman—why not? It wasn't love, it was diplomacy. He'd be all charm, so she would come to him, binding herself with each surrender. He'd be her guide, his tutorial hand light at the base of her spine, the energy radiating...Oh, I knew that pleasure. He'd show her the twenty towers of the Kremlin. But not the grave of Seryozha Makarov, hard by the Kremlin wall. He'd walk her into Red Square, tell her to close her eyes, and he'd position her before St. Basil's Cathedral. "Now look." Her gasp, her joy. As if he'd built it for her. They'd stand, hand in hand as he relayed the story—how after it was completed, Ivan the Terrible put out the eyes of the Italian builders, so that they'd never again construct anything so beautiful—astonishing her with our cruelty, our sense of iron destiny.

That fist in my ribs would not stop.

And she'd beg him to bring her to Petrograd. She'd heard so much about it from him when they were together in London. But now she was here, he'd discourage her. How he loved a side deal. Me, his redheaded mistress in Petrograd, and Adela, his English wife in Moscow. And London. And the world. No wonder he didn't want to get me a passport.

I could smell him in my hair, on my hands. I felt his kisses even now. He'd filled me with such visions of the future. While all the while, it was just the mirrored box of a magician's act, gently lit in fantasy light. Worlds and worlds. In this world, there were nightclubs and silver dresses and impossible sex morning and night. In this world he adored me, was going to protect me, was going to get my papers, we would have another child. Then, in a world parallel to it, one floor up or one floor down, there were his wife and Sir *Gram*, contracts and copper and Lady Stanley and her gum boots. In that life I was simply a sensual memory, a city he could visit when he had time.

Ukashin had taught us the spiral of worlds, the vertiginous layered dimensions of cosmic reality. People had dimensions as well, stories in which they were heroes, stories in which they were the devil himself. In one of those worlds I could cut his heart out and eat it raw, still beating. In another I could bludgeon him to death with a bottle of wine. In a third, I'd strangle him with a silk stocking. In a fourth, lie sobbing and screaming on the floor. And in a fifth, just an empty room. Table, bed, chairs. A phone ringing with no one to answer.

He returned that evening, arms full of packages. He dropped a book on the table, and a wrapper of sweet peas, fish in newspaper, a loaf of good bread. He kissed me on the head as if I were a child. "What a day! Let me put these away." He bustled into the kitchen. I didn't follow him. Didn't wrap myself around his ankles like a cat. He returned in a moment, a bottle of vodka pressed to his chest, two pink glasses pinched between forefinger and thumb. He set them on the table, filled them, collapsed into the other chair. His long hard day, poor dear. He lifted his glass. "To the Bolsheviks. Long may they rule." Those dear happy eyes, turned up at the corners, though hers had been green, and his were lying blue. He nudged my vodka toward me. "They just gave us the all clear to bring the *Haarlem* into Petrograd. Grain for the Volga, Marina."

Grain for the Volga. I examined my glass, its narrow facets. How many facets did he have? Sparkling, and each a little different. "When were you going to tell me about her?"

He cocked his head to one side, as if puzzled. Whatever could I mean? The *Haarlem*? His face registered not the slightest shock. What a gambler. When he hadn't a card worth a tinker's damn. If only his father had been so good, he wouldn't have lost their fortune.

"I know, Kolya. She called. Adela."

He went white, then red, respecting all factions. "What did you tell her?"

Now I wished I'd told her everything, instead of taking the coward's way out, hanging up. "I told her that her husband was a liar and a thief. That he was already married and that she should jump in some English lake."

He drank down his vodka, traced his brow with the glass. "I was going to tell you, I swear. That very first day. But I couldn't. Then you told me about Antonina—"

691

"Iskra."

"How could I tell you? When? Standing by her grave?" An automobile sputtered along outside the open window. "I just want you to be happy, Marina. I didn't want to complicate it." He always wanted to make everyone happy, that was his weakness. Truth was an unfortunate orphan tugging at his coat, trying to get his attention as he pushed it away with his foot.

"But you did—complicate it."

He stretched out his hand to me, but I wouldn't take it. "Be reasonable. I didn't know I'd be coming back. I had to start over, and England isn't so easy for foreigners. Even with my sterling references." He smiled, weakly. "Sir Graham invited me to a holiday weekend at his estate. There were three daughters, the younger two married, but this one was left over." He shrugged, sticking out his lower lip, as if it was nothing. "People get married, why not this girl? Good as anyone. Important family, sweet temper. No beauty but that was fine."

"How are her teeth?" I drank down my vodka and poured myself another. The curtains sighed in the mellow light of early autumn.

"Not bad," he said with a wry smile. "Then this trade agreement changed everything. I saw a chance to come back. It's what I'd been waiting for, a triumphal return. The lion rampant. Rawr." He was trying to make me laugh, unsuccessfully. Dragging his chair closer, our knees touching under the table, he threw his arm over the back of my chair, leaning in, knowing that just the smell of him disarmed me. "You're still married, aren't you?" he said. "Does it make any difference to me? Did it ever?"

Of course it didn't.

"So why should this be a big deal? Have you suddenly become a moralist?" His eyes glinted, knowing he'd made a good point. "It was necessary, to become part of Sir Graham's world. It was my ticket home."

It was insane, pretending he'd done it all for me. "Tell me one thing. Do you love her?"

"Don't be absurd. Don't even think about her," he said, even softer. "There's you and me, and that's it. Always."

I wasn't going to listen. "So you thought I'd just sit here waiting while you went down to Moscow and greeted your English wife? Wait for you to drop by when you want a good fuck or some nostalgic chitchat?"

"Oh, and you are such a good fuck," he said, pushing up my skirt.

"Don't touch me."

His hand dropped. He pushed himself away. His face grew hard, something I'd seen before, when he dropped the charm. It was always shocking to see it, the coldness below the warmth. "Well, that's how it is. Without this *situation*, I wouldn't be here. We'd never have seen each other again this side of the grave." But now he remembered who he was talking to. This wasn't a business negotiation. He softened, leaned forward, took my hand. "Don't get off the train, Marina." As I had in Tikhvin, which I'd regretted for so long. "Let it be what it is, imperfect but—my God, who gets to have what we have?"

There was no doubt about that. I could have lived my whole life with Anton and never seen a half second of the passion I felt every time this man and I were together.

"Have I ever cared who else stumbles into the picture? That oaf Genya, whoever else you're fucking these days. Poets, sailors. It doesn't matter to me. You're mine, I'm yours. Please, for God's sake, don't get off the train again. It's taken so long to get here."

I had to put some distance between us. He was making too much sense. I got up, marched unhappily behind him, like some prosecutor. "Tell me the truth, Kolya. No more lies. You haven't applied for my papers, have you?"

He gazed up at me with his sheepish guilty-boy face, that winning pout, eyes lit with hope for forgiveness. He wanted us all, me *and* her, *and* Sir Graham's millions, and copper and marble and for everyone to love him. I'd never known a greedier man. He reached back, trying to catch my dress, but I moved away. He stroked the edge of the tabletop as he would stroke my leg. "I'm not returning to London," he said. "We're opening offices in Moscow. You want to come to Moscow? There's a housing shortage, but I can find you something…"

"What would you do with your precious Adela?"

"Sir Graham goes back to Nottingham soon. I can't see her staying alone in Moscow, when I'll be traveling so much. Overseeing the concessions." His smile, as if we were both in on the joke.

"Still wanting it all." I poured a last vodka and drank it off, hoping it might soften the fist between my ribs.

"Who doesn't?" Now he was looking at me directly, hands on the table. "Don't you? What do you want most of all? Tell me, if you even know."

Once, the answer would have been so simple. I would have said: *You*. To be together under any circumstances.

Once, I might have said: *Just to be known*. Accepted as a poet. By a Blok, a Gorky. And now I was. Part of the House of Arts, not just the building at 59 Moika. The secret society of artists that knows no walls.

Once, I might have said: *Revolution*. Freedom and justice, all the promises the Bolsheviks had made come true. I might even have said: *For Kronstadt to hold*, for the people of Russia to have risen up in the sailors' defense.

I might have just said: *I want the impossible*. Iskra back, and Seryozha, my father, Volodya home from the war. Maryino and fireflies, summer rain. To start over.

But now I just wanted to walk across the Troitsky Bridge without screaming. Never to be cornered again. Really, just to be completely forgotten. To go about my business without looking over my shoulder.

He was waiting for an answer—tapping one of his Egyptian cigarettes on its pretty box, putting it between his lips, lighting it with his battered lighter made from a shell cartridge. I was sure she'd given him a gold one for a wedding gift. *All my love, Adela*. But he didn't want to show it to me. What did I want? He wasn't talking about impossible things. He wanted it to be something he could give me. Besides fidelity, a life together, a real life of washing out clothes in a basin and hanging them by the fire, making dinner over a Primus stove, getting under the thick covers on winter evenings. Kolya Shurov didn't want a life with me. He just wanted moments, like candies stuffed with brandy, like Roman candles, like arias. Exquisite moments of passion, of playfulness, of beauty. But life was all the rest.

We gazed at each other, like two old warriors sitting on shaggy horses at a crossroads filled with skulls.

"Your problem is, you don't know what you want." He pushed the box of cigarettes and the lighter away from himself, rose and stood next to me, smoke trailing up from his hand on the chair back. "I know who I am, what I want. I want that tightrope walker. I knew *that* girl. But who are you now? The revolutionary? The adventurer? The poet? Or this"—he gestured to me with his cigarette—"sanctimonious little wife? I don't know who I'm talking to anymore."

Adventurer, that's what Arkady had called me. But I'd lost my taste for adventure. At one time, I'd have been dazzled to be a man's *mistress.* How romantic it would have sounded! Now it seemed like the hard heel of a stale loaf of bread. Politics was a failure, idealism had drowned itself and lay like Ophelia in the water weeds, the surface floating with pages from my Cheka file.

What did I want? A new baby? If I asked in my truest heart, what I wanted was—sails. Open water. The freshness of the wind. That formless airy unwritten thing—the future.

Freedom. More than courage, more than poetry. More than fame, or love. To love Kolya would always mean this: a storm, followed by wreckage, then a few days of startling blue sky while you hammered the roof back on the house, just in time for the next storm.

I could smell salt in the air.

She will never be with anyone. My mother's curse.

Perhaps it was true. And if it was, there was nothing to be done about it. I was not afraid of being alone. I would take—white sails.

I gazed at my great, my one true faithless love, whom I'd wanted since he was a boy of twelve and I a freckled six-year-old. I hadn't even started school yet when I'd set my heart on him. Now he was mired in a loveless marriage and hopes of gain, Sir Graham this and Chicherin that, immaculate pale suits and two-toned shoes... My dear, my dear, he thought he had it all, and me as well, his dog on a little leash. *NEPman with Lapdog.* I wondered what Chekhov would make of this.

I lit one of his Egyptian cigarettes, and considered what he was offering.

If I had a certain strength of mind, I could do as he proposed. Live in his flat, write my verses, I could hold poetry evenings here as Galina Krestovskaya had once done. And have my love whenever he came through town. We would dance on tables and smash our plates, set fire to the bedroom.

But I was not so strong. The heartache would break me. If only I didn't love him the way I did, like a forest fire, I might hold on to myself, *live with it.* But I could smell the coming dampness. I felt the dark gathering in the corners of the bright and pretty room. I had waited so long for this — just to taste that sweet mouth, feel his body in my arms, urgent, irrepressible. To sleep with him at night and wake with him in the morning. Kolya wanted everyone to be happy, but he made everybody miserable in the end. "Get me out of here, Kolya. On your Dutch ship. I want to be on it when it leaves."

"What happened to your glorious future?" he asked, letting the smoke wreathe his hair. "You used to argue with me, heaping abuse on my capitalistic endeavors. Where's your revolutionary spirit?"

What irony — Kolya Shurov, proponent of Communism? There's a role reversal. But I could not stomach a future built on mines in the Urals and the graves of Kronstadt. Without Blok, without Gumilev, without Gorky. The only sound would be the trumpeting of the triumphant rabble. There might be money, copper, and railroads, but where would our voices come from? No sounds could escape the collapsing star. That's what Blok meant when he said there were no more sounds.

I turned away from him, moving to the window, gazing at the

sunset blush outside the thin curtains. Down in the square, one or another of our watchers would be waiting for us to leave for dinner. I would remain a person of interest. I would not avoid a prison camp, an ugly death. The airlessness closed in on me even before the breathing curtain. Unless I was prepared to do more or less what Genya was doing, my cries would never be heard. I remembered the day I sat on the embankment watching *The Mystery of Liberated Labor*. I understood even then that the revolution had passed into the realm of myth, had become a religion, codified, with hierophants and heretics.

"You ask me what I really want," I said, watching the man in the straw hat in the shadow of a linden tree. "I want a passport, a visa. And a berth on the *Haarlem* when it leaves. That's what I want. You can do this for me, Kolya."

He came to me then, pulled me to him, that intoxicating smell, the slight give of his flesh, his breath against my neck. "Give me some time. A few weeks. We've waited our whole lives for this."

And then I knew he wasn't going to help me. *A few weeks* meant *never*. The *Haarlem* would be gone. Winter would come, and then spring. The air turned to chlorine gas, it made my eyes smart. He loved me, he wanted me, and he wasn't going to let me get away. He could, but he wouldn't.

This sweet failed life. Soon the birds would be flying south, the winds turning cold. And I was trapped, trapped by my love. This was why Akhmatova had not left. It wasn't her nobility at all. It was that life caught you. You lived one day after the next, and fought the rupture.

66 *Hey, Little Apple*

Makar was there, right where he said he'd be, outside the Little Brick, in the old neighborhood near the Poverty Artel. Such a long time ago. Music spilled out onto the street, a neurasthenic band braying a version of "Yablochko." *"Hey, Little Apple, where are you rolling? Not to Lenin, not to Trotsky, but to my sailor of the Red Fleet."* I leaned against the building, had to catch my breath. *"Hey, Little Apple..."* Had it become just a tune? Didn't people remember the words anymore? Or perhaps there were new ones now.

The boy was selling something to a worker and his flushed girl-friend on their way home for a late-night tryst. I waited until they were done before I approached him. "Hey, Makar," I said. "How's business?"

"Ne plokho." He shrugged. But he touched a bulging pocket. He must be cleaning up.

"Listen, I need you." I pulled him to one side, out of the light from the streetlamp, and spoke into his dirty ear. "I need to talk to your Finn."

The orphan frowned, folding his heavy brows until they formed an unbroken line. "What Finn?"

"Your friend. The fisherman. Who brings the necessary, to capture the white sea."

The boy laughed, startled that one of his old orphanage matrons would make a dirty joke. "What do you want with him?"

"That's between me and him," I said.

He shook his head, lipped his faint moustache. "That's not how it goes. I set something up for you, I get a piece. You can't cut me out."

"I want him to take me to Finland."

Makar's eyes opened wide, gave me a look of admiration that I would venture such a bold move. And perhaps pride that I trusted him with such an illegal activity. Well, who else did I have these days? My rich boyfriend had gone down to Moscow to show his wife around. There would be no visa, no first-class ticket or even a berth on a cargo ship bound for Amsterdam. I would have to take it into my own hands.

"Maybe I'll go with you," he said. "I was never on a boat before. I've just been here."

"Let him know. I'll be back tomorrow night." I turned my face from the streetlight so I wouldn't be seen.

"Wait, just a minute. Wait there." The orphan disappeared through the curtain of the Little Brick, into the din.

I waited on the street corner through several rounds of crude advances. "Come on, kitten, I'll pay your ticket." "*Milaya*, you've been waiting for me all your life." "How much for a quick one? We can go in that courtyard. Fifty thousand? I'll get a scumbag—what do you say?" The inflation was prodigious. A match was two hundred fifty rubles now.

Eventually the boy emerged from the rust-colored curtain, leading a tall, ginger-haired man who didn't look much like a fisherman—too tall, too slouchy, with a red beard, a long sharp chin and long nose. His eyes were very dark under pale brows, level and dangerous, like the barrels of two guns.

"This is her," Makar said. To me: "This is the Wolf."

So this was what had replaced Arkady von Princip, a lean, voracious redheaded Finn of twenty-five or so with a fresh scar through one pale eyebrow. He held his sharp chin in his hand. "The kid said you want to take a tour," he said.

"How much?" I said.

He looked at me closely, squinting at my dress, my boots. I'd changed back into my old clothes—if I'd worn the things Kolya had bought me, the price would be double. "A million," he said.

I was blown backward as if in a strong wind. "Where is this tour going, Africa?"

"Sestroretsk." Just over the border.

"That's not far enough. I could walk there and keep the million," I said.

"So walk." The Wolf turned to go back into the nightclub.

"You really a fisherman?" I called after him.

"Fisher of men," he said. And laughed and stepped back toward me. "And you, you're really a teacher?"

"In the school of many sorrows," I said. "How about Helsinki?"

"Two million," he said.

What a disgusting fellow. "It's not *that* much farther."

"I have no need to go to Helsinki. It's more complicated all around."

A million, two million—it made my head swim. Everything was so expensive now—yet, the new people had bathtubs of money—for restaurants, for nightclubs, and beaded dresses and silk stockings. How in the world could I raise that kind of money? A million. He might as well have said ten times that. "I don't like Sestroretsk. It's too close. Too many eyes on the border."

"I know a customs officer," he said. "My brother Ahti. You know who is Ahti?"

I shook my head.

"The God of Water. It's good luck for us, Sestroretsk."

I didn't like it. I especially didn't like the brother. Too many heads to get ideas. Like taking my money and dumping me right back into Russia—why not? Or worse, into the hands of the Russian border police. Or into the sea. No, I could see it as clearly as if I were Vera Borisovna. "How about Kuokkala?" The former Russian artists' colony on the gulf a couple of miles northwest of Sestroretsk, a place I actually knew. My Uncle Vadim once rented a dacha there, next door to the artist Repin.

The Wolf considered it, rubbing his chin.

I wondered if the painter had remained after that coast was returned to Finland. Seryozha had adored that old man, as did Vera Borisovna. We went visiting as often as she would allow it. My brother in particular had been fascinated by a half-finished portrait of a young man in a black suit smoking a cigarette.

"Nothing's going on in Kuokkala. Sestroretsk, that's where you want to be. Catch the train for Vyborg."

Those afternoons at Repin's, painter of *The Volga Boatmen,* and the famous portrait of the barefoot Tolstoy. All of us had posed for him. Those pictures, where had they gone? Sold for grain to the Volga? My mother, knocking sweetly on his door—she had the perennial entrée of beautiful women everywhere. Seryozha watching the artist with the same concentration with which the artist studied him. Surely there were still some Russians left in Kuokkala. If I couldn't get to Helsinki, I'd rather land on familiar terrain. Somewhere without the Wolf's brother.

The Finn gazed at me, stroking his little beard. "I like you, Teacher. You find two more people, I'll let you go for eight hundred thousand."

"Each?"

"No, just you. For them it's the regular price. But it's a bargain. People will cross you on foot for two million, and you'd have to take the train, hide in the woods. This is a hundred percent safer."

"I don't know anyone else," I said.

The Wolf sighed. Makar was back, stuffing cash into his pocket. "So when do we go?"

"Thursday," said the Finn.

Three days to collect a million rubles. But I had an idea how I would get it.

Our brass bed was the big seller of the day. I felt I was killing swans, selling it. That bed was our love, where he'd hoped we'd spend the months and years ahead. We would never sleep in it again. *Forgive me, Kolya.* But I'd told him plainly. I could not be his toy. I could never put my life in his hands after that duplicity. I watched the two metalworkers break the bed into parts—footboard, headboard, frame, and springs. All around me, the empty places where our love nest had been feathered. It was so soon, but if I waited, it would be too late. *Don't hesitate,* Arkady taught me. In a few months, I'd be accustomed to our lives—the comings and goings of Mrs. Shurov, waiting for visits. Perhaps I'd buy cocaine through the Wolf. Drink. Make interim arrangements. It would be the death of me.

The metalworkers didn't want the mattress. I could sell that separately. They would cut up the brass for rings and pins, belt buckles. The iron they'd do God knows what with, the springs they'd sell individually to upholsterers.

"They'll make four times what they paid," said Makar, counting out the cash and handing it to me. My little assistant was proving his worth. The wad of Kerenskys was growing as thick as a Bible. A couple bought the rugs, Makar talked the price up. I sold the curtains, the pillows, the mirrors, the pink champagne glasses. The groceries went to a woman wearing the ugliest hat I'd ever seen, someone the orphan knew from a brothel near the Little Brick. Sugar and sardines, quail eggs, salt and caviar. He counted the money twice, held it up to the light. She'd wanted the wine and the brandy, the whisky and the vodka, but didn't have enough money. "Put it away for me?" she purred to Makar. He looked at me quizzically, as if asking the adult what to do, but crossed his eyes when he did it. *No.*

"I have another customer," I said.

"How much? I'll double it."

How much would this nonexistent customer give us for bottles of vintage wine and cognac, English whisky and vodka? "A hundred thousand," Makar said.

"You little runt," the woman replied, resetting her hat. "Go jump off a bridge."

He looked to me again, shrugged. I touched my eyebrow, meaningfully. We would have been a good team, Makar and me. Who could have imagined *this* in the days when I told the boys the story of Shinshen, and Iskra and Maxim were still alive?

In the end we came down to eighty. "If you can be back in a half hour."

"I'll be right back. Don't sell any of it, promise me."

Where did these people come from? How had they survived the war ready to set up shop as soon as the season changed? Such strange times. Yes, perhaps it would all end well, just as Kolya hoped. But I felt the lid descending, the last door closing. Kolya had too much faith in himself, which was fine for him, but I could not make a life out of hope. Makar counted the money, smoking his dirty *chinar*—I'd given him a box of Egyptian ovals but he must have sold them. "Sure you want to leave?" he asked. "We could make a fortune together, and live like kings." He handed me a pile of cash. "Here's another hundred thousand. How much do we have altogether?"

"Almost a million and a half." I'd sewn myself a wallet I could wear under my clothes, where I kept the bulk of the funds. He was an impressive salesman. I should introduce him to Kolya. I'd told him if he could find enough traders to empty the Preobrazhenskaya Square flat in two days, I'd give him ten percent. I'd been skeptical, but he said, "Give me one day." All day yesterday, he'd brought people up to the flat, and today was even richer. How could an orphan know so many people with money to burn? I supposed that's what you got when you moved from newspapers to *galoshy*. Two million would get me all the way to Helsinki. But I would be happy with Kuokkala, and had other plans for that extra cash. In just two more nights the moon would be dark. That's when the Wolf did his fishing.

The portable phonograph and two pairs of silk stockings sold to a NEPman, Makar's best condom customer, so he said. The man also bought the pretty dishes. He counted out the money with a flourish before his moonfaced girlfriend as my partner played lookout, watching for bandits. "How about the telephone?" he asked.

I hadn't thought about it. Private phones were still rare. Kolya used it for work, but it was a traitor. *Don't answer the phone.* "Two hundred thousand," said the boy without blinking an eye, a boy who'd never held a thousand rubles of his own.

"Little swindler. I can get one for eighty," the man said. "Real Ericsson, straight from Sweden."

"So get one," the kid said.

I was scared sick with what the Cheka might be thinking about all this coming and going in the apartment of the *Angliysky* spy Nikolai Shurov, furniture and rugs leaving out the front door in his absence. But the birds were flying, I had no choice. I had set my course.

In the end, he didn't buy the telephone. But the woman came back for the liquor, with a bosomy girl in tow carrying two canvas bags. Did she want the telephone?

"I'm tapped out," she said, as she filled her bags with bottles and handed them to the girl to lug home. "For God's sake don't drop them, Mila, whatever you do."

The girl meekly carried the bags away.

We sat eating in the emptying flat when a knock on the door made us jump. Makar pressed his ear to the wood.

"It's me, idiot." A man's voice. "Open the fucking door."

He let in a burly man with a salt-and-pepper beard and heavy black eyebrows. I almost dropped my glass when I saw him, caught it before it fell. A face I never wanted to see again. Borya, Arkady's lieutenant. Saint Peter at the gate. He wasn't nearly the man he'd been, but who was? I still had the scar on the palm of my hand. Would he remember me, the girl locked in the room overlooking the Tauride Gardens, the one he almost threw out the window? Or that night in the woods when they shot at me as I ran?

He spat sunflower seeds onto the parquet, denuded of its rugs. "My friend says you have some goods to off-load. Let's see what you've got."

"I remember you," I said.

He gazed at me, not trying to place me. "Yeah, so what?"

"How about a telephone?" Makar said.

The big man glanced at the machine on the wall in its black lacquer case, curled his fat lip, shrugged. "How much?"

"Two hundred," Makar said.

"Stop wasting my time," he said. "You're on my list, *malysh*."

Something was wrong with his leg. He was sparing it. "What happened to you?" I asked.

He fixed me with a terrible gaze, an Evil Eye stare. "What do you think, shit for brains?"

Arkady. The men deserting him, he must have shot him, struck him, beat him. But this was the world I was moving back into. The world where anything was possible. "Listen, I'll trade you that phone for a gun. Something small. And ammunition. A straight-up trade. Something that won't blow up in my hand. Can you do it?"

Makar stared at this woman, his little comrade matron. He didn't know me after all. Borya laughed, a small and joyless snort. *Can I do it?* Yes, I'd asked the right man. He turned to Makar. "Ten tomorrow."

I lifted the telephone down from the wall, held it out. The big man took his knife and cut its throat.

"You still out on Kamenny? St. John the Baptist?"

He hoisted the phone under his arm. "The kid knows where."

67 *The Émigré*

I stood out on Nevsky in the dark, watching Anton in his lit window. I knew he'd be up. The other passengers already asleep, only a window here and there still glowing in the velvet night. He didn't sleep soundly, and so preferred to work until he was exhausted, then slept hard, grinding his teeth, well into the morning. I wondered if he could see me down here, though I knew the reflection of himself and his own flickering lamp in the window glass would be his only view. I wanted to touch him, to put my cool hand on his hot brow, lead him to safety. Soon this whole ark would list, would founder, and drown in the rising waters of control and mediocrity. I watched and waited, but I saw no one. I was betting the Cheka didn't have enough manpower to surveil the House of Arts all night. Not for one girl poet, one insignificant nobody.

I slipped into the sleeping house through the Bolshaya Morskaya entrance. I wondered what the Cheka had been looking for in my room, searching my papers that night. Some link between me and Gumilev and Pasha. *Actively helped create counterrevolutionary content...* Something on which they could base a case against me. Or strengthen the one against Nikolai Stepanovich. And yet, what corroboration did they really need? Their law wasn't the foundation of a civil society, it was simply pretext, as easy to shift as a pair of slippers.

As I quietly threaded my way through the halls, I wondered again why Gumilev had picked me to teach at the sailors' club. We weren't close, I wasn't one of his students, there were certainly more masculine poets than me. Was it because I was expendable? Because we didn't have any connection? Or had he seen something else in me, something more incendiary? Or was it just luck? I remembered how he'd pretended indifference to the sailors' plight during the siege. He was telling me, *Don't moan, don't wring your hands. Watch, hang on to yourself.*

Up the stairs and down the hall, the route I traveled in my dreams. These halls, these doors, the heaven of my poet's life. Here was Khodasevich, there Kuzmin, a light wheeze. And Inna...I prayed that anyone who saw me now would wait until tomorrow to gossip about it. One more day, and the dark face of the moon would turn to this earth, and I would be gone. They had an informer here—how else would they have known about Pasha? But I doubted anyone would be energetic enough to call the ravens tonight. Human torpor, that great Law of Laws. One more day, and I would be gone. In Finland, or robbed and thrown overboard by the Wolf into the deep and silent waters of the gulf.

When I got to Anton's, I silently pushed open the door and I found him just where I'd seen him from the street—at his desk, lantern fluttering, working in a haze of foul tobacco. When he saw me, he stopped his pencil, cigarette dangling from his mouth. Whiter than usual, the color of paper. He stood as if levitating, the smoke still rising.

"Turn off the light," I said softly.

He doused the lamp.

I walked to him in the illumination from the street. He was just a silhouette, tall and thin. Under my shoes, sunflower husks—up to his old tricks. I pulled him away from the window, plucked the burning cigarette from between his fingers, took a puff and ground it out on the floor. I kissed him, his ashtray breath. He seized my hand, pressed it to his mouth. "Marina," he breathed into it. "I saw you at the funeral." He held me as if he thought he might break me, one arm around me, the other hand buried in my hair. "Are you real?" he whispered, his unshaven cheek against mine. "I wanted so much to talk to you that day. It's been absolute hell, knowing you were somewhere, but not being able to see you.

Where've you been all this time, at the orphanage? Why didn't you contact me?"

"Shh...shh...shhh..." I pressed my mouth to his, to stop his questions. What did it matter where I'd been? What mattered was where we were going.

"I saved all your things," he whispered into my hair. "Your coat, your books...Look." He handed me a folded piece of paper. The lock of Iskra's hair. "It was on the floor." Then he clasped me again, overcome with emotion, hurting me in his awkward grip. "Come back, Marina. There haven't been any more searches. I think it's over for now. They've made their point."

It would never be over. Whether it was a matter of weeks or years, they'd be back. And back and back.

He stroked my hair, rubbing his face in it. We sat on the sagging bed in the dim room the color of the inside of a jar. The bedding emitted a lonely, sad smell. I turned the small packet of her hair over and over in my hands. "I've missed you so much," he whispered. The squeak of the bed as he crossed his long legs. I could see his profile as he turned his head to the window. "Every night since you left. I've sat in that window. Hoping you'd see me."

"I have."

"Sometimes, I think I see you. But it's the way a woman walks, or holds her head. A word someone says in the street. But you're always just out of reach, rounding a corner, disappearing into a shop. I've been out of my mind." He laughed, an unnatural, forced laugh. "Like a tormented girl suffering over a crush. My writing is crap. *Zhili, razdavili...*" *We lived, we crushed.* "Look what you've done to me! I've become Semyon Nadson."

"I'm leaving, Anton," I said. "And I want you to come with me."

The big house creaked, stretching in its sleep. "Leaving Petrograd?" he whispered. How bewildered he sounded.

"Leaving the country," I said.

The bed squeaked. He scratched, turned toward the window. I could see him in profile, his sharp nose, his hair a messy haystack in silhouette. "When?"

"Tomorrow night. I've got the money. Everything's set." I took his hand, dry and papery.

"Tomorrow? So fast?" He took both my hands. "What about *Anvil*? The first issue's scheduled for October. Eikhenbaum's even contributing an essay." Pleading with me. "It's not just a Living Almanac anymore. They're giving us print. You know what this means? It's the future of Russian literature. Petrov-Vodkin's doing the cover." He had a life, right here, that's what he was telling me. He didn't want to go. I hadn't imagined he'd refuse.

"Think about Gumilev," I said. "It's not going to stop."

I could hear him breathing, a rapid pant. There was a catch in his lungs from all the smoking. "Gumilev was taunting them. Wearing his crosses, talking about restoration. He forgot they could bite."

Anton thought there was a difference between Gumilev and me, Gumilev and him, Gumilev and the rest. There was no difference. We were all only as good as our freedom to think. "There's a boat leaving tomorrow night," I said. "I've got enough money for both of us. By the end of the week, we'll be in Finland, Anton. We'll be free."

He sucked in a breath. It rattled as he let it out. He stood, walked to his desk, and slumped into the chair. I could see his body against the window, hands rolling another stinking *makhorka*. The scratch of the match lighting his face, the slope of the nose, the small unhappy mouth. "We've got the Blok memorial coming up. We're just planning it. Akhmatova's coming—she's got a whole new book coming out, she's writing like mad. She and Shileiko split up—"

"Anton, are you listening to me?" Was I shouting? I lowered my voice. "Blok is dead. We lost. It's over."

He sat in the chair, smoking and pulling on his forelock as he did when he was unhappy. He blew a stream of smoke up to the ceiling. "Have you thought about what it would be like, being an exile?"

I hadn't given it a thought. "I only know I can't be here."

"It's going to be like being adrift on a raft. We'll be people fallen out of time. Cut off." His smoke painted arabesques in the windowlight. "We'll become ridiculous. Who would we write for? Other émigrés? People on the same small, crowded raft? Soon we'll be the only ones who can understand our antiquated tongue. Growing old, dying a bit more every day. While all around us, people will be writing in living languages. Who would publish us? We'd be as useless as vestigial tails." He'd thought about this far more than I'd imagined. "I don't want to be a French writer, Marina. A German writer, Swedish, Portuguese. I'm Russian—I don't *translate*. If only we were painters, or musicians, it would mean nothing. We could walk down the Champs-Elysées. But we aren't. I can't leave."

"But if we stay, what then?" I whispered urgently. "We'll have journals and books, memorials for the dead, but we won't be able to *say* anything. We'll be speaking in code, for people who can understand us. And there'll be fewer and fewer. We'll be exiles in our own country."

He started to pace, smoking, footsteps crunching the layer of sunflower-seed shells into powder. "What would we do abroad? How would we work? How would we live?"

"We'd find something. There's always work of some kind."

"Who do we know in Finland? I hate Finland. What's in Finland? Trees. I don't even like trees. They give me hay fever. We don't speak the language, what would we do, raise reindeer?" He was getting hysterical.

"We'll do whatever we like," I said. "It's not the Transbaikal. It doesn't have to be Finland. We can live anywhere."

"A couple of exiles. Foreigners. We'd always be foreigners—subject to suspicion. And here, they'll forget about us. Unknown there, forgotten here—we'll cease to exist." He waved his hands like he was dissipating smoke. *Poof, we're gone.*

"If we stay, we'll cease to exist," I said. In a pool of blood. "And you know what? If I'm forgotten, so be it." I sat cross-legged on the sagging bed.

"It's not the same for you," he said. "You have English and French and German, you could start over like that." He snapped his fingers. "What are you, twenty-one? You're a baby. Me, I'm already going bald."

He was what, twenty-nine? "Your French isn't so bad. You'd pick it up fast if you spoke it every day. They have bald people in France. You could set up a press, publish what you like."

"You know that's not the way it'd be." I could see his outline, clutching his hair in his hands. "We'd be broke and friendless, misunderstood by everyone, starving in some freezing room."

"Just like the Poverty Artel. We'll still be the Transrational Interlocutors of the Terrestrial Now."

"It would be a desert." He picked up a thick pile of papers from his desk, and shook it at me. "I'd die without this. In the West, who would I be? Just another Russian crackpot. Ivan the Futurist. A joke. Nobody would understand a thing about new prosody, about our new poets. Nobody needs a lousy translator of Apollinaire in France, do they? I'd be superfluous. The new superfluous man." He leaned against the window, his lanky frame transformed into just a pair of legs. "Always the extra man. Well, I finally found a place for myself here. I'm known. I'm on the board of the House of Arts now, right along with Chukovsky and Shklovsky."

He'd come up in the world. Even if it meant Gumilev and Blok had to die.

"I'm from Orel—do you know what that means? A schoolmaster's son from Orel? I *know* what it's like to be circling the outer planets. This"—he gestured to Nevsky Prospect out the window—"this is my place in the world." He laid his forearm on top of his head, an awkward gesture that was as much a part of him as his stinking tobacco. "We're going to have a reading at the end of September. Sasha and I are designing the poster. I can't leave. People depend upon me."

Pacing, haloed in smoke, he was not talking to me anymore but arguing with himself. "Russian literature depends on us. How can we just leave? What's going to happen to it if everybody runs for the doors? We're opening the gallery again, we're going to sell prints, the concert section's starting up. It's going to be…"

Then he remembered me. "Don't leave, Marina. You're panicking. This is all going to blow over. You'll see." He was running out of arguments.

"It's not going to blow over," I said quietly but firmly, and hooked his sleeve as he passed by me. "Anton, stop it."

"My French stinks!" He waved his arms in the air. "I know you think I'm a coward. But I'm just an ordinary man. Nothing scares you, that's the problem. You don't know what life is like for the rest of us. This is my world. This!" I could see his arm shoot out. His voice rising again. "This room, this desk, the hall outside. The canteen. Sasha and Shklovsky and Eikhenbaum. Russian poetry, Russian problems, the Russian mind—that's my dowry, that's my bank account. Yes, there's no more Gumilev, there's no more Blok. It's horrible, like having our lungs cut out, but this means it's up to us, our generation, to keep it alive."

I smelled his fear, felt his frenzied piling up of obligations and reasons into a barricade, fortifications around his position. He was throwing everything he had onto the pile. As afraid of the unknown as I was afraid of the known. Maybe he was more of a poet than I was. I remembered when Kolya asked me what it was I really wanted, *poetry* wasn't my answer. *Freedom* trumped even that.

"Look, look, look," he said, kneeling before me, taking my hands. "We've been through the worst. Everything's going to take off now. It's our moment. They're allowing private publishing again. There'll be paper. We can sell our books, make a living. Stay, Marina, please." He sat on the bed next to me, wrapping his arm around my shoulders. In my new state of cleanliness, I could smell him—strong, acrid. "Who's going to understand your poems in the West? You're Russian—you're no *Jack London*. Out there, you're just some beautiful girl who thinks she speaks better English than she does. Here, we *know* you." He stroked my hair. "We *admire* you. We want to hear what you have to say. Your verses speak to us, they feed us. We need you to understand—for us. Look at Akhmatova—is she leaving? No. And Gumilev was her *husband*. But she's going to stay and live our life along with us. She's even got

711

a new poem, I heard it the other night—I'm not a fan, you know, but who do they have like this?

> *Dark is the road you travel, Wanderer—*
> *the bread of strangers smells of wormwood...*
> *While here, wrecking our youth's last days*
> *within the blaze's blinding smoke,*
> *we all have steadfastly refused*
> *to dodge a single savage stroke.*
> *We know that, in the final count,*
> *each hour will be justified...*
> *But no one has wept less than us—*
> *no one's more plain or full of pride."*

How stern she was, how absolute. But I wasn't Akhmatova. Russia would eat me in a casual bite. Should I let myself be eaten, then, so I could be simpler and more filled with pride? There was nothing simple about the Cheka, and your tears flowed like the Nile.

We sat, side by side. I could hear him sniffling. "So that's it? Going to shut the door behind you, like leaving the hospital? 'Thank God that's done'?" He launched himself back to his feet, punching the air, kicking the chair.

"Shhh, you're going to wake them."

"The future's just opening up. Can't you wait? You need to be part of it. We need you." He couldn't even say *I need you.*

He was going to stay in the ward and wait for death. Because he was a coward, and because he loved Russia, and lacked the imagination to see how there might be other lives, that the future here might be more full of ravens than he could imagine.

Well, I would eat my bread scented with wormwood. Wanderer, be my name.

68 *The Wolf*

The boy and I waited for the Wolf on Krestovsky Island, the deserted south shore of the Little Nevka. The islands, where all dark deeds went unpunished. My pocket once again armed, this time with a gun I'd purchased that day from Saint Peter in his lair on Pharmacists' Island, along with three boxes of ammunition. I'd long ago learned my lesson, made the old thief fire it himself in an overgrown park with a weedy pond, so I could be assured it wouldn't blow up in my hand. Makar had taken me there. He'd wanted to fire it too. How he admired himself as he weighed it in his hand, his eyes alight in a way that saddened me. I didn't want to shepherd him any further into a life of crime. As if my actions could have had any effect on such an outcome.

I myself fired a round, and felt unjustifiably pleased to have hit the rusted can at about twenty paces. Not that I was going to fight a duel. If I needed to fire it, it would be in close quarters, say, in a rocking boat on the Gulf of Finland, or on a tumbledown dock on the Little Nevka in just a few minutes.

The boy paced in the tall grass in the last rays of the sun, his hands behind his back, jumping on the balls of his feet. He was half out of his mind with excitement. I'd brought a satchel packed with food, the few things Anton had saved from my room—a comb, a couple of books, my sheepskin coat and fox-fur hat. Brought my new clothes as well, the green dress and the blue. In the hem of the green one, I'd sewn the earrings Kolya had given me, the little emeralds. *Esmerelda.* That was the girl he loved, the tightrope walker. But the tightropes were higher these days. Two million rubles, half in my bag for the smuggler, the rest stashed away under my clothes—enough to get me to Helsinki, if they even honored our Kerenskys there. I sat with my sheepskin draped over my shoulders, though it was still early fall, the gun loose in its pocket. Crickets began singing in the birches. But winter would come soon enough. Fifteen miles and we'd be in Finland. If it was winter I could walk it over the ice. But I could not wait.

"It's so quiet here," said the boy. "Spooky."

Volodya and Kolya used to play tennis up here on Krestovsky with their gymnasium friends. This whole island had once been the property of a single family, the Belosselsky-Belozerskys. They had owned mining concessions, and all the streets were named for their mines. I watched the last streak of sun fade from the horizon, and we sat in the gathering dark, listening to the water lick the shore, the splash of an occasional fish. The boy chattered away to fill the unfamiliar silence, like the nervous little kid he was. "After we drop you, we're going to Sestroretsk to meet the Wolf's brother. I'm gonna be *in*. Maybe I'll end up being partners with them. I could do this all the time." He tipped his head back and howled as he imagined a wolf howl would sound. I clapped my hand over his mouth.

"Cut it out. This is not a joke." He really was so very young.

Now he looked ready to cry. He lowered his voice. "Sorry." He managed to be quiet for all of two minutes. "Just think, last week I was selling *Pravda* and sleeping in a water duct. Now I got two hundred *tisich* in my pocket." Two hundred thousand rubles—probably about one hundred prewar rubles, but a fortune for an orphan of thirteen.

"Better keep quiet about it," I said. "Your Wolf might get ideas."

"*Nyet*. Him and me are buddies." He was pulling up grass from around his feet. "I'm his best salesman. He'd be cutting his own throat, wouldn't he?"

I didn't want to disappoint him by saying that the smuggler wouldn't have to look far to find boys who would do more for less. "As far as he's concerned, you're just in it for the ride, understand? Don't tell him about the money."

"How dumb do you think I am? Wait'll I get one of those little *stvoli*." A pistol. "Nobody'll push me around then. I'll be *Nat Pinkerton*."

I couldn't say I was a good influence on him. I worked my fingers

714

through the sheepskin's fatty curls. The stories this coat could tell, my old friend. How many nights had it sheltered me? I'd tucked Iskra up into its warmth. I'd wrapped it around my father. A gun once again in its pocket. I'd always thought of faith as a positive thing, but faith was a blindfold—you walked along the edge of a cliff at all times. The crickets thrummed in the bushes, knowing their time was growing short. Overhead, the sound of flying geese heading south filled the twilight. A sea wind rinsed the stones. I was as anxious to be gone as the boy. At last, the stars emerged—first in the east, then scattered throughout the sky. With no lights to outshine them, no clouds to blur them, they seemed more populous than the city itself. How lonely we were by comparison.

Finally, the sound of a motor. Not sails after all. Coming not from the sea but up the Little Nevka. I lit the lantern. The motorboat pulled up to the dock. The Wolf, in knitted cap and leather coat, manned the tiller, while another man hunched over on some crates, smoking a pipe. The Finn brought it up neatly to the old dock, jumped off, tied it loosely to the post.

"Got the *babki?*" he said. *Little cakes.* The money, the dough.

"Who's that?" I wanted to know.

"None of your business is who," said the Wolf.

"I don't know him. Maybe he's Cheka," I said.

"Maybe he's Joulupukki, the Yule Goat," said the Wolf. "It's my boat. Give me the *babki.*" He held out his hand, snapped his fingers.

I took out an envelope, that brick of paper notes, and counted out half, put it back in my bag. The rest of my money was neatly secreted in a pocket under my dress, money he didn't need to know about. "That's half. You get the rest when we land."

"I thought you had more people," said the smuggler.

"No, it's just us," I said.

"Just you," he said. "Not the kid."

Makar protested, rising to his knees. "We had a deal—"

"I changed my mind."

"But you promised!" I could hear the tears in his voice. He might be a streetwise orphan, but he was still a child.

"I promised nothing. Now beat it. Get back to work."

"But you promised!"

"Did I tell you to beat it? Maybe you're hard of hearing." He pulled out a nasty-looking knife, a blade about six inches long. "Can I help clean out your ears?"

Suddenly I felt the boy's hand plunge into my pocket and before I could stop him he'd pulled out the *stvol*. He was up, pointing it at the Wolf. "Want to clean out my ears, asshole? Go ahead. Try me."

Oh God, was he going to ruin this? "Give it to me, Makar. It's mine. Don't do this. It's fine. We'll take you, I promise."

But he wasn't listening to me, he had eyes only for the Wolf, who'd wounded his pride. "Come on, fucker," he said, laughing. "My ears, I'm not hearing very well."

"You're dead, Makar," spat the smuggler. "Nobody pulls a *stvol* on me."

I was going to lose my captain, my ship, my chance to get away. All of it because of this newly sprouted little man. "Just put it down," I urged the orphan. "Everybody calm down. It's going to be okay."

Makar clearly didn't know what he was going to do next, hopping from one foot to another, giggling. And neither did the Wolf, standing with his hands half up. He obviously could not believe one of his own street boys would produce a firearm and train it on him. It still all might have sorted itself out, except that the man on the crates lurched for shore, or maybe just for cover, and the movement startled Makar. He fired, striking the Wolf in the shoulder. The tall ginger-haired thug came at him with the knife, and the boy kept firing until both men lay dying, and the woods were full of sound.

The noise radiated out and out, rolling across the water. The faces of the men, pale in the dark. Startled, eyes open. I blew out the lantern.

I wanted to vomit. I only hoped the strange man was one of the Wolf's colleagues and not another citizen hoping for escape. I waited in the dark for my senses to return to me. I waited for shouts, for running footsteps, arrest. I wanted to run, but where? Back to Petrograd? No.

Makar sat next to me in the darkness. "He was going to cut me out."

Was that an apology? "You didn't have to shoot him."

"I didn't know what the other one was going to do."

"Give me the gun."

It was hot and I could smell the sulfur. By touch, I reloaded it from the box of ammunition in my other pocket, the cylinder almost too hot to handle, then I returned it to its home. *Luck has not been your friend.* So what were we going to do now?

Makar was crying. "We were going to be partners." This poor crazy kid. His big chance just a fantasy. Nobody likes having to look at themselves in the spotlight and see the gull, the fool. What the Wolf didn't know about the human heart. I felt like crying myself, but I patted his leg. We had to pull ourselves together. We had to think.

"What's in the crates?" I asked. Trying to sound practical. "Go look."

He stumbled over to the boat, shook a crate. "Vodka, I think," he sniffled. "He shouldn't have tried to cut me out. He shouldn't have done that."

I couldn't begin to count the ways this thing was going wrong. All of my hopes had been pinned on the ginger-haired man now dead or dying on the dock. After a while, I relit the lantern, gazed down at the victims. The Wolf on his back, his pale eyes staring. The blood-soaked shirtfront black in the faint light. The other man lay draped, half in, half out of the boat. He didn't seem like a smuggler, but how did a smuggler look? He wore city clothes, a black coat, shirt, dark pants. Dark hair. His cap had come off along with the top of his head. No satchel, no luggage.

Makar was already searching the dead men. From the smuggler he produced a lighter, some cigarettes, gold coins that flashed like fire between his fingers and disappeared. He held out my bills, which I took and replaced in my bag. He wrestled and rolled the Wolf out of his jacket, put it on. He took off his mismatched boots and slid the man's sturdy ones over his bare feet. They were enormous. He took his belt and cap and grinned, as if he hadn't just killed two men. "Pretty nice, eh? I never had a leather jacket before." The Wolf's knife he also kept.

"The other one. Who is he? Does he have a labor book?"

He checked the man's pockets. A few rubles, a lighter, a bag of cheap tobacco. No labor book. No papers. Nothing to indicate whether he'd been an innocent man whose life we just ended, or a smuggler, or both. All of my volition had drained from me. I felt as weak as an invalid. Nevertheless, we had to get rid of the bodies. Two splashes, we didn't even bother to weigh them down. "Sorry," I said as the passenger sank into the little Nevka.

Breathe. Breathe in calm, breathe out chaos. Breathe out wanting to throw that kid into the Nevka.

"Are you mad at me?" he asked.

I didn't know whether to laugh or grab him by the throat. "Do you know how to drive a boat?"

"How hard could it be?"

We examined the vessel. One bullet had gone through just below the oarlock on the starboard side, but the bottom seemed untouched. The motor? I lifted the lantern but it was hard to tell. Well, I couldn't go back to Petrograd and I couldn't stay here. I'd said my goodbyes, I'd *sat on my luggage,* so to speak. I climbed into the boat and the boy followed me. Now I was grateful Anton hadn't come. Panic was a disease that spread faster than cholera. He would be accusatory by now— *This is what leaving gets you*—on his way to venomous hysteria. Makar was still a child, he would follow my lead. He held the lantern, peering over my shoulder as I explored the boat's mechanisms.

The tiller jutted out from the frame. The skiff's motor had a kind of spool and a handle—a crank of some sort. The petrol tank was easy to identify, and a flat metal tongue poked out from under the spool. I shifted it from left to right, but nothing happened. I felt like a monkey looking at a gramophone. If it had sails, I could get us to Finland. Damn this kid, and that dead bastard Wolf. All the boy wanted was respect, how hard would that have been, just to include him? They'd both be alive, and we'd be on our way.

The boy knelt in the bottom of the boat, holding the lantern so I could see the motor's levers and spool and not my own shadow.

Please, Theotokos, help this poor sailor. I grabbed the knob on the spool. Clearly, it was designed to be spun. "Well, here goes."

It only rotated a half turn, but when it sprung back it cracked my knuckles hard enough to break them. I yelled as the motor sprang to life, the spool racing around like a fishing reel. How noisy it was! The boat lurched and strained against the rope.

"Slip that off," I said, trying to ignore the fiery pain in my hand. I held on to the boy's belt as he leaned out and slipped the rope from the mooring. Then we were chugging out into the dark channel of the Little Nevka, the motor spluttering and stinking. He looked down into the water as we left. "We did have a deal, motherfucker." And he spit into the slow current.

"Kill that lantern," I said.

He did as he was told. I took the tiller and headed west.

The sea roughened as we left Krestovsky Island and entered the gulf, waves slapping the bottom of the small skiff. "Hey, is it supposed to do this?" Makar grabbed the sides.

"It's fine," I said, hoping it was true.

The wind was cold. I was happy for my sheepskin and my hat. I turned north, trying to follow the shore. We struck something, there was an ugly scraping against the hull.

"What's happening?" Makar cried. "Watch out!" But there was nothing to watch out *for* on this moonless night, that was the point. I had to do it by feel. I pulled off the rock or whatever it was, turning out deeper into the gulf. All I could see were stars, thick above us, and the dark mass where the trees were pasted against them on the starboard side. As I steered away from the hazards of the shore, I noticed the tree-line shadow diminish. When I came experimentally closer, I watched it rise up again. If I could just follow the line of darkness, I could navigate without running up on anything.

There was a bit of a chop, but it wasn't terrifying, except when a wave lifted and dropped us unexpectedly, and the boy cried out. I found that by turning the lever to the right I gave the engine more petrol; turning it left slowed us down again. Better to go slow, save fuel, and arrive closer to dawn when I could see the shore better.

There was also the problem of the dead smugglers. And the boy. The liability of him was becoming more clear, and in any case I couldn't take him to Helsinki with me.

"I never had a leather coat before. It's so warm." The Wolf's pelt, with its blood and bullet holes. "Can I steer?"

I tried not to think *bad luck boy.* If it hadn't been for him I wouldn't be out here tonight, trying to steer by a dark strip against a vast sky of stars. But there was no such thing as luck, only fate, which could not be outrun. "Come over here, then."

The boat shifted. I heard him fall to the deck. "Careful!"

I wondered if he could even swim. He crawled to me on hands and knees, and I slowly moved over on the bench, gingerly balancing our weight, helping him settle himself. With him and me in the stern, the boat rode differently, nose up, striking the water more forcefully, I could feel the roughness in the tiller. "This is how you steer." I put his hand on the stick, and my uninjured one—the left—on top. "It goes the opposite of how you think. If you want to go left, push right."

I guided our hands until he could feel the boat turning, then guided them back to the center. He laughed, as excited as a child. "Look, I'm doing it!" *Captain Kidd.*

As we bounced along the waves, wind in our ears, I studied the star-filled sky, located the Great Bear, or as they said in the West, the Big Dipper, and counted the five spans from its head and foot up to Polaris, the North Star, as Aristarkh Apollonovich had once taught me. North, off to the left above the line of trees. We were heading west-northwest. "See that star all alone, about halfway up above the trees?"

"Sure," he shouted back. "Or maybe the one next to it." Smart-ass.

"See the Great Bear?"

"Sure, they teach us all about that at the Higher Orphan Academy."

So I taught him the rudiments of navigating by constellations, the certainties of the night sky. Though he was skeptical, he needed me, and the comfort of believing in me outweighed his doubt. I taught him to recognize the Great Bear—"They thought bears had tails?" It didn't inspire confidence. I taught him that the night sky was like a big wheel, and as the night wore on, the stars would turn, all but Polaris. I drew the wheel on the back of his tiller hand, then traced its turning, like opening a doorknob, then poked the center of the wheel. "That's the one we steer by. The North Star."

I taught him to count the distance from the bear's foot to his ear. "Can we call it a wolf?"

Better the wolf should be up in the star-filled heavens than pulling a knife on us here in the boat. I saw a theme emerging in the poem of our voyage. "Why not?"

Thank God we had the stars, a clear night. I never thought I would have to do this in earnest but the sky proved true, and there was Polaris halfway up the sky, above the starless line of trees. "If you can find it, you'll never be lost." A funny thing for me to say, who was more lost than anyone.

"It's like that statue...the guy on the rock, down by St. Isaac's. Just sits there, doesn't change."

The *Bronze Horseman*. "That's Peter the Great."

"Yeah. Let's call him Peter." *Peter*. It's what we called Petersburg. My own fixed star, which lay farther and farther behind us.

"Now look to its right. Farther up, see the upside-down *M*? That's Cassiopeia, the queen on her chair." We were going to devolve back to the first men, who told their stories about the stars. "The Wolf chases the Queen around the North Star."

"Peter, you mean."

"So sometimes you'll see the Wolf upside down, and no Queen, because she's beneath the horizon. Sometimes you'll see the Queen and no Wolf. But *Peter* will always be there. He's the ringmaster."

Call him Kolya. "Steer a little to the left." He began steering right. Just like the Bolsheviks. "The other left."

He corrected course. "Maybe the *M*'s Marina."

Marina, running from the wolf, in an endless circle around the ringmaster? I preferred the other story. "See the space where there aren't stars? That's the shoreline, the trees. Keep Peter where he is and we'll follow that line until we get to Finland. Keep the trees about there, so you can see the stars."

"You just figured this all out?" His voice awed that someone could observe something so simple and find a way to use it.

"Steady as she goes." Cradling my damaged hand, I crab-crawled forward and settled in against the crates. Immediately the ride smoothed with the extra weight in the bow. I sat back against the crates and watched the Milky Way, imagining riding that celestial road. The sky was immense and far away, and we were very small in a tiny boat, navigating like ancient men had always done.

"What are you going to do when you get to Finland?" he shouted out over the engine's clamor.

"Got an old friend in Kuokkala." Maybe. I hoped Makar wouldn't want to come with me. I didn't want to be responsible for this unpredictable orphan who had just killed two men and stolen their boat. "How about you?"

"Maybe I'll sell off that vodka and go back to Petrograd, be the new Wolf."

He made me laugh. In less than an hour he'd gone from panicked weeping to planning to take over the Finn's *bizniss*. "Don't forget the brother in Sestroretsk. They might recognize the boat and come after you."

"Don't you worry about me," he called back, his voice full of swagger. "Fuck the Wolf. And his brother."

I fingered the ammunition boxes in my pocket as Makar spoke into the wind, feeling his way along the handholds of his imagination. "You know, the Wolf wasn't going to let me in on anything. Son of a whore just wanted me to be his donkey, sell scumbags in front of the Little Brick. Now his suppliers can talk to me. Or maybe

I'll go to his competitors—even better. That guy you called Saint Peter, he knows things. He can't even walk. He could use a partner."

"You be careful." How could I tell him what I knew about the big man with the salt-and-pepper hair? "That is a really bad man."

But who could tell what would happen to Makar. Maybe he would end up being the new king of Petrograd—what did I know? Maybe he would become a commissar of foreign trade. I was through with predictions.

"First thing, they'll try to knock me off," he shouted. "I'll need a gun." He was already planning how to take over the Wolf's business. "I come back wearing his coat, I'll need more than talk, you know?"

He wanted my pistol, that's what he was saying. "No. You're asking for trouble."

"I've got money now. I'll go back to Saint Peter."

What do you want, Marina? Maybe I had a deal for him. "What if we get there—if we get there—I let you have it. The boat, the gun, the whole thing. Just do me a favor when you get back." If the boat held, if the gas held, if fortune favored.

"You know I will," he said. "*Stvol* or not."

I thought of Anton, alone there, unprotected, with his ideas about the future. "There's a man, a poet, his name is Anton Chernikov. He's one of the eggheads at the House of Arts. Tall, pale, dark hair, grumpy. They'll be hosting a Blok evening at the end of the month. Find him, and just...be his friend. Will you do that for me? He'll need a friend, even if he doesn't know it. Give him a little money, check on him from time to time, agreed?"

"He's your boyfriend?"

"No. My boyfriend's the one whose flat we just robbed."

He started to laugh and I joined him, as the Wolf chased me across the sky.

I leaned against the crates of vodka, gazing up at the stars, thinking how Kolya would feel to see our flat, what I'd done to it—all that was left was the red-and-pink wallpaper. He'd certainly know my answer to what he'd proposed. If he'd loved me less selfishly, I'd

Janet Fitch

be aboard the *Haarlem* tonight, instead of risking my life out here
with the unpredictable Makar, a good chance of drowning before we
ever reached Finland.

"Marina, something's happening. The trees are gone."

I sat up. I could see stars all the way down to the horizon. A light
blinked on shore. I knew where we were. Lisy Nos. The Fox's Nose.
Right across from Kronstadt. If Pasha had run, this was where he
would have come ashore. "The coast comes to a bend here," I
shouted. "Turn right. Steer toward Peter. And stay away from the
shore."

We were out of Neva Bay and into the Gulf of Finland, the deep
water. When the shoreline turned west again we'd be at Kuokkala.

Now the boat rocked heavily on the swells, rolling in sideways.
We wallowed in the troughs, not enough to capsize us but enough
to upset our skipper. "This is making me sick," Makar said. "You
steer." But I couldn't stand up.

"Just zigzag a bit," I shouted back. "Try not to let them come at
you sideways."

He did as I asked. The small boat still rose and fell, but more like
a horse at a canter, not wallowing in a sick-making way. "You know
a lot," he said. "How come you know so much?"

"Because I'm old," I said. "You'll catch on. Maybe you should go
back to school. You could go to the Rabfak." The Workers' University.

"Eh. Schoolteachers and me don't get along," he said.

"Read books. And talk to smart people. That's school too."

"Your friend—he's smart like you?"

"Very smart." Smart enough not to have come. Anton would
have been suicidal by now. The death of the two men on Krestovsky
would have been enough to have him running for home. He knew
himself, I had to give him that. He knew his limitations, as I never
did. I thought to mention that if the boat flipped over, the boy
should cling to it, but I figured that would panic him more than help.
He had pretty good instincts, except for the quick trigger finger.

The rocking was pretty rough, though, even with him zigzagging into the swells. How far was the shore? I imagined five hundred yards. Less. I could swim that—I hoped. Kick off my boots, lose my sheepskin, and hope there were no odd currents. Appear naked on the shore of what might be Finland or might still be Russia, new-born. Perhaps one of those crates of vodka would float.

"Look," he said. "Is that it?"

A light, way up ahead, a couple of streetlights, a small town. A lantern moving on shore. Sestroretsk, it had to be. "Cut the motor." Someone waiting for the Wolf, gazing out to sea.

"How do I do it?"

Oh damn. Carefully, I crawled back, keeping my weight low and in the center, rejoining him in the stern. I didn't dare touch the motor's spinning reel. My right hand still throbbed with pain, but I managed to light the lantern, keeping it low, beneath the sides of the boat, shielding it from shore. I pushed the throttle all the way left. It slowed and sputtered but wouldn't quit. The motor could be heard a quarter mile.

Makar pointed to a square button, a piece of metal painted red. "What's that?" A wire connected it to a cylinder. I pressed and held it—and merciful Virgin, the engine shut down.

Without the motor roaring, how silent it was. Just the swells and the beat of the waves. "Find an oar," I said quietly. By the low lantern light I picked up the other, placed it in the starboard oarlock. "Put it in the lock and for God's sake don't drop it." The wind had fallen off. It had been of our own making. Makar took his oar and dropped it into the port lock. He missed, but managed to grab it before it fell. "Sorry."

"If you have to let go, remember to pull it into the boat first," I whispered. "I'm going to turn us around now, so don't row until I say so. Coming about." I pulled on my oar, turning the boat in the cold and the spray. Then we began rowing, propelling ourselves backward, stroke by stroke. Now I was the one closest to the lights on the shore, my right hand twanging. I wondered if I could really swim to shore if I had to. We were ridiculously off rhythm. If he kept pulling after the waves lifted us, we were going to get nowhere.

"Ti MORryak, ti kraSIvi sam saBOYu..." I started to sing, low. *"You sailor, you are so handsome, and only twenty years old...* Sing with me. *Love me with all of your soul..."*

"I don't know it."

It was such an old song, I thought everyone knew it. But he was an orphan, he knew street songs, the songs of the *besprizorniki*. In a low voice, I taught him "You, Sailor"—he picked up the refrain right away, the sailor's part. *Across seas, across waves, now here, but tomorrow there.*

We approached Sestroretsk, dipping the oars quietly, and now I was thankful for the swells, the breaking of the waves on shore. We were close enough to hear a dog bark across the water. Silently now, we pulled. I found a star I could keep the stern of the boat trained on, dead opposite Peter. I saw someone on the dock with the lantern, but they could not see us. It was only after the lights were very small that I dared speak again. "Be careful here on the way back," I said.

"Across seas, across waves, now here, but tomorrow there," he sang.

"We can turn the motor on if you like." Though my hand hurt just thinking of it.

"No, this is nice," he said. "How much farther?"

"Not far. A few miles."

"I'll row. You go sit down, and watch Peter and Queen Marina."

I handed him the port oar, making sure he had it firmly before I let go, and crawled back to the crates, where I could rest and watch Polaris. He started a new song, an orphan's song about how everyone hated him, how he would die alone.

I crammed my fox-fur hat deeper onto my head, wrapped my coat tighter, listening to Makar sing, lulled by the rhythm of his rowing.

It was nice like that. I felt free. Just a few last hours in this boat, neither Russia nor Finland, neither past nor future, not here nor there, just me and the kid on the black, star-dotted water. I could hardly imagine how I might remember this hour in the years to come, how I would tell this story.

"Think you'll stay in Finland?" the orphan asked.

"I don't know what I'm going to do in twenty-four hours," I said.

If you'd asked me yesterday, I would have said Buenos Aires wasn't far enough. But the reality was beginning to set in, the gravity of what I'd done. Never to see Russia again. Everything I knew and loved, behind me. *I just pray I'm buried on Russian soil*, Avdokia had once said. I didn't think she got her wish. And I certainly would not see a Russian grave, not Tikhvin Cemetery, not Novodevichy with Iskra.

Russia was a book whose cover was closing, and ahead lay the scent of wormwood and the bread of exile.

I suddenly saw them, our great poets, like a forest of tall trees, just as they'd been the day of Gumilev's requiem at Kazan Cathedral.

> *While here, wrecking our youth's last days*
> *within the blaze's blinding smoke*
> *we have all steadfastly refused*
> *to dodge a single savage stroke.*

I was glad of the dark, that Makar couldn't see my face right now. Abandoning Russia. As I had abandoned everything.

I gazed up into the bristling stars, rocking in the waves and the pull of the oars, and wondered if somewhere there was another nursery on another Furshtatskaya Street, where another three girls stood over a different basin of water, and other wax was poured. I wondered what my fate would look like in that other world, whether I'd still be rowing here with Makar, the dead bobbing in my wake, the living going on nobly, holding up the domes of the cathedral without me.

As I fled, to hide in the West, shucking my burden, dodging the blows.

The oars slowed. Makar was tiring. Just as well. No point in arriving before dawn.

"Sing us a song," he said. "It's nicer that way."

What should I sing him?

How about "Do Not Awaken My Memories"? Varvara's joke that evening outside Belhausen knitwear factory, where we had distributed her illegal pamphlets so long ago. She'd lost her way, trying to steer a straight course by a crooked star.

All my songs died in my mouth, tragedies of parted lovers and faithless ones, women seeing soldiers off to war. How could I sing them now? I would have to break into the vodka and drown myself. All of our songs so bitter. Ironic—how I had once loved to pose as the melancholy girl singing Russia's soulful tunes. I'd gloried in them—before I myself had felt the sorrow that had given them birth. Now that I felt them truly, I was unable to bring myself to sing them. They were too sharp. They would shed too bright a light now that I had been that woman watching the road, and also the faithless one, had known love's flashing steel, the spear of longing. I was still bleeding from it.

Fleeing Russia, I was more Russian than I'd ever been.

But why should I allow my grief to rob me of my songs? I argued with myself. These songs were mine. I paid for them. I would own them as I pleased.

Quietly, unsteadily, I began to sing "The Wide Expanse of the Sea." The splashing of oars matched my voice. *"The sea stretches wide, the waves they roll far...Far from our land, far from our land we go."*

I thought of the lucky people somewhere, who'd lived their lives unbroken by circumstance. They must look in the mirror and, seeing themselves old, feel a jolt. Bewildered when grandchildren paged through their albums and laughed at the photographs, the old-fashioned clothes and hairstyles. Those people had become exiles without even knowing it. But I would not be surprised. The doors were already swinging shut, my clothes going out of style on my back.

And I would never return to my own native land, back to the one place that had ever mattered, the fixed point around which my whole life revolved—the House of Arts, that fraternity of the Word, the ship on the Moika Canal. Anton, my friend, lover, editor, in his window. *Don't go, we need you*...It would all take place without me, the autumn season at the House, the Blok memorial and all the memorials to come...the new issue of *Anvil* would have a poem of mine, but after that—nothing. I would never see them again—Kuzmin and Chukovsky, Mandelstam, Inna Gants. New poets would arrive and they would never know my name. And how long until the ones I knew forgot me? *Remember that girl who lived on Slezin's floor, Anton's girlfriend? Whatever became of her?* I would disappear like a rock falling into water, as if I were already dead.

Eventually, inevitably, the stars turned in their great circle, and the shore began its shift, the line of trees not just to the east but also ahead. "We're almost there," I told the boy. "Let's stop here, take a rest."

I found the anchor in the bow of the boat and gently dropped it, the rope playing out until it caught and held.

Rocking on the swells, wrapped in my sheepskin and scarf, I thought about what Anton had said. Was it true, my life as a poet was over? If so, it was already done. I was cut off and already withering, severed from the living Russian language. Events would take place this fall without me, the writers coming together, that family of art, and I would be alone, more alone than I'd ever been in my life. Without lovers, friends, family, child, country.

When Iskra was coming, the midwife made me say goodbye *as if it is your last day on earth. Forgive them.*

I said goodbye. To the poets who knew me, and to the generation whose names I would never know, and who wouldn't know mine. Goodbye to Russia, my native land, Mother Blackearth, with your orphans and your lunatics, your poets and rivers and graveyards. And Petersburg, to your waters and your graces and your sins. Goodbye to the kind ones, who kept my nose above waterline, to those who loved me, the living and the dead. And goodbye to you, my dearest, my fox, my folly, and my fate...I forgive you. We could not be other than what we were. I loved you more than anything, my dear, except freedom.

The boat rocked on. The boy was quiet, sleeping or just thinking his orphan thoughts of fame and manly triumphs. The stars burned on, the sea air rich with the salt of the seven continents, bitter with every tear that had ever been shed, bright with every slice of starlight.

I'd said goodbye to so many things in these last years. But whatever Anton said, whatever Akhmatova thought, they were wrong about this: I would remain a Russian poet to the end. Not her most faithful child, certainly no pillar for her cathedral, but hers nonetheless. Her own blood and bone pitched outward into the world—not a pillar, but a seed. I would float on the waters, carrying her songs, and sing them wherever I washed ashore.

One by one, the stars blinked out. Gradually the sky paled, the celestial ink fading to gray. Ahead, the beach at Kuokkala emerged from the formless dark, its pinkish sands just discernable against the line of trees. Small waves rushed in, striking the land with a soft hiss. And strange joy arose in me, an unexpected lightness. I had imagined nothing but grief, perhaps a noble stoicism. But I could feel my sails unfurling, catching the light of early dawn. This stateless tramp, this seed, with nothing to my name but a couple of dresses, a pair of earrings, a wad of Kerensky bills of uncertain value, and ten thousand lines of Russian verse.

I shook Makar awake. "It's sunrise. Time to go." The boy stretched and yawned as I hauled in the anchor.

Acknowledgments

No book is born on its own. Many midwives were at play in the writing of this novel. Always, thank you to the heroes of my writing life, my writing group, David Francis, Rita Williams, and Julianne Ortale, whose unfailing support saw this project through. To my daughter, Allison Strauss, my infinite gratitude for your sharp eye and unfailing judgment. To my tireless editor, Asya Muchnick, at Little, Brown, who unflinchingly shouldered Marina's epic journey, as well as the entire team at Little, Brown for believing in this project. Thank you to Karen Landry, for shepherding this through the production process, and master mapmaker Jeffrey Ward, whose Civil War map graces these pages. And undying gratitude to my agent and champion Warren Frazier at John Hawkins and Associates, ever in my corner. And ever, William Reiss.

Translation is a generous art and these translators personify the spirit and the calling. Depthless thanks to Boris Dralyuk, friend, mentor, and sounding board, who created original translations for much of the Russian verse that appears in this novel; to Brendan Kiernan, PhD, for his original translations from *Notes of an Eccentric;* and to the other translators who so kindly allowed me to use their work: Peter France, Antony Woods, and the estate of Stanley Mitchell. Deep thanks to Natalya Pollock for her oral translation of Olga Forsh's novel *Sumashedshiy Korabl'* (*Crazy Ship*), and to teacher and translator Dr. Judson Rosengrant, my literary Virgil into the manners and mores of the Russian intelligentsia.

And I am humbly grateful to the Likhachev Foundation of St. Petersburg, Russia. The Likhachev Fellowship enabled me to do research with some of the most prestigious cultural institutions in St. Petersburg. Thank you Alexander Kobak, Elena Vitenberg, Inna Sviderskaya, Anna Shulgat, Sasha Vasiliev, and Ksenia Kobak, for your generosity and care. Many thanks to the Akhmatova Museum's director Nina Popova, Tatyana Poznakova in the Education Department, and Masha Korosteleva; at the Museum of Political History, Alexey Kulegin and Alexander Kalmykov; at the Museum of the City of St. Petersburg, Irina Karpenko; and at the Museum of the Peter and Paul Fortress, Julia Danidelova. Special thanks to Eireene Nealand, translator and friend, for alerting me to the Likhachev Fellowship, and for introducing me to contemporary St. Petersburg poets. Thank you Tobin Auber, for your warm welcome and unique insider views, and Andrey Nesteruk and his parents for their memorable tour of hidden St. Peterburg.

Research was the oxygen in the water of this novel. I thank the eminent Russian historians Alexander Rabinowitch and Arch Getty, social historian Choi Chatterjee, and art historian John Bowlt, as well as the H-Russia List-Serv. Much gratitude goes to the USC libraries, where a large part of this research was done, and to Reed College, whose 2007 alumni trip under the guidance of Dr. Rosengrant began my research, and whose alumni support services allowed me essential access to the JSTOR digital library.

Novelists not only require the world, they also require retreat from the world, and this book found many a kind harbor in the years of its writing. Many thanks to those who offered me shelter and the gift of time—David Lewis and Liz Sandoval; Eduardo Santiago and Mark Davis; Brett Hall Jones, Louis Jones, and the Hall Family; Andrew Tonkovich and Lisa Alvarez; Jan Rabson and Cindy Akers; Wendy Goldstein and Sharon Smith; Chris Nicholls and Lorca Moore; and the Helen R. Whiteley Fellowship at the University of Washington Friday Harbor Laboratories.

I want to thank my father, Vernon Fitch, who first put Dostoyevsky into my restless teenaged hands, sparking the flame that down through the years resulted in this book, and my mother, Alma Fitch, an irresistible force, who taught me that girls can do anything. Eternal memory.

Acknowledgments

Most of all, I want to thank my husband, Andrew John Nicholls, for his boundless good humor, astute judgment, and willingness to read so many drafts, calm so many storms, cheer me when it looked impossible, and who taught me to celebrate prematurely whenever possible. I love you more than I can say.

For an overview of the books that shaped my understanding of the revolution and other insights into Marina's world, please visit: www.janetfitchwrites.com.

About the Author

Janet Fitch's first novel, *White Oleander,* a #1 bestseller and Oprah's Book Club selection, has been translated into twenty-eight languages and was made into a feature film. Her second novel, *Paint It Black,* hit bestseller lists across the country and has also been made into a film. Her third novel, *The Revolution of Marina M.,* begins an epic journey through the Russian Revolution. She lives with her husband in Los Angeles.